W9-BMS-002

ALSO BY TOM CLANCY

TOM CLANCY
FLASH POINT

DON BENTLEY

BERKLEY
New York

PRINCIPAL CHARACTERS

UNITED STATES GOVERNMENT

JACK RYAN: President of the United States

MARY PAT FOLEY: Director of national intelligence

ARNOLD "ARNIE" VAN DAMM: President Ryan's chief of staff

SCOTT ADLER: Secretary of state

ROBERT BURGESS: Secretary of defense

THE CAMPUS

JOHN CLARK: Director of operations

DOMINGO "DING" CHAVEZ: Assistant director of operations

DOMINIC "DOM" CARUSO: Operations officer

GAVIN BIERY: Director of information technology

LISANNE ROBERTSON: Former director of transportation

JACK RYAN, JR.: Operations officer/senior analyst

USS *DELAWARE*

COMMANDER CHRISTINA DIXON: Skipper

SENIOR CHIEF PETTY OFFICER BILL DAVIS: Sonar technician

LIEUTENANT COMMANDER DAN YOUNG: Executive officer

P-8 POSEIDON

LIEUTENANT TOM MCGRATH: Pilot-in-command

LIEUTENANT JUNIOR GRADE JACK STEWART: Copilot

LIEUTENANT COMMANDER VINNIE SHORTS: Naval flight officer

CHINESE CHARACTERS

FEN LI: Chief executive officer of the HAZ Corporation

AIGUO WU: Member of the Central Committee of the Communist Party of China

PRESIDENT CHEN: President of the People's Republic of China

OTHER CHARACTERS

DR. CATHY RYAN: First Lady of the United States

ISABEL YANG: Potential Campus helper

MASTER SERGEANT CARY MARKS: Operational Detachment Alpha 555

SERGEANT FIRST CLASS JAD MUSTAFA: Operational Detachment Alpha 555

MARIO REYES: CIA asset

PROLOGUE

VICINITY OF PARACEL ISLANDS
SOUTH CHINA SEA

LI JIE WATCHED AS A WAVE BROKE OVER THE BOW OF HIS SHIP. THE green foam scoured away the paint flecking from the *Dragon*'s discolored deck. To Li Jie's seasoned eye, the frothing sea was a harbinger of what was to come. An omen of both the approaching storm and the violence brewing on his vessel.

Keeping his left hand on the wheel, Li Jie used his right to touch a button on the digital display mounted in the dashboard in front of him. A swirl of angry reds and oranges filled the LCD screen as the weather radar rendered the looming storm into abstract art. As predicted, the typhoon was shaping up to be a monster. But while the sea was rough going now, Li Jie planned to have his precious cargo tucked safely back in Zhanjiang Port before the worst of the storm hit.

The same could not be said of the Vietnamese fishing trawler wallowing through the choppy seas two points off his bow and three hundred meters distant.

"Are you certain the boat is dead in the water?"

The question came from behind Li Jie, but he didn't turn to answer. Ostensibly, this was so that he could keep his eyes on the unforgiving waves, but the raging sea was not the only danger Li Jie feared. The slip of a woman with her bone-white hair and voice as quiet as the grave terrified Li Jie in a way that thirty years of plying his trade on stretches of the world's most dangerous oceans did not. The sea might be a fickle mistress, but even at her worst, she could claim the lives of only those who sailed upon her waters. The same could not be said of the woman. A single whisper from that unassuming voice could render Li Jie, and his entire family, ash.

"Yes," Li Jie said, toggling the monitor to yet another display. "This feed is from our passive sonar array. The trawler is not emitting engine noise. Her power plant is completely offline."

Li Jie gestured as he spoke, tracing the nonexistent Doppler returns with his index finger. On the surface, there was no reason why Li Jie's vessel would possess a passive sonar at all, let alone one sensitive enough to detect and classify targets more than one hundred kilometers distant.

But there was more to the *Dragon* than met the eye.

Though the *Dragon* was registered as an ordinary Chinese-flagged cargo ship, she was anything but. Beneath the *Dragon*'s purposely rusting exterior was a surprisingly robust power plant capable of sending the vessel knifing through the water at greater than twenty knots and up to almost thirty in a pinch. The massive diesel engines also drove a pair of generators responsible for satisfying the *Dragon*'s prodigious electrical requirements. This appetite for power ran the gamut from banks of software-driven receivers designed to suck RF signals from the air to a suite of cleverly disguised electro-optical sensors that could surreptitiously observe and record activities from kilometers away.

But all of that was just window dressing compared to what the *Dragon* carried in the specially configured compartment deep within her hull. This fifteen-by-fifteen-meter space housed a deep-sea submersible hardened to withstand the steel-crushing water pressure at depths of greater than eight thousand meters. In his five years of captaining the *Dragon*, Li Jie had used the two-man minisub to tap undersea fiber-optic lines, install surveillance devices in enemy ports, monitor undersea weapons tests, and, in one case still discussed in the hushed tones the exploit deserved, beacon an American *Ohio*-class boomer submarine.

Still, as impressive as these exploits might be, they were but footnotes to the mission the minisub had just undertaken. A mission so secretive that for the first time in Li Jie's tenure aboard the *Dragon*, the crew had been joined by a platoon of men commanded by a single woman.

Armed men.

If the hard-looking warriors had hailed from the People's Liberation Army Navy Marine Corps, Li Jie would have still been uneasy, but not terrified. The Marine Corps' Jiaolong Commando Unit, or Sea Dragons, were easily recognizable in their black uniforms and were often tasked to guard Chinese vessels from pirates. But the twenty men now crowding Li Jie's berthing with their assortment of weapons and gear did not hail from any branch of the military. Instead, they were a detachment from a private security company known only by the English initials HAZ.

The men were mercenaries.

Killers for hire.

And while Li Jie and his crew had performed what at first blush had been deemed an impossible mission with the ease and professionalism for which they'd become known, the operation was not yet complete. As the woman with the quiet voice had made clear, until the *Dragon* was safely back in harbor and the contents of the ship's vault transferred ashore, Li Jie and his crew were on war footing.

"Have they seen us?" the woman said, her quiet voice the whisper of steel on leather.

Li Jie paused, considering his answer.

While his years of clandestine service had taught him the need for secrecy, at his core, Li Jie was still a sailor and the thought of being caught powerless in a typhoon's path was the stuff of nightmares. And yet, at the end of the day, a nightmare was still just a dream while the woman and her contingent of killers were very much a reality.

"I don't know," Li Jie said as another wave crashed over the *Dragon*'s bow. For a moment, the frothing water blurred the windshield, washing away the image of the stricken ship. Then the laboring windshield wipers did their work and the fishing trawler returned. "We're jamming across the electromagnetic spectrum as per your instructions, but we've detected no RF energy emitting from the trawler. If she has a radar, she isn't using it, and her radios seem to be down as well. Could be that she's a ghost ship. Either way, without enough power for steerage, she won't last long in this storm."

The last sentence filled Li Jie with a sense of trepidation, but he added it nonetheless. He was a third-generation sailor and would always be the boy who'd learned about the sea while working alongside his fisherman father. Seeing the lifeless trawler wallowing in the waves clawed at his soul in a way that a non-sailor could never understand. In that moment, the ghost vessel wasn't a Vietnamese-flagged ship. Instead, it represented his uncle and father desperately trying to bring the engines online before the South China Sea claimed another victim.

The slight woman with the bone-white hair and the power of life and death in her soft voice tapped long, elegant fingers on the faux-wood dashboard. Her emotionless eyes tracked the ailing trawler. She'd begun to speak when a signal light flashed from the trawler's bridge, interrupting her.

ENGINES DISABLED. TAKING ON WATER. NEED ASSIS-
TANCE. URGENT.

As heartbreaking as the plea was, Li Jie didn't bother translating the flashes for the woman. The fishermen had just sealed their fate. Indeed, the slight woman was already speaking into the small radio she kept fastened to her belt. The radio that linked her to the hulking, scarfaced warrior who commanded the mercenary contingent. After a final flurry of words, the woman released the transmit button and returned the radio to her belt.

A moment later, light again split the darkness.

But this time, the light carried something far more lethal than mere words.

A series of flashes rippled across the trawler's waterline as armor-piercing warheads detonated. The crippled vessel listed to the right, her watertight compartments flooding. In less time than it took for Li Jie to breathe a prayer to the ancestors on behalf of the fishermen's souls, the trawler disappeared into the swirling water.

"Survivors?" the slight woman asked.

Li Jie dutifully played the *Dragon*'s infrared sensor across the maelstrom, searching for the telltale white thermal signature of a warm human body amid the churning black waves. He thought he'd caught a glimpse of gray during the first sweep, but the sensor's second revealed only the raging sea.

Satisfied, Li Jie toggled the display back to the weather radar.

"None," Li Jie said. "The storm is almost upon us. I respectfully suggest that we make for port."

"Agreed," the woman said. "And I respectfully suggest you get us home in one piece. More than just our lives depend on your nautical skills."

Li Jie gave a curt nod as he advanced the twin throttles, sending the *Dragon* lurching forward. But behind his carefully cultivated blank face, Li Jie was shaking. He breathed a second prayer to the ancestors.

This time, the soul he bargained for was his own.

1

"ENTSCHULDIGUNG—WO IST DIE FAKULTÄT FÜR MATHEMATIK?"

Jack Ryan, Jr., did in fact know the way to the mathematics department, but not because he was an aficionado of the Pythagorean theorem. In fact, Jack's last math class had been under the tutelage of Father O'Neil, whose love of equations and variables was rivaled only by his adoration for the writings of St. Thomas Aquinas. Jack had escaped the class with a C-plus, much to the chagrin of his surgeon mother, who took a dim view of any mark less than a B.

Jack's familiarity with the University of Regensburg's quaint campus was not the result of a newfound thirst for knowledge or a desire to right his past collegiate wrongs characterized by too much time on the football field and not enough in the library. Neither had Jack's familiarity come from strolling along the campus's network of pedestrian paths under the azure sky and brilliant German sunshine. No, Jack knew where the math building was for the same reason he was seated at a section of tables in the cobblestone-paved common area that formed the university's heart.

Jack was running a surveillance operation.

But he couldn't say this to the cute blonde dressed in a white half-shirt, black Lululemon leggings, and white cross-trainers. While Jack hadn't thought much of college math, there were certainly some aspects of the higher-education experience he'd found enjoyable.

"Sorry," Jack said with a smile. "I'm not a student."

The girl smiled back, and Jack's grin widened.

At six foot two and two hundred twenty pounds, Jack was a big boy. Now that he was closer to forty than twenty, he had to hit the gym harder to maintain his athletic build. But his blue eyes were still bright, his face unwrinkled, and his brown hair thick and curly.

Judging by the coed's reaction, Jack must not be aging too terribly.

He still had it.

"Of course not," the girl said, laughing, as she switched to German-accented English. "You are much too old to be a student. I thought you might be visiting your child for parents' weekend?"

Or perhaps not.

"Nope, no child," Jack said, fighting to keep his grin from withering. "Just here for a conference."

"Oh," the girl said, her face reddening. "Sorry. Could you tell me where the mathematics building is located?"

"Sure," Jack said. "Quickest way is through there." He turned in his chair to point to the doors of the University Student Office behind him. "It'll be the first building you see on the other side."

"Danke," the girl said.

She offered Jack a final smile that reeked of pity before heading into the building.

Jack gritted his teeth as he waited for the other shoe to drop. As jolting as it had been to learn that he could no longer pass as a college student, he knew the worst was still to come. As if on cue, a feminine voice echoed from a Bluetooth-equipped combination transmitter/ receiver lodged deep in the canal of his right ear.

"Do we have a med kit?"

"Why?" Jack said, instantly alert.

"Thought you might need something for your bruised ego."

The raspy tone engendered images of raven hair and vanilla-scented olive-toned skin. Unlike Jack, who was seated at a flimsy metal table with a doner kebab wrapped in aluminum foil for company, his coworker and girlfriend, Lisanne Robertson, was lounging in the grass on the south side of the University Student Office. In fact, if they'd been the only two operatives on the net, Jack might have broken protocol long enough to tell the Lebanese American woman how he'd accidentally mixed salt into his coffee after seeing her in "college attire."

Jack didn't.

This was partly because he was still trying to navigate the pitfalls of working clandestinely with someone who was also a love interest and partly because he and Lisanne weren't alone on the net.

Not by a long shot.

"Don't sweat it, Jack. We all get old."

The high-pitched voice belonged to Gavin Biery.

Like Jack and Lisanne, Gavin was an employee of The Campus, an off-the-books intelligence agency. Unlike Jack and Lisanne, who were paramilitary officers, Gavin was The Campus's director of information technology, and its resident hacker. As such, he was perched in his comfortable chair at The Campus's Alexandria, Virginia, headquarters rather than in Germany.

Since the operation the three operatives were currently running had been billed as surveillance only, Gavin had asked to accompany his teammates. Jack had turned down the portly keyboard warrior. Gavin brought more to the fight ensconced in his climate-controlled IT labyrinth than he would deployed to the field.

Not to mention that he looked far less appealing in summer wear.

"First of all, I'm not old," Jack said. "Second, I need everyone focused on the task at hand. Coffee break is coming up."

"Whatever you say, pops," Lisanne said, her husky voice raising goose bumps across Jack's skin.

Before catching his flight to Munich, Jack had been called in for a sit-down with his boss and The Campus's director of operations, John T. Clark. Clark's operational history was both long and distinguished, beginning with his time as a SOG veteran and Vietnam-era Navy SEAL. In the ensuing years, Clark had worked as a CIA paramilitary officer and served as the original Rainbow Six. He and Jack's father had met in the jungles of Colombia during a CIA-helmed counter-drug operation gone wrong.

Now Jack's father was the President of the United States, and Clark was Jack's boss. When John Clark talked, Jack listened, even on the rare occasions when he didn't agree with what his boss had to say.

This had been one of those times.

Jack and Lisanne had been honest with their brothers- and sisters-in-arms when their relationship had firmly left platonic territory. While this wasn't a surprise to most of their compatriots, Clark had counseled the pair on what this meant from an operational sense. In short, it changed things. Contrary to the movies, operating with someone with whom you were romantically involved was difficult.

Serving objectively as that person's team leader was nearly impossible.

Jack hadn't disagreed with Clark's assessment. Who was he to argue with someone who'd been hunting his nation's adversaries while Jack had still been in diapers? Still, this was not an operation, per se, as much as a tactical test-drive. A test-drive of Isabel Yang's utility as well as a demonstration for a rather unique bit of software Gavin had been tinkering with for the last several months. It would also serve as a trial run for Jack's ability to operate with Lisanne in the field. As Campus work went, you couldn't get much more vanilla than an academic conference held in the sleepy German town of Regensburg.

Milk run were the exact words Jack had used with Clark.

"I've got movement on Socrates's phone," Gavin said.

Socrates was Isabel Yang's call sign.

Yang was a twenty-six-year-old Ph.D. student who was being groomed as a Campus helper. The Campus's black side numbered less than twelve people, and the flat organizational chart and lack of bureaucracy was one of the organization's selling points. Unlike traditional members of the intelligence community, Campus operatives were not limited by findings, statutes, or authorities. Jack Ryan, Sr., and his friend and Campus founder, Gerry Hendley, were the North Stars when it came to deciding what was in and out of bounds as it pertained to sanctioned operations. Though not a history professor like his father, Jack Junior was an adept enough student of the antiquities to know that this arrangement was not a recipe for success.

But that was a problem for another day.

Jack's near-term concern lay with The Campus's manpower, or lack thereof. Nimble organizations were great at the type of missions that required a scalpel, but more and more often, Campus work tended toward the sledgehammer variety. With multiple teams operating simultaneously around the globe, the lack of depth in nonoperational departments like logistics, recruiting, and human resources was beginning to show. Even among the door-kickers, Campus personnel were stretched painfully thin. To make matters worse, the entity had no formal accessions process. This meant The Campus had no standardized way to vet and onboard potential new talent.

Enter Jack's thought on helpers.

The Mossad was a shining example of how to do more with less. As a country of only about nine million people, Israel was constantly required to punch above its weight. The tiny nation's intelligence service was no exception. As a way to even the scales against its much-better-funded and -manned counterparts, the Mossad had developed a network of helpers that spanned the globe. These men and women weren't operatives as much as they were people in unique positions or with unique skill sets who could fill logistical or intelligence gaps for active Mossad operations.

People like Isabel Yang.

In addition to her qualifications as an academic who spoke three languages and could pass for half a dozen nationalities, Isabel was an Army brat. Her Chinese American father had been a Green Beret assigned to the 10th Special Forces Group when he'd been killed in Afghanistan. Isabel's patriotism ran deep. Jack had first made her acquaintance during an operation in South Korea, and he'd been impressed with her mettle. Now they were taking the next step in the agent/handler relationship.

Isabel was attending the academic conference hosted by the University of Regensburg at The Campus's behest. A conference also attended by three influential Chinese scientists whose work spanned both military and civilian applications. The conference was now entering its second day, and while Isabel had confirmed the presence of the Chinese scientists, she had yet to meet them.

Jack was hoping this would change today.

"Roger that, Gavin," Jack said. "Can you confirm she's heading toward the break area, over?"

"Stand by," Gavin said.

Geolocating someone with their phone was old news. What once took the power of the NSA's supercomputers could now be done with one of the many publicly available apps. But the utility of this capability vanished once someone was inside a structure.

Until now.

Gavin had been toying with the idea of using the accelerometer in a target's phone to judge the direction and distance of their movement, but he'd struggled with how to baseline the algorithms. Everyone's stride was different, and this made it difficult to judge how fast and far someone was moving once the accelerometer triggered.

Then Gavin had had one of his famous breakthroughs.

Rather than attempting to baseline a target independently, he would use the phones surrounding the target phone to measure the distance it covered. He'd developed an app that would allow him to use phones connected to a single Wi-Fi router as a miniature GPS constellation. Code-named PARSEC, the invention worked pretty well in the shakeout exercise Jack had run at a mall near Alexandria.

This was its first operational test.

"Confirmed," Gavin said, sounding like a kid on Christmas morning. "Socrates is moving with the targets toward the break area."

"Roger that," Jack said. "Lisanne, you ready?"

"You bet," Lisanne said. "Video and audio feeds are great."

The tobacco-cessation efforts that were all the rage in America had yet to take hold in much of the rest of the world. The Chinese scientists were no exception. Thus, the common area outside the mathematics building had proven to be a popular hangout for those who preferred nicotine to caffeine for their afternoon pick-me-up. The courtyard offered a breath of fresh air along with the all-important receptacle for cigarette butts.

After watching the targets eschew the conveniently located coffee shop for the smoking area on day one, Jack had adjusted his plan in two ways. One, he'd repositioned Lisanne and her goodies. Two, he'd suggested to Isabel that she take up smoking.

Unsurprisingly, the first directive had been much better received than the second.

Isabel was a fitness fanatic who viewed smoking as only slightly less risky than taking a dip in the cooling reservoir for Chernobyl's reactor. Even so, by the second day of the conference, the scientist had come around to Jack's way of thinking. The trio of Chinese scientists kept to themselves in the auditorium and hadn't attended any of the socials scheduled by the university's faculty for the visiting scholars.

It was the smoke pit or nothing.

As a backstopped member of academia, Isabel's legend was perfect. She was not an intelligence operative, and nothing in her background would suggest otherwise. As such, her assignment was simple—engage her Chinese counterparts in small talk. Jack hadn't even wanted Isabel to attempt to garner an email address or contact method—that would be too obvious. Instead, he'd told her to be who she was—an accomplished academic at a conference. This strategy was designed to account for Isabel's inexperience and Jack's desire to use a nonthreatening environment to get the scientist's feet wet.

Unless Jack missed his guess, he wasn't the only shark circling the conference. Other intelligence operatives were probably likewise prowling for interesting contacts, and as a bona fide scientist, Isabel was the perfect dangle to identify other intelligence officers and their interests.

But Jack hadn't explained this part of the plan to Isabel.

Though the scientist had acquitted herself well during their first interaction in South Korea, she was a novice operative and Jack wanted her to behave as such. Intelligence officers were adept at spotting people who were something other than what they claimed to be. Isabel would be most effective if she didn't know she was being used.

At least that's what Jack told himself.

"Okay," Lisanne said, breaking into Jack's thoughts. "I've got eyes on three Chinese scientists plus two minders and a couple other members of the tobacco club. Waiting for face shots."

With her outfit, Lisanne should have no trouble enticing the men to look her way. Dressed in what passed for college casual, Lisanne was wearing a cream-colored tank top, cut-off jean shorts, and flip-flops. Though she was almost a decade older than most of the college students, Lisanne wore her age well. She'd pulled her raven hair into a ponytail, added oversized aviator sunglasses to mask her face, and mimicked the short shorts, tight tops, and painted toes that seemed to be the university's female uniform.

Jack thought Lisanne beautiful in operator garb, but when she was dressed to impress, his girlfriend truly was a heart-stopper. Today her outfit of choice showcased miles of tan skin, and her long, brown legs looked especially appealing against the white blanket she'd spread across the grass. Normally an operative's job was to vanish in plain sight. To assume the Gray Man persona. For Lisanne, this was impossible. Pretty could be downplayed and attractive figures could be hidden beneath layers of bulky clothes, but Lisanne's most noticeable feature couldn't be masked.

Her missing left arm.

In a Campus operation gone wrong, Lisanne had sustained a grievous gunshot wound that had required the amputation of her arm and almost cost her her life. In any intelligence organization but The Campus, this would have spelled the end of Lisanne's operational career.

But The Campus wasn't just another intelligence apparatus.

Knowing that she needed them far more than The Campus needed her, John Clark had given Lisanne the time and space to flesh out her new role. While her time as a gunfighter was over, she and Jack both believed that there were ways in which she could still contribute.

Today was a good example.

Lisanne would have turned heads with both arms. With one missing, everyone noticed her. Jack intended to use this to the team's advantage. With her iced coffee, laptop, collection of books, and notebook, Lisanne looked like any of the other students lounging on the grass. Except that her messenger bag contained a combined camera and parabolic mic wirelessly linked to her laptop. If people were going to look at Lisanne anyway, Jack intended to leverage their curiosity to obtain facial and voice prints of the Chinese team for The Campus's biometric database.

So far, his idea had paid off nicely.

Male scientists stared at Lisanne for obvious reasons. Their female counterparts gave her missing limb a second, and usually sustained, glance.

All the while Lisanne captured valuable intelligence.

Lisanne Robertson took the notion of a *dangle* to the next level.

"Say cheese, boys," Lisanne said.

Jack unwrapped his doner and took a monster bite.
He was further removed from the action than he would
have liked, but as his earlier encounter with the inquisi-
tive student had proven, Jack did not look as if he belonged. At least not in Lisanne's easy manner. As such,
he was running command and control of the operation,
not a job he relished. Then again, he was enjoying the
sunshine between bites of the world's best doner with a
half-empty glass of pilsner to keep him company.

There were certainly worse ways to earn a living.

"Okay," Lisanne said, "I've got high-resolution shots
of each target scientist and my mic is capturing the audio. I'm sending you the raw feed, Gavin."

"Confirmed," Gavin said. "I'll run the audio through
a translation app I borrowed from a friend at the agency.
The software's a beta version, so I'm not sure we'll get
anything useful, but it's worth a try."

As with all conversations with Gavin, Jack found this
one insightful, as much for what the keyboard warrior
did say as for what he didn't. For instance, Gavin had
pointedly left out which agency the software had originated from or how he'd borrowed it. Then again, as Ding
had told Jack on multiple occasions, if you know you're
not going to like the answer, don't ask the question.

"Lisanne," Gavin said, "I'm showing Socrates heading for the smoke pit. You should see her any minute."

"Tally," Lisanne said. "She just popped out of the
building. And look at this girl—she's got a cigarette in
her mouth but seems to have forgotten her lighter. Heading over to the Chinese scientists now."

Jack set the remains of the doner on the metal table and dusted off his hands. He envisioned what was happening as he listened to Lisanne's play-by-play. In addition to making the acquaintance of the Chinese, Gavin had pushed for a slight escalation to Isabel's tasking. The hacker extraordinaire had been fiddling with a program he called HOUDINI, which was designed to compromise a user's phone. Currently the app used a device's Bluetooth port to gain entry, as this protocol was often less heavily encrypted than Wi-Fi or cell networks.

The tool had worked pretty well in testing, the only limitation being that the target phones had to be within Bluetooth range. With this in mind, Gavin had asked to try his new creation out on the Chinese scientists' phones with Isabel serving as the delivery vehicle. Jack hadn't seen the harm, since it wouldn't require anything more of the scientist than what she'd already committed to doing. She'd engage in small talk with her fellow researchers while Gavin worked his magic.

Simple.

Or so Jack hoped.

"Tracking," Gavin said. "Lemme see what we've got here. Okay, I'm showing three Xiaomi 12S Ultra phones. Doesn't even look like they have standard government encryption. This is gonna be a cinch."

Jack smothered a smile at Gavin's response. The IT guru almost sounded offended by the lack of a challenge.

"Let's just get it done, pal," Jack said. "Like Ding says, sometimes you just wake up on the right side of the bed."

Actually, Jack was pretty sure that fellow Campus operative and Rainbow cofounder Domingo "Ding" Chavez had said nothing of the sort, but his mentor was a font of knowledge. Besides, when Jack attributed something wise to Ding, no one on the team pushed back.

Usually.

"On it, Jack," Gavin said. "Penetration in process."

Gavin hummed an accompaniment to his clacking keyboard, seemingly oblivious to the awkward silence his pronouncement had just produced. Jack was in the process of keying the transmit button to say something—anything—to move the word *penetration* out of everyone's head when Lisanne beat him to the punch.

"This is interesting," Lisanne said, her tone all business. "Two minders have just joined the scientists. Counting Isabel, the group now numbers six."

Jack fumbled with his cell phone, willing it to display the video from Lisanne's sensor. Her camera/mic package had the ability to stream its pickup to any number of devices, but Jack decided not to use this feature. Live video and audio required a large data pipe, and Jack hadn't wanted to spike any SIGINT receivers the Chinese might be employing or, worse yet, allow them to potentially compromise the feed. Based on the threat analysis, there was no reason to suspect that the Chinese were employing any such countermeasures, but in the profession of espionage, caution was the word of the day.

"How's Socrates handling the newcomers?" Jack said.

"Like a champ," Lisanne said. "After getting a light from Target 1, she hung around to shoot the shit. She didn't even break stride when the two minders joined the party. This girl's a natural."

After spending a hair-raising afternoon with Isabel in Seoul dodging a North Korean kill team, Jack was inclined to agree. Still, it was nice to have his judgment independently verified. The recruitment process really was a courtship of sorts, and becoming blind to your asset's shortcomings was a pitfall all handlers had to avoid. Though Isabel was something in the gray space between fellow operative and agent, Jack was the one running her. As such, he wanted to make sure he kept both eyes wide open during her evaluation phase. Even so, Jack was confident that if Isabel had the tactical sense to escape a trio of DPRK commandos, she could handle making small talk with Chinese academics.

"Hey, guys, I'm seeing something weird here," Gavin said. "My spectrum analyzer is picking up fluxes across the entire band. It's like—"

Gavin's transmission ceased, mid-sentence.

Jack's first feeling was one of annoyance. Though the computer ninja was hell on wheels when it came to the digital universe, his situational awareness often suffered when he had to transition from the world of ones and zeros to one populated by flesh and blood. Case in point, it would have been nice if Gavin had led with what exactly he was seeing.

With a start, Jack realized what his subconscious was trying to tell him.

Spectrum fluxes.

Electronic interference.

Loss of comms.

Someone was jamming Gavin's transmission.

"Lisanne, this is Jack, do you read me?"

Silence.

"Lisanne, are you there?"

Nothing.

So much for a milk run.

2

"I HAVE A QUESTION," SERGEANT FIRST CLASS JAD MUSTAFA SAID.

Master Sergeant Cary Marks sighed, preparing himself for the inevitable. Cary had traveled the world with the man sitting across the table from him. And while the locales might change, one thing remained constant—his companion always had a question.

"What?" Cary said.

"Are we in heaven?"

Cary didn't answer.

At least not right away.

This wasn't so much because of annoyance, though his comrade certainly could be annoying. No, Cary's hesitation stemmed from a much deeper root—he wasn't sure how to reply. While Haidplatz plaza didn't have streets of gold, Cary thought heaven might look a lot like Regensburg, Germany.

"If this is heaven, one of us is in the wrong place," Cary said.

"Why? Because I'm a Muslim and you're a Christian?"

"No," Cary said with a smile, "because Saint Peter has a strict policy when it comes to admitting Green Berets— only one through the Pearly Gates at a time."

Jad chuckled. "I should have known better than to talk theology with a Presbyterian."

"Baptist," Cary said.

"To-may-toe, to-mah-toe," Jad said. "Anyway, what I'm trying to say is that if this isn't heaven, it's gotta be pretty close."

On this, Cary agreed.

The two men were located in the outdoor seating area of a tiny Italian restaurant that specialized in amazing food and even better beer. Remnants of a margherita pizza lay between them, along with two glistening glasses of Radler. The pizza had been devoured with unabashed vigor, while the beers had been carefully nursed. Contrary to Jad's sentiments, this was not heaven or even a vacation.

This was work.

The type of work that did not mix well with alcohol.

But if eating great pizza and drinking even better beer was what passed for a standard day in their new gig, Cary could get used to it pretty quickly.

"You don't miss the sand fleas in Syria?" Cary said.

"I miss getting after it with the boys," Jad said, dusting off his hands, "but take a look around. It feels like we're guest-hosting on the Travel Channel."

Cary chuckled, but he didn't disagree.

Cary and Jad were both members of the 5th Special Forces Group, which was located in Fort Campbell, Kentucky. The two men were Green Berets, members of Operational Detachment Alpha, or ODA 555, also known as Triple Nickel. Triple Nickel was famously the home of the horse soldiers—Green Berets who'd embedded with the Northern Alliance and called down air strikes from horseback during the initial invasion of Afghanistan.

While these legendary exploits had been before Jad and Cary's time, the two men had certainly done their part to add to Triple Nickel's illustrious unit history. From multiple deployments across the Fertile Crescent, to a recent op in South Korea that had begun as a training exercise and nearly ended in war, team sergeant and sniper Cary, along with his trusty spotter Jad, had visited many foreign locales.

Physically, the two Green Berets couldn't have been more different. Cary Marks was a blue-eyed, blond-haired farm boy from New England whose vowels gave away his Yankee roots under stress. Jad Mustafa's dark complexion and SoCal surfer accent lent themselves to kidding from his teammates, who often accused him of being a closet SEAL.

Jad's affinity for hair gel and fashionable clothes didn't help.

Even so, the men's differences in skin color and ethnicity had ceased to matter long ago. As with most combat veterans, Cary and Jad were brothers in a way that transcended birth parents or family lineage. They'd gone into harm's way side by side more times and in more places than Cary could count, but this was the first operational assignment that could have been featured on the Travel Channel.

Coincidentally, it was also their first assignment with The Campus.

Or maybe not so coincidentally.

"Do you think all Campus trips revolve around beer and pizza?" Jad said.

Cary chuckled.

Next to his wife and kids, the New Hampshire boy had spent more time with the Libyan American surfer than he had any other human being. Much of that time had been while huddled beneath a sniper's hide site with an M151 spotting scope and Barrett Advanced Sniper Rifles for company. Two assignments ago, while observing a cult of apocalyptic Shia militants, the snipers had saved Jack Ryan, Jr., from being nailed to a cross. One assignment ago, Cary and Jad had reunited with Ryan to prevent the Korean peninsula from going to war. Once again, the pair of Green Berets had saved Jack's life, and this time he'd made them an offer they couldn't refuse.

Literally.

After confessing that he shared both a name and bloodline with the President of the United States, Jack had invited the commandos to meet his mother and father and partake of a meal in the Executive Residence. During after-dinner cigars, Jack's father had asked the pair if they'd ever considered coming over to the dark side.

Triple Nickel had just rotated back from an operational assignment in South Korea and was due some home station time to train, refit kit, and reacquaint themselves with their families. As the team sergeant, Cary's plate was full, so his first inclination had been to decline. But one did not tell the President of the United States no, especially a president with Jack Ryan, Sr.'s credentials. That said, Senior didn't think much of the arm-twisting method of recruiting. Instead, he'd suggested that the two men accompany his son on a shakeout of sorts.

A two-week operation in beautiful Bavaria.

Three days into the two-week mission had Cary reassessing his previous hard no. While he'd loved his time as a Green Beret, Cary had been a team sergeant now for almost ten years. He'd been passed over for promotion to sergeant major twice, meaning that his Army career had plateaued. This, coupled with his aching knees and perpetually sore back, meant that Cary's days of humping a ruck were coming to a close. Perhaps the cloak-and-dagger world wouldn't be such a bad way to spend the handful of years remaining until he was eligible to retire to the family maple syrup farm in New Hampshire.

Perhaps.

"Before you get too attached to cappuccinos and crumpets, remember that the first time we linked up with Jack you caught a bullet," Cary said. "The second time, we almost started a nuclear war."

"Eeh," Jad said, shrugging. "Those are what we call operational hazards. Speaking of which, the fräulein a table over has been eyeing yours truly and—Wait a minute, boss."

At the mention of the word *boss*, Cary's thoughts focused like the closing of a steel trap. Cary had become attuned to his fellow Green Beret's mannerisms at an almost subliminal level. When Jad said *boss*, the time for bullshitting and ass-grabbing was over. This was usually the moment when Cary moved his rifle's selector switch from safe to fire. Except that neither Cary nor his spotter were carrying firearms.

Apparently even unicorns-and-rainbows missions had drawbacks.

"What've you got?" Cary said.

The two men were at the northern end of a triangular-shaped plaza, facing south. The cobblestone common area was dominated by a large statue with a tiered circular base and bounded by multistory buildings featuring coffee shops, restaurants, and a quaint gasthaus. Though not as well known as her more famous Munich or Nuremberg siblings, Regensburg was everything a tourist would want in an old European city, as the crowd thronging the plaza attested. Travelers of all ages frequented the restaurants and bars, and the statue at the plaza's center was a popular spot for the all-important selfie.

That said, Cary and Jad weren't at Haidplatz for beer, pizza, unicorns, or selfies. Instead, the pair were focused on the hotel on the opposite side of the plaza that was situated between another pizzeria and a Thai eatery. The five-story gasthaus embraced its stereotypical heritage with a flat façade broken by narrow windows and a pair of massive wooden doors that could have been at home on a medieval castle. To be precise, the two commandos weren't focused on the building as much as they were on the occupants in a series of rooms on the gasthaus's third floor.

Chinese occupants.

As per the mission brief, this was an exercise more than an operation, but Jack's team at the University of Regensburg weren't the only potential Campus members on their shakeout cruise. Cary and Jad had been assigned the enviable task of monitoring the hotel in which the Chinese scientists and their minders were staying. On the whole, it was a boring assignment, but in the largely unglamorous life of a sniper, boring was par for the course. Since the hotel had a single entrance and exit, the two commandos had a fairly easy task. But as per Jad's earlier comment, in this business easy and boring existed just a hairsbreadth away from complex and terrifying.

"Bob and Jim just exited the hotel carrying duffel bags. Something's going down."

Cary tended to agree with his spotter's assessment, but he also wanted to ensure they weren't jumping to conclusions. The Green Berets were well versed in establishing a target's pattern of life, but their experience in a metropolitan area like this was admittedly limited. Even so, Chinese men vacating their hotel in the middle of the day was not normal.

"Reposition," Cary said to Jad as he tossed a pair of twenty-euro notes on the table. "I'll call it in."

"Roger that," Jad said.

The Libyan American left the table, heading for the restaurant's interior. Cary turned slightly in his chair to better see the plaza and, more important, the two targets code-named Bob and Jim.

Surveillance was the ultimate game of cat and mouse. Oftentimes, a surveillance target employed his or her own set of watchers in the form of a countersurveillance team to identify the opposing force. A triggering event was a tried-and-true way to force the surveillance team to react and thereby inadvertently identify themselves.

Since Cary's team consisted of just two people, Jad had to reposition to cover the mobile Chinese team. But Jad was walking into the restaurant away from the Chinese targets rather than following them outright, in the hopes of confusing potential countersurveillance assets.

"Scepter, this is Reaper, over," Cary said at a whisper.

Like the rest of the Campus team, Cary and Jad were equipped with low-profile receiver/transmitters. Since the surveillance operation the Green Berets were running was separate from Jack's efforts at the college, Cary had stayed off the other Campus team's net. But if Cary was right and the Chinese men really were abandoning the hotel, the two efforts were about to intersect.

A white Sprinter van weaved through the narrow streets before stopping just to the west of the pizza shop. The sliding cargo door opened, revealing a dark interior.

Jim and Bob angled toward the vehicle.

Showtime.

3

JACK'S FIRST URGE WAS TO START WALKING TOWARD LISANNE.

He didn't.

At the moment, Jack knew just one thing—his team's communications had been compromised. If the loss of comms could be attributed to a hostile intelligence service, as opposed to atmospheric interference or just plain bad luck, what he did next would be very important. Gavin's observation regarding signal interference across the frequency band suddenly took on much greater significance. Jack wasn't an RF expert, but even he knew the difference between targeted and broad-spectrum jamming. One was possible only if you knew the exact frequency on which your adversary was operating.

The other was employed when you had to blanket an entire frequency band.

The jamming could be happening because someone suspected an ongoing operation but didn't know for sure. If Jack leapt to his feet and made for Lisanne at the exact moment his team lost connectivity, that suspicion would fast become a certainty.

Caution was the word of the day.

Jack's phone buzzed with a text from Lisanne.

Trouble!

Or not.

Jack stood, pausing as he thought. The lack of a comforting bulge at his right hip had never felt more apparent. This operation was just one step above a training exercise. Though the team was running surveillance, they had neither the mission brief nor the perceived need to go kinetic. Jad and Cary hadn't been officially transferred over to The Campus's operational logs, Isabel was a civilian, and Lisanne had just one hand.

Getting into a gunfight was not an option.

Jack's gaze drifted to the red lines bisecting his left forearm. The scars were a memorial from the last time he'd encountered a Chinese MSS operative unarmed. The locale was Tel Aviv rather than Western Europe, but the experience had been far from pleasant. Shaking off the morbid thought, Jack thumbed a message to Lisanne with one hand while yanking open the door leading to the Student Office with the other.

Coming.

Jack hit send and then pushed through the lobby, dodging milling groups of college kids. Passing through a common area adorned with the requisite coffee shop as well as tables and nooks set aside for studying, Jack exited the southern side of the building to a raised walkway.

To his right, a pedestrian path meandered westward

through a series of grassy areas shaded with beech trees. To the left, the same pathway led east before intersecting a north/south-running fairway that paralleled Jack's walkway back to the Student Office to the north while bisecting the mathematics building to the west and a parking garage to the east. A grassy common area abutted the parking garage, bounded by a pond separating the Student Office from the university proper. A striking woman was stretched out on a blanket amid a pile of books on the grassy area's eastern edge.

Lisanne.

If she'd noticed Jack's arrival, Lisanne gave no sign.

To be fair, her attention was probably focused on the mathematics building to her west, or, more specifically, the smoking area where Isabel Yang was presumably trying to make small talk with a trio of Chinese scientists. Jack couldn't see the outdoor courtyard from his vantage point, as the building's eastern corner and a clump of trees blocked his sight line. But Jack did notice a pair of BMW motorcycles racing north along the pedestrian path, heading straight for the building.

Not good.

Both drivers were helmeted and wearing head-to-toe leather in the manner common to German motorcyclists, making it a challenge to determine their identity. Not to mention their intentions. Judging by the way the students scattered at the riders' approach, motorbikes roaring across the university's green space was not a regular occurrence.

Abandoning all pretenses of blending in, Jack sprinted

along the walkway and darted to the left, vaulting down the steps leading to the eastward-bound path.

"Reaper, this is Scepter," Jack said as he ran for the building. "We've got trouble."

The answering silence seemed to confirm Jack's suspicions. The motorbikes' appearance and the corresponding loss of comms was not a coincidence.

Something was about to go down.

Something bad.

Lisanne stood, but Jack ignored the raven-haired beauty, focusing on the math building instead. Lisanne had one arm, no way to communicate, and no weapon.

She wouldn't be much help with whatever happened next.

The pair of bikes arrived at the smoking area about fifteen seconds before Jack. As Jack spun around the corner, the bikes came to a halt. A scrum of Asian men from the smoking area walked someone into the grass. Jack caught a glimpse of a youthful Asian man in his early twenties with close-cropped hair and black Buddy Holly–style glasses. The man's escorts pushed him toward the nearest bike. He was clearly hesitant, but after a less-than-friendly shove, he climbed behind the driver.

Jack tried to make sense of what he was seeing.

Was this a kidnapping?

He didn't think so, at least not in the traditional sense. A person could not be compelled to stay on a motorbike. But just because he voluntarily climbed on the machine didn't mean the Asian man was doing so of his own free will. Renditions came in all shapes and sizes.

If snatching someone off a dark street and throwing a bag over their head was one end of the extreme, coercing a person to leave was on the other. Every fiber of Jack's being screamed that what he was witnessing was some form of a rendition.

But what could he do about it?

With the passenger now aboard, the bikes accelerated away from the smoking area in a cloud of exhaust, heading north before veering west—toward Jack. In an instant, Jack understood. The pedestrian path the motorcyclists were following passed a parking garage before intersecting Universitätsstrasse, a large north/south street. Once there, the autobahn in the form of west/east-running Highway 3 was only five hundred meters south.

The kidnappers were as good as gone unless Jack did something.

Something stupid.

As the bikes roared toward him, Jack eyed the pavement below, computing angles. The motorcyclists would have to slow as they passed beneath the pedestrian bridge in order to weave through an assortment of tables. Their most likely course would bring them alongside the stairwell to Jack's left, which presented Jack with an opportunity.

A slight one.

Dashing down the concrete stairs two at a time, Jack reached the edge of the staircase just as the bikes roared past. He let the first one carrying the reluctant passenger speed by.

Then he vaulted into the air.

For a long moment, Jack saw nothing but concrete. He had just enough time to consider how ridiculous he would look belly-flopping onto the pavement when the second bike appeared exactly where he hoped it would.

Well, almost exactly.

Rather than follow the lead cycle's path, the second bike had offset slightly to the right. This meant that instead of landing on the rider's back, Jack was hurtling toward the beckoning concrete.

Jack was a big man.

Not linebacker-sized for sure, but large enough to put his mass to use. He'd intended to clothesline the motorcyclist. Unfortunately, his trajectory wasn't the only thing Jack had misjudged. The rider shot beneath him in a blur of leather and a blast of engine noise. Jack missed the chance to take his opponent out at the throat, so he improvised.

Grabbing a fistful of leather jacket, Jack opted for a collar tackle instead.

It was an effective technique.

Highly effective.

The bike went in one direction and the motorcyclist in the other. The man hit the concrete with an audible *thump* as the BMW careened into the grass and fell on its side. Jack landed mostly upright, taking the impact with bent knees.

The rider wasn't as lucky.

The man's helmeted head bounced off the ground, and he lay still. Jack debated flipping up the motorcyclist's dark visor for a look at his face, but the sound of the first BMW's fading motor cemented his course of action. Running to the sputtering bike, Jack lifted the motorcycle, swung his right leg over the frame, and shot after the lead bike.

Even though interdicting the second rider had taken just seconds, the first bike had already gained a sizable lead. After navigating the outdoor seating area, the driver had opened up the throttle. The rider looked to still be accelerating, leaving Jack at yet another crossroads. Jack could attempt to overtake the nimble bike by following the same path or make up time by off-roading to an intercept point farther to the south. But if Jack guessed wrong and the biker went north instead of south, he'd lose the pair completely.

An oblivious student made Jack's choice for him.

The man stepped from the building's awning, directly into Jack's path. With earbuds in place, eyes locked on his phone, and finger busily scrolling, the student was in another world. If Jack continued his current trajectory, the man would remain there.

Permanently.

Cursing through clenched teeth, Jack leaned the bike to the left as he downshifted. The engine's RPMs skyrocketed and the BMW screamed, finally breaking through the student's electronics-induced stupor. The kid's eyes jerked from his cell to Jack, widening as his mouth opened into a silent *O*. Jack flashed past the still-frozen student, rolling on more throttle as he swung his weight back to the right. The BMW fishtailed, but Jack kept the bike upright and on the path.

Mostly.

Deviating around the student required steering the BMW into the grass, and the motorbike's tire tore a chunk of sod from the perfectly manicured lawn. The good news was that Jack was still atop the bike and the hapless student was unharmed. The bad news was that he was now committed to the path leading south, while his quarry had chosen the branch heading north. Slaloming through a copse of trees, Jack burst through the foliage onto a north/south-running pedestrian path that formed the westernmost boundary of the campus.

Jack braked hard, then planted a foot on the ground as he added gas, pivoting the bike around his leg. This maneuver worked well with the lighter dirt bikes Jack liked to ride with his younger brother, Kyle, but it was more difficult on the heavier BMW. Jack added even more gas as the turn faltered, and the bike quivered beneath him, the one-hundred-plus-horsepower engine screaming. Jack shot out of the turn like a stone slung from David's sling. He barreled down the pathway toward his rapidly disappearing quarry. Leaning over the handlebars, Jack squinted his eyes against the blasting wind and stinging grit.

The kidnapper was about one hundred yards away, but the bike's brake lights flashed red as the driver weaved between a stand of trees in an impressive display of ridership. Jack knew from his pre-mission reconnaissance that the stretch of land to his west consisted of a thick forest and the occasional fallow field. In other words, that direction should be clear of hapless students. With the area in front of him open, and the common area to his right similarly empty of pedestrians, Jack dropped the hammer.

The bike surged as the BMW's suspension cushioned the off-road ride.

Up ahead, the bike Jack was pursuing fishtailed around the western edge of a multistory structure, vanishing from sight. Jack pushed his motorcycle beyond his comfort zone, cycling through the gears as fast as he could shift. He couldn't for the life of him figure where the kidnappers were going. Jack would have turned left instead of right, roaring south down Universitätsstrasse and the quick getaway represented by Highway 3. Heading in the opposite direction was counterintuitive.

Then Jack understood.

He was thinking about the escape as if the passenger was a willing accomplice rather than a kidnapping victim. The captive had been coerced aboard the bike, but each moment he spent behind his kidnapper was another moment he could reassess his decision. The kidnappers had used motorcycles in order to quickly evacuate the victim from campus. But the bikes were not a viable long-term transportation solution. The lead motorcyclist was taking the Asian man somewhere specific.

Or to someone specific.

If memory served, the structure the kidnapper had just rounded was the university's cafeteria. A parking lot ran along the building's western side. A parking lot sheltered from view from the rest of the university by the building's bulk with ready access to Universitätsstrasse, as well as a number of west-running smaller roads that dumped into an even larger traffic artery—Highway 93. The kidnappers intended to use the parking lot to transfer the Asian man to another vehicle.

Jack redlined the engine, transforming the trees to his left into one continuous blur. If the kidnappers made the transfer before Jack arrived, they were as good as gone.

Using the track chosen by the other motorcycle as his guide, Jack plowed across the lawn rather than attempt to follow the footpath's ninety-degree turn to the left. The BMW groaned in response, but Jack downshifted, keeping the bike upright as he added more torque to the rear tire with a liberal application of throttle. The bike tore massive ruts into the manicured grass, but Jack stayed on course, perhaps for too long. He off-roaded across the lawn, zipped between two trees, and picked up the path just as it made another ninety-degree turn, this time to the north.

As he rounded the corner, Jack saw everything.

The BMW he'd been pursuing was idling next to a white Sprinter van. The van's sliding cargo door was open and two beefy Asian men were muscling the much-less-compliant victim. Jack's screaming engine drew the group's attention. Which made him realize that he'd been focused exclusively on staying with the fleeing motorcyclist, to the detriment of planning what he'd do once he caught him.

Jack cut left, paralleling the stone wall bounding the parking lot with the intention of blocking the van's exit to the north. He wasn't sure exactly how that was going to play. In a game of chicken, Jack's motorcyle was no match for the five-thousand-pound Sprinter.

Then again, maybe Jack's presence would be enough to thwart the men. Up until this point the kidnappers hadn't broken anything but the speed limit. Jack's gut said that the Asian man had been abducted, but he didn't know for sure.

Perhaps this was all just a big misunderstanding.

Or, judging by the kidnappers' submachine guns, perhaps not.

4

CARY REPOSITIONED HIS PHONE, ACTIVATED THE RECORD FEATURE, and engaged the digital zoom as he tried Jack again.

"Any station vicinity Scepter, this is Reaper, over."

Still nothing.

"Reaper 2, this is Reaper 1," Cary said. "Are you receiving my Scepter transmissions, over?"

"One, this is 2, that's a roger," Jad said. "Want me to try?"

Cary considered the request.

If the two men had been using radios rather than cells to communicate, it would have made sense for Jad to give Jack a call. But as the reception bars at the top of Cary's phone's display clearly indicated, interference was not the reason for Jack's silence. At least not on Cary's end. Besides, the two Chinese men were loading their bags into the van.

Cary wanted Jad focused on the task at hand.

"Negative, 2," Cary said. "We've got bigger fish to fry. You in position, over?"

While the plaza offered an exit to the east in the form of a narrow street, the walkway's tight confines serviced mostly pedestrians. The occasional delivery van braved the winding turns and outdoor seating areas, but vehicular traffic was minimal. With this in mind, Cary had gambled that when the Chinese watchers departed the hotel for good, they would use the western access point. This side street, while also narrow, was at least straight, and it emptied into a large intersection known as Arnulfsplatz, or Stephen's Place. Five separate roads sprouted from Stephen's Place heading in every cardinal direction, making it an ideal jumping-off point.

Since the van's nose was pointed west, Cary thought he'd guessed correctly.

"Come on, boss," Jad said. "I'm fast, but I'm not the Flash. Besides, Mom always said not to run on a full stomach."

"If only Mrs. Mustafa could see her boy now," Cary said, getting to his feet. "Bob and Jim are in the van and the door's closing. Pick up the pace, soldier."

As per their plan, Jad had exited the restaurant through a side door and was now hauling ass west. The speed at which he traveled down the street wasn't so much driven by how fast Jad could run as it was by how quickly he could move without looking out of the ordinary. All of their planning would be for naught if a countersurveillance team identified Jad before he was in position to interdict the van with the Chinese men.

On the other hand, the men had cleaned out their hotel room. They weren't coming back, and if the van made it to Stephen's Place and disappeared, the Green Berets would not have a chance to reacquire the Chinese team.

The cargo door slammed shut, and the van edged forward.

"Van's moving," Cary said.

"Fifty more meters," Jad said.

The huffing between his words suggested that the Libyan American was now all-out sprinting. Cary needed to buy Jad time, even if it meant burning himself in the process. Fortunately, he'd planned for just such a contingency. A bike rack sat at the edge of the plaza where the cobblestones met the street. A bike rack directly along the van's route of travel.

Reaching into his pocket, Cary fingered a key fob and depressed the unlock button.

No set of corresponding car doors unlocked.

Instead, the mountain bike closest to the road jumped as its rear tire detonated with a sharp *crack*. The popping tire caused a ripple through the crowd as people instinctively turned toward the noise. Cary had also added a little bit of dust to the small explosive for a better visual, and the combination of sound and sight caught everyone's attention.

Including the van's driver.

The Sprinter's brake lights illuminated as the vehicle screeched to a halt. The dust settled a moment later to the accompaniment of nervous laughter from the crowd.

Bike tires didn't spontaneously explode every day, but it was an understandable event. The Sprinter's driver seemed to come to the same conclusion. After a brief pause, the vehicle smoothly accelerated west.

"Two, this is 1," Cary said. "Bought you all the time I could. Hopefully it was enough."

"Of course it was," Jad said, no longer huffing. "I'm a Green Beret, not a SEAL."

Cary smiled as he headed toward a café on the opposite side of the plaza and the car parked by its entrance. His stride was quick but measured. Jad would pick up the van and have the eye as the surveillance turned mobile until Cary was in position to help. Though he wanted to link up with his fellow commando as soon as possible, Cary was still determined not to give away his presence to a potential countersurveillance team.

So far, everything was going to plan.

Except for the eyes Cary felt on the back of his neck.

LIFE AS A GREEN BERET HAD TAUGHT CARY MANY THINGS, NOT THE least of which being when to trust his lizard brain. The career Cary had chosen was often more suited to his primal instincts than to the intellect he'd spent his life developing. In Cary's line of work, the maxim "kill or be killed" was not just idle posturing.

This sentiment was doubly true for a sniper.

Every time he lay in a hide stalking a target, Cary had to remain conscious of the fact that a man or woman with similar abilities could very well be on the opposite side of the battlefield hunting him. With this in mind, Cary worked hard to stay in tune with his subconscious. Though he was as willing as the next operator to make use of all the technology his nation put at his disposal, Cary knew that the primitive portion of his mind should not be discounted.

Especially in moments like this.

Cary slowed as he approached the car, trying to give the impression that he was just another tourist enjoying the amazing Bavarian weather. He wanted to avoid conveying anxiousness with an impatient stride. Even though he knew that the Chinese team and his fellow Green Beret were moving farther away with each passing second, Cary practiced tactical patience. This was yet another lesson he'd learned while slithering on his belly. A sniper's success or failure almost always came down to the stalk, not the shot.

Cary paused as he transitioned from cobblestone to pavement, shooting a quick look up and down the street before crossing. The German propensity to follow rules was even more pronounced in motorists, but accidents still happened. Case in point, a black Audi revved its engine and accelerated out from a parking spot just to Cary's left. Cary reflexively took a step back as the station wagon zoomed by, and his surprise provided him with an ample excuse to peer into the vehicle's cabin.

A pair of fit men occupied the front two seats.

Cary wasn't the only one interested in the hotel.

"Two, this is 1," Cary said as he opened the door to the Volkswagen hatchback. "Status, over?"

"One, this is 2. I'm mobile. Where do you want me to set up, over."

Cary considered his response as he dropped into the driver's seat, fastened his seatbelt, shut the door, and cranked the tiny motor. In no scenario could a two-man surveillance team keep eyes on a mobile target for long. If this were a traditional operation, Cary would have at least four mobile teams at his disposal. The large number of participants allowed the team leader to flex the team to any cardinal direction the target chose, while rotating the participants through the "eye" position at regular intervals. This helped to prevent the target from identifying their pursuers. A moving surveillance with just two members couldn't do any of this.

Fortunately, Cary had a couple aces up his sleeve. One, he knew the Chinese team's destination—the University of Regensburg. Two, Cary had guessed the route that they would take and had a plan to interdict them. The university was just three kilometers south of the hotel, but a large railway station formed a natural barrier along the most likely direction of travel.

The railway station featured almost two dozen east/west-running tracks. Only two roads bridged across the station—Kumpfmühler Strasse to the west of the hotel and Galgenbergbrücke to the east. Of the two, Kumpfmühler was the more direct way, so Cary had assumed the Chinese operatives would take it. So far that bet was paying off, which meant that it was time to place another. Jad was on a motorbike, meaning the Green Beret was incredibly mobile, but also very recognizable.

Accordingly, the two men had decided that the spotter would stage ahead on the Chinese team's route rather than tail them directly. Cary would close ground with the intention of taking over eye duties from Jad once the Chinese team was committed to the university's winding streets. Now Cary had to decide where to position his spotter, in the hopes of interdicting the moving Chinese operatives without burning the surveillance.

"Two, this is 1," Cary said as he accelerated through a traffic circle bordered by a collection of quaint shops and restaurants before turning south on Neuhausstrasse. "Recommend you stage vicinity Grisham, over."

"One, this is 2, acknowledge Grisham, over."

Grisham was the parking lot of a tobacco shop located just on the southern side of the railway station. Since the shop sat at an intersection of three roads that led to the university, it formed a natural choke point. If it were Cary in the driver's seat of the Sprinter van, he would execute a surveillance-detection route, or SDR, after exiting the bridge to identify any pursuers following him across the channelizing terrain. By arriving at the parking lot ahead of the van, Jad could shadow it through either of the three routes without arousing the team's suspicion.

At least that was the theory.

After a tight turn by the Theater Regensburg, Cary accelerated south, passing the iconic Bismarckplatz on his left. As per his earlier reconnaissance, the pedestrian area was crammed with people, forcing Cary to balance his desire to close distance with the Chinese team with the requirement to drive slowly enough to dodge any wandering and perhaps inebriated tourists. In another couple hundred meters, Cary would be through the most congested part of the town.

A pair of flashing brake lights announced a traffic snarl in the form of several Germans making use of a crosswalk. Cary took his foot off the accelerator, allowing the vehicle to decelerate. A moment later the brake lights resolved into the Audi station wagon. With a curse, Cary realized he'd forgotten to inform his spotter about the new addition to their surveillance.

"Two, this is 1," Cary said. "Be advised, we've got at least one new player in the game. A dark Audi station wagon broke station shortly after the Chinese team left the hotel. The occupants are two military-aged males. Currently at the intersection of Schottenstrasse and Wiesmeierweg proceeding south, over."

"One, this is 2, roger all. Do you have a plate, over?"

As if tuned to the Green Berets' frequency, the Audi accelerated away from the crosswalk just as Cary got close enough to read the plate. "Two, this is 1, I've got a partial Sierra, Alpha, Delta, over."

"One, this is 2," Jad said. "Got it. How do you want to play this?"

Cary turned the problem over in his head.

Jad was asking whether Cary intended to blow by the Audi so that he could continue to close the gap with the Sprinter van. While this was the more conservative play with respect to the Chinese, if the two men inside the Audi were on a surveillance mission as well, doing this meant Cary would risk burning himself. Though the art of surveilling a target was a constantly evolving practice, one tenet remained unchangeable—seeing the same person or vehicle across multiple locations and times equated to a surveillance team. Cary had gotten a good look at the Audi's occupants, so tradecraft dictated that he assume the men had also gotten a good look at him in return. If the Audi's passengers saw him again, they would assume that Cary was a fellow espionage practitioner.

"Two, this is 1," Cary said, maintaining his interval with the southbound vehicle. "I'm on the most direct route to cross the railway station. I'm going to stay with the Audi, but not attempt to pass him. No change in your task—lock down that Sprinter van once he hits the south side of the bridge. If the Audi's still in play, we'll deal with it then."

"Roger that, boss," Jad said. "I'm set up at Grisham and oriented north time now. I've got line of sight to the south side of the bridge only. No sign of the van."

"One copies all," Cary said. "Bridge is about a klick south of my current location. You should be seeing the van in the next thirty seconds, over."

"Standing by," Jad said.

Ideally, Jad would be able to observe the entire length of the bridge, but finding a location that would allow him to do so hadn't been possible. The street swung to the southwest after exiting the bridge, bisecting two grassy areas heavily populated by thick stands of trees. In the trade-off between observing the bridge and observing the intersection south of the bridge, Cary had chosen the intersection. Setting up on the south side of the choke point would allow Jad to follow the van through several likely avenues of approach without giving away his presence.

This was the better tactical solution.

Even so, Cary would have loved to have eyes on the Chinese team right about now. Unfortunately, the Audi was keeping its distance, which meant Cary had to do the same.

Then Cary understood why.

Like the Green Berets, the Audi's occupants were professionals. This meant that unlike he and Jad, the two men ahead of him were most likely part of a larger surveillance effort, so they had no need to get closer to the Sprinter van.

This revelation did nothing to ease Cary's irritation.

But it did present an opportunity.

"Two, this is 1," Cary said. "Change of plan. I'm going to blow past the Audi and proceed to King to see if I can reestablish comms with Scepter. If the Chinese team is heading toward Scepter, I'll be able to acquire them. If not, I'm going to collapse onto Scepter's position to see what's happening there, over."

"One, this is 2," Jad said. "Copy all. Be advised, I tried to establish comms with Scepter from my location and was unsuccessful. Something doesn't feel right, boss."

"Agreed, 2," Cary said. "Ending surveillance time now."

Jad's transmission solidified Cary's resolve. While he didn't like abandoning the surveillance, Cary believed that larger forces were now in play. As a young Green

Beret, Cary had been the beneficiary of countless bits of wisdom doled out by his crusty seniors. Some aspects of that sage advice had been more useful than others, but one slogan had proven true time and time again. In an operation, there was no such thing as a coincidence. The Green Berets had lost communication with Jack's team at the same moment the Chinese men had vacated the hotel.

The game was afoot.

Cary pressed the accelerator to the floor.

German motorists weren't perfect, but they were much more likely to comply with traffic laws than their American contemporaries. This was especially true of the most sacrosanct traffic law of them all—the left lane was only for passing. Cary put on his left blinker and slid into the adjacent lane as he continued to add speed. The Volkswagen's underpowered engine voiced its displeasure with a sound that was more a squeal than a growl.

There were many things Cary loved about Europe.

Shopping cart–sized cars wasn't one of them.

Up ahead, the Audi crested the north side of the bridge.

"One, this is 2. The Sprinter just came off the bridge. Currently stopped at a light. Intersection of Kumpfmühler and Friedenstrasse, over."

"Roger that, 2," Cary said, barreling onto the bridge. "I'm gonna turn east at the intersection, then south on University before heading east toward Scepter's last known location, over."

"Two copies all. Be advised, Sprinter is moving through

the intersection . . . heading east on Friedenstrasse. I say again, east on Friedenstrasse, over."

The Chinese were taking the shortest route to the university. Cary had guessed correctly. The Audi edged into the fast lane, blowing by the slower-moving traffic.

Cary closed the distance further.

He was now only fifty meters from the station wagon.

The operation might just go according to plan after all.

Then the Audi's tire ruptured.

5

ONE MOMENT THE STATION WAGON WAS ZIPPING ACROSS THE bridge.

The next, its rear driver's-side tire blew in a cloud of smoke and chunks of rubber. Cary covered the brake with his foot, not yet knowing whether stopping in the current lane or accelerating into a different one would be the correct response. The effects of losing a tire at a high rate of speed could range from inconvenient to deadly, depending on the driver's reaction.

The Audi fishtailed for a millisecond as the car yawed right.

This was the moment of truth.

Steady hands and slow braking equaled an inconvenience.

The brake lights burned red, and the car jerked left as the driver overcorrected.

Then the station wagon was airborne.

Cary cursed as the car hurtled over the concrete-and-metal barrier separating the road from the elevated pedestrian walkway that ran the length of the bridge. The Audi's undercarriage snagged on the barrier, and the car rotated, smashing against concrete. For an instant Cary thought the station wagon would continue its roll, tumbling over the railing. But in a miracle of physics, the car balanced on the tubular steel, teetering toward the precipice, but not falling.

Yet.

Braking, Cary nosed his car to the left, blocking the fast lane as he activated his hazard lights. The groan of steel on steel greeted his arrival as the Audi rotated, its hood dropping toward the beckoning tracks. Cary slammed the transmission into park, hurtled the barrier, and ran toward the stricken car.

The metal tubing had embedded in the Audi's roof, preventing the car from falling, but also acting as a fulcrum. With the heavy engine and the weight of the passengers both located in the section of car closest to the drop, Cary knew it was only a matter of time before the Audi plunged over the side.

"Two, this is 1," Cary said as he sprinted for the Audi. "Forget the van—I need your help. Now."

"One, this is 2, roger that. What's up?"

"The Audi went off the road," Cary said. "They're balanced on the side of the bridge and—Fuck!"

As Cary drew even with the Audi, he could see beyond the vehicle for the first time. Or, more specifically, he could see what waited on the pedestrian walkway beyond the car. A man dressed in motorcycle gear stood next to an idling bike.

A man cradling a submachine gun.

His helmet's visor was open, revealing dark eyes that widened at Cary's sudden appearance. The submachine gun came up to the man's shoulder in one fluid movement.

Cary dove for the concrete as a burst of automatic fire ripped through the air.

"One, this is 2, say again, over."

"Gunman on the pedestrian walkway, east side of the bridge," Cary said, crawling toward the car on all fours. "He's facing north and doing his best to fill me full of holes, over."

"Two copies all. Sit tight, over."

Though Cary had the utmost faith in his spotter, he would be doing nothing of the sort. The gunman didn't have a direct bead on Cary, but he knew that advantage wouldn't last long. The shooter was already advancing toward the car. Covering the last few feet to the Audi in a crouch, Cary drew even with the driver's-side door as the automobile let out another long groan.

Cary paused, his fingers just short of the door handle, as he deliberated what effect he might have on the vehicle's equilibrium. The last thing he wanted to do was accidentally send the Audi slipping onto the tracks twenty feet below. Then an explosion of glass made the decision for him. If Cary did nothing, the shooter would kill the men inside the car and him along with them.

Better to go out swinging.

Wrenching open the door, Cary came face-to-face with the car's occupants. Both men were unconscious. Judging by the angle of his limp head, the passenger's neck was broken. While he wanted to help the crash victims, Cary knew his first task lay with neutralizing the shooter. Cary patted the driver's midsection and waist as another burst of automatic fire raked the car.

The passenger's body jerked as several rounds found their mark.

Cary resisted the urge to duck out of the Audi. If he didn't find what he was looking for, Cary would be sharing the passenger's fate. After a moment of pure terror, Cary's questing fingers touched the unmistakable hardness of a plastic polymer grip. Stripping the Glock from the man's holster, Cary sighted around the edge of the car and fired a quick pair at the still-advancing gunman. The gunman jerked but didn't fall. Instead, he took a knee and fired a more prolonged burst at the precariously perched SUV.

The shooter was wearing body armor.

Perfect.

"Two, this is 1," Cary said. "Be advised, the gunman's wearing body armor, over."

"Two copies all," Jad said. "Thirty seconds."

In addition to a penchant for getting on each other's nerves, the many long hours Cary had spent shoulder to shoulder with his best friend had yielded a much more valuable trait—trust. Cary didn't ask Jad what the fellow Green Beret was planning because he trusted his spotter.

Well, that and the fact that the car let out a prolonged groan as the hood dipped ever lower.

Cary didn't have thirty seconds.

After taking a steadying breath, Cary leaned around the car's bumper, using the vehicle frame to steady his arms. He found the crouching figure with the pistol's stubby front sight post and dropped the hammer. In the space of five seconds, Cary emptied half the magazine, scoring multiple hits to the gunman's torso with little effect.

At least little deadly effect.

As was often the case in gunfights, Cary's rapid, controlled, and accurate fire shifted the fight's psychological balance. With its longer barrel, higher rate of fire, and greater magazine capacity, the gunman's submachine gun was vastly superior to Cary's Glock, especially in a short-range engagement such as this one.

But head knowledge was not the same as heart knowledge.

The shooter gave in to his fear, crouching behind a metal barrier as Cary's 9-millimeter rounds kicked up concrete and pinged off steel. With a final flurry, Cary expended the remainder of the magazine. Tossing the pistol to the ground, he spider-crawled to the still-open driver's door even as the vehicle teetered toward the tracks. With a gunman intent on his death and the Audi threatening to drag him over the side, no one would have faulted Cary for just standing aside as fate took its course.

But Green Berets weren't much for standing aside.

Reaching into the wobbling car, Cary triggered the seatbelt release, hooked the driver under the armpits, and yanked. For a moment Cary thought he'd signed his death warrant. Like an overbalanced teeter-totter, the rear of the car rose as the nose tipped, pulling Cary into the air.

But rather than letting go of the driver, Cary doubled down.

Grabbing two fistfuls of the man's shirt, Cary jerked, throwing his weight into the effort. The driver slid free from the cabin just as the vehicle cartwheeled over the side to the accompaniment of shrieking steel and shattering glass. The man's slacks snagged on the door as the car fell, and the fabric parted with a rip, leaving Cary lying on the concrete with a pantsless man on his chest.

One of the things Cary loved most about being a Green Beret was the job's variety. No two days were ever the same. But right about now, Cary was thinking that a dull day or two might not be such a bad thing.

Cary rolled the man to the side, ignoring the concrete exploding just inches away. Cary sheltered the unconscious driver with his own body as he slid a spare magazine from the holder strapped to the man's belt, but Cary's fingers were moving too slow. He'd never get the driver's Glock back into action before the gunman fired the killing shot. Cary braced himself for the inevitable.

It never came.

Instead, his earbud crackled with a familiar voice speaking with an unfamiliar British accent.

"Tally-ho."

Cary was certain his spotter followed up the radio transmission with something equally idiotic, but he couldn't hear over the roaring of a 500cc engine. Jad appeared behind the shooter, streaking down the pedestrian walkway with all the speed the motorcycle could muster.

The gunman turned, raising the submachine gun.

Cary knew how this would end.

His spotter had made a valiant attempt to save Cary's life, but until he closed the distance to the shooter, Jad's weapons consisted of just shock and awe.

They weren't enough.

Scrambling to his feet, Cary charged the gunman, intending to bury his shoulder in the man's unprotected back. But even as his feet churned, covering the fifty yards separating them in distance-eating strides, Cary understood the futility of his effort. As with the precariously perched car, physics was not on his side.

The distance was just too great.

Even so, Cary continued his headlong rush.

Green Berets weren't much on quitting, either.

With less than five feet separating Cary from the gunman, something unexpected happened. Jad pulled a wheelie. As wheelies went, the stunt wasn't going to win any awards. Rather than the ramrod-straight form common on social media videos, Jad's wheelie was more parody than trick. The front tire hung in the air at an oblique angle as the bike wobbled from side to side.

But it was a wheelie all the same.

The psychological effect on the gunman was both immediate and pronounced.

While standing firm in the face of a racing motorcycle took some courage, Cary had to believe the gunman's distance from the bike and the submachine gun tucked into his shoulder helped to even the odds. His brain understood the danger posed by the four-hundred-pound machine, but it wasn't immediate. That assessment changed dramatically when he was confronted by a massive black tire hurtling toward him.

The shooter hesitated.

And then Cary was on him.

Cary piled into the gunman, driving from his legs as he envisioned his left shoulder snapping the man's spine in two. While he didn't quite manage that, the Green Beret drove the shooter into the ground, face-first. The submachine gun skittered across the pavement and Cary wound back his right hand with the intent of launching a hook into the man's kidney that would leave him pissing blood.

He didn't get the chance.

Instead, Cary found himself on the receiving end of a pointy elbow. Cary saw the blur of motion in time to get his arm up, but he didn't fully mitigate the blow. The gunman had twisted, throwing the elbow blindly but violently, and as was often the case in hand-to-hand engagements, naked aggression won the day. The elbow strike snapped Cary's head to the side. He'd diverted the killing strike from his temple, but the bone-on-bone contact still rang his bell. Cary sagged, fighting to maintain consciousness as the world spun. The man squirmed from beneath him, and Cary raised arms that felt like wet noodles in an attempt to shield himself from the kick he knew was coming.

Once again, physics was not on his side.

Then Jad was beside him.

The bike's roar rattled Cary's fillings as his spotter dumped the motorcycle to join the fray. The gunman's dark eyes hardened. Then he vaulted over the railing into space.

With a groan, Cary grabbed hold of the railing and pulled himself to unsteady feet. He peered over the edge in time to see the gunman scrambling down from the crushed car onto the stone-lined rail yard.

"Oh, no you didn't," Jad said.

Cary turned to see that his spotter had appropriated the gunman's submachine gun. Jad was taking the slack out of the trigger when a shouted command rang through the air.

"Halt."

Turning, Cary saw a flood of blue as an army of *polizei* advanced on the Green Berets. An army equipped with a variety of sidearms, all of which were pointed at the Americans.

"Let him go," Cary said, "and put the gun down. Nice and easy."

Jad gave a pained sigh, but he did as he was told, setting the submachine gun on the ground. "I was really looking forward to putting one into that douchebag's cranium."

"Cheer up," Cary said as he sank to his knees with his hands over his head, "I'm sure we'll be back on the street in no time."

"Think so?"

"Nope," Cary said. "But after that sad attempt at a wheelie, I figured you could use the encouragement."

If Jad had an equally witty reply, he didn't voice it. Perhaps because it was hard to speak with a *polizei*'s knee in your back. As Cary's arms were wrenched behind him to a chorus of shouted German, he had a final thought.

With Jack Ryan, Jr., no operation was ever routine.

6

SUBMACHINE GUNS WEREN'T DESIGNED FOR LONG-RANGE ENGAGE-
ments. Unlike traditional assault rifles, the Chinese
CS/LS06 was not equipped with a long rifle barrel because the pistol ammunition it fired didn't have the
requisite gunpowder to engage a target at ranges greater
than about one hundred yards.

That was fine.

In fully automatic mode, the CS/LS06 spit out a
mind-numbing eight hundred rounds per minute, and its
distinctive top-mounted helical magazine carried fifty
9-millimeter rounds. The weapon was perfect for situations when the work was up close and personal.

Situations like this one.

The gunman extended the weapon. Jack threw himself from the bike, aiming for the bushes to his left even
as he cradled his head between his forearms. He registered the spitting sound of a suppressed weapon firing on
automatic and then was tumbling through the brush.

Limbs cracked as Jack's superior mass and acceleration made short work of the landscaping.

Until he encountered a beech tree.

Jack had the sense of colliding with something large even as his head pinballed in the fortress he'd created with his arms.

Then everything got hazy.

Jack came to in phases.

Sound intruded into the mental morass in the form of unfamiliar voices that dragged him from his half-consciousness. Then his nerve endings prodded him the rest of the way awake as his battered body reminded him why motorcyclists wore protective equipment.

Jack opened his eyes and groaned.

He was flat on his back, staring into a cloudless blue sky. That was the good news. The bad news was that everything hurt.

Everything.

With deliberate slowness, Jack wiggled his fingers and toes. He wasn't paralyzed and nothing seemed to be broken. On the not-so-positive side of the ledger, Jack was once again looking down the barrel of a gun. Two guns, to be precise. And the guns in question, Heckler & Kochs if Jack were to guess, belonged to a pair of German *polizei*. Jack breathed a sigh of relief that sounded suspiciously like another groan. German *polizei* were known for their professionalism.

He was in good hands.

The officer closest to Jack's head popped off with a stream of largely indecipherable Deutsch. Jack knew a bit of the language, but the man's Southern Bavarian accent was giving Jack a run for his money. Or perhaps it was his pounding head. Either way, Jack's brain wasn't doing such a good job rendering the sound into something understandable.

"Sprechen Sie Englisch?" Jack said as he moved to touch his face, trying to determine if the sticky sensation along his right cheekbone was blood or sap. Unfortunately, the second policeman did not respond favorably to Jack's unexpected movement. In a blur of motion, the *polizei* snared Jack's wrist and pinned his limb into an arm bar.

"On your stomach," the German said, transferring the arm bar into a respectable shoulder lock.

Jack complied, hissing through gritted teeth.

Besides their professionalism, the German *polizei* were famous for something else—making short work of those who chose not to follow their instructions. That Jack hadn't understood didn't seem to make any difference. The operative portion of Jack's brain evaluated the joint lock's effectiveness even as he rolled onto his stomach. His combatives instructors had been some of the best in the business. This guy could give them a run for their money.

Or maybe that was just his bruised ego talking.

Between the tiny spots of light still dancing in his vision and his pounding head and aching body, Jack wasn't in a position to make trouble for anyone.

"Keep your pants on," Jack said. "I'm complying."

The policeman responded with the compassion Jack

should have expected from a German law enforcement officer. The man ratcheted Jack's arm so that it was nearly vertical, handcuffed one wrist, and then quickly secured the second. Only after he'd securely latched the metal bracelets did the *polizei* inquire about Jack's health.

"Can you stand?" the officer said in accented but understandable English.

"Not sure," Jack said, "I—"

Before he was finished speaking, Jack was hauled to his feet.

In addition to being efficient, the men were strong. Very strong. The sudden change in orientation set the world to spinning, and Jack staggered, allowing the officer closest to him to catch his weight. Then the two *polizei* were propelling Jack toward their patrol car.

As he walked, Jack got his first look at the scene of his short-lived engagement with the kidnappers. The parking lot was empty and there was no trace of either the kidnapper's motorbike or the Sprinter van. Jack's bike lay against the stone wall that had saved his life, while a trail of crushed branches marked his inglorious dismount.

"Why am I being arrested?" Jack said.

The German on his left replied with a string of Deutsch. Once he paused, his partner took over.

"Englisch, bitte," Jack said, but the policemen seemed to have lost their multilingual talents as quickly as they'd earlier found them. With a final blast of incomprehensible instructions, the man on Jack's left opened the rear passenger door, while the one on the right pushed Jack inside.

Then the door slammed shut and he was alone.

"Good afternoon."

Or maybe not.

Jack struggled into a sitting position. The front passenger seat was occupied by a man with close-cropped gray hair and glasses. A man who didn't seem at all surprised that Jack had just been dumped into the rear of his car.

"Who are you?" Jack said.

"That question is not relevant," the man said in German-accented English, "but I will tell you. You may address me as Hans."

Jack couldn't see the man's face, nor did Hans make any effort to turn around. Instead, the man kept his head down as he fiddled with something in his lap, apparently waiting for Jack to lead the conversation.

"Nice to meet you, Hans," Jack said. "Why have I been arrested?"

"Who said you have been arrested?" Hans said. "This is just a casual conversation between fellow professionals."

"Then why the cuffs?" Jack said.

"Because ours is a unique profession."

"I don't follow," Jack said.

"Of course you do," Hans said, "but to avoid the tedium of the cat-and-mouse game that is sure to follow, let me cut to the chase, as you Americans like to say. I am a member of the Federal Office for the Protection of the Constitution's Department 4, which means I focus on counterintelligence. You are an American intelligence officer illegally operating in my country. I am prepared to overlook this illegality so that we can engage in a candid conversation."

"While I'm in handcuffs?" Jack said.

"I said I would overlook the illegality," Hans said. "Not forgive it. One of my men is dead. Another is fighting for his life. Count yourself fortunate this conversation is being conducted in such a civil manner."

"I'm not responsible for what happened to your men," Jack said, squirming to take the pressure off his hands. The combination of the steel clasps biting into his wrists and his body weight driving the handcuffs into his flesh was cutting off his circulation.

"Not you directly," Hans said, "but the two team members of yours I have in custody suggest otherwise. At a minimum, you could have brought me into your operation. Perhaps things would have turned out differently."

Jack kept silent as he thought.

While it was clear that Hans was a member of BfV, the German equivalent of the FBI when it came to counterespionage investigations, everything else felt murky. As Jack's jammed communications could attest, the Asian man's rendition was not a random kidnapping. The technology, tactical coordination, and weapons the kidnappers had employed aside, the abduction had a brazen quality that wasn't usually practiced by traditional intelligence operatives. The event had gone down in broad daylight in the middle of a college campus, not some Karachi back alley. An operation this flashy meant one of two things—either the participants were amateurs or the rendition fell into the category of high risk/high reward.

Jack was betting on the latter.

"What do you want?" Jack said, hunching forward.

"Vengeance," Hans said, adjusting the rearview mirror so that he could see Jack eye to eye. "When this conversation concludes, I will have the distinct pleasure of informing a young mother of two that she is now a widow. I'll then make a trip to the Regensburg hospital to watch a man fight for his life. This travesty occurred because my government allowed it."

"How so?" Jack said.

"In 2016, China became our largest trading partner," Hans said. "Today, the combined value of imports and exports exchanged between our two nations exceeds two hundred fifty billion U.S. dollars. The politicians who run my nation have decided to avert their eyes from some of the more unsavory aspects of our Chinese relationship in order to keep euros flowing into our coffers. My supervisor will expect me to sweep what happened today under the rug."

"Will you?" Jack said.

"A man is dead for the crime of doing his job," Hans said.

"Then go after the kidnappers," Jack said.

"You do not understand," Hans said. "We knew the abduction was going to take place."

"How?"

"The Chinese told us."

Jack shook his head, certain he'd misheard. "The

Chinese told you that they were going to kidnap one of your citizens, and you did nothing?"

"Not our citizen," Hans said. "The man who was taken was Chinese. His name is Wang Lei. He'd been living in Germany for the last five years as an expat. As you can imagine, this means little to the Chinese Communist Party."

Jack nodded.

The CCP's rendition program was infamous. Targets for the Ministry of State Security, or MSS, snatch teams ran the gamut from billionaires wanted for fraud to dissidents. In years past, the Chinese had limited these renditions to countries more willing to turn a blind eye, but as of late, the MSS had extended their operational portfolio to Western nations. Rumor had it that one rendition had even taken place on U.S. soil, though Jack couldn't imagine his father tolerating such an act.

Even so, it was one thing for an MSS team to clandestinely persuade a Chinese national to leave the country in their company. It was something else entirely to announce that a rendition would be taking place to the host nation. If what Hans was saying was true, the Chinese had significantly upped the stakes, especially since a member of the team had greeted Jack with a burst from his submachine gun.

"You're just going to let this stand?" Jack said.

"I am talking to you," Hans said.

"Look," Jack said, "I'm as sympathetic to the plight of Chinese dissidents as the next guy, but this isn't my fight."

"You are wrong," Hans said. "The kidnapped scientist is a Chinese citizen, but his brother, Zhang Wei, is American. An American scientist."

Now Hans had Jack's attention.

"You think the Chinese kidnapped Wang Lei as leverage over his brother?" Jack said.

"Perhaps you should ask him," Hans said.

"What do you mean?" Jack said.

"Zhang Wei just happens to be in town."

7

MARIO REYES HATED FISH.

The taste of their rancid flesh, the feel of their slimy bodies, and most of all their smell. The odor seemed to crawl up his nostrils and take residence in his sinuses, coating the passages with oily sediment. The smell made him want to vomit, and once he'd had the misfortune of inhaling it, fish stench would stay with him for days, soiling every meal and desecrating every experience.

This was a problem.

Mario lived and worked just kilometers from one of the largest fishing ports in the world. His family were fishermen, and his customers almost all made their living on the sea.

Mario was surrounded by the thing he hated most.

No, that wasn't quite true.

While Mario absolutely detested fish, his greatest hat-red was reserved for the place at which they were collected—Navotas Fish Port Complex.

The place where he was now headed.

Mario paid off the cab with a handful of Philippine pesos and waved the man away. As a successful banker who financed a good portion of the fishing fleet that called the port home, Mario did not have to take public transportation. His driver, Alejandro, would have been happy to chauffeur Mario to the port in his stately Range Rover, or if Mario had been craving a little adventure, he could have made the trip in his Bentley Continental GT. Mario did neither, precisely because of the stench now assaulting his nasal passages.

Business might dictate that Mario had to visit the fishery, but he endeavored to bring as little of it home with him as possible. This was why the tires of Mario's luxury cars would never turn onto Palengke Street. It was also why he was dressed in faded jeans and a T-shirt rather than the suit he normally wore to the office. No amount of washing would rid his garments of the essence of fish that would become embedded in their fibers after even a single visit.

"Ginoo, ginoo."

Mario ignored the child beggar as he angled past the rusted buildings belonging to various fishing companies, stepping over the ever-present puddles. As a boy, Mario had crewed his father's boat, as was expected of each of his four male siblings. But while his brothers had accepted the nautical life as their eventuality, Mario had not. If anything, his stomach-churning sessions on the water had instilled in him the drive necessary to escape this life. With every backbreaking day, every evening spent gutting the catch, Mario had vowed that this existence would not be his.

He would escape the ocean.

He'd half succeeded.

Mario was not a fisherman, but the sea still funded his livelihood.

"Magandang araw."

Mario nodded at the greeting shouted from a storefront.

Even at this hour, the complex teemed with activity. Workers in T-shirts, shorts, and the obligatory rubber boots were sorting fish, arranging overflowing buckets, spraying down the constantly bloody concrete, and scrubbing away offal-filled puddles. Mario was a recognizable figure to many of the laborers.

While he'd detested the way in which his father had made a living, Mario had adopted the man's work ethic. Unlike many of his contemporaries, who were content to pore over spreadsheets from the comfort of air-conditioned offices in the Makati Central Business District, Mario preferred to see his investments with his own two eyes. With his slim build and ordinary features, there was nothing imposing about Mario, but dockworkers made way when they saw his salt-and-pepper hair all the same. Though if he were to be truthful, Mario would have to admit that some of this deference stemmed more from his business associates than from his banking prowess.

Associates like the man Mario was coming to see.

"Mar, it is good to see you."

As if summoned from Mario's thoughts, a figure stepped from the shadow enclave offered by the salt-stained overhang. Rail-thin, with dark eyes and a commanding voice, the man's given name was Ramon, but his friends called him Mon Mon.

Everyone else used the honorific Mr. Garza.

Like Mario, Ramon had been raised on a fishing boat, but while Mario had pursued a somewhat legitimate path to wealth at the prestigious Asian Institute of Management, Mon Mon had earned his degree in the port's hard streets and dark back alleys. He was dressed in the collared shirt and slacks of a businessman, but his business made the gutting of fish seem like a pleasant pastime.

Mon Mon was *mambubutang*. A gangster and the undisputed lord of the port.

He was also Mario's cousin.

"Good to see you, Mon Mon," Mario said, accepting an offered handshake.

Though the majority of Mario's business was legitimate, completely honest businessmen were rare in Navotas. Like ports the world over, the complex was a center of gravity for smuggling and the organized crime that went with it. Corruption was a long and storied tradition in the Philippines, and criminal tendrils reached from the dockworker charged with off-loading contraband all the way up to the office of the president and its occupant. Unlike many, Mario had made the decision to focus on lawful commerce for the most part, but there were still aspects of his trade that required interaction with the darker side of life and the people who inhabited it.

People like Mon Mon.

"You as well, cousin," Mon Mon said.

Though handshakes in the Philippines were traditionally soft, as with much of the rest of Asia, Mario could feel the bones in his hand shift beneath his cousin's grip. Mon Mon was fascinated by all things Western in general and American in particular. He was an aficionado of gangster movies and loved surprising the unwary with a handshake that would leave the recipient with a reminder of the encounter for days.

Mario gripped his cousin right back, giving as good as he got.

They might be family, but Mon Mon was a predator, and predators sought out weakness. Mario wanted to ensure that his relative found none here.

"Come in, come in," Mon Mon said after the squeezing contest was over. "There's something I need you to see."

Mario nodded and followed the taller man into the warehouse, even as he steeled himself for what might be waiting. Mon Mon had offered Mario access to his greater criminal organization on multiple occasions, and each time the banker had declined. While he was happy to finance his cousin's fleet of boats, including some that were clearly built for smuggling rather than fishing, Mario drew the line when it came to outright criminal ventures.

Seeming to recognize that access to a legitimate

source of cash was to his advantage, Mon Mon had accepted Mario's refusal with grace. But each time he turned down an overture, Mario couldn't help but think that one day he'd be presented with an offer he couldn't refuse.

Perhaps today was that day.

"It's over here," Mon Mon said, shepherding Mario through the dimly lit room. "One of my crews found it tangled in their nets. I didn't know what to do with it, but I thought you might."

Part of Mario's worry about being strong-armed into Mon Mon's business dissipated, replaced by another concern. As a private banker, Mario did more than just extend much-needed capital to the fisherman who plied the ocean. His successful business had garnered him a reputation.

A standing in society.

Mario was a fixer of sorts.

Not the sort of fixing that came via envelopes stuffed with cash. Instead, Mario traded favors. As someone who ran a mostly clean enterprise, Mario had stature and the political clout that accompanied it. He knew people and was often sought out for his influence as much as for his money.

Mario followed his cousin to a relatively dry corner of the warehouse, where a trio of men were clustered around a workbench. At a word from Mon Mon, the fishermen stepped aside, and Mario caught his first look at what had dragged him down to the fishery at this hour of the night.

He froze.

The object lying on the scarred wooden planks was not a dead body, as Mario had feared. Neither was it crates of contraband or drugs. Instead, the single light above the workbench illuminated a long, cylindrical metal tube. The cylinder looked vaguely like a missile of some sort, with skin painted the gray color of the sea, a nose cone at the front, a pair of finlike wings mid-body, and a tiny propeller protruding from the rear.

Mario's hesitation reflected his worry that Mon Mon's fisherman had uncovered some sort of munition, but a second look disabused him of that notion. The cylinder was too narrow to be a bomb. Nor did its propeller seem large enough to drive the device to high speeds like a torpedo. Mario was still no closer to understanding what he was seeing, but he was also confident that it wasn't going to kill him.

Reasonably confident.

"What is it?" Mario said, turning to Mon Mon.

"Not sure," Mon Mon said, "but the crew found this."

Mario followed Mon Mon's pointing finger and discovered that *this* seemed to be an access panel. The waterproof metal casing enclosing the panel was open, exposing a series of ports, a small LCD screen, and several rubber buttons. Mario looked closer, examining the stenciled lettering above the ports. He couldn't make out the words, but he certainly knew the language.

Mandarin.

"What do you think?" Mon Mon said.

Instead of answering, Mario took out his cell phone and began snapping pictures. He captured the entirety of the cylinder, but devoted most of his attention to the access panel and the Mandarin characters. Only after he was satisfied with his work did Mario turn back to his cousin.

"I think you've discovered something potentially valuable . . . to the right person," Mario said.

"Do you know such a person?" Mon Mon said.

"I might," Mario said, thinking of a certain American. An American who paid Mario for information about the goods and people that moved clandestinely through the Navotas port. "Who else knows about this?"

Mon Mon gestured toward the trio of men. "The fishing crew and these guys. All men I can trust."

Mario had his doubts about that. If even half of the rumors about his cousin were true, Mario knew that Mon Mon was not the sort of boss who inspired loyalty. Fear was a great motivator, but only until something more terrifying came along. According to Mario's contact in the Philippine National Police, another gangster might very well be vying for Mon Mon's turf.

But Mario didn't say this.

Instead, he nodded.

"I'll put out some feelers," Mario said. "Give me a day or so. In the meantime, my advice would be to keep a tight watch on this thing."

"This is my warehouse," Mon Mon said. "Nowhere in Manila is safer."

Mario nodded again, declining to argue the point.

Instead, he opened his Signal app and selected a text thread. He typed out a quick message, attached the photographs, and hit send. He thought about admonishing the American to hurry, but didn't.

This device, like his cousin's tenuous hold on the market, was not Mario's problem.

At least that's what he told himself.

8

JACK SAT BENEATH A LEAFY CANOPY, STARING AT A FIELD OF DEATH as he considered his options.

None of them were good.

Jack had spent the last hour or so putting distance between himself and the kidnapping debacle. Fortunately, the BfV officer, Hans, had seemed to be just as ready to be rid of Jack. After delivering his cryptic remark, Hans had gestured at one of the *polizei* standing respectfully just out of listening distance. Or maybe not so respectfully, based on the look the German officer shot Jack.

Jack understood.

Truces between rival intelligence services were all well and good, but local law enforcement often had to deal with the repercussions when these cease-fires didn't turn out as planned.

Repercussions like newly fatherless children.

The officer had opened the passenger door and helped Jack out of the cruiser. *Helped* might have been too strong a word, as the strapping German kept Jack from falling, but he wasn't exactly gentle about it. An iron fist clamped down on Jack's biceps in a none-too-subtle reminder of how the police officer wanted this interaction to conclude.

After a deluge of German from Hans, the officer relaxed his grip.

Slightly.

Once he was certain Jack was standing, the man unfastened the handcuffs.

"You are free to go," the *polizei* said, though his flinty blue eyes suggested otherwise.

Jack nodded as he massaged his wrists. He turned to have a final word with Hans, but realized he was wasting his time. The BMW smoothly accelerated away from the curb, leaving Jack to ponder what exactly the BfV operative hadn't said as much as what he had. Jack needed time to think, but this wasn't the place. He'd struck out north, walking along the sidewalk that paralleled Universitätsstrasse until he'd come to the Oberer Katholischer Friedhof, or Upper Catholic Cemetery. Only after losing himself among the sea of tombstones had Jack felt secure enough to grab a bench shaded by a cluster of trees and consider his next steps.

During their brief interaction, Hans had insinuated much, but offered little proof. Maybe the intelligence officer had evidence linking Jad and Cary to Jack and maybe he didn't. Either way, Jack wasn't going to make the man's job any easier by touching base with his team within electronic or audible earshot of the *polizei*. Stirring the pot was a tried-and-true counterespionage technique. Jack was determined to create space between himself and anyone possibly associated with the German government before reestablishing communication with his folks.

Jack did a quick visual sweep of the cemetery as he pulled out his phone.

Though sitting on a bench surrounded by gravestones was a bit morbid, the cemetery was a great location for regrouping after a potentially burned operation. People were expected to linger, the groomed grass and vegetation offered unobstructed sight lines, and the sprawling complex had multiple ingress and egress points from all four cardinal directions.

In the pre-Internet days, tombstones were a valuable source for information that could be turned into aliases. A wayward spy could find a deceased member of the appropriate sex and of a similar age and use their personal data to craft a cover identity. Though computer algorithms now rendered this kind of subterfuge moot, the cemetery's physical attributes still made the location a desirable stop for fellow espionage professionals. Cathy Ryan loved to say that the more things changed, the more they remained the same.

Once again, the world-class ophthalmic surgeon was prescient.

Thumbing the weather app on his phone's home

screen, Jack waited two seconds before pressing and holding the down volume button as he cycled the phone's mute button.

A moment later a hidden encrypted chat window appeared.

As per Campus standard operating procedure, or SOP, Jack was diverting to the briefed alternate means of communication. In this case, it was a secure app Gavin had designed with low-profile operations in mind. As with his decision to vacate the university, Jack was switching to backup comms out of an abundance of caution. Other than the brief interruption due to what was probably broad-spectrum jamming, Jack had no indication that his team's secure radio transmissions had been compromised.

But in the profession of espionage, safe always beat sorry.

The first message in the text stream was from Lisanne.

Continuing the mission with Socrates.

Exactly the correct decision.

The Chinese researcher's kidnapping had been one hell of a triggering event. Though Jack didn't believe any of the MSS operatives had remained on station, that didn't mean his adversaries hadn't employed another means of low-profile surveillance. If he were in their place, Jack would have positioned a few cameras to capture the crowd's reaction to the kidnapping with the hopes of identifying members of the opposing team. To Lisanne's credit, she'd instantly understood this predicament and had elected to stay put after the dust had cleared rather than exit the university, as Jack had done.

Brains and beauty.

Which brought to mind the admonishment his mother had delivered to her wayward son.

Marry that girl before someone else does.

With a smile, Jack found himself considering just that. Which only served to reinforce a different set of instructions conveyed in John Clark's gravelly tone.

Do not work with someone you love.

As if a Chinese direct-action team and a kidnapped scientist weren't enough to worry about. Another message popped up on the message stream.

Reaper elements are PZ clean.

So Jad and Cary were also now clear of the *polizei*.

Though the Green Berets were new to The Campus, they were hardly strangers to low-profile operations. China fell within the mission set of the 5th Special Forces Group and the men had been training for the looming conflict with the Asian powerhouse by practicing their tactics, techniques, and procedures in denied environments like South Korea. Rather than head back to the university, the commandos had taken up residence in a coffee shop in Regensburg proper. Jack's team had reacted to the unexpected event like pros.

Now they just needed instructions.

Instructions from him.

With a sigh, Jack thumbed in a response.

Scepter acknowledges all. Anticipate change of mission. Stand by for instructions.

Replies from Lisanne and the commandos popped up moments later.

Now that he'd reestablished communication, Jack was truly out of excuses to avoid what needed to be done next. In the past, Jack had often lived by the maxim that it was better to beg for forgiveness than to ask for permission.

Now he was a team leader.

As a singleton operative, Jack might have been able to rationalize rash decisions. This was no longer the case. Responsibility went hand in hand with the autonomy that had been granted to him. His butt was no longer the only one hanging in the breeze. Clark had trusted Jack with overseeing this operation. He would not betray that trust. Jack did the time conversion in his head even as he selected Clark's number. Noon Germany time equated to six a.m. in Alexandria, Virginia.

Here's to hoping Mr. C. had already consumed the day's first cup of coffee.

9

"CLARK."

"Hey, Mr. C.," Jack said. "It's me."

The familiar exchange brought the ghost of a smile to Jack's lips. How many times had he and John Clark begun a conversation this same way? Then Jack's gaze settled on the rows of tombstones and his mirth faded. Jack's adventures might begin innocently, but they seldom ended that way. For a moment, Jack was lying on a dark, rain-soaked North Korean hillside, body to body with Jad and Cary as bullets snapped by his head.

Jack and The Campus had been lucky more often than not.

But even the best luck eventually ran out.

"Junior? Can you hear me?"

With a start Jack realized that Clark had been talking while he'd been woolgathering. Never a good thing to do with the former Rainbow commanding officer, especially at six a.m.

"Yes, sir," Jack said, "sorry about that. I need to give you a sitrep and get authorization for a follow-on mission."

"A second training iteration?" Clark said.

"No, Mr. C.," Jack said. "Real-world. Here's what went down."

For the next several minutes Jack brought his boss up to speed. To his credit, Clark allowed Jack to finish without interruption. Jack was asking permission before embarking on one of his infamous crusades, and Clark was calmly listening.

The end times must really be near.

"That's where we stand," Jack said, transitioning from the sitrep portion of the conversation. "I recommend we flex to the brother and interview him."

"You think the Chinese are going to attempt to rendition a U.S. citizen?" Clark said.

Jack sighed. "Based on what I've seen in open-source reporting, I wouldn't think so. Then again, the op I just witnessed wasn't exactly clandestine. It also fits with Tel Aviv."

Jack eyed the scars on his forearm as he spoke.

"The FBI's had Dr. Schweigart on their radar since she returned from Israel," Clark said. "She was under constant surveillance for the first several months, but the counterintelligence agents assigned to her case saw zero Chinese activity. My understanding is that she gets random check-ins from the local field office, but as far as the Bureau's concerned, the matter is closed. More important, your father raised the issue directly with the Chinese president. Mary Pat said that your old man spelled out to Chen in no uncertain terms what would happen if the MSS attempted something like this again."

Dr. Rebecka Schweigart was a scientist with a doctorate in applied physics. A scientist whose expertise in material science had yielded a series of coatings that could be tuned to either scatter or transmit RF energy. In layman's terms, she'd discovered stealth in a bottle. The MSS had attempted to co-opt Becka in order to gain access to her research. When she'd refused, a Chinese paramilitary operative had tried to kill her. Jack had stopped the assassination attempt, and his father had escalated the issue.

Case closed.

Unless it wasn't.

While Jack understood his father's propensity for straight talk, he thought this might be something different. The Chinese were famous for playing the long game. While targeted assassinations were off the table as long as the elder Ryan was President, that didn't mean the Chinese Communist Party had renounced their intentions to steal American technology.

In fact, Jack expected that the opposite was probably true.

"I'm wondering if this might be a different approach to the problem posed by scientists like Dr. Schweigart," Jack said. "We know Zhang Wei is a scientist, but not much else until Gavin finishes his research. Still, I wouldn't be surprised if the American is the real target. The BfV officer I talked with intimated as much."

"The Chinese are using the kidnapped brother as leverage? For what? So the American will defect?" Clark said.

"Maybe," Jack said, "maybe not. It depends on the nature of Wei's work. If he is working on something sensitive, maybe the CCP wants him to remain in place."

"To act as a mole?" Clark said. "I guess that's a possibility."

"Fits with the idea of the Chinese playing the long game," Jack said. "Maybe the MSS figures the American's access to technical programs is worth more than his knowledge. We won't know for sure until I talk with him."

"Someone needs to talk with him," Clark said, "but I don't think it's you."

"Why not?" Jack said.

"Between the FBI legate, CIA officers, and the DIA, there are no shortage of qualified people already in-country to interview the scientist. Campus assets are finite—it's my job to make sure they're used appropriately."

"You have something else for me?" Jack said.

"For your entire team," Clark said. "I think you should head for Manila."

"Why?"

"Not over the phone," Clark said. "Check your secure Campus email."

Jack paused as something occurred to him.

Mr. C. had said *I think*.

"Hey, Mr. C.," Jack said, the words feeling strange on his tongue, "just so I'm tracking, are you asking or telling me to drop the scientist?"

Contrary to what Jack expected, the ensuing silence was neither ominous nor lengthy. If anything, Clark's voice conveyed a sense of confusion.

"Son, you're a team leader now," Clark said. "I don't make a practice of telling my team leaders what to do. If you think interviewing the scientist is the best use of your team, do it. You're the on-the-ground commander. I'm just a has-been in the rear with the gear."

Jack knew that Clark was no such thing, but he also greatly appreciated the sentiment. As team leader, the tactical decisions were Jack's, with the expectation that responsibility for the outcomes of those decisions accompanied Jack's newfound autonomy. After taking a breath, Jack gave his answer.

"Roger that, Mr. C.," Jack said. "We're pulling up stakes here. I'll be en route to Nuremberg Airport with the team in under an hour and connect with Gavin to get high-side access to your email summary. We're headed for Manila."

"Good hunting," Clark said. "Out here."

Clark disconnected, leaving Jack feeling like his dad had just tossed him the keys to his '65 Mustang.

Jack just hoped he brought the old girl home in one piece.

10

COMMANDER CHRISTINA DIXON FACED A TOUGH CHOICE.

This was not a novel situation.

The thirty-seven-year-old petite blonde had been facing tough choices ever since the Naval Academy recruiter had shown up unannounced at the championship lacrosse match during her junior year of high school. The match in which Christina had scored three goals and in the process cemented an offer to play for the mecca of college lacrosse—Johns Hopkins University. A school known for its academics as well as athletic excellence. A school her mother and father had both attended. A school Christina had set her sights on as a six-year-old wearing her father's Hopkins lacrosse jersey while watching his alma mater advance to the NCAA Final Four.

At the conclusion of the match, the Hopkins coach had approached Christina with the full ride she'd been expecting. It shouldn't have been a hard decision. And perhaps it wouldn't have been, had it not been for the naval officer in pressed whites waiting on the sidelines. A naval officer with an offer—play lacrosse for the Naval Academy instead.

A tough choice.

In a decision that surprised Christina and shocked her parents, she'd forsaken Johns Hopkins for Annapolis, and in so doing committed herself to years more of hard choices. A degree in political science rather than premed. Submarines rather than aviation. Fast attack rather than boomers. Now, fifteen years later, Christina's hard choices had borne fruit. As the captain of a *Virginia*-class attack submarine, Christina was one of the fewer than one hundred female submarine officers and the only one to command her own boat. She was quite simply at the very top of her game, enjoying the benefits of a succession of hard choices that had begun on a lacrosse field as a seventeen-year-old girl.

Now she faced what was perhaps her hardest choice to date.

"Status," Christina said, the word both a question and a command.

Captaining a submarine was a daunting task.

Unlike her surface-warfare contemporaries, Christina did not take her orders in the form of coded light signals from an admiral ensconced in the bowels of an aircraft carrier. She wasn't part of a larger fleet maneuvering across the ocean in a thundering display of American warfighting power. Instead, Christina was a lone wolf. A nuclear-powered predator, prowling the ocean's depths in search of hostile submarines. As such, Christina was given an astonishing amount of leeway in the manner in which she accomplished her mission.

Except she was now on the precipice of discarding the orders she'd received from COMSUBPAC, or Commander, Submarine Force, Pacific, altogether.

"Contact S-47 remains the same," the senior chief said as he eyed the sonar display. "Bearing 270, range two thousand yards. Speed holding steady at seven knots. Contact appears to be paralleling our course."

The ever-changing "waterfall" on the senior chief's monitor could have been a look into the Matrix, for all the sense it made to the uninformed. The display represented the sounds and bearings to contacts discovered by the sub's very capable sonar systems, but the readings were not easy to decipher. Fortunately, Senior Chief Petty Officer Bill Davis was in charge of the boat's contingent of enlisted sonar technicians. As such, he was an expert on the high-powered computers that rendered the array of acoustic inputs garnered by the USS *Delaware*'s multiple sonar sensors into intelligible data.

Unlike its predecessors, the *Delaware* featured both low- and high-frequency towed sonar arrays as well as optic arrays mounted to the hull to complement the traditional bow-mounted passive/active spherical sonar. Lots of attention was paid to a *Virginia*-class submarine's ability to operate undetected in the ocean's depths, and for good reason. But fewer people understood the advances in the sub's ability to detect and classify targets.

Targets like the one currently shadowing them.

"Put-up-or-shut-up time, Senior Chief," Christina said. "What are we looking at?"

Bill pushed back the glasses precariously perched at the end of his nose before answering. The gesture was one any middle-aged submariner might make. Contact lenses were impractical on a submarine, so many of the older crew members relied on readers.

But Christina knew her sailors well enough to understand that this was not what Bill's gesture signified. Bill Davis was a rarity. An enlisted technician who'd earned both an undergrad and master's degree from the Ohio State University before joining the Navy. Bill wasn't waiting to render judgment because he wanted to look at the screen one more time.

He was cautious because he was a scientist and scientists didn't like to be wrong.

Unfortunately for Bill, the mystery contact had been proving them wrong all morning.

"I don't think it's noise, Captain," Bill said, his diction slow but firm. "We've run three diagnostics on the sensor packages. Each test came back clean. I've cross-referenced the anomaly using two of our sonar arrays independently. If I didn't know what I was looking for, I doubt I'd have noticed it among the background noise."

"It's not marine life?" Christina said.

Bill shook his head. "That was my guess at first, too. But let me show you this."

Bill's fingers flew across his keyboard.

Unlike the *Los Angeles*–class submarines in which Christina had cut her teeth, the *Virginia* system architecture was one hundred percent digital and therefore interconnected. At her captain's station, Christina could pull up any of the ship's systems in the form of configurable pages, much like the multipurpose displays that had transformed aircraft cockpits from analog to digital.

Truthfully, Christina had found the new flexibility a bit too captivating. With the entirety of her boat at her fingertips, she had to resist the urge to bypass her people in favor of searching for the answers to her questions herself. The USS *Delaware* might be one massive computer, but it was also a submarine that displaced almost eight thousand tons of water, not a hobby drone.

"Here's an example of some faint biologicals the system picked up earlier," Bill said, breaking into Christina's thoughts. "The amplitude and frequency match, but the variability doesn't. Living organisms are unpredictable when studied at this level of detail. Even a person pacing back and forth across the floor would look widely divergent to our algorithms. Not so with the anomaly. It's too regular. Has to be man-made."

"What do you think, XO?" Christina said, turning to the lanky man standing beside her.

Unlike Bill, who could have easily been mistaken for a lecturer at a leading university's computer science department, Lieutenant Commander Dan Young was a sailor's sailor. Though he'd also earned an undergraduate in engineering, Dan had eschewed the technical path followed by ship engineers for the command track. He was a ship driver through and through, as evidenced by the rendition of the Jolly Rogers on his right biceps. Though he would never swing from a rope with a cutlass clenched between his teeth, Dan epitomized the killer instinct necessary to successfully command a fast attack sub.

His thoughts were always a useful counterpart to Bill's more deliberate musings.

"If you'd asked me an hour ago, I'd have said the anomaly was whale farts or a glitch in Senior Chief's Matrix," Dan said.

Her XO voiced his opinion with the calm, steady tone Christina had come to expect, but he'd also deliberately caged his tone low enough that his comments wouldn't carry beyond their ad hoc command circle. This wasn't because Dan was unsure of his opinion as much as that he didn't want to inadvertently cast suspicion on Bill's judgment. Though she'd worked hard to keep her command team unified, Christina knew that fissures between crew members were unavoidable.

Faced with a choice between the gregarious pirate and the analytical scientist, the sonar technicians would undoubtedly throw their lot in with Dan. Charisma was a good quality to have in an XO, but not at the expense of doubting another leader's opinions. Dan recognized the situation for what it was, and he moderated his personality accordingly. Christina had recommended Dan for command during his last fitness report, and she intended to reaffirm her comments at the earliest opportunity.

"But now?" Christina said, asking the inevitable follow-up question.

"Now I'm not sure," Dan said. "I think the professor's onto something, but I don't know that it's worth jeopardizing our mission to pursue it."

And there it was.

The crux of the decision Christina now faced.

At almost three and a half billion per copy, *Virginia*-class submarines were much too valuable to send on pleasure cruises. Case in point, Christina was about to transition her boat into the mission profile that they would adhere to for the next several weeks. At 1.4 million square miles, the South China Sea was the earth's largest sea and one of the most heavily contested waterways on the planet. It was also arguably the most strategic. One-third of the world's cargo transits through its waters, while untold amounts of untapped oil and gas reserves were waiting to be discovered in its depths. Guaranteeing freedom of navigation through the sea would have been an essential task for the U.S. Navy for these reasons alone, but there was a much more succinct explanation for the *Delaware*'s presence.

China.

China claimed the entire South China Sea, the islands that populated it, and its natural resources both known and still to be discovered. And the Chinese weren't content just to pursue these claims through international courts and governing bodies. Firm believers in the precept that possession was nine-tenths of the law, the Chinese Communist Party had been working overtime to make their territorial aspirations a reality. A series of man-made islands now populated the maritime shipping lines, serving as island redoubts for a plethora of Chinese military hardware. Everything from listening devices to advanced radar to fighter jets and land-to-sea missiles sprouted from the islands' sandy shores.

The unseen hardware prowling the ocean's depths was just as deadly.

In 2015, the Chinese Navy eclipsed the size of its American counterpart. By 2021, the Chinese fleet was on track to grow by the size of the entire French Navy every four years. What in 1996 had been a force of less than sixty ships was now a power to be reckoned with, a claim reinforced when China fielded its first domestically built aircraft carrier in 2019.

China commissioned its first domestically produced diesel submarine, the Type 039, in 1998. Less than ten years later, the Chinese made an exponential jump by manufacturing the nuclear-powered Type 094 ballistic missile submarine. In their early attempts to field submarines as quickly as possible, the Chinese had committed the cardinal sin of sacrificing submarine stealth for manufacturing speed. Fielding quiet subs was as much art as science, and the developmental process couldn't be expedited. In their rush to field operational subs, the Chinese had cut corners, and these shortcomings showed. The PLA's nuclear submarine force was easily detectable by their American adversaries, negating much of the advantages intrinsic to a submersible boat.

Until now.

If Christina's hunch was correct, she may have just happened on a new Chinese vessel.

A craft with stealthy characteristics that rivaled her own boat's.

Or perhaps exceeded them.

"How good a track do you have on the anomaly?" Christina asked.

Bill scrunched up his face, again vying for the most accurate answer possible. While the man was an exceptional engineer, the rapidly changing environment intrinsic to a fast attack submarine didn't always permit long deliberations and exact solutions.

Christina made a mental note to address this with the senior chief later.

"Using the arrays independently gives me a pretty good tracking solution," Bill said, running his index finger along the squiggly lines populating his monitor. "If we break contact, I don't know that I'll be able to pick her up as easily. I know this sounds counterintuitive, but I have to know where to look. I've got my sonar techs writing algorithms that should help refine our search parameters, but until we have a chance to vet them, I'd say our chances of losing the anomaly are fifty-fifty."

Bill's explanation did make sense.

A number of years ago, Australian researchers had made waves in the scientific community by claiming to be able to track American B-2 stealth bombers. This was true, after a fashion. Scientists hadn't been able to identify the bombers in real time, but after juxtaposing their data with flight logs showing the departing aircraft, they'd been able to point to radar returns that showed disturbances in the air caused by the massive flying wings.

The findings hadn't amounted to much, as the returns denoting the B-2s had been far below the noise threshold filtered out by the radar's algorithms, but the lesson had been driven home all the same. Even the best stealth could be rendered useless if you knew where to look. Right now, Bill knew where to look, but that would soon change if Christina adopted her assigned mission profile.

If.

Christina had an opportunity to flesh out a possible threat to the entire U.S. submarine force, though pursuing the opportunity meant deviating from her orders to patrol across the warren of interconnected deep-sea trenches that crisscrossed the South China Sea.

She judged the risk worth the reward.

"Officer of the Deck," Christina said, the plan coming together in her mind as she spoke, "come to new course 090, maintain current speed and depth. Stand by for additional course and speed changes. Over the next sixty minutes, we're going to see what contact S-47 can do."

"New course 090, maintain current speed and depth, aye," the officer of the deck echoed back.

Lieutenant Brian Andrews was still a junior officer, but he had the makings of a good bubblehead. Ship's scuttlebutt claimed that Brian was working on a novel in his spare time. If young Mr. Andrews was half as good a writer as he was a submariner, Christina thought she might just be reading one of his novels someday.

"I want to gather as much data on S-47 as possible in

the next hour," Christina said. "Senior Chief—come up with a test protocol. Dan—work with him. At the end of sixty minutes, I want to shed this contact and continue with our patrol."

"Aye, Captain," Dan said. "We're on it."

It turned out that shedding S-47 took a bit of doing. The wily mystery contact stayed with the sub through several course changes across a range of speeds and depths. Though she didn't express as much to the crew, Christina began to grow concerned. At the forty-five-minute mark, she rigged the sub for ultra-quiet and then executed her most radical course change yet, doubling back on the path she'd followed.

The final turn did the trick.

As the *Delaware* slipped through the ocean tracking north by northeast, S-47 maintained its current course and speed heading south. Christina watched Bill's waterfall display until the contact disappeared for good.

"Have we lost it, Senior Chief?" Christina said.

"Aye, skipper," Bill said. "We might be able to pick out the contact later after reconstructing the data, but this is the best we're going to get in real time."

"Officer of the Deck," Christina said, "you have the conn. I'm going to craft a message to headquarters letting them know what we've found. I don't imagine they're going to be happy."

Christina had no idea how prophetic her words would prove to be.

11

ZHANJIANG PORT, CHINA

GREEN-TINGED WATER BATTERED THE LAUNCH, SPRAYING SALTY foam across Fen Li's rubber slicker. The small craft rolled and pitched beneath her like a drunken elephant, and she fought to keep the contents of her stomach where they belonged.

She did not like boats.

Detested them, actually.

And now the sum of her future was tied to the ocean.

"As you can see, we are ready to embark at a moment's notice."

Fen shifted her attention from the roiling water to the man standing in front of her. With her bone-white hair and slight figure all but swallowed by her poncho, Fen knew she must look even smaller than normal.

Diminished.

Her soft voice was no help.

Compared to the fire hydrant–shaped man who stood on the swaying bridge with thick legs as if he were part of the launch, Fen more resembled a willow battered by the wind. Which was why Haoyu was at her side. As if he could hear her thoughts, Fen's second-in-command edged closer to the launch's captain, his muscular frame more than a match for the sailor's swarthy build.

"If I gave you the order now," Fen said, her voice competing against the crashing waves and the small craft's growling engine, "the ship would be moving in how many minutes?"

Ship seemed too pedestrian a descriptor for the vessel that towered above the launch. Its official name was *Maochong*, Mandarin for "caterpillar." This was more an homage to the ship's purpose than to its ungainly appearance. At forty meters wide and over two hundred long, *Maochong* displaced seventy thousand tons. The vessel boasted a crew of almost two hundred, and its onboard generators could power a small town.

But it was the *Maochong*'s profile that made the ship unique. In addition to a massive crane and a decking full of girders and other support equipment, the center of the vessel sported a multistory skeletal structure that resembled an oil rig.

But the *Maochong* did not drill for oil.

The ship collected something much more valuable.

Fen rolled up the sleeve of her slicker, revealing a large waterproof sports watch. The brand was American, but like everything else of significance, it was manufactured in China.

"Not minutes," the *Maochong*'s captain said, squaring his chest. "Seconds. Give the order, and we will be heading to sea within thirty seconds."

Fen eyed the captain, searching for signs of subterfuge.

In this endeavor, timing was everything. The excavation site was in the vicinity of the Paracel Islands, approximately five hundred and sixty kilometers southeast of Zhanjiang Port. The *Maochong* would require at least two days to make the journey, and more time still to employ her special cargo. This was the window within which Fen would be required to operate.

Begin too soon, and the entire endeavor would be compromised.

Start too late, and the opportunity would be missed.

The captain endured Fen's scrutiny, his gaze revealing nothing. He appeared ready to back up his words with action.

Was Fen ready to do the same?

Fen dipped her hand into the raincoat's oversized pocket, her fingers touching a piece of China's future.

Her future.

Though only about the size of a walnut, the black polymetallic nodule held a mixture of ten different elements, including manganese, cobalt, nickel, and other rare earth metals. One enterprising entrepreneur had termed the nodule *a battery in a rock*, and Fen found the description apt. In a world consumed with an ever-growing appetite for stored electricity, the unassuming chunks of rock were pound for pound one of the most valuable materials on earth.

Or, in this case, under the earth's ocean.

Just months ago, Fen had financed a voyage to obtain samples from a newly found deposit of polymetallic nodules in the Paracel Islands. As the rock in her pocket could attest, the seabed concentration was one of the richest ever discovered, and, more important, the depth of the deposit was not prohibitive. While no walk in the park, the nodule deposits were well within the operational envelope of the *Maochong*'s specialized collection equipment. There was just one problem—the waters in which the deposit was located were claimed by someone else.

Actually, several someone elses, if Fen were being precise.

But she had a plan for that, too.

Fen's phone vibrated.

After checking her watch a second time, she withdrew her cell. As always, Fen's operatives were precisely on schedule. This was one of the many benefits of employing former military. Schooling her features to remain blank despite her racing heart, Fen read the one-word text.

Success.

Looking from her phone to the sailor, Fen arrived at a decision.

"Launch your vessel, Captain," Fen said.

This time, she didn't even try to hide her smile.

12

MARY PAT FOLEY LOOKED AT HER DESK WITH A SIGH.

The director of national intelligence was in her sixties, making her one of the older members of President Jack Ryan's administration. Her nutmeg-brown hair had long ago transitioned to gray, and Mary Pat had resisted the urge to color it. She was an intelligence professional who worked alongside politicians. Though many of her colleagues had succumbed to the youth-obsessed culture of politics, Mary Pat was happy to be the exception. She kept her figure trim, but Mary Pat's wardrobe still skewed more toward function than flattery. As was the case on most days, the dark-colored pantsuit, plain blouse, and functional flats she was wearing would probably not turn many heads.

That was fine.

Mary Pat wore her age as a badge of honor. The lines on her face spoke to the hard-won wisdom she'd accumulated over decades of service to her country. She was older than most federal employees and had come of age in an era still ruled by pen and paper.

Her desk reflected this truth.

While Mary Pat certainly had the obligatory laptop and desktop computers along with a tablet and a secure cell phone happily humming in close proximity to her workspace, these capable tools were not her preferred method of ingesting and analyzing the reams of information that found their way to her on a daily basis. As the DNI, or director of national intelligence, Mary Pat sat atop the eighteen agencies and organizations that called the intelligence community home, but her current posting was just the latest stop in her long and illustrious career. Mary Pat got her start in the Central Intelligence Agency and had spent her formative years running and recruiting agents behind the Iron Curtain.

That her boss, President Ryan, had also cut his teeth in the same organization was no coincidence. Back then, chalk marks, dead drops, and brush passes were a way of life, not the lexicon from a bygone era. Forty years ago, computers had been new, bulky, and not entirely secure. For that reason, case officers consumed information in the form of hard-copy documents.

In the ensuing decades, technology had progressed by leaps and bounds, and the profession of espionage with it. Today, analysts debated whether the once-fearsome

Russian Bear was even capable of swallowing one of its smaller next-door neighbors, let alone all of Europe. Communications between agent and handler happened via unbreakable encryptions, and data was displayed in link charts produced by machine-learning algorithms.

Even so, the relationship between handler and asset was still decidedly analog, as was the woman who'd spent most of her career running agents. Mary Pat still thought best with honest-to-goodness paper between her fingertips, but the three documents currently dominating her workspace were defying her legendary intellect.

With another sigh, the nation's top spy eyed the chipped mug taunting her from the far side of her desk. In a nod to his boss's predilections, Mary Pat's assistant, Sam, kept a constant supply of her favorite coffee brewing in a metallic monstrosity known as a silver bullet. Like her preferred method of consuming data, the percolator had been state-of-the-art at about the same time F-14 Tomcats had prowled the skies in search of Soviet MiGs to splash. Be that as it may, the coffeemaker functioned just fine. That it was stocked with Folgers, rather than one of the legions of craft coffee preferred by her younger workforce, only added to Mary Pat's mystique.

At least that's what she told herself.

A glance at the clock provided Mary Pat with the motivation required to resist the percolator's siren song. Though she was still more than mentally capable of doing this job, physically Mary Pat was no longer the previous century's cocksure case officer. Back then she'd subsisted primarily on coffee, takeout, and, when the occasion merited, nicotine. Now she had to watch her caffeine intake past noon lest she pass the night staring at the ceiling as Ed, her husband of forty years, snored beside her. Sleep had ceased to come easy for Mary Pat long ago. With the weight of the world on her shoulders, the last thing she needed was a chemical boost for her insomnia.

Which brought her back to the three documents.

Mary Pat loved her husband, but her devotion to John Patrick Ryan ran a close second. The current occupant of the Resolute desk embodied everything the Founding Fathers had imagined in a politician. Like Cincinnatus of old, Jack had come to political office reluctantly, with plans to return to civilian life as soon as possible.

In the ensuing years, Ryan had just as reluctantly come to terms with the notion that events beyond his control had extended his original *as soon as possible* longer than planned. Despite his years in the Oval Office, Jack still hadn't developed a liking of Washington or the creatures that inhabited it. As he was wont to remind Mary Pat on an almost daily basis, once his term was up, Jack was done with D.C.

But while Ryan was the embodiment of a servant leader, he was not divine. More than anyone besides Cathy Ryan, Mary Pat understood the current commander in chief's all-too-human limitations. Jack might have earned his spurs in the same Agency as Mary Pat, but he was not a clandestine officer.

At least not officially.

Jack had begun his intelligence career as an analyst,

and he naturally defaulted to this role even now. Because
of her boss's predilections, Mary Pat took extra care
when selecting what topics to bring to his attention. This
was not because she was worried about his capacity to
comprehend the complexity of rapidly evolving world
events. The opposite was true. Jack loved raw intelligence
and he relished dissecting the President's Daily Brief, or
PDB, in excruciating detail. Jack's intellect was a powerful force, and Mary Pat took great care in deciding on
what she allowed it to focus. Unlike the relationship between previous DNIs and their Presidents, Mary Pat personally reviewed the PDB each day before it went to Jack.

That this resulted in more work for her was a given,
but Mary Pat had long ago accepted this as the price of
doing business. Jack Ryan was brilliant, but he still required guardrails. Normally, she had an almost innate
sense of what was important and what was not. Or, more
specifically, what intelligence required a decision from
the nation's chief executive, and what fires could be
fought by the other capable members of his team.

Not today.

Today, the seemingly disparate information vexed
even Mary Pat's legendary intellect. Though the topics at
hand didn't seem related, Mary Pat's gut said otherwise,
and over the course of a clandestine career that read like
a spy novel, Mary Pat had learned to trust her instincts.

The topics summarized in the documents were three:
the sinking of a Vietnamese trawler, the discovery of a
Chinese glider, and a startling report from an American
fast attack submarine. While these events were each sig-

nificant in their own right, they would not normally rise to Mary Pat's level. She had the inevitable job of keeping watch over the entire world. Even more so than the man she served, Mary Pat had to be capable of separating the signal from the noise. Her staff of tireless analysts and seasoned case officers did an exceptional job at this, but here Mary Pat had added her own ironclad rule—if something happened in the South China Sea, she wanted to know about it.

Immediately.

And all three of these events had occurred within the confines of the globe's most important waterway.

The average American could be forgiven for not understanding why a stretch of water almost seven thousand miles distant merited such fuss. After all, why would the Western world care about the boundary squabbles of Asian nations? As the multiple foreign wars of the last twenty years could attest, the United States had more than enough to keep its military busy without nosing around for additional trouble.

And this was the trap that swallowed most of the uninformed. A South China Sea that could be safely navigated without fear of Chinese encroachment was critical to maintaining an independent Taiwan. An independent Taiwan was essential for national security reasons. Sixty-five percent of the world's semiconductors were produced on the island nation. When it came to the kind of advanced chips that were essential to defense applications, the percentage jumped to close to ninety percent. Everything from common household appliances to the rockets that carried astronauts to outer space were dependent on a tiny country not much bigger than the state of Maryland.

Thriller novelists had long theorized about the devastating effects that an electromagnetic pulse, or EMP, might wreak on a targeted nation's economy. And while Mary Pat agreed with the potential for disruption, by some measures an EMP device that detonated above the United States might prove less catastrophic than a Communist Chinese invasion of Taiwan. Chips damaged by an EMP could be replaced, but if China developed a stranglehold on the world's supply of high-tech microprocessors, Armageddon might well ensue. Optimistic estimates put the time that it would take to stand up replacement factories on U.S. soil at years. Mary Pat thought these predictions a bit too rosy. The United States had won World War II in part by depriving Germany and Japan of the natural resources required to manufacture replacements for their combat losses.

With control of Taiwan, China could very well do the same to America.

Picking up the nearest document, Mary Pat read the enclosed summary for the fourth time. At first blush, the sinking of a Vietnamese trawler, while tragic for the people involved and their families, was hardly the sort of event that merited the DNI's attention. Even in the twenty-first century, life as a commercial fisherman was still a treacherous endeavor, and the crews that plied the South China Sea were no exception.

But this was no ordinary sinking.

A member of the crew had survived, and the tale he told was interesting. According to the fisherman, his boat had been sunk by a Chinese vessel. In the South China Sea's congested and contested waters, this was also not a terribly unusual occurrence. Rubbing was racing in that part of the world. Sometimes captains jostling for position took things too far.

But if the survivor was to be believed, this was not that.

The fisherman claimed that his ship had been sunk by munitions fired by men on the Chinese vessel. RPGs, by the sound of things. Always eager to extract leverage from its much larger neighbor, the Vietnamese government had lodged a formal complaint with the international maritime court. China denied the altercation had taken place. The entire occurrence might have faded away were it not for the enterprising work of an analyst in the National Reconnaissance Office. While the woman hadn't been able to retrieve imagery of the alleged attack, she had narrowed down a list of Chinese vessels that had potentially been in the area.

One of the vessels had set off alarm bells for Mary Pat's staff.

The *Dragon*.

Officially registered as an oceanic research platform, the ship was classified by the CIA as dual-use. Like countless other similar vessels, the *Dragon* could indeed be used to gather data and conduct seabed extractions. But the CIA was convinced the vessel's real purpose was not so benign: clandestine undersea work. In practice, this area of specialization could run the gamut from tapping undersea cables to attempting to recover American hydrophobic sensors or even shipwrecks. When the *Dragon* put to sea, American intelligence analysts paid attention. If the dual-use ship really had played a part in sinking a Vietnamese trawler, it served to reason that her crew was on a secretive mission.

A secretive mission in the South China Sea.

Setting the paper summarizing the incident aside, Mary Pat examined the second piece of the puzzle—flash traffic from the USS *Delaware*.

Jack Ryan was a naval specialist. While this wasn't Mary Pat's area of expertise, it didn't take a tactician to understand the importance of the sub's message. For a period of time, an unknown contact had tracked the world's premier stealth platform. The analyst who'd prepared the estimate had included a short synopsis of another event in which an unexpected surprise had upended the U.S. submarine community.

Prior to fielding their own high-speed nuclear submarines, the U.S. Navy believed that American carriers could easily outrun the Soviet submarines sent to hunt them. This thinking was abruptly turned on its head after an encounter between the USS *Enterprise*, an American aircraft carrier, and a Soviet November-class nuclear submarine sent to tail her. Over the course of two days, the *Enterprise*'s captain slowly increased his ship's speed until the engines were firewalled at thirty-one knots.

The Russian sub kept pace, with power to spare.

This was the moment when the U.S. Navy realized

they needed their own high-speed nuclear-powered submarines to combat their Soviet adversaries. The technical innovations that followed ushered in an era of American submarine dominance. The USS *Delaware* was an apex predator. A submarine so silent that it made less noise under way than its predecessor had emitted while tied up in port. The *Virginia* class of submarines were undetectable.

Or so American intelligence had believed.

Now Mary Pat had powerful evidence to the contrary.

If the *Delaware*'s skipper was correct, her boat had been tracked through a series of evasive maneuvers. If the unknown contact was of Chinese origin, the balance of power in the South China Sea had just shifted.

Which brought Mary Pat to the final piece of information—the Chinese glider.

Setting aside the *Delaware*'s flash traffic, Mary Pat examined the only summary to include images. The pictured object wasn't anyone's idea of sexy. The glider was long and cylindrical, more resembling a fifties-era rendering of a rocket ship than a modern weapon of war. But retro look or not, the glider represented an opportunity that was impossible to ignore.

Gliders in their simplest forms were unmanned sensors propelled by the rising and falling of columns of water in the same way aerial gliders used thermals to stay aloft. This revolutionary design meant that while the sensor couldn't travel fast, the glider could make its way through the ocean without a motor, allowing the device's internal power to be devoted to sensors and communication devices. While first conceived as tools for long-duration oceanic research, gliders had quickly been apportioned for another task—sub hunting.

Constellations of distributed data-linked gliders could slowly prowl the ocean's depths, searching for what was previously unfindable. But the glider's unique method of propulsion was also its Achilles' heel. With a top speed of no more than three or four knots and limited maneuvering abilities, a glider was vulnerable to any number of ocean hazards, including shifting currents and manmade obstructions.

Obstructions like fishing nets.

A CIA asset originally recruited to monitor weapons shipments flowing into and out of Navotas Fish Port Complex, located in Manila, had found something else instead.

A Chinese glider.

Mary Pat had considered asking the U.S. State Department for assistance with recovering the glider, but quickly abandoned the idea. The attitude of the Filipino government toward America was, in a word, unfavorable. Rather than asking State to potentially burn a diplomatic bridge, Mary Pat decided to solve the problem in-house. Recovering the glider was a job for a clandestine organization, but which one?

She didn't want to use acknowledged CIA officers to retrieve the device, for the same reason she didn't want to ask the Filipino government for help. If the operation went awry, the Filipino president might see returning the glider to China as a double win. In one fell swoop he could both thumb his nose at America and ingratiate himself with the Chinese. Not to mention the diplomatic fallout that would come from acknowledged CIA paramilitary officers conducting a clandestine operation on Filipino soil.

Fortunately, The Campus existed for situations such as this.

Though the intelligence entity's original charter had imagined its command structure as separate from the U.S. government, this distinction had slowly eroded. From a practical standpoint, The Campus's utility relied on its ability to glean actionable intelligence from U.S. sources. After all, even the world's best operators weren't worth much if they didn't know where to point their rifles. But this was only part of the reason. The more practical thinking behind incorporating The Campus under the DNI lay with Mary Pat's boss.

Jack Ryan, Sr., wasn't much for plausible deniability.

While the President understood the need to operate out of sight as much as the next CIA officer, Jack would never hang a clandestine operative out to dry in the name of political expediency. After once finding himself on the receiving end of just such a policy in the Colombian jungle, Ryan had made it clear to Mary Pat on more than one occasion what he thought of such nonsense.

But in this case, using The Campus was the correct play. Clark and his merry band of marauders could slip into the country using legends, secure the glider, and slip back out with no one the wiser. If word of the operation leaked, the Filipino president might suspect that the operation had been helmed by U.S. operatives, but he wouldn't be sure. More important, he could say as much to his Chinese counterparts with a straight face. Mary Pat had signed off on Clark's OPLAN to retrieve the glider hours ago, but if anything, the flash traffic from the USS *Delaware* made the endeavor even more urgent.

The Chinese had something cooking in the South China Sea.

Something new.

A look at this glider might just help the smart men and women at the Naval Research Laboratory better understand what America was up against.

And then there was the sinking of the Vietnamese boat.

That heavy-handedness seemed way out of proportion. A fishing trawler had crossed paths with a Chinese vessel that had probably been engaged in espionage. So what? What had been compelling enough to order the deaths of a dozen fishermen and risk the potential political ramifications that came with the killings? Mary Pat frowned as the opening scene to the movie *Heat* came to mind. The sequence in which a crew of hardened bank robbers execute defenseless guards to ensure there are no witnesses to the crime.

What was the crew of the Chinese vessel afraid the fishermen had witnessed?

Mary Pat shook her head.

Chasing hypotheticals was never a winning strategy. The Chinese were up to something in the South China Sea. As to what, she wouldn't yet hazard a guess. Neither would she put it on her boss's plate. After Clark did what he did best, she'd have a better understanding of the lay of the land. Until then, she'd concentrate on the world's other dumpster fires.

They weren't exactly in short supply.

13

"YOU'RE AWFULLY QUIET UP THERE."

Jack looked from the road to the Green Beret seated behind him.

"Something wrong with being quiet?" Jack said.

"For normal people, no," Jad said. "But you're our team's version of an officer. When the officer gets quiet, bad things happen."

"Hey, now," Cary said from the front passenger seat. "That's a bit rough."

"Come on, boss," Jad said. "You were thinking the same thing. You're just too polite to say it."

"You're not?" Cary said.

"Nope," Jad said. "We had dinner with Jack's old man. Promised him we'd keep Junior here safe. That's hard to do when he doesn't let us in on whatever he's cooking up."

"I can actually hear you," Jack said, "because I'm sitting right here."

Jack changed lanes to make way for a marauding BMW.

"Good," Jad said. "Then lay it on us. You'll feel better once you get the craziness off your chest. Trust me."

"He's right," Cary said with a sigh. "Between the two of us, Jad and I have served with half a dozen team leaders. The sooner you tell your NCOs what you're scheming, the better chance we have of keeping you out of jail."

Cary smiled as he spoke, but Jack still felt the gentle but firm truth beneath the man's levity. In the brief but admittedly intense time they'd known one another, the two Green Berets had saved Jack's life at least twice. This trip was supposed to be a reset. A chance for the commandos to feel out Jack and The Campus without the distraction of a real-world op. Instead, Cary and Jad had just been in a gunfight.

Not exactly what the pair had signed up for.

"Okay," Jack said with a sigh of his own. "I was thinking about making a detour."

Reaching into his pocket, Cary withdrew a handful of euros and tossed them over his shoulder.

"You're just a sore loser," Jad said as he collected the fluttering bills.

"What's with you two?" Jack said.

"We had a bet," Cary said. "I said you'd wait until we had the airport in sight. Jad figured it'd be sooner."

"What would be sooner?" Jack said.

"Your decision to ignore your boss and interview the American scientist."

Put that way, Jack suddenly wasn't such a big fan of the choice he was contemplating.

"I'm not ignoring my boss," Jack said. "I was just thinking that since Edelweiss Resort is only an hour southwest of Munich, we could head down there, talk to the scientist, and still make it back to the airport in plenty of time."

"Whatever lets you sleep at night," Jad said.

Jack vented his irritation by flooring the accelerator, but he'd no sooner put on his left turn signal than another vehicle roared by, this time a Honda. Of all the cars available to drive in Germany, Jack was stuck behind the wheel of something that made a Prius look sporty.

"Easy there, team leader," Cary said. "Jad's just busting balls. Besides, it's kind of a compliment."

"Yep," Jad said.

"How so?" Jack said.

"Men like us don't stop when there's still a thread to pull," Cary said. "My partner's jackassery aside, you're engaging in a common Green Beret practice."

"What's that?" Jack said.

"Developing the situation," Jad said. "It's a fancy doctrinal term for poking a hornet's nest to see what flies out."

"That's a dumb analogy," Cary said. "Of course hornets fly out of a hornet's nest. Developing the situation is more like shaking a tree to see what falls from the branches."

"Only if cinder blocks grow on your tree," Jad said. "This is not our first operation with young Mr. Ryan. We both know there's a high likelihood someone's gonna get stung in the ass before this is over."

"Again, right here," Jack said, but he was smiling as he spoke.

The Green Berets were correct.

Jack was usually more of a hornet's nest kind of guy, but not this time. Hans had given Jack a parting bit of information. The American scientist, Zhang Wei, was registered at Edelweiss Lodge and Resort, a hotel located in the mountainous region near the German/Austrian border. The child-friendly facility was part of the U.S. Army Garrison's Bavaria installation and was intended for U.S. service members, Department of Defense civilians, and their dependents. Aside from a possible run on chocolate ice cream, Jack wasn't worried about a catastrophe befalling the hotel.

Besides, Clark would probably thank Jack for conducting the interview. Campus resource requests ran through Mary Pat, who was already a busy woman. Every time a Campus operative needed help, the DNI had to figure out a way to disguise the tasking so that the paperwork trail didn't inadvertently point back to an organization that didn't officially exist.

The Campus was great at conducting nimble operations in denied environments. It was not so good at liaising with clunky government bureaucracies. The more Jack thought about it, the more it made sense for him to have a quick talk with the American scientist before Jack left Germany. He'd send a summary of the interview to Clark from the airport and then board the flight to Manila. If Clark then decided that the scientist merited official attention, he could pass along the request and a copy of Jack's summary to Mary Pat.

If not, no harm no foul.

But that still left a couple blanks that needed to be filled in.

"What do we know about this guy?" Jad said.

Once again, the Green Beret seemed to be reading Jack's mind.

"The short answer is not much," Jack said, "but that's about to change."

"You bringing Lisanne into the loop?" Jad said.

Jack eyed the Green Beret in the rearview mirror before replying. The commando fit the definition of tall, dark, and handsome. He also happened to be showing way too much interest in Lisanne's well-being for Jack's taste.

"No," Jack said, resisting the urge to once again step on the gas. "The three of us are burned, but she might not be. Since she's Isabel's handler, Lisanne will stay in place until the conference is over. It's time for you guys to meet my secret weapon."

After ensuring that his cell was linked to the car's Bluetooth system, Jack selected a contact from his favorites. The sound of ringing echoed through the speakers. By the fifth ring, Jack was beginning to second-guess his dramatic lead-up. Though they were willing participants in this operation, Cary and Jad were not Campus members, as John Clark had made perfectly clear. The director of operations saw this as more of an exchange program than an onboarding of two new shooters. Even so, Jack liked the two men and was already gearing up for the discussion he knew was coming.

The one that would center on adding the men to The Campus's roster.

Unfortunately, that bit of convincing would have to go in two directions.

Jad had not been exaggerating with his earlier comment. At dinner, the senior Ryan had uncharacteristically made his case for The Campus directly to the Green Berets. Jack thought this was partly due to his father's innate ability to spot talent and partly because he knew that the commandos were responsible for saving his son's life. Jack Ryan, Sr.'s sales pitch had hit its target. Cary and Jad had both agreed to a Campus overseas exercise.

But Jack knew the men were far from convinced.

In addition to setting aside promising Army careers, the commandos would now be going into harm's way absent the combat multipliers to which they'd become accustomed. Hitting an objective with Campus shooters meant sneaking and peeking in the dead of night without the comforting drone of an AC-130 gunship's four turboprop engines providing the mood music. There were no 160th Night Stalker Little Birds waiting to wreak vengeance on the enemy and no QRF of amped-up Rangers ready to kick down doors and take names. Working for The Campus was sexy, but decidedly different than playing with the hard men and women who made up Special Operations Command. With this in mind, Jack wanted to be able to expose the Green Berets to The Campus's brand of operational magic.

Assuming, of course, his chief combat multiplier actually answered his phone.

On the eighth ring, Jack got his wish.

"Jack? Is that you?"

As always, Gavin's voice seemed rough, as if he'd just woken. Though the plump keyboard warrior's hours tended toward the nocturnal, Jack knew this wasn't the case today. Gavin had just been helping with Jack's operation on the University of Regensburg campus. He should be wide awake.

Unless Gavin had decided to engage in one of his famous power naps.

"Yeah, it's me, buddy," Jack said. "Got a minute?"

"Sure," Gavin said. "I was just trimming my tree."

Jack hit the mute button a millisecond before snickers echoed through the car.

"Uh, Gavin?" Jack said.

"What? Oh, come on, Jack. I'm talking about my bonsai tree. I'm testing for my aikido green belt tonight. Trimming my tree always gets me in the martial mood."

This time Jack wasn't quick enough with the mute, but he covered the sounds of laughter with several well-timed coughs.

So much for impressing the commandos.

"You okay, Jack?" Gavin said.

"Fine, buddy," Jack said after loudly clearing his throat. "Just had something go down the wrong hatch. I need your help."

"Help watching your back?" Gavin said. "I think that Green Beret Jade has the hots for Lisanne."

"It's Jad," Jad chimed in from the back.

"You sure?" Gavin said.

"Positive," Jad said. "I was there when my momma named me."

This call was giving new definition to the term *shitshow*.

"Sorry, buddy," Jack said. "Should have mentioned that the Green Berets are in the car."

As one part of Jack's mind was furiously trying to figure out how to do damage control, the other portion made a note of the fact that while Jad had corrected his name, he hadn't said a thing about Lisanne.

Interesting.

"Hey, Gavin," Cary said, stepping into the fray, "nice to meet you. And for what it's worth, my son has a couple bonsai trees, too. He's a big fan of *Cobra Kai*."

"No kidding?" Gavin said. "Man, when Elisabeth Shue made a guest appearance I—"

"Sorry to interrupt," Jack said, "but we don't have much time. We're on our way to interview Zhang Wei, the American brother of Wang Lei, the Chinese kidnap victim. I was hoping you'd run us through what you've found."

"Sure, Jack," Gavin said. "Sure. So I queried the usual open-source sites and put the info into a targeting package that I sent to your Campus high-side account. Bottom line, Zhang Wei specializes in machine learning."

"What does that mean?" Jad said.

"Is that Jade again?" Gavin said.

"Close enough," Cary said.

"Thought so," Gavin said. "I have a way with names and voices. Anyway, think of machine learning as data pattern analysis on steroids. Scientists develop algorithms that allow machines to make determinations about data sets. For instance, imagine you're a company that manufactures brackets and one of your products keeps failing. You know something's going wrong in the fabrication process, but you're not sure what. Machine-learning algorithms would analyze all the data you've amassed on brackets that failed or passed inspection and draw conclusions. Oftentimes, these conclusions point in directions you wouldn't normally consider."

"Are there military applications?" Jack said.

"Tons," Gavin answered. "Data analysis is analogous to the concept of stealth back in the seventies. It's the new frontier. Machine learning at its best can both draw conclusions from vast data sets and teach the computers how to better solve problems."

"Can you unpack that one for old Jade?" Jad said.

"Certainly," Gavin said. "Everyone knows that computers do a better job of analyzing fingerprints than humans. A good algorithm might examine the arches, loops, and whorls in closer detail than a human bioinformatician. But that's only part of the equation. Machine learning can analyze all the positive identifications made by human technicians and discover novel ways to identify a fingerprint's owner. The machine learns."

"Tracking," Jad said.

The Green Beret sounded impressed, and Jack began to relax. For all his quirks, Gavin really was a force to be reckoned with. Maybe the hacker was winning over his audience after all.

"Any specifics on Zhang Wei's work?" Jack said.

"Sorry, no," Gavin said. "His dissertation and thesis are pretty standard fare, but then his résumé falls off."

"What do you mean?" Jack said.

"After getting his Ph.D., Zhang Wei published several papers but then abruptly stopped. His LinkedIn profile shows some postdoc work for a couple of the Silicon Valley usuals, but the last entry was from almost five years ago. I called the company's HR department and learned that he hasn't worked for them in two years."

"Government lab," Jad said.

"That's what I'm thinking," Gavin said.

"What do you mean?" Jack said, feeling a little irritated at the exchange.

"Academics have a saying—publish or perish," Jad said. "If a scientist has stopped publishing it usually means one of two things. Either they're no longer working in the field—"

"Or they've taken a job with a government lab doing the kind of work that you can't talk about," Gavin said.

Jack glanced at Jad in the rearview mirror only to see the Green Beret grinning back at him.

"He's an Echo," Cary said, answering Jack's unspoken question. "That's the equivalent of having a degree in RF engineering. Jad knows a thing or two about scientists. The smartest Green Berets are always Echoes."

"*And* best-looking," Jad said, his smile even wider.

"Okay," Jack said. "Any idea why our boy's vacationing at Edelweiss?"

"Not positive," Gavin said, "but the fact that he was even able to make a reservation also suggests he works for a government lab. Since the resort is on a military base, you have to be a service member or government civilian, or sponsored by one, to gain access. As to why he's at Edelweiss, the resort's security camera footage from the last several days shows Zhang Wei in the company of a brunette. He eats breakfast with her every morning. His reservation for a single room began two days ago, but he also has a reservation for an additional room beginning tomorrow."

"The day the conference at the University of Regensburg ends," Cary said. "Does the brunette have a ring?"

"Stand by," Gavin said, "let me check."

"You have access to the video in real time?" Jad said.

"Of course," Gavin said. "I compromised the system and mirrored the hard drives after Jack asked me to poke around. By the way, the hotel's got a special going for the next three days in case you guys are interested. Also, yes, the girl has an engagement ring but no wedding band."

"How in the hell were you able to—" Jad said.

"Geek out with your fellow keyboard ninja on your own time," Cary said. "I think the second room is for Wang Lei. Maybe Zhang Wei wants to introduce his fiancée to his brother."

"Or maybe the Regensburg conference provided the

excuse for a family vacation to Europe," Jad said. "Both scenarios make sense. So what's the play?"

"Meet with Zhang Wei, tell him what happened to his brother, and see what he knows," Jack said, feeling a bit like he was a passenger on a freight train that was barreling off the tracks. "Gavin, can you book us rooms? That way we don't have to dodge security."

"No problem," Gavin said, his keyboard clattering. "Mountain or parking lot view?"

"Mountain, for sure," Jad said.

"Got it," Gavin said. "Oh, man, those are a bit pricey. Do the three of you want to split a room?"

"Gavin," Jack said.

"Sorry, Jack," Gavin said, "but Mr. C. is always on me about operational costs. Okay, three rooms booked with mountain views. Zhang Wei's dossier is in your inbox. I've still got no hits on Wang Lei or his kidnappers."

"Hits from where?" Jad said.

"The German closed-circuit television network," Gavin said.

"The BfV shares CCTV feeds with The Campus?" Jad said.

"Not so much shares as they don't stop us from taking it," Jack said.

"My digital kung fu is strong," Gavin said.

"Gavin," Jack said.

"Sorry," Gavin said, "but it seemed to fit. Anything else?"

"Nope," Jack said. "Thanks, buddy."

"No problem," Gavin said. "Good luck."

"We don't need luck," Jack said. "This is just a friendly interview."

"Sure it is," Gavin said with a chuckle. "Do you remember when—"

Jack hung up.

"Huh," Jad said, leaning forward. "Do your calls always drop like that?"

"Only when the Chinese are jamming them," Jack said.

"Maybe we should get some hardware before the knock and talk," Cary said.

"It's an interview," Jack said, redlining the engine. "There will be no shooting."

"Wanna bet?" Jad said.

Jack did not.

14

NINETY MINUTES LATER, JACK PULLED INTO THE RESORT'S PARKING lot.

The Edelweiss was a resort in every sense of the word. Nestled at the base of Germany's tallest mountain, the facility boasted acres of pools, restaurants, health clubs, and other amenities. Unlike his father, Jack had never served in the military. As a result, he'd always assumed that military resort hotels would be poor imitations of their civilian counterparts. One look at the Edelweiss's rustic interior had him reassessing this opinion. With its leather couches, exposed stone, and plethora of wood furnishings, the main lobby more resembled a high-end Austrian hunting lodge than a hotel for military families.

Walking up to the counter, Jack thought through how he was going to play the interaction. At first, he'd intended to check in and then walk up to Zhang Wei's room and knock. But this approach didn't sit right. Too passive. Besides the ticking clock associated with his pending departure from Munich, there was something else bothering Jack.

The kidnapping of Zhang Wei's brother felt wrong.

Though the operatives who'd executed the rendition were no doubt professionals, the operation was off. Rushed. The smart play would have been to wait until after the conference instead of snatching their target in broad daylight like an action sequence from a Bourne movie. A quiet but forcible conversation in a crowded bar or, better yet, a surreptitious entry to the man's hotel room would have accomplished the same goal with none of the associated fanfare.

A paramilitary team conducted an overt rendition for one reason only.

Timing.

There had to be some sort of operational constraint tied to time. A reason why burning the several hours it would have taken to set up a snatch at a far less circumspect location wasn't feasible. This was the only explanation that made sense, but if so, this line of thought raised still more complications. The Chinese team had announced their presence in the most dramatic way possible—by killing a member of the German intelligence service. Germans, like most anyone else, do not like having their asses handed to them in their own backyard. Politicians might attribute the incident to the cost of doing business, but Jack thought the German populace would be out for blood.

Jack needed to discover Zhang Wei's location. Quickly. This was the type of information that a luxury hotel's staff knew about their guests. Withdrawing a set of credentials from his pocket, Jack opened them for the woman behind the check-in desk to see.

"Afternoon," Jack said with a smile. "I need to speak with one of your guests."

The credentials were a new addition to the Campus kit. A nod to the reality that the operatives employed by the off-the-books intelligence organization were no longer tasked with just sneak-and-peek operations. More and more often, field hands like Jack found themselves in situations where they had to not only explain their unlikely presence, but also compel the assistance of bystanders.

Hence the credentials.

The black billfold contained a picture of Jack, a false name, and the emblem of a real but unpopular governmental entity—the Department of Agriculture. This was seen as a compromise of sorts. While the DoA's special agents did have investigative authority, the agency embodied none of the FBI's or CIA's sexiness. Nobody would want to tell their friends about the time they were interviewed by the Department of Agriculture.

At least that was the theory.

As Jack had hoped, the person behind the counter was American. She eyed the offered credentials and compared Jack's photo to his face.

Then she spoke.

"I can't give out room numbers," the woman said, her dark eyes daring Jack to disagree, "but I can call a guest for you."

"That would be great," Jack said. "I'm looking for Dr. Zhang Wei."

On a whim, Jack pulled up a picture of the scientist on his phone and slid the device across the counter. The woman paused in the act of dialing as she eyed the image.

"I can still call his room if you like," she said, "but I think you just missed him."

"Missed him?" Jack said, his smile growing more forced.

"Yes," the woman said. "He asked me for directions to the Eibsee Hotel on his way out about ten minutes ago. The hotel's located on a lake fifteen minutes from here."

"Sure it's him?" Jack said.

"Not positive," she said, "but we don't have many Asian guests."

"Thank you," Jack said. "Can you call his room anyway?"

"Love to," she said, but the tone of her voice suggested otherwise.

As the woman dialed, Jack ran a quick search on Eibsee Hotel with his phone. After reviewing the results, he understood the woman's tone. Edelweiss was beautiful, but it was no Eibsee Hotel. That resort sat nestled on the eastern side of a glacier-fed lake bearing the same name. Its outdoor seating pavilion was feet away from the glistening water. If the handful of images posted to Google were any indication, the place could have doubled as a set for a remake of *The Sound of Music*.

Stunning didn't really do the place justice.

"No answer," the woman said, placing the phone back in its cradle.

Her self-satisfied tone gave Jack an idea.

"With your aptitude for faces," Jack said, "you might be in the wrong line of work."

The woman smiled. "I'm taking a semester off from school to travel. This isn't my permanent career field."

"What are you studying?" Jack said.

"Accounting."

"If balance sheets ever start to feel boring, give me a call," Jack said, placing his business card on the counter. "We're always looking for good people, and the work can take you to exotic places. Thanks again for the help."

"Just a minute," the woman said as Jack was turning to go. "Do you want me to give you a ring if he comes back?"

"That would be great," Jack said.

The woman was punching his number into her cell as Jack exited the hotel, proving once again that his mother was right—you could catch more flies with honey. This should have come as no surprise, because Cathy Ryan was usually right.

About everything.

15

"REAPER ELEMENTS, THIS IS SCEPTER, RADIO CHECK, OVER."

"Scepter, this is Reaper 1," Cary said. "Read you loud and clear, over."

"Scepter, this is Reaper 2," Jad said. "Got you Lima Charlie as well, over."

"Roger that," Jack said.

Defaulting to the call signs they'd used during the North Korean operation was natural, but the brevity codes also brought with them a slew of emotions. Jack had been in plenty of tight spots, but the North Korean mission might just take the cake. In the ensuing weeks, he'd awakened more than once from dreams in which shadowy figures were overrunning his foxhole.

"Scepter, Reaper 1 has eyes on Sheldon. He's sitting alone at a table on the white side of Schnitzel, over."

Jack sighed.

If the Reaper and Scepter call signs dredged up bad memories, the brevity code words the Green Berets had selected for this mission were formulating new ones. Since Zhang Wei was a scientist, Jad had promptly christened him Sheldon, after the character in the TV show *The Big Bang Theory*. Not to be outdone, Cary had decreed that the Eibsee Hotel was Schnitzel, while the surrounding buildings were Brat, Wurst, and Spätzle. If nothing else, the radio traffic was sure to gin up an appetite.

"Roger that, Reaper 1," Jack said. "Reaper 2, any uninvited guests, over?"

Their proclivity for strange radio protocol aside, the Green Berets would make great Campus operatives. The two men were both snipers and had more time surveilling high-value targets than most shooters spent cleaning their weapons. Even though the pair were absent the rifles and spotting scopes they normally carried into battle, the commandos had wasted no time preparing a plan of action centered on Jack's engagement with the American scientist. If he'd been operating solo, as was usually the case, Jack would have thought nothing of ambling up to Sheldon and introducing himself.

Jad and Cary had vetoed the idea.

Though there was every reason to believe that the MSS direct-action team they'd tangled with earlier was long gone, this wasn't a gamble the Green Berets were prepared to take. In truth, Jack was grateful for the commandos' presence. Though night terrors might haunt Jack's dreams, real life had turned out differently. The three of them had survived an encounter with a well-trained and numerically superior force. An encounter

Jack knew would have turned out much differently absent the Green Berets. Jack considered the ferocity and precision with which the snipers dealt out violence a fair trade for their quirks.

Most days.

"Scepter, this is Reaper 2, that's a negative on uninvited guests. I've got line of sight to the red and green sides of Schnitzel and a pretty good view of the woods to the black side. No Hermans in view, over."

The hotel really was the perfect spot for a clandestine meeting.

The western, or white, side of the resort featured a wraparound deck that served as the outdoor seating area for the hotel's restaurant just steps away from the glacial lake's rocky beach. The beach continued to both the north and south. Cary was perched in the pavilion of a second restaurant about one hundred meters southwest of the hotel's south, or green, side. From here, the team sergeant had an unobstructed view of the wraparound deck as well as a marina that occupied the space between the two buildings.

As the team's spotter, Jad had chosen to position himself on the high ground.

Literally.

In a nod to the Zugspitze peak that dominated the surrounding terrain, the Germans had erected a cable car that ferried tourists to the summit. The cable car station was a contemporary glass-and-metal monstrosity that more resembled a modern art museum than the rickety conveyances of old.

After conducting his initial recon, Jad had settled into the second-floor observatory and made good use of the floor-to-ceiling windows. Not only did his observation post offer an excellent vantage point, it also gave him a reason to use a hastily acquired set of Steiner binoculars. Though most of his fellow tourists were focused on the mountain, a good many were also marveling at the liquid-blue lake.

Perfect cover.

"Scepter copies all," Jack said. "Entering Schnitzel now."

Though the hotel's facilities were officially closed to non-patrons, the reviews Cary had perused on Google as Jack drove suggested that this rule was not strictly enforced. After all, euros were euros whether they came from hotel guests or from outsiders. Jack figured that as long as the restaurant wasn't too crowded, the hotel staff would be content to look the other way.

Now it was time to put this thesis to the test.

After mounting the steps, Jack breezed through the lobby as if he had somewhere to be. Which he did. The lanky fräulein manning the pedestal spit out a burst of German as Jack made eye contact. He responded by smiling and shaking his head as he pointed to the beckoning restaurant's deck.

"Meeting someone," Jack said, never slowing his stride.

The hostess seemed on the verge of objecting when a couple entering behind Jack demanded her attention. The woman opened with a deluge in German that her male companion accentuated with a word here or there.

It didn't take a linguist to understand that the pair were unhappy.

Jack quickened his step and then he was past the hostess and into the restaurant proper. A second hostess attempted to check his progress, but Jack was most of the way toward his goal and had no intentions of stopping. Once again, he played to the American stereotype, speaking loudly and slowly as he strolled on by.

"Heading back there," Jack said, gesturing toward the deck.

The woman muttered something in German, but nodded.

Jack navigated the tables and passed through a set of double doors to the outdoor terrace. He hesitated on the far side, as much to take in the incredible view as to search for Sheldon.

The outdoor dining area sat on a cobblestone plaza that also served as the roof for a recessed meeting room. Balconied hotel rooms began on the second floor and continued overhead, leaving the dining area open to the elements. Tables were set apart from one another with collapsible umbrellas to offer shade. But it wasn't so much the eating area as the expanse of blue beyond it that stole Jack's breath.

Thanks to his father and mother, Jack had been a world traveler long before his employment with The Campus. In fact, some of his earliest memories involved toddling through London museums during Jack Senior's tour with MI5. But as grand as these sights had been, the view of Lake Eibsee was in a category by itself.

The dining area was bounded by a waist-high railing that made the lake look like an infinity pool. The still water mirrored the surrounding lush, green hillside in startling detail. Had he been here under other circumstances, Jack would have gladly ordered a plate of currywurst and passed the afternoon soaking up the beauty of God's creation.

But he wasn't here under other circumstances.

Sheldon sat alone at the far right of the patio, close to the railing. One look at the scientist confirmed Jack's suspicion that Sheldon wasn't having a good day. A plate of *Jägerschnitzel* sat untouched in front of Sheldon with a scandalously full stein for company. Even the smile from the pretty blond fräulein who topped off Sheldon's water went unnoticed.

The scientist had a lot on his mind.

Jack could sympathize.

"Reaper elements, this is Scepter," Jack whispered. "Eyes on Sheldon. Sitting alone at the northwest corner of the patio, over."

"Scepter, this is Reaper 1, roger that," Cary said. "He's obstructed by the column, but I've got eyes on the rest of the patio, over."

The column Cary was referencing was one of four spaced evenly across the deck. They stood about fifteen feet high, and their bases were lodged in planters offset by bushes. A tarp covered each column. Jack didn't have the slightest idea as to their purpose—perhaps they were heaters or misters, or maybe just a funky piece of German art.

That didn't matter.

What did matter was that the column closest to the lake was hiding Sheldon from Cary. Even in picturesque Germany, no operation ever went as planned.

"This is Reaper 2," Jad said. "Brat, Wurst, and Spätzle are still clear. I've got the hustle and bustle you'd expect, but no suspicious singletons and no Hermans."

Herman was the brevity code word denoting potential Chinese operatives. Unlike their time on the Korean peninsula, Jack knew that he and the team had the advantage in homogeneous Germany. Unless the Chinese hitters were decked out in motorcycle gear again, they would be easy to spot against the sea of Caucasians. No Hermans equaled good news as far as Jack was concerned.

"Scepter copies all," Jack said. "I'm going in."

16

JACK HAD NO TROUBLE NAVIGATING THE MAZE OF TABLES. THIS TIME
of the afternoon, the seats were less than half full. It was
too late for lunch and too early for dinner. With the sun
blazing from a blue sky, the lake crystal clear, and the
mountains beckoning, Jack figured that the hotel's patrons were busy enjoying the great outdoors.

This suited Jack just fine.

The conversation with Sheldon would be enlighten-
ing, which meant the fewer ears snooping, the better.
Sheldon made eye contact with Jack and then looked
away, his gaze traveling across the lake. Jack logged the
man's reaction as he considered what it meant. The seat
across from Sheldon was empty, but the table held an
extra place setting and menu.

Sheldon was waiting for someone.

"Look sharp," Jack murmured. "Our guy's expecting
company."

As Jack passed the final table separating him from

Sheldon, the scientist eyed him. Sheldon's dining area was set apart from the rest of the patio. No doubt the isolation was intended to facilitate intimate conversations out of earshot from the rest of the diners. A place for lovers to talk. Sheldon watched as Jack approached, and his previously blank expression changed to irritation.

"Is this seat taken?" Jack said.

Running agents was all about relationships. To be an effective handler, you had to convince your asset that you genuinely cared about them, not just what they could do for you. This was especially true during the initial meeting between handler and agent. In this first date of sorts, the asset always made judgments about their handler's capability, veracity, and compassion. Nobody wanted to work for a boss who cared about the results at the expense of his people. This was doubly so for the world of espionage. Jack could have just taken a seat, but by first asking Sheldon if the chair was occupied, he afforded the scientist the illusion that their budding relationship was on equal terms.

"No," Sheldon said, his face wrinkling in confusion. "I mean, not yet."

Though Sheldon was slender, he had a runner's or cyclist's toned build rather than the skinny frame that came from diet alone. His hair was thick and black and swept away from his forehead in an unruly cowlick. His bronze face sported faint tan lines around his eyes. Jack assumed the marks came from sunglasses worn while running or biking, giving credence to his guess that Sheldon was an endurance athlete.

Actually, it wasn't much of a guess.

Scientists tended to prefer solitary athletic activities, with swimming, cycling, and running topping the list. Sheldon's narrow shoulders eliminated swimming. Based on the monstrous sports watch that occupied a quarter of the scientist's left wrist, Jack bet on trail running. The mountains surrounding Edelweiss were riddled with pedestrian footpaths, making this the perfect vacation destination for someone like Sheldon.

Well, almost perfect.

"Great," Jack said, settling in across from the scientist, "because I need a few minutes of your time."

"Sorry," Sheldon said, "but do I know you?"

"No," Jack said, "but this isn't about me. It's about your brother."

Jack had rehearsed his opening several times during the drive to the hotel. He wasn't going for smooth or conciliatory. Jack was trying to provoke a reaction. His time was limited, and Jack needed to get to the heart of the matter quickly. He wanted to know if the scientist knew about his brother's abduction. If so, Jack then wanted to ascertain whether the kidnappers had already given Sheldon instructions in the form of a task Sheldon had to complete before his brother would be released.

Judging by Sheldon's face, the scientist definitely knew his brother had been abducted. Fear warred with anger, and Jack found himself updating his appraisal of Sheldon. Most people were sheep, and fear was an appropriate reaction for a herd animal. Anger, on the other hand, suggested that Sheldon had some fight in him.

This would be a welcome development.

"What do you know about my brother?" Sheldon said.

"Not much," Jack said, "but I want to help."

Reaching into his pocket, Jack withdrew his credentials. He opened the leather case and angled it so that Sheldon could read them while using the far side of the table to shield the creds from the rest of the patio.

Sheldon leaned forward, brow furrowing as he studied the document.

"Department of Agriculture?" Sheldon said, frowning. "Why am I not talking with the FBI or State Department?"

"Because I'm here and they're not," Jack said. "I saw your brother get taken, but I couldn't stop it. I'm assuming his kidnapping has something to do with your work. Is that correct?"

Sheldon shook his head. "I can't talk about what I do. You need to leave. Now."

The anger Jack had seen earlier was still there, but now a different emotion superseded it. Sheldon's thin fingers drummed out a staccato on the tablecloth as his gaze slipped over Jack's shoulder. The scientist had chosen the seat offering a view of the entire dining area as well as the rocky beach.

He was definitely waiting for someone.

"What were the kidnapper's instructions?" Jack said.

Sheldon's eyes hardened as his cheeks flushed.

"The Department of Agriculture investigates missing scientists?"

"You work for a government lab," Jack said, "right?

Then I'm sure you can connect the dots. I'm guessing your brother was targeted because of you. If you insist on dealing with the kidnappers alone, I won't stop you. But I wouldn't recommend it."

"What are you offering?" Sheldon said.

"Help," Jack said. "Tell me what they said to you. I'll do what I can to get your brother back, but you have to be honest with me."

Sheldon looked at Jack without speaking.

Jack wondered what the other man saw.

Working for a government lab didn't make Sheldon a covert operative by any stretch of the imagination, but it did mean the scientist probably rubbed shoulders with some interesting people.

People like Jack.

While Sheldon wasn't overly impressed with the Department of Agriculture creds, he could guess their purpose, even if his conclusion probably pointed him toward the wrong agency. Jack's clothes were rumpled, his face scratched, and his knuckles bruised. This was not the look you'd want for your financial adviser. But if you were facing the sort of rough problem that could be resolved only by equally rough men, Jack's appearance might just be perfect interview attire.

"They told me to come here," Sheldon said.

"To the hotel?" Jack said.

"No," Sheldon said, shaking his head. "To this exact table. They even told me on which side to sit."

The hair on the back of Jack's neck stood up.

This was a setup.

Jack froze, unsure whether to get off the X and risk triggering the ambush or to remain in place and coordinate his next steps with the Green Berets.

Then the glass carafe next to his right hand exploded.

17

CARY MARKS WAS PONDERING HIS POOR LIFE CHOICES.

Though he was overlooking a glacier-fed lake reflecting a mountain, he was not happy. As much as he loved the feel of a cool breeze against his face and the warm sun on his neck, Cary found himself almost longing for the close confines of a sniper hide site. This was not because Cary missed lying in the dirt or the smell of his own body odor. No, Cary was unhappy for just one reason—his sixth sense said that things were about to go sideways, and he was armed with nothing but harsh language.

Well, that and his Special Forces can-do attitude.

Maybe he was just being paranoid.

"Reaper 1, this is Reaper 2," Jad said. "This doesn't feel right, over."

Or perhaps not.

So as not to disturb Jack's meeting with Sheldon, the Green Berets were utilizing a separate radio channel. The

Campus operative had just relayed that he was entering the restaurant. If something was going to go wrong, Cary expected it to be soon.

"Concur," Cary said. "What are you thinking?"

The pavilion Cary had chosen as an observation post was a little over one hundred meters straight-line distance from the hotel's outdoor seating area. The lakeshore doglegged to the southeast for about fifty meters before curling back to the southwest, forming a small inlet. This geography offered Cary an unobstructed sight line across the expanse of water. He had no trouble identifying Jack as the Campus operative emerged from the restaurant's interior, crossed the outdoor seating area, and settled into the seat across from Sheldon.

So far so good.

"Our boy has his back to the action," Jad said. "His table is the closest to the beach."

"Meaning he's a big fat target," Cary said, completing his spotter's thought. "I don't like it, either, but I'm not seeing any sign of trouble. You?"

The pavilion where Cary was seated was about half full of guests, most lingering over beers or glasses of wine. Though a variety of languages were being spoken, every face was Caucasian. In theory, this meant they were not the people Cary was hunting.

In theory.

But theory did nothing to quiet the tingling running down Cary's neck.

"One, this is 2," Jad said. "I've got nothing here, but I think I might have picked a bad spot. This is a fantastic venue for observation, but not for interdiction. If something happens, I'll never get to you in time. I'm going to reposition, over."

The Special Operation Forces sniper training class was known as the Special Operations target interdiction course. *Interdiction* was code for shooting, and Cary agreed with Jad's assessment. Perhaps they'd both been looking at the situation wrong. Cary had chosen his spot for the pavilion's unobstructed sight line to Jack, as well as the surrounding area. But in this case, perhaps he needed to think like a fellow sniper. If Cary was going to take a shot, it wouldn't be from the crowded pavilion. Instead of a countersurveillance mission centered on Jack, maybe he and Jad needed to transition to a counter-sniper profile focusing on the areas that a fellow shooter would pick to construct his hide site.

"Good copy, 2," Cary said. "Let me know once you're in place. I'm going to reposition as well."

Cary looked over his shoulder to signal the waitress, only to have his plans shift once again. The previously empty table ten meters behind Cary was now occupied by a man.

An Asian man.

Well, shit.

Cary took in his fellow diner's appearance as he let his eyes slide over the potential shooter in search of the waitress. When his gaze naturally intersected with the Asian man's, Cary didn't shy away from the eye contact, but neither did he prolong it. There was no flash of recognition in the man's eyes, but that might not mean much. The operatives who'd kidnapped Sheldon's brother were professionals.

Professionals didn't make rookie mistakes.

The pretty waitress smiled at Cary and started toward him. Which complicated things. Since he was weaponless, Cary was already at a disadvantage. He didn't want to be both weaponless and surrounded by potential hostages or targets.

"Beer," Cary shouted.

The waitress's smile disappeared, and she gave a tight nod. Her reaction didn't make Cary feel great, but better a disappointed girl than a dead one. Now Cary had to worry only about his new Asian friend. His interaction with the waitress had given Cary another opportunity to eye the potential shooter. While the man was sitting alone, he now had a cell phone pressed to his ear. This threw Cary for a loop. If the guy really was a shooter, he'd want both hands free.

Why was he on the phone?

Because he wasn't the shooter.

Swearing, Cary keyed the transmit button as he finally understood what was happening.

His teammate beat him to the punch.

"One, this is 2," Jad said. "I've got—"

The unmistakable cough of a suppressed rifle interrupted Jad's transmission. A moment later the crinkling of shattering glass echoed across the water. Jack spilled from his seat but appeared to be unhurt. Hopefully.

While Cary was worried about the Campus operative, his primary concern was seated behind him. Jad had eyes on the shooter, which meant the Asian man on the pavilion with Cary could be only one thing.

The spotter.

18

ACCOUNTING FOR WIND DRIFT WAS ONE OF THE MOST CHALLENGING
aspects of distance shooting. The outdoor dining area
was a nightmare of swirling vortices. The breeze blowing
off the lake had to be significantly different from the air-
flow at the top of the parking lot where the shooter was
located. This meant the Asian man behind Cary must be
feeding the sniper wind information.

Which meant he was an enemy combatant.

Grabbing his stein, Cary whipped the mug at the
Asian man.

Though beer mug throwing had not been a part of
the curriculum covered in the Special Forces Qualifica-
tion, or Q, Course, Cary was uniquely qualified in this
aspect. Like most members of the Special Operations
community, Cary had been a high school athlete. A
pretty gifted one. Though the oblong glass wasn't designed with aerodynamics in mind, Cary had been a
catcher with a reputation for throwing out runners at

second. From that perspective, accurately chucking a glass projectile twenty feet was child's play.

Or so Cary had thought.

But a stein didn't quite fly the same way a baseball did. No matter. The glass projectile had a bit more umph behind it.

The stein bounced off the table and cartwheeled into the Asian man's chest. Other than soaking him with the sudsy remains of Cary's brew, the projectile did no noticeable damage.

The same could not be said of Cary's size twelve shoe.

Or, more accurately, the disruption his shoe caused when it impacted the table.

Cary kicked the table with everything he had, snapping his hips and waist into the blow. The table's edge slammed into the Asian man, hitting him in the solar plexus. He folded over, the phone tumbling from limp fingers. Not one to look a gift horse in the mouth, Cary threaded his fingers through the man's black hair and bashed his face against the table three times. Strictly speaking, the first two blows were enough to finish the job, but in Cary's experience, anything worth shooting once was worth shooting twice.

Or three times.

The man slid from his chair in a limp puddle.

While part of Cary's mind realized that he'd received his last smile from the cute waitress, the other more rational section was fervently hoping that the man was armed. This was both so that Cary could better come to his friends' aid and because he desperately wanted to be-

lieve that he hadn't just beaten an innocent man senseless.

After a frantic pat-down, Cary found a bulge near the
man's waist. Stripping the pistol from the Asian's pants,
Cary racked the slide, chambering a round. Or, to be
more specific, chambering a second round as the one already in the chamber cartwheeled through the air.

Fine.

Racking the slide was quicker than press-checking the
pistol.

What was not fine was the sight greeting Cary as he
stood, pistol in hand. Several of the more courageous
bystanders were now converging toward him. Apparently, slamming a man's head repeatedly against a table
was frowned upon in Germany.

Cary was both sympathetic to their cause and impressed by their bravery. However, as the sound of scuf-
fling echoing from his earpiece coupled with another
rifle report could attest, he was out of time. So he persuaded the would-be vigilantes to step aside with the elo-
quence for which Green Berets were known.

"Back the fuck up," Cary said, pointing the pistol at
the nearest bystander.

Between Cary's exquisite language skills and the pistol's
gaping black maw, the crowd got the message. Would-be
heroes edged back, retreating into the restaurant.

Which was exactly the direction Cary needed to go.

"Avalanche, avalanche, avalanche."

The person who'd last uttered those three words in
succession had been Cary. At the time, he'd been in a

fighting position overlooking a Syrian compound populated by a cult of apocalyptic Shia militants. Jad had been critically wounded, and the two snipers had been in danger of being overrun by militants.

This time, Jad was calling for help.

The beautiful surroundings suddenly didn't seem quite so picturesque.

"Coming, brother," Cary said, not bothering with radio protocol.

Then he jumped off the deck.

19

THE PAVILION WAS ONLY ABOUT TEN FEET ABOVE THE GROUND, BUT Cary's drop zone consisted of the loose gravel that made up the lake's beach. Not exactly the softest landing place, but it beat piling into a concrete runway with sixty pounds of gear strapped to his back.

Mostly.

Though Cary kept his knees bent and together in his best approximation of a parachute-landing fall, the gravel did him no favors. The loose rocks churned under his weight, bruising his feet and torquing an ankle. But those were concerns for another day. His best friend and team-mate had just called an avalanche.

Cary had shit to do.

Turning toward the road leading to the parking lot that serviced the cable car, Cary took off at a dead sprint. The sounds of grunts and the deep *thunk*s of flesh impacting flesh still coming from his earpiece added fuel to the fire, hitting his nervous system like a jolt of epineph-rine.

Jad was fighting for his life.

Cary reached the top of the drive in five or six distance-eating strides, leaving him with a decision. The pavement spiraled to the right, climbing up the incline toward the cable car station. That's where Jad had origin-ally set up, but Cary didn't think his spotter was there any longer. The platform didn't have line of sight to the patio, and it was way too crowded. Passengers were still queued up outside the glass lounge, waiting for their chance to ride to the summit. Germans had a deserved reputation for stoicism, but moms were still moms. Cary couldn't imagine that the women shepherding small chil-dren would still be passing out snacks and sippy cups if Jad was wrestling a shooter just feet away.

The gunman was elsewhere.

Looking to his right, Cary settled on the wood line cascading down from the hill to the lake's rocky shore. That was where Cary would set up. Good lines of sight, secluded, and multiple egress avenues.

His decision made, Cary took off running.

"Heading into the trees," Cary said, transmitting in the blind.

The answering silence was ominous.

Cary tried not to read too much into Jad's non-response. His partner wasn't Superman, but he was one hell of a fighter. Cary would put Jad up against any single opponent.

Except Jad probably wasn't fighting a single opponent.

Adrenaline surged through Cary.

These guys were professionals. Professionals wouldn't emplace a sniper without security. Jad must be going hands-on with two bad guys.

Two armed bad guys.

The odds no longer seemed quite so promising.

Transitioning from grass to forest, Cary resisted the urge to stop and listen for sounds of the fight. Instead, he followed the rolling terrain toward the summit, trusting his tactical sense. He didn't have time to stop. If Cary chose wrong, Jad was a goner. If he was right, but took too long to get in the fight, Jad was just as dead.

Clambering up a stony outcropping, Cary caught movement to his right.

Three figures struggling.

Cary was too far away to identify the writhing shadows, but he knew he needed to end this.

Now.

Cary paused as he sighted along the pistol's short barrel.

The distance to the pile of bodies was too great. He couldn't distinguish Jad from the other two.

Cary changed tack.

Pointing the pistol at his feet, Cary fired three rapid shots.

The pistol's report was incredibly loud in the forest's stillness.

The sound of gunshots broke up the scrum. Two of

the men stopped fighting and looked toward Cary, giving the third an opportunity to roll off the rocky ledge and onto the unforgiving ground below.

Jad.

The sight of his best friend's limp body tumbling to the ground broke something in Cary. He rushed forward, firing as he moved. While he didn't give in to his animal instinct to run, Cary covered the ground at a pace faster than he could accurately shoot. But just as he moderated his urge to sprint, Cary also restrained his desire to empty the pistol's magazine in a span of seconds.

Instead, he maintained a constant, though rapid, rate of fire.

The rounds kicked up dirt, tore bark from the trees, and sparked off boulders. At least one bullet hit home, judging by the puff of fabric that flew from the assailant on the left's chest. The strike spun the man, but didn't put him down.

Which meant they were wearing body armor.

Cary's day had just become much, much worse.

He dashed the last ten yards, his pistol now just a glorified noisemaker. Cary added his voice to the mayhem, shrieking a battle cry that would have done his Scottish ancestors proud. In a close engagement between numerically equal forces, sometimes raw aggression really could carry the day.

At least that's what Cary was hoping.

A final burst of speed put him on top of Jad just as his pistol's slide locked to the rear. Dropping the gun, Cary scooped up his spotter and dragged the limp man under the shelter offered by the cliff's craggy overhang. The two assailants occupied the high ground and presumably still possessed ammunition for their weapons. They held all the cards.

All the cards but one.

Positioning.

The terrain sloped down from Cary while the cliff offered overhead shelter. To finish him off, the gunmen would have to clamber down the slope, exposing themselves. As Cary's pounding heart could attest, the gradient grew much steeper on the far side of the shelter, meaning that a grenade dropped from above would probably roll down the hill before detonating. By the same token, the jutting and jagged overhang would limit the shooters' ability to point their pistols over the edge and just spray and pray.

By dragging Jad into the rocky redoubt, Cary had become a cornered wolf. Now his hunters had to decide if they were willing to flush Cary out, knowing what it would probably cost them in the process. Judging by the fading sound of crackling leaves and snapping branches, Cary didn't think they were ready to pay that price.

With a shuddered sigh, Cary turned his attention to his spotter. After verifying that the other Green Beret was breathing, Cary slid his fingers across Jad's torso, looking for bullet wounds. Finding nothing, he eased his spotter over and performed the same triage across his back.

Still nothing.

Rolling Jad faceup again, Cary expanded his efforts,

now looking for blunt-force injuries that might have caused an obstructed airway, broken bones, or internal hemorrhaging. A massive red welt covered the top of Jad's face, but while the blow was undoubtedly painful, it didn't look serious.

"Jad," Cary said, lightly slapping his friend's face, "come on, brother."

"What?" Jad said, his eyes fluttering open. "What happened?"

"You got your ass kicked and fell off a cliff," Cary said with a smile.

"Bullshit," Jad said as he struggled to a sitting position. "I was conducting a tactical withdrawal. What about the bad guys?"

"I saved the day," Cary said, "like usual. Can you walk?"

"I'm a Green Beret," Jad said, his words losing some of their earlier slur, "of course I can walk. Find my knife and we're out of here."

"You have a knife?" Cary said.

"You don't?"

"Jack said not to bring any weapons."

"Have you met Jack?" Jad said.

Great point.

"Got a spare?" Cary said.

"Help me up," Jad said. "Then we'll address your stunning lack of preparedness. What's our fearless leader up to, anyway?"

That was a very good question.

20

THE SOUND OF THE SHATTERING CARAFE SURPRISED JACK EVEN AS A flood of water spilled across the table. For an instant he sat rooted in place, his tired brain not connecting the dots. Then Jack registered the sharp *crack* that had accompanied the crinkling of the glass.

The sound a high-velocity rifle makes as it transits the sound barrier.

Lurching out of his seat, Jack reached across the table as a second *crack* sundered the air. This time the bullet's miniature supersonic boom was accompanied by another sound. The deep *thunk* of a projectile striking flesh.

Sheldon spun out of his chair.

Jack dove on top of the scientist even as additional rounds peppered the table and patio. Stone slivers scored grooves down Jack's face as invisible death rained down around him. That Jack hadn't been hit was nothing short of a miracle. But miracle or not, Jack knew that his luck was too good to last.

He wanted to radio the Green Berets, but his phone was nestled in his front pocket, giving new meaning to the phrase *so close but so far away*. Digging for the device would entail arching his back or flaring his elbow, neither of which went with his current plan of becoming one with the patio. Several times Jack heard a buzzing indicative of lead projectiles passing inches from his face. Any movement meant putting a body part into the real estate currently occupied by rifle rounds.

No, thanks.

But staying put wasn't an option, either, as the hammer blow to his hamstring attested. The impact sent pins and needles racing the length of Jack's leg. He groaned in pain. Steeling himself, Jack peered down the length of his body.

No blood.

Must have been a ricochet. He had to do something to change the equation.

Fast.

Looking to his left, Jack saw one of the mystery columns.

Perfect.

Sliding off the still-convulsing Sheldon, Jack grabbed the scientist by the legs and dragged him toward the row of columns. Progress was mind-numbingly slow, but by edging along the ground Jack was staying out of the sniper's sight line. The same couldn't be said of his fellow diners. Shrieks echoed as customers milled across the patio, unsure how to escape the unseen onslaught.

Jack was torn. He wanted to do something to help, but getting up would put him squarely in the line of fire.

Then he had an idea.

After positioning Sheldon at the base of the column, Jack worked his way up the slender metal until he found what he was hoping to see—a crank for a massive umbrella. Jack grabbed the handle and began to turn it with both hands, spinning the bracket as fast as he could. At first, his efforts yielded only a series of metal shrieks.

Then, little by little, the umbrella began to unfurl.

As Jack cranked, the bullets seemed to come faster. The earlier drizzle was now a full-fledged hailstorm. Taking this as a good sign, Jack cranked faster. The sniper must be rushing his shots in response to his disappearing target. After a couple dozen rotations, the massive umbrella partially unfurled like a peacock spreading its feathers.

The metal rainstorm became a pitter-patter, suggesting that either Jack's scheme had worked or the gunman was approaching the end of his magazine. Or, better yet, maybe his two Green Beret friends had finally entered the equation. Either way, Jack had done all he could to help the restaurant's patrons. For the first time, he turned his attention to Sheldon. Unlike in the movies, getting struck by a rifle round moving at several thousand feet per second was not insignificant. Even if the bullet entered an area of the torso devoid of vital organs, the round's impact sent a shock wave convulsing through the victim's abdominal cavity, rupturing organs and inducing massive hemorrhaging.

Jack started to rip away Sheldon's red-stained shirt but stopped, his hands hovering above the scientist's chest. Whether or not Sheldon's torso wound was survivable was no longer a concern. At some point during the chaotic last few moments, the scientist had sustained a second injury. Most of the left side of his skull was missing.

Jack slowly withdrew his shaking hands and keyed the radio instead.

"Any Reaper element, this is Scepter," Jack whispered, conscious of his surroundings.

The gunfire might have ceased, but screams still filled the air. Even so, Jack was still cautious. Everything up until now would be a muddled mixture of sensory inputs for the survivors. This wouldn't be the case for much longer. Jack didn't want to give a German bystander a reason to remember him when the *polizei* began to ask questions.

"Scepter, this is Reaper," Cary said, sounding a bit winded. "Reaper 2 and I are egressing toward Wurst. We stopped the shooters, but they got away, over."

"Roger that," Jack said. "I'll meet you there. Sheldon took a round to the head. He's gone."

"Reaper copies all," Cary said. "You'd better beat feet. I can see flashing lights at the turnoff to the lake. You've got three minutes. Maybe less."

Jack ground his teeth. He hated abandoning Sheldon. Even though he didn't know the man, Jack felt somewhat responsible for the scientist's death. Maybe if he had moved faster, Sheldon would still be alive. Jack's instincts had been correct, but being right counted for nothing when the man you were trying to protect was now missing half his skull. But staying with Sheldon would help no one. At the very least, Jack would be taken into custody and questioned. Maybe he could leverage Hans as a get-out-of-jail-free card, but that would take time.

Time that Jack didn't have.

It was just as likely that the BfV officer would throw Jack in a cell. Unlike what had happened at the University of Regensburg, this time a civilian was dead. Maybe more than one civilian. Germany didn't have active-shooter events, and there was no way this catastrophe was going to be swept under the rug. Someone would have to take the blame, and that someone might just be an American intelligence officer who was conducting an unauthorized operation on an ally's soil.

"Roger that," Jack said. "Egressing now. Meet you at the rally point."

"You sure?" Cary said. "We can pick you up at Wurst."

"Positive," Jack said. "I don't want to chance you getting caught inside the *polizei*'s perimeter. Everything's still chaotic here. No one's gonna notice one more person running for cover."

While Jack hoped that was true, there was only one way to find out. Already the screams and cries were beginning to quiet. If he wanted to leave before the inevitable lockdown, he needed to get a move on. Jack took one more look at Sheldon's disfigured face, emblazoning the scientist's features in his mind. Someone needed to avenge the scientist's death.

Jack had a feeling he was that someone.

Jack was getting to his feet when he had a thought. Patting down the man's pants, Jack found the scientist's cell phone and slipped it into his pocket. Then he turned and followed the rest of the crowd from the restaurant just as police sirens echoed up the drive.

Jack stayed with the flow of bodies until he reached the woods.

Then he jumped on a trail heading toward his Green Berets and vengeance.

21

"WHAT NOW, BOSS?"

Though the question came from the car's backseat, Cary, who was driving, looked to Jack as well. Both Green Berets seemed a little less taken with life as a Campus operative than they had at the beginning of their German adventure.

Jack understood.

He felt the same way.

"Decision time," Jack said.

In a seeming first for the events of the last several hours, Jack's egress from the hotel and the linkup with Cary and Jad had gone according to plan. Maybe at some point running away wouldn't be the only part of the mission that went like clockwork.

After he'd belted himself into the front passenger seat, Jack had signaled Cary to drive. The Green Beret complied, heading northeast on A 95 at a comfortable one hundred and thirty kilometers per hour. Once they'd put a good twenty kilometers between themselves and the site of the shooting, Jack knew it was time to settle on the next step. He'd been turning options over in his mind when Jad had voiced his question.

Now was as good a time as ever to let his comrades in on his thinking.

They'd more than earned a vote.

"Here's the deal," Jack said, eyeing the sign announcing the rapidly approaching turnoff for Highway B 472 and the Austrian border. "The way I see it, we've got a couple choices. Mr. C. wants us to catch a flight to Manila out of Munich. Staying on A 95 will get us there. I'm thinking the smarter play is to head for Austria and fly out of Salzburg under new identities instead. But getting our hands on new legends is going to take time, and the delay might affect Clark's operational timeline. There are risks with either course of action."

"The kind of risks that get us arrested by airport security?" Cary said.

"Security?" Jad said. "Hell. The Germans have CCTV all over Munich Airport. We'll be lucky to get out of parking. Jack's been in two gunfights in a country with less than one hundred gun-related homicides per year. The *polizei* probably have his picture on continuous loop."

"To be fair, Jack's not the only one who's been dropping bodies," Cary said.

"From what I could see, you shot the shit out of some trees and not much else," Jad said.

"I shot what needed shooting," Cary said, "and for the record, I was aiming at those trees."

"The guy I stuck with my knife probably lived," Jad said. "His leather coat stopped the blade."

"Wait," Jack said, trying to regain control of the conversation, "you brought a combat knife into Germany?"

"Sure did," Jad said, unclipping a Spyderco from his belt. "And it's a good thing. My partner shoots like my grandma and doesn't run much faster."

"I said no weapons," Jack said.

"I've needed a gun every time I've been in the same zip code as you," Jad said. "Today was no different. Those last two jackwagons came pretty close to punching my clock."

"Not that close," Cary said. "I was there."

"The goose egg on my forehead begs to differ," Jad said. "Here's the thing, Jack, your daddy might be President, but that damn sure doesn't make you king. From now on, if I go somewhere with you, I carry a Glock. Even if it's to grab a beer with your pops. If his Secret Service detail has a problem with that, they can pry my piece from my hairy fingers."

Jack had been in combat with the Green Berets enough times to appreciate Jad's tactical prowess, but he wasn't sure who would win that dogfight. That was neither here nor there. Jack's first operation as a bona fide team leader had not exactly been an unqualified success. The mission was blown, his team had been split, and the two remaining members were at each other's throats.

This op needed a hard reset.

Starting with him.

"This is on me," Jack said, "all of it. You two have

already been through way more than you signed up for. Our asses are hanging in the breeze, we've got no in-country support, and I severely misjudged the threat environment. Twice. Option three is that we head for the U.S. consulate in Munich so you guys can get off this runaway train."

"Now you're trying to get rid of us?" Jad said. "That's pretty messed up, isn't it, boss?"

"Very messed up," Cary said, nodding, "especially after what his daddy made us promise."

"And who says no to Jack freaking Ryan?" Jad said.

"Not me," Cary said.

"Wait," Jack said, eyeing Jad in the rearview mirror, "my dad made you promise something?"

"Yep," Jad said, "the moment you left to take a piss."

"Very persuasive, your old man," Cary said.

Jack fought the urge to ask the obvious question for as long as he could.

He lasted two seconds.

"What did he make you promise?" Jack said.

"Should we tell him, boss?" Jad said. "Seems like a breach of trust to me."

"Definitely a breach of trust," Cary said, "and loyalty seems pretty important to Jack freaking Ryan."

"Very important," Jad said.

"You're not gonna tell me?" Jack said.

"How about this?" Cary said. "Let's finish dealing with the shitbirds who tried to kill us. After we've helped them see the error of their ways and are safely back on

American soil at an alcohol-serving establishment, we'll reconsider your request."

"And not just beer," Jad said. "Gluten makes me bloated."

For a moment Jack was truly lost. Even as the turnoff for B 472 grew closer, he couldn't for the life of him understand what the two Green Berets were trying to tell him. He glanced at Cary, and though the commando was staring straight ahead, his lips were twisted into a ghost of a smile.

Then Jack got it.

"I take it you guys are okay with a detour to Austria?" Jack said.

"Are all spooks this slow, boss?" Jad said.

"I think what my spotter is trying to say," Cary said, exiting onto B 472, "is that we've been knocked down twice now. Maybe it's time we started doing the tackling. Did I get that right, Jad?"

"Sure enough," Jad said.

"Then buckle up," Jack said as the car angled east toward Austria. "The rest of the flight's gonna be bumpy."

"*Bumpy* as in more guys trying to kill us?" Jad said. "Or *bumpy* like you're making this up as you go?"

"What did my dad say?" Jack said.

Jad sighed.

Sliding down in his seat, the commando closed his eyes.

"Wake me up when the turbulence is over."

22

FEN LI STARED AT THE FLAT-SCREEN TV ENCOMPASSING THE FAR wall.

Like the rest of her office, the TV was sleek, ultra-modern, and stylish, as befitting a chief executive officer of Fen Li's status. As was always the case, the touch-screen TV displayed a China-centric map of the world populated by a collection of colored pins. Each pin represented an active contract Fen Li's collection of former intelligence and paramilitary operatives were currently servicing. Although the vast majority of the pins corresponded to projects associated with the Chinese Communist Party's expansive Belt and Road Initiative, which spanned large portions of Africa and Asia, or maritime fleets sailing through the pirate-infested waters of the South China Sea, the map did contain a few surprises.

One such surprise was located in Europe.

Germany, to be precise.

Unlike its compatriots, the pin marking a German city near the Austrian border was colored red. If she'd been of the mind, Fen could have crossed her office and tapped the red pin, bringing up a summary of the failed operation. There was no need. In a departure from the operational leeway she normally imparted to her subordinates, Fen had personally monitored the Germany operation.

Perhaps not closely enough.

Fen's slender fingers found the walnut-sized polymetallic nodule that served as the only decoration on the otherwise empty glass slab that formed her desk. The nodule resembled nothing so much as a brick of partially charred charcoal, but like Fen, the rock was more than it seemed. The collection of ore would guarantee both the future of the company Fen had founded and her ascension into the upper echelons of the Chinese Communist Party.

Her coconspirator and benefactor had promised as much.

China might be a Communist nation, but it was as beholden to capital as any Western democracy. Maybe more so. In the last several years, the Party had made monstrous monetary bets on its trillion-dollar Belt and Road Initiative. Bets that had so far netted rather dubious returns.

And then there was Chinese real estate.

Between twenty and thirty percent of China's gross domestic product was tied to its property market, and Chinese real estate sales were a bubble about to burst.

Western analysts were likening the business practices of China's largest property developers to a Ponzi scheme, while influential figures within the Chinese government were estimating that up to eight hundred billion yuan might be required to stabilize the market. Taken together, these signs pointed to a Chinese economy on the brink of collapse.

But not if Fen Li had her way.

The longer Fen's cadre of hired experts pored over the data she'd collected during her clandestine exploration of the Paracel Islands deposits, the rosier their predictions became. Fen had at her fingertips the power to alter not just her own future, but China's as well.

Assuming, of course, she succeeded where her team in Europe had failed.

Fen stared at the offending red pin, considering.

The conservative play would be to let her benefactor know about the setback in Europe and request additional resources. But this course of action came with its own risks. The deal she'd negotiated with her coconspirator depended in no small part on her assurances that she would bear the risks of their joint endeavor, allowing him to share in the rewards. If she asked for additional help, he would undoubtedly see this for what it was—an opportunity to revisit the terms of their agreement. The entirety of the company she'd spent her life building was tied to this effort. Fen had no intention of trading it away to a bureaucrat who'd faced nothing more deadly in his political career than the occasional paper cut, while Fen's prior life in the Ministry of State Security had whitened her hair and broken her body.

Fen's gaze moved from the touchscreen TV to the digital clock mounted above it.

The *Maochong* was already more than halfway to the Paracel Islands. Though the Germany operation had not gone as Fen would have liked, her coconspirator had already given her the means to address the shortcoming, and the pieces of her plan were falling into place.

The opportunity she'd been chasing was still right in front of her.

Fen needed only to be brave enough to seize it.

Setting aside the nodule, Fen withdrew a cell phone from her purse and made a call. The number she dialed did not belong to her benefactor. She'd succeeded thus far by relying on herself rather than the largesse of others.

Fen did not intend to change course now.

23

TURNS OUT THAT IT WAS QUITE SOME TIME BEFORE THE TURBULENCE was over.

Crossing from Germany into Austria was about as difficult as driving from Indiana to Ohio, but what came next was considerably more taxing. While all three men had traveled to Germany under their true names, Jack had wanted to flex as many Campus assets during the surveillance exercise as possible. This meant spinning up the document-creation folks to manufacture an alternate set of passports for the team. Unlike weapons, alternate documents could be easily concealed in specially designed compartments within each teammate's luggage and just as easily disposed of if the need arose.

When it came to traveling clandestinely, Canada was the country of choice for American spies. There was no pesky accent to master, and outside of a couple major cities, almost no one knew anything about Canada. Also, unlike their American neighbors, the stereotype of Canadians as polite, nice people was both accurate and complimentary.

Unfortunately, the team's passports were still in their luggage, which was resting comfortably in their Regensburg hotel rooms. While it was possible to get replacement documents into Austria through the CIA's Vienna station, Jack was hesitant to make use of this connection. Every interaction with a legitimate member of the intelligence community put The Campus's status as an off-the-books organization at risk. Sure, Clark had run some joint operations with Mary Pat's blessing, but these needed to remain the exception rather than the rule. If this were truly an emergency, Jack would have no problem making the necessary request. While his time in Germany had been far from the idyllic shakeout operation he'd imagined, as Campus activity went, this did not yet qualify as an emergency. But if Jack were being honest, he'd have to admit that operational security took a backseat to his biggest concern.

John T. Clark.

Jack had given his boss a sitrep like an adult and Mr. C. had treated him as such. Rather than reining Jack in like he had countless times before, Clark had deferred to Jack as the on-the-ground team leader. That the team leader in question was the most junior member of The Campus had not been discussed. Clark had afforded Jack the same level of autonomy and discretion he would have allotted his second-in-command, Ding Chavez.

And how had Jack rewarded Clark's trust?

By executing an on-the-fly operation that had resulted in the murder of their only lead and undoubtedly delayed Clark's operation in Manila.

Jack sighed as he probed his half-empty espresso for answers.

With its stunning architecture, cobblestone streets, and scenic Salzach River, Salzburg was every bit as beautiful as the travel brochures claimed, but Jack was looking forward to an even more captivating sight.

And here she came.

Though she'd traded her half-shirt for a tank top and her cut-offs for a white denim skirt, the wardrobe change had done nothing to diminish Lisanne's presence. Her hair fell loose in a raven curtain around her shoulders and the pair of aviator sunglasses shading her eyes only added to her mystique. Like the jean shorts, her skirt showed off miles of brown, toned legs, and the white fabric only served to highlight her olive complexion. Jack's stomach fluttered as he heard his mother's voice.

Marry that girl before someone else does.

Judging by the attention directed Lisanne's way from the café's male diners, Austria contained no shortage of *someones.*

"Hey," Jack said, getting to his feet.

Once again, his lips twisted into the goofy grin he could never quite rein in around Lisanne. He was a grown man and a covert operative. A world traveler who brought justice to his nation's enemies from the shadows.

But one look from this girl reduced Jack to a lovestruck teenager.

"Hey yourself," Lisanne said.

She leaned in for a quick hug, and Jack pressed his face against the warmth of her neck, reveling in the hint of vanilla.

Her smell.

His face tingled, and Jack broke the embrace with effort.

"Any trouble?" Jack asked as he seated Lisanne before returning to his side of the table.

The dark-haired beauty shook her head.

"No," Lisanne said. "I grabbed the luggage from both rooms. The suitcases went into a dumpster, but I've got the passports and IDs. I rented a car under my alias and took the scenic route into Austria. No sign of surveillance, but I didn't have time to run a full SDR. Where are the boys?"

"Buying supplies," Jack said as he processed Lisanne's update.

The next flight to Manila left soon. Jack had booked separate tickets under the assumed names he, Jad, and Cary were using. Then he'd tasked the Green Berets to purchase appropriate travel attire and the usual accoutrements. People who flew internationally without baggage attracted attention. The kind of attention Jack couldn't afford. So while the commandos ran errands, Jack had read through the research Gavin had forwarded while waiting for Lisanne to courier their new identities.

She'd agreed to Jack's request, but had been reluctant to leave Isabel. The scientist couldn't be linked to the rest of the Campus operatives, so there was no reason to suspect that Isabel was in danger. Then again, this morning there'd been no reason to suspect a gang of Asian operatives was about to conduct an extreme rendition in broad daylight, either.

Even so, the mission was no longer on the Regensburg campus. The center of gravity was in Austria with Jack and the Green Berets. But traveling to Salzburg had presented its own challenges. Normally Lisanne would have engaged in a long and circuitous SDR. These twists and turns were designed to ferret out surveillance, and the technique worked very well when done correctly.

But Jack didn't have time for Lisanne to conduct the SDR correctly. Clark had made it abundantly clear that the operation in the Philippines was time-sensitive. Jack had missed his flight in Munich. He couldn't afford to miss the one leaving from Salzburg. In the constantly evolving risk-versus-reward calculus, Jack had decided that speed was more important than security.

Accordingly, Lisanne had come straight to Salzburg.

With a larger team, she could have still accomplished a modified SDR by positioning Campus operatives ahead of her intended route to conduct countersurveillance, but there were no more bodies to draw from. As the leader, Jack bore the responsibility for the current state of affairs. In his defense, he'd had no intention of running an actual operation when he'd settled on the manning roster back in Arlington, but in the profession of espionage, results, not intentions, were what mattered.

That was a topic for later.

At present, Jack needed to focus on getting to Manila as fast as possible. But first he had to have a talk with Lisanne. A talk he was dreading. Jack opened his mouth, but Lisanne spoke first.

"I'm not going, am I?" Lisanne said.

"No," Jack said, shaking his head. "This operation has unexpectedly gone kinetic twice. I'm not taking you to a potential gunfight, Lisanne."

Lisanne nodded, but her soft brown eyes turned hard.

"Are you saying that as my team leader or my boyfriend?" Lisanne said.

Jack sighed, but Lisanne pressed an index finger to his lips before he could reply.

"Sorry," Lisanne said, "that was a cheap shot. It's not you I'm mad at. It's this."

She punctuated the *this* by raising her arm.

The one that ended in a stump.

"I'm a Marine, Jack," Lisanne said, "and a former police officer. I'm not the kind of girl that slinks offstage once the shooting starts. At least I didn't used to be."

Jack threaded his fingers through Lisanne's.

"Lisanne Robertson, you're still the same girl you've always been," Jack said. "You're a warrior. A fighter. Losing an arm doesn't change who you are. But it does change the way you contribute."

"I know," Lisanne said, squeezing Jack's hand. "I know. But that doesn't make it any easier. I don't think I can keep doing this."

"What?" Jack said.

"Pulling back every time things get bad."

"Is that the only thing that's wrong?" Jack said.

Lisanne stared back at him for a long moment without answering.

Before, her eyes had seemed like shards of iron.

Now they were filling with tears.

Jack swallowed.

"I don't know," Lisanne said. "Probably not. I love being with you, but I can't figure this out. One minute you're my boyfriend. The next my team leader. Between my injury, my role in The Campus, and whatever the hell it is we're doing, I feel lost."

"What do you want?" Jack said, dreading the answer.

Lisanne hiccupped, half laughing and half crying.

She let go of Jack's hand to brush away her tears.

"What I want doesn't matter," Lisanne said. "Two men are dead, and a scientist has been kidnapped. You're about to hop a flight to the other side of the world, and we're having the relationship talk. This just isn't working, Jack. Your passports are in the satchel under the table. Good luck."

Without waiting for a reply, Lisanne got to her feet, turned, and walked away.

A thousand and one thoughts flooded Jack's mind as he watched the woman he loved melt into the crowd. As was par for the course for this operation, he had no idea what to do next, but he knew one thing for certain.

Lisanne was right.

This wasn't working.

24

"JUNIOR—SO GOOD OF YOU TO JOIN US."

Jack paused at the apartment's threshold, not quite believing what he was seeing. The décor was exactly what Jack would have expected of a safe house the world over. The three-room dwelling's white walls were bare and the gray tile floors relatively clean. Furniture was cheap but functional—a couch with sagging cushions, a brown love seat with a couple cigarette burns, and a scarred end table. A no-frills kitchen was to the right and a living room with an ancient TV perched on a particleboard entertainment system to the left. A narrow hallway led from the living room, presumably to the bathroom and bedroom.

But while the apartment's décor was not unexpected, the people occupying it certainly were. Seated on barstools ringing the kitchen's small island were Ding

Chavez, Dominic "Dom" Caruso, and the person who'd greeted Jack—John T. Clark.

Clark didn't look happy.

To be fair, neither did the rest of the Campus team.

JACK AND HIS TEAM HAD SPENT MUCH OF THE LAST TWENTY-FOUR hours traveling. Salzburg offered multiple flights to Manila, but no direct options. Quite a few of the layovers occurred in German cities, and Jack rejected these outright. Though the legends he and the Green Berets were flying under had never been used, Jack took Jad's comment about German CCTV capabilities to heart.

With this in mind, Jack had chosen a different flight for each of them. He and Cary were flying Turkish Airlines with separate departure times but similar arrivals, and Jad scored a Lufthansa ticket. The three operatives had navigated layovers in Istanbul, Doha, and Abu Dhabi before reconnecting in Manila.

It hadn't been anyone's idea of fun.

Jack had passed the travel time by reviewing the information he'd received from Gavin and assessing what had gone wrong with the Sheldon meet. As much as he didn't want to believe it, Jack was stuck with the conclusion that somehow his team had been burned. Whether that was due to surveillance Jack hadn't detected, sloppy tradecraft on their part, or some other reason he'd yet to identify, the conclusion was the same.

Jack's team had been made, and now an American was dead.

Jack had decided not to attempt to update Clark on what had transpired or even that he and the two Green Berets would be arriving at Manila later than expected. Until Jack better understood what had gone wrong in Germany, he intended to operate under the assumption that all of his communications protocols had been compromised. The safe house in Manila would have a means to securely contact Clark.

Until then, Jack would remain dark.

On the few occasions when he wasn't obsessing about the blown operation, Jack found himself replaying the scene at the café with Lisanne. Each time he arrived at the same conclusion. The correct response as a team leader was in direct conflict with the correct response as Lisanne's boyfriend. Jack suspected that this was the exact quandary Clark had been trying to warn him about. With very rare exceptions, lovers did not make for good field partners. If you loved someone, the mission would always come secondary to their safety.

For proof of this adage, Jack looked no further than his father.

Jack Ryan, Sr., was the epitome of a manly man. He'd once slithered into a Soviet submarine to face down a KGB operative in order to prevent World War III. On another continent, Ryan had interrupted a family outing in order to stop an IRA assassin from murdering a British royal.

In the submarine Ryan had at least been armed with a pistol.

In London, he'd had nothing but his fists.

Jack's father was no stranger to violence, but even he had recognized the necessity of stepping down from the presidency after a paramilitary group kidnapped Cathy Ryan. It just wasn't possible to maintain objectivity when a person you loved was in the hands of evil men.

But the dustup with Lisanne was about more than just Jack's dual role as her team leader and boyfriend. Jack had finally proven himself to be not just the equal of any Campus operator, but also leadership material. After his escapades in Syria, and then the Korean peninsula, Jack had been given his own team.

This was a new development.

On previous operations, Jack had utilized Campus support assets like Gavin, but he'd often worked apart from his fellow Campus shooters. Aside from the occasional phone call to Clark, usually asking for forgiveness rather than permission, Jack had been the master of his own destiny rather than the junior member of an accomplished team. He'd enjoyed the autonomy and hadn't relished the idea of returning to the Campus fold. The pseudo-training exercise in Germany had been a way for both Jack and Clark to understand what Jack's future with The Campus might hold.

Not much, from where Jack was sitting.

Germany had been a dumpster fire. Now Jack's boss had flown into the field to clip Jack's wings. Unexpectedly finding Clark, Ding, and Dom in the safe house angered Jack, but his fellow operatives weren't the real source of his fury.

He reserved that honor for himself.

―――

"WE EXPECTING A PARTY?" CARY SAID, EYEING THE APARTMENT'S occupants.

"Reason one hundred and twelve why I will never again go anywhere with you unarmed," Jad said, closing the safe house door behind him.

With a start Jack realized that this was the first face-to-face meeting between the Green Berets and the larger Campus crew. While Clark had approved Jack's Germany mission, the director of operations had wanted to keep the commandos and Isabel separate from the clandestine Campus team. The senior Ryan's invitation to the commandos aside, Clark was the ultimate arbitrator of Campus membership. Until Clark was certain about the two men, their involvement would be operationally siloed. An off-the-books organization could remain clandestine only if the number of outsiders who knew it existed was kept to a minimum.

Cary and Jad had been fine with this arrangement. They'd now gone to war with Jack twice, and the elder Ryan was one hell of a salesman. But knowing that the shadowy organization you were loosely affiliated with employed other operatives and coming face-to-face with them in a dingy apartment that reeked of fish and garbage were two very different things.

The Green Berets weren't in combat mode, but they weren't all smiles and sunshine, either. Cary had posted to Jack's right while Jad had slid to his left, preparing to dominate the room. Like rival packs of wild dogs meeting on a crowded street, the five operatives sized one another up, instinctively doing the kind of battlefield calculus that was as natural as breathing to those who lived by the gun.

With a sigh, Jack interposed himself between the two groups.

"Hey, Mr. C.," Jack said. "Wasn't expecting you. Cary and Jad, this is my boss, John Clark, his 2IC, Ding Chavez, and Dom Caruso, my cousin and fellow shooter. Gents, meet Cary and Jad. Cary's the team sergeant for ODA 555, and Jad is his teammate."

"Triple Nickel," Ding said with a smile and an outstretched hand. "That's no 3rd Battalion, 17th Infantry Regiment, but your outfit's reputation isn't too shabby."

"Please," Jad said, returning Ding's handshake. "From what I hear, you ninjas are only one step above SEALs."

"What's that about SEALs?" Clark said.

The former Rainbow Six was smiling, but there was iron in his voice.

"Sorry," Jack said, "I probably should have added that in addition to serving as the first Rainbow Six, Mr. C. was also a Vietnam-era SOG member and Navy SEAL."

Jack expected embarrassed silence.

He should have known better.

"Well, shit," Jad said, eyeing Clark, "guess I stepped on it again, huh?"

"Par for the course," Cary said, offering Clark his hand. "Honored to meet you, sir."

"Honor's all mine," Clark said, his smile now genuine. "Triple Nickel has one hell of a legacy. Glad to have you both on board."

"Our pleasure," Jad said, taking his turn at hand-shakes. "Working with Jack is always interesting."

Just that quickly, the moment of levity passed.

Clark and Ding both turned to the junior-most member of the team.

"I don't doubt that for a minute," Clark said. "Jack, can you give us the CliffsNotes version of what happened? I haven't had a chance to read your sitrep."

"That's because I didn't send one, Mr. C.," Jack said. Even though he appreciated his boss offering him a way to save face, Jack wasn't having it. Leaders faced the music. "Once I had a chance to review Gavin's data dump on Zhang Wei, I didn't like the idea of leaving the scientist to someone else. Wei normally lives and works in America, but he just so happened to be in Germany on the day his brother was kidnapped. I didn't believe it was a coincidence that Wei was staying at a hotel less than two hours from Regensburg. These factors seemed to indicate that interviewing Zhang Wei might be time-sensitive, so I deviated from the itinerary you and I discussed. Based on our scheduled departure from Munich, I should have had plenty of time to debrief Wei and still make our flight to Manila."

"I'm guessing *should* is the operative word?" Clark said.

Jack nodded. "Things didn't go as planned. We found Zhang Wei, but the kidnappers had already contacted him and set up a meet. As he and I were talking, somebody put a bullet in his chest."

Clark shook his head. "Did you learn anything?"

"No," Jack said, "but Cary and Jad got up close and personal with the team who killed him."

"They were good," Cary said. "Professionals. The shot wasn't exceptionally difficult from a distance perspective, but it was very technical. The change in elevation from the rock outcropping where the shooters were situated to the target's location at the base of the lake was significant."

"High-angle shooting," Clark said, nodding, "and I bet there was a breeze coming off the lake that made the target's ambient conditions quite a bit different from the shooter's."

"Exactly," Jad said. "You a distance shooter, too, Mr. Clark?"

"Call me John," Clark said, "and no, I'm just a dabbler compared to you guys. I do my best work with a knife."

Jad smiled, waiting for the punch line.

There wasn't one.

"Jad and Cary saved my bacon," Jack said, stepping into the void. "Jad interdicted the sniper and spotter bare-handed until Cary showed up."

"Not exactly bare-handed," Jad said. "I had my trusty Spyderco. Besides, saving Jack's bacon seems to be part of the job description."

This time, everyone laughed.

Everyone but Jack.

"You two are going to fit in just fine," Ding said.

"Agreed," Clark said. "What happened next?"

"We went head-to-head with a direct-action team twice in one day," Jack said. "You taught me not to believe in coincidences, Mr. C. Somehow, we were blown, which meant that I had to assume everything else was blown, too—our identifications, travel plans, maybe even comms. So I called another audible. We changed legends, hopped across the border to Austria, and jumped on a flight out of Salzburg. Sorry I've been out of the loop, but going dark seemed better than potentially burning what's happening here."

All eyes turned to Clark.

After a long moment, Jack's boss slowly nodded.

"That was the right play, Junior," Clark said. "We can debrief in more detail later, but you handled the exfil correctly. Jad and Cary, this hasn't been the shakeout cruise you two signed up for, but we could still use your help. You boys up for a bit more action?"

Jad shot a look at Cary, and the older Green Beret cleared his throat.

"We're more than happy to lend a hand," Cary said, "but I have a condition."

"We," Jad said. "We have a condition."

"Sorry, Jad," Cary said. "We have a condition."

"Spit it out," Clark said.

"We want guns," Cary said. "Fists and knives only go so far."

"We can accommodate that," Clark said with another smile. "The back room's stacked with Pelican cases. I'm sure you'll find something in there that will wet your whistle. We'll get you both kitted out as soon as we finish running through the concept of the operation."

"Fantastic," Cary said. "Then we're all yours. Assuming our team leader agrees."

While Jack appreciated Cary's vote of confidence, he wasn't sure he'd earned it. Their training, rather than Jack's leadership, had been what kept the Green Berets alive. Though Clark had been generous with his assessment of Jack's exfil, he hadn't addressed the previous events.

Jack could read between the lines.

Mr. C. didn't like the choices Jack had made.

But setting his performance as a leader aside, there was an even bigger elephant in the room. Ding was Clark's second-in-command, and Dom was also senior to Jack. While he'd been a notional team leader up until this point, Jack's time at the helm had come to a close.

"I'm a big believer in battle-rostered teams," Clark said. "You three have operated together and are familiar with each other's idiosyncrasies. I don't intend to disrupt that. This op calls for two elements. Ding, Dom, and I will be the main element. Jack, you and the Triple Nickel boys will be in support. Everyone good with that?"

"Suits me just fine," Cary said. "As long as we have guns."

"Lots of guns," Jad said. "With Jack, more is always better."

25

NAVOTAS FISH PORT COMPLEX
MANILA, PHILIPPINES

"SCEPTER, THIS IS REAPER, WE ARE SET. GOOD SIGHT LINES TO MAC-beth. Objective is clear. Nothing to report, over."

"Reaper, this is Scepter," Jack said. "Copy all. Charlie Mike, over."

"This is Reaper, continuing mission, over."

Jack eyed his cell phone to ensure he had the correct channel selected, then pressed the transmit button. Keeping separate nets for each team made sense, but the constant changing of channels was going to be the death of him. Jack had his audio set up so that he could listen to both nets at the same time, but he could still transmit on just one.

"Trident element, this is Scepter, over."

"Scepter, this is Trident, go ahead, over."

Hearing Ding's voice using a SEAL call sign made Jack smile. But once the Green Berets had suggested operational call signs from the North Korea mission, Clark had latched on to the SEAL call sign. Jad had an impressive repertoire of frogman jokes, but being John Clark still counted for something. Jack also couldn't help but notice that the normally free-spirited Green Beret tempered his SEAL jokes around Clark. As Ding had once confided to Jack, if even half the stories about Clark were true, Rainbow Six was one bad mama jama.

And the kicker was that all the stories Jack knew were true.

"Roger that, Trident," Jack said. "Reaper element is in position. Good sight lines to Macbeth. You are cleared to proceed, over."

"Trident copies all," Ding said. "We are Phase Line Bravo, inbound, over."

"Roger all," Jack said, "call Phase Line Alpha."

Jack examined the imagery on his cell phone as Ding replied with two clicks of the transmit button. Phase Line Bravo was a straight line stretching west from the intersection of the west/east-running Pescador II Road and the north/south Radial Road 10. As the support team leader, Jack had two very important functions. One, he served as the information conduit for the Green Berets, who were arrayed in sniper overwatch position approximately five hundred meters northeast of Objective Macbeth. This required Jack to maintain overall command and control of the operation while Clark, Ding, and Dom were focused on the objective.

Two, Jack was the single person QRF or quick reaction force.

Neither task was insignificant.

Jack shielded his phone from a pair of teenagers strolling by as he confirmed Phase Line Bravo's location. Though the two boys looked harmless, Jack had long ago learned that youth did not equal innocence. In fact, the opposite was often true. Criminals frequently employed children as lookouts, errand boys, messengers, and, for the truly depraved, killers.

The closest teenager, a thin kid of about fifteen, gave Jack a hard glare, but kept walking. This close to the docks, hard glares were probably a way of life. And while he'd done his best to conceal his American appearance with a ball cap, shades, and bulky clothing, Jack was obviously not Filipino.

This made him different.

On the seedy side of Navotas Fish Port, different was not good.

To be fair, Jack thought his surroundings weren't too far from what he would find in any industrial port. Be it Baltimore or Hong Kong, shipyards tended to attract a certain clientele. People accustomed to manual labor and a hardscrabble approach to making ends meet. The honest work available here was likely to be both backbreaking and dangerous.

The dishonest work doubly so.

Navotas Fish Port was one of the largest fish centers in Asia. Over three hundred tons of seafood were unloaded onto its docks daily from the fleet of more than fifteen commercial fishing vessels that called the port home. The sprawling complex was located on the west side of Highway R-10 and bounded by thick, head-high brick walls that separated the port proper from the nearby series of parks, greenbelts, and pedestrian areas.

Ports were by nature centers of gravity for a nation's criminal element. Navotas was no exception. Within a stone's throw of the brightly lit promenade and the leafy landscaping of Navotas Green Zone Park were the dingy warehouses, crumbling slips, and rusted derelicts of a working port. It was to one such warehouse, code-named Macbeth, that Clark, Ding, and Dom were now headed.

"Trident is approaching Phase Line Alpha."

"Roger that," Jack said.

He switched channels and relayed the information to the Green Berets as he shifted position to get a better view of the multilane R-10 behind him. Phase Line Alpha denoted Tioco Street, a small thoroughfare that branched to the east, just north of Pescador Park, Jack's current position. Unlike the Navotas Green Zone Park on the western side of R-10, the park's title was a bit grander than its facilities deserved.

Jack was seated on one of several concrete benches carved into a length of planters that separated the park from R-10's busy traffic. The park itself consisted of a series of basketball courts surrounded by rust-colored iron fencing. The courts were filthy from a combination of debris from the surrounding vegetation and the dirt and grit kicked up by the constant vehicular traffic just meters away. The court was pockmarked and uneven, with sections of discolored concrete spreading across the ground like liver spots. Tagalog graffiti tags marked most of the concrete barriers, and only one of the four street-lights pointed at the court still functioned.

While not a place he'd want his children congregating, the lengthening shadows and unoccupied basketball court provided a perfect place for Jack to sit unobserved. The bench also gave him an unobstructed view of Phase Line Alpha, which would prove critical for what was about to happen. As if on cue, a dark-colored four-door sedan motored by. At first glance, there was nothing to set the car apart from the rest of the traffic teeming down R-10.

Nothing but the car's occupants.

"Trident is Phase Line Alpha," Ding said, just as the vehicle drew abeam to Tioco Street.

Activating its left turn signal, the car pulled a U-turn across traffic, heading for the collection of rusted buildings that marked the start of the waterfront on the western side of R-10. Jack relayed the information to Jad and Cary as he watched to see if any other vehicles would follow the Campus operatives west.

Traditionally, provocative actions like U-turns were avoided when conducting an SDR. The name of the game was to make the surveillance team continuously second-guess whether the target of their attention was attempting to link up with a spy for a clandestine meet or just going about the normal business of their day. A U-turn is the equivalent of a flashing red light, announcing that the game was afoot.

Usually.

But in the Philippines, as in many Asian countries, the rules of the road were a bit different. Here, traffic signs weren't so much absolutes as suggestions, and aggressive maneuvers like a U-turn were more the rule than the exception. The location of the waterfront also helped. Even though traffic up and down R-10 was constant, there were no cross streets or stoplights to allow motorists to cross the road.

This limitation made Jack's post a perfect spot to identify a surveillance team.

He watched a parade of motor scooters and cars pass even with the basketball court as Clark's taillights vanished into the warren of alleys leading to the waterfront on the western side of R-10. After a minute or two spent observing the street, Jack felt good. No one was following Clark.

So far so good.

"Scepter, this is Reaper, I think we've got something."

Or not.

26

MARIO REYES EYED THE TWO MEN IN FRONT OF HIM, UNSURE WHAT he was seeing. On the one hand, they looked as he'd expected—hard. Not the kind of testosterone-induced bulkiness common among Mon Mon's thugs. While the pair appeared fit, they weren't bodybuilders. In fact, the opposite was true. Their physiques looked almost desiccated. As if everything superfluous had been scoured away. More than muscle and bone, the men had the appearance of steel and iron.

The sense of hardness extended to the men's expressions. While not hostile per se, they radiated intensity from across the courtyard. The pair had the feel of men who were familiar with violence, but their mannerisms were absent the posturing practiced by local thugs or wannabe gangsters.

They were clinicians.

Professionals.

Soldiers.

Whatever the correct descriptor, the men's body language and bearing suggested that they'd been schooled in the art of death and were well versed in its many facets.

But they were also old.

After he'd sent the pictures of the device to his American contact, Mario had received the expected reply. The Yankee contact was very much interested in whatever Mon Mon's fishermen had pulled from the ocean. He would send men to collect it and pay a finder's fee—half up front and half upon delivery. Negotiations on the finder's fee amount were quick, which was to say nonexistent. Mario had proposed a rather exorbitant sum and the American had agreed. Instantly. This had made Mario both happy and a little sad. As a banker, he understood the truth of negotiations—leaving money on the table was second only to paying too much.

But that was a matter for later.

Mario had secured double the amount he'd promised Mon Mon and made his American friend happy in the process. And while Mario was no sycophant for the Yankees, he was a realist. In a world as ever-changing as Mario's, an American intelligence operative was a friend worth cultivating. After concluding the business aspect of their endeavor, the American had sent Mario a series of straightforward instructions. His collectors would arrive at the fish market at a certain time, and Mario was to shepherd them to Mon Mon's building and transfer the device into their custody.

Simple.

Except that Mario had expected his visitors to be, well, younger.

"Mario?"

Mario nodded.

The question had come from the elder of the two. The man was easily in his sixties, and Mario would have figured him too old for this type of work. Then Mario had a disturbingly different thought. Perhaps even at sixty the older man was still deadlier than operatives half his age. Staring into the man's ice-blue eyes and weathered face, Mario hoped this question remained unanswered.

"Yes," Mario said.

Like most Filipino businessmen, Mario spoke the international language of commerce—English. But Mario was willing to bet that if he hadn't, the man's brown-skinned comrade would have been able to engage him in several other tongues.

"Good," the man said. "I'm Clark. This is Chavez. You have something for us?"

Chavez was easily a decade and a half younger than Clark, but his thick black hair was still streaked with gray. Though shorter than his comrade by half a foot, Chavez's wide chest and heavy shoulders made up for his lack of stature. And then there was the man's intensity. Chavez's face was wrinkled with laugh lines, but the operative exuded purpose like a potbelly stove emitted heat.

These were not men to be trifled with.

Mario nodded, a sense of unease settling in his gut. The two operatives were not old hands about to be put out to pasture, but neither were they the junior muscle Mario had expected. Mario could only assume that the device was more valuable than he'd realized.

He should have asked for more money.

Maybe he still could.

His intended words died on Mario's tongue. The same sixth sense that helped him sniff out the real estate deals his competitors missed encouraged him to be happy with what he'd negotiated and bring this encounter to a conclusion. Quickly. Men such as these were not used for routine operations. Best to part ways with the device before trouble had a chance to manifest.

"Will your friend be joining us?" Mario said, pointing to the men's car. The driver was clearly visible behind the wheel, watching through the grimy windshield.

"No," Clark said.

Clark's tone brokered no argument.

Fine.

Mario wanted this business concluded as quickly as possible. His finder's fee was growing smaller by the second.

"No problem," Mario said, opening the building's metal door to usher the pair inside. "You'll be on your way shortly."

The building's interior suggested otherwise.

27

"Roger that, Scepter," Cary said. "I've got five military-aged males southwest of Macbeth where the boardwalk abuts the pier. They're hunkered down between two moored fishing boats and a panel van. Probably out of sight of Trident. I designate this group Charlie 1, over."

"Scepter copies all," Jack said. "Passing info to Trident. Continue to observe and report."

Cary replied with two clicks of the transmit button as a red diamond-shaped icon labeled *C-1* appeared on Jack's phone.

Like the operation Jack had conducted with the Green Berets in North Korea, each of the Campus team's Android devices was running a version of the military software app known as ATAK. Designed to provide disparate end users with a common operating picture, ATAK was capable of merging a large number of sensors and operators. In addition to streaming live video from an ISR platform, the app also allowed operational graphics inputted by one user to be shared across the entire network. This meant that Clark's team would instantly know about the men Cary had designated Charlie 1.

Assuming, of course, that the assault team was paying attention to their phones.

"Trident, this is Scepter," Jack said. "Approach to Macbeth is clean from my vantage point. Be advised that Reaper has designated five military-aged males southwest of Macbeth. They are designated Charlie 1, over."

"Scepter, this is Ringside," Dom said. "Acknowledge all. We didn't expect this place to be deserted. As long as Reaper has eyes on Charlie 1, you are cleared to reposition, over."

"This is Scepter, roger all," Jack said, getting to his feet.

If Dom was transmitting using his Ringside call sign, Clark and Ding must already be in contact with the Filipino asset and therefore unable to talk. Time to get this show on the road. Taking his life in his hands, Jack found a break in traffic and shot across the street as children braved the stream of motorists without a second glance. An expat friend of Jack's claimed that traffic in Asian countries relied more on vehicular flow than rules.

Maybe the kids were better at surfing that flow than Jack was.

Or maybe they were just clueless.

Either way, Jack was coated in sweat by the time he reached the western banks of R-10. The teenager who'd paced him across the street had never once looked up from his phone.

Maybe Jack was getting old.

While the paved pedestrian paths, well-lit benches, and immaculate landscaping of the Navotas Green Zone were a far cry from the more austere park across the street, Jack wasn't changing positions for the scenery. The northern end of the Green Zone was only about five hundred meters from Macbeth. Better still, while the manicured portion of the greenbelt ended a hundred meters or so from the west-leading street Clark had followed to the dock, the thick brush did not.

Jack intended to make his way through the brush until he came to a particularly thick section of foliage he'd identified using satellite imagery. From there, he would shimmy up a neem tree and boost himself over the wall into a west/east-running alley that paralleled the route Clark had driven. Clark said that the Filipino asset had already agreed to a price for the Chinese glider, but Jack wanted to be close by just in case the man decided to renegotiate the deal.

By force.

Moving through the underbrush, Jack monitored his pace count, marking the steps until he reached one hundred meters. Distinctions that seemed obvious on overhead imagery were often less so when viewed from a person's vantage point. The pace count provided Jack with a rough idea of when to start looking for his ticket over the wall.

He needn't have been worried.

Like an old man's gnarled fingers, the tree's twisting limbs reached over the crumbling stone exactly where Jack had expected to find them. With a quick glance to ensure he was alone, Jack unzipped his backpack, revealing a folded Heckler & Koch MP5.

After using the weapon in North Korea, Jack had developed a certain fondness for the submachine gun's accuracy and concealability. It would never match an M4's ability to reach out and touch someone, but the weapon was ideal for in-close work. This variant sported an integrated suppressor, and the compact submachine gun clipped nicely into the single point sling Jack was wearing beneath his unbuttoned shirt.

Clark and Ding were carrying concealed pistols, while Dom had a second MP5 on the car seat next to him. As the designated snipers, Cary and Jad were each equipped with HK416 rifles featuring under-barrel 40-millimeter grenade launchers. Not the weapons the Green Berets traditionally carried, but Jad had pronounced them adequate for the task at hand.

Jack shimmied up the tree, crawled out on the limb that spanned the wall, and dropped to the far side. The hiss that greeted Jack once he hit the ground was unsettling, but it did not belong to a coiled cobra, as he'd first feared. Instead, Jack found himself eye to eye with a crouching orange cat.

The feline was hunched over a fish carcass, ears flat against its head, teeth bared.

"Keep it," Jack whispered, taking his bearings as he slowly stood.

The cat hissed again before returning to its meal.

Jack hoped the rest of the mission went as smoothly.

"Scepter, this is Reaper," Cary said. "Military-aged males vicinity of Charlie 1 are moving southwest along the pier, away from the red side of Macbeth, over."

More good news.

In sticking with Cary and Jad's convention, Macbeth's four sides had been delineated by color. White was the southern side and the entrance to the building Ding and Clark intended to use. Black was the rear, or northern, section of building that abutted the dock and water. Green was the eastern side closest to R-10, while red was the western section facing the extended pier that ran along a boneyard of rusting fishing boats. If the men were moving away from the red side, they might be returning to a fishing boat. At the very least the military-aged males were putting distance between themselves and Macbeth, as well as the alley where Jack was hiding south of the white side.

Things were definitely looking up.

"Scepter, this is Ringside," Dom said. "We've got trouble."

Jack swore.

28

IT WASN'T THE BUILDING THAT GAVE MARIO PAUSE.

The dank structure still reeked of fish, and seawater puddled across the filthy concrete. The lights provided a weak counterpart to the thick darkness. A single lamp dangled above the stainless-steel fish-cleaning station, casting a sickly yellow circle on the device's de facto cradle. Everything was as Mario expected it to be.

Everything but the cluster of men gathered around the device.

Men with Danilo at their center.

"What's this?"

As before, the question came from the older of the pair. Clark. As before, Mario detected an undertone to the man's comment. But if before there'd been only a hint of steel, Mario could now sense the entire bared blade.

"This is Danilo," Mario said, "my cousin's lieutenant. His fishing crew recovered the device."

While Mario tried to keep his own tone light, there was no getting around the sense of menace permeating the air. Danilo's group seemed to be as surprised to see Mario and the Americans as Mario was to see them. On closer examination, Mario realized that the five men were not from Mon Mon's usual band. Though they wore the standard dock uniform of short-sleeve shirts and shorts, the ink crawling down their forearms bore no sign of the smiling skull that symbolized Mon Mon's clique.

"What is going on, Danilo?" Mario said, switching to Tagalog.

Mon Mon's lieutenant didn't speak English and Mario sincerely hoped the Americans weren't conversant in Tagalog. He had a terrible feeling that whatever was going to be said next would not make the Americans happy.

"Change of plans," Danilo said. "Mon Mon decided to sell the device to another interested party."

Mario's relationship with Danilo was strained at best. Though he felt genuine affection for his cousin, Mario could not say the same about most of the men who shared Mon Mon's life. Danilo was a criminal, plain and simple. His closely cropped bristly hair and narrow skull brought to mind a wire brush. His beady eyes and elongated nose made him look more weasel than man, a likeness Mario thought the thug's actions merited. Mario had never cared for Danilo, but like it or not, the thug was Mon Mon's man.

Mario took a closer look at the tattooed thugs, trying to make sense of what was happening. Then he saw dragons spiraling down their arms, tails encircling the English characters *14K*. Mon Mon was a bit craftier than Mario had given him credit for. The newcomers were from the 14K triad, a Chinese organized crime syndicate known to act as a criminal arm for the Chinese Communist Party. Mario's cousin was trying to kill two birds with one stone. By giving the glider to 14K, Mon Mon would cement an alliance with a powerful criminal enterprise and thereby counterbalance the pressure from upstart Filipino gangsters eager to move in on his turf. At the same time, Mon Mon's actions would endear him to the Chinese Communist Party, potentially providing his fleet relief from CCP's relentless efforts to crowd Filipino fishermen out of the best South China Sea fisheries.

Not a bad play at all.

If Mario discounted the operatives standing behind him.

"I'm sorry," Mario said, turning to the Americans. "My cousin has decided not to part with the device after all."

As he made eye contact with Clark, Mario realized three things. One, judging from their expressions, the Americans understood exactly what was happening. Two, they didn't seem inclined to just walk away. Three, Mario had positioned himself between two groups of killers.

"Did you get that?" Clark said, directing the comment to his Hispanic companion.

"Most of it," Chavez answered. "My Tagalog's a little rusty, but from what I can tell, the short guy's decided to sell our product to other buyers."

Clark nodded and then turned back to Mario.

"Tell your cousin we'll pay him double what the other guys are offering."

"I'm sorry," Mario said, already knowing how this would end, "but I don't think—"

"Tell him."

Clark hadn't shouted the command, but his words crackled through the air all the same. Mario nodded, swallowed, and pulled out his cell phone.

"What are you doing?" Danilo said.

"Calling my cousin," Mario said, dialing Mon Mon's number.

The triad member standing closest to Danilo reached for his waistband.

Then all hell broke loose.

29

"Scepter, Ringside," Dom said. "Ding just kicked off the Alamo signal."

Abandoning any pretense of stealth, Jack took off like a lightning bolt.

This was the part of Campus operations for which Jack found himself growing increasingly less fond. Though they'd always operated on the very edge of what was possible, Jack now viewed the exploits of his fellow Campus shooters through the lens of his experience in North Korea. In that theater, Jack had been in the company of a SEAL team with the two Green Beret snipers in reserve.

While the mission had certainly unfolded differently than the operations order had foreseen, Jack had been able to fall back on the capabilities of the twelve rough men and the combat multipliers that came with them once violence became inevitable. Campus operators had no lack of grit, but sometimes quantity really was a quality all its own.

"Ringside, this is Scepter," Jack said, answering Dom's transmission. "Copy Alamo. I'm moving to Lear time now. Can you pass us a sitrep, over?"

Clark had anticipated the need to communicate without the use of voice or text transmissions. Accordingly, he and Ding had configured their phones to act as emergency transmitters. Pushing one set of buttons transmitted an audio tone known as Alamo—code for things were not as expected inside the warehouse. A second combination broadcast Custer, the brevity code signifying that the Campus operators were fighting for their lives. In Jack's experience, these two radio calls often went together like peanut butter and jelly.

"Scepter, this is Ringside, nothing yet," Dom said. "They just stepped inside and . . . Hang on a minute. Clark just triggered continuous broadcast."

This feature was the primary reason why Jack and his Green Beret snipers were on one channel while the entry team and Dom used another. While Clark and Ding couldn't mutter to themselves in a room full of hostiles, they could switch their microphones to continuous transmission. The mics were designed to pick up just the vibration of the speaker's voice, so they weren't capable of relaying ambient noise, but they were better than nothing.

"Okay," Dom said, "sounds like they've got company inside the warehouse. Clark just asked what was going on. Then he offered to pay double for the glider. I think this op's about to go sideways."

Of that, Jack had no doubt. The only question was whether this was the kind of sideways that would be resolved with words or with bullets. Based on his luck thus far, Jack was betting on bullets.

"Copy all," Jack said, huffing as he hurtled down the trash-strewn alley. "I'm almost to Lear. Break, break— Reaper, this is Scepter. Get ready to execute the contingency plan, over."

Lear was a loading dock just to the southwest of the warehouse, which would allow Jack to stage almost on top of Macbeth while still remaining out of sight. From Lear, Jack needed only to hop a small wall separating the adjacent building from the target warehouse. In other words, it would position him close enough to help if things got loud.

At least that was the idea.

But as much as Jack loved the thought of riding to Clark's rescue, he knew that he and Dom would probably not be enough manpower to turn the tide of the battle. For that, Jack would need the Green Berets.

But there was a problem with that scenario.

The Army commandos were in a hide site about three hundred and fifty meters northeast of Macbeth. Not an insurmountable distance, but they'd have to cross a section of harbor to get to Jack. The overland path meant traversing a bridge and then doglegging east down the same alley that Clark and Ding had used to reach Macbeth. Two Honda Click scooters stood ready at the base of the building Jad and Cary were using as a hide site for just that purpose, but the Green Berets' response time would still be measured in minutes rather than seconds.

Minutes in a gunfight could be the difference between life and death.

With that in mind, Jack had briefed a contingency plan. An option to call the snipers forward if things started looking hinky. Since this course of action meant that the Green Berets would have to abandon their overwatch position, leaving the assaulters blind, Jack wanted to use it only as a last resort.

Based on Clark's transmission, it was last-resort time.

"Scepter, this is Reaper," Cary said. "Be advised, I've got a small watercraft approaching Macbeth from the black side at a high rate of speed. The cabin is enclosed, and the deck is empty, so I don't have a head count on passengers, but it's headed right for the dock, over."

Jack swore even as he ran faster.

This was the exact reason why the snipers were positioned where they were. Their hide site allowed the Green Berets to both cover the assault team and maintain surveillance on the rear of Macbeth. Jack was torn. Should he order the commandos to fold up shop and augment his admittedly scarce QRF, or keep watch on the boat? Staying on the boat was the more conservative play. After all, it was John Clark and Ding Chavez inside that building, not a couple of rookie operators. To Jack's way of thinking, there wasn't much the Rainbow CO and his team leader hadn't weathered.

Jack keyed the transmit button, intending to tell Cary

and Jad to remain in place, when Dom stepped on his transmission.

"Scepter, this is Ringside. Custer, Custer, Custer, over."

Sometimes Jack really hated being right.

30

JACK RESISTED THE URGE TO ASK DOM FOR AN UPDATE. CLARK HAD just called Custer. One of the most lethal men Jack knew thought his life was in danger. The specifics did not matter. Jack was singularly focused on getting himself and as much combat power into the fight as quickly as possible.

"Ringside, Scepter, copy Custer," Jack said. "Break, break, Reaper, this is Scepter. Divide forces. One of you stay on the boat, the other moves here. Now."

"Reaper acknowledges all," Cary said. "Reaper 1 on the way."

Jack took comfort in Cary's radio call, but he still had business to attend to. Grabbing the wall, he vaulted over the side, landing in an ankle-deep puddle of motor oil, seawater, and God knew what else.

But that was not his concern.

Instead, Jack ran for the door on the red side of Macbeth.

A blur to his right demanded his attention.

Jack was in the process of bringing his HK onto target when he realized the blur was Dom racing for the same door. In the excitement, Jack had forgotten that Dom would be stacking with him. If Clark and Ding were already in a gunfight, it made no sense for Dom and Jack to enter behind the two men, potentially placing themselves in the fatal funnel formed by the white side door.

"One coming in," Jack hissed.

Dom jerked, suggesting that Jack wasn't the only one who'd let adrenaline cloud his thinking.

But that was a topic for later.

Since he'd made it to the entrance first, Dom took the number-one position in the tactical stack. With his HK tucked into his shoulder and the whole of his focus centered on the rust-streaked door, the former FBI agent looked every bit the warrior he was. Jack slid around the big man, taking up a position opposite his cousin. With a stack of just two, it fell to Jack to act as the breacher. In a perfect world, Jack would have waited for Cary's arrival before entering, since a stack of three would be exponentially more deadly. But as the sound of gunfire echoing in the building could attest, this was not a perfect world.

Jack met Dom's gaze, and his cousin nodded.

Jack turned the door handle.

Locked.

Shouldering his HK, Jack aimed where he imagined the bolt to be and squeezed off a three-round burst. As breaching techniques went, this one was a bit unorthodox, but the flimsy metal siding would offer no resistance to the 9-millimeter rounds. Hopefully the locking mechanism wouldn't fare any better.

The muzzle blast reflected off the wall, buffeting Jack in the face.

No matter.

Speed and violence of action were now the names of the game. The aluminum buckled under Jack's onslaught, and the shattered remains of the bolt loomed like a snaggletooth in a jack-o'-lantern's leer through the jagged hole the 9-millimeter rounds had created.

Jack grabbed the door handle one-handed, cranked, and yanked.

Metal shrieked, but the door swung open.

Dom flowed through the entrance, and Jack tucked in behind him.

Chaos reigned inside.

Since he'd entered from the left, Dom button-hooked in the same direction. Normally, this would have been Jack's cue to orient right.

Normally.

But as he was in the process of sweeping right, Jack remembered Clark and Ding and corrected his turn. If his Campus teammates were behind Jack, logic dictated that the threat was in front of him.

One look confirmed his hunch.

The building's interior was dingy, dimly lit, and rectangular. It was also filled with men intent on killing one another. At first, Jack wondered why Clark and Ding hadn't handled the situation already. Though the cluster of tattooed men to Jack's left numbered at least five, they were also grouped together. With just a flimsy metal table stained with fish blood for cover, the gangsters were caught in the open. The two senior Campus operators should have made short work of them.

Then the crack of a semiautomatic rifle knifed through the air, and Jack understood.

A loft ran the length of the far wall. Jack imagined that the space was used to store equipment and nets out of reach of the corrosive mixture of fish offal and salt water that coated the floor.

It also contained a pair of snipers.

Jack tracked the red holographic dot from his EOTech reflex sight onto the first man as he thumbed the MP5's selector switch to single shot. As soon as the crimson circle settled, Jack began squeezing the trigger as he advanced forward with a smooth rolling gait at serious odds with his thundering heart. Though moving toward the scrum of men felt counterintuitive, Jack knew remaining stationary equaled death. Besides, an adversary advancing triggered a primal response. The snipers' brains might know that Jack couldn't reach them, but their hearts wouldn't be so sure.

Jack's first aimed pair went low, sparking off the grating. The third and fourth found the mark. His ears registered bursts of fire as Dom and the rest of the Campus team engaged the men crouched behind the fish table, and Jack saw a sniper's limp body fall from the loft.

Without halting his steady fire, Jack shifted to the second shooter.

When employed correctly, suppressive fire had a devastating effect on an opponent's psyche. Unlike the rapid bursts associated with scared men, a consistent rain of bullets suggested an adversary calmly in control of the situation. Even though Jack didn't have a clear shot at the second sniper, the continuous stream of 9-millimeter rounds rattling the loft's floor and boxes the sniper was using for cover did the trick. The man scrambled up to a crouch, no doubt intending to retreat.

He didn't get the chance.

Jack put four quick pairs into the crouching sniper.

Then he turned back to the floor.

Dom had been busy.

Of the five guys who'd been on their feet when Jack had breached, three were now down. One was still standing, weapon in hand, while his partner was beating feet for the door. Panning his sight left, Jack put an aimed pair into the standing gunman just as Dom did the same. The shooter spun, sprawling the length of the fish table before sliding to the ground. Jack tracked right, centered his red dot on the fleeing man's back, and pressed the trigger twice more.

Then he was out of targets.

"Clear front," Jack said.

"Clear side," Dom echoed.

"Clear rear."

Jack turned toward the unmistakable sound of Clark's voice and got his first look at his fellow operatives. What he saw wasn't encouraging. John Clark was standing tall, apparently no worse for the wear. Ding Chavez was a different story. The onetime Rainbow team leader was sprawled against the wall, his SIG still gripped in one hand as a scarlet circle spread from his right shoulder.

"Ding," Jack said, moving toward his mentor even as a voice crackled across his earbud.

"Scepter, this is Reaper 2, the boat's still closing in on the dock. Fifteen seconds, over."

Jack turned to see Clark's eyes were locked on him. Jad must have switched to the assault team frequency on his own accord. The Green Berets were some pretty switched-on dudes.

"You and Dom take a look at that boat," Clark said. "Mario will help me get Ding to the car."

For the first time, Jack registered the presence of their asset. The Filipino man was pressed up against the wall, trying to be small. To his credit, the banker stood in response to Clark's command, even though his skinny legs were quivering. The asset had gumption, no two ways about it.

"On it," Jack said.

Jack ran across the floor, trying to ignore the puddles of red. He was no stranger to gunfights, but the close quarters of this one had him rattled. His body was now reacting to the combat-induced adrenaline dump, and Jack had that jittery, high-on-coffee feeling.

"Scepter, this is Reaper 1, five seconds," Cary said.

"Roger that, 1," Jack said as he pushed open the building's black side door. "We have one Eagle WIA. Rally on the red side of Macbeth to assist with the casualty, over."

"Reaper 1 copies all."

Jack had hesitated in the doorway while speaking with

Cary. Coordinating multiple parts of an operation over the radio often required a team leader to stop and visualize the moving pieces. Until Dom tapped him on the shoulder, Jack hadn't even realized he'd paused. With a start, Jack moved toward the water, his eyes locked on the boat speeding toward him.

But apparently not fast enough.

Dom shoved him in the back, sending Jack stumbling.

Then the world exploded.

31

THE OCEAN'S ROARING DRAGGED JACK FROM THE DARKNESS. AN
all-consuming sound that washed against his pounding
head in skull-crushing waves. Then came the burning sensation of salt in his eyes. Sputtering, Jack tried to push
himself upright, only to slump back into the water.

Nearly drowning did the trick.

With a cough, Jack edged out of the surf and attempted to make sense of his surroundings. He was lying
in shallow water near the dock, but couldn't for the life
of him remember how he'd gotten there. Then his addled
brain identified what he'd previously mistaken for crashing waves.

Ringing.

His ears were ringing.

From an explosion.

Dry-heaving, Jack rose to unsteady feet. The shallows
were covered in debris—pieces of wood, bits of steel, and
the ever-present fish offal.

And something else.

A body.

With a curse, Jack realized that the floating form he'd mistaken for a piece of the dock was actually a person.

A person facedown in the water.

Dom.

Jack hooked the big man under the shoulder blades and hauled him toward shore. The distance wasn't more than ten or so feet, but it still took Jack an eternity. The concussion-induced vertigo made it hard to stay upright, and the silt-covered shoreline clung to his feet. Jack fell twice during the short trek even as he pushed his wavering legs to go faster. Dom wasn't in good shape, but there was nothing Jack could do until they reached dry land.

The growl of an outboard motor announced the return of Jack's hearing. He turned to see a boat speed away in a cloud of diesel smoke. Jack tracked the craft's progress for half a second before shifting his attention to Dom.

The watercraft wasn't his concern.

Jack had his hands full right here.

With a final tug, Jack dragged Dom onto the slimy beach and dropped to his knees beside his cousin. What he saw wasn't good. A length of jagged steel protruded from the operative's leg. The metal shard was buried deep in Dom's flesh, perhaps lodged in his thigh bone. But Jack was more worried about his cousin's blood-matted head. Dom's skull seemed intact, but head trauma can cause swelling in the brain. If this was the case, Dom would need surgery to relieve the cranial pressure, else he might suffer brain damage and death.

Jack's cousin needed medical help.

Now.

"Any station this net," Jack said. "Scepter has an Eagle down on the black side of Macbeth. I say again, Eagle down."

A familiar voice answered Jack's radio call, but the ringing in his ears hadn't completely subsided. He couldn't make out the words. Rather than ask the caller to identify himself, Jack ripped open the cargo pocket on Dom's right leg.

As Jack had hoped, Dom had followed Campus SOP by carrying the low-profile first aid pouch Ding had put together in response to lessons gleaned from the nation's two decades of combat in Iraq and Afghanistan. The unobtrusive pouch carried the bare minimum—several one-handed tourniquets, a package of QuikClot Combat Gauze, and a small pressure bandage. Nowhere close to the contents of a standard first aid kit, but God willing, enough to save Dom's life.

"Dom, can you hear me?" Jack said.

His cousin's rising and falling chest let Jack know that Dom was still breathing, and a quick check of the carotid artery confirmed a weak but stable pulse. But that was the only good news. Jack fit a tourniquet above the shrapnel wound, twisted the rod until the arterial bleed stopped, and locked it.

Dom didn't so much as moan.

The Campus operative was in trouble.

Shaking out the pressure bandage, Jack eyed Dom's head wound. He'd need to lift his cousin's head to apply the bandage, but Jack was loath to do so. Without a way to first stabilize the operative's neck, moving Dom's head could aggravate a spinal injury, potentially paralyzing him. Jack keyed the radio, intending to transmit his request for help a second time, when a hand grabbed his shoulder, shaking him.

"We've got to go, Jack. Now."

Jack looked up to see Cary.

"Help me stabilize his neck," Jack said. "I've got to bandage the head wound."

"No time," Cary said even as the Green Beret's fingers moved across Dom's neck. "His spine feels intact. We can move him to the car and treat him there. Besides, I need you calling the shots, not playing medic."

"Why?" Jack said. "I'm the junior Campus member."

"Not anymore," Cary said, grabbing Dom beneath the shoulders. "Ding's concussed and in and out of consciousness. You're it."

"What about Clark?" Jack said, his leaden tongue barely able to form the words. "Is he . . . ?"

"No," Cary said, "but they have him."

The Green Beret inclined his head toward the vanishing launch.

Clark was on the boat?

Why?

What was happening?

"I don't understand," Jack said.

"I'll explain in the car," Cary said. "Grab his legs. We have to go. Now."

The Green Beret lifted Dom's torso, and Jack grabbed his cousin's limp legs. Together the two men started up the slippery bank, splashing through water as the sound of sirens drifted across the bay.

This was really happening.

In the space of seconds, Clark had been kidnapped, Ding concussed, and Dom incapacitated.

Someone had just gutted the entire Campus.

Everyone was down.

Everyone but Jack.

Jack had thought he'd known what it meant to be the team leader.

He hadn't.

32

"JACK. JACK!"

The words seemed to be coming from far away. Jack made eye contact with Cary in the rearview mirror.

"He's crashing, Jack."

Part of Jack's mind realized that the Green Beret's constant use of his first name was intentional. Though he didn't want to admit it, Jack knew that he was dangerously close to slipping into shock.

Clark kidnapped, Ding incapacitated, Dom crashing.

Each of those hard truths hammered against his psyche, and Jack found himself mentally reaching for that soft, warm feeling beckoning from just out of sight. He wiped blood from his cheek with the back of his left hand as he kept his right firmly on the steering wheel.

Perforated eardrums.

Fantastic.

He wanted to blame his injuries, but Jack knew they weren't the source of his lethargy. For the first time in his operational career, Ding, Clark, and the rest of his Campus brethren were out of the mix. Jack was the only operator still standing.

The one in charge.

Time he started acting that way.

Jack adjusted the mirror to better see the scene unfolding behind him.

The seven-person Mitsubishi Xpander was packed. Mario sat beside Jack in the front passenger seat, staring into space. The banker had helped Jack load the glider into the storage area behind the Mitsubishi's rear seats, but had said nothing of substance since.

Ding was behind Mario, slumped against the door. The Campus's second-in-command appeared to be concussed, and he was drifting in and out of consciousness. At the moment, Ding's eyes were closed, and his hastily bandaged shoulder was soaked with blood.

The Xpander's remaining seats had been laid flat, and Dom was stretched across them. Cary and Jad were crouched next to the unresponsive operator, and the pair began CPR as Jack watched.

His cousin was dying and there was nothing Jack could do.

Closing his eyes, Jack rubbed the bridge of his nose as he sorted through the ambush's final milliseconds. Jack remembered pausing in the building's doorway to answer Cary's radio transmission and his cousin shoving him out of the warehouse.

Then, nothing.

But it was to the pause that Jack kept returning. His

inadvertent hesitation had forced Dom to do the same. Then something had registered with his cousin. Maybe the sound of the bomb's relay closing, or perhaps a tingle from the sixth sense that all operators develop over time. Regardless of its source, Dom's premonition had caused him to act, shoving Jack clear of the warehouse. Dom had borne the brunt of the bomb's concussive shock wave because of Jack's inaction.

He might have just killed his cousin.

"Jack!"

"On it," Jack said.

His voice sounded rough, like he'd been gargling with shards of glass. With an effort, Jack turned from Dom's still form to the Filipino. The confident banker Jack had seen in Mario's asset picture was gone. In his place was a creature more mouse than man. Someone who looked like he wanted to run from this car of blood and death at the earliest opportunity.

Jack understood.

"Mario," Jack said, keeping his diction slow and his pronunciation clear, "we need your help."

People loved to make fun of how Americans defaulted to speaking slowly and loudly when conversing with foreigners, but there was actually a method to this madness. Stress affected mental acuity. Judging by his trembling hands, Mario was barely hanging on.

"No," Mario said, shaking his head, "I've done enough."

"That ambush was preplanned," Jack said. "Either your cousin set you up or his organization is in the middle of a corporate restructuring. Neither spells good news for you. Until we figure out which way the winds are blowing, you need us, and we need a doctor. Someone trustworthy and discreet."

Mario shook his head even more violently.

"I am a banker, not a—"

"An important banker with important friends," Jack said, talking over the man. "Friends who owe you favors. Call in some of your markers. I need a well-equipped clinic and doctor or my friend will die. But it needs to be private."

"You do not understand what you are asking," Mario said.

"I do," Jack said. "And I think I also understand you. I used to be in finance, too. You're a banker. You make deals for a living. Believe me when I tell you this will be both the easiest and potentially most lucrative deal you've ever closed. Your cousin's organization is experiencing a hostile takeover, and your name is on the balance sheet right next to his. Help us and we will protect you and your family."

"What if we want to go to the United States?" Mario said.

"Pack your bags," Jack said.

"I have a very large family," Mario said.

"Get us a private clinic and a doctor, and I don't care if you want to bring half of Manila," Jack said. "But if my friend dies while we're dithering about the price, I'm going to be unhappy. Very unhappy."

Mario thought for a moment.

Then he slowly nodded.

"Turn right there," Mario said, pointing at the next stoplight. "I'll call ahead."

Jack turned at the indicated intersection and floored the accelerator. For once, he was grateful for the chaos of Manila's traffic. The sea of cars and motor scooters gave him something to focus on besides the Green Berets' increasingly frantic efforts.

Or the phone call he'd have to place once they reached the clinic.

33

HER RINGING DESK PHONE STARTLED MARY PAT.

This was not because she was unused to receiving calls. To the contrary, even though her number wasn't exactly publicly available, the DNI received countless phone calls every day. Or at least she would, were it not for the tireless work of her dutiful assistant, Sam.

At first, Mary Pat had pushed back against the notion that her phone calls needed to be scheduled. She wanted to be available to anyone at any time. It had taken her less than a week to see the error of her ways. While she wanted to believe that she was still a field hand rotating through another obligatory desk job, Mary Pat knew in her heart this wasn't true. As much as she wished otherwise, her days of midnight asset meets in Gorky Park were long gone. Mary Pat was now a bureaucrat and the system recognized her as such. The ability to get the DNI on the phone was something of a status symbol among the Washington elite, and Sam guarded Mary Pat's calendar like Cerberus barring the gates to Hades.

If her desk phone rang unexpectedly, it rarely heralded good news.

The number displayed on the caller ID caused Mary Pat's fingers to freeze inches from the beckoning handset. The usual name or string of digits had been replaced by the word UNKNOWN. While Mary Pat was as vulnerable to spam calls on her personal cell as the average American, this wasn't the case for her office line. To bypass Sam's legendary vigilance, a caller needed to enter a series of numeric codes at an unacknowledged prompt. The people who knew these codes were already stored in Mary Pat's phone under names or identifiers. In her many years as DNI, Mary Pat had never received a call from an unknown caller.

Until now.

Wrapping her fingers around the black plastic, Mary Pat lifted the handset to her ear.

"Hello?"

"Mary Pat? It's me. Jack."

"Jack?" Mary Pat said, not bothering to hide her surprise. "Why are you calling?"

"It's bad, Mary Pat," Jack said. "Really bad."

Mary Pat listened without interruption as her oldest friend's son spoke. At the end of his update, she had just one thought—he was right.

It was bad.

Really bad.

"MP—I WASN'T EXPECTING TO SEE YOU TODAY."

John Patrick Ryan stood from where he'd been seated behind the Resolute desk with his back to the windows overlooking the Rose Garden. In two quick strides, he rounded the desk's corner to greet one of his dearest friends. Mary Pat accepted a hug from the most powerful man in the world as her mind raced. She'd thought through a handful of potential approaches during her thirty-minute commute from her office at the Liberty Crossing Intelligence Campus to the White House before discarding each one. This was the danger of serving with a friend. On the one hand, she would follow the man into the fires of hell without a second thought.

On the other, she'd become fiercely protective of him. Next to Cathy Ryan, Mary Pat had the most up-close view of the sacrifices the man in front of her had made while occupying the world's most sought-after office. Everyone knew that the office prematurely aged its occupant.

Very few understood the toll it took on a person's soul.

"Thank you for seeing me so quickly, sir."

The President's grin retreated at the word *sir*. Though they'd already been fellow warriors for decades before the genesis of Ryan's unexpected political career, Mary Pat still paid him the honorific his office deserved.

In public.

In private, Jack insisted she do otherwise.

With the title of commander in chief came great power and even greater isolation. As Jack had explained to Mary Pat early in his first term, only a handful of people outside of his family still saw him as a person rather than the President. Mary Pat fit that bill, and the price Jack requested for their ongoing friendship was the use of his first name. As she did with nearly everything her friend asked, Mary Pat had agreed. But even though the Oval Office held just the two of them, Mary Pat wasn't here to talk to her friend.

She needed the President.

"Out with it, Mary Pat," Jack said. "No secrets between us. You know that."

Mary Pat did know that. She also knew that her friend was still recovering from a trauma the depths of which he had yet to fully process. Decades ago, the love of his life had been nearly killed by an assassin from the Irish Republican Army. Jack had once told Mary Pat that seeing Cathy lying bloody and unconscious in a hospital bed was the lowest point in his life.

Mary Pat no longer believed this to be true.

A year ago, Cathy Ryan had been kidnapped and held hostage for twenty-four hours. Those hours had taken a spiritual toll on the President. As she'd expected from a man with a moral compass as unwavering as John Patrick Ryan's, her friend had relinquished his presidential duties.

But what happened next had been far worse.

Instead of the President, Jack Ryan had become just another man. A man helpless to do anything as the woman he loved languished in the hands of monsters. Fortunately, Cathy had been rescued, and though her physical injuries consisted of nothing more serious than bumps and bruises, the psychological injuries were considerably more serious. Jack's wife had been moments from death. As someone who'd been forced to confront her own mortality on more than one occasion, Mary Pat knew that the First Lady had left a piece of herself in the forsaken house where she'd been held hostage.

Now Mary Pat was worried that Cathy's husband might have done the same.

"Your immediate family is safe, sir," Mary Pat said.

The President's response was instantaneous, both confirming her suspicions and making her feel like a fool for not leading with this statement. Jack Ryan had been an intelligence analyst long before he'd taken up politics. She should have known that he would have understood the purpose of her visit the moment she'd walked into the room unaccompanied.

For an instant, Mary Pat saw the man, not the President. The relief projected in her friend's shining eyes and the hitch in his shuddered breath. Ryan had once offered her the role of vice president. Though she'd turned down the job, Mary Pat had revisited that decision more than once during her ever-more-frequent bouts of insomnia. After witnessing Ryan's reaction, she knew she'd chosen correctly. Risks to her person were part of the job, but she was not cut out to wonder if every bearer of bad news meant the death of someone she loved.

"Then what?" Ryan said.

"The Campus," Mary Pat said. "There was an ambush. Your nephew, Dom Caruso, is in a coma. The prognosis is uncertain. Clark is wounded and missing, and Ding is incapacitated. Junior is a bit banged up, but overall he's fine. He called me with the sitrep."

Another shuddered breath.

"Tell me," Ryan said.

Mary Pat nodded as she structured the information she was about to relay. Dom was family. Clark wasn't family, but he was about as close to being part of the Ryan clan as someone could be. Clark, Jack Senior, and Ding were the original three amigos. First comrades-in-arms, then friends, then something much, much more. The President didn't share blood with the former SEAL, but when it came to Jack Senior's sense of honor, this was probably a distinction without a difference.

"The Campus was on an unacknowledged operation to recover a Chinese undersea glider," Mary Pat said. "We think the sensor platform might be part of a new distributed network the Chinese are fielding in the South China Sea."

"To detect submarines," Ryan said.

Mary Pat nodded. Jack had made a name for himself as the lowly analyst who'd unraveled the mystery of the *Red October*. Now he might be the leader of the free world, but he would always be a navalist at heart.

"Yes," Mary Pat said, "and according to some flash traffic we received from the USS *Delaware* during her patrol in the South China Sea, it might be working. I used The Campus because the glider was in Manila and—"

"You didn't want to put the CIA in the position of stealing something from a sometime American ally," Jack said, waving for Mary Pat to continue. "I get it. I don't like it, but I get it."

Mary Pat knew this last statement was less of an indictment of her methods than of the world writ large. Jack Ryan would have made an excellent knight of the round table. Words like *honor*, *right*, and *wrong* were not abstract concepts to him. While Jack was not so naïve as to believe in the absolute ascendancy of U.S. foreign policy, he was very much in the Reagan camp when it came to his thoughts on American exceptionalism. The United States, while far from perfect, had done more to lift the world from darkness than any nation since the dawn of history. Jack Ryan understood the need for a deniable agency like The Campus, but he didn't have to like it.

"Yes, sir," Mary Pat continued. "In any case, the glider seems to have been used as bait."

"For The Campus?" Ryan said. "How?"

This question had bedeviled Mary Pat since she'd received the younger Ryan's call. If Jack Junior had the right of things, the operatives in the warehouse were waiting for someone. No, that wasn't right. They weren't just waiting—they'd set up a kill zone. An ambush.

"Uncertain," Mary Pat said. "Initial indications point

that way, but I don't know that I'm ready to open that particular can of worms. However, based on the available intelligence I feel comfortable stating that Clark and his team walked into an ambush set for Americans."

"What happened?" Jack said.

"An asset led Clark and Ding into the warehouse where the glider was being stored. Junior was not part of the entry team, so he isn't certain what happened next. At some point Clark triggered a duress signal. Dom, Junior, and two non-Campus personnel responded."

"Who?" Ryan said.

"A pair of Green Berets," Mary Pat said. "Cary and—"

"Jad," Ryan said, running his hands over his face. "That's a hell of a shakeout tour for those boys."

Mary Pat paused to see if her boss would elaborate.

As a former active-duty Marine, Jack Ryan, Sr., did not have the abstract view of battle that most of his predecessors brought to the Oval Office. He made it a point to know who paid the ultimate sacrifice on their nation's behalf, especially if their deaths resulted from an operation he'd ordered. That he knew the names of the two pseudo–Campus personnel wasn't unusual. Mary Pat did find it surprising that her boss was better read in than she was on the organization she notionally controlled. Perhaps once this was over, it was time to more cleanly delineate The Campus's chain of command.

"Yes," Mary Pat said after it became obvious Ryan wasn't going to say anything more. "Cary was still en route and Jad was providing overwatch from a sniper hide site, so Jack and Dom entered the building and helped eliminate the threat. At that time, Ding was the team's only casualty."

"And then?" Jack asked.

"Things get fuzzy," Mary Pat said. "Jad reported a boat approaching the pier at a high rate of speed. As Jack and Dom were exiting the building to get eyes on the boat, a bomb inside the warehouse detonated. Jack was thrown clear, but Ding, Clark, and Dom sustained shrapnel wounds. Dom coded en route to a medical facility. He's still touch and go."

For the first time, Ryan reacted as an uncle rather than the commander in chief. While Mary Pat knew that her friend had heard the news of his nephew's predicament when she'd first relayed it, the analytical portion of his mind had been sorting, cataloging, and processing the information. Only now, after his formidable intellect had hashed through the implications of a state-sponsored attack against an undeclared intelligence organization, could his feelings catch up.

Ryan's face fell and his right hand trembled.

Mary Pat looked at her friend, torn. Should she offer comfort or wait silently as Ryan sorted through his grief? In the end, she stood rooted in place. There would be a time for grieving.

This was not that time.

"Clark?" Ryan said.

The President's voice was a bit unsteady, but the blue eyes he directed at Mary Pat were unflinching. This was not her friend. This was the commander in chief of the most powerful nation on earth.

"Jad reported that a team from the boat entered the building," Mary Pat said. "Cary arrived at the same time from the opposite direction. He engaged the team. In the ensuing gunfight, the attackers left Ding but took Clark."

"Clark was alive?" Jack said. "You're sure?"

Mary Pat nodded. "Very much so. Jad had a clear view of the men hustling Clark onto the boat. He wasn't going willingly."

"Of course he wasn't," Jack said. "Who did this, MP?"

"Sir, we're not—"

"Best guess. Who?"

Mary Pat sighed.

Just as she'd known that she needed to give this update to her boss alone and face-to-face, she'd also understood that he'd want a name. Someone or something to paint a bull's-eye on. This was John Patrick Ryan.

But she still hesitated.

While it was true that the Ryan she'd known most of her life wasn't prone to flying off the handle, she wasn't sure that the person standing in front of her was still that man. Evil men had once again come for those he held dear. His nephew was at death's door, and one of his oldest and dearest friends was missing. No one would expect the President to step aside during this crisis, and Mary Pat wasn't convinced this was a good thing. Would the futility and fury spawned by Ryan's helplessness during Cathy's kidnapping influence his decisions this go-round?

Mary Pat met her boss's gaze and knew her internal deliberations didn't matter. The duly elected President of the United States had asked her a question. She was duty-bound to answer.

"My best guess is the Chinese," Mary Pat said. "Junior was working on something in Europe that went sideways. A Chinese scientist was renditioned, and his American brother killed. The perpetrators were Asian. The Chinese are up to something. Something big."

Jack slowly nodded. "Okay. What's your recommendation?"

"Let me run with the Clark issue for now. I'll handle the fallout from the operation and sync with Junior. I know you'll want to talk directly with President Chen, but you need more than I have right now. Give me the time to work this so that when you do make that call, you'll be dealing from a position of strength."

"How long?" Jack said.

Mary Pat had war-gamed this question as well. Clark was in trouble, and The Campus was shattered. Whoever had set this into motion had a plan, and they were executing it. Mary Pat had precious little time to play catch-up. But if she didn't ask for enough time, she risked coming back to Jack with nothing. She knew how that would play. Position of strength or not, Ryan would get the Chinese president on the phone and let the chips fall where they may.

As much as the President might espouse otherwise, Dom and Clark were personal.

"Four hours," Mary Pat said.

"You can have two," Jack said. "In the meantime, I'm

going to be talking with Arnie and the secretary of defense."

"I thought you were giving me time?" Mary Pat said.

"Oh, I am," Jack said. "But not much. *Si vis pacem, para bellum.*"

Mary Pat wasn't a Latin scholar, but she still knew the translation.

If you want peace, prepare for war.

34

"IS THERE ANYTHING ELSE YOU REQUIRE?"

"No," Fen Li said without looking up from her computer.

The questioner was the boat's captain. A hard man accustomed to a hard life. As a member of the Filipino Islamist group Abu Sayyaf, the captain probably considered himself a soldier for Allah.

Fen did not.

While the Abu Sayyaf terrorist organization had gone through many incarnations, the man standing before her was a pirate, plain and simple. Whether the captain kidnapped victims and ransomed captured ships in the name of Allah or just old-fashioned greed was not important to Fen. She just needed him to honor the agreement she'd brokered with his superiors.

Years of guarding Chinese ships against the menace posed by the Filipino pirates had given Fen a new perspective on how to mitigate the Abu Sayyaf problem.

She'd reached a mutually beneficial agreement with the terrorist group's leadership that allowed ships carrying her mercenaries to pass through their waters unmolested. In exchange for generous payments, the pirates also permitted Fen to hire their crews from time to time for *special* assignments.

Assignments like this one.

Fen had already been in a foul mood by the time her launch had rendezvoused with the captain's boat. Saying that things had not gone well in Manila was a bit of an understatement. The captain's reaction as she'd climbed aboard his boat in the company of her paramilitary team and their hostage had further rubbed salt in her wounds. Though he hadn't questioned her authority outright, the man's body language spoke volumes. Fen Li had a feeling that before this part of the operation was over, she would have to assert her dominance in a more dramatic fashion.

But that was a task for later.

First she needed to provide her coconspirator with an update.

"You're sure?" the captain said, moving into the cramped cabin.

Rather than answer, Fen Li drew the QSZ-92 pistol from where it was secreted against her back and laid the weapon on her bunk with one hand as she continued poking at her laptop's keyboard with the other. Like the upper echelons of the Chinese Communist Party, Abu Sayyaf pirates didn't seem to think much of women leaders.

No matter.

The captain would not be the first headstrong male she'd had to put in his place. With respect to the Chinese Communist Party, Fen believed that her polymetallic nodules would go a long way toward leveling the playing field. In the captain's case, Fen was prepared to employ a more visceral solution.

The captain took a step closer.

With a sigh, Fen reached for the pistol.

"There's no cause for that," the captain said with up-raised hands. He backed out of her cabin and closed the door behind him, but not before his eyes lingered on her salt water–soaked T-shirt for entirely too long.

She waited for the captain's retreating footsteps to fade and then slipped in her earbuds and activated her satellite phone's encryption program. Like most Chinese technology, the app was based on software pilfered from a number of different nations. Also like most Chinese technology, the encryption worked, but not as well as its Western counterpart. That said, Fen Li was currently on a fishing trawler motoring through the ocean at ten knots. While the powers of the American NSA bordered on the mythical, the agency was not omnipresent. In a world full of emerging threats, a call placed from a small boat in the middle of nowhere had to rank pretty low on the NSA's target list.

At least that's what Fen told herself.

Entering in a number she'd memorized long ago, Fen pushed the call button and listened as the phone rang. The recipient answered almost immediately.

"Wei?"

"It is done," Fen said, relishing the unexpected rush that accompanied her words.

"The target has been neutralized?"

"No," Fen said, picturing the big American even as she started down the word path she'd rehearsed in the launch countless times during the bumpy ride to the Abu Sayyaf fishing trawler. "That was not possible."

The answering silence was brief, but still caused Fen to shiver. The voice on the other end of the phone had as much as Fen riding on the outcome of this operation.

Perhaps more.

While he rewarded success extravagantly, he was just as thorough when it came to failure.

"If the American is still alive, how exactly is your mission a success?"

"I have something better than a dead American," Fen said.

"What?"

"A live one," Fen said.

"Explain."

Fen took a breath.

Her presentation was almost as important as the information itself. Her coconspirator did not have her tolerance for risk. If her voice betrayed even the slightest hesitation, he would sense it. She needed to project a calm certainty that was starkly at odds with her thundering heart.

"In March of 1984, the Americans suffered one of the biggest blows ever visited upon the Central Intelligence Agency. It was not from a blown operation or asset, or the discovery of a mole. No, the cause was much simpler—a kidnapping. Beirut chief of station William Buckley was kidnapped by Hezbollah. From the moment of his kidnapping until his body was discovered fifteen months later, the entirety of American collection efforts in the Middle East was thrown into chaos."

"Because they were afraid he was dead?"

"No," Fen said, "because the Americans knew he was alive. Several proof-of-life videos were released. Each showed the effects of Buckley's torture. He was the chief of one of the world's most important intelligence stations, and his terrorist captors were extracting his secrets one by one. Though they would never publicly say it, by the end, his Agency brethren were secretly hoping that each videotape would show Buckley's dead body. The man I captured is Buckley's modern equivalent."

This time the ensuing silence didn't feel as daunting. It was almost as if Fen could hear her coconspirator's thoughts as he ruminated over her words.

"What about the son?"

"What about him?" Fen shrugged. "Would his death have immobilized his father? Undoubtedly. But this is better. Not only is my captive privy to some of the most closely guarded secrets in the American intelligence community, he is also one of the President's closest friends. The death of a man's son is a horrible thing, but it also carries with it a finality. The President would have had to recuse himself as he did when his wife was captured, but eventually he'd come to terms with the tragedy and return. Perhaps emerging stronger. But this is something else. Imagine knowing that your friend is being taken apart by savages, piece by piece, even as he spills your most closely guarded secrets. I promised you that I'd distract the American President. With this man, I can do something better."

"What?"

"Cripple the entire government," Fen said.

"How?"

She outlined her plan in the terse no-nonsense manner her coconspirator expected.

"How do you know it won't have the opposite effect? That Ryan won't leverage everything in his power to rescue his friend."

"I fully expect him to," Fen said. "Either way, we win."

There was no pause between Fen's pronouncement and the man's reply.

"Proceed. I will see to my part."

He disconnected without waiting for Fen's reply.

That was fine.

Fen had work to do.

35

"HOW'S HE DOING?" JACK SAID.

The diminutive Filipino woman had just draped her stethoscope around her neck after a prolonged session of listening to Ding's chest. As far as Jack was concerned, this was the universal signal that a healthcare professional was now ready to discuss their prognosis.

"Stable," the doctor said, removing her glasses to rub the bridge of her nose. "I'm keeping him sedated since he's intubated. His heartbeat is steady, but I'm worried about his head wound."

Jack was also worried about Dom's head wound.

Among other things.

Surrounded by machinery and sprouting tubes of all shapes and sizes, Dom looked frail. Diminished. Thanks to the ventilator, his chest was now rising and falling with machine-inspired regularity. The shrapnel in his thigh had been removed and his leg bandaged and immobilized, but the contusion on Dom's head could still be concealing a ticking time bomb.

"I don't think there's bleeding on the brain," the doctor said, breaking into Jack's thoughts, "but I can't tell for sure with the equipment I have on hand. If you'd let me take him—"

"No hospitals," Jack said, shaking his head. "I appreciate what you've done. Help is coming."

The doctor, Maria, nodded, but Jack could see she wasn't happy. He understood. Dom wasn't her only surprise patient. Ding lay propped up in an adjacent bed. While his injuries were not nearly as severe as Dom's, Ding had suffered a gunshot wound as well as a nasty concussion. His periods of lucidity were lengthening, but Ding wasn't going to be kicking in doors and shooting bad guys in the face anytime soon.

When it came to The Campus, Jack was still the senior operative on the ground.

"I cannot keep my clinic closed for much longer," Maria said, hands on her hips.

Though the woman was barely five feet tall, her personality added a sense of gravitas to her short stature. Her dark hair was collar-length and graying at the sides, while her face bore the laugh lines of a woman in her late forties.

But her current expression wasn't humorous in the least.

"Don't worry," Jack said, holding up his hands in surrender, "we'll pay you for your time."

"I am not worried about money," Maria said, her expression growing more severe. "I am worried about the people you are forcing me to turn away. They need me, and I need to be open for them."

Jack understood.

After Jack had communicated the need for an isolated medical facility to Mario, the banker had suggested an address deep within the Tondo slums. He'd assured Jack that while the neighborhood wasn't great, the medical care was top-notch and the presence of law enforcement nonexistent. Maria's clinic delivered on all counts, but now Jack realized that his presence was costing her something more meaningful than revenue.

Purpose.

"I'm sorry," Jack said, meaning it. "We'll be out of your hair soon. My people should be here in thirty minutes or less."

Maria's frown didn't magically transform into a smile, but Jack saw something different in the doctor's eyes all the same.

Resignation.

One did not run a medical clinic in one of Manila's highest poverty neighborhoods with aspirations of getting rich. Neither did one return to said clinic day after day and remain an idealist. While he knew she was most certainly a valued member of the community, Jack thought Maria was no stranger to navigating circumstances beyond her control.

"I know we're keeping you from doing good work,"

Jack said, "but I promise it will be worth your while. Make a list of medical supplies and medicine that are hard to come by. I'll make sure you get them."

"What about equipment?" Maria said, unfazed by Jack's offer. "I could use a new X-ray machine and a portable ultrasound."

If his horrifically injured cousin wasn't lying just feet away, Jack might have smiled. Though she looked like a stiff wind might blow her over, Maria had grit. The kind of determination that allowed the doctor to face down Manila criminals and gun-toting Americans with equal vigor. Jack had a feeling that his mom would like this lady.

Hell, Cathy Ryan might just want to pay her a visit.

"Add them to your list," Jack said. "I'll see what I can do."

Maria gave a quick nod and then headed for the door leading to her small waiting/administrative area, where Mario, Jad, and Cary were parked. No doubt she intended to use the remaining time before the CIA extraction team arrived to fill as many sheets of paper with supplies and equipment as possible.

The door swung shut behind her, leaving Jack alone with his two friends.

Jack had flown to Germany what seemed like a lifetime ago, convinced that he had the stuff to be a team leader.

Now he wasn't even sure if he was truly operator material.

"Is Dom your first?"

Jack nearly jumped out of his skin.

Turning, he found Cary standing behind him.

"First what?" Jack said.

"First man you might lose."

"He's not the first Campus operator to die," Jack said.

"That's not what I asked," Cary said. "Is he the first man *you* might lose."

This time Jack understood. There was a difference between serving on a tactical team and leading one. As a leader, you were responsible for your team's successes.

And failures.

"Yeah," Jack said.

Cary nodded and squeezed Jack's shoulder. "I'd tell you it gets easier, but it doesn't. Everyone thinks that inspiring men to follow you into combat is the hardest part about being a leader. It's not. The hardest part is looking at yourself in the mirror after a teammate dies on your watch."

Jack stared at Dom's still form.

"I could say it wasn't your fault," Cary said, "but you're not ready to hear it. And maybe what you're thinking is true. Maybe you are responsible for Dom. But trying to assign fault right now is bullshit. What we do is messy. I lost my first soldier in a training accident while practicing fast-rope insertions. It was our third run of the day, and the team was firing on all cylinders. The Black Hawk flared, and the crew chief kicked out the rope just like he had twice before. Chris was the first one out the door, just like the previous two runs. Except this time, he missed the rope. One minute he was standing next to me. The next, his lifeless body was crumpled on the concrete sixty feet beneath us."

Cary paused to clear his throat.

Then the Green Beret continued.

"Wish I could tell you that Chris was the only guy I lost," Cary said. "He wasn't. If you stay in this business, Dom won't be the last guy critically injured or killed on your watch. It's a shitty deal, but we live in a shitty world."

Jack nodded.

The Green Beret hadn't said anything particularly profound. No earth-shattering conclusions, no life-changing wisdom. Even so, the commando's words carried a weight because they'd been spoken by someone who'd lived them. Someone who'd stood over the body of a fallen comrade. This was not to say that Jack was absolved of his guilt or responsibility. The events of the assault and subsequent ambush would be dissected in unflinching detail during the post-mission after-action review. Corrective actions would be instituted, and if merited, blame would be assigned.

But not today.

Today, The Campus had taken a broadside, and Jack was the only operator still on his feet. Someone had targeted Jack's brothers, and that same someone now had Clark.

This could not stand.

"All right," Jack said, turning from his stricken teammates to Cary. "How are we looking?"

"Jad and I are fit to fight," Cary said. "But I thought we were exfiling with the Agency extraction team along with Dom and Ding?"

"Not anymore," Jack said. "Someone just punched us in the face. We're gonna punch them back."

36

"BEGIN," FEN SAID, KEYING THE TRANSMIT BUTTON ON THE WALKIE-talkie.

Though she was perfectly capable of performing the needed tasks herself, Fen had decided to delegate the duties. Nothing in this entire endeavor, from the work in Europe to the aborted ambush on the dock, had gone as expected. While she'd been in the espionage business long enough to know that no operation ever went completely as planned, this one was in a class all its own. Fen's mother would look at the results and tell her wayward daughter that the ancestors were angry.

Then again, Fen's mother had been blaming angry ancestors for every slight both real and imagined for as long as Fen could remember. But just because Fen didn't agree with her mother's diagnosis of the cause for her trouble didn't mean that she disputed the truth. Something had gone very wrong, and Fen was taking nothing else for granted.

Especially the man strapped to the chair below her.

Though not constructed with interrogations in mind, the Abu Sayyaf fishing trawler hadn't required many modifications to fit the purpose Fen envisioned. A couple additions to the refrigerated compartment where the fish were normally stored and Fen had exactly what she needed—a climate-controlled room, a chair mounted to the floor with freshly drilled screws, and a drain to catch by-products from the coming work. As an added bonus, an observation deck of sorts provided a vantage point through reinforced glass into the compartment. While the observation deck was undoubtedly intended to provide fishermen with a means to determine how much space remained in the cavernous container, Fen found that the deck also doubled as a fine place to observe and direct the effort.

Her mother's take on divinity aside, Fen had no intention of being anywhere near the man secured to the chair. That he was never leaving the boat alive was a foregone conclusion. That he would depart this life without taking a few of his captors with him was less so.

As if he could hear her thoughts, the man stirred as the Filipino pirate Fen had designated as the interrogator approached. In truth, the term *interrogator* put too much stock in the man's meager abilities. An Abu Sayyaf member to his core, the man was a blunt object in every sense of the word.

Though Fen guessed the man at barely thirty, his bristly hair was streaked with gray. Likewise, his frame was whip-thin and he walked with a limp. These features, combined with the length of scar tissue that bisected his right cheek, seemed to add credentials to his pirate persona. Religious notions aside, the man was a thug who made his living robbing and murdering sailors unwary enough to slip into his web.

No matter.

For what Fen had in mind, a blunt instrument was exactly the right tool for the job.

Fen studied the man strapped to the chair as the pirate strode toward him.

John T. Clark.

The paramilitary officer's résumé was extensive. Portions of Clark's history were still shrouded in mystery, even from the voracious Chinese digital warriors employed by the Third Department of the People's Liberation Army's General Staff Department. Known as 3PLA to Westerners, this organization was the Chinese equivalent of the American National Security Agency, and it had been focused like a laser for the past year on ferreting out everything there was to know about just one man—John Patrick Ryan, Jr.

The American had originally come to Fen's attention due to what was thankfully an anomaly in her company's storied operational history—a failed contract. Unlike other Chinese private security companies, the organization Fen had built specialized in conducting clandestine operations in denied environments. While her mercenaries could be found guarding ships in the South China Sea or securing Chinese road and belt infrastructure projects in third world countries, the bulk of Fen's revenue did not come from these jobs. Instead, Fen had become a wealthy woman by serving as an unacknowledged instrument of Chinese foreign policy in places where the Ministry of State Security, or MSS, and PLA feared to tread.

Places like Israel.

A little over a year ago, Fen had received a contract to kill an American scientist on Israeli soil. Dr. Rebecka Schweigart had a Ph.D. in applied physics and the formulation for something known as stealth in a bottle—an appliqué coating capable of providing a radar-attenuating outer layer to everything from vehicles to aircraft.

Like many of the best American researchers, Dr. Schweigart was a university professor with her own private laboratory. But unlike many of her peers, Becka had refused both Chinese investment dollars and lucrative offers to participate in one of the many Chinese Communist Party–sponsored talent recruitment plans. After a Chinese graduate student at Becka's university had stolen test data from the appliqué's preliminary evaluation and provided it to her MSS handler, a decision had been made. If Becka wouldn't work for the Chinese, she wouldn't be allowed to work at all.

Enter Fen and her company.

Except the operation in Israel had gone tragically wrong due to the intervention of a single man—John

Patrick Ryan, Jr. Fen had spent her life in paramilitary organizations, and she recognized a fellow operative when she saw one. In the most basic terms, the American was her competition.

Fen was determined to learn more.

After reading the operation's after-action review, Fen had tasked her formidable organization with uncovering everything there was to know about the paramilitary operative who was at that point just an unknown American.

That's when Fen hit a brick wall.

Or a blank page, to be more precise.

To begin her effort to flesh out the operative, Fen had turned to her benefactor and now coconspirator, Aiguo Wu. Aiguo was an influential member of the Central Committee of the Chinese Communist Party. A member with his sights set on the office of general secretary and the nation's presidency. As with most successful business leaders in China, Fen had worked to cultivate relationships within the Central Committee. These power brokers were the men, and on rare occasions women, who shaped China's future.

In Aiguo, Fen had found a kindred spirit. Someone with a bold vision for the betterment of China. Aiguo had been impressed with the white-haired woman whose company of mercenaries undertook the operations deemed too dangerous by her competitors and government alike. Aiguo was soon steering sizable government contracts Fen's way, making her company a veritable extension of the MSS and the Chinese military. Fen reciprocated by awarding her benefactor a stake in her company and then using his status as a shareholder as a mechanism to award Aiguo generous kickbacks for each contract she received.

Was the practice corrupt?

Of course.

But it was also the way business was done in China.

So it was to Aiguo that Fen had presented her request for more information about the unknown American. Aiguo then tasked the 3PLA hackers to develop a complete profile of the mystery man. While Israel was a notoriously hard country to penetrate, Chinese investment in Israeli infrastructure projects and technology companies had risen dramatically in the past several years. As a result, it hadn't taken long for 3PLA to obtain images of Ryan from hacked Israeli CCTV networks, and details about the American's arrival from airport computers. But when the Chinese cyberwarriors tried to link this data to digital fingerprints in the greater World Wide Web, they found . . . nothing.

Ryan was for all intents and purposes a ghost.

But in the twenty-first century, no one can remain a ghost for long. Eventually the 3PLA operatives formed a mosaic of Ryan's life piece by digital piece. Fen still recalled the absolute shock she'd felt after the Chinese hackers stumbled upon Ryan's true identity.

But with that discovery came opportunity.

What had begun as an effort to identify and potentially settle the score with an adversary had morphed into something much, much bigger. Aiguo had been the one to bring the rumored polymetallic nodule repository in the vicinity of the disputed Paracel Islands to Fen's attention. As was typical with their arrangements, Fen bore the financial burden of verifying the repository's worth and would be responsible for mining the nodules, while Aiguo provided her with bureaucratic cover. But to stake a claim and begin harvesting the nodules, Fen would have to ensure the rest of the world was distracted.

Or, more precisely, that the world's policeman was distracted.

And nothing distracts a father like the death of his eldest son.

After obtaining Aiguo's blessing, Fen began to build a target package on Ryan. Using everything from airport surveillance cameras to passive biometric sensors, the MSS and 3PLA worked hand in hand to construct a link chart with Ryan at its center and his accomplices as spokes in the wheel. Through machine learning and data pattern analysis algorithms pilfered from laboratories and university campuses around the world, including some very nice code sequences from the United States, Chinese cyberwarriors were able to connect Ryan to other, previously unknown operatives.

One of those was John T. Clark.

But unlike Ryan, Clark had been a member of several acknowledged American entities, including the CIA, the U.S. Navy, and the Rainbow counterterrorism organization. As such, much of his personal and operational history was readily available, thanks to the 2015 Chinese hack of the United States Office of Personnel Management. This benign-sounding entity was the digital repository for the personal information of every American who held a security clearance. For an intelligence service, the data pilfered during this digital penetration represented an operational gold mine.

A gold mine Fen put to use.

The operation against Jack Ryan, Jr., in Germany had been a work of art. The perfect dangle coupled with the operational excellence for which Fen's mercenaries were known.

And it had failed.

Which had led to Manila.

After getting a hit on Jack via a CCTV camera in the Salzburg Airport, Fen was able to determine that he was heading to Manila, where three other individuals in Ryan's link chart were already gathered. Clark was one of the three. From there it hadn't been too difficult to determine the *why* behind the Americans' visit. Like any other intelligence service worth its salt, the MSS had contacts within the Filipino underworld that owned the territory around the nation's largest port. It helped that the criminal who had discovered the glider was both greedy and not particularly bright.

In Fen's experience, this wasn't an all-too-unusual combination.

Still, setting up the ambush ahead of the arriving Americans had taken some doing. After her team's failure in Germany, Fen decided to personally supervise the

Manila operation, and she'd perhaps gone a bit over-board. She'd intended to finally rid herself of Ryan by detonating the bomb hidden in the warehouse, then check the results of her work. With the scattering of Triad, Filipino, and American bodies at the scene, she was certain the Filipino police would draw some very interesting conclusions.

Once again, Fen's operation hadn't gone according to plan.

Like a cat with nine lives, Ryan had somehow survived the explosion. Not only that, an unseen sniper and the arrival of a second gunman had prevented Fen and her Abu Sayyaf help from finishing the work the bomb had started. But she had not retreated empty-handed. In the confusion of the warehouse gunfight, she'd stumbled upon Clark and decided to capture rather than kill him.

But her up-close view of the operative had left her unimpressed.

Clark was old.

Too old for the field, in Fen's estimation.

Perhaps she was about to do the Americans a favor.

The pirate ripped Clark's hood off with one hand while holding a filleting knife in the other.

When trying to decide how to frame this first video, Fen's eyes had settled on the rusted knife lying in a neglected corner of the compartment. She'd instantly known that the weapon was perfect for what she had in mind. Though the crew had tried to talk her into one of the freshly sharpened hunting knives they preferred to use when beheading their captives, one look at the curved blade and blood-soaked wooden handle convinced Fen otherwise. She wasn't concerned with how well the knife parted meat. Fen wanted to inspire fear, and the brown-speckled blade did that in spades.

Clark's head lolled to the side, seemingly lifeless.

For an instant, Fen was worried that she'd lost her American prize. The pirate had no such concerns. With the contempt of someone for whom violence is a way of life, he smacked the prisoner across the face with a lazy backhand.

Or at least he tried to.

If Fen hadn't been watching what unfolded, she wouldn't have believed it. The exact millisecond before the pirate's hand impacted Clark's face, the operative's eyes opened.

Along with his mouth.

Lurching forward, the man Fen had been convinced was too old for field work clamped on to the pirate's fingers. The terrorist screamed and dropped his knife in shock. Fen expected this to be the end of the prisoner's rebellion.

She was wrong.

Like a terrier worrying a rat, Clark ground through flesh and bone as he shook his head from side to side. The pirate's shriek became a high-pitched keening. Instead of punching the American in the jaw with his free hand, the pirate grabbed his own wrist and tried to pull his fingers free.

Were it not so sickening, Fen might have laughed.

The cocksure pirate was now in a tug-of-war with an angry grandfather. The drama played out long enough that Fen began to wonder whether the old codger might succeed in biting through the pirate's fingers. Then one of the pirate's contemporaries came to his senses. With a roar, a scraggly bystander belted the prisoner in the head with the butt of his AK-47. Blood splattered against the steel wall along with bits of flesh, not all of which belonged to Clark.

Either way, the pirate had his hand back.

Or what was left of it, anyway.

The pirate cradled his mangled fingers to his chest, his streaming eyes burning with rage. He shouted something in Tagalog to his companion, the words coming too fast for Fen to translate.

No matter.

She had a pretty good idea what had just been said.

Ending the video recording with one hand, she brought the walkie-talkie to her lips with the other. Her voice echoed through the hold just as the second pirate raised his AK-47. Clark's head lolled against his chest, but this time Fen didn't think the operative was faking. Fen issued rapid-fire instructions. The man with the Kalashnikov looked from her to his comrade, who was still dripping blood onto the metal decking. The wounded pirate shuddered, but shook his head all the same. Fen knew what the Abu Sayyaf terrorist wanted to do, but she couldn't permit Clark's execution.

Not yet.

The American would most certainly die in the dank metal tank that smelled of fish.

But first, Fen had more videos to shoot.

37

LIEUTENANT TOM MCGRATH WONDERED FOR THE THOUSANDTH TIME what he had done to deserve to be this lucky. While most of his flight school classmates spent their non-flying time wedged into the unaptly named staterooms the Navy black-shoe non-aviators grudgingly afforded their pilot comrades, Tom had never set foot on a ship.

Okay, that wasn't exactly true.

Tom had spent most of the summer between his junior and senior years of college experiencing all the Navy had to offer alongside thousands of other Reserve Officers' Training Corps midshipmen. Over those several months, Tom dove to the depths of the ocean in an *Ohio*-class submarine, stood watch aboard a *Ticonderoga*-class cruiser, and had the ride of his life in the backseat of an F/A-18 Hornet. He'd even spent some time at the range with SEAL Team 10.

After returning from this nautical whirlwind, Tom had just two thoughts.

One, he wanted to fly.

Two, he never wanted to set foot on another boat.

Fortunately, the Navy had an aerial platform that matched both of these requirements—the P-8 Poseidon. As the replacement for the venerable P-3 Orion, the P-8 was big. Huge by the standards of naval aviation. The twin-engine aircraft was actually a retrofitted Boeing 737—a passenger plane much too large to land on an aircraft carrier. By competing for the jet, Tom eschewed the sexy fighters most of his classmates chased in favor of something that would allow him to sleep in a bed far from the ocean's swells. For those reasons alone, Tom would have considered flying the Poseidon an even trade.

But that was before he'd actually become certified on the aircraft.

Much to his surprise, Tom loved piloting the lumbering jet. He loved the exotic locations, long-duration flights, and the crew comradery. Most of all, Tom loved the mission. Like its predecessor, the P-8 was a multipurpose platform. Though designed with finding and killing submarines in mind, the jet was also capable of conducting anti-surface warfare, and intelligence, surveillance, and reconnaissance missions.

And nowhere were those capabilities more needed than Tom's current duty assignment—the South China Sea.

"Foreign military airplane, you are approaching my military secure area. Please turn around immediately to avoid intercept."

Tom reached for the radio toggle to lower the volume. Chinese radio transmissions seemed to have just one level—loud.

"Right on schedule."

The comment came from Lieutenant Junior Grade Jack Stewart, Tom's copilot. The two men were battle-rostered together and had logged more time side by side over the last month than they had apart. Though the P-8 was in-flight refuellable, the men and women who operated the jet were still governed by the Navy's crew rest requirements, which dictated how long a crew member could perform flying duties. This meant that the P-8 had to be based somewhere near the area of operations. In this case, that somewhere was Clark Air Base, located in the Philippines. Even pre-positioned, the distance to their northernmost patrol area in the South China Sea added three hours of commute time to their four hours of station time.

This translated to a lot of cockpit time with Jack.

But long stretches of straight and level flight still beat living on a boat.

"I am a United States military aircraft conducting lawful military activities outside of national airspace," Tom said after keying the radio. "I am operating with due regard in accordance with international law."

"Military aircraft, turn away now."

The Chinese radio transmission could have originated from any of the dozens of islands, both real and artificial, that dotted the South China Sea. The Chinese had created the artificial landmasses as a means of enforcing their infamous "nine-dash line," so named for the roughly drawn graphic denoting the area of the South China Sea the Chinese considered their own.

In no surprise to anyone, it equated to most of the body of water.

The man-made islands were of varying sizes, but all were militarized in some form or another. The larger ones sported runways, hangars, and missile batteries, while even the smallest housed sensor arrays and communication antennas. The islands acted as nodes in a fixed Chinese sensor network, and one thing an enemy sensor network did not want was a P-8 flying nearby.

"Who do you think we're getting today?" Jack said.

Tom smiled as his eyes moved across the flat-panel displays that made up his digital cockpit. For the last week, a Chinese fighter had intercepted the P-8 each time Tom had voiced his intentions to ignore the radioed warning to remain clear of Chinese-claimed airspace. These interceptions fell into two categories, depending on the Chinese aviator. The first and preferable pilot Jack had termed Ice Man. When Ice Man was at the fighter's controls, the interception of Tom's P-8 was done smoothly and by the book. Though the J-16 fighter ventured a bit closer than Tom would have preferred, the Chinese pilot never put the P-8 in any danger.

The same could not be said of the second Chinese aviator.

Pilot number two had nearly torn the nose off the Poseidon the first time he'd intercepted the American plane. Tom was a firm believer in the adage that the amount of calm a good pilot projected needed to be inversely proportionate to the amount of crazy happening in the cockpit. But seeing a twin-engine Chinese interceptor flash past your windshield at better than four hundred knots tested the resolve of even the best aviator.

His second encounter with the Chinese aviator hadn't been much better.

This time, the nimble J-16 had attempted to jostle the much bigger P-8 with jet wash by lighting its afterburners while passing from below the Poseidon to above in a maneuver known as "thumping." As coffee cups and checklists bounced across the cockpit, Jack had wondered aloud whether the Chinese pilot had a death wish.

This comment led to the pilot's nickname.

Kamikaze.

That the Japanese moniker would have surely infuriated the Chinese aviator only added to the call sign's allure. But gallows humor or not, Tom was desperately hoping that it was Ice Man, not his homicidal countryman, who joined their flight today.

His hopes were in vain.

One second Tom was verifying the waypoints on the active route, the next he was reaching for the yoke and throttle as the P-8 bounced the way his old Ford Fiesta had when he'd hit the speed bumps in his high school's parking lot at fifty miles per hour. A wailing siren announced that the abrupt turbulence had caused the autopilot to disengage, further adding to the fun.

"Holy crap," Jack said.

"Language," Tom said as he stabilized the aircraft and reengaged the autopilot, silencing the siren.

Jack famously bucked the *cursing like a sailor* naval tradition. For Tom's devout copilot, uttering the word *crap* was the equivalent of dropping the f-bomb. Like an aircraft's automated flight controls, Jack wasn't easily rattled.

"What in the hell was that?"

This time the question came over the crew intercom from Lieutenant Commander Vinnie Shorts. The former Annapolis football player was not a pilot, nor was he particularly careful with his language, a condition that Tom suspected went hand in glove. Vinnie was the naval flight officer in charge of the aviation warfare operators who handled the Poseidon's plethora of sensors in the cabin located behind the cockpit. Tom might be the pilot-in-command, but Vinnie saw the two aviators as nothing more than glorified bus drivers. He and his team did the real work, and Vinnie was not pleasant when his work was interrupted.

"Kamikaze," Tom said after toggling the intercom switch.

"That was one hell of a jolt," Vinnie said. "What did he do this time?"

"Not entirely sure," Tom said, even as he scanned the sky for the fighter's fleeting form. "If I had to guess, I'd say he cut across our flight path at just under Mach 1."

"I wouldn't bet on the *under* part," Jack said.

"Where's he now?" Vinnie said.

"I don't have a visual," Tom said. "Anything on sensors?"

Unlike its cousin the E-2 Hawkeye, the P-8 was not built with aerial surveillance in mind. The Poseidon was a sub killer, plain and simple. But over time that mission set had been expanded along with the suite of sensors needed to fill the jet's newer roles. In addition to the acoustic sensor used to ferret out submerged submarines, the aircraft boasted a multimode maritime radar as well as a forward-looking infrared, or FLIR, turret. While both of these sensor platforms were meant to monitor sea-based targets, they could be directed against aerial contacts in a limited fashion.

"Stand by," Vinnie said. "Lemme see what we can find."

Tom added his own eyes to the search mission, but as before, he saw nothing but open sky. Not for the first time, he wondered whether this is what his World War II–era Army Air Corps predecessors had felt while piloting bombers over the skies of Europe.

"Want me to call it in?" Jack said.

"Good idea," Tom said to his copilot. "I'm gonna keep an eye on the flight controls. Everything feels fine, but that shock wave was a doozy."

"Roger that," Jack said.

Out of habit, Tom eyed each of the six electronic display units that made up the P-8's digital cockpit. He lingered on the screen showing the readings for the Poseidon's two engines before cycling through the navigational and primary flight displays.

Everything seemed in order.

"Charlie Main, this is Badger 15," Jack said. "We have a—"

"Tom," Vinnie said, talking over Jack, "the fighter's right—"

A rumbling as the Poseidon buffeted through unseen turbulence drowned out Vinnie's words. No matter, Tom no longer needed the sensor's help to find the Chinese fighter plane. The J-16 was just outside his windscreen. The twin-engine jet was so close that Tom reflectively put his hand to his face to shield his eyes from the glowing engine exhaust.

"Holy shit," Jack said.

Tom grabbed the yoke and edged it forward as he added right rudder for trim, trying to slide his aircraft below the jet wash he was certain would be coming his way after the J-16 lit its afterburners.

He was half right.

Something was coming, but it wasn't engine exhaust.

The air ignited as a stream of flares and glittering clouds of chaff erupted from beneath the J-16. Flares and chaff that Tom was forced to guide his plane through as he tried to descend. The countermeasures were meant to deter enemy missiles, but Tom thought that flares burning at two thousand degrees Fahrenheit and chaff composed of millions of tiny aluminum fibers would probably have a detrimental effect on his jet if either hit the Poseidon in the wrong place.

"Shit fire," Jack said. "Number one engine is out."

Like the number one engine, for instance.

38

AS WITH MOST COMMERCIAL JETS, THE BOEING 737 WAS DESIGNED to fly with just one engine if necessary. The number of modifications the P-8 had over its commercial sibling were too numerous to count, but in their bones the airplanes handled similarly. Under normal circumstances, the loss of an engine, while serious, was not a life-threatening emergency.

These were not normal circumstances.

As if summoned by Jack's cry, the engine display unit heralded some rather ominous news. The number one engine was not only no longer producing power.

It was on fire.

Glancing down at the cluster of red switches located aft of the engine start levers in the center of the instrument console, Tom confirmed that the switch labeled *1* was illuminated.

The number one engine was toast.

"Engine fire, number one engine," Tom said, reciting

the emergency procedure from memory. "Disengage auto throttle."

Tom settled his right hand on the number two engine's thrust lever, preventing Jack from inadvertently performing the emergency procedure on the engine that was still producing power. This technique was known as "guarding" the power lever. It reflected the bitter truth that even the most experienced pilot could misidentify a power lever during the adrenaline-saturated environment of an actual emergency. All too often, simple pilot error caused aviation incidents to progress from manageable emergencies to fatal ones.

"Auto throttle disengaged," Jack said.

"Thrust lever engine one, confirmed closed," Tom said.

"Confirmed," Jack said.

"Engine start lever, number one engine, confirm cut off," Tom said.

"Confirmed," Jack said.

"Engine fire switch number one engine," Tom said, "confirm and pull."

"Pulling," Jack said.

Tom watched as Jack pulled the illuminated fire switch. Then Tom's eyes tracked to the ENG OVERHEAT light. It was still illuminated.

Engine one was still on fire.

"Rotate engine fire switch to the stop and hold for one second," Tom said.

Jack complied, and the ENG OVERHEAT light extinguished.

The engine fire was out.

Progress.

Except that the controls still didn't feel quite right.

"We've got an issue with number two," Jack said. "EGT is close to redline."

EGT stood for exhaust gas temperature. It was a measure of the jet engine's internal temperature. A redlining EGT meant that the combustion chamber was abnormally hot. This could happen for a number of reasons, but troubleshooting the malfunction's cause wasn't important at the moment. If left unchecked, the high temperature would eventually damage the engine, perhaps permanently.

At the moment, a damaged engine ranked pretty low on Tom's priority list.

He was more concerned with keeping his jet in the air.

Like everything else aboard the Poseidon, control of the engines was relegated to a computer. In this case, the computer in question was aptly named the Electronic Engine Control. In addition to ensuring that the correct air/fuel mixture was achieved for each desired power state, the EEC helped to ensure the engine itself remained undamaged by regulating the amount of fuel allocated to it.

While this was a great idea in theory, this bit of electronic wizardry was in the process of biting Tom in the ass. To keep the engine from overheating, the EEC was decreasing the amount of fuel that flowed into the combustion chamber. This in turn limited the amount of thrust the engine produced. Judging by his jet's rapid rate of descent, engine number two was not generating enough thrust to keep the underside of the Poseidon from making the acquaintance of the frothing salt water ten thousand feet below.

Not good.

"What's going on up there?" Vinnie said.

"Might have to ditch," Tom said. "Secure the cabin."

To his credit, the normally verbose sensor operator replied with a succinct "Aye, aye" before dropping off the net. Nothing focused a conversation like the possibility of an unplanned swim in an angry ocean.

"How's it feel?" Jack said.

Tom shook his head. "Like she doesn't want to fly. I can't maintain altitude."

"EGT's not coming down," Jack said. "I think we're fixing to lose engine two."

Tom eyed the engine display unit as he reduced the throttle for the number two engine another quarter inch to idle. The effect on the troubled engine should have been immediate.

It was not.

If anything, the internal temperature on the belabored engine continued to climb.

Tom had two choices. He could try to baby the engine and limp closer to shore at the risk of a fire potentially engulfing the rest of the aircraft, or he could accept that the engine was gone and set the best possible conditions for ditching while he still had altitude to play with. Tom ran through the possible ramifications of each choice even as the EGT inched upward and his altimeter spooled downward.

Decision time.

"We're ditching," Tom said, his voice sounding surprisingly calm even to his own ears. "You get the mayday call, I'll tell the crew."

"Roger that," Jack said, reaching for the radio transmit button. "Mayday, Mayday, Mayday, we are a U.S. Navy P-8—"

Tom tuned out Jack in favor of triggering the intercom toggle.

"We're ditching," Tom said. "You've got ten minutes."

"Ten minutes, aye," Vinnie said. "Crew is strapped in. We're sanitizing the bird."

Like its predecessor the P-3, the P-8's innocuous-looking fuselage contained a few surprises. Though the former passenger plane lacked a B-2 stealth bomber's intriguing shape or a Spectre gunship's protruding weapons, the Poseidon held some of the nation's most closely guarded secrets. Between its array of cutting-edge sensors, libraries of submarine-related data, and the algorithms that fused the two together, a P-8 falling into Chinese hands would be the equivalent of handing an adversary a stack of classified documents.

That wasn't going to happen.

Part of the work would be done by Vinnie and his cadre of sensor operators as the technicians wiped hard drives and destroyed valuable data. As the pilot-in-command, Tom bore overall responsibility for the aircraft. This obligation did not end once the jet was on the ground, or, in this case, water. It would fall to Tom to ensure that the aircraft was configured in a manner that would not allow the Chinese to exploit the crash site. While everyone else abandoned ship, Tom would be focused on scuttling the plane.

But that was a concern for later.

At this moment, Tom cared about just one thing—flying his stricken jet.

"I think we need to start the APU," Tom said.

"Why?" Jack said. "That's not part of the emergency procedure."

"The emergency procedure didn't imagine us losing both engines," Tom said. "No engines means no power to the flight instruments or hydraulic pumps. Kind of hard to fly without those."

"Tracking," Jack said, "starting the auxiliary power unit."

"Cockpit, this is cabin," Vinnie said. "We've got flames outside the number two engine cowling."

"Roger that," Tom said, easing the nose over. "Steepening my dive. Assume crash positions."

"Assuming crash positions," Vinnie echoed.

"Passing through five thousand feet," Jack said as he locked his harness in preparation for impact.

"Five thousand feet," Tom echoed.

He steeped the dive angle even more, knowing that he was on borrowed time.

A modern jet engine was constructed from a multitude of exotic materials. Metals and alloys designed to withstand the high temperatures and rugged environments that formed the engine's performance window. Some of these components burned at temperatures that were almost impossible to extinguish. If the number two engine cooked off, the wing and its thousands of gallons of jet fuel would not be far behind.

Tom needed to get this bird on the water.

Now.

"EGT is still climbing," Jack said. "Slipstream isn't helping."

For a moment Tom was confused by his copilot's comment. Then he understood. Jack thought Tom was diving in an effort to blow out the flames or at the very least cool down the engine. Normally not a bad plan, but the words ENG FAIL displayed in amber on the EGT indicator told a different story. The engine temperature was now beyond what the sensor was capable of reading.

Tom was now officially piloting a flying bomb.

"One thousand feet," Jack said.

"We're gonna bring her in hot," Tom said. "Give me forty degrees of flaps."

Normal landings were conducted as close to the aircraft's stall speed as possible. This was because the plane's velocity affected the force at which the 138,000-pound metal bird impacted the runway, and passengers, not to mention the millions of dollars' worth of sensitive equipment on the jet, preferred soft landings to a controlled crash.

But not in this case.

As if reading Tom's mind, the jet shuddered in response to a deep *thump*.

"Number two engine is completely engulfed," Vinnie said. "Flames are spreading to the wing."

"Roger that," Tom said. "Brace for impact."

"Five hundred feet," Jack said. "Airspeed's looking good."

If able, Tom would have promoted his copilot to pilot-in-command on the spot. Anyone who could speak that calmly while riding right seat in a dead-stick bird trailing flames certainly had the decision-making skills and maturity required to be the one calling the shots. But Tom didn't have the mental capacity to give Jack even a simple attaboy.

He was too focused on the rapidly approaching ocean.

"Impact, impact, impact," Tom said as he eased the yoke backward, attempting a flare.

Salt water exploded across his windshield.

39

"SORRY I'M LATE, SIR," MARY PAT SAID, HURRYING INTO THE SITU-ation room.

Though the underground bunker was held at a constant temperature and humidity, the air always felt oppressively cold to her, regardless of the time of year.

Today was no exception.

"No apologies, Mary Pat," President Jack Ryan said. "I'm the one who called the unscheduled meeting. Or I guess it's more accurate to say the Chinese did."

Ryan rose as he spoke, indicating the vacant chair to his right. Mary Pat smiled her thanks. John Patrick Ryan might be the leader of the free world, but he was still a gentleman, and always behaved as such. No amount of private chiding about the pecking order inherent in their official roles would ever stop her friend from standing when she entered the room and then personally pouring

her a cup of coffee. Normally, Mary Pat welcomed the
subtle reminder that she and the President had been
friends long before he ascended to the nation's highest
office and, God willing, would remain so long after he
left.

But not today.

Today, Mary Pat had to show her friend something
that would pierce his soul and then ask him to set aside
his justified emotional response in favor of his responsibilities as commander in chief.

Not an easy proposition.

"What did I miss?" Mary Pat said as she settled into
her seat.

Mary Pat could normally make a pretty good guess at
what she was walking into based on who the President
had asked to attend the meeting. Today, the chief of staff,
secretary of state, and secretary of defense were all in attendance, along with some minor staffers. Admiral Billings was the naval representative, and it was clear from
the illuminated flat screens along the walls that he had
been about to brief Ryan in her absence.

Or perhaps had already started, seeing that the Power-
Point slide showed an enlarged image of the South China
Sea with the nine-dash line superimposed. Though Jack
was a stickler for holding briefings only after the intelligence community, usually in the form of Mary Pat, was
in attendance, sometimes this wasn't an option. The ability to monitor events occurring halfway around the globe
in real time meant that decisions had to be rendered
quickly. Other times, briefers attempted to address the

President in Mary Pat's absence for less charitable reasons.

In an administration with a foreign policy as muscular as Ryan's, the military and intelligence communities often jockeyed for position. The two decades spanning the war on terror had altered the uniformed service in many ways, not all of them good. Case in point, Mary Pat was seeing more and more flag officers adopt attitudes reminiscent of their political counterparts.

Though she had no desire to ever serve beyond her current role, Mary Pat had been a fixture in government for too long. Many D.C. insiders were convinced that she was angling for a post-Ryan political future. If only they knew. Not only had she turned down the job of vice president, but nightly Mary Pat had to contend with her husband Ed's bedtime musings about what their life would be like after the Ryan administration. As of late, these soliloquies had become far less subtle. Ed had also been a career CIA case officer and was no stranger to selfless service.

But he was a grandfather.

A grandfather who understood that the time he and his wife had to spoil their grandchildren was finite. Ed wanted Mary Pat to retire and enjoy the fruits of their labor. The last several years had been hard. Hard enough that Mary Pat found herself slowly coming around to her husband's way of thinking. But even so, something kept her in this chair.

John Patrick Ryan.

Until her dearest friend finished his term, she would

endure this purgatory with him. This was their final battle, and Mary Pat intended to remain shoulder to shoulder with her comrade in arms until its conclusion.

"Go ahead with your presentation, Admiral," Jack said.

The reprimand was subtle but noticeable, as the admiral's reddening complexion could attest. People who tried to outmaneuver Jack Ryan did so at their own risk.

"Yes, sir."

A fresh-faced Navy lieutenant whose nameplate read CAINE advanced the slide, seemingly oblivious to the power struggle playing out around her. Or at least Mary Pat hoped the pretty brunette was oblivious. When Mary Pat had been the woman's age, she'd been focused on running agents in East Germany one step ahead of the murderous Stasi. Office politics had been the furthest thing from her mind. What did it say about the current state of things that Mary Pat saw the Cold War as the good old days?

Maybe Ed was right.

"Approximately fifteen minutes ago, a P-8 Poseidon transmitted a mayday call after nearly colliding with a Chinese J-16 fighter," Admiral Billings said. "The transmission included the aircraft's GPS coordinates, which placed it here." The flat screen now reflected a rendering of the P-8's flight plan showing the crash site as a section of the South China Sea, roughly equidistant from Hong Kong, the southwestern tip of Taiwan, and the northwestern corner of the Philippines, along with a stock picture of the Chinese twin-engine, dual-seat multirole fighter.

"We knew this would happen," Bob Burgess said. "The Chinese have been playing with fire. It was only a matter of time before one of their fighter jocks pushed things too far."

Mary Pat found the secretary of defense's sentiment understandable. In fact, she agreed with his assessment. But this was a time for clarity, not emotion.

"What's the status of the P-8?" Ryan said.

Of course this was the first question her boss would ask. Ryan was certainly not naïve to the human cost of his policies, but he treasured each man and woman under his command. Service members who fought and died at his behest would never be relegated to sterile casualty reports.

This was exactly what had Mary Pat worried.

"The aircraft's emergency location transmitter activated, indicating that the jet impacted the water," Admiral Billings said. "In addition to GPS coordinates, the data burst from the Poseidon contains information from a mini black box of sorts. Based on the aircraft's speed and rate of descent, we believe the ditching was survivable."

"Survivors?" Ryan said.

Lieutenant Caine shook her head. "Unknown at this time, sir. We're scrambling every ISR asset in the area, but the P-8 was at the outermost limit of its patrol. It will take time to get friendly eyes overhead."

"What about satellite coverage?" Ryan said.

The question was directed at Jason Jackson, the liaison for the National Reconnaissance Office. Though

Mary Pat sat at the pinnacle of the intelligence community, her position was created more to ensure that all of the organizations that fell under her umbrella operated in a synchronized fashion. She didn't manage individual intelligence community members. That responsibility rightfully resided with the respective agency's director.

But she was very much interested in Jason's answer.

"I can have my folks take a look at the coordinates," Jason said, "but I suspect it's probably a bit outside our birds' current tracks. The P-8's mission profiles are built with this in mind. The jets fly patrols meant to fill in the gaps from our nonterrestrial coverage."

"Why can't we change orbits?" Ryan said.

"We can, Mr. President," Jason said, "but I'll need to run the numbers on the impact to the satellite's life expectancy."

Though Jason had been in his role for several months, his answer indicated he still didn't understand how his boss thought. At least not completely. Jason's response made sense from a dollars-and-cents perspective. Satellites reached orbit with a finite amount of maneuvering fuel. Once that propellant was expended, the satellite was committed to an orbit. Even if their new position was advantageous to the analysts who handled their collection priorities, the satellites would eventually fall back to earth without the periodic propellant boosts required to maintain their eternal fight against gravity.

The cost of manufacturing a spy satellite could easily approach a billion dollars and take up to a year and a half of assembly time. They were not assets to be trifled with.

But Jack Ryan was suggesting just that for the sake of seven women and men who may or may not already be dead.

Ryan's comment helped to remind Mary Pat why she still resisted Ed's entreaties.

"Rescuing the crew is my top priority," Ryan said, locking gazes with Jason. "I don't care about the bird's life expectancy. If repositioning an orbit will allow us to get eyes on that crew, do it. Now."

Ryan hadn't raised his voice, but his message had been delivered. Unequivocally. A rustling enveloped the table as attendees reached for secure cell phones and tablets to dash off messages or to make inquiries. Ryan might be a shoo-in for Mount Rushmore, but he was also very much human. When aroused, his Irish temper was legendary.

No one wanted to be the next exemplar of the Ryan Doctrine.

"What about the 7th Fleet?" Ryan said.

Secretary of Defense Burgess nodded as if he'd expected the question.

Good.

"The bulk of the carrier task force is about four hundred nautical miles away from the crash site. That's pretty close to the maximum range for our fighters. The alert F-18s have already been launched, along with several slower-moving search-and-rescue platforms. Even at supersonic speeds, it's going to take a bit for our birds to get overhead. Once they arrive, the Hornets will only have a few minutes before they'll need to break station to link up with their tankers."

"We have a Poseidon crew potentially treading water, and you're telling me we can't do anything but twiddle our thumbs?" Ryan said. His voice was still even, but a flush was building at the base of his neck.

Never a good sign.

"There is one other option," Burgess said. "The USS *Delaware* is on patrol nearby. She can intervene, but doing so will compromise her mission profile. Several PLA Navy frigates are heading toward the P-8's crash site. I expect that entire section of ocean will soon be crawling with ships."

Expending the propellant on a billion-dollar satellite to find Americans was one thing. Exposing a three-and-a-half-billion-dollar submarine was something else. Stealth was a submarine's greatest asset. Using the *Delaware* to rescue the crew would not only give the Chinese a look at one of America's most secretive weapons systems, it would also compromise the sub's purpose in the South China Sea.

The cost-benefit analysis for such an action was much, much different.

But not for Ryan.

"Rescue that crew by any means necessary," Ryan said. "Am I clear?"

"Yes, sir," Secretary Burgess said.

"Good," Ryan said. "Scott, I want you to get me on the phone with President Chen. When one of his submarines was disabled, I gave him space to recover it. He's about to return the favor."

Mary Pat knew that was coming. Ryan was a Boy Scout through and through. His absolute sense of right and wrong was one of his best traits, but his unwavering moral compass could also be a blind spot. Because he always acted with integrity, the President believed that, given the chance, others would do the same.

Providing a counterbalance to Ryan's better angels was part of Mary Pat's job.

"Understood, Mr. President," Secretary of State Scott Adler said, "but I'd ask that you let me relay the message. My counterpart can yell at me first, setting the conditions for a second call between you and President Chen. One in which he graciously agrees to your terms. Allowing the Chinese to save face might permit us to steer through this mess without escalating the situation further."

The flush that had begun at Jack's neck was now creeping toward his ears, but the President still nodded. Even at his angriest, the analyst at Ryan's core allowed him to dissect and analyze arguments without emotional interference.

Usually.

"Okay, Scott," the President said, "but the clock's ticking. The Chinese caused this mess, and my patience is wearing thin."

Left unsaid was the reason for Jack's impatience. The P-8 crew wasn't the only reason Ryan looked like he wanted to pummel the Chinese with his bare hands. Mary Pat knew that Clark was at the forefront of the

President's mind, and if proof that the Chinese were behind Clark's kidnapping and Dom's attack surfaced, all
bets were off.

"Yes, sir," Scott said. "I'll get my counterpart on the
phone as soon as we're done here. Give me thirty minutes. An hour, tops."

"Thirty minutes is better," Jack said. "Bob—I need
everyone in the region to understand the severity with
which we view what happened. Have our naval assets in
the area start steaming toward the projected crash site."

"Which ones?" the secretary of defense said with a
frown.

"All of them," Ryan said.

Silence greeted the President's words as the secretary
of defense and Admiral Billings exchanged glances. Finally, the admiral bit the bullet.

"Sir, even if the USS *Ronald Reagan* sprinted ahead
with minimal escort, it would take the carrier thirteen
hours to get to the crash site," Billings said.

"I understand," Ryan said. "This action is separate
from the rescue. It's about displaying our intentions to recover those crewmen. Period. We are juggling with dyna-
mite. The Chinese must not misjudge our commitment,
and nothing says commitment like seven U.S.-flagged
warships sailing in the same direction."

Mary Pat wholeheartedly concurred. The last time she
remembered this large a naval effort was almost forty
years ago when a certain Soviet submarine had gone
missing.

She decided to keep this observation to herself.

"Anything else?" Ryan said. After surveying the silent room, Ryan nodded. "Good. Get after it, people. We've got Americans in the water."

Wisely, no one bothered to point out that the assembled group had no idea if this were true. Jack Ryan was an optimist, and he expected those he surrounded himself with to adopt the same attitude. Until proven otherwise, he believed that the P-8 crew had survived the crash, and that U.S. forces would rescue them. Though he was pissed, Jack was also in the zone.

This was her friend at his best.

Mary Pat hoped this remained true after he heard her dark news.

40

"SIR, CAN I HAVE A MINUTE OF YOUR TIME?" MARY PAT SAID.

Jack looked over at her, his blue eyes taking in her countenance.

"Of course," Ryan said. "Do we need anyone else?"

"No, sir," Mary Pat said.

"Okay," Ryan said. "Arnie, wait for me in the Oval Office, please."

"Yes, Mr. President," Arnie van Damm said, shooting Mary Pat an irritated look.

The President's chief of staff obviously wasn't happy at being excluded, but he didn't press the issue. Among the President's inner circle, only Cathy Ryan rated higher than Mary Pat. Arnie had been with Jack for ages, but he'd never bled with the President.

Mary Pat had.

The room emptied in a collection of rustling papers, swishing fabric, and clicking heels.

Then it was just the two of them.

"What do you have, MP?" Ryan said.

Mary Pat unpacked a secure tablet from her messenger bag, powered it on, and progressed through the myriad security protocols. Only once the screen was replaced by a paused video did she turn her attention to the President.

"Jack," Mary Pat said, laying her hand atop his, "you need to prepare yourself. Clark's alive, but it's not pretty. Okay?"

Ryan's eyes hardened, but he slowly nodded.

Mary Pat squeezed Jack's fingers and then pressed play.

The video was horrible, and not just because of the creepy lighting and shaky video. The audio captured every *thunk* and highlighted every scream. Mary Pat had watched the sequence three times at her desk and once more on the drive over. It had turned her stomach, but the sound quality was excellent. She thought she could even make out the sound of finger bones snapping as Clark savaged the guard's hand before the former SEAL was beaten senseless.

Then it was over.

"Again," Ryan said.

"Jack, I—"

"Again."

The President hadn't raised his voice, but Mary Pat still jerked. It wasn't the volume that had startled her. It was the tone. Jack was speaking with a Marine's command voice.

Biting her tongue, Mary Pat pressed play. This time

she didn't watch, and that might have been a mistake. Without the savage images to distract her mind, the visceral audio was all the more prominent.

Bile unexpectedly burned its way up her throat.

Mary Pat placed a hand to her mouth, fighting the urge to vomit.

"I'm sorry, MP," Ryan said. "I'm sorry."

"Not your fault, Mr. President," Mary Pat said, shaking her head. "I'd be more worried if watching this didn't make me vomit. I'm sorry for distracting you."

Ryan squeezed her arm.

"You didn't distract me, MP," Ryan said, "you reminded me to be human. I just learned that seven people crashed into the ocean because they flew a patrol on my orders. Before that I had to tell my sister that another one of her sons might die in service to our nation. Now this with Clark. The urge to just turn off my emotions is almost irresistible."

"You're the commander in chief, sir," Mary Pat said. "Maybe that's the right call."

"I know what you mean," Ryan said, "but I don't agree. There's a reason why a person instead of a computer sits behind the Resolute desk. The best leaders acknowledge rather than suppress the emotional aspect of their decisions. It's what keeps us human."

Mary Pat understood Jack's point, but she still worried. A commander who placed too much emphasis on his troops' lives often drifted into indecisiveness or decisional paralysis. While she agreed that the President should not rush into conflict, neither should he dither once it became obvious that a conflict was unavoidable.

But Mary Pat did not say this to the President. Instead, she nodded and gave him space to process what he'd just seen. She needed Jack to be on his A game for what she had in mind. This was why she'd chosen to show him the video in private. In front of his staff, Jack needed to be the President of the United States. But here, in this unguarded moment, he could shed his mantle of responsibility and react like a grief-stricken friend.

Briefly.

"Who has Clark?" Ryan said.

Mary Pat placed both hands flat on the table as she prepared to deliver the second piece of bad news. "The short answer is that we're not sure," Mary Pat said. "The video popped up on one of the Abu Sayyaf You-Tube channels. Analysts are working on the digital forensics now. Preliminary data suggest that the video was uploaded from a hilly area of Basilan Island in the southwestern part of the Philippines. It's a known Abu Sayyaf stronghold and would further seem to suggest that Clark is being held by the Islamic terrorists."

"But you don't think so," Ryan said.

Mary Pat paused to gather her thoughts.

This was why summarizing intelligence was more art than science. The very best briefings combined facts with the analyst's intuition—a perfect pairing between man and machine. But the balance required to walk this tightrope was not easily attained. Too much intuition and the briefer could inadvertently supplant raw intelligence with their own biased suppositions. Too few human inferences and the intelligence could be reduced to meaningless data points, bread crumbs that were interesting on their own but led nowhere.

"I think there's more here than meets the eye," Mary Pat said. "Clark could very well be in the hands of Abu Sayyaf, but this doesn't fit the group's normal pattern. Yes, they engage in piracy and kidnapping, and yes, Abu Sayyaf has conducted operations in Manila. It's also not a stretch to think that the organization wields influence in one of Asia's busiest ports, but this is still a departure from their usual MO. What happened to the Campus team occurred in two parts. First, a gunfight between rival elements both interested in the Chinese glider. But the second half of the engagement is the most troubling. That pre-positioned bomb combined with the kidnappers' presence points to something preplanned. An ambush. I'm beginning to believe this, taken with the kinetic action in Europe, points to an operation meant to target The Campus itself."

"Then why the video of Clark?" Ryan said, gesturing at the tablet. "Why not just put a bullet in his skull? For that matter, why go to the trouble of kidnapping him in the first place?"

These were the same questions that burned through Mary Pat.

Questions she couldn't answer.

There were moments when she wished that her boss

hadn't spent his formative years working for the world's premier intelligence organization.

"I don't know yet, sir," Mary Pat said, "but I will find out. I promise."

Jack eyed her for a long moment before sighing.

"I believe you, MP," Ryan said, "but what about Clark?"

"Let me work Clark," Mary Pat said. "My sense is that everything we're seeing in the region is related. A Campus member was critically injured and one of your oldest friends was kidnapped. I don't think that's a coincidence."

"Meaning what?" Ryan said.

Though his voice was still calm, Ryan's tone changed. He knew where she was heading, and he didn't like it.

"Less than a year ago you were forced to step aside because your wife was kidnapped," Mary Pat said. "I told you then, and I still believe now, that voluntarily relinquishing your duties was the right call."

"But?"

"But the world's bad guys were watching. And learning. If we assume that The Campus has somehow been penetrated, then we should also assume that the same bad actors know about your ties to Junior, Clark, Ding, and Dom. You are a formidable President who acts decisively and wisely on the world stage."

"Unless I'm put in a position where I can't," Ryan said.

Mary Pat nodded. "Attacks on our loved ones affect us at a visceral level, no matter our station in life. You mitigated that to some extent when Cathy was kidnapped by stepping aside, but what if you hadn't? What if you'd stayed in power and your anxiety about your missing wife had interfered with your ability to make unbiased decisions?"

"What are you saying, Mary Pat?" Ryan said. "That I should step aside because Dom's in a coma and Clark's been kidnapped?"

"No, sir," Mary Pat said, shaking her head, "I'm not. But I do think that you need to be aware that your decision-making ability might be the ultimate target of whatever is happening here."

"What is happening here?" Ryan said. "So far, I've got a P-8 in the water and not much else. If your theory's correct, what am I missing?"

"I don't know, sir," Mary Pat said for what felt like the hundredth time. "But forewarned is forearmed. That's why I want you to let me handle Clark while you focus on what's unfolding in the South China Sea."

As if Mary Pat's comment reminded him of what was happening outside of the Situation Room's sterile atmosphere, Ryan glanced at his watch. "By now Scott should have the Chinese ambassador on the phone," Ryan said. "If history is any guide, it'll be my turn in about forty-five minutes. I'll take your advice, but I need you to produce, Mary Pat."

"Understood, sir," Mary Pat said. "I have assets in place to work the Clark situation, but I'm going to need something from you."

"What?"

"Authority. Clark's clock is ticking. We need to be able to leverage every asset under our control and merge their taskings and output seamlessly. No barriers, artificial or otherwise."

Ryan frowned as she spoke.

Then he understood.

"The Campus," Ryan said. "You want to bring it under the intelligence community's official umbrella?"

"Semantics, Mr. President," Mary Pat said. "I don't care about org structures or federal charters. Neither am I concerned with get-out-of-jail-free passes. I want your approval to integrate The Campus as I see fit. If I'm right, someone has already penetrated the veil of secrecy surrounding the organization. If I'm wrong, well, we can cross that bridge when we come to it."

Ryan looked back at her, for once his expression unreadable.

Then he slowly nodded.

"Okay," Ryan said, "do what you have to do."

"Thank you, Mr. President," Mary Pat said, collecting her things. "Unless you have anything else, I need to get to work."

"Just a warning, MP," Ryan said.

His tone made Mary Pat freeze mid-gesture, her fingers hovering above the secure tablet. "Sir?" Mary Pat said.

"I'm not prepared to let one of my oldest friends get tortured to death," Ryan said. "I'll give you time and space, but if another video comes in, all bets are off. Understood?"

"Yes, sir," Mary Pat said. "We'll get Clark back."

As the President stood, Mary Pat hoped that she hadn't just lied to her friend.

41

"YOU NEED TO SEE THIS, SKIPPER."

Commander Christina Dixon looked from the paper she'd been reviewing to the anxious face of her executive officer. Even though the entire boat was one sprawling computer network, Christina still preferred to review the daily department statuses in paper form rather than on her networked tablet. Christina had been a child of the digital age, but she still found flipping through the status update and adding comments with her ever-present government-issued black Skilcraft pen comforting.

From the look on her XO's face, she was about to need some comfort.

"What have you got, Dan?" Christina said.

Rather than speak, Dan handed over a printout. This was another bad sign. If Dan wanted her to read the message for herself, Christina had a feeling that things were about to get wonky.

She was right.

A P-8 had just gone down and the *Delaware* had been tasked to investigate. No, that wasn't quite right. The orders were not vague, but they offered room for interpretation, as was normal for a submarine captain. While the *Delaware* was instructed to make for the crash site at best possible speed, what Christina was supposed to do next was not specified. This was because her boat was the biggest single weapon in her nation's arsenal when it came to deterring potential Chinese aggression, and this deterrent depended on her ability to skulk in the waters surrounding Taiwan undetected.

The very rumor of her presence affected Chinese behavior in the same way that a single hidden sniper caused havoc in a platoon of thirty men. Every Chinese vessel had to wonder if the *Delaware* was lurking just out of sight with a targeting solution fed to its contingent of Mark 48 torpedoes or twelve Tomahawk cruise missiles. But Christina's advantage vanished the moment she abandoned her stealthy profile. If her enemies detected her, the battlefield calculus changed.

The *Delaware* was still a dangerous predator, but far less so once exposed.

"How far?" Christina said.

"Twenty miles."

At her patrol speed, the transit would take Christina several hours. Several hours that the crash survivors would have to brave the elements and contend with potentially life-threatening injuries. On the other hand, the *Delaware* could get to the crash site a whole lot faster, but traveling that quickly would increase the sub's ambient noise. This in turn would render the *Delaware*'s passive sonar less effective and potentially make Christina's boat easier to detect.

Decision time.

"Officer of the Deck," Christina said, "plot an intercept course for the crash site. Make your speed twenty knots."

"Plot an intercept course for the crash site and make my speed twenty knots, aye, Captain," Brian said.

"Make sure the navigator takes into account where the currents and wind might have pushed the survivors," Christina said. "If there are American sailors in the water, we need to get to them before the Chinese do."

After listening to the officer of the deck acknowledge her orders, Christina turned to Dan. "Send a reply to the message. Tell COMSUBPAC that *Delaware* is responding."

"Aye, aye, Captain," Dan said.

Though his eyes gave away his thoughts, Dan was smart enough not to voice them. Christina was the commander of a 7,800-ton nuclear-powered machine of war. She was afforded far more latitude on how to best employ her boat than her surface-based peers. Even so, her reply had just pushed that latitude to the max. It was customary for a captain to be more specific when describing her intentions.

Christina had not been.

Contrary to what Dan might think, this was not due to bravado. Christina still wasn't sure what she intended to do if she discovered survivors at the crash site, and with her boat churning through the ocean at twenty knots, she had less than an hour to decide.

Time to start thinking.

42

"LISANNE, CAN YOU GUYS HEAR ME?" JACK SAID.

"Yes," Lisanne said. "Gavin and I have you loud and clear."

Lisanne's raspy voice sent a shiver down Jack's spine.

Though he hadn't had the chance to follow up on their last conversation, Jack had still arrived at the answer to a question he hadn't realized he'd been asking. Jack was not going to let the raven-haired beauty walk out of his life, unlike the many girls who'd preceded her. Whatever it took, he was going to win Lisanne back and keep her.

Unfortunately, this bit of relational insight couldn't have come at a worse time.

"Great," Jack said, talking past his anxiousness. "Here's where we stand."

Jack took a deep breath, more because he wasn't exactly thrilled with his team's current situation than to steady his nerves. Then again, as his surgeon mother liked to say, more than one thing could be true at the same time. Jack could be both a ball of nerves at the sight of Lisanne's pretty face on his laptop screen and less than happy that he, Cary, Jad, and Mario had traded the gloomy confines of Maria's clinic for the equally gloomy confines of an apartment located on Manila's rougher side.

"Mary Pat sent a CIA extraction team for Ding and Dom," Jack said. "Ding is being evaluated at the embassy. Dom was stabilized and is being medically evacuated back to the States. He's still in a coma."

This time, his pause wasn't an attempt to delay the inevitable.

While Jack knew turning down the extraction team's offer to bring them all in from the cold was the correct decision, he still felt guilty that he wasn't accompanying his cousin home. Cary's earlier words had done much to put the Campus operator's injuries into perspective, but Jack was close to his aunt. He should have been with her when she received her critically injured son.

But that would be something Jack would have to deal with later. Right now, the sum of his efforts was focused on Clark. Until The Campus's director of operations was back in friendly hands, everything else would have to take a distant backseat.

Including sorting out his relationship with Miss Robertson.

"Where are you?"

The question came from off-screen, but Jack recognized Gavin's high-pitched voice.

"We're in a safe house, Gavin," Jack said. "Sort of."

After the Agency extraction team had departed, Mario had tried to do the same. While Jack had felt sympathetic to the Filipino's plight, he couldn't let Mario leave. Mario was their only in-country contact. His connections to the city's underworld were the Campus team's best shot at understanding who took Clark, and where the kidnappers might be now.

Jack asked the banker to stay with the team in return for providing Mario's family sanctuary at the U.S. embassy, which was located on Manila's waterfront within walking distance of Mario's home. Since he'd been unable to reach his cousin Mon Mon, the banker was still unsure whether Danilo had been operating in accordance with his boss's instructions or had decided to strike out on his own. Either way, Mario wanted his family safe until he understood which way the wind was blowing.

Jack had readily agreed.

After he received confirmation that his wife and children were safe on embassy grounds, Mario had jumped back on board with both feet. With a handful of calls, Mario secured the location of a recently repossessed property in return for Jack's request for a safe house and the combination to the keyless-entry pad.

This was where Jack and his meager team were currently holed up.

"What do you need?" Lisanne said.

That was a very good question.

Jack took in the dingy apartment as he considered his response.

With buzzing overhead lights, a dripping sink, and grime-encrusted floors, this wasn't the worst safe house he'd occupied, but the two-bedroom flophouse was certainly in the running. That said, the toilets flushed and something approaching cold air blew from the air conditioners.

As far as accommodations, the team was set.

Weapons and kit were in a similar state of tolerability. While not equipped for war, Jack and the Green Berets had the weapons they'd used during the last firefight and were still green on ammunition, thanks to the commandos' foresight. Before leaving the first safe house, the Green Berets had pilfered The Campus's Pelican cases, loading up their backpacks with as much ammunition as the two men could carry.

Jack had laughed at the time.

He wasn't laughing now.

With logistics taken care of, there was just one thing Jack still required—a target.

"I need Clark's location," Jack said. "Mario reached out to his sources at the dock, but no one knows anything about the shooters who kidnapped Clark, where they came from, or why the warehouse was rigged to blow."

"Then we've got our work cut out for us," Lisanne said.

"Yep," Jack said, resisting the urge to contradict his teammate's assessment.

After making the decision to stay operational, Jack

knew that he'd need all the help he could get. This meant looping Lisanne and Gavin into the mix. Lisanne would act as the effort's operations officer while Gavin worked on fleshing out the intelligence picture. The pair would become the effort's de facto support cell, enabling Jack and his pipe hitters to do what they did best—shoot bad guys in the face.

At least that was the theory.

"What do you have?" Lisanne said.

"That thing," Jack said, tilting the laptop so Lisanne could see the Chinese glider lying on the floor.

Though he knew the sight of him, Jad, and Cary carting the glider up a flight of steps from their car must have resembled something from a *Saturday Night Live* routine, Jack wasn't letting the Chinese contraption out of his sight. Though he still didn't know why the glider was so important, it was apparently worth killing for. This made it too valuable to leave in the car's trunk.

Especially in this part of town.

"I took a look at the images you sent of the glider's control panel," Gavin said. "The data port looks like a standard USB would fit. Can you plug it into your laptop?"

Jack looked at the screen as he waited for Gavin's laugh to signify that the keyboard warrior was kidding.

It didn't come.

"You want me to connect my computer to the torpedo thing?" Jack said.

"Got a better idea?" Gavin said.

Jack did not.

Even so, exposing his laptop to a piece of Chinese military tech didn't seem like a great idea. Then again, Gavin had a point. Ideas weren't exactly beating down Jack's door.

"Okay," Jack said, unrolling a cable before plugging it into the port Gavin had indicated. "Just for my edification, what exactly are you looking for?"

"Beats the hell out of me," Gavin said, unwrapping a piece of bubble gum and popping it into his mouth. "I'll know it when I see it."

This seemed thin to Jack, but Gavin had worked larger miracles with less.

Besides, what was the worst that could happen?

"Hey, Gav," Jack said as the laptop's hard drive began to whir, "how sure are we that this glider doesn't contain a warhead of some kind?"

"Definitely not a warhead," Gavin said, smacking the gum. "I've been researching these babies. That little propeller on the end is more for altitude control than propulsion. The intel I've seen suggests that the glider can do two knots. Maybe three or four, tops. That's way too slow to chase down ships."

Jack exhaled the breath he hadn't realized he'd been holding.

"On the other hand," Gavin said, "I guess an anti-tamper device isn't out of the question. We should probably watch for that."

Jack jerked his hand away from the glider.

"When you say 'watch for that,' what specifically should I be looking for?" Jack said.

"What?" Gavin said. "Oh, you mean the antitamper device? I really don't know, Jack. Maybe see if the LCD screen on the glider's control panel shows a countdown or something. That's how it happens in the movies."

Jad muttered something that sounded like Arabic while Cary began reciting the 23rd Psalm.

Jack felt tempted to join in.

"How we doing, Gavin?" Jack said instead.

"Good, thanks for asking. Though headquarters is out of cold brew again. I gotta see somebody about that."

"I'm talking about the glider, Gavin," Jack said. "Or, more specifically, the glider's antitamper device."

"Oh, that," Gavin said. "The good news is that I've powered up the device's hard drive and have begun to image it. Since nothing's exploded, I think we're in pretty good shape. Though I guess the real test will come when I finish. I mean, if it was me, I'd configure the electronics so that an unauthorized intrusion would arm the device. Then I'd wait for the hard drive to be almost completely imaged before I detonated the anti-personnel device. You know, to draw the suckers in?"

Jad switched to English and the Green Berets finished the Psalm's final stanza in unison.

"How close are we to being done?" Jack said.

"Geez, Jack, I'm not a miracle worker. This data's encrypted, so it's going to take me a while to see what we're looking at. First I'll need to—"

"The hard drive, Gavin," Jack said. "How close are we to being done imaging the hard drive?"

"Oh, that? If nothing happens in the next five seconds, we should be good. I think—"

A chime reverberated through the room.

A chime originating from the glider.

43

JACK GRITTED HIS TEETH, WAITING FOR THE BRIGHT FLASH OF LIGHT that would precede an audience with the Almighty. If the situation wasn't so dire, it would be the start of a really good joke. A Muslim, a Catholic, and a Protestant find themselves at the Pearly Gates . . .

Then the chime sounded again.

And again.

With a shuddered breath Jack realized that the sound wasn't coming from the glider.

It was originating from his back pocket.

The one holding his burner phone.

Withdrawing the cell with shaking fingers, Jack answered.

"Hello?"

"Jack?"

"Yes?"

"It's Mary Pat. Are you all right?"

Jack wasn't quite sure how to answer.

"Hey, Mary Pat," Jack said. "I'm good. Just kind of in the middle of something."

"Can you talk?"

Jack eyed the icon on the laptop displaying Gavin's progress. The status bar had crested ninety percent and was still rising. If Gavin's prediction about the potential antitamper device was on point, things could become interesting real soon. On the other hand, Jack had a feeling that the DNI wasn't giving him a ring just to shoot the breeze.

"Sure," Jack said as the bar pushed through ninety-five percent, "but we might get cut off unexpectedly."

"No problem," Mary Pat said. "I'll make this quick."

Jack doubted the spymaster would be faster than electrons traveling through the glider's wiring at the speed of light, but he supposed that didn't matter. What was going to happen was going to happen. Mary Pat had more than enough to worry about without adding a Chinese antitamper device to her list.

"Okay," Jack said, "shoot."

"It's imaged," Gavin said from the laptop, "but don't unplug the dongle from the glider. Sometimes the antitamper devices are wired into the control port. This thing could still explode. Maybe."

"Jack," Mary Pat said, "what exactly are you doing?"

"Not me specifically," Jack said, disconnecting the dongle from his computer. "Gavin's doing the heavy lifting. I'm just providing him with access to the Chinese glider we captured."

"Did he say something about it exploding?" Mary Pat said.

"You know Gavin," Jack said. "He's a worrier."

"With good reason," Gavin said. "I—"

Jack hit the laptop's mute button as he prepared for the tongue-lashing he was certain he was about to receive from the nation's intelligence chief.

"It's actually good he's on the line," Mary Pat said, "because what I'm about to say involves him as well. Can he hear me?"

"Just a minute," Jack said. The entire conversation was beginning to feel like a game of telephone. Muting Mary Pat, Jack activated the laptop's mike. "Mary Pat's on the cell. I'm going to put her on speaker so she can address us all. Until then, keep the line clear, please."

"Of course," Gavin said, sounding slightly offended. "I won't say a word."

Jack strongly doubted that, but enough was enough. Between Clark's kidnapping, the war in gangland that might or might not be brewing, the Filipino police who had to be crawling all over the dock by now, and the antitamper device that might or might not exist, it was long past time to get this show on the road.

"Okay, Mary Pat," Jack said after unmuting his phone, "you're on with the group. Cary and Jad are here with me. Lisanne and Gavin are connected via my laptop."

"Great," Mary Pat said. "Hello, everyone. I want you each to know that while I feel for your injured team-mates, we can do nothing more for them. The same isn't true for Clark, so I'm going to spend our precious time on him. Agreed?"

"Agreed," Jack said as Cary and Jad both nodded.

While what Mary Pat had said might have been obvious, Jack appreciated that she'd taken the time to address the elephant in the room. Ding was doing fine, but Dom was still touch and go. This was not just another day at the office, and Jack was grateful to Mary Pat for not pretending otherwise.

"Okay," Mary Pat said. "Here's how this is going to go—as of this moment, The Campus is officially part of the U.S. intelligence community, reporting to me."

"Why?" Jack said.

"Because we have neither the time nor the resources to pretend otherwise," Mary Pat said. "The South China Sea might as well be a pool of gasoline waiting for a match. This is the closest we've been to war with the Chinese in my lifetime. A J-16 fighter just brought down an American P-8, and Chinese frigates are racing toward the crash site. The President has directed all available conventional assets to focus on recovering the P-8's crew. I might be able to vector a Ground Branch team in your direction or possibly one of the special mission units, but that's going to take time. Until then, if getting Clark back requires a kinetic operation, The Campus has the job."

Jack swallowed as he recognized the significance of Mary Pat's words. As of this moment, The Campus consisted of exactly three gunfighters.

But that was a problem for later.

Right now, Jack needed just one thing—actionable intelligence.

"Understood," Jack said, "but we've got nothing on the people who took Clark."

"You've got nothing *right now*," Mary Pat said. "That's about to change. Since The Campus is now an official member of the intelligence community, the floodgates are open. I'm signing an emergency intelligence finding that will authorize linkage between The Campus's hardened IT network and our own. Gavin and Lisanne will have access to everything we have—ISR feeds, source reporting, the works."

"Even the NSA's haul?" Gavin said.

"Everything," Mary Pat said.

Jack clicked and muted Gavin's mike before he could reply. The jubilant expression on the keyboard warrior's face would have been laughable had the situation not been so dire. Gavin looked like a little kid who'd just been handed the keys to the toy store. In a way, Jack supposed he had. After spending most of his career engineering work-arounds and second-rate apps meant to mimic the U.S. government's true capabilities, Gavin now had access to the real thing.

But as much as he appreciated what Mary Pat was doing, Jack was also a realist. To have a chance of finding Clark, the Campus team needed a starting point from which they could venture into the unknown. Without this, the resources put at their disposal might prove to be nothing more than a distraction.

"Thanks, Mary Pat," Jack said. "That will be a huge help. But the best flashlight in the world isn't worth much if you don't know where to shine it. Do you have anything we can use? Anything to help us narrow down who took Clark and where they might be?"

The sigh that echoed from the phone was answer enough.

"Precious little, I'm afraid," Mary Pat said. "Something has been uploaded to one of the Abu Sayyaf group's social media accounts. A video of Clark being tortured."

"How bad is it?" Jack said.

"Not as bad as it could be," Mary Pat said. "Clark got the shit beat of out him, but he's still alive."

"What do we have on the video?" Jad said.

"Excellent question," Mary Pat said. "The analysts on this side of the Pacific determined where the video was uploaded. The metadata attached to the file suggests Basilan Island, which is in the southwestern part of the Philippines about five hundred miles from Manila, but this only tells us where the file joined the Internet."

"Not necessarily where it was shot," Jack said. "Besides, there's no way the people who took Clark could have covered five hundred miles this quickly."

"Exactly," Mary Pat said.

"Hey, Jack," Jad said, "looks like Gavin wants to talk."

Jack glanced at his laptop to see Gavin with his hand raised like a schoolchild. The image should have made Jack smile, but the hopeless feeling in the pit of his stomach wouldn't allow it.

"Sorry, Gav," Jack said, unmuting the laptop.

"No problem," Gavin said. "Can you ask Mary Pat to send me the source video? I've got an idea."

"Of course," Mary Pat said. "In fact, I'll do you one better. I'll provide you with my assistant Sam's direct line. Anything you need, he'll get. Anything. He'll be your one-stop shop for all the resources the intelligence community has to offer."

"Fantastic," Gavin said. "Right off, I know we're going to need to—"

"Hey, buddy," Jack said, "Mary Pat's time is valuable. Unless you have something specific for her, let's hold all that for her assistant."

"Right," Gavin said. "Got it, Jack."

As if on cue, the sound of a phone ringing echoed from Jack's handset.

"That's my office line," Mary Pat said, "which means I need to take it. Anything else, Jack?"

"Yes," Jack said, the question forming even as he spoke. "Dad said you were the best intelligence officer he's ever worked with. If you had to guess, where would you place Clark?"

The phone rang twice more before Mary Pat spoke.

"The water," Mary Pat said. "There are thousands of fishing boats and commercial vessels that ply that stretch of ocean. If Clark was my high-value target, that's where I'd stash him. Good luck, Jack. I've got to go."

Mary Pat ended the call.

For a long moment Jack stared at the dead phone as if it might spring back to life. It didn't. Dropping the device into his pocket, Jack turned to confront his team's waiting faces.

His team.

His Campus, really.

"Gavin," Jack said. "You tracking everything Mary Pat said?"

"On it," Gavin said. "I need some time to review the video. I also want to take a peek at what we recovered from the glider. I've got the beginnings of a plan, but I need time to flesh it out."

Time was in rather short supply, but Jack didn't say that. Ding had once told Jack that understanding what motivated your team was one of the most important aspects of being a leader. Gavin didn't need motivation to work faster.

But maybe Jack could help in a different way.

"Lisanne," Jack said, "I need you to battle-captain this. Grab any ISR assets you can. Hell, commandeer anything you think would be useful. I'm not counting on Mary Pat's special mission unit or paramilitary operators riding in to save the day. That said, taking down a ship with three people is a hard act. A platoon of SEALs would be great right about now."

Jad opened his mouth but then slowly shut it.

"Cat got your tongue?" Cary said.

"No," Jad said, shaking his head. "I feel obligated to make a SEAL joke, but I just can't. If Lieutenant Brandon Cates and his fellow frogmen walked through the door right now, I might just hug them."

People chuckled, but the laughter sounded forced.

Jack had done some crazy things in his Campus career, but taking down a boat with just three shooters was a nonstarter. But that was a problem for later.

First, he needed to find the boat.

"I understand," Lisanne said.

She held Jack's gaze for a beat before giving a quick nod.

Jack knew she really did understand, both the specified tasks he'd given her and the implied one—keep Gavin on track. He thought he might have seen something else in her brown eyes. Something suggesting that all wasn't lost between them. But determining whether the olive branch was real or imagined would have to wait.

"Thanks, guys," Jack said. "Ping us once you get something."

Gavin and Lisanne both nodded. Then the call ended, leaving Jack alone with two Green Berets and a Filipino banker who looked as if he was questioning his life choices.

Join the club.

"Where's this leave us?" Cary said.

"With time to fill in a couple holes in our plan," Jack said.

"Only a couple?" Jad said.

"Ease back on the negativity," Cary said. "He has a plan. I feel better already."

Jad snorted.

"Go on, Jack," Cary said. "Tell us the plan."

"First we need to get a boat," Jack said.

"Great," Cary said. "Where do we get one?"

"I was thinking someone else could help with that," Jack said.

Three sets of American eyes centered on Mario.

The little man muttered in Tagalog, but he didn't argue.

Progress.

44

"LOOKS A WEE BIT CROWDED UP THERE, SKIPPER," DAN SAID.

Christina had to steel her expression as she took in the digital navigation plot.

Her XO's gift for understatement was on full display once again. The digital nav plot was a horizontal electronic display akin to a huge Microsoft Surface. In *Virginia*-class submarines, the chart tables of old were gone. The digital nav plot incorporated nautical charts as well as all the contact information from sonar in a single moving map. But digital or not, Christina had never seen a nav chart so crowded in her fifteen years in the silent service. A dozen separate surface contacts cluttered the display, and several were heading her way.

"Officer of the Deck, what's the range to the suspected crash site?" Christina said.

"Two miles, Captain."

Christina had sounded general quarters fifteen minutes ago, and while she had every confidence in her crew, the nav plot suggested that the next several minutes were going to be a handful. Then again, sailors didn't vie for a spot on a nuclear-powered fast attack submarine because they wanted a sleepy cruise spent turning circles in the ocean. Judging by the no less than three Chinese frigates steaming toward the projected crash site, the USS *Delaware* was about to have action aplenty.

"Periscope depth," the officer of the deck said.

"Up periscope," Christina said, the buzz of energy the simple-seeming command elicited more pronounced than usual.

Nothing more symbolized life as a submariner than standing with your face pressed against the viewfinder as the optic broke through the waves fifty feet above. As a little girl, Christina had watched all the classic submarine movies with her father. From oldies like *Run Silent, Run Deep* to more contemporary films like *Crimson Tide*.

Now Christina was living her dream.

Sort of.

In a first for U.S. submarines, *Virginia*-class boats no longer featured a traditional periscope with mirrors and lenses. Instead, the USS *Delaware* sported a photonic mast that was connected to monitors in the sub's control room via fiber-optic cables. This eliminated the old periscope viewing well, instead providing the captain with high-resolution, color, or infrared images displayed on a television screen for everyone to see. While the improvements certainly made her boat much more lethal, Christina was more than a little nostalgic for the old days.

The view from above the water drained the levity from her thoughts. The seas were at state four. To the uninformed, this designation meant very little, but to a sailor, sea state four meant that the seething foam could reach heights of eight feet. The swells now looked to be closer to four and a half feet. While a frigate could handle these waves with ease, smaller pleasure crafts would have a hold full of seasick passengers.

But Christina wasn't looking at a pleasure craft.

Instead, she'd spied an orange raft crammed with people in flight suits who were doing their best to keep from being tossed overboard. But that wasn't the worst of it. A black form loomed just ahead. Christina activated the mast's digital zoom, already knowing what she would see.

A moment later, the menacing hull of a warship swam into view.

But not just any warship.

The vessel was a Type 054A Chinese frigate screaming toward the survivors.

Things were about to get interesting.

45

COMMANDER LIXIN WANG OF THE CHINESE PEOPLE'S LIBERATION Army Navy eyed the digital display prominently located in the bridge of the Type 054A frigate he commanded.

It was an honor to serve as the *Xuchang*'s skipper. Its 2017 commissioning made the warship one of the newest in the PLA's fleet, and her nerve center reflected this modernity. From here, Lixin could watch the returns generated by the *Xuchang*'s target-acquisition and fire control radar while simultaneously plumbing the ocean's depth with both active and passive sonar. He could also target a variety of threats in the air, on land, in the sea, or even under it. The *Xuchang*'s portfolio of weapons ran the gamut from 76-millimeter guns, to antisubmarine rockets, to cruise missiles capable of destroying either ships or land-based targets.

But it was not a warship or enemy aircraft that was

currently giving Lixin pause. No, that honor belonged to an orange raft that was barely weathering the pounding waves.

"How long until we're alongside?" Lixin asked.

"Fifteen minutes, sir."

The answer came from Lieutenant Yan Zhang, Lixin's executive officer. Lixin had sailed with the man for the last eighteen months. Together, they'd stalked pirates, enforced Chinese sovereignty in the disputed islands, and shadowed American warships across the South China Sea.

But like Lixin, Zhang seemed more nervous than usual.

Perhaps it was because he also understood what was at stake.

"Increase speed to twenty-seven knots," Lixin said.

"Make my speed twenty-seven knots," the officer of the deck said before relaying the order.

With her four 7,600-horsepower Shaanxi diesel engines, the *Xuchang* was capable of holding this speed almost indefinitely. But under emergency conditions, the four-thousand-ton frigate could accelerate to over thirty. Sustaining that blistering pace for too long risked damage to the vessel's drive shaft and screws, but in this case, Lixin was comfortable with the gamble.

Perhaps because the consequences of failure were far greater.

The deck vibrated beneath Lixin's feet as the *Xuchang*'s power plant responded. While Lixin hadn't detected a competitor in his race to snare the Americans, that didn't mean someone wasn't out there, unseen. Though he wasn't privy to the geopolitical events unfolding in this stretch of ocean, Lixin understood two things—a Yankee spy plane had crashed, and he had been ordered to secure the survivors. It stood to reason that if the PLA Navy's South Sea Fleet command was willing to task every available vessel with recovering the stranded crew, the Americans would be just as eager to get to their countrymen first.

Lixin could not permit this to happen.

His orders had been unambiguous—capture the crew at all cost. Though even a message as black-and-white as this one developed shades of gray when confronted with the ocean's reality. Lixin wasn't so much worried about convincing the survivors to come aboard—the weather would do that for him. No, Lixin was concerned about something more treacherous than surging tides or rogue waves.

The American Navy.

What should Lixin do if an American vessel attempted to rescue the survivors? His orders hadn't addressed this contingency, and Lixin was willing to bet the omission was purposeful. No matter. While Lixin had no control over the fickle nature of the bureaucrats in Beijing who held his life, and that of his crew, in their hands, he could control one thing—getting to the survivors first.

"Is the helicopter ready?" Lixin said, eyeing Zhang.

The man shook his head.

"Not yet, Comrade Captain," Zhang said. "The crew is still troubleshooting a hydraulics issue."

Any sailor worth his salt knew that naval aviation was unreliable at best, and the single Z-9C helicopter the *Xuchang* carried was doubly so. The rotorcraft was a derivative of the French Eurocopter Dauphin. The original version had been a licensed production, while this *improved* iteration was a Chinese design made from mostly Chinese-sourced components. Lixin was not an aviation expert, but in the eighteen months he'd been in command of the *Xuchang*, the aircraft had spent the majority of its time in the hangar.

Today was shaping up to be no exception.

Lixin eyed the tactical display as the range between his ship and the presumed location of the stranded aircrew continued to shrink. Less than ten minutes remained until he'd have the Americans off the side of his ship, but Lixin had an uneasy feeling that this would be too late. Though his suite of multimillion-dollar sensors had not detected any Yankees, Lixin's sailor intuition said otherwise. With the usually large number of surface contacts in this stretch of ocean, zeroing in on a nearly silent American submarine would be even more difficult than usual. Lixin's sonar operator had developed a promising track just minutes ago, only to lose it amid the sea of ambient noise.

Lixin needed to get to the crash survivors.

Now.

"Instruct the engine room to firewall the diesels and start the timer on the engine's transitory torque," Lixin said. "Also, tell the aviators that their aircraft will be leaving my ship in ten minutes. The helicopter will either fly under its own power or be pushed from the deck. The pilots will be strapped inside in either scenario."

"Yes, Captain," Zhang said, his expression carefully blank. "Anything else?"

"Sound general quarters," Lixin said.

Zhang's normally stoic face registered a fleeting reaction. Nothing drove home a captain's singular purpose like his ship's weapons stations preparing for action. With both his surface-search and over-the-horizon radars radiating, Lixin knew that any hidden Americans would see him coming.

Good.

Hopefully his actions would also demonstrate his depth of purpose. In ten minutes' time, the undoubtedly soggy crash survivors would be aboard his frigate. Whether that happened with or without a fight was up to their countrymen.

46

"THOUGHTS?" CHRISTINA SAID, EYEING THE TACTICAL DISPLAY.

"We've got two choices," Dan said. "Either convince the frigate to back off so we can surface and rescue the crew, or . . ."

"Watch as the Chinese take our brothers and sisters hostage," Christina said, finishing her XO's thought.

Dan gave a slow nod.

Christina looked from the tactical display to a second video screen, this one showing a loop of the video recorded while the photonic mast had been above the waves. Though she'd spent most of the time ogling the approaching frigate, Christina had also quickly panned the optic across the raft. Now the results of that scan played out in front of her.

Seven crewmen.

Christina wasn't sure how many souls had been on board the P-8, so she didn't know if the crew had suffered any fatalities. But she did know who was responsible for their predicament—the Chinese.

Just as they had been more than twenty years earlier.

"Hainan was before my time," Dan said, reading her thoughts.

"Mine, too," Christina said, "but an Academy classmate's brother had been part of the crew."

On April 1, 2001, a Chinese J-8 interceptor collided with a P-3 Orion on patrol in the South China Sea. The PLA pilot had perished, and the American crew had come close to dying as well. Displaying extraordinary airmanship, the Navy pilots brought the heavily damaged aircraft down safely against all odds.

But that was only the beginning of the ordeal.

With his plane badly damaged, the aircraft commander had made the difficult decision to land on Hainan, a Chinese-controlled island. The Chinese promptly seized the multimillion-dollar spy plane and imprisoned its crew. Over the course of ten days, the aviators were repeatedly interrogated and were released only after the American government sent two humiliating letters of apology to the Chinese.

In the ensuing years, relations with China had only grown worse. This newest encounter between an American and Chinese plane might become a flash point for the entire region. Christina didn't believe the American crew battling the sea above her would fare any better than their predecessors. In fact, there was good reason to think they might not be released anywhere near as quickly.

Or at all.

Once more Christina considered her options.

Below the sea, the *Delaware* was a force to be reckoned with. Seventy years after the launch of America's first nuclear submarine, the U.S. fleet had reached mythical status. Apart from a brief period of time when the Soviet Union came close to achieving technological parity, no vessel could operate as clandestinely as a U.S. submarine. And the Soviets' success with their *Typhoon-* and *Akula*-class boats had been during the late eighties, with advances largely stolen from the U.S. Navy, thanks to an American father-son espionage ring. In the ensuing years, diesel submarine technology had become much quieter, and the Chinese were now fielding nuclear-powered submarines of their own. But at this moment, Christina still reigned supreme.

Until the *Delaware* surfaced.

There was no way to rescue the stranded aviators without giving away her position. As soon as Christina surfaced, her modern marvel of technology became just another boat. No, that wasn't right. In truth, the *Delaware* would be rendered less than just another boat. While the sub still had the use of her four torpedo tubes, in a surface fight, the Chinese frigate hopelessly outclassed the *Delaware*.

Which meant Christina needed to set the conditions for the rescue now.

"Up scope," Christina said. "Prepare to verify the range to the Chinese frigate with active sonar. Use just one ping."

"Prepare to verify range with just one ping, aye," the officer of the deck said.

Christina caught Dan's gaze and the question in his eyes was obvious. *Did she know what she was doing?* Employing active sonar against another vessel was tantamount to an act of war. Then again, so was kidnapping a downed naval crew under the guise of rescuing them.

Did she know what she was doing?

Christina wasn't really sure.

Only one way to find out.

"Sonar, standing by," the officer of the deck said.

With a deep breath, Christina eyed the image of the Chinese frigate.

Then she spoke.

"Ping them."

47

LIXIN HAD ALWAYS ASSUMED THAT THE NOISE OF A SHIP CRACKING around him would be the most terrifying sound he'd ever hear.

He'd been wrong.

One moment, he'd been listening to the roar of his overstressed engines. The next, the striking of a giant tuning fork reverberated through his ship's hull. The sonar ping rang with such energy that Lixin could have sworn his fillings were vibrating.

"Report," Lixin bellowed.

"Undersea contact, bearing 070, range two thousand meters."

Lixin looked at his first officer, who nodded.

The submarine was just beneath the bobbing American raft.

"Are torpedoes in the water?" Lixin said.

"Negative, Captain," Zhang said. "No sounds from the torpedo outer doors opening, either."

Which meant the Americans might have already opened the torpedo hatches in preparation to fire. Or the torpedo doors could still be closed, which would communicate something else entirely. The single sonar ping was obviously meant to convey a message. Modern submarines had no need to use active sonar to acquire a target, especially American submarines.

So the ping was what?

A warning to back off?

This was probably what the submarine's captain intended to communicate, but in a scenario this serious, Lixin was not prepared to operate off assumptions. Even now, he imagined standing in front of the South Sea Fleet commander explaining his actions. He doubted the fish-faced vice admiral would take kindly to one of his frigate commanders abandoning the American prize in response to a single sonar pulse.

Lixin couldn't afford to blink.

Besides, the submarine captain might lose his nerve first. While the single sonar ping had revealed the sub's location, the vessel was still far from helpless. The American captain could fire a spread of torpedoes at Lixin's ship. Even if the fish missed, the submarine could use the opportunity to crash-dive in the hopes of hiding beneath a sonar-confounding thermal inversion layer. But to recover the stranded crewmen, the sub would have to surface, thereby stacking the terms of the engagement in Lixin's favor.

Would the sub captain trade the safety of his boat for the helpless aviators?

Lixin didn't know.

If the situation were reversed, Lixin certainly wouldn't countenance such a choice. But Americans were different. Unpredictable. Either way, Lixin wasn't backing down.

The American viper had just rattled its tail.

Now it was time to see if the sub commander was willing to strike.

48

"CHINESE FRIGATE IS STILL ON AN INTERCEPT COURSE," DAN SAID. "He's increased speed slightly. He'll be on station in five minutes."

Five minutes.

In the time it took to brew a pot of coffee, Christina would be face-to-face with a Chinese warship capable of reducing her boat to an oil slick. While Christina had never played chicken in a speeding car, she had stared down disaster more than once.

As the goalie for her lacrosse teams, Christina had learned that nothing brings the world into focus quite like the sight of an attacker barreling down the field at you with the ball in her lacrosse stick's pocket and nary a defender in sight. From her first game as a child to her last at Annapolis, Christina had never backed down from a confrontation, regardless of her opponent's size.

She wasn't going to start today.

"Prepare to surface," Christina said. "We're going after our aviators."

"Prepare to surface, aye," the officer of the deck said.

"Blow ballast and open the outer doors to torpedo tubes one and two," Christina said.

Once again the officer of the deck, Lieutenant Andrews, repeated the command without pause, but she thought Brian stood a little straighter as he bellowed the words. For sailors who made their living hunting submarines, there was just one sound more recognizable than the gurgling of compressed air forcing water from a sub's ballast tank—the ominous grinding as the steel outer doors that protected the torpedo tubes opened. Christina had just done the equivalent of telling the approaching frigate that while she didn't want any trouble, she wasn't leaving without her fellow sailors.

She just hoped the Chinese captain received her message.

49

LIEUTENANT TOM MCGRATH HAD SEEN BETTER DAYS.

He'd ditched his jet into choppy water with a landing that might not be considered smooth, but could charitably have been termed functional. In the ensuing chaos, his crew had followed the ditching drills to a T. Survival rafts had been inflated and lashed together, and the able-bodied had helped the injured abandon ship. All seven crew members had made it out of the jet alive. Just as important, the aircraft had been configured to sink, taking the multitude of secrets and sensitive equipment housed within its innocuous-looking fuselage to a watery grave.

And sink it had.

Perhaps too well.

The jet went under faster than anyone had expected. Tom had taken a turn with one of the raft's small paddles, frantically trying to keep the bobbing craft clear of the swirling vortex created by the massive aircraft. He helped to prevent his crew from following the P-8 into the ocean's depths, but this was where Tom's streak of good luck ended. With an abruptness that was all too common for this part of the world, weather conditions had changed. The sea hadn't exactly been placid before, but the waves had been manageable.

No longer.

As the wind kicked up, the frothing water responded, coiling into undulating mounds that threatened to swamp the fragile survival raft. A rogue wall of water had nearly tossed Jack over the side, prompting Tom to order the crew to tie themselves into the supposedly capsize-proof raft. After an hour of battling the elements, Tom had emptied his stomach of the granola bar he'd snacked on earlier, as well as everything he'd eaten in the last week.

Then salvation had arrived.

Except it hadn't.

"Definitely a Chinese frigate," Jack said, confirming Tom's suspicions. "I can see her ensign."

The sight of the gray-hulled warship had buoyed the spirits of the waterlogged survivors, until Tom thought the ship's silhouette looked a little too familiar. In a bad way. Since the bag containing the survival equipment was lashed to a carabiner next to Jack, he'd asked his copilot to find the binoculars and take a look. Jack had complied, losing a couple odds and ends from the bag in the process, but rendering a judgment all the same. The question Tom now faced was a hard one—which was the better option, the Chinese or the sea?

"That's what I thought," Tom said. "Anything on sat-com?"

Jack shook his head. "I think our ELT is beaconing, but I can't get anything on the voice channel."

Tom nodded, disappointed but not surprised.

The waterproof radio was designed to send out a stranded crew's location via satcom radio, but that frequency band was notoriously spotty during inclement-weather conditions. The cloud cover and moisture-saturated air played havoc with voice transmissions, but the data burst containing their GPS coordinates probably had enough juice to burn through.

Probably.

"What are you thinking?" Jack said.

The copilot pitched his voice so that only Tom could hear.

Tom understood.

While their two nations were not at war, Tom knew that the Chinese warship did not represent rescue. At least not in the traditional sense of the word. Tensions hadn't been nearly as high twenty years ago, and the Chinese had still squeezed the maximum propaganda out of the situation. If the choice was between survival and boarding the frigate, he would come down on the side of his fellow sailors, but Tom wasn't sure he was there yet.

"Let me see the radio," Tom said. "Maybe the problem's operator error."

Jack snorted, but handed Tom the transmitter.

Both men knew that Jack was much better with radios of any sort. Some pilots just had a gift when it came to the finicky contraptions, and Jack had coaxed more than one wayward receiver to accept the daily cipher or reset its GPS time long after Tom had given up. But the look Jack gave Tom suggested that he understood the true purpose of Tom's request.

Tom's responsibility as aircraft commander had not ended with the ditching. For better or worse, until the Americans were back in friendly hands, he was in charge. As such, the decision about what to do when the Chinese frigate pulled alongside also resided with Tom. Before he potentially ordered his crew to stay in their waterlogged raft, he wanted to give the radio a try.

After accepting the transmitter, Tom made a show of inspecting the collapsible antenna, seating the battery, and scrolling through the various presets. But a show was all it was. As he'd suspected, Jack had done a far more thorough job troubleshooting the device than he could have. Deciding that he'd delayed the inevitable long enough, Tom lifted the device skyward and depressed the transmit button.

Just as a random wave smashed against the raft.

If he hadn't been tied in, Tom was certain he would have gone over the side. The radio wasn't so lucky. One moment he'd been about to speak, the next his hands were empty.

Tom didn't know whether to laugh or cry.

The erupting ocean answered the question for him.

50

THE SURFACING SUBMARINE DIDN'T RESEMBLE SO MUCH A HUMAN creation of metal and steel as a black leviathan. Though Lixin's sonar operator had communicated the Americans' intent, seeing the monstrosity rocket out of the water was still a surprise.

One moment there had been nothing but green-tinged swells.

The next, an obsidian structure loomed above the ocean.

"Orders, Captain?"

Lixin stared at the image rendered by the frigate's high-definition cameras as he thought. The second sound his sonar man had relayed had been equally unambiguous—the outer doors to the Americans' torpedo tubes opening. The submarine was all but assured to lose a fight with the *Xuchang*. Lixin had an array of weapons he could rain down on the helpless sub, and now that he knew its location, several more that could follow the boat into watery depths if the submarine attempted to crash-dive.

But still he hesitated.

Though he wanted to pretend otherwise, Lixin understood the significance of the Americans' gesture. The submarine had opened its torpedo doors but had yet to flood the tubes. Like the single active sonar ping from earlier, this was a show of restraint.

A wolf baring its teeth but not yet lunging for the kill.

But would the American actually fire?

Lixin's aviation comrades had been getting the better of their American counterparts for decades, as the bobbing orange survival raft demonstrated. Perhaps it was time Lixin took a page from their playbook.

"Captain?" the officer of the deck said.

"Maintain current course and speed," Lixin said.

Time to see what the American sub captain was made of.

"WHAT IS HE DOING?" DAN SAID.

Christina could forgive the waver in her normally steadfast XO's voice. He was standing next to her in the cramped confines of the *Delaware*'s sail, surrounded by the sub's assortment of electronic masts. Unlike the conning towers of old, which once housed the mechanisms needed to steer a submarine, the sail on a *Virginia*-class attack sub served as an observation post only. The section of steel was exposed to the elements with only a chest-high metal rail to grip as the boat wallowed in the crashing waves.

But Dan's inflection wasn't driven by the sea.

No, that honor belonged to the Chinese frigate bearing down on them.

The warship had to be making close to thirty knots, as evidenced by the frigate's frothing white bow wave. Worse still, the looming hull was pointed directly at Christina's boat. Viewing the pixels that represented the Chinese warship on the *Delaware*'s tactical display had been concerning, but seeing the monstrosity with her own two eyes brought a new level of urgency to Christina's decisions.

"Trying to get our attention," she said. "Officer of the Deck, come right to course 075 degrees."

The officer of the deck echoed Christina's orders as Dan scrambled down the ladder leading to the submarine's external deck to lend a hand. The *Delaware*'s sailors had already secured the survival rafts to the submarine, but three of the naval aviators were still struggling to board the sub's slick exterior. Like a matador turning inside a charging bull, Christina's abrupt course change was meant to buy time for the crew members to board by slipping the submarine past the frigate.

Unfortunately, Christina's boat was not the nimble dancer on the ocean's surface that it was below the waves. The *Delaware* simply could not turn quickly enough, and the Chinese frigate's bow was still on a path to bisect the *Delaware*'s hull.

The Aldis lamp on the Chinese ship's bridge flashed out a message in Morse code.

ENGINE PROBLEM. UNABLE TO CHANGE COURSE.

In an instant, Christina understood what her Chinese counterpart was attempting. By communicating that he was experiencing maneuvering issues, the frigate's captain was laying the groundwork for a plausible defense.

A defense for a looming catastrophe.

The homicidal maniac was going to try to ram her.

"Officer of the Deck, prepare to crash-dive," Christina said.

"Prepare to crash-dive, aye," the officer of the deck echoed.

Two sailors remained on the *Delaware*'s hull—Dan and one of the injured aviators.

Christina looked from her struggling XO to the looming frigate.

It was going to be close.

"FIVE HUNDRED METERS TO THE SUBMARINE, CAPTAIN," ZHANG said.

"Sound the collision alert," Lixin said.

As Klaxons echoed through the bridge, Lixin ground his teeth. He'd fully expected the Americans to abandon their downed aviators in the face of his mad charge.

They hadn't.

In fact, the opposite had proven true. First one, then both of the officers manning the sub's sail had abandoned their post in favor of aiding their stricken crew members as they clambered aboard the submarine's slippery deck. The final three were scrambling up the ladder to the sail now.

A blond woman was in the lead.

Zhang met Lixin's gaze from across the room, the question in his eyes obvious.

Lixin shook his head.

His instructions from the vice admiral had been unambiguous. Lixin knew that every command he issued had been recorded and would be analyzed in painstaking detail at the conclusion of this engagement. Even so, this was a no-win scenario. The American submarine was designed to withstand the ocean's crushing depths. The HY-100 plate steel that formed the sub's pressure hull was more than a match for the sheet metal that made up the *Xuchang*'s exterior. A collision between the two vessels would more than likely split Lixin's frigate in two.

But there was still a chance.

In the South China Sea, collisions between competing vessels were a way of life. Accordingly, the *Xuchang*'s bow had been purposely reinforced with a blend of proprietary alloys. While this makeshift battering ram hadn't been constructed with submarines in mind, Lixin thought that his bow might just be able to inflict enough structural damage to render the American vessel incapable of diving. With the sub trapped on the surface, the balance of power would rapidly shift as additional Chinese frigates joined the fray. It was a desperate gamble born of a desperate man, and Lixin had no idea if his ploy would succeed.

But he was certain of one thing.

For the sake of his career and perhaps his life, he could not back down now.

"One hundred meters," Zhang said.

The submarine was now close enough for Lixin to see the top of the sail in detail. Two of the three remaining sailors disappeared inside, leaving only the blond. She paused for a split second, looking into the frigate's camera as if locking gazes with Lixin.

Then the sail was empty.

A series of geysers erupted the length of the hull as the submarine flooded its ballast tanks, and the obsidian structure began to slide beneath the water's oily surface.

"Fifty meters," Zhang said.

"Brace for impact," Lixin said.

A second, more dire-sounding, Klaxon gonged through the ship.

Lixin gripped his chair's armrests.

Then the *Xuchang*'s hull plowed through swirling water that had only moments ago held a submarine.

51

"MA'AM?"

Mary Pat looked up from the stack of papers on her desk to see Sam standing in the office doorway. She'd been so absorbed in her work that she hadn't heard him approach. If she were being honest, that wasn't the only reason Mary Pat felt out of sorts. Rather than return to her office at Liberty Crossing, she'd appropriated a spare workspace in the West Wing for herself and Sam. She knew the decision to remain close to Jack was the correct one, but the new digs came at the expense of the familiarity of her own space and the proximity to her full staff.

Not to mention her secret stash of Folgers.

"Is it another video?" Mary Pat said, taking in Sam's drawn face.

Her voice caught in her throat as she asked the question.

Contrary to what she'd told the President, Mary Pat didn't know how many more of those videos she had in her. Jack Ryan kept her beside him over the years because he trusted her implicitly, but the situation with Clark had her second-guessing herself. How long would she be able to continue to render impartial counsel when she knew he was being tortured?

"No," Sam said, taking the question as an invitation to enter. "I'm sorry, I should have led with that. And here, I brought you this."

This turned out to be a mug.

A mug full of Folgers, by the smell.

Where Sam had managed to locate the brew, Mary Pat didn't know, but she gratefully accepted it all the same. Gesturing for him to continue, Mary Pat took a sip. She could almost feel the caffeine flood her tired brain.

How long had it been since she'd slept?

Just as she needed to be aware of her blind spot with regard to Clark, Mary Pat had to ensure that she was well rested enough to provide the analysis Jack required. The steaming mug would prolong her crash, but even Folgers couldn't hold off her exhaustion indefinitely.

"There's been some action in the South China Sea," Sam said, handing Mary Pat a tablet. "We got to our downed aviators first. The *Delaware* pulled them out of the drink right under the nose of a Type 054A Chinese frigate."

"That's good news," Mary Pat said, scrolling through the offered tablet. "Did grabbing our folks cool the region's temperatures at all?"

Sam shook his head. "Unfortunately not. If you check out the last slides in the deck, you'll see what I mean."

Mary Pat swiped her way to the end of the presentation and swore.

If anything, the situation in the disputed body of water had worsened. In the last update, a handful of frigates had been heading toward the suspected crash site. Now it looked as if the entire Chinese fleet had put to sea in one giant armada, but instead of the crash site, the warships were congregating on an even more sensitive target.

Taiwan.

"The President's called a meeting with the principals," Sam said. "I've been sifting through analysis from across the intelligence community and bouncing it off what DoD is seeing. The consensus is that this is a show of force, not a prelude to an initial invasion."

Mary Pat nodded.

She'd arrived at the same conclusion. While the number of conventional forces churning toward the Taiwan Strait really was astounding, an invasion of Taiwan wouldn't begin with a massed flotilla. While that had worked at Normandy, the days of achieving surprise with a massive amphibious assault were over, especially in a section of ocean as heavily monitored as the one hundred miles separating Taiwan from mainland China. Smart money said an invasion would begin with a bombardment of Taiwanese defenses and airstrips by a combination of ballistic and cruise missiles launched from the mainland.

This was not that.

Which led to the more obvious question: *What in the hell were the Chinese doing?*

"It's like they're showing off," Sam said. "Trying to save face after we beat them to the P-8 crew."

"Or trying to get our attention," Mary Pat said, mumbling as she paged through the slides.

"Why?" Sam said.

Another excellent question.

"My dad was an amateur magician," Mary Pat said, thumbing back to the beginning of the presentation. "He said that magic was really about just one thing—controlling where the audience looked."

"Watch the right hand while the left hides the rabbit?"

Mary Pat nodded. "Are there any slides that show imagery farther south? Like, say, around Hainan?"

Sam leaned over Mary Pat's shoulder, scrolling through the presentation at something approaching light speed. "Try slides six through eight," Sam said. "What are you looking for?"

"Remember that Vietnamese trawler?" Mary Pat said. "The one that the Chinese sunk."

"Sure."

"What were the coordinates for that?"

"Much farther south," Sam said. "Vicinity of the Paracel Islands, if I remember correctly."

"Do we have imagery for any of the major southern Chinese ports?"

"Not in the presentation," Sam said. "But I can get it."

"Do it," Mary Pat said. "Run it back to the time of the trawler's sinking."

"We already looked for that," Sam said. "Between the weather and the uncertainty of the trawler's position, we weren't able to find anything."

"I know," Mary Pat said, getting to her feet. "I'm more interested in what happened *after* the trawler sank. See what you can find of the entire area. Time-lapse shots. If a Chinese ship really did sink that trawler, I want to know where it put into port."

Sam frowned. "Okay, but that's thousands of square miles and might be hundreds of vessels. We're not even talking a needle in a haystack. It's more like sifting through a coffee can of nails to find the short one."

Mary Pat arched an eyebrow.

"What?" Sam said defensively. "My dad was a farmer. He didn't believe in wasting nails."

"Or anything else, I'd wager," Mary Pat said. "You're right, the data set is too big, and we don't know what we're looking for. But that's okay. We're not the ones who are going to find it."

"Come again?" Sam said.

"This is a problem for the boys and girls in analytics," Mary Pat said. "I keep getting updates on the new machine-learning algorithms they're applying to the NSA's metadata. Find someone to put them to work on the satellite imagery using the Paracel Islands as the southern boundary. Bookend it from the time the trawler sank until now, but pay special attention to maritime activity starting with the attack on the Campus team in Europe. Time-stamp significant events like Clark's kidnapping, and the downing of our P-8."

"Wait," Sam said, "you think the Chinese crashed our plane on purpose?"

"I don't know if that was the pilot's intent," Mary Pat said, "but I think the interaction was meant to cause an international incident. A distraction to make sure we're looking at the magician's empty right hand instead of the floppy-eared bunny in his left. The USS *Ronald Reagan*'s carrier strike group was already heading north toward the P-8's crash site. Now they're probably pivoting even farther north toward Taiwan. So where's nobody looking?"

"The Paracel Islands," Sam said.

"Where a Vietnamese trawler was sunk and we still don't know why," Mary Pat said, grabbing a legal pad. "Tell the computer nerds to put up or shut up. Find me the rabbit, Sam. Oh, and check in with Gavin. If another video drops, I've got to be able to tell the President we're closer to finding Clark."

"But we aren't," Sam said as Mary Pat made for the door.

"Then get on it," Mary Pat called over her shoulder. "Don't make me a liar."

52

IN WHAT SHOULD HAVE BEEN NO SURPRISE TO JACK, THE BOAT MA-
rio found . . . was not a boat. Though, strictly speaking,
Jack supposed the craft could be classified as one, since it
floated and was for the most part seaworthy. This was
where the similarities ended. Unlike most any other craft
that called the Manila Yacht Club home, Mario's boat
did most of its traveling without ever touching the water.

Because it flew.

"Anyone else feel like we should be scouring the water
for Japanese submarines?"

The question came from Jad.

The irreverent Green Beret seemed capable of finding
humor in just about any situation, but in this case, his
question could have been literal. While the Grumman
HU-16 Albatross the men were riding in had been first
manufactured in 1949, four years after the end of World

War II, the aircraft's exterior and twin radial engines reminded Jack of the Allied seaplanes famous for rescuing downed American aviators and scouting for the Imperial Japanese Navy.

Jack just hoped that the Grumman's flight instruments were a bit more modern.

"I was thinking more of smugglers," Cary said from the other side of the cabin. "Didn't Jimmy Buffett crash one of these?"

"Yeah," Jad said, "but he swam out. Almost wasn't so lucky a couple years earlier in Jamaica. Authorities thought he was a drug runner and shot up his plane."

"Never happened," Cary said.

"I'm a surfer from SoCal," Jad said. "You're a farm boy from New Hampshire. Which of us is more qualified on this subject?"

"Boy, I came out of the womb a Parrothead," Cary said. "Besides, the Granite State is the SoCal of New England."

Jack thought Jad had a point, but he didn't weigh in on the Libyan American's side of the argument. This was somewhat because when it came to rhetorical skirmishes, Jad seldom needed help. But the real reason was a bit more dire.

Jack wasn't entirely sure he hadn't lost his mind.

"This is fun and all," Jad said, "but maybe we should talk about how long we're going to keep burning holes in the sky."

And there it was.

Though Jack was tempted to attribute Jad's grouchiness to the roaring engines, the turbulent flight, and the plane's less-than-five-star accommodations, he knew this wasn't the case. As a sniper, Jad was quite conversant on the topics of boredom and unpleasant living conditions. Over dinner with Jack's father, the Green Berets had recounted a time when they'd set up a sniper hide site in an Iraqi trash pile. A hide site they occupied for twelve hours in one-hundred-and-twenty-degree heat in order to get a bead on a troublesome Shia militia leader.

Jad wasn't grouchy because they were bouncing around the sky in a World War II–era plane. He was grouchy because the three men were soaring over a one-and-a-half-million-square-mile expanse of water looking for a boat for which they had no description and were not entirely sure existed. Meanwhile, Clark's clock continued to tick down as the Chinese Navy conducted maneuvers within shooting distance of Taiwan.

Jack didn't necessarily disagree with the Green Beret's assessment.

But he had absolutely nothing else to go on.

THINGS HAD BEGUN PROMISINGLY ENOUGH. JACK HAD REQUESTED a boat. Something fast enough to run down Clark's captors' several-hour head start, but with enough endurance to hang with the target vessel as Jack's meager crew developed the situation. It didn't take Jack long to realize that those two constraints were in conflict. Fast boats typically didn't have great endurance, while a fuel-efficient trawler would never make up the lost ground.

Enter the seaplane.

Though he didn't much care for fishing, Mario loved exploring places off the beaten path. When you lived on an island nation, air was the best way to do that. Mario was an aviation enthusiast, and the HU-16's top speed of over two hundred knots coupled with its almost three-thousand-mile range and ability to land on the open ocean made the Grumman seaplane perfect for the job.

With his mode of transportation now secured, Jack had transitioned to his next task—figuring out where to look for Clark. This was also easier than he'd anticipated. If the Chinese were behind Clark's kidnapping, it made sense that they would move the former frogman some-where they considered secure. Over the last several years, Chinese territory had edged steadily closer to the Philip-pines, thanks to the series of Chinese-made islands that now dotted the South China Sea.

Jack thought the handful of disputed reefs and shoals located in the vicinity of the Spratly Islands approximately five hundred miles southwest of Manila were a good place to start. More important, this section of ocean also hosted the over-one-hundred-and-twenty-ship-strong Chinese maritime militia.

Though the Chinese government claimed otherwise, the militia had become one of the CCP's most reliable means of enforcing its maritime goals. Comprised of Chi-nese citizens who received training from the People's Lib-eration Army and worked as sailors, fishermen, or other marine-related vocations, the fleet was a perfect tool for bullying and intimidating would-be encroachers into

Chinese fishing waters and maritime territories. While the militia vessels lacked overt martial capabilities, the swarming tactics employed by the vessels were impressive.

Jack thought the fleet would provide excellent cover for whatever the Chinese kidnappers had in mind for Clark. If his boss was still on the water, finding him among the maritime militia would be the equivalent of trying to identify a single grain of sand on a beach full of sediment. Jack and his team had to locate Clark's boat before his captors made it to the protection offered by the militia or, worse, Chinese soil in the form of one of the man-made islands or reefs.

Using the assumption that the kidnappers were making for friendly territory at a trawler's or freighter's best possible speed, Jack had worked with Mario to draw up a possible search grid. Then Jack and the Green Berets had moved their kit and equipment into the Grumman and taken to the air.

Unfortunately, what had seemed like a fairly straightforward plan while poring over nautical charts on the ground was considerably less so bouncing through the choppy sky. Located four hundred or so miles southwest of Manila and about six hundred miles due east of Ho Chi Minh City, Vietnam, the fisheries surrounding the Spratly Islands were some of the richest in the world.

And the most contested.

China, Vietnam, the Philippines, Taiwan, Malaysia, and Brunei all laid at least partial claim to the islands and surrounding waters. With each of these nations jockeying for position, Jack had no shortage of potential targets. Even after narrowing down their search parameters to vessels heading toward the Spratlies from Manila to meet the timeline Jack and Mario had agreed on, the three men had identified half a dozen potential ships.

And these were just the boats they could see.

Though Jad and Cary had spent years perfecting their search and observation skills, combing the ocean with just binoculars was a daunting task. Conducting a truly effective search required multiple radar-equipped ships and aircraft. The ocean distances were simply too vast and the potential targets too small for Jack to feel comfortable believing that his team had identified all the boats that could be carrying Clark.

As plans went, this one was not shaping up to be one of Jack's finest.

"GAVIN SAID HE MIGHT HAVE AN IDEA HOW TO FIND CLARK," JACK said, lowering his binoculars to rub tired eyes. "I want to be in position to take advantage of whatever he comes up with, but you're right. I don't know that this is getting us anywhere. I'm going to talk to Mario about putting us down in the water to save fuel. Then I'll check in with Gavin."

"Any idea what Gavin is doing?" Cary said.

Jack shook his head. "It's usually better not to ask. Trying to follow his thought process while he's working his digital magic is like watching a puppy chase its tail. But I will say this—Gavin always comes through."

This was true.

What was also true was that Gavin's idea of coming through didn't always line up with Jack's.

"No worries," Cary said. "I actually wouldn't mind a little time on the water. It will give us a chance to re-zero our weapons."

Cary gestured to the HK416 rifles secured to the bulkhead, and Jack nodded. Though both men had used their rifles during Clark's kidnapping, the snipers were fanatical about maintaining their rifles' zero. The atmospheric conditions on the ocean were similar but by no means identical to what the men had encountered in Manila. Before attempting any high-precision shots, the Green Berets would want to confirm that their long guns were performing as expected. Of course, the world's most accurate rifle didn't count for much without a target.

Jack was about to make his way to the cockpit when his pocket vibrated. Pulling out the pulsing cell, he examined the caller ID.

Gavin.

"Speak of the devil," Jack said, angling the screen so that Cary and Jad could see.

53

MARY PAT HEARD HER BOSS'S VOICE THROUGH THE THICK DOOR DI-
viding the Oval Office from the reception area just outside. He didn't sound happy. Mary Pat exchanged glances
with the Secret Service agent who opened the door for
her. Their eye contact lasted for no more than a second
or two, but his gaze communicated volumes.

Things were not going well.

"President Chen, that is simply not true."

Ryan's tone seemed almost robotic. Devoid of feeling.
As someone who'd seen the President experience the entire spectrum of emotion, Mary Pat recognized the warning tell for what it was. When John Patrick Ryan spoke
this way, he wasn't just angry.

He was incandescent.

Ryan looked up as Mary Pat walked in, but for once

he didn't rise. Probably because it was taking every bit of his control not to reach through the telephone centered on the Resolute desk in front of him and strangle the Chinese president. Arnie van Damm was seated in his usual spot on the couch to the President's right, and his suit looked somehow more wrinkled than normal. Ryan's chief of staff leaned forward as Ryan spoke, as if worrying that he'd need to physically restrain the President.

It wasn't an unrealistic concern.

To Mary Pat's practiced eye, Ryan looked like a caged animal. His fists were clenched and planted on either side of the phone and his torso was hunched forward as if the desk itself were holding him back. Perhaps another reason why he'd elected not to stand.

The door closed with an unusually loud *thump*, and it added a sense of finality to Mary Pat's arrival. Ryan made eye contact with her and raised his eyebrows. Though he hadn't said a word, she knew what he was asking.

Do you have anything?

Bitterness flooded Mary Pat's mouth as she shook her head.

Ryan gave a quick nod, but his shoulders still slumped.

She'd come up short. Though Mary Pat knew that Ryan understood the fickle nature of intelligence-gathering, that didn't make his look of defeat any easier to bear. Her friend had been counting on her and she'd failed him.

Oblivious to the exchange, Arnie scooted over on the

couch, making room for Mary Pat, but she remained where she was. Though she'd never been a naval officer, Mary Pat had to believe that this is what it felt like to be on the bridge in the middle of combat. On a ship of war, only the captain was permitted to sit.

"The incident between our aircraft occurred because your spy plane was in Chinese territory."

While President Chen spoke English, the voice on the phone was young and female, meaning it belonged to a translator. This was normal practice for a high-stakes conversation, but it still added a sense of surrealness to the event. Ryan was engaging in a discussion that could be the prelude to all-out war, and he could neither hear nor see his adversary.

The President's face flushed at the reference to the P-8.

While the *Delaware* had successfully rescued all seven crew members, one of the aviators had sustained a broken arm in the crash sequence and a one-hundred-fifty-million-dollar spy aircraft had been lost, to say nothing of the *Delaware*'s altered mission profile. These were not insignificant events to Ryan, and while he might be persuaded to meet the Chinese halfway if they acknowledged their own culpability in the incident, he would not be sending a letter of apology like his predecessor.

But at the moment, the downed aircraft was the least of anyone's concerns. Clark was still in captivity, and a large portion of the Chinese fleet was conducting maneuvers on Taiwan's doorstep. A single misstep by anyone could turn what was now a diplomatic impasse into a shooting war, and Mary Pat had nothing to offer her boss to tilt the conversation to his advantage.

"We obviously see this event differently," Ryan said. "I vehemently disagree with your characterization of what happened. Your aircraft intercepted mine in a dangerous manner which disregarded all established international norms. Your pilot then compounded an already precarious situation by deploying chaff and flares into my aircraft's flight path. This provocative act resulted in the destruction of the airplane and nearly caused the deaths of seven Americans. I do not take these actions lightly, Mr. President, but neither do I want the regrettable actions of one pilot to offset the trust you and I have built together over our long and mutually beneficial relationship."

There it was.

The lead-up to a gentle reminder Ryan intended to deliver about the leeway he'd granted the Chinese president so that he could recover his stranded submarine. Except rather than being dealt from a position of strength, Ryan's hole card more resembled a Hail Mary. A last-ditch plea for restraint rather than a face-saving off-ramp for President Chen.

This wasn't going to work.

Mary Pat's cell phone vibrated.

She flipped over the device to see a text from Sam.

Outside. Now.

Catching the President's eye, Mary Pat held up her index finger.

Ryan frowned but nodded.

One minute.

Her boss would stall for sixty seconds in the hopes that his top spy had come up with a way to save the day.

Not for the first time, Mary Pat was glad she'd worn flats.

It was damn hard to run in heels.

54

"The missing piece," Sam said.

For the first time, Mary Pat registered her assistant's appearance.

At barely thirty, Sam normally dressed like an academic twice his age, probably in an attempt to offset his youthful countenance. If this was his purpose, Sam was failing. His black curly hair, perpetually pale skin, and unlined face brought to mind one of Peter Pan's Lost Boys in spite of the corduroys, sweaters, and sport coats Sam favored. But though his dress was a bit eccentric, Sam's attire was always spotless and completely put together.

Not today.

Today, Sam could give Arnie a run for his money. His shirt was half untucked, with one sleeve rolled up to his elbow and the other drooping around his wrist. His hair resembled Einstein's tangled mess, and his eyes sported dark circles. Somehow, Mary Pat had completely missed that she wasn't the only one going without sleep. She needed to do better by Sam.

But that was a thought for later.

Mary Pat had sixty seconds to keep the South China Sea from erupting.

Everything else would have to wait.

"How did you get answers so soon?" Mary Pat said. "I know that AI algorithms are good, but they're not magic."

"Not AI," Sam said, his curls bouncing as he shook his head. "I did it your way. I looked for the rabbit instead of watching the empty hand."

Mary Pat had no idea what Sam was talking about.

Neither did she have time for him to explain.

She could feel the seconds passing by one by one like the gong of a clock.

"Bottom-line me," Mary Pat said. "The boss is on the phone with the Chinese president. I've got less than a minute."

"No problem," Sam said, turning his tablet so Mary Pat could see. Though his hands were shaking from nerves, too much caffeine, too little sleep, or all of the above, his voice was clear and steady. "This is the *Maochong*, Mandarin for 'caterpillar.' It left Zhanjiang Port two days ago, around the same time Junior ran into trouble in Germany. It's been steaming southeast ever since and is currently in the vicinity of the section of ocean where the Vietnamese trawler was sunk."

Mary Pat frowned as she considered the *Maochong*.

The ship was an odd-looking vessel, without a doubt. It vaguely resembled a container ship, but instead of aluminum shipping containers, the ship's deck was covered in metal scaffolding. A pair of industrial-sized cranes sat at the stern and what looked like an oil-drilling rig was located midship.

"Does it drill for natural gas or oil?" Mary Pat said.

"Close," Sam said. "Based on the equipment lashed to the deck, we believe the *Maochong* is designed to vacuum up polymetallic nodules from the ocean's floor."

Mary Pat shook her head.

"You're losing me, Sam. What does this have to do with what's happening in the South China Sea?"

"Everything."

Sam began to speak. His explanation took slightly longer than the thirty seconds Mary Pat had remaining, but once he finished, she understood.

Everything.

"Okay, Sam," Mary Pat said, interrupting her assistant with an upraised hand, "I've heard enough. You're coming with me."

"Where?" Sam said.

"To backstop me when I brief the President."

"I . . . I can't," Sam said, his white skin somehow growing even paler. "I'm just an analyst."

"Not anymore, kid."

55

"SORRY FOR THE INTERRUPTION, PRESIDENT CHEN," RYAN SAID.
"We had technical issues on our end and the call dropped. Can you hear me?"

"Yes, I hear you," the female interpreter said.

As she entered the Oval Office with Sam in tow, Mary Pat noticed two things. While still behind the Resolute desk, Jack Ryan was now standing. Two, judging by the mortified look on Arnie's face, there had been no technical difficulties. Unless of course you counted Jack Ryan's index finger. She'd asked her boss for one minute, and rather than improvising, the leader of the free world had hung up on his Chinese counterpart.

Mary Pat didn't know whether to laugh or cry.

As the Oval Office door closed behind her, Ryan pointed at Mary Pat as his eyebrows shot toward the roof. The question was as obvious to her this time as her boss's silent inquiry had been earlier.

Do you have the goods?

Mary Pat nodded.

Then she pointed to herself.

To his credit, the President didn't hesitate.

"Good," Ryan said. "The next person you'll hear speaking is my director of national intelligence, Mary Pat Foley. She has some late-breaking information that I think might help shed some light on what's happened thus far. Mary Pat."

Ryan stepped back from the phone, offering her the floor. In that moment, Mary Pat knew that regardless of what she told Ed, she was never leaving this man's side.

Mary Pat loved her husband, but she adored Jack Ryan.

"Hello, President Chen," Mary Pat said, staring down at the phone. "I apologize in advance for any confusion. My assistant will be sending over a summation to my Chinese counterpart of what we discuss, along with the relevant images and data, immediately after this call. We have evidence that a Chinese company named HAZ has mounted a concerted and deliberate attack against American intelligence officers, and that this company, in conjunction with the Abu Sayyaf group, is holding and torturing one of those officers now. We believe the purpose of these attacks is to lead our two nations to the brink of war."

For once, Mary Pat was glad that this was not a video teleconference. Never known as a superb poker player, Arnie sat with his mouth hanging open and his fingers gripping the couch. From the other side of the phone, Ryan looked at her as if she'd lost her mind, which Mary

Pat wasn't entirely sure she hadn't. Beside her, Sam was almost quivering, whether from a caffeine high or because he was in the Oval Office face-to-face with the President for the very first time, or maybe even because he wasn't quite as sure of the conclusions he'd laid out for her as he'd let on.

For both their sakes, Mary Pat prayed it wasn't the latter.

The silence from the other end of the phone seemed to last an eternity.

Mary Pat knew that she'd just done the equivalent of emptying a dump truck into Chen's lap, but even with the translation and the inevitable checking of her facts, the quiet seemed to stretch. Ryan's infamous index finger hovered over the mute button, as if he couldn't decide whether to push it and ask Mary Pat for a more detailed explanation or press on and damn the torpedoes.

His calloused forefinger was descending toward the button when the silence was broken.

"Why would HAZ want us to go to war?" said the interpreter.

Mary Pat exhaled the breath she was holding as quietly as possible. As a case officer, Mary Pat had become adept at war-gaming the direction a conversation would most likely flow. Sometimes crash meetings between an asset and her handler lasted less than a minute. In sixty short seconds, the CIA officer had to garner intelligence, communicate a tasking, and reassure her agent.

While it had been a while since she'd whispered instructions to the Cardinal of the Kremlin, anticipating a person's thoughts was something Mary Pat still did well. In a first for the last several hours, something had gone according to plan. President Chen had asked the exact question she'd hoped for, and like a slugger stepping into a fastball, Mary Pat swung for all she was worth.

"Great question, Mr. President," Mary Pat said. "I should have been more precise with my language. I don't believe the person responsible for this situation intends for us to go to war. I think they want us focused elsewhere long enough for them to stake a claim on the deposit of polymetallic nodules located in the vicinity of the Paracel Islands. The same location the Chinese-flagged ship *Maochong*, which departed from Zhanjiang Port two days ago, is steaming. My assistant is emailing you pictures of the *Maochong* now. As you can see by the twelve-meter-long, twenty-five-ton undersea robot secured to the *Maochong*'s deck, the ship is specifically designed to harvest the nodules."

Mary Pat debated going further, but didn't.

This conversation was a cross between a prisoner interrogation and an asset debrief. The key was to give enough information to convince the Chinese that she knew exactly what was going on, while at the same time holding the evidence close to her chest. Which, in truth, wasn't much more than what she'd already said. Sam was good, but he wasn't omniscient. He'd laid out several startling coincidences that hinted at something bigger. Ironclad proof this was not, but Mary Pat had learned long ago that in both espionage and poker you played the hand you were dealt.

The silence stretched for a beat, broken only by the sound of Sam's frantic typing as he emailed the appropriate images and a brief summary of their findings to the Chinese. Sam hit a final key, and the email was sent to the accompanying sound of a chirping bird. Sam's face flushed scarlet, making him look even younger. Mary Pat would have found the entire episode adorable were the stakes not so high. Still, the kid recovered admirably enough. Sam tapped a couple more keys and then made eye contact with Mary Pat and nodded.

The email had been received.

"As you can see from what we've sent you," Mary Pat said, "the *Maochong* was rented by a front company associated with HAZ. As I'm sure you're aware, HAZ provides military contractors for hire and enjoys close ties with the Chinese Communist Party."

The last statement was deliberately provocative, and Mary Pat succeeded in getting attention. Everyone's attention. The President locked gazes with her, his lips twisted into a slight frown, while Arnie looked as if he was going to throw up. Sam's mouth soundlessly opened and closed, giving him the appearance of a curly-haired beached fish.

But the biggest reaction came from the disembodied female voice.

"Are you saying my government had something to do with this?"

And just like that, Mary Pat was in.

"Of course not, sir," Mary Pat said. "We all know that if the Chinese government were to have sanctioned an undersea mining effort without first requesting a permit through the United Nations' International Seabed Authority, the seven other exploration permits held by Chinese companies could be summarily revoked and awarded to other nations, potentially sacrificing years of work and billions of dollars. Based on the magnitude of what is at stake, we can only assume that this endeavor was undertaken by rogue elements within the HAZ Corporation without the Chinese government's approval or knowledge."

Mary Pat surveyed the room as she finished speaking. Arnie still had both hands dug into the leather couch like he was holding on for dear life, and Sam's fingers were drumming a nervous rhythm on his tablet, but Mary Pat cared about only one man.

The one standing behind the Resolute desk.

John Patrick Ryan's expression was still grim, but as he locked gazes with Mary Pat, the President nodded. The gesture was slight, but noticeable. An acknowledgment from one professional to another.

She'd done it.

"President Chen," Ryan said, "this is President Ryan. I will speak plainly. I would like to request your help with two things. One, our two nations have been tricked into an escalation that could prove deadly. I certainly don't want that to happen, and I don't believe you do, either. If you will terminate the live-fire exercises you are currently conducting in the Formosa Strait, I will instruct my carrier strike group to return to their previous patrol."

Mary Pat felt herself nodding along with the President's words. Providing an avenue to save face was important when dealing with any foreign leader. With the Chinese, this concept was paramount. By referring to the Taiwan Strait by its Chinese name and offering to vacate the contested section of ocean, Ryan was doing just that.

"What is your second request?"

This time, the voice was male, older, and spoke with perfect Oxford English.

President Chen himself.

Ryan took a steadying breath and leaned closer to the phone. "The man being held by the rogue members of HAZ is a friend of mine. I'd be very grateful if you could help me get him back."

56

"HEY, GAVIN," JACK SAID. "WHAT HAVE YOU GOT?"

Jack pushed a sleeping bag off the lower of two bunk beds mounted to the Grumman's bulkhead and took a seat on the soft mattress. Though he didn't want to admit it to the Green Berets, the seaplane was actually growing on him. As air travel went, the aircraft was still a far cry from first class on an international flight, but its furnishings had a campy feeling that brought to mind family trips in a rented RV.

"Jack—tell me you've still got the Chinese glider."

Jack's muscles tensed despite the memory-foam bed. Gavin was an incredible asset when leveraged correctly, but Jack had learned long ago not to expect the keyboard warrior's mannerisms to reflect the angst Jack felt while operating at the tip of the spear.

This was not because Gavin didn't understand the life-or-death nature of Jack's work.

He did.

But with rare exceptions, Gavin labored in a world of ones and zeros far away from the smell of cordite or the ear-ringing cacophony of a gunfight. Gavin was naturally more relaxed because the stress he faced on his side of the phone, while not inconsequential, was just not in the same league as the pressure under which Jack operated. So when Gavin's normally laissez-faire phone voice was replaced with one full of urgency, Jack paid attention.

"Yeah, we've still got it," Jack said.

The glider's winged shape peeked out from the nest of blankets Jad and Cary had created to cradle the Chinese device.

Jack wasn't sure what had possessed him to keep the submersible. Maybe it was because the price paid to obtain the device made it too valuable to leave behind. Once Gavin had finished mirroring the device's hard drive, its worth was probably minimal, a sentiment echoed by the Agency extraction team. Even so, Jack couldn't abandon it. To do so would suggest that Dom had been critically injured for nothing more valuable than a disposable sensor.

While this might be true, Jack couldn't bring himself to believe it.

So the glider had gone with them down to the marina and into Mario's seaplane.

"Thank goodness," Gavin said, his voice even squeakier than usual. "That thing's going to lead us to Clark."

Jack got up from the bed and crossed the narrow cabin until he was standing over the glider. In the aircraft's dim lighting, the device was somehow even less impressive than before. With the dongle from Jack's laptop still dangling from its USB port and shadows crawling along its fuselage, the glider more resembled a prop from a B science fiction movie than Clark's salvation.

"Help me out with this, buddy," Jack said. "I'm not seeing how this hunk of junk is going to help us find Clark."

"Two things," Gavin said, his words coming faster in response to his growing enthusiasm. "One, I confirmed Clark's on a boat. Whoever uploaded the video didn't do a great job of sanitizing the ambient noise. I had to run the raw file through several software filters, but I was able to grab enough background sound to both confirm the video was shot on a boat and develop an audio profile that will allow us to find it."

Jack paused as thoughts of what sounds Gavin must have filtered out came to mind.

Sounds of Clark being tortured.

"Audio profile?" Jack said, pushing his anger to the side.

There would be time to feel all of this.

Later.

"Yeah," Gavin said, oblivious to Jack's struggle, "in the same way submarine sonar operators develop profiles that allow them to identify ships based on the noise they emit. We now have the acoustical fingerprint for the ship where Clark is being held."

"You did this yourself?" Jack said.

"Not hardly," Gavin said. "I'm good, but not that good. But when Mary Pat said that she was opening the intelligence community's floodgates, she wasn't kidding. Turns out there are some pretty smart people at—"

"Okay, Gavin, I got it," Jack said, keenly aware that the Grumman's radial engines were devouring fuel at an alarming rate. "And this glider's what—gonna listen for Clark's boat?"

"Of course not," Gavin said, his tone almost offended at Jack's ignorance. "Its sensors have an extremely limited range. The glider would never be able to—"

"Gavin," Jack said.

"Sorry, Jack. I should have explained this better. That glider is part of a distributed network of sensors that spans a chunk of the South China Sea. Since your glider was discovered by Filipino fishermen working in the same portion of ocean where the people who have Clark are currently hiding, it's logical to assume the rest of the glider fleet is located in the same general area."

"And this glider gives us access to the entire submerged network?" Jack said.

"Not exactly. Communication through the water is extremely difficult. We believe that the gliders surface periodically like porpoising whales to data-burst the data they've gathered to an autonomous sea drone."

"A what?" Jack said.

"Think of the gliders as worker bees," Gavin said, "and the sea drone as the hive's queen mind. The sea drones are uncrewed high-endurance autonomous vehicles that collect and analyze data from the glider network before passing the finished product back to China via satcom. Naval intelligence thinks one of these sea drones actually tracked a *Virginia*-class submarine a couple days ago as the boat transited the glider network."

"And we're going to use our glider to sync with the sea drone in the hopes that we can leverage the sensor network to find Clark's boat?" Jack said.

"That's what I've been trying to say," Gavin said.

Jack looked from the glider to the two other members of his three-man assault team. As professional soldiers were wont to do, the Green Berets were making use of the downtime by giving their rifles a little TLC. Both men seemed completely engrossed in the process of oiling and cleaning their weapons, but Jack wasn't fooled. Cary had wiped down his already spotless bolt carrier three times, while Jad was unloading and reloading the same magazine over and over like a glitched factory automaton. Jack was never going to be tapped for a job at the Navy Research Laboratory, but even to him what Gavin was proposing was thin.

Then again, so was the idea of taking down a boat full of terrorists with three men.

One problem at a time.

"Okay," Jack said. "What do we do?"

IN WHAT SHOULD HAVE BEEN NO SURPRISE TO JACK, GAVIN WAS A little iffy on how to transition his idea of hacking into the Chinese equivalent of Skynet from theory to reality. After a bit of brainstorming that seemed a bit too off-the-cuff for Jack's taste, Gavin had provided a set of maritime coordinates where he wanted Mario to land. The designated section of open ocean took into account a number of data points, including estimates for Clark's current location based on the length of time that had elapsed since the kidnapping and the target ship's probable speed, the distributed glider network's likely area of coverage, and the vicinity of the as-of-yet-unseen sea drone based on the *Delaware*'s reporting.

Jack had been wrong earlier.

This wasn't thin.

It was ludicrous.

But they had nothing else.

Twenty minutes later, the Grumman was bobbing on the ocean's swells. The seaplane's port-side hatch was open, and Cary and Jad were holding the glider above the water as Jack plugged his laptop back into the device. He'd already connected the computer to a satellite phone–enabled Wi-Fi hotspot and ceded control of the laptop to Gavin.

At this point, Jack really was no more than a monkey.

"See if any of the LEDs in the glider's access port are lit, Jack," Gavin said. "I'm not getting anything."

Jack stood corrected.

A monkey would probably at least have the good humor to enjoy the situation. Jack knew enough to be worried, but too little to do anything more helpful than follow Gavin's increasingly terse commands.

With a sigh, Jack set the laptop on a bench seat and joined the Green Berets.

In perhaps the first bit of luck in a long time, the cable connecting the laptop to the glider was long enough that Jack had been able to remain inside the aircraft while the commandos wrestled the glider partially out the hatch. The intent was to provide the device's satellite antenna a block of clear sky while keeping the contraption out of the surf.

The Green Berets were succeeding.

Mostly.

While the nubs that Gavin was certain contained satellite aerials had unobstructed access to the overcast sky, the ocean wasn't being terribly cooperative. The sea state had increased, and the Grumman was now waddling from side to side as waves broke against the fuselage, soaking the Green Berets. This had seemed funny when Jack had been warm and dry inside the seaplane.

It was considerably less humorous now.

"Gavin wants to know if any of the LEDs are illuminated," Jack said.

"Hell if I know," Jad said.

For all his professions of being a lifelong SoCal surfer, Jad seemed to have a particularly low tolerance for cold salt water. But Jack wisely kept this observation to himself. Leaning past the men, he examined the access port.

A pair of dark LEDs stared back at him.

"No lights, Gavin," Jack said as he verified that the USB adapter was snug in its port.

"Okay," Gavin said. "My best guess is that this thing has some kind of standby mode that shuts down all non-essential systems in case the glider accidentally beaches itself. Its microprocessor acknowledged receipt of the executable file I just uploaded, but the device's peripherals are still powered down."

"English, Gav," Jack said, ducking back inside the aircraft just as another swell crashed against the seaplane's underwing pontoon float.

"The glider powers itself down if it's out of the water for too long," Gavin said. "I think you guys need to disconnect the laptop, close the glider's access port, and hold the device in the ocean for a couple minutes. Once the glider's microprocessor detects seawater, it should power the sensors and transmitters back up."

Ignoring the word *should*, Jack asked the obvious question, even though he already had a feeling he wasn't going to like the answer.

"Exactly how long do we have to keep the glider in the water?" Jack said.

"No idea," Gavin said. "I would assume the device powers up pretty quickly. Five minutes?"

"Two minutes in the water it is," Jack said.

"You've got to be shitting me," Jad said.

As Jack had expected, the commandos had been monitoring his side of the conversation. As he'd also expected, they were less than thrilled with Gavin's prognosis.

"Come on, Jad," Jack said, "you're always saying that whatever a SEAL can do a Green Beret can do better."

"And with less hair gel," Cary said.

"You boys really know how to take the fun out of an interservice rivalry," Jad said. "Okay, how we doing this?"

"I'll help you two once I get this USB cable stashed,"

Jack said, unplugging the dongle and then closing the glider's waterproof access port. "Between the three of us, this should be no problem."

"Waves are picking up. We need to take off before they get much bigger."

The comment came from Mario, who was still seated in the Grumman's cockpit. Jack had heard their aviator slide open the cockpit window, but he'd assumed the banker was going to offer an encouraging word or two.

Apparently not.

"How much time?" Jack said.

"I need to start the engines in three minutes," Mario said.

"No problem," Jack said, tossing the laptop onto the bunk bed.

From inside the cabin, the aircraft's swaying was even more apparent. They needed to get this show on the road. Cary and Jad appeared to be of the same mind. The two Green Berets had already muscled the nose of the glider into the water, and Jack grabbed the aft end.

The glider was heavy and awkward. Fortunately, once the forward half was in the sea, the aft end was much easier to handle. With a minimum amount of muscle strains and cursing, the trio got the device into the ocean and oriented parallel to the Grumman. Jad latched on to a dorsal fin–shaped antenna that was positioned midway down the glider, while Cary held on to one of the wings.

"Okay, Gavin," Jack said. "It's in the water."

"Two minutes," Mario yelled.

A surge of seawater smacked the glider against the Grumman's fuselage. Cary narrowly got his hands out of the way in time, but then had to dive headlong for the slippery wing as the glider began to slide away. Jack caught the Green Beret by the belt buckle, just as Cary's fingers closed around the wing.

"This gives new meaning to the term *shitshow*," Jad said between clenched teeth. He'd grabbed hold of the dorsal fin when Jack had been forced to let go, and his arms were shaking with the effort.

"One minute," Mario said.

"How we looking, Gavin?" Jack said.

"Uh . . . I don't . . . Wait. Wait!"

"Gavin, I swear to God," Jack said, "if you don't—"

"It's working, Jack," Gavin said. "It's working. The peripherals are powering back up. I can see the GPS receiver trying to acquire satellites. Huh. That's weird."

"Gavin?"

"Some kind of secondary processor is powering up. Looks like it's—Pull it in, Jack. Pull the glider back in!"

Jack was only flesh and blood. As such, it took a moment for his human brain to comprehend Gavin's instructions and then form words of his own.

The glider was under no such constraints.

One moment the device was docilely floating next to the Grumman.

The next, the tiny propeller at the glider's aft end roared to life.

Apparently, tiny was in the eye of the beholder. Up

until that moment, Jack would have sworn that the multi-bladed length of glittering steel was more ornamental than functional.

That assessment changed the moment the propeller started turning.

The glider rocketed out of the men's hands and into an approaching swell. Then the nose dropped and the stubby shape knifed into the ocean's murky depths like a homesick demon.

"Fuck," Jack screamed. "Fuck, fuck, FUCK!"

"That about covers it," Cary said.

"We are leaving," Mario said, "right now."

"Where'd the glider go?" Gavin said.

"Judging by its trajectory, I'd say straight to hell," Jack said, slumping against the bulkhead. Jad took a seat on the opposite side of the cabin as Cary closed the fuselage hatch to the sound of the Grumman's starting engines.

"What are you going to do now?" Gavin said.

Jack didn't have a clue.

57

"I'M SORRY, JACK. REALLY, I AM."

Jack didn't answer.

At least not right away.

Though the Grumman's takeoff had been decidedly less smooth than their earlier departure from a relatively placid Manila Bay, the turbulent air and squeamish feeling in Jack's stomach were not the reason for his silence. No, Jack wasn't answering Gavin for a much more basic reason—he didn't trust that he could speak without losing his shit. Clark was probably getting the hell beat out of him at this very moment, and the only potential clue to his whereabouts was now at the bottom of the sea.

Jack was way past Gavin's heartfelt sorry.

Okay, that wasn't really fair.

Yes, the glider's unexpected departure was undoubtedly linked to something Gavin had accidentally done, but it wasn't like the hunk of plastic and steel held the GPS coordinates to Clark's location somewhere in its computer brain. The whole bit with the glider had been a long shot. Besides, Gavin had been following the same playbook Jack had used for years. When you have only one card left in your hand, lay it on the table and hope for the best. This time, that strategy hadn't been enough.

Besides, Jack knew Gavin wasn't the real target of his anger.

That honor belonged to him.

"Jack?"

"I'm here, buddy," Jack said. "Look, man, it's not your fault. Without your glider idea, we had nothing. We're in no worse shape than when we started."

Technically, that wasn't true. The gas the Grumman's engines were devouring and the minutes that were elapsing were both finite resources. The situation was definitely worse off than it had been, but Jack didn't say this to Gavin. He needed the computer ninja on his A game, and berating Gavin for this mistake wouldn't help. As much as Jack wanted to curl up in one of the bunk beds and let someone else take a shot at being in charge, he couldn't. He had to lead, even if at this moment leading consisted of nothing more than ensuring his teammates didn't quit.

"I just wish I had something left," Gavin said. "Another idea."

Jack's lips were forming the words to another platitude when his thoughts jumped off the train he'd been riding and onto another headed in the opposite direction.

"Hey, Gav," Jack said, "what about that software app you were playing around with back in Germany? The one you were trying out on the Chinese minders?"

"What, PARSEC? That's meant to—"

"No, not the *Star Wars*–sounding one," Jack said. "The other."

"Oh," Gavin said, "you mean HOUDINI. Sure, I was using that to try to penetrate the minders' phones and—"

"What about the kidnappers on motorcycles?" Jack said. "Would it have penetrated their phones, too?"

"Huh. That's a great question, Jack. But why would I—"

"The kidnappers in Germany and the operatives in Manila work for the same organization," Jack said. "If your HOUDINI penetrated their phones, then you'd have access to their contacts and call histories. Figure out who they called and then who those people called. Build out the entire bad-guy network. Then figure out if any phone associated with that network is pinging a satellite or Wi-Fi connection from somewhere in the South China Sea."

The long pause at the end of his diatribe suggested to Jack that he was onto something. He resisted the urge to prompt Gavin, instead giving the hacker room to think. A patch of turbulence sent the aircraft lurching one way and Jack's stomach the other.

Right about now, travel by seaplane didn't seem quite as charming.

"That's not a half-bad idea, Jack," Gavin said, "but I don't have the resources to do that kind of computing."

"The hell you don't," Jack said. "You heard Mary Pat—the walls are down. The entire intelligence community is at your disposal. Get her assistant Sam on the phone and explain what you need. He'll have the NSA's supercomputers at Fort Meade crunching data in no time."

"I'm on it, Jack. I'm on it."

Gavin ended the call.

"That sounded promising," Cary said.

Jack looked from his phone to the Green Berets seated across the cabin from him.

"After what just happened, *promising* isn't a very high bar," Jack said.

While he had been talking with Gavin, the commandos had reassembled their weapons and readied their kit. By the looks of things, the men had also taken a turn with Jack's HK.

"Do you think Gavin will be able to find Clark?" Cary said.

Jack shook his head. "I don't know."

"Honesty's good," Cary said.

"Yeah," Jad said, "we can work with that. What's the play if Gavin's keyboard magic fails?"

"We pick a boat and hope for the best," Jack said.

"Seriously?" Jad said.

"You wanted honesty," Jack said.

"Not that much," Jad said.

"We know Clark's on a boat," Jack said, "and based on the math we did earlier, we have a pretty good idea which subset of ships could be holding him. Let's do high-level recons of each one and sketch up takedown plans. At this point, that's all we can do."

"Agreed," Cary said. "I'll sync with Mario. I just hope that Gavin works faster than this bird's engines burn fuel."

So did Jack.

58

"IT IS OVER."

Fen stared at her phone, as if it was the device itself that had betrayed her. Though she recognized the words that had just been spoken, she could not comprehend their meaning.

"I don't understand," Fen said, trying to keep the concern from her tone.

"It is simple," Aiguo Wu said. "The Americans have seen through your ploy."

Though confined spaces had never bothered Fen, her cabin's dingy walls suddenly seemed to be collapsing. Her gaze drifted to a dirt-colored section of ceiling, the discoloration reaching down the steel like clutching fingers. Surely a fishing trawler's filthy cabin was not where the struggle for both her future and that of her nation would end.

"How?" Fen said.

"How is not important," Aiguo said. "At Ryan's request, President Chen has agreed to provide Chinese assistance rescuing the American operative you're holding captive. Jiaolong commandos have been tasked with securing your pirate ship. I suggest you not be present when they arrive."

"What of the nodule deposits?" Fen said.

"I do not know how to say this more plainly," Aiguo said. "Your plan has failed. The Americans know everything. President Chen has ordered the *Maochong* to return to port. Your corporate offices are being raided even now. I'm telling you this out of respect from one professional to another. Disappear while you still have the chance."

Fen could disappear.

Like every successful corporate CEO in China, she knew that her existence depended on maintaining favor with a mercurial Chinese Communist Party. While her alliance with Aiguo had provided Fen with some level of protection, she'd also fashioned her own safety net in the form of offshore bank accounts and falsified passports. As a former intelligence operative, Fen knew how to hide. If she took Aiguo's advice and disappeared for a time, perhaps her benefactor might be able to facilitate her return at some point in the future.

But Fen didn't believe in running.

"No," Fen said. "I will stay the course."

Then she ended the call.

She would not abandon her plan.

She would finish it.

While this venture certainly would have enriched her, Fen hadn't embarked on it for money or power. Her nation's rivalry with America had driven it to the brink of economic collapse. With Clark as her captive, Fen still had a chance to strike a crippling blow to China's most dangerous adversary.

She intended to take it.

59

JACK'S CELL VIBRATED.

He pulled the device from his pocket and checked the caller ID, hoping for Gavin.

He saw Mary Pat's number instead.

"Hey, Mary Pat," Jack said.

"They're gonna kill him, Jack. They're gonna kill Clark."

Jack's first instinct was to ask Mary Pat whether she was sure, but he bit back the response. She was the director of national intelligence and a former CIA case officer.

She was sure.

"How much time do I have?" Jack said.

"Not enough," Mary Pat said. "Another message just went up on the Abu Sayyaf group's social media site teasing a final video. An execution video. Whoever is running this from the Chinese side must not have had as tight a leash on their coconspirator as they thought."

Mary Pat's words battered Jack, but he refused to feel their weight. He had a job to do. A job that required clear eyes and a full heart. A job that would permit no emotional attachment to the victim. In this moment, Clark was not his friend or mentor. The Campus operative was just a nameless, faceless American hostage.

A hostage Jack intended to rescue.

"Can I count on any help?" Jack said.

As much as he fought to keep his voice calm, some of his emotion must have leaked through. Jad looked up from where he was fiddling with his rifle, and Cary reached for his body armor. The two Green Berets had to know that they were facing insurmountable odds, but the commandos were kitting up just the same.

Jack's chest burned with pride.

"No," Mary Pat said. "The Chinese have grudgingly offered assistance, but we're a long way from fleshing out what that would actually look like. Our special mission unit shooters are en route, but their plane is still hours away. You're it, Jack."

Mary Pat's words were comforting in a way. While Jack would have traded his left eye for Brandon Cates and his merry band of frogmen, introducing newcomers into his tactical stack now would be more hindrance than help. As recent events had made clear, Campus operators weren't invincible. But when it came to a gunfight, Jack would much rather be standing next to operators he'd already shed blood with than an unknown team. Besides, knowing that his resources were limited to the people in the Grumman helped to bring the tactical situation into focus.

The unknowns were gone from the equation.

This would all come down to Jack and his boys.

"Okay," Jack said, "I'm on it."

"Jack?" Mary Pat said.

"Yeah?"

"Take them to the woodshed."

Mary Pat ended the call.

Jack speed-dialed Gavin's number.

"Jack," Gavin said, "I was just about to call you. I—"

"Sorry to interrupt, buddy," Jack said, "but it's decision time. We have to hit a target. Now. What do you have for me?"

"I need more time, Jack," Gavin said, his voice quaking. "I've got some promising leads, but—"

"They're going to kill Clark, Gavin," Jack said. "Right now. I'm not asking for perfect. I just need your best guess."

Jack kept his tone calm, even though his stomach was quivering.

This was it.

The moment of truth.

"But what if I'm wrong?" Gavin said. "Last time I was wrong, we lost the glider. This time one of you could come home in a body bag."

"Listen to me, Gavin," Jack said. "I'm the team leader, and this is my call. Mine. Whatever happens is on me, not you. Now give me your best guess. Please."

For a long moment, Jack was worried that Gavin would refuse to answer.

Then a sigh echoed from his phone.

"Okay, Jack," Gavin said. "Here's what I think."

Gavin read aloud a string of coordinates, which Jack compared to the nautical chart stretched across the table he'd appropriated as a workspace. Though not exact, the coordinates corresponded to one of the trawlers he and the Green Berets had marked as a potential target.

They were in business.

"Great job, Gav," Jack said. "I'll give you a ring once we have Clark."

Jack ended the call.

"What's up, boss?" Jad said.

Until now, Jad had reserved the title of *boss* almost exclusively for Cary. That the Green Beret was now applying it to Jack meant something. But Jack wasn't going to take a victory lap quite yet. He might be making progress, but Jack had a feeling he'd be right back at square one once the Green Beret heard what he intended.

"We're going after Clark," Jack said.

"I'm down with that," Cary said. "Who's in the assault team?"

"You're looking at them," Jack said.

"You just had to ask," Jad said.

"Got it," Cary said. "Who *else* is in the assault team?"

"I guess they breed them big *and* dumb in New Hampshire," Jad said.

"We're it," Jack said, "so the good news is that we

won't have to worry about coordinating with unfamiliar units during the assault."

"I don't think I want to hear the bad news," Jad said.

"What's the plan?" Cary said.

"Not so much a plan as a concept of the operation," Jack said.

"Told you," Jad said.

"Told me what?" Cary said.

"That he was an officer," Jad said. "Only officers spew that kind of bullshit."

"Right here, guys," Jack said. "I'm right here."

"Better lay it on us," Cary said. "The sooner you finish talking, the sooner we can get to shooting."

Jack couldn't help but think that there was a strange sense of logic to the Green Beret's words. Maybe they really were gelling as a team. Or maybe he was losing his mind.

Only one way to find out.

"Okay," Jack said. "Here's what I'm thinking."

60

ANTEL ANDANG DID NOT PUT MUCH STAKE IN THE MIRACULOUS.
Though he espoused the same Muslim faith as his crew-
mates, when it came to day-to-day living, Antel was practical. He survived through kidnappings and theft. That
the imam had given him sanction for the bloody work as
long as he donated ten percent of his take to the mosque's
coffers meant very little to Antel. In the years he'd been
plying his trade on the Sulu and Celebes Seas off the
coast of the Philippines, Antel had witnessed plenty of
strange sights, but he'd never seen Allah personally weigh
in on his behalf.

Until today.

One moment, Antel had been standing watch on the
bridge. The next, the heavens opened and a bucket of
money fell into his lap. Not a literal bucket of money,
perhaps, but pretty close. Antel had been a pirate his en-

tire adult life. As such, he'd developed a finely tuned sense for what was going to make him rich versus what equated to just another headache.

The plane bobbing on the water in front of his ship had dollar signs written all over it.

Antel had heard the twin-engine aircraft before he'd seen it. While his aviation experience was admittedly limited, he knew motors, and the ones powering the airplane were struggling. The sound of the sputtering engine had him looking skyward through the bridge's dirty windows just as the plane had limped into view. Between the dense, white smoke pouring from the craft's cabin and the misfiring engine, Antel didn't think the aircraft could make it very much farther.

Apparently, the pilot shared his view.

The plane made a tight turn around Antel's ship and then came in for a landing. The craft bounced across the waves before settling into the water, its engines coughing a final time and then dying. While the pilot appeared to have set down in the nick of time, landing the seaplane in no way abated smoke pouring from the cabin's open window.

If anything, the noxious cloud grew thicker once the cabin door opened.

A small raft was thrown out the door by unseen hands, automatically inflating after splashing into the seawater. Then two men leapt into the rolling surf and pulled themselves into the raft. Without pause, the pair began paddling toward Antel's vessel as if their lives depended on it.

Judging by the smoke still billowing from the airplane, perhaps they did.

One of the men, American by the look, uncapped a flare and began waving the device at Antel as the second continued to paddle.

As if the pirate could have missed the stricken plane's arrival.

"Throw down the cargo net," Antel said to a trio of deckhands as he eased his trawler closer to the pair, "and help them aboard."

While the airplane might be a lost cause, the two crew members certainly weren't. Anyone wealthy enough to travel by airplane was wealthy enough to be ransomed. And if Antel was wrong, disposing of their bodies in the ocean would be no great chore.

Perhaps Allah really did look after those who looked after themselves.

61

"LOOKING GOOD, BOSS," JAD SAID. "YOU'RE REALLY SELLING IT."

"LOOKING GOOD, BOSS," JAD SAID. "YOU'RE REALLY SELLING IT."

Jack responded with two clicks of the transmit button. Sound traveled easily over the open water, and he didn't want to accidentally alert the pirates that all was not as it seemed.

Besides, Jad was right, they were really selling it.

Jack liked to think that Mario was furiously paddling because he, too, believed in the tactical genius of Jack's plan. But this probably wasn't true. Jack had promised the banker that once Jack got aboard the trawler, Mario's role in their rescue operation would be complete. This was most likely why the Filipino was paddling like a madman.

That was fine with Jack.

With four-foot swells battering his meager raft and a boatload of armed pirates towering over him, Jack was also ready to conclude this phase of the rescue.

"Okay, Scepter," Cary said, his tone all business, "I've

got movement in the bridge. I need that guy outside to guarantee the shot, though, over."

Shooting through glass was always an iffy proposition.

The silicon-based barrier altered a projectile's trajectory in unpredictable ways, making it difficult to achieve target effect with the first shot. This was doubly so with the light 5.56-millimeter round the Green Berets' HK416 rifles fired. Jack needed the pirate standing watch on the bridge dead, which meant that he had to get the terrorist to move to his side of the glass.

With a sigh, Jack eyed Mario and settled on what he had to do.

62

Cary didn't answer. After working this long with Jack Ryan, Jr., Cary considered Jad's question rhetorical. But to be fair, right about now Cary was half convinced that they'd all lost their minds.

"I said we needed the pirate out of the bridge," Cary said. "He's getting him out of the bridge."

"By stripping Mario naked?" Jad said.

"Maybe he's a Method actor," Cary said.

"Or maybe his luck has finally run out."

"Call the shot," Cary said.

This was less because Cary needed a wind call and more because he wanted his spotter focused on something other than the theater of absurdity playing out in front of them.

"Winds from the northwest at three miles per hour," Jad said, his voice now all business. "Range is one hundred fifty meters."

Most civilian hunters could manage such a shot with an off-the-shelf rifle and a plain-Jane optic. A Special Operations–trained shooter like Cary could have made the shot with iron sights and an ancient M-16. Since the Green Beret was equipped with an HK416 and a SIG Sauer Tango6T rifle scope, taking out the pirate should have been the equivalent of Babe Ruth stepping up to the plate in a slow-pitch softball league.

But as with everything associated with Jack Ryan, Jr., the devil was in the details. In this case, the two Green Berets were not on solid ground firing down at an unsuspecting insurgent. Instead, the men were huddled on a makeshift shooting platform recessed in the Grumman's cabin, peering through recently removed windows as the aircraft bobbed in the swells.

And then there was the smoke.

On the positive side of the ledger, there was actually nothing wrong with Mario's seaplane. The Grumman was not in danger of sinking, and its engines still functioned just fine. On the negative side, Jack knew that he had to give the pirates a reason why he and Mario would abandon a perfectly good airplane for the open ocean.

Smoke grenades provided the answer.

And while Jad had tossed the munitions as close to the open ramp as possible, the air inside the cabin was still getting a bit stuffy as acrid chemical fumes brought tears to Cary's eyes. This kind of suck wasn't in the same league with rotting garbage heaps in Iraq, but neither was the pending hundred-meter shot a walk in the park.

Cary centered the red cross representing his round's

point of impact on the pirate's head and waited. If Jack floated all the way to the side of the trawler without convincing the pirate to show himself, Cary would shoot through the glass and hope for the best. He debated offsetting the aiming reticle to try to account for the deflection imparted by the glass, but didn't. Trying to guess how his first shot would break was a fool's errand. Better to aim where he wanted to hit, with the intention of sending a second bullet chasing the first if necessary.

"Lookee there," Jad said, "our boy just might win an Academy Award after all."

A cargo net cascaded down the trawler's side, offering Jack and Mario a way to board the ship. But Jack's frantic actions must have convinced the pirates that he was in need of help. Though not exactly known as the Florence Nightingales of the sea, the pirates were probably also loath to let a potential payday slip through their fingers. Cary's target left the bridge to join a cluster of sailors, even as another pirate grabbed hold of the cargo netting and began to climb down toward Jack's raft.

That was good.

What was not so good was that Cary now had multiple targets to engage.

"Get on your gun," Cary said, adjusting the plan on the fly. "I'll take the man closest to the bridge. You have his friend."

"Thought you'd never ask," Jad said, trading his binoculars for his HK. "What about the Crow on the cargo net?"

"He belongs to our fearless leader," Cary said.

63

"SCEPTER, THIS IS REAPER, TARGETS ACQUIRED. BE ADVISED, YOU have one Crow climbing down the cargo net toward your boat. He's yours. We will initiate on your go, over."

Jack nodded, too busy doing chest compressions on a perfectly fine Mario to click the transmit button. Or at least the banker was mostly perfectly fine. If given the choice, Mario would probably rather not be lying in a puddle at the bottom of the raft with his shirt off.

To Mario's credit, the most reluctant member of Jack's team was doing his best to sell Jack's performance. Then again, since getting kidnapped by Islamic terrorists turned pirates was the alternative, Mario probably didn't have much difficulty finding his motivation for the role. Jack continued to thump on Mario's chest as he played out how the engagement would flow. The raft had drifted slightly, and Jack's back was now to the ship, so he couldn't see the pirate scrambling down the net.

But the Green Berets could.

"Scepter, Reaper, Crow is ten feet above you."

This time, Jack didn't bother to nod. He simply waited, visualizing the coming fight like he was choreographing an action scene. In a manner of speaking, that's exactly what he was doing. Jack would need to surprise and silence the pirate in concert with the two snipers. Two snipers who were bobbing on the ocean one hundred yards away in a smoke-filled airplane.

Just once, Jack wished for something easy, but as his SEAL friends loved to say, the only easy day was yesterday.

"Scepter, Reaper, Crow is—Shit."

This was not the update he'd been expecting. Jack was about to turn when the raft quaked beneath him, answering his unasked question. Rather than climb the rest of the way down, the pirate had jumped the remaining five feet.

So much for a carefully synchronized operation.

"Tayo," the man shouted.

"Thank goodness," Jack said, turning toward the pirate. "He's having a heart attack. I—"

The pirate didn't seem to be one for bedside manners. With the casual disregard one might show a buzzing mosquito, the pirate reversed the short-barreled AK-47 he was carrying, and butt-stroked Jack in the head.

Strike two for Jack's choreography.

The blow rang Jack's bell. He stopped himself from face-planting into the rubber, but he was in no position to administer a killing strike with the folding knife he was palming. Jad's folding Spyderco knife. A scream from Mario helped clear his cobwebs, and only then did Jack realize what was happening. The pirate's solution to Mario's cardiac arrest was simple—shoot the patient.

The pirate was tightening his finger on the trigger when Jack struck, burying the blade into the tender portion of the man's inner thigh. Jack missed the femoral artery, but he got the pirate's attention all the same. The AK-47 fired, but the burst went wide. Unfortunately, not wide enough. The rifle's chatter was greeted with an immediate *hiss* as the stream of 7.62-millimeter rounds punched through the raft's flimsy rubber frame.

But that was a problem for later.

The entirety of Jack's attention was focused on preventing the pirate from firing a second, more lethal burst. Snapping his hand up the man's thigh, Jack grabbed a fistful of testicles and twisted. The pirate's scream turned decidedly high-pitched, but the AK-47's looming maw continued tracking toward Jack's face. Jack dropped the Spyderco and reached for the metal barrel, trying to redirect the rifle.

His efforts were wasted.

The distance was simply too great.

And then Mario was there.

The Filipino tackled the pirate, bearing him to the raft. The rifle fired again and the report buffeted Jack's head with unseen fists. No matter. He was still alive. Jack celebrated his continued existence by grabbing the Spyderco and plunging the knife into the man's neck and ripping.

Blade work was rarely clean.

This was no exception.

After a string of savage thrusts that coated Jack's hands to the wrists in blood, it was done. The guard was dead, and Jack and Mario were alive and unhurt.

Relatively speaking.

Unfortunately, they were also passengers in a shot-up and sinking lifeboat.

"Scepter, this is Reaper, if you're done fiddle fucking around, you might want to get moving. Your kill wasn't exactly silent. Besides, your boat's sinking."

Sometimes Jack didn't know whether to laugh or cry.

Without bothering to reply, Jack grabbed hold of the cargo net and began to climb.

64

FEN LI LOOKED AT THE DECKING ABOVE HER, TRYING TO PLACE THE source of the unusual sound. That it was a motor of some kind she had no doubt. The trawler's metal walls were vibrating with the engine's deep bass, but it sounded . . . wrong. As if it were running roughly or perhaps not firing on all cylinders. The roar crescendoed, and Fen clutched her phone for support, preparing for the worst.

Then the rumbling began to subside as whatever it was passed by.

"Check on that," Fen said to Haoyu in Mandarin.

To his credit, her second-in-command didn't argue. Instead, the hulking mercenary gave a brisk nod and then slithered up the ladder leading topside, leaving Fen in the refrigeration compartment with a single Abu Sayyaf pirate named Radullan and Fen's prisoner, Clark. Gone were the days of Fen issuing instructions from the safety of the observation deck. This needed to be done perfectly, which meant she intended to do it herself.

"What was that?" Radullan said.

Like his compatriots, Radullan was Filipino, small, and skinny. But unlike his fellow pirate, who was now short several fingers, Radullan had reacted quickly and decisively to Clark's earlier outburst. He would be a worthy partner in this final endeavor.

"Probably nothing," Fen replied. "Either way, Haoyu will handle it. You and I will finish the work here."

Radullan looked from Fen to Clark and back again. "How?"

"I'm stronger than I look," Fen said.

The pirate shrugged and set to tying one end of the rope he was holding into a noose as Fen tossed the other through the metal loop secured to the ceiling. She didn't know the piece of metal's intended purpose. Nor did she care. The circular section of steel looked as though it would bear Clark's weight, and that was all that mattered.

The rope's coarse fiber irritated her skin, and for a moment she considered what it would feel like cinched across her own throat. If done correctly, hanging was a quick and relatively painless method of execution. The victim's falling body weight drew the noose tight, snapping their spine.

Death was nearly instantaneous.

Clark's execution would not be done correctly. Fen and Radullan would hoist the American into the air and let him hang until the noose collapsed his windpipe and his brain died from lack of oxygen.

This would make for extremely good television.

After watching Clark piss himself as his face turned ever deeper shades of blue, Jack Ryan would be infuriated, and infuriated people made mistakes.

Deadly ones.

"Ready?" Radullan said.

"One moment," Fen said.

She'd need both hands to help the pirate hoist the American into the air. Looking around the compartment for a place to stage her cell phone, she spotted a small shelf running the length of the far wall. She configured her phone to auto-record as she crossed the bloodstained decking and placed the device on the ledge.

After a several-second trial run, she reviewed the results.

Perfect.

Clark and his chair were centered in the frame. The zoom would capture him as the rope dragged him upward, while keeping her and Radullan out of the image. Or at least her, anyway. Perhaps it would be better if the Americans were allowed to see the pirate. Ryan's coming rage would need a target.

After deleting the trial run, Fen set the countdown feature on her phone and placed the device back on the shelf.

Then she turned back to Radullan.

"It is time."

65

JACK SCAMPERED UP THE CARGO NETTING, TRYING NOT TO THINK
about what might be waiting to greet him on the trawler's deck. He'd intended to use the Green Berets' suppressed rifles to effect a silent boarding.

Or at least nearly silent.

As anyone familiar with firearms knew, while the soda
can–shaped suppressors dampened the rifles' report, they
could do nothing about the distinctive *crack* a high-
velocity round made as it transited the sound barrier. But
that was fine. The ocean's ambient noise combined with
the constant background chatter of a working boat ought
to go a long way toward masking the shots.

That had been the theory, anyway.

But since Jack's pirate had gone full rock 'n' roll with
his AK, stealth was out the window. Now the steady bar-
rage of rifle fire coming from the seaplane provided Jack
with some much-needed confidence. He might still be

outgunned and outmanned, but his Green Beret friends were doing their best to level the playing field.

"Reaper, this is Scepter," Jack said, pausing just below the lip of the boat's steel side. "How am I looking?"

"Scepter, Reaper, wait one."

Jack hesitated, clutching the swaying rope with gloved fists. Two cracks echoed from across the water.

Then a form tumbled over the gunwale and splashed into the ocean.

"Scepter, Reaper, you're clear over the ledge. Be advised, we're going to reposition one at a time onto the seaplane's roof. This will give us better visibility of the boat, but you'll be down a rifle until we're both set, over."

"Roger that, Reaper," Jack said. "Good shooting."

Once again Jack found himself thanking his lucky stars for the commandos. The snipers had elected to operate from inside the seaplane for better concealment and cover. While transitioning onto the roof would undoubtedly offer the shooters better sight lines, it would also make the pair easier to see. But as always, threats to their person didn't seem to factor into the Green Berets' decision-making process.

Their job was to cover Jack.

If they could do their job better from the airplane's roof, moving was a foregone conclusion despite the tactical risk.

Jack might be boarding the ship by himself, but he wasn't alone.

Jack hoisted himself over the gunwale and landed on

the deck in a crouch. He brought his MP5 up to his shoulder, panning the EOTech's crimson circle across the deck. The cabin door to Jack's left swung open, revealing a bearded face. Jack fired twice, but the first shot did the job. The man fell forward, his rifle clattering off the deck. Jack stalked toward the door, keeping the crimson circle floating in the space the man's head had just occupied.

Based on a bit of quick research, Lisanne had estimated the trawler probably had a crew of six or so, along with room for another handful of passengers. Judging by the bodies sprawled across the decking, Cary and Jad had been doing a fine job thinning the herd, but that was still a huge imbalance in comparison to Jack's one-man rescue operation.

Fortunately, he had a plan to address that.

Or, more accurately, Cary had a plan.

After closing the distance to the still-open door, Jack conducted a quick peek around the corner, leading with the MP5's muzzle. The passage was dimly lit and stank, but was mercifully empty.

For now.

"Scepter is inside," Jack whispered as he flowed down the hallway. "Execute Phase Two."

"Roger that," Cary said. "Fire in the hole."

The ship's thick bulkheads kept Jack from hearing the beginning of Phase Two, but there was no mistaking its culmination. An explosion echoed the length of the hall as dirt and grit drifted from the shuddering bulkhead. Though Jack had been skeptical when Cary had first explained his idea of a distraction, he was now sold. The 40-millimeter grenades the Green Beret was lofting from the M320 launcher mounted to the bottom of his HK416 were nowhere near powerful enough to do serious structural damage to the trawler, but they made a hell of a bang. Hopefully this would be enough to give what remained of the crew something to focus on for the next several minutes.

Something that wasn't Jack.

Up ahead, the passageway swung ninety degrees to the right. The narrow corridor didn't offer enough room for Jack to ease around the corner using the slicing-the-pie method of clearing the space, and neither did he want to take the time for a quick peek. By firing high-explosive grenades into the top of the ship's superstructure, Cary was calling attention to himself in an unmistakable way.

Time was of the essence.

Crashing the corner, Jack dominated the space.

Or at least he would have dominated the space, had there not been a burly Asian man sprinting toward the door with the same idea. The fighter hit Jack like a locomotive. Both men fell to the floor in a tangle of limbs and automatic weapons.

While Jack was certainly familiar with the notion of fighting in an elevator, he'd never been in an environment this restrictive. His fingers reflexively went to the MP5's plastic stock, but there was no way he was getting the submachine gun into the fight. With one shoulder wedged against the bulkhead, the other pressed flat against the deck, and the HK smashed against his chest by a combination of the Asian man's weight and AK-47, Jack needed to think creatively.

So he used his head.

Literally.

Jack headbutted the fighter in the face with the short, quick strike he'd practiced countless times in the Campus fight house. It didn't go so well. Rather than crunching the man's nose or rearranging his grille, Jack's forehead connected with the fighter's head. The skull-to-skull contact made Jack see stars, but it also created space between the combatants.

Space Jack filled with his right elbow.

Though the angles and body position were once again not in Jack's favor, he didn't try for a perfect strike. Rather than gunning for the temple or jaw, Jack plowed his body's hardest bone into the Asian man's neck. His first hit landed high, almost at the man's jawline, but his second impacted lower on the neck in brachial stun territory. The fighter slumped, but Jack drilled him twice more. The shots disrupted the flow of the blood to the man's brain, inducing a blackout. A blackout made permanent after Jack secured his MP5 and shot the fighter twice in the chest.

As with most hand-to-hand combat scenarios, the entire episode had been both brief and brutal. Getting to unsteady feet, Jack took a breath even as he combat-reloaded the MP5. He'd been lucky, no two ways about it. A misplaced shot or a quicker reaction on the fighter's part and Jack could have been the one on the floor with two holes in his chest.

Jack stared at the dead fighter. The hulking fighter looked Asian. Chinese, if Jack had to bet. Which meant that maybe Jack was on the right boat after all.

Things were finally starting to go his way.

"Scepter, this is Reaper."

"Go for Scepter," Jack said, seating the new magazine.

"You need to hurry. Our diversionary attack has been a bit too successful, over."

"Reaper, Scepter," Jack said, "it's already been a long day. Spell it out in black-and-white, please."

"The fishing trawler's on fire, over."

Of course it was.

66

BETWEEN THE EXPLOSIONS ROCKING THE SHIP AND THE SOUNDS OF automatic rifle fire, Fen knew things weren't going well, but that was okay. She had one task left in this life to complete, and by her ancestors, she would complete it.

"Quickly," Fen said, "throw it around his neck."

Radullan gave a long look at the hatch leading from the compartment, but he didn't abandon her. Instead, the pirate shrugged and finished the noose, checking the loop with two quick tugs to verify his handiwork.

Then he turned toward Clark.

The American watched the pirate approach with an expressionless face.

It was difficult to anticipate how a man would approach death, no matter how well you knew them. Some who Fen had thought were warriors cried like children when the moment came. Others faced the eternal with a stoicism that defied description.

And then there was Clark.

Though the man was handcuffed and his chair bolted to the floor, the American's empty expression still gave Fen chills. He wore a look of foreboding. A darkness reminiscent of an angry storm cloud moments before lightning erupted from its roiling mass. Clark more resembled the executioner than the condemned.

But it was Clark's eyes that most troubled her. As they locked gazes, Fen didn't see fear.

She saw death.

Suppressing a shiver, Fen ran her end of the rope through a pulley mounted to the bulkhead. Clark had to weigh at least ninety kilos. Even with Radullan's help, it would be no small task to get him airborne. She would take all the mechanical aid she could get. After giving the rope a yank to ensure it had fed through the pulley mechanism correctly, Fen turned back to Clark and nodded at Radullan. The pirate had learned his light-fingered compatriot's lesson.

As agreed, the pirate snapped a fist into Clark's jaw, torquing the American's head to the right. Dazed, Clark slumped. The pirate looped the rope over the American's neck and drew the noose tight in one practiced motion.

Next, Radullan bent to release the set of cuffs securing Clark to the chair. As before, the pirate's motions were practiced and smooth. The same could not be said of the cuff's locking mechanism. Whether the key had been bent, the keyhole rusted, or the ratchet coated in condensation, Fen didn't know. When the handcuff didn't immediately release, the pirate went to one knee, resting his shoulder against the back of Clark's chair as he continued to work the key.

Though nothing in Clark's appearance suggested that the American had emerged from his punch-drunk twilight, Fen's stomach still clenched.

Something wasn't right.

Fen opened her mouth to shout a warning when a steel-on-steel shriek announced the handcuffs' release. She jerked the slack from the rope, intending to put tension on Clark like he was a dog on a leash.

It was the wrong decision.

Exploding upward, Clark propelled himself backward. The rigid chair acted as a pivot point, the screws securing it to the floor preventing it from tipping. Clark flopped over the chair into the still-kneeling pirate. Fen tugged the rope for all she was worth, putting her entire fifty-kilo weight into the endeavor. The rope snapped tight, jerking Clark toward the ceiling, but the American's girth was too much for Fen to bear.

Then she understood why.

Though he had crashed into the pirate with the grace of a boulder rolling off a cliff, Clark had not missed the opportunity offered by the collision. In the fraction of a second the two men were entangled, Clark had wrapped his legs around Radullan's neck. Though her initial adrenaline-fueled movement had indeed jerked Clark skyward, Fen had unwittingly provided additional tension for Clark's choke. Tendons stood out on the American's neck like steel cables as he fought the noose even as he thrashed Radullan from side to side.

Fen's arms shook with the effort of bearing the weight of both men, but she didn't dare let go. Despite Clark's best efforts, the noose was cinching into his throat, and his face was beginning to redden. The American was tough but not invulnerable. If Fen could keep tension on the rope, Clark's weight would do the hard work for her. Her screaming back and arm muscles begged for relief, but Fen held tight. As Clark had twice demonstrated, he was as dangerous handcuffed as most men were free.

A lesson Radullan was relearning.

As often happens when people are put in a fight-or-flight situation, the pirate engaged his muscles rather than his brain. Radullan spasmed as he tried to pry Clark's legs from his neck. His fists battered the American's thighs with ineffective strikes. The solution was easy for Fen to see, but Radullan's fear and rage prevented him from arriving at the same conclusion.

"Stand," Fen said as her slender arms shuddered beneath the strain. "Stand up!"

Something in Fen's tone must have cut through the pirate's mental fog. Just as Fen's arms were about to give out, Radullan gathered his feet and stood. Fen resisted the urge to allow slack into the rope. Instead, she kept the line taut, maintaining pressure on Clark's neck as the now standing pirate forced the American to bear most of his own weight with his quivering legs. For a long moment the fight devolved into a contest of wills—Fen's as she ordered her screaming arm and back muscles not to give way, and Radullan as he stood and pushed down on the American's torso.

Clark was stretched in one direction by the tension on his neck and a second by his body weight. The pirate took a stumbling step toward Fen, and the American swayed like a rope bridge, anchored at one point by the noose and the other by his leg lock on the pirate's neck. Fen gritted her teeth even as she voiced her agony in a guttural moan.

Something had to give.

Clark broke first.

Releasing his leg hold on the pirate's neck, Clark caught the chair with his feet, relieving the pressure on his neck. Like an anaconda tightening its coils, Fen jerked the slack from the rope as she screamed at the pirate.

"Help me!"

The latch activating the pulley's ratchet taunted her, just centimeters away. If she could trigger it, the American's weight would be borne by the locking mechanism instead of her quivering muscles. But now that she had the tiger by the tail, Fen couldn't let go. For a long moment, Radullan swayed on his feet. Then, like a dog shedding water from its coat, the pirate shook his head from side to side.

Finally, his dark eyes settled on Fen.

With a shout, Radullan charged toward her.

67

AN UNSEEN SENSE OF URGENCY PROPELLED JACK DEEPER INTO THE bowels of the boat. He sprinted down dingy corridors and hurtled blindly through turns. A feeling he couldn't quite explain but nonetheless believed told him that time was running out. Though explosions still rocked the trawler and the smell of smoke lay heavy on the air, Jack didn't think the vessel's deteriorating condition was the source of his distress.

He'd never responded to an active-shooter scenario, but Jack imagined this must be what the first law enforcement officer on the scene felt. An overwhelming sense that if he did not get to his destination quickly, the horror he would find would prove unbearable. A tiny part of Jack's mind was thankful that it wasn't a classroom full of helpless children he was rushing to save. Nonetheless, desperation still roiled his stomach.

The Campus was still reeling from the aftereffects of the warehouse ambush. The close-knit organization wouldn't be able to weather the loss of yet another teammate.

Neither would Jack.

So he ran.

Ran like a man possessed.

Jack still carried the MP5 in the high-ready position, but he no longer bothered with clearing corners or stacking on closed doors. His carelessness might very well result in his own death, but Jack didn't slow. Like a captain was expected to go down with his ship, Jack was coming home with John T. Clark or not at all.

A shadow stretched across the wall.

Jack brought the MP5 up to his shoulder, taking the slack out of the trigger. A millisecond later, a man rounded the corner. Jack fired a burst into the man's chest and then trampled his still-twitching body without breaking stride.

Speed.

Speed was everything.

Jack dropped the MP5, letting the sling catch the submachine gun as he pumped his arms. For a moment, he was back in high school, running the hundred-yard dash as his father looked on from the stands. His breath came in shuddering gasps as the balls of his feet pounded against the metal decking. Jack surged down the corridor.

He was out of time.

Like a runner sliding into second, Jack skidded around the final corner. As per the blueprints Lisanne had provided for the trawler, a ladder stood in a dingy corner. A ladder leading to the fish-refrigeration compartment.

Grabbing the rungs, Jack slid into the darkness. For the first time, he heard what before had been too faint for anything but his subconscious to notice.

Screams.

Screams coming from inside the compartment.

Jack slammed onto the deck and turned toward the compartment's door.

The screaming stopped.

68

RADULLAN GRABBED THE ROPE WITH DIRTY HANDS AND PULLED. Though the stringy pirate was not the epitome of strength, equal parts adrenaline and anger must have fueled his effort. With one enormous yank, Clark lurched toward the ceiling. The American's toes were now just above the chair, but those millimeters might as well have been kilometers.

Clark's legs thrashed as the rope bit into his neck.

With a shaking hand, Fen threw the locking mechanism.

The gears engaged, and the strain from her muscles vanished.

It was over.

With a shuddering sigh, Fen turned toward Radullan, a smile on her face.

Then the door exploded inward.

69

JACK ENTERED THE ROOM LIKE A BREACHING CHARGE.

Shouldering aside the door, he swept the compartment, his focus narrowing to the EOTech's holographic circle. The red dot in the middle of the circle centered on a figure hanging from a rope.

Jack registered the limp body even as he forced himself to ignore it.

Buttonhooking right, Jack came face-to-face with two combatants—a man and a woman. Jack thumbed the MP5's selector switch to fully automatic and hammered the trigger. As the submachine gun spit bullets, Jack panned the muzzle from person to person. This was not the way he'd been taught to engage targets, but once again Jack was trading speed for precision.

He registered both figures crumbling, but he didn't pause to administer safety shots. Instead, Jack emptied the remainder of the magazine into the wall-mounted pulley. Jack had spent much of his Campus career learning to temper his brute-force instincts. To become more scalpel and less sledgehammer.

But sometimes a sledgehammer was just what the doctor ordered.

Bullets sparked off the metal until the MP5's magazine ran dry, and the bolt locked to the rear. The pulley was battered, but still clinging to life. Grabbing the end of the rope, Jack yanked it away from the wall like he was starting a lawn mower.

The ratcheting mechanism gave way in a metallic scream.

Then Clark's weight and life were in Jack's hands.

Desperate to relieve the killing tension from Clark's neck, Jack released the rope. Clark crashed into the chair, his limp form falling to the deck.

Jack crossed the room with two distance-eating strides.

Wedging his fingers beneath the noose, Jack worked the rope from Clark's neck. Clark's face was purple, his eyes closed, and his chest unmoving. A reddening welt encircled his throat, and Jack pressed two fingers into the hollow of his friend's jaw.

Nothing.

Tilting back Clark's head, Jack gave two quick rescue breaths before starting chest compressions. Usually, compressions were more important than breathing. Without a heart to pump the oxygenated blood from the lungs to the brain, the victim would quickly die. Some studies had even shown that a person might gasp or begin breathing on their own during chest compressions without the help of rescue breathing.

But that didn't take into account a person who had been hung.

Jack's greatest fear was that the rope had crushed Clark's windpipe. If this were the case, performing a tracheostomy might be the only way Jack could save his friend. Time slowed as Jack's mind raced, trying to recall the steps in the process. Mike Houtz, an emergency medicine physician at Johns Hopkins, had provided a trauma refresher course for Campus operatives several months ago. He included a block of instruction on how to perform an emergency trach, but the classroom conditions were significantly different than what Jack faced now.

Jack eyed the swelling around Clark's neck. Jack had a knife, but he would have to stop compressions while he did the surgery. Then again, if Clark wasn't breathing, he'd die from oxygen starvation.

What to do?

With a start, Jack realized he was mumbling.

No, not mumbling.

Praying.

He was praying the rosary.

Jack stopped compressions and flicked open the Spyderco with a metal-on-metal *whisk*. Pressing his fingers against Clark's throat, Jack felt the confirmation he needed.

A pulse.

Clark had a pulse.

With a shuddering breath, Jack probed the base of Clark's neck with one hand, his blade held ready in the other. To do a tracheostomy, Jack needed a hollow tube or needle to insert into the incision he was about to make into Clark's throat.

He didn't have one.

Maybe he could hold the incision open with his fingers.

"Please, God," Jack whispered, "don't let him die."

With a hand that was steadier than he would have imagined, Jack pressed the tip of the blade against Clark's throat and began to apply pressure.

"Get that away from my neck before I kill you."

Jack jumped, nearly impaling his patient.

Clark's voice sounded like a rusty hinge, but it was still recognizable.

"You weren't breathing," Jack said.

"Getting your throat cut is a great motivator," Clark said. "Do I smell smoke?"

With a start, Jack realized that the air now tasted of soot.

"Probably," Jack said. "The boat's on fire."

"Why am I not surprised?" Clark said. "What do you say we get the hell out of here?"

That sounded just fine to Jack.

70

WHILE JACK WAS IN VIOLENT AGREEMENT WITH CLARK'S SUGGES-
tion to abandon ship, the task proved to be more work
than Jack expected. To be fair, getting beaten by terrorists and then hanged tends to take it out of you. Clark
was now more dead weight than operator, and that made
escaping from the ship's bowels an interesting proposition, to say the least.

And then there was the fire.

Thick, clinging smoke hung in the air, turning the
already poorly lit corridors into a murky twilight. Since
the ladder Jack had used to descend into the subdeck
now served as a reverse chimney, he had to drag Clark to
the opposite side of the hold, where a second ladder
awaited. Thankfully, the air there seemed a bit cleaner,
but the climb was no shorter and Jack had his doubts
about Clark's ability to scale the steel rungs.

"Hey, Mr. C.," Jack said, leaning Clark against the
ladder. "Can you climb?"

"What am I, an invalid?" Clark rasped. "Of course I can climb."

It became readily apparent that Clark's ability to climb was in the eye of the beholder. Yes, Clark could transition his body from one steel rung to the next, but at the pace he was moving Jack figured they'd both be dead long before they made it to the top. The only question was whether their deaths would be due to smoke inhalation, burns, or drowning after the trawler capsized.

"Let me give you a hand," Jack said. "Sit on my shoulders."

"I've got this, Junior," Clark said.

"I know," Jack said, "but I need you to have something left when we get to the top. Getting off this dump is gonna be a lot harder than getting on."

Whether it was from Jack's face-saving effort or that after ascending barely two rungs Clark was forced to confront the reality of his battered body, Jack didn't know. Neither did he care. The important thing was that Clark settled on Jack's shoulders.

For an instant, Jack felt his lips twist into a smile.

If only his Campus brothers and sisters could see them now. John T. Clark, the man who had once ended a man's life with his bare hands, now sat on Jack's shoulders like a teenager about to play chicken-fight at the local pool.

Then Jack started up the first rung and the situation didn't seem quite as funny.

Clark was a big man, and he must have been even more spent than Jack figured. Though The Campus's director of operations was grabbing hold of the rungs, he wasn't doing much to hoist his body. The first three or four rungs went okay, but by the sixth, Jack's legs were trembling. He didn't dare stop to rest for fear that Clark would insist on finishing the climb under his own power.

But that was only part of Jack's concern.

His greater worry lay with the billowing smoke rising from the compartment beneath him and the heat radiating from the passage's metal walls. The ship was going up in flames. As much as Jack respected his boss, Jack had no intention of spending his last moments in the bowels of a fishing vessel with Clark for company.

Summoning a final burst of resolve, Jack cleared the last several rungs.

Or at least he would have.

With just one rung remaining, Jack nearly lost his grip. This wasn't because his legs felt like Jell-O and his arms were trembling. No, Jack almost lost his grip due to a distraction.

The distraction of Clark firing the HK Jack had handed him at the start of the climb.

The MP5 coughed four times, but in the steel confines of the ladder well, the already loud reports sounded like thunderclaps. Jack swayed on the ladder, gripping the rungs so tightly that his right forearm began to spasm. Though the pain from the muscle cramp was intense, it was nothing compared to his pounding eardrums.

"Clear," Clark called. "Let's go."

Ignoring his quivering limbs, Jack summitted the last rung, spilling Clark onto the decking next to a dead pirate. An AK-47 lay beside the man, who sported a rapidly expanding crimson circle in the center of his chest. After enduring multiple beatings and a near hanging, John T. Clark could still put a four-shot grouping into a man's chest one-handed.

Jack might be a pretty good operator, but there was still only one Rainbow Six.

Resisting the urge to rest, Jack looped Clark's arm over his shoulder and staggered down the hall, triggering the radio transmit button as he moved.

"Reaper, this is Scepter, two coming out."

"Scepter, this is Reaper, good to hear your voice. Confirm you are exiting the port side, over?"

Jack knew he had definitely entered the ship's super-structure on the port side, but after backtracking through the rat's nest of passageways to avoid the smoke and pirates, he was no longer sure which side of the boat he was on.

"Mr. C.," Jack said, defaulting to the sailor, "are we on the port or starboard side?"

"Starboard," Clark said. "Definitely starboard."

The SEAL devolved into a fit of coughing after answering, preventing Jack from asking any follow-up questions, like *How in the world would you know that?* Maybe sailors were just born with the ability to tell port from starboard. Like homing pigeons, but with boats.

The smoke must be getting to him.

Clearing his throat, Jack keyed the transmit button.

"We're coming out the starboard side, Reaper," Jack said.

"Roger that, Scepter," Cary said. "Stand by. We need to reposition."

The plan had been for Mario to paddle back to the seaplane and fire up her engines after Jack boarded the ship. No small feat in a sinking raft. But unless one of the Green Berets was now piloting the Grumman, the banker must have made it. Just when he was about to bask in the feeling of goodwill that came from knowing an operation was proceeding according to plan, Jack faced another curveball.

A pirate peeked around the far corner.

Or at least Jack assumed it was a pirate. All he saw was the muzzle of an AK-47, but that was more than enough for Jack to get the picture.

Especially once the muzzle started spitting fire.

Fortunately, the pirate had adopted the pray-and-spray methodology, while Clark went with the aim-and-shoot plan. Unsurprisingly, Clark's method was more successful.

Another pirate toppled to the decking as Jack lost another year off his life.

"Negative, Reaper," Jack said. "We're coming out now."

Jack dragged Clark toward the hatch at the far end of the corridor. The one opening to the ship's starboard side.

He hoped.

If he objected to being treated like an invalid, Clark didn't say so. Or maybe with a submachine gun in his hands and his Irish temper flaring, The Campus's director of operations was in his happy place. Either way,

Jack kept his head down and his legs pumping and he tried to ignore the MP5's coughing as Clark covered their retreat. That was a little easier said than done, especially when a bullet sparked off the wall to his left before ricocheting around the corridor, sounding like hail on a tin roof.

Apparently, there were still a couple pirates left alive.

And they didn't seem happy.

Jack got to the hatch just as Clark's measured fire ceased.

"I'm Winchester," Clark said.

Jack didn't bother replying. Instead, he kicked open the door, dragged the SEAL through, and closed the hatch behind him even as a flurry of rounds impacted the steel, buckling it outward.

They'd made it.

Sort of.

What Jack saw wasn't encouraging. While this section of the trawler was clear of pirates, it didn't take Jack long to understand why. With the exception of a length of decking leading off the boat like a gangplank, everything was on fire.

Everything.

"Come on," Jack said, helping Clark to the edge. "Time to abandon ship."

Except they couldn't.

Jack looked over the side of the boat only to see the ocean in flames. The fuel leaking from the stricken vessel had ignited, turning the roiling sea into something resembling a scene from Dante's *Inferno*.

The two men were stuck.

Jack turned back toward the hatch just as a piece of flaming superstructure crashed to the decking, barring their way.

There was no going back and no going forward.

"Well, shit," Clark said.

The two innocuous words carried with them a world of meaning. Jack had known from the moment he'd started his paramilitary career by plunging a syringe loaded with poison into a terrorist that there was a high likelihood his life would end violently. Those who lived by the sword really did often die by it. But even so, Jack would have never imagined that *Well, shit* would be the last words he heard.

Come to think of it, though, that phrase might just make a fine tombstone epitaph.

"Scepter, this is Reaper, we're coming from the stern. Get ready to jump."

Jack turned to look behind him and was rewarded with a glorious sight.

Like an angel escaping hell's lake of fire, the Albatross bounced across the flaming water. Cary and Jad stood on the aircraft's massive wing as the seaplane pulled even with the boat. The port engine's three-bladed propeller wasn't turning, but between the heaving trawler and the licking flames, this would be no walk in the park—a sentiment reinforced by the chatter of Jad's rifle as he swept the deck of pirates.

"Jump," Cary screamed.

The Green Beret stood at the edge of the wingtip,

ready to grab tumbling bodies, but Jack knew Clark wasn't going to be able to make the leap.

"Go ahead, Junior," Clark said, as if reading Jack's thoughts. "I'll be right behind you."

"Sure thing, Mr. C.," Jack said.

Then he grabbed his mentor by the back of his belt and the scruff of his neck, took a running step forward, and hurled The Campus's director of operations into space like Jack was tossing a hay bale. To his credit, Clark landed like a cat—an old angry feral cat, but a cat all the same. Clark crashed to the wing on all fours, and Cary grabbed the SEAL, hauling him to safety.

Before he could change his mind, Jack followed his boss.

Jack wasn't nearly as graceful.

Whether it was a sudden shift in the waves, a gust of wind, a miscalculation, or just tired legs, Jack smacked into the top of the wing in a full sprawl. Then he skidded off the slick canvas like an egg sliding out of a skillet.

One moment Jack saw Cary's horror-stricken face.

The next he was tumbling into space.

Or at least he would have been if not for the portside underwing float. Jack caught the bright yellow, bullet-shaped pontoon between his legs, halting his fall and bruising his thighs. The ensuing jolt rang the length of Jack's spine, promising another visit to his long-suffering chiropractor.

He didn't care.

The pain radiating from his groin meant he was still alive.

Jack wrapped his aching legs around the float as he gripped the vertical nacelle with his arms.

"You actually made it!"

Jack looked up to see Cary peering at him from the top side of the wing.

"Get us the hell out of here," Jack said.

Cary nodded and then vanished. A moment later, the aircraft yawed to the right, bouncing across the ocean as Mario powered away from the stricken trawler. With the wind in his face, salt spray coating his clothes, and the knowledge that Clark was safe somewhere above him, Jack had a final thought.

Maybe the German college student had been right.

Maybe Jack really was getting too old for this shit.

Nah.

EPILOGUE

THE BREEZE ROLLING OFF THE OCEAN TOUSLED LISANNE'S HAIR, framing her face in strands of midnight. The last of the day's light traced golden fingers across her olive skin and the faint hint of her perfume teased at Jack, promising more if he could just close the six inches that separated them.

Those six inches might have been six miles.

Though candlelight played along crystal glasses, the wine they held hadn't been touched.

"Why are we here, Jack?" Lisanne said.

The question, while not accusatory, was tinged with sadness. A sorrow the twin of which resonated in Jack's chest. They were seated side by side at a table draped in white linen on the second-floor deck of one of Old Town Alexandria's most exclusive restaurants. As per Jack's arrangement with the owner, the couple had the deck to themselves, but the softening twilight had done little to bridge the chasm between them. Their table was positioned to offer a view of the harbor, and Lisanne had done Jack the favor of keeping her focus on the horizon as she'd spoken.

Even so, her question still burned.

Viewing Lisanne only in profile didn't make the tear trickling down her cheek any easier to bear.

Jack reached for Lisanne's hand, but she deftly moved her fingers out of reach.

"Words, Jack," Lisanne said. "It's time for words."

He'd endlessly practiced the words he wanted to say, but they were now lodged in his throat. Clark was no worse for wear and Ding's through-and-through gunshot wound was healing, along with his concussion, but Dom wasn't so quick to mend. The Campus operator had just been weaned from the ventilator the previous evening. Surgery had been initially required to ease the cranial pressure brought on by the swelling of Dom's brain, but the procedure had been complication-free. After Dom had a battery of tests and several weeks of recovery, his neurologist was now confident that he hadn't suffered permanent brain damage.

That was the good news.

The not-so-good news was that the piece of metal shrapnel embedded in Dom's thigh had shattered his femur. Correcting the damage had required multiple surgeries. The orthopedic surgeon expected the Campus shooter to regain full use of his leg, but a long regimen of physical therapy awaited.

Judging by what Jack had just seen, the road back to recovery would not be easy.

To celebrate Dom's discharge from ICU and the accompanying visitor privileges, Jack, Lisanne, and several other Campus members had gathered in Dom's small hospital room a few hours ago. While Jack was no stranger to wounded men, the sight of Dom's battered and bruised body shook him to his core. From the dressing on Dom's shaved skull, to the still-healing trach stoma, to the mass of bandages on his thigh, the Campus operative was clearly a man who'd come within a whisker of making the trip home from Manila in a body bag.

Adara Sherman's reaction had been even more profound.

The normally even-keeled woman had wrapped her arms around Dom and sobbed. After Adara's tears continued unabated for several minutes, the rest of the group had quietly withdrawn to give the couple privacy. Lisanne must have seen Jack's look of confusion. On the elevator ride down to the hospital's entrance, she'd whispered something that had rended his soul, her devastating words in stark contrast to the husky voice he loved and the warmth of her breath.

Several months ago, Adara had miscarried Dom's baby.

Jack and Lisanne hadn't spoken during the trip from the hospital to the restaurant. To his mind, the silence had been warranted.

Then.

Not anymore.

Lisanne was right.

It was the time for words.

"Look," Lisanne said, still staring at the horizon, "neither of us are in the right headspace for a relationship talk. Why don't I just get an Uber back to my place? This will keep."

"No," Jack said, "it won't."

With a sigh, Lisanne turned to face him.

"Damn it, Jack," Lisanne said, her eyes dark pools, "can you not be noble just once? I'm trying to give you an out."

"Lisanne Robertson," Jack said, whipping away her tears with his thumb, "I don't want out. I want in. All the way in."

"What are you talking about?" Lisanne said.

"You were right," Jack said. "What you said in Austria was right. The way we've been doing things hasn't been working. I want our relationship to change. Completely."

For a moment Lisanne looked at him in silence, her confusion evident.

Then her eyes widened.

"Are you out of your mind?" Lisanne said, leaning back in her chair. "We just came from Dom's hospital room."

"I know," Jack said. "Believe me, I know. But here's the thing. I finally feel like I am in my right mind. Do you know what my mom said to me after she met you the first time?"

Lisanne shook her head.

"Marry that girl before someone else does."

"Jack, I—"

"Just let me get this out," Jack said. "Okay?"

Lisanne slowly nodded.

She looked equal parts bewildered and horrified. As if wondering whether Jack had lost it.

Not exactly how he'd pictured this moment.

"I'm not saying this because of what happened in Manila or even because of my mother," Jack said. "I'm saying it because I thought I'd lost you in Salzburg. Forever. In that moment, I didn't care about the mission, or gaining Clark's respect, or even living up to my old man's reputation. I only cared about growing old with you. I don't mean the rest isn't important. It is. I've spent my life trying to prove that I'm good enough. That I deserve to be part of The Campus for my skills, not just because my last name is Ryan. But whether it's tomorrow or in twenty years, one day I'll leave The Campus. When that time comes, I want to go home to you. Does that make sense?"

"Nothing about this makes sense," Lisanne said, her words coming slowly, "but I understand what you're saying. I think. And I know you're being sincere, but we're not normal people, Jack. Know what I learned in Salzburg? That two people who love each other can't do this kind of work. At least not together. But I'm not sure I know how to do anything else. Are you willing to go back to a desk and spreadsheets?"

"I don't know," Jack said.

Jack didn't know.

He'd finally achieved what he'd most wanted. His actions in Manila had cemented Jack's status as a Campus operator and team leader. More important, he'd earned the respect of John Clark and Ding Chavez. The two men who'd shaped him more than anyone but his parents. Instead of the annoying little brother who'd been allowed to tag along at Dad's behest, Jack was now their peer.

He should have been happy.

He wasn't.

The image of Adara sobbing into Dom's chest cycled through Jack's thoughts on repeat.

Cary was right. If Jack continued down this path, there would be more tears. More pain. More hushed words and more gatherings with subdued comrades. Perhaps one day he would be the one lying in a hospital bed.

Or a grave.

This was the way of the warrior. To pretend otherwise was to ignore the reality he'd just experienced. For as long as he could remember, Jack had relentlessly pursued a life at the tip of the spear. This quest had become the singular purpose for which he'd subordinated all else.

But no longer.

"I don't know," Jack said again, "but if that's what it takes to have a life with you, I'm willing to try. I hope we'll be lucky enough to have kids and grandkids. That someday we'll retire and watch the sun rise over cups of coffee. But I can't promise any of that. Our days are numbered, and our lives are fleeting. I don't know how many tomorrows we have, but I do know that I want to spend each of them with you."

Jack took Lisanne's hand again.

This time, she didn't pull away.

Getting down on one knee, Jack removed a ring from his pocket. The ring that Cathy Ryan had helped him choose. Opening the box one-handed, Jack presented the sparkling diamond to the woman he loved.

"Lisanne Robertson," Jack said, "will you marry me?"

Lisanne's eyes welled up with tears.

Then she spoke.

"Yes."

Ready to find
your next great read?

Let us help.

Visit prh.com/nextread

Penguin
Random
House

A LITTLE BIT WILD

"Jude," she whispered.

He ignored her plea and kissed his way along the line of the fabric. Her hands tightened in his hair, and pleasure pulsed into his veins. She wanted this. She wanted *him*.

Jude eased one hand beneath her robe and curled it over her shoulder so that he could feather his thumb across the very top of her breast. She shivered and arched into his body.

This was a more difficult exercise in control than he'd imagined. And Marissa was showing no restraint at all.

Jude closed his eyes and counted to twenty; then, telling himself he could stop when he needed to, he finally pressed his lips to the thin fabric that covered her breast. He closed his mouth over her nipple, and Marissa gasped in a high, sweet voice.

He wanted so badly to tug her gown down and see the miracle of her naked body. He wanted to strip her bare and taste every inch of her skin. Then he wanted to bury himself deep within her for hours.

But more than anything, he wanted Marissa to think she couldn't live without him, as he was beginning to think he couldn't live without her. . . .

Books by Victoria Dahl

TO TEMPT A SCOTSMAN

A RAKE'S GUIDE TO PLEASURE

ONE WEEK AS LOVERS

A LITTLE BIT WILD

HIGHLAND BEAST
(with Hannah Howell and Heather Grothaus)

LORDS OF DESIRE
(with Virginia Henley, Sally MacKenzie,
and Kristi Astor)

Published by Kensington Publishing Corporation

A Little
Bit Wild

Victoria Dahl

ZEBRA BOOKS
KENSINGTON PUBLISHING CORP.
http://www.kensingtonbooks.com

ZEBRA BOOKS are published by

Kensington Publishing Corp.
119 West 40th Street
New York, NY 10018

All Kensington titles, imprints, and distributed lines are
available at special quantity discounts for bulk purchases
for sales promotion, premiums, fund-raising, educational or
institutional use.

Special book excerpts or customized printings can also be
created to fit specific needs. For details, write or phone the
office of the Kensington Special Sales Manager: Attn. Special
Sales Department. Kensington Publishing Corp., 119 West
40th Street, New York, NY 10018. Phone: 1-800-221-2647.

Zebra and the Z logo Reg. U.S. Pat. & TM Off.

ISBN-13: 978-1-4201-0483-7
ISBN-10: 1-4201-0483-7

First Printing: August 2010

10 9 8 7 6 5 4 3 2 1

Printed in the United States of America

Chapter 1

Lincolnshire, 1847

The man above Marissa York groaned loudly, his breath shuddering over her cheek.

She turned her head and frowned at the wall as the room spun slowly around her. *Goodness.* This wasn't going well at all. Thankfully, it seemed it was nearly over.

After an endless summer of pretending to look for a husband in London, Marissa had thought to treat herself to a night of forbidden pleasure. It was her family's first house party of the hunting season, after all. Everyone else was having a rollicking good time, and Marissa had thought to find some fun too. But instead she'd found clumsy fumbling, not to mention a bit of discomfort and lots of grunting. Perhaps this was why girls were ordered to keep themselves pure for marriage. No matter how unfortunate the consummation, there was no turning back afterward.

"My love," Peter White sighed into her ear. "My sweet, sweet Marissa. That was beautiful. Perfect."

"Perfect?"

"Oh, yes."

She stretched her neck, trying to ease the strain on her back. "Um, could you please . . . arise?"

"Of course, I'm sorry." He pushed up to his elbows. Unfortunately, though this eased the weight on her chest, it pushed his bottom half more thoroughly against her. Everything down there felt rather . . . squishy.

"Mr. White, please? Get up?"

He gave her a sly grin. "Don't you feel silly calling me Mr. White right now?"

"No."

"When we are married, I hope you will call me by my Christian name, at least in—"

"Pardon?"

He leaned down to press a kiss to her nose. Marissa wiped it away.

"I'll speak to your brother tomorrow," he purred.

"You will do no such thing! Now get off. It's taking you more time to dismount than you spent riding."

Finally, the stubborn fool seemed to sense that she wasn't limp with gratitude at his rutting. He drew back, squishing even more firmly into her.

"Oh, just get off me, you great dolt!" she cried.

He gasped, "Marissa!" as shocked horror took over his face.

And that was when she heard the footsteps in the hall. Her eyes went wide. She pushed at his chest. And the door opened.

Marissa held her breath. It was dark. The light

from the hallway might not have reached them. If they just kept quiet . . .

Peter White cleared his throat. "If you would close the door, please. We require privacy."

Before her shock could twist into anger, the shadowed figure shifted. "Pardon me?" Her brother's voice.

Oh, no. Not her brother.

The door flew fully open, and Marissa had to squint against the light from the hall, so she could only assume they were now visible. Her heart sunk down to rest on her spine. "No," she breathed.

"Marissa Anne York!" her brother bellowed just before he lunged for the man atop her.

Mr. White was finally off her, but she could hardly summon a feeling of thankfulness. The shadows of the two men merged into one large beast that lurched into the darkest corner of the room. Vases shattered. A table crashed into the wall.

"Stop!" Marissa screamed, hoping her shout would put an end to the fight and stop time as well. If she could only go back to a half hour earlier when she'd finished that last glass of wine and let Mr. White coax her into this room . . .

Tempted to jump up from the couch and sprint to her chambers, Marissa instead chose the more daunting path. She tugged her skirts down and pushed unsteadily to her feet to face her brother. "Edward! Stop. *Please.*"

"You foul bastard," her brother's voice huffed.

A loud thump of flesh on flesh made Marissa flinch. The chaos ceased, and suddenly only the sound of the two men panting emerged from the dark. She could do nothing but stand there and shake.

"Edward?" she breathed.

Broken glass slid against the wood floor. One of the shadows rose up and started toward her. Marissa backed away, afraid of her brother, only because she couldn't *see* him. He would never hurt her, no matter what she did. But he looked like a goblin coming at her from the dark.

Or perhaps it was Mr. White, and her brother lay unconscious on the floor.

"Edward?"

The shadow shifted at the last moment, her brother's snarling face finally coming into the light, and he moved past her. Glass rattled. A match struck.

Light swelled slowly over the room. When it reached the farthest corner, she saw that Mr. White wasn't unconscious at all, but sitting up with a hand pressed to his eye. At the sight of him, Marissa had to tamp down an urge to fly at his face and do further damage. Easier to be furious with him than with herself.

A shadow cast itself from the hallway, and Marissa glanced up to see her cousin Harry standing there.

"What in the world is all the ruckus?" Harry asked. Oh, this was only getting worse. How many others had heard?

"Marissa," her brother said, that one word full of worry and hurt and confusion and fury.

She wrapped her arms around herself and turned slowly toward him. "I apologize." Her voice was steady, just as she meant for it to be. "I did not mean for you to see that."

"*See* it?" he barked.

A maid appeared at Harry's side, her apron clutched in her hands.

"Harry," Edward said carefully. "Please wait for me in the study. And *close the door.*"

This situation would have to be handled very carefully. Her family was not known for coolness or rationality. Impetuousness flowed in their veins like blood, and she'd clearly gotten her own share of it. But now she'd need to choose her words carefully. "Edward. I'm sorry. Obviously, I acted as . . . I was not—" She was interrupted by the worst possible statement.

"We shall marry immediately," Mr. White said from the floor.

Her brother was already nodding.

Marissa shook her head to counter him. "We most certainly will not."

Glass shifted and clinked as Mr. White moved. "If you'll give me a few moments to . . . arrange myself, Baron York, I will meet you privately in—"

"No!" she protested. "There will be no meeting! I have no intention of marrying Mr. White. None at all."

Her brother turned toward her, his green eyes bruised with hurt and disappointment. "You can't mean you dallied with this man without even a hope of marriage?"

"That's exactly what I mean. And if I'd have considered the idea before, I certainly wouldn't now. Do you see any evidence of gratification on my face? I wouldn't marry that eager hound for anything."

Edward's eyes snapped back toward Mr. White. "Did he force himself on you?"

"No, no. He only failed to meet even the lowest expectations of performance."

"Perfomance?" her brother sputtered. "What could you know of—"

"Here now!" Mr. White said. "I won't tolerate this. We shall be married as soon as we can possibly manage. Baron York, do you have any means of arranging a special license?"

"Oh, for God's sake," Marissa interrupted. "I won't marry him! I can't possibly make it any more clear." Whispers floated in from the hallway on the tail end of her words.

Mr. White, having apparently *rearranged* himself, strode forward to put a hand on her shoulder. "With all due respect, Miss York, you have no choice but to marry me."

"Excuse me?"

"I've taken your virtue. The maids are already talking. You're mine now, darling."

"Yours?" She jerked her shoulder from his grasp and stepped away to glare at him. "I most certainly am not."

Edward cleared his throat. "Let us worry about our own servants, Mr. White."

"Of course. And the talk will be meaningless once the vows are exchanged. Miss York is understandably beset by emotion. Let's discuss this man to man, Baron. She isn't thinking logically."

Marissa drew herself up in outrage. "On the contrary, I am thinking quite logically. It's very clear to me that I'd rather enter a nunnery than spend the rest of my nights suffering your grunting efforts between my legs, Mr. White. Now I'd like to have a private conversation with my brother, if you don't mind."

Her brother choked on horror, but Mr. White's

face went red with a different emotion. "I have had you, and you *will* marry me, young lady."

Too late, she realized what he'd meant earlier when he'd first snuck his hand beneath her skirt. "Finally," he'd breathed. "You'll be mine." She'd thought he meant a more temporary ownership. She should have known better. He'd already proposed twice.

Her brother took a step forward. "White, I need to speak with my sister. Please await me in my study."

Anger creased his flushed forehead. "You can't mean to indulge her. She made her choice when she laid herself down on that couch, sir. I won't let her call off now."

Her vision narrowed until all she could see was Peter White's face. One eye was already swelling. She focused on the undamaged one, wondering how much strength it would take to create a matching set. "You won't *let* me? I've told you twice now that I won't be your wife."

He had the nerve to smile at her. "If you meant that, you should have stopped me. We will be married. You've no choice."

"White," her brother growled, "Marissa is twenty-two and can't be forced to anything."

Mr. White scoffed. "She might already have a belly full of me. And as the head of the household, it's your job to protect her from her own foolishness. When word gets out that—"

Edward took another step, drawing menacingly close to the other man. "How would word get out?"

"There are forty guests in your house right now, Baron. Surely one of them will hear the tale. Your cousin saw it firsthand. You would not want it put about that your sister is a trollop, would you?" Triumph gleamed in his eyes.

"You awful cur," she whispered. "You *planned* this."

Edward's hand shot out and wrapped around Peter White's cravat. "You *did* plan this, didn't you?"

"I mean to give her my *name*. My devotion. There is no harm done here. She should be honored. My grandfather is—"

She'd heard his speech about the glory of his bloodlines before, so she was relieved when Edward cut it off with a blow to Mr. White's jaw. The man stumbled back, clutching his chin with both hands before he fell to his rump.

"Get out of my house," Edward growled.

"You can't be serious!"

"Go!"

White shook his head. "I'm in love with her."

Marissa gasped in offense, but Edward just pointed at the door. "Get out of my home, and if you breathe a word of this to anyone, I will hunt you down and kill you."

Mr. White watched him carefully, clearly considering whether Edward could or would commit murder. He looked doubtful. Marissa was sure she did too. Edward had a wicked temper, but it cooled quickly. He was known as the mature one in the family. Once Mr. White was away, he was probably in little mortal danger. Unless . . .

Edward smiled. "And if I can't find you, I'm quite sure my brother Aidan can. He'll enjoy the hunt, vicious ruffian that he is."

Well, Aidan was another matter entirely. Even Marissa cringed at the thought of him finding out about this. And he would.

Peter White rolled his shoulders and pressed his

fingers gingerly to his jaw. "This is absurd. You're both upset. I'll take my leave for now, but I shall return in a few days' time. I love you, Marissa."

"Oh, I'd wager you love the idea of my five-hundred pounds a year," she snapped. Mr. White ignored her and stalked from the room.

She'd wanted him to go, but now she was alone with her brother. Shame welled to her skin like blood. Her throat tightened. "I'm sorry," she managed to whisper.

"Marissa, what . . . ?" His shoulders slumped. "How could you have done this?"

"I'm sorry! I shouldn't have! I was bored, and I've had too much wine, and I . . . there's no man I've even come close to falling in love with, and I suppose I was . . . curious." That was mostly the truth, anyway, with only a few details left out.

"Ah, 'Rissa," her brother sighed. "You've gone and done it this time."

"I was stupid. I know that. But I swear he wasn't nearly so awful beforehand. I rather liked him until this."

Her brother watched her closely, sadness etched on his face in deep lines.

"What is it?"

"I won't try to make you marry him. He's a cad. But—" He reached for her hand and held it between both of his. "You'll have to marry someone now."

"What?" she yanked her hand away. *"Why?"*

The door suddenly burst open, and her mother stretched her arms wide, filling the room completely, despite her short stature. "What has happened?" she wailed.

Marissa shook her head. "Nothing. Everything's wonderful."

Her brother waved their mother inside and slammed the door. "Everything is not wonderful. Everything is a mess."

In a highly predictable gesture, the dowager baroness pressed her palm over her heart. "What's happened? Is it Aidan? What has happened to my sweet, sweet boy?"

"It's not Aidan. It's Marissa. She is compromised."

The baroness gasped so loudly that the sound echoed through the room.

"Oh, why did you tell her?" Marissa sighed.

Edward was busy leading their mother toward a chair, where she folded into a graceful faint. Another highly predictable gesture.

He stood straight and dusted off his hands as if he'd just completed a task. "She might have grown suspicious when we arranged your hurried wedding completely out of the blue."

"There's no reason for me to marry!"

"Marissa, don't act even more a fool than you already have. It's clear from what I witnessed that you could very well be pregnant. We must find you a husband immediately."

"That's absurd!" But before she'd finished speaking the words, fear rushed over her on a dark wave. She hadn't really thought of that. The mechanics of pregnancy were a vague cloud of rumor and overheard tidbits she'd collected for years. "I thought . . . the first time . . . isn't it impossible?"

"No, it's not. And I rather wish you'd approached me with any questions about marriage and breeding before this happened."

"Oh, no," she groaned.

The line of Edward's mouth turned down. "You will either marry that scoundrel or you'll marry someone else. A wedding will help dispel any rumors, and it will go a long way toward distracting from an early birth. And *apparently* you need some way to occupy your time. Being a wife should take care of your boredom."

"But . . ." Her jaw began to tremble, so she clenched it shut for a count of ten. "But I do not wish to leave here. This is my home."

The anger left his face as if it had been swept away by a hand. "I know. I don't wish you to go either. We shall find someone who will bring you home whenever you wish. Someone biddable."

"Well, who else would marry a ruined woman and accept a bastard?" she whispered. "Someone biddable and . . . henpecked."

"Marissa . . ."

Her mother groaned dramatically, eyelids fluttering. The swoon was about to come to a gasping end.

Panic swarmed through Marissa's chest. She couldn't argue her brother's point. She hadn't meant to bring her family shame. She hadn't meant anything at all by it. But if Peter White spread the tale it would be awkward. And if she was pregnant, there could be no choice. But if he didn't and she wasn't . . .

"Edward, it will take time to find a willing and acceptable match, won't it? Decent men do not hang about at crossroads just waiting for a ruined woman to take them home."

"Ah . . ." he started.

"Harry will never tell a soul. And if there are to be

permanent consequences, we should know within two weeks. Two weeks would be quick enough! If you must orchestrate a betrothal, let us prepare for it and then forget it entirely when I'm proved, er . . . unripened."

A blush flared up his neck. "I . . . is there no one you are fond of? No one who would make an offer?"

"I was rather fond of the gentleman in question before this evening. He's an excellent dancer, and his coat always fits perfectly. But now . . . no. No one."

Her brother muttered something that sounded like, "His *coat*," just as her mother's eyes fluttered open.

"Marissa," she sighed. "How could you? Why would you do something so *awful*?"

Awful. Yes, her mother had that right. "I don't know," she replied honestly. There had been wine and secret kisses, and it had seemed rather exciting when they'd stumbled into this room together. Then it had deteriorated into something more easily described in scientific terms than poetry. "Idiot," she bit out.

"Yes, you are an idiot!" her mother cried.

"I meant Mr. White."

"Mr. White," her mother said. "Hm. He *is* an excellent dancer. And a handsome fellow. He does bring in a fair income. Yes, he'll make a perfectly good husband."

Edward waved her off. "We'll discuss this later, Mother. Right now I have to think. Where is Aidan when I need him? He's supposed to be here, and he probably knows some likely fellows."

"Please don't tell him," Marissa pled. Somehow,

she wasn't the least bit surprised that her words preceded the entrance of a footman by mere seconds.

"Mr. Aidan York has arrived, my lord," the servant said, bowing. "He sends apologies for his tardiness and bids me tell you he'll descend as soon as he's washed and dressed."

"Perfect," Edward murmured. "I won't tell him until White has had time to pack and flee. Otherwise we might have a murder on our hands."

"Murder!" their mother gasped, then slumped back into the chair, presumably unconscious, though not so unconscious that she couldn't eavesdrop, of course.

Marissa glanced around to see if there was a chair close enough for her to faint into as well, but there was only the couch, and she'd had enough of that. There was nothing to be done but take a deep breath and live with the consequences of what she'd done.

A moment later she realized there was one more thing she could do. The wine in her stomach began a war with the anxiety now coursing through her body. Head spinning, Marissa leaned over to peer closely at the gold-hued Oriental rug beneath her feet. And then she was sick all over it.

"Did I thank you yet for the invitation?" Jude Bertrand asked half-jokingly as he followed Aidan York down the curved staircase.

Aidan tossed a glance over his shoulder and said nothing, though he raised an amused eyebrow.

Jude had, in fact, thanked him several times already. For some reason, being on the York estate filled Jude with buoyancy. The house was large and airy, the windows looking out onto wild meadows and swaths of forest. The land enchanted him, and the family . . . well, oddly enough, the family reminded him of his early childhood. Decidedly strange, as his early years had been spent in what had essentially been a French whorehouse.

Chuckling at the odd comparison, Jude ran his hand down the banister, remembering his stay here last year and a certain strawberry-haired hoyden's slide down the wood. She'd thought no one else awake at that early hour, and Jude hadn't disabused her of the notion. He'd simply watched her slide down the banister, and then he'd continued on his way, marveling that no one else seemed able to see the wildness inside her.

He was greatly anticipating seeing her again.

When they reached the first floor, Aidan York nodded to a few of the guests but continued on toward his brother's study. Jude followed. The door was closed when they reached it. Raised voices could be heard vibrating through the wood, but Jude felt no surprise. The York family was surprisingly dramatic for such an established peerage.

Aidan didn't seem surprised either. He simply gave a perfunctory knock and walked into chaos.

The dowager baroness had draped herself across a settee and was weeping loudly into a lace handkerchief. The baron, Aidan's older brother, paced in front of the fireplace, his red face giving him away as the source of the shouting. A cousin was there too. Harry, maybe? He looked decidedly morose.

Jude raised a hand in greeting to the mob.

"Aidan," barked Edward. "Thank God you're here!"

Then his gaze shifted to Jude. "Jude, *you* can't be here. I'm sorry."

"Oh. All right then." He had spun halfway back toward the hall when Aidan's hand stopped him.

"Don't be melodramatic, Edward." His dry voice was a direct contrast to his brother's. "Of course Jude can stay. Now, what seems to be the latest crisis?"

Edward shook his head. "You don't understand. This is serious. And a very private matter."

"Don't tell me you've fallen in love with the upstairs maid?"

The baroness finally roused herself. "Aidan! Don't be disrespectful." She cocked her head toward Jude, and he offered her a small bow while she studied him. "I'm sorry, Mr. Bertrand, but you'll have to . . ." She stopped and frowned. "Then again, perhaps Mr. Bertrand could be of use to us. He does bring a certain . . . perspective."

Jude raised his eyebrows at that, wondering what she could mean.

"Yes!" the cousin exclaimed. "His mother!"

Ah. Jude nodded. His *mother*. Had Edward gotten a mistress pregnant? "If I can assist you in some way, I'd be happy to. And I was raised from the cradle not to tell tales, of course."

But Edward was shaking his head. "The matter is too sensitive." He tossed a glare in his mother's direction. "As you well know."

Aidan shook his head and crossed the room to the brandy decanter. "This is ridiculous. I'd trust Jude with my life. If he can help you, just spit it out, old man." He collapsed into a chair, so Jude wandered toward the sideboard and poured himself a drink as well. He should have excused himself, but he was more than a little curious now.

He supposed Edward's whisper was meant to be discreet, but it easily filled the whole room. "It's about our sister!" he hissed.

Jude froze and spun back to face the York family. "Marissa?" he asked.

All eyes turned toward him.

"Ah . . . I mean Miss York, of course."

When Aidan rose to his feet, the attention in the room shifted to him. "What about Marissa?" His mouth had stiffened to a thin line.

"Now Aidan," his mother said.

"What about Marissa?" Aidan shouted.

Edward took a deep breath and quietly said, "She's been ruined."

Silence fell over the room. Everyone held their breath and watched as the tips of Aidan's ears turned red. Not a good sign.

The baron held up both hands. "The damage is done. We need to find her a husband, and quickly. Perhaps Jude can help—"

"Who was it?" Aidan ground out. "Was she hurt?"

Jude stepped forward, serious now, but Edward was already shaking his head.

"No, she was drunk. And foolish. But not hurt. And the so-called gentleman is gone now."

"Who?" Aidan bellowed.

Edward winced and swallowed hard. "Peter White."

A flurry of muttered threats erupted from Aidan, and then the whole story was told in fits and starts, while Jude listened and thought ugly thoughts about Mr. White. A pretty, arrogant fellow. And apparently a scoundrel. "Cowardly ass," Jude muttered while Edward explained why Marissa could not marry Mr. White.

"But," Edward rushed on, "she must marry somebody. The servants are talking already. And if that fellow has planted his seed . . ."

The baroness's hands fluttered. "This is horrible. Impossible. What if Mr. White insists? It would be his child, after all."

Harry shook his head. "I can feel no sympathy for him there. He had a child by the carriage maker's daughter, and he harbors no tender feelings toward that babe. Cannot even be bothered to set up an income." Harry looked stricken at his own words. "I'm sorry. I should have known he could come to no good. I shouldn't have invited him."

Edward shook his head. "That's not your burden. But now . . . we must all endeavor to find her a decent gentleman."

"Oh, the torment!" the baroness wailed. "Our Marissa must go to someone kind and respectable. An established man who will treat her well and . . . and accept the child as his own."

Aidan threw up his hands. "Well, who the hell would do that?"

They all shook their heads sadly and stared at each other.

Jude waited a moment, poking through the swirl of thoughts inside his head to be sure his first instinct was correct. He wasn't a man given to doubting himself, so it took only a few moments to find peace with his decision. Before chaos could begin to rumble through the room again, Jude stepped forward and inclined his head. "I would."

For a moment, no one reacted. No one even

looked at him. Then Aidan glanced toward him with a frown. "You would what, Jude?"

"I would marry your sister."

That got everyone's attention.

"You?" the baroness snapped.

"Yes, me."

"But you're . . ."

Jude smiled. "A bastard?"

"Well," she answered, "*yes*. Granted, I thought you might offer a perspective or perhaps advice, but . . . a natural-born husband . . ."

"Ah, but I'm the natural son of a duke. The *acknowledged* natural son of a duke. And how else would you land a duke's son in this situation? I don't have a title to protect, so I needn't worry about having an illegitimate heir. And I didn't receive my father's name, so I'm not even concerned about passing that on."

He watched the wheels turning behind the baroness's eyes. "You make an interesting point," she conceded.

Aidan shoved his hands into his pockets and glared. "Why would you want to marry my sister? Do you even know her?"

"Of course I know her. I've been here for, what, four parties now? Then again, I'm not entirely sure she knows me."

Aidan grunted in acknowledgment. They both knew that Jude was not the type to attract notice from gently bred young women. He was large and not elegantly made. His features were neither refined nor comforting. Sheltered young girls edged away from him.

But certain types of women—those who'd been

unhappily married for a dozen years, for example—those women eyed him with avid hunger in their eyes. He looked like a brute, and a brute was just what they wanted.

"So," Aidan continued in a doubtful tone, "you may have sat across from her at dinner on occasion. That still doesn't answer my question. Why would you marry her?"

"I like her."

"Marissa?"

Jude laughed at the doubt in his friend's voice. "Yes, Marissa."

"She hardly seems your type."

Yes, he had a known weakness for rather naughty women. Jude raised an eyebrow. "Apparently she is exactly my type."

Aidan huffed, then rocked back on his heels to stare at the floor.

Actually, Marissa had caught his attention the first time Jude had seen her. There was that brightness in her green eyes. Not merriment, but . . . *transgression*. It had always been disorienting, being surrounded by people who seemed to consider her the last bastion of calm and propriety in the York family. Yes, she was graceful and tall and lovely, but could no one else see the way her eyebrows twitched any time she overheard a double entendre? Did no one notice the way her eyes traveled over men's bodies when she watched them dance?

The girl liked wine and dancing and pretty men. She rode her horse too hard and was constantly slipping free of her shoes to stroll barefoot on the grounds. Wildness lurked just beneath her skin, and Jude could feel it every time he passed too near.

But because Marissa York raised her chin to a haughty angle when she walked, she was seen as proper. Because she did not faint or yell or laugh as loudly as the rest of her family, they considered her staid. In comparison to the other Yorks she might be a paragon of control, but it was the passion she was trying to keep contained that interested Jude.

He glanced up from his thoughts to find the family exchanging meaningful glances. "Shall I leave you to discuss this?" he offered, and Edward slumped with relief.

"Thank you, Jude," he said. "Go have a drink. We need to talk. And I'd caution you to consider this more carefully."

Shrugging, Jude turned and let himself out of the study. He didn't need to consider it further. If he could persuade her to give up her affection for pretty boys, Marissa York would make a fine and naughty wife. But pretty boys congregated in droves at these parties. Jude had set himself up for a serious challenge.

Chapter 2

Marissa waved her hands in helpless frustration as her maid pulled hard on the corset strings. The morning sun mocked her with its cheery brightness as it slanted past the window. Marissa glared at the light, her legs burning with the need to move, to pace, to run to the door and fling it open. "Oh, do hurry," she whispered, clasping her frantic hands together to stop their useless shaking.

The night before, she'd thought she would never sleep. Terror and regret had fought a war for her attention after she'd been sent to her room, and the battle had left her restless. She'd tossed and turned, then paced miles across her chambers, trying to think of a way out of this horrid situation.

No one had come to speak with her, and she'd been too mortified to request an audience. The waiting had been sheer torture.

But in the end, she had slept, and she'd slept too late.

This morning, she found that regret had won the night's battle, and now she felt sick with it.

What had she *done*?

Edward's terse note glared white against the dark wood of the dressing table. The writing was spiked with anger, vastly unlike his normally careful hand.

Marissa was wanted in his study immediately. Her fate awaited her. If only she'd been awake and dressed when the footman had delivered the note, she would be there already.

The maid finally drew a dress over her head, and Marissa breathed a sigh of relief as she stared down at the somber shade of pale gray. Perhaps her brother was feeling regret too. Perhaps he'd changed his mind.

My God, how stupid she'd been. How foolish and reckless. It must have been the wine. Yes, the wine. And the fine cut of Peter White's new coat. And as he'd danced, his trousers had tightened over his thighs, revealing every line of their . . . *elegance.*

Men's legs were just so lovely. Slim and strong and exposed in a way that ladies' legs never were. How could they expect that girls should not be affected by the sight? Gentlemen obviously intended to be admired, the way they flashed their thighs about, hardly covered at all in the tight cloth of their trousers.

What hypocrites they were, showing off their bodies and expecting her not to look. Or touch.

Still, she shouldn't have given in to temptation, for it hadn't been worth it. Not as it had been worth it before. Before, there had been much more than fumbling and regret. There had been . . .

Marissa sighed even more deeply, certain she'd never experience such deliciousness again.

"There you are, miss," the maid said. She was new,

and betrayed her nervousness by giving one last tweak to the sleeve of the dress.

Marissa nodded. She liked this new girl, but if her old maid hadn't run off two weeks before, Marissa would have someone to talk to. As it was, she felt like an island.

Though Marissa was free to descend to the study, she stared at the door. Aidan must know by now. He hadn't come to her room last night, which likely meant he was too furious to talk. Edward never frightened her, but Aidan . . . he was a different sort of man these days, and she worried that she would burst into tears the moment he turned his disappointed glare on her.

He'd once been joyful and charming, but then he'd suffered his own private scandal. The girl he'd loved and meant to marry had died. His anger and guilt over the wretched circumstances had changed him. Now her handsome brother was as cold as he'd once been charming. Marissa did not want to face him.

But it was time to pay the piper, so she gave herself a somber nod and set off for the study.

She expected to find Edward there, of course. And she feared she'd find Aidan as well. But she did not expect a whole room full of gentlemen, all looking toward her as she stood frozen in the doorway.

To be fair, there were only four of them, her brothers and her cousin and another man who looked vaguely familiar. She had the brief impression that perhaps he was a groundskeeper, but she could not puzzle that out now, for Edward was walking toward her with a grim set to his mouth.

Her eyes rolled with a touch of panic, and she

caught sight of her mother in a corner chair, but her mother would offer no refuge. Her eyes were closed, and she'd pressed a cold compress to her head.

Marissa would face the men of her family alone.

"Marissa." Edward kissed her cheek and took her hands as if she were made of the thinnest glass. "Are you well?"

"Yes, quite."

"You're sure? You do not feel . . . injured?"

"Not at all." She pushed up on her toes to whisper in his ear. "Is Aidan very angry with me?"

"I believe he's angrier with that scoundrel White."

She snuck a peek over his shoulder to find Aidan staring out the window, his jaw clenched so hard that the muscle jumped in a secret rhythm. "He won't even look at me. Edward, I'm so sorry. Have you . . . surely you have reconsidered your proposal? I'm certain there's no reason to worry."

"On the contrary, I have found a likely husband for you."

"Pardon?" She stepped back in shock, her heels crossing the threshold so that she stood half in the hallway, as if stepping the last six inches into the study would be an acceptance of this mad plan. "Where could you possibly have found a man who'd marry me?"

"Right here, as it turns out."

"Here? In the district?"

"Here, in our house."

"But who?"

He gestured toward the room. "Mr. Jude Bertrand."

"Mr. Bertrand?" she repeated too loudly. Panic was beginning to set in. Edward hadn't changed his mind at all. He was moving matters forward at a dizzying pace. "Who is Mr. Bertrand?"

A figure moved from Aidan's side. It was that groundskeeper fellow, stepping toward her, his wide mouth crooked in a half smile as he approached. He stopped a few paces away and made a passably elegant bow. "I am Jude Bertrand," he said, turning the surname into something French and exotic.

"Should you not present him?" she snapped at her brother, meaning to insult the presumptuousness of this man who looked like a servant dressed in gentleman's clothes.

"Miss York, my apologies," the man said, rising now to meet her gaze. "But we have already been introduced. Twice."

"Oh." She pressed her hand to her chest, briefly mortified by her own rudeness. "I apologize, Mr. Bertrand. I must have . . ." The words trailed off as she realized how meaningless all these pleasantries were. She slid her eyes toward Edward, trying to convey her alarm.

This man was not suitable. Not at all. He was big and rough-looking, built for mucking out stables or loading freight onto a ship. He was not a gentleman. Not by far.

"I . . ." She gave up subtlety and raised her eyebrows at her brother.

He smiled. "Marissa, Mr. Bertrand is a good friend of Aidan's, and he has generously offered to . . . be your escort for the next few weeks. Would you allow him to accompany you to the breakfast room this morning?"

Had she driven her brother to madness? Marissa

gave her head a frantic shake. "I would rather a moment to speak with you in private!"

Mr. Bertrand offered another bow. "Of course, Miss York. I'll excuse myself." Again, it was a perfectly elegant bow, but each time he rose, he seemed to grow bigger. He was taller than either of her brothers, and his shoulders looked to fill the whole doorway when she stepped aside to let him pass. Not a groundskeeper then, but a blacksmith. Yes, she could picture him perfectly in a leather apron, hand grasping a great hammer.

Utter madness.

Cousin Harry rose, tortured regret twisting his mouth. "I can't help but feel responsible. Peter White was my friend, after all. I apologize to all of you for inviting him."

"Nonsense," Edward said. "Aidan and I knew him as well. It's no more your responsibility than ours. Please don't give it another thought."

Harry didn't look convinced. "I wish it were as simple as making him step forward as a gentleman. I'd be gratified by the opportunity to persuade him."

Marissa closed her eyes to try to find some calm, but when she opened them, she found that Aidan had crossed the room and now stood before her. She'd been wrong to think he would wound her with a glare. He looked at her with disappointed pity in his eyes.

Tears gathered in her throat like a tightening fist. "I'm sorry," she whispered. "But can we not reconsider this plan?"

Edward shook his head. "It is enough of a risk to wait the month out. I have given you that, 'Rissa. It's more than our father would have done."

"But that man . . . he is entirely inappropriate. I would not even trust him to see me across the street, much less give the rest of my life to him."

Aidan finally spoke. "Jude Bertrand is a gentleman and a good friend. I would not have let him offer otherwise."

"He looks as if he were dragged from the smithy's hearth!"

"Marissa," Aidan bit out, and she finally saw the scorn she'd feared to find in his eyes. "You sound like a silly, spoiled chit. A decent man has offered to help solve a problem that your thoughtlessness created. Perhaps instead of acting like a rude child, you could treat him with a bit of graciousness."

Anger rose up to cover her hurt. "I don't even know him!"

Aidan leaned toward her and pointed a finger at her chest. "Here is what you need to know: He's smart. He's decent. I've never seen him mistreat a woman. And he is willing to marry you and accept another man's babe as his own firstborn child without a moment's hesitation."

"He . . ." She threw up her hands in frustration. "And what kind of man would *do* that? He must be a grasping, prideless fool who wants nothing more than to elevate himself with a convenient marriage!"

Edward crossed his arms. "Marissa Anne York, you forget yourself. Need I explain to you the kind of vile words others would use about you if the truth gets out? Your disdain is sadly misplaced."

Her anger left her as suddenly as it had appeared to prop her up, and she felt the full force of her brothers' scorn. Her shoulders slumped, and she pressed a hand to her forehead. "I'm sorry. I'm sure he is a fine man, it's just that . . ."

"As these things seem so important to you," Aidan interrupted, "understand that Jude Bertrand is the acknowledged son of the Duke of Winthrop. Jude needs no elevation, Marissa. Not from the ruined sister of a baron, certainly."

Marissa closed her mouth so quickly that her teeth clicked.

Aidan's own teeth looked ready to crack under the pressure of his clenched jaw. He shook his head in weary disgust. "You are no longer a child. You've made sure of that. You will marry Jude or you'll marry Peter White, but Mr. White will not make a very good husband with his throat cut out, I'm afraid."

"Aidan," she whispered, starting to reach for his arm, but he stepped away from her. "It's not fair. You'd never be forced to marry a girl who—" Horrified with what she'd been about to say, Marissa cut off her own words. "I'm sorry."

For a moment, his eyes went dark with pain, but he gentled his expression with a smile. "Life is unfair, little sister, but Jude is a good man. I wouldn't have it otherwise."

She nodded, knowing that was true. He finally reached for her, pulling her close for a tight hug before he kissed her cheek and let her go. Marissa wanted to cling to him, but she could see he was already far away, his eyes looking into the past. "If you'll excuse me . . ."

He would take one of his long rides now, and be gone for hours. Her friends all thought his brooding irresistibly romantic, but Marissa couldn't share their admiration for his sorrow.

She stared at the closed door of the study for a long moment.

"I agree with Marissa," her mother said in a wobbling voice. "That Mr. Bertrand has a frightening appearance, and he moves like a thief. I still don't see why she can't simply marry Mr. White. He's lovely and handsome, and his sister is married to George Brashears. Do you remember Mr.—"

"She can't marry him," Edward cut in on a sharp note, "because he deceived her into giving up her virtue in a deliberate attempt to force her into marriage. Does that seem lovely to you?"

"Well . . . if he claims to be in love with her . . ."

Both Edward and Marissa glared furiously at her, and their mother finally lay back in the chair with a martyrlike sigh. "I suppose you must be right, Baron. Oh, this is all so difficult to accept! My poor family!" And she was gone into one of her swoons again.

Marissa turned back to Edward. "The acknowledged son of a duke. He's natural born then?"

"Yes."

She started to raise both hands to plead with him, then thought of what Aidan had said. She lowered her hands. "I have never even spoken with him, Edward."

"He's visited us four times, but if he doesn't make a pretty turn in the ballroom, I suppose you do not see him."

The awfulness of that truth swept over her like an icy breeze. Gooseflesh sprang up on her skin. And yet, what could she say? She liked to dance with handsome gentlemen. She enjoyed their flirtatious attention and the excitement of stolen kisses. And when there was no music or dancing to be had, she preferred that they disappear into their smoky male habitats and leave her alone with her friends.

It was no different for the men, so far as she could tell.

"I'm sure he is perfectly nice—"

"You'll find out soon enough. Jude will spend time with you this week. Enough time that no one will talk if a betrothal is announced a fortnight from now."

Protest bubbled inside her. She wanted to scream a denial. Fall to her knees and beg. Shout at the world to leave her be.

But her brothers were right. She was not a child anymore, not by even the most liberal definition. So Marissa folded her hands together and nodded. There would be time for another solution, if one was needed at all. This was not the end. Jude Bertrand was not her husband.

Yet.

Chapter 3

Mr. Bertrand stood at the end of the hall, hands clasped behind his back as he stared out a narrow window. Sunlight should have streamed through the glass, but the wide span of his back blocked every single ray. If he did dance, Marissa should not like to be the girl whose slipper he trod upon.

Yet as rough a figure as he cut, she could see no other reason to believe that Jude Bertrand wasn't a gentleman. It may have taken yards of fabric to cover those shoulders, but the lines of the coat were impeccable. His hair might look a bit coarse, but it was trimmed straight and neat at his neck.

He shifted, and his hair glowed in the sun, revealing that the dark shade was not true brown but auburn, and Marissa found herself cringing to think that it must have been quite red in his youth. What a little ruffian he would have looked. Red-headed and coarse-featured. What a little ruffian his *children* would be. And with her own red hair, there would be no escape from it.

She'd meant to approach him with determination, but her feet slowed at that thought.

Perhaps Mr. Peter White was not such an awful choice, after all. He was witty, and he kept a merry crowd of friends.

She stopped, intent on escaping without notice, but Mr. Bertrand cocked his head and turned toward her.

"Miss York," he said solemnly.

When their eyes met, she blushed, thinking of what he must know about her. "Mr. Bertrand," she murmured.

He smiled, and his smile, at least, was pleasant, despite the vulgar width of his mouth. "Have you decided if I may escort you to the breakfast room?"

The question recalled her earlier rudeness. *If* I may escort you. But in truth, he wasn't asking about breakfast. He was asking if she might marry him at the end of the month. If he could pretend to be her suitor. Because she'd lost her virginity the night before on the couch of the sewing room. Her cheeks burned with heat. "Of course, Mr. Bertrand. I'd be honored."

He nodded, but the tilt of his mouth made clear that he found her answer amusing.

"This is overwhelming," she explained. True enough, but she knew that much of her discomfort was because she could not picture marrying a man like him. She liked handsome, elegant, finely made men. Jude Bertrand was . . .

Marissa could not bring herself to call him ugly, not when he was treating her so fairly. But his face was wide and looked hewn from stone, with an old break in his nose as if the sculptor's chisel had slipped. His cheekbones were high and broad, and the wicked angle of his eyebrows added menace to his masculine features. That and his unrelenting largeness . . .

When he walked toward her, Marissa snuck a peek at his thighs. The muscles strained at his trousers in a vulgar display. He was made for the battlefield or the shipyard, not the ballroom.

Still, when he offered his arm, she took it, aware of a hint of spice in his scent.

His arm was too solid beneath her hand. More like the wood of a banister than the flesh of a man. She supposed that might be comforting if she knew him, if he were charged with the duty of caring for and protecting her. But he was a stranger, so she felt nothing more than a vague anxiety and kept her fingers light against his sleeve.

"I apologize," she murmured as he led her through the doors of the breakfast room. "I'm sorry I did not know you earlier."

"You needn't apologize. I didn't expect I'd drawn your notice."

Marissa glanced around the room, noting that one guest was leaving, and only one other, her elderly Great Aunt Ophelia, remained. Marissa leaned a little closer to Mr. Bertrand. "I don't understand why you're doing this."

"Are you not hungry?"

"I mean this," she protested, waving an impatient hand. She lowered her voice. "Why did you volunteer to court me?"

He stopped their slow progress toward the buffet and angled his body toward her. "Because I like you."

"You just said yourself that you don't even know me!"

"No, Miss York. I said you didn't know me. But I have liked you from the moment we met."

Shocked, Marissa drew back so that she could more easily see his expression. His mouth offered her that crooked smile again, as if he knew some secret about her. And so he did. "You have never even asked me to dance."

"Would you have said yes?"

No. She knew she would have found an excuse not to dance with him, and a sharp stab of guilt left her angry. "Are you saying you were too cowardly to ask, for fear I might say no?"

"On the contrary. I was brave enough not to interfere with your clear affection for graceful young boys."

"My . . ." Marissa stared at him, her lips parted in shock. Surely he couldn't mean that he'd noticed her secret. No, he only meant that she liked to dance with elegant gentlemen.

Just as she snapped her mouth closed, Mr. Bertrand winked and tilted his head toward the sideboard. "Shall we break our fast, Miss York?"

Relieved to have time to puzzle out this strange conversation, she nodded. But her relief faded a bit when he picked up a plate and gestured her ahead of him.

He was on his best behavior, it seemed, and meant to serve her breakfast. A lovely effort, except that gentlemen were notoriously stingy when it came to filling her plate. She was a lady. Her appetite was meant to be dainty.

It wasn't.

But she took a deep breath and pasted on a smile because ladies did not snatch plates from gentlemen's hands in order to get another ration of bacon. She could always sneak back for more when he went riding with the other men.

He stood still next to her, both hands holding the plate at waist level. She glanced toward the kipper fork.

"Please," he murmured, nodding his head toward the dish. "I wouldn't presume to know your tastes just yet. Allow me to play footman." He held the plate out to clarify.

Marissa's heart beat fast in surprise as she carefully served herself one kipper and then a tiny spoonful of stewed apples. When she reached the bacon, she slid two slices onto the plate, then darted a look at him.

Mr. Bertrand raised an eyebrow, offering that same secret smile. As if he knew her.

Or perhaps that was just the way a smile looked on a mouth so unfortunately wide.

Marissa bit her lip and added three more slices, staring at the blunt thickness of his thumb as she did so. When she looked up again, his smile was wider.

What an odd man. She served herself more generously with the remaining dishes.

He followed her to the table, delivering her plate with a little bow before he filled his own.

When a footman approached with tea, Mr. Bertrand requested coffee instead. "Would you prefer coffee, Miss York?"

Would she? She started to say no, but paused when her tongue touched the roof of her mouth.

Half the male visitors preferred coffee, but all the ladies drank tea. She'd tried a sip of coffee once, and it had been awful. Bitter and harsh. She hadn't liked it . . . and yet she wanted it again, if only to be daring.

Marissa glanced to her steaming cup of respectable tea and shook her head. "No, thank you."

Disconcerted by his smile, Marissa took a bite to buy herself a moment of quiet. She was supposed to be getting to know this man, yet every moment with him left her more confused.

She did not want to like him. He was taking advantage of an awful situation. He was unattractive and strange. She would not like him just because he offered her an extra portion of bacon and a sip of a daring drink.

Her aunt excused herself before Marissa was halfway through her plate. "Have a lovely morning, Aunt Ophelia," Marissa called out loudly. The half-deaf woman waved an irritated hand.

They were alone.

Marissa decided to be up-front, because she was simply no good at prevarication. "Mr. Bertrand, this is obviously a delicate matter. I find it difficult to address, and yet I have no choice, due to my own . . . poor choices."

His voice remained as calm as if they were speaking of the weather. "I assure you that you may speak freely. I'm quite aware of the circumstances and am entirely unfazed by them."

"But . . . I don't understand you. How can that be?"

"Miss York, your brother may have told you that my father is the Duke of Winthrop? As lofty as my father's title is, my mother is not the most respectable of women."

"Well, I assumed . . ."

"She is a paid companion."

"To whom?"

"To whichever gentleman she deigns to love at the moment."

"Oh!" she yelped. "I thought . . . oh, I see."

"She loved my father for a good many years, but he was not her only gentleman admirer, and she was not his wife. So when I tell you that you may speak freely with me, I am not being polite. You were with a man last night, and he is even less appealing a suitor than I, and so here we are."

You were with a man. . . . Her heart beat so hard that he must be able to see her pulse in her throat. He could undoubtedly see the scarlet blush climbing her cheeks. There was no hiding behind euphemisms. He knew that she lain down and raised her skirts and allowed Peter White to . . . do that. "I'd had too much wine."

"As is often the case in these situations."

"Mr. Bertrand," she snapped, "I am trying to discover your motives."

"I've already confessed my motives. I like you, Miss York. Is that not enough of a reason?"

"No! It makes no sense. You know nothing of me but this awful thing I've done. What could you possibly like so much that you would be willing to marry me?"

He finished his coffee, watching her over the rim of his cup as he swallowed.

"Well?" she demanded.

Mr. Bertrand set the cup down, the proportions

of it ridiculously small in his wide fingers. He politely raised his napkin to his mouth, the white linen calling attention to his tanned skin. No wonder she'd thought him a groundskeeper. It was likely he was related to one or two.

But regardless of his base beginnings, there was nothing subservient in his eyes as he leaned toward her. His eyes radiated all the confidence of a duke as he met her gaze.

"I like you, Miss York, because you are wicked, and there can be no finer a blessing for a man than a good and wicked wife. Wouldn't you agree?"

His words were so shocking that Marissa could not comprehend them for a moment. Wicked? He'd called her wicked? Blood rushed in her ears as the offense sunk in.

"How dare you? You are absolutely—"

He pushed back his chair, interrupting her tirade. "I'm sure you are correct. No need to continue. Consider me chastened. Now if you'll excuse me, I'm dreadfully late for the hunt." He bowed as if he weren't being rude, and murmured, "Miss York," as though he had a right to address her with such warmth in his voice.

Marissa gawked at his wide back before it disappeared through the door. For a long moment, she just sat there, stunned, but nothing could keep her still for long. Marissa clenched her jaw and stood to serve herself a second helping of every dish.

She'd been wrong about him being a gentleman. Very wrong indeed. And if he thought she would tolerate him even an instant longer than she had to, Jude Bertrand wasn't as wily as he seemed.

Chapter 4

Jude pulled on his finest evening coat, ran a hand through his hair, and met his own happy eyes in the mirror. Unfortunate face or not, he'd managed to get under Marissa York's skin this morning. He wagered that no one had ever called her wicked before, and she would deny the label to her last breath. But the truth always proved more tenacious than a lie. His words would be hooked in her thoughts precisely because she suspected she truly was wicked.

Yes, he was far from pretty, but he had no doubt that Marissa had been thinking of him all day. She'd probably rehearsed an outraged speech she meant to deliver as soon as she got him alone. He'd be happy to oblige by finding them some privacy. After all, he thought her outrage a lovely thing.

A knock sounded abruptly on the door of his chambers. "Yes?"

Aidan York opened the door and gave him a once-over. "I can't believe you're going to be my brother," he growled.

"Don't worry. I'll put in a good word for your

import business with my father, if that's what you're after."

Aidan snorted, but then he frowned at the ceiling. "Actually, since you brought it up . . ."

Jude clapped him on the shoulder and turned him toward the hallway. "Best get your sister to the altar before we talk cozy alliances. I believe she finds this an imperfect match."

"Yes. That could be a problem."

"I've no doubt Marissa prefers charming boys, but there's no changing that. My job is to convince her that she might be looking for something entirely different in a man."

"I see." Aidan tossed him a warning look. "You know she plans to call off if there is no child and no scandal."

"I don't mean to fix my place by guaranteeing one or the other, if that's what you mean."

"Good. Unwise as she may have been, she's a good girl, and I won't see her suffer."

Jude arched an eyebrow at the implication that marrying him would be suffering, but he held his tongue. He also refrained from mentioning that he suspected Marissa was anything but a good girl. Older brothers weren't inclined to welcome that sort of speculation, and apparently even less inclined to notice bad behavior.

"She complained to Edward about you again, you know. Said you were unacceptable."

"The story of my mother, I'm sure."

"You told her the truth?"

"I did."

Aidan paused at the top of the staircase, frowning

down at his shoes. "Will she visit your mother at Christmas, do you suppose?"

Jude thought of Marissa sitting in his mother's parlor, taking tea with the beautiful, improper women who always gathered there. She would love it, and so would Jude. "I would not do anything to offend her," he answered carefully.

"See that you do not. But . . . if you do go, might I tag along? That woman your mother calls Kitten . . ."

Jude was halfway down the stairs and still laughing when he caught sight of a new guest. His laugh ended on a low groan. "What the hell is Patience Wellingsly doing here?"

Aidan glanced toward the woman below, and his face hardened. "Christ."

Jude raised an eyebrow. "I thought you found her amusing."

"I did, yes."

Jude had no problem reading between the lines of those three words. Aidan was notoriously popular with the ladies. And he was also notoriously averse to any relationship that lasted longer than a week's time. Upon spying Patience, Jude had assumed she would be a problem for himself, as she'd been hinting at an affair for months now. But it seemed she'd prove more of a problem for Aidan.

"So . . ." Jude ventured.

"I presumed a friendship at the end of the Season would prove conveniently limited. I see I was wrong."

The woman, forty years old and still stunningly beautiful, glanced up then, and her renowned blue eyes widened as they touched first on Jude and then on Aidan. Her smile welcomed them both, and though her face bespoke her intelligence and her warmth, her eyes warned of tenaciousness. When Patience wanted something, she usually got it. Jude had sidestepped that trap, but Aidan apparently hadn't.

"How long will she be here?" Jude murmured.

Aidan shook his head. "I didn't know my mother had invited her. She'll stay the week, I would imagine."

"Well, I'd appreciate if you'd keep her busy. Don't want her interfering with my courtship."

"Sod off," Aidan answered, though his lips barely moved. They reached the last step, and Patience stepped forward. "Mr. York, what a pleasure to see you again. And dear Mr. Bertrand, how have you been?"

Jude's irritation toward her softened. He hadn't minded her pursuit this summer. She was amusing and interesting. But she was known to fall madly in love at the drop of a hat. Even her husband had joked about it when he was alive. Aidan, equally well known for loving no one, had been foolish to get involved.

Jude bowed over her hand, offered an honest compliment on her beauty, and quickly excused himself. He felt the red-hot burn of Aidan's glare burrowing through his shoulder blades as he walked away, and Jude stretched his shoulders back with a smile. He was under no obligation to help his fool of a friend. He had wooing to do.

Unfortunately, Marissa had not been standing at the bottom of the staircase, arms crossed and foot tapping out her impatience. Was she actively ignoring him? Only one way to find out.

Jude made his way first to the drawing room and then to the music room. Dark notes greeted him as he drew close to the threshold, and he was hardly surprised to see Marissa at the piano, coaxing out the angry tune. When she looked up to see him smiling, her fingers banged harder.

"Marissa!" Lady York screeched. The music stopped, and the last notes rang through the room. Lady York cleared her throat and tempered her volume. "Do play something a bit gentler, dear."

The other guests shifted, some hiding smiles.

"I don't feel gentle tonight, Mother. Perhaps you would care to play?"

"Oh, I couldn't!" Lady York trilled, already pushing forward in her seat. "I haven't . . . well, all right. If you insist. Mr. Bertrand, would you accompany me? You have such a lovely deep speaking voice."

His chin jerked up in shock. "Er, I must excuse myself, madam. I've been told my singing voice evokes thoughts of dying wolves. But please allow me to escort you to the piano."

He delivered her safely to her seat, and she protested that if he didn't sing, she would have to sing herself. After a bit of coaxing, she acquiesced with a giggle of delight. Even the slightest acquaintance could see that Lady York loved performance above all else, and she launched happily into a romantic song about a knight and his fair maiden.

Jude's fair maiden glared from the settee as he walked toward her.

"Miss York," he said quietly.

She did not offer her hand.

"You look beautiful this evening." She did. The faint red of her hair glinted in the candlelight. He wanted to lean down and press a kiss to the top of her head, but her glare warned that she might box his ears if he did. And the other guests might find it shocking as well.

"You called me wicked," she hissed.

Jude grinned. Oh, yes. She'd been stewing all day. "May I?" He took a seat before she could say no, and Marissa sat straighter so that her shoulders would be an inch farther away.

"Your dress is the exact color of a lake on a cloudless day. Stunning."

"Sir, you cannot insult me and then carry on as if we are to be friends."

"Did I insult you?"

"Obviously."

"I did not intend to. I find wickedness to be a personal grace. Naughtiness is even better." He leaned closer, and she could not inch away without drawing attention. "Wouldn't you agree, Miss York?"

She stood so quickly that the breeze she created raised his hair. He stood with a bit less haste. "Shall we stroll about the garden? It's an uncommonly warm evening."

"Dinner will be served soon."

"Then I promise not to stroll you all the way to London."

She was breathing fast, nearly panting with anger, and Jude cast an admiring eye at the state of her neckline. Modest enough, but straining to contain her emotions.

"I believe," he said so low that she angled her head to hear him better, "that we have important matters to discuss. In private." He offered his arm, and Marissa cast a quick look about the room before she took it.

"A few minutes. Nothing more."

A young buck watched with a patently confused frown as Jude led Marissa out of the room. Jude smiled easily back.

When they stepped from the hallway through the patio doors, Marissa took a deep breath and let go of his arm. "You are insufferable," she growled. "To ask if I am wicked. As if I were a naughty child."

"Oh, Miss York. I assure you I meant nothing of the sort."

"What did you mean, then?"

Jude clasped his hands safely behind his back so he would not be tempted to find out just how naughty she was. "How many men have you kissed?"

She drew breath for at least three seconds, the air wheezing inside her tight throat. "Mr. Bertrand!" she finally managed on a strangled gasp.

"More than a few, I'd wager. As I have kissed more than a few women. Mouths are enticing things, are they not?"

She shook her head hard, just once, as if she needed to clear a thought. "I will not have this conversation with you. I am a lady, sir."

"Yes, you are," he murmured, watching her chest rise and fall in the dark light of dusk. "And unlike other gentlemen you may know, I would not dream to tell you that ladies do not like to kiss. Or do not like to think of men. Or cannot be tempted by a pretty turn of leg."

Her breathing slowed. She stood quiet, still as a statue in the deepening night. "I . . . is this what you meant to speak of? This is ridiculous."

"No, actually. I meant to find a moment of privacy so that you could say all those things to me that are swirling inside your head. You're angry?"

"I . . . yes. No. I am simply . . ." She took another deep breath, and set her shoulders back. "Mr. Bertrand—"

"Jude, please."

A few seconds ticked by before she relented. "Jude. You must see that we are incompatible."

"I do not."

"But you are older than I and—"

"I am thirty years old. Your friend Mr. White is twenty-seven, I believe."

"Oh. Mr. White. Yes. Well, I suppose you seem much older than he."

"Indeed I do."

"And you are so very different. And while I truly appreciate you stepping forward to assist me, I wish to explain my plans."

"Your plans?"

"Yes." Nodding, she folded her hands together and began to pace a short path across the stones and back. "I do not expect there to be a scandal. And if there is not a scandal, then there is no reason to proceed with this charade."

"But there may very well be a scandal. Or a babe, at least."

Her body jerked to a stop, and her hand opened against her stomach. "No. I'm sure there's not."

"You've bled?"

"My God, how can you speak of such things?"

"I've spent a great deal of time with women who concern themselves with the subject."

"Well, I do not normally concern myself with such topics and do not wish to speak of it. Not with you."

"I understand. But you may always speak openly with me. If you have any questions, anything that you've wondered about, do not hesitate to ask. You're an intelligent woman, Miss York. You must be eaten up with curiosity."

"About what?"

"About men and wickedness."

"No!" she gasped. "No, I am not! And regardless, I have no intention of marrying you, so it would be entirely inappropriate."

Jude stepped closer, arms burning with the impulse to touch her. He fisted his hands tighter. "How about we strike a deal? I will step aside with grace and goodwill if your wishes prove true. Despite my heartbreak, I will smile and kiss your hand and bid you farewell. But in the meantime, we will be betrothed. Truly."

"But . . . but I don't even like you."

"Truly, Miss York, can you not at least pretend I might have tender feelings?"

"I'm sorry! I'm only being honest. And what do you mean, 'pretend'?"

"Pretend. That you like me. That you trust me. Pretend that you may speak your most intimate thoughts. 'Tis all I ask."

Head cocked, she stared at him with a frown. "Have you no pride?"

"Ha. On the contrary. I have far too much. Why, look at me. Who am I to presume to court you? A big, ugly bastard son of a French courtesan? How could I possibly win your heart?"

Though he grinned to soften his words, Marissa looked more upset than ever. She didn't seem to realize that he'd drawn close enough to see her expression clearly, despite the dark.

"Do not look so sad for me, Miss York."

"I don't think you're ugly."

"Yes, you do."

When she shook her head, he finally let his hands free and raised one arm toward her. He slid the edge of one finger along her jaw, paying close attention to the detail of her skin. Soft and fine and warm against his, and the hitch in her breath added weight to his blood so that each beat dragged through his heart. "You are too beautiful for me," he whispered.

She started to shake her head, then froze when his thumb brushed her mouth.

Jude rested the pad of his thumb on her bottom lip, memorizing the feel of her breath rushing over him. "You are. People will talk when they see us together."

"Jude—"

"They will whisper and frown, and you will blush with mortification. But I will not mind, Miss York. Do you understand?"

"No," she breathed.

His thumb must have inched forward of its own accord. Her top lip brushed it when she spoke. Her breath came faster. Jude stared at her mouth with the fascination of a hungry predator. "I am not a boy. I have not been a boy for a very long time. And I was never pretty, so there is no point in wishing it so. But there are great advantages to loving a man. You will decide for yourself which you prefer. Boy . . . ?"

A tiny shift of his thumb and it was resting at the seam of her mouth.

"Or man?"

When her lips parted, he felt a torturous hint of heat and moisture and promise. He dragged his thumb gently across her mouth until he reached her cheek.

Her breath came faster. She leaned toward him. Jude smiled. "Now shall I escort you to dinner?"

"Pardon?" The word was all gentleness and night. Her eyelids dipped in a sleepy blink as he touched the sensitive skin beneath her ear.

"It's time for dinner, *mon coeur*."

"Is it?"

When he dropped his hand, Marissa frowned and stepped away, as if recalling that she did not like him.

"Come, we must put on a show."

She hesitated for only a moment, her eyes sweeping up and down his body for one last evaluation. Then she laid her hand on his and let him take her to dinner. This time, her fingers rested more easily against him, and Jude walked into the dining room with a smile that set that young buck's teeth on edge.

The boy would probably ask Marissa to dance at least twice tonight, and Jude would watch happily from the side. He did not mind Marissa entertaining herself, so long as her evening ended with him.

Chapter 5

The music room had been cleared for dancing, as the ballroom was too large for so few people. Marissa's mother perched impatiently in a chair near the piano, waiting for the gentlemen to wander in. The musician at the piano played a happy tune, but Marissa watched her mother frown. Lady York did not approve of leaving the men in the dining room with their port. She felt their absence postponed the merrymaking, and she went to much trouble to keep the house lively in the evenings.

Lady York took pride in having the merriest house party in the country, and it went on for nearly a week instead of the traditional three days. The York estate was well known for hosting country dancing and traveling plays during the hunt. She hired musicians every night, and organized card games and charades if there would be no dancing. But there would be dancing tonight.

The music room was large enough to accommodate quite a few couples, and the fiddler was ready, but they were missing twenty or so gentlemen.

Finally the low notes of male conversation rumbled into the room, and the first few men stepped in.

Jude was not among them. Marissa craned her neck, but did not see him in the hallway either. She had no idea why she was looking for him. He'd been seated across from her at dinner, after all, so she'd gotten her fill of looking. Still, conversation had been impossible, and Marissa had found herself wondering what he'd said to the lady on his right that had made her laugh so. And why had the woman on his left stared at him with such bright eyes and touched his sleeve every few minutes to draw his attention?

It made no sense. He wasn't handsome or elegant. He didn't offer a title. Then again, he *was* interesting. Intriguing, even.

For instance, what had he meant about being a *man*? Peter White was hardly a boy at twenty-seven.

"Miss York," a voice said from close by, making Marissa jump as she twisted in her seat.

A gentleman stood there, but he wasn't the one she'd been watching for. "Mr. Dunwoody," she said, offering a wan smile. Mr. Dunwoody had been high on her list of potential lovers earlier in the week. Alas, White had been less polite and more persistent.

"Miss York, may I sit with you?"

"Yes, of course. How was your hunt this morning?"

"A bit slow, I'm afraid." He launched into a description of the disappointing ride. Marissa nodded politely and shifted her feet. Unlike her mother, she preferred that the men linger over their port with a bit more tenacity. If they spent a full hour discussing their unfortunate male topics amongst themselves, perhaps they'd have exhausted the tales by the time they joined the women.

"But," he finished his story with a deep breath, "I wished to inquire if all was well with you?"

The muscles of her neck went stiff. "Yes, of course. Why wouldn't they be?"

"You seem . . . not yourself today."

"Mr. Dunwoody," she said with a brighter smile. "I hope you are not telling me I look unwell."

"No! No, of course not, Miss York. You are radiant as ever. Your eyes are the loveliest shade of green, and your hair . . . an indescribably delicate red."

His cheeks went pink as he spoke, and Marissa couldn't help but notice the sculpted bow of his mouth. Such fine lips he had. A bit narrow, but perfectly proportioned to his slim face. She had tried to tempt him to kiss her, but he had grown flustered and nervous.

She smiled more widely. "I hope you will still beg a dance tonight."

"I will! Absolutely, I will. In fact, might I commit you to the first dance?" He raised his hand, drawing her attention to his long fingers. Her waist tingled at the thought of his hand touching her there.

"That would be lovely, sir."

He smiled in answer, but it faded quickly. "Um. I inquired after your well-being because I had heard that you and Mr. White argued last night."

Her skin ceased to tingle and turned to ice instead. This might be it. This might be the moment when she realized that she had no choice but to marry Jude Bertrand.

Dunwoody cleared his throat. "I can't help but notice that he has since departed. I hope that whatever happened, your feelings weren't injured. He seems a nice enough fellow, but perhaps overconfident."

"Oh . . ." He looked sincere, not curious or sneaky. He might truly believe there'd been only an argument. So Marissa nodded. "We argued, yes. And in my anger, I asked him to leave. I regret that now, of course. It was impetuous."

"I'm sure you had your reasons, Miss York. I've never known you to be rash."

Marissa forced a smile. Mr. Dunwoody was the type of man she would rather marry. Quiet, gentle, and handsome . . . and apparently unaware of her flaws. But perhaps not biddable enough to accept another man's child? Still, he seemed to like her, even if he'd never mentioned a future.

He cleared his throat, and she had the brief, mad thought that he might propose then. "Do you know if Miss Samuel is expected this week? I know you are close friends, and I'd heard her mother has recovered from the illness that kept them from London."

"Oh, I think . . ." Her words faded away as she realized what he must mean. He admired Elizabeth Samuel. Perhaps he even thought he loved her. As well he should. Beth was her best friend and a wonderful person. This solved the mystery of why Mr. Dunwoody had never kissed her. "Yes, she promised she would try to come. I'm sure she'll arrive any time now. Have you written to her?"

He flushed again. "I did not feel it proper. We only met once. ""

"Well, I'm sure she'll be happy to know she's been in your thoughts."

The music paused for a moment, then started

again with a chorus of swirling notes. Mr. Dunwoody's elegant fingers touched her arm, and he smiled brightly. "The first dance?" he asked, and Marissa rose to dance with him.

He swung her around in a lively jig, and soon enough others joined them. By the time the dance was over, Marissa was laughing and struggling to catch a full breath at the same time. Mr. Dunwoody's hand settled on her back with a steady touch, but she told herself not to enjoy it. He liked Beth, and Marissa could only be glad.

As he led her back to the settee, his smile grew strained. "Who is that man?" he murmured.

She looked up and saw that Mr. Bertrand had finally arrived. Arm resting on the mantel, he spoke with Aidan, but his eyes watched her. She expected jealousy, and yet his eyes sparkled with laughter.

He made no sense to her.

"That's Mr. Bertrand, a friend of the family." *And perhaps my husband.* As always, he was bigger than every other man in the room. He drew her eye even as she thanked Mr. Dunwoody for the dance.

When she saw that Jude was moving toward her, the hair on her neck rose with awareness.

"Miss York," he murmured. "You're a beautiful dancer."

"Thank you. Do you dance, Mr. Bertrand?"

"I'm capable of it."

She waited from him to request her hand, but he merely stood politely. Marissa's heart shrank with disappointment. She couldn't marry a man who could not dance. Dancing was one of the joys in her life. Dancing and riding and reading novels. And on special occasions, letting men do thrilling things to her body.

Boys, Jude's voice seemed to whisper in her ear. Marissa jumped with shock, her gaze traveling down to his hands.

"Well," she said, "If you'll excuse me, I owe my cousin a dance."

"Of course. I'll enjoy watching your grace from afar."

Flustered, she hurried toward the other side of the room, though she had no idea where Harry was or whether he might want to dance. But as she crossed the room, she caught sight of one of the maids hovering in the doorway. The girl's eyes widened when she saw Marissa, and she tilted her head toward the side before disappearing.

Having a bit of experience with the situation, Marissa followed.

"Miss," the girl said as soon as they were alone in the passage. "A note."

"From whom?"

"'Twas left at the kitchen door, miss."

Nerves sizzling with excitement, Marissa hid the note in her skirts and hurried toward the next closed door. The sewing room. She hesitated before it, then shrugged away her misgivings and stole inside. The sconces were lit, as if her brother no longer trusted the darkness of unused rooms. Guilt overtook her for a moment, but she tried to look at the room with clear eyes. There was no ghost couple here, replaying her misadventures of the night before. There was no stain of her innocence on the couch. It was just a room.

Hands trembling, she opened the note.

My Darling,

Despite my rash words, I would not ever see you come to harm. Please forgive my behavior. My passion for you misrepresented itself as rudeness. I love you.

Pray, reconsider your refusal of my offer. I would spend every night as I spent that brief hour in your arms.

"Hour," she muttered. It had been hardly thirty minutes in all, and yet it had felt an eternity.

I am humbled by the gift you granted me. Please be my wife.

For a moment, she thought affectionately of Mr. White's legs. Of his closely shaven jaw and tender hands. Those hands had looked so promising, and yet they'd delivered so little pleasure. His thighs hadn't brought much pleasure either, but at least he hadn't marred her face with a stubbled chin.

Could she marry him?

Her mind rebelled at the thought. Perhaps dancing wasn't as important to her as she'd believed. She did not give Mr. White's proposal another moment of thought. Instead, she folded the note with a sigh and was turning to leave when she saw that she wasn't alone. Jude lounged in the doorway. "Oh! I was just . . ."

"He isn't blackmailing you, is he?"

She realized then that the mysterious smile was finally gone. In its place was ice and warning.

"No! No, it's nothing like that. He only says he loves me."

"Ah. Are you inclined to forgive him?"

"Of course not!"

The iciness melted into a satisfied smile. "Good." He sauntered in and wandered toward the couch. "So, Miss York, this is the site of innocence lost."

"Mr. Bertrand!" she gasped.

He winked and dropped onto the couch, patting the seat beside him. "It's Jude, remember?"

"Jude," she mumbled.

"So, tell me something, Miss York. Was it worth it?"

Her body hovered in a strange place, half cool with horror and the other half churning with an odd excitement. This man sat there and said these outrageous words as if they were perfectly acceptable. As if they shouldn't offend her. As if she would *want* to speak of them.

She eyed the cushion next to him.

"It can be enjoyable, you know."

"I know that," she snapped, before dropping down beside him.

"Was it?"

"No," she huffed.

He stiffened beside her. "He wasn't rough?"

"Oh, no! He was only . . . unimpressive." As soon as the word left her mouth, Marissa realized how inappropriate it was. How should she know of such things? "I mean—"

But Jude was laughing beside her. "Unimpressive, eh? Well, that is a tragedy, but perhaps a welcome one for a lady's loss of innocence."

"How so?"

Jude leaned back and stretched his arms across the back. "It can be painful, and I would hate to think of you in pain."

"Well, there was a bit of discomfort, but I rather

think that was due to him squishing me." She snuck a glance at Jude. "Now that I think of it, you look unfortunately heavy."

He tilted his head in such gracious acknowledgment that she felt churlish. "I can assure you I've not yet squished a lady. Not even once."

Interest prickled through her with a feeling like all the hair on her body standing at attention. "So . . . are you very experienced, then?"

"Experienced enough."

"What does that mean? Among gentlemen, I mean. There is an entirely different standard from what I can gather."

He settled one ankle on his knee, and his thigh ended up very near her hand. "It means that I have had practice at bringing women pleasure."

Pleasure. The very prize she'd been seeking to reclaim ever since that fateful night two years before. Pleasure. And aching. And surprise. A knot low in her belly seemed to acquire weight. She squeezed her thighs together. She hadn't thought Jude Bertrand could make her feel that way with his inelegant largeness.

But his words were so . . . *plump* with confidence. Not arrogance. Just assuredness. *He* had no doubt he knew how to bring pleasure, and so she had no doubt as well.

"Is it—" Her voice emerged a bit cracked, so she cleared her throat and tried again. "Is it a secret then? The way to bring a woman pleasure?"

"From what I've heard from women, yes. It seems a knowledge gained by only a happy few. Still, I'd say it's a more important skill than jumping a hedge, for instance, and yet so many husbands spend far more time learning of horses. You wouldn't want one of those husbands, would you, Miss York?"

"I-I'm sure I don't know what you mean."

"Really? I'm sure you do." He settled more firmly against the back, stretching enough that his thigh inched closer to her, his knee brushing her skirts. "There is more than one way, you know."

"More than one way to what?"

"Pleasure a woman."

Her pulse took up residence between her legs. "Is there?" she squeaked.

"Indeed. And of course men are pleased in countless ways. We are easily deciphered creatures. No depth to us at all."

Oh, but that wasn't true. She did not know any more of men's pleasure than she knew of her own. Did they like the same things? Did they feel the same sensations? Marissa stared straight ahead, hands fisted in her lap. She should not encourage him. She should not lay a hand on his thigh or lean toward him for a kiss. Then he might think she truly desired his attentions, when all she really wanted was pleasure.

The faint shush of fabric behind her told her he had moved his hand. And when he dragged one finger down her neck, Marissa shivered and closed her eyes, trying to hold back a sharp sigh.

"May I call you Marissa when we are alone? We are pretending, after all." His touch circled to the side of her neck as his thumb brushed her spine.

Marissa felt the tightening of her nipples as gooseflesh flowed down her body. She knew that was a place that men might touch during lovemaking. "Yes, of course."

"This is nice. Here, in the quiet, with you."

"Mm." She dared not say more.

"But your dance partners will be looking for you. Marissa."

A faint French accent molded her name, the same as it molded his own when he introduced himself. "Mm," she murmured again, concentrating on his hand at her neck. It was hot and surprisingly light against her. She imagined it moving toward her neckline. . . .

"Shall we?" his quiet voice brushed over her as his palm snuck heat into the nape of her neck.

Marissa arched carefully, curving her spine more fully into his hold. For a moment, his fingers felt heavier, and tension stretched between their bodies like a visible cord. His thigh tensed, pressing his knee against her. Was he leaning forward? Would he brush his mouth over the exposed skin of her shoulder? Her lips parted to allow deeper breaths. "Yes," she whispered . . . and Jude stood and straightened his coat.

"Then please allow me to escort you to your eagerly awaiting beaus."

"To what?"

He offered a hand, and she took it automatically, letting him help her to her feet.

"But I don't feel like dancing now."

"Then we shall talk."

"What in the world would I talk to you about?"

He huffed a laugh. "Why, anything you might talk to anyone else about."

Disgruntled by her misunderstanding of his intent, Marissa scowled. All men ever wanted to discuss was horses and government. "Oh, you'd like to hear of my gardening, would you? Or I could regale you with tales of the latest novel I read. Perhaps I shall tell you of my plans for the little pillow I'm stitching."

"Absolutely." He walked her slowly from the room.

"I am not appeased by polite murmurings and the glazing of eyes, Mr. Bertrand. But if you care to speak of horseflesh, I will hang on your every word, I'm sure."

"My God. You have a low opinion of men, don't you?"

"On the contrary, I like men. They are polite and helpful and necessary for dancing. And men are so handsome and *different,* aren't they?"

"Not all of us, clearly, but I'll let that go. You know, my mother enjoys gardening, and I used to spend hours helping her."

She studied his face to see if he was humoring her, but he looked earnest.

"She grows herbs in her small yard, and roses along the walk."

"Really? I have never grown herbs. Cook won't let me into her plot, but roses . . . roses are a puzzle. So easily upset and yet so strong and hardy."

"Like men?"

Her laughter escaped so suddenly that she put her fingers to her lips to quiet the sound. "Yes! Like men!"

"A laugh," he drawled. "And a common subject. We are like two peas in a pod, Miss York. Will you grant me a favor? Let me borrow the last novel you finished so that we may discuss it."

"You wouldn't like it. It's melodramatic and over-wrought."

"Then it will remind me of you, so I'm sure I'll enjoy it a great deal."

"Me?" she gasped, rounding on him just as they entered the music room. "I am not the least bit melodramatic! I am well known as a calm and composed woman, Mr. Bertrand."

"My mistake," he said, bowing over her hand to take his leave.

She felt the faint brush of his mouth on her knuckles, and then he left her. Her frustration bubbled over, and Marissa stomped her foot before realizing the gesture could be interpreted as melodramatic. Or overwrought. Two things she most decidedly was not.

Her composure was often remarked upon by the people of her circle, and she wasn't going to let Jude ruin her calm. A servant passed, and Marissa snatched a glass of wine from his tray and sipped it as quickly as she could manage. Only to help her composure, of course.

She forgot all about dancing and glared at Jude Bertrand's wide back. He was insufferable, and she could only pray to God that she did not end up married to the man. He'd drive her mad before the first year was out.

Chapter 6

Marissa woke with a tense neck and an aching head. She nurtured the pain into anger as she sipped her tea. She glared at her own reflection as the new maid brushed and styled and dressed her. One stupid, drunken mistake and she'd forfeited all control over her own life. She'd had so little control in the first place and had held onto it with stingy determination.

Of course, she'd known that she would marry, but Marissa had been in control of *when*. She'd known she would have to leave her home, but only when she was ready. And she'd known that her life would be spent with a husband, but *who* . . . the *who* had been up to her.

If nothing else, she would at least snatch that one tiny piece back. *Who.*

When her most modest dress was buttoned up and smoothed down, Marissa set off to battle with the baron.

Angling her chin ridiculously high, she pushed open the doors to Edward's study and swept in. Her family had at least taught her how to make a grand entrance.

"Ah, Marissa," Edward said, glancing up from his papers. "Would you close the door behind you? We need to speak."

"We most certainly do."

"So you've heard?"

Marissa's chin inched in. "Heard what?"

"Mrs. James Ready asked to speak with me this morning. She had heard there was an *incident* between you and Mr. White, and she was concerned that it might have been something 'nefarious.' She worried that her daughter might be exposed to the rumors. Millicent is a few years younger than you."

All the anger drained from Marissa's muscles as if a hole inside her had opened up. Her chin inched down. Her knees lost feeling.

"I managed to assuage her by bringing her into my confidence. I fed her the same story we gave the servants. That you argued with Peter White over a minor jealousy, and it was nothing."

"Oh," Marissa breathed. "Oh, that is good."

"Millicent hasn't behaved strangely toward you?"

"Not at all."

Edward's head dropped, and the sight of his bowed neck stole the rest of the strength from her legs. Marissa lowered herself carefully to a chair.

"Still, I cannot stop all the stories. I'll do my best, but . . ."

She nodded, and kept slowly nodding until the movement faded to nothing. It finally hit her. She had done this not just to herself, but to her family. To Edward, who had never done a sorry thing in his life. And to her mother, who might enjoy the fainting, but would not like hearing malicious laughter. And to Aidan, who had heard enough whispered gossip to last a lifetime.

She could not complain. She could not stomp her foot and demand to be accommodated. If she needed to marry, she would marry Jude Bertrand and be grateful for his generosity.

Or at least not resentful.

Edward offered a wan smile. "I'm sure all will be well, 'Rissa. What did you wish to speak with me about, if not Mrs. Ready?"

"Nothing. 'Twas not important."

"It seemed important."

"No."

His eyes dropped to his desk. "I hoped it was something concerning that note you received last night."

Shock jolted through her. "He *told* you?"

"Who? Jude? No, the housekeeper told me. She is aware that you have behaved in an impetuous way and is eager to keep you from scandal. It was from Mr. White, I presume?"

"He asked me to marry him," she murmured, surprised at the relief that coursed through her. Jude hadn't betrayed her trust.

"You haven't changed your mind about him?"

"No! Whatever happens, I won't marry Mr. White."

"Good. But you will tell me if he contacts you again?"

She considered the question for a long moment before nodding.

"Oh, and Aidan is eager to discover his whereabouts. If he gave a direction, please don't reveal it to Aidan. A murder trial wouldn't help the situation."

She left the library without another word, and went upstairs to offer her false fiancé an olive branch.

Jude removed his coat and crumpled it into a ball as the distant echo of gunshots hovered in the air. He lay back on the shaded grass, propped the coat behind his head, and cracked open the book that had been delivered to his room that morning.

As soon as the pages had been laid in his hand, Jude had sent word that he would miss the morning hunt, and he'd hied himself off to the garden to read. It was a beautiful morning, surprisingly warm, and Marissa York was softening toward him.

But perhaps softening was the wrong word. Tension was what he was after, and her body fairly snapped with it.

He stared at the first page of the book without seeing it. Instead he thought of Marissa. She was pretty, but more than that, she was fascinating. Her ill-hidden wildness. The way she spoke of men with simultaneous affection and disdain. Her hot temper and cool words.

Neither her activities nor dress marked her as any different from other young women of society. And yet, beneath that façade of normality, something else burned. Something hot and fierce.

Jude had admired her from afar, but now that he was close . . . he was enchanted.

But his goal was to pique her interest, not to follow her about like a lovesick pup. She had enough of that kind of attention. So much that she didn't see it. There were at least two young men vying for her eye at the York estate, but she saw them as dance partners and nothing more.

Marissa was bored and restless and spoiled, and she didn't even know it.

Jude slid the note free from the pages of the book and smiled at the curls of her signature. So deceptively delicate. She had everyone fooled. But not him.

He saw the meaning behind her simple words. *A story of admirable emotion,* it read. And she certainly was.

The book was part of her puzzle, so he forced himself to focus on it, and before long he was swept up in the rush of dialogue and drama. Soon enough, the sun's shadow had crept far down his legs when Jude looked up to see a woman in the garden. Marissa. She hadn't noticed him yet, and he didn't dare disturb her solitude.

Instead, he watched her. She moved quickly through the grassy walks of the garden, snapping off dried heads. It was unnecessary, he knew. The rose bushes would be pruned soon in preparation for winter, so a few dead blooms meant nothing, but the exercise must relax her, pointless as it was. Her face looked peaceful and younger.

She must be frightened about her future, but she had yet to let it show. He'd seen her angry and happy and disapproving and joyful. And now peaceful. But never scared.

His mother would like her, and he had no doubt the two women would meet someday. Marissa was not the kind of lady who would pass up the chance to meet a true-life courtesan. The meeting would likely be kept secret from the rest of society, but Marissa wouldn't be able to resist. Jude wasn't sure he could've said that of any other woman of the ton.

She looked up then, and her body froze when their eyes met. Jude raised the book high enough so she could see it, and her shoulders relaxed. Much to Jude's surprise, she walked toward him with a smile.

"Good morning, Marissa."

Her cheeks were pink from the sun, and her smile uncharacteristically soft as she sank down to the grass beside him. The skirts of her yellow dress belled out around her before she patted them down. "You're not riding."

"I had a book to read."

"And what do you think?"

"It's admirably emotional. And enjoyably over-wrought."

"Cheeky."

He laid the book on the grass near her foot. Her bare toes curled quickly beneath the yellow fabric. Jude stared for a moment, wishing he'd noticed her naked feet sooner. "I think Wendell is a bully and Chloe a bit soft in the head. But Danielle makes the story worthwhile."

Her eyes lit. "Truly?"

"What did you think of it?"

"Well." She tugged a piece of grass from the lawn and twirled it. "My fingers itched to slap Chloe into some sense, and I yearned for Danielle to give Wendell a good set-down. But it gets much more lively when the handsome gentleman moves in next door."

"Oh, my. A handsome gentleman. I'll have to keep reading then."

She plucked another blade of grass. "I have news. One of the guests heard talk about me, but I think Edward convinced her that Mr. White and I only argued."

"And what of Mr. White? Will he spread tales when he realizes your feelings haven't changed?"

"I don't know. I hope not. It cannot flatter him either."

"I'm sure he'll leave his own name out of it."

Marissa shook her head, and one tendril of her hair escaped the braid to caress her face. "I'm hopeful he isn't so spiteful. And I'm certain there will be no other . . . consequences. And if there aren't . . . what will you do?"

"Me? I suppose I will simply go back to being a bachelor."

"I would not have hard feelings between us."

When she dropped the second blade of grass, Jude reached idly for her hand, aware of her surprise when her fingers twitched against his. But she didn't pull away. "There will be no hard feelings on my part. I accept you on your own terms, Marissa."

"That's odd. For a man."

"Perhaps." He stroked his thumb along her palm, and her fingers curled as if to keep him close.

"It is very strange that you know such an intimate embarrassment about me. I'm at a disadvantage."

"Ask me anything then. I'll answer truthfully."

Her sharp glance made clear that she'd been hoping he would make that offer. When he slid his fingers in between hers, she responded by holding tight.

"So . . . your mother is a companion."

"Yes."

"That must mean . . . the household must have been unusual. Did you live there?"

"In my early childhood, yes. And then I sometimes

spent summers with her later. It wasn't so strange, really."

"Oh."

She stared down at their hands, her cheeks delightfully pink.

"Is that what you wished to ask me?"

"I just . . ." Her words came quickly, as if she were afraid to breathe. "I just thought you must have *associated* with them. The women."

"I see. Shall I tell you the story of how I lost my innocence, then?"

"Yes! That's what . . . yes, it only seems fair!"

"I agree. Well, I was far younger than you. Only sixteen. As you suspected, she was a friend of my mother's."

Marissa's green eyes widened, and her hand tightened around his thumb as she leaned toward him. "A courtesan?" she breathed.

"Yes. I'd been in love with her for two miserable years. She was the most beautiful, ethereal woman I'd ever seen. I wrote her poetry and made calf eyes at her. I was insufferable, I'm sure. But she finally decided I was old enough. She granted mercy and took me to her bed. By God, I thought I would never stop loving her after that."

She laughed. "But you did?"

"A young boy's fancy is nothing if not convenient. I was in love with the neighbor's new kitchen maid not three weeks later."

"Ah, so you fall in love often?"

He slowly raised their clasped hands to his mouth and pressed a chaste kiss to her knuckles. Marissa watched his mouth closely, as if she were waiting for more. "I have since learned the difference between lust and love. Men are easily distracted by lust."

"But not women?" She kept the words light, but he heard the edge of worry in them.

"Some women as well. It is nothing to be ashamed of, Marissa."

"I am not beset by lust! It's only that I like to dance."

"Of course."

She yanked her hand away. "It's true!"

"I'm sure that's why you evaluate your partners' legs so carefully. To be sure they will step lightly."

Her eyes went so wide he could see the white all around. "I enjoy fashion! And beautiful fabric!"

"Come, Marissa. Tell the truth. What you enjoy is ogling men's limbs."

Color rushed to her face so quickly that Jude worried she might grow dizzy and tip over. He put a hand under her elbow to steady her.

"There's no need to lie," he said softly. "Not to me."

She drew in a slow breath. Then she set her shoulders back and nodded. "Yes, I like to look at them."

"There, that wasn't so hard, was it?"

"I don't understand how I can be the only one! They walk around with their legs just . . . out. They wear trousers so snug, and everyone pretends that we're not supposed to look as they strut about like peacocks, and—" She cut off her own rant and drooped as if her strings had been cut.

Jude raised an eyebrow. "I'm rather disappointed not to be included in your diatribe. You haven't snuck a peek at my legs yet, Miss York?" He crossed his ankles and watched her eyes slide down his body. He wore riding breeches and boots, and he knew she would look.

"I have. You are very . . . strong."

Despite her disapproving tone, Jude felt a coil of satisfaction warm his chest.

"They look very hard."

His thighs tightened at the shock of her words. "Are men's legs not supposed to be hard?" When she shrugged, her gaze skittering back to his legs, Jude's heart beat faster. "All that looking and no touching?"

"Hardly any at all," she sighed miserably.

Jude's nerves sang with awareness, but he kept his expression calm. "Ah, but you are betrothed now. In theory."

She finally looked up at him, brows tightening even as her mouth curved up. "Jude Bertrand, are you inviting me to explore your limbs?"

"Would a gentleman encourage that sort of thing?" He stretched his arms high, then folded them behind his head and closed his eyes. "But if I were to take a nap, I suppose I'd be at your mercy."

"Jude," she whispered. "I can't. What if someone sees?"

"Shush. We're in the shade, and I'm asleep." But he wasn't asleep. He was tense with painful anticipation. Would she dare? He was mad to even suggest such a thing, and yet he could never stop himself from goading her.

When he realized he was holding his breath, Jude made himself breathe.

"Of the two of us," Marissa murmured, "I'm not sure who is the more scandalous." And then her hand touched his thigh.

It was an innocent touch, if such a thing could be. A gentle laying of a hand just above his knee. And yet a faint tremor shook his bones. The touch stayed tentative and light for a very long time. When he offered no response, she shaped her fingers to his leg.

"You're very solid." Her hand inched up, a shocking slide of faint pressure.

He'd be a damn sight more solid in a few minutes if he let this continue.

She squeezed him lightly, testing his give. "I prefer you in breeches, I think."

"Mm."

The supple buckskin warmed beneath her hand. When she slid her touch toward the inside of his leg, Jude felt his cock thicken. *Christ*.

He tried counting to ten. He tried thinking of hunting. He tried to recount the names of all his childhood tutors. But when she made a little humming sound and slid her hand slowly higher, Jude dragged his foot up and propped himself up on his elbows. She jerked her arm back.

"Thought I heard something," he said, and the words set her head turning back and forth to try to locate the nonexistent intruder. On another day, in another place, he'd let Marissa explore his thighs as much as she liked. But not here in the garden. Not when the very thought made him throb.

Goading Marissa York could prove a very dangerous exercise indeed.

Chapter 7

Marissa hurried down the stairs, surprised by her eagerness to see Jude again. After luncheon, he'd asked if she'd like to ride to the old church, and Marissa had happily accepted. Her mother was busy gathering up players for the next stage drama, and Marissa was not in the mood for bad acting.

But her leaf green habit lightened the weight on her heart, and the thought of a ride through the warm autumn with Jude . . . it sounded almost as lovely as dancing.

Lovelier perhaps, because when Mr. Dunwoody stepped into the hall, stopping her rush, Marissa felt nothing but regret. "Oh, Mr. Dunwoody. Good afternoon." He wore riding breeches just as Jude did, as the men all rode during the day. But Mr. Dunwoody looked very different in his. Elegant, of course. Or just . . . ornamental?

She shook the thought from her head as Dunwoody offered a friendly bow. "I'm off for a ride," she explained with an awkward wave toward the corridor.

"Oh, of course. Forgive me for keeping you. I only wished to ask if I might escort you into dinner tonight."

For a moment, her brain told her to say yes, to cultivate a relationship with anyone but Jude. But she'd made a decision today, and she'd honor it.

"I'm flattered, Mr. Dunwoody, but I fear I've already committed myself."

"Ah. I see. A new suitor, perhaps?" he teased. His words pricked her with both excitement and guilt.

"I . . ." Her blush worked to the advantage of the story they were weaving, but it was entirely genuine, all the same.

Mr. Dunwoody smiled wider. "I'm relieved to see you looking more yourself. And, uh . . . no word from the Samuel family as of yet?"

That erased her awkwardness, and Marissa matched his grin. "They must arrive today."

Marissa was still smiling when she swept out the front door to find the groom waiting with her horse. Her smile didn't falter until she saw Jude, mounted and waiting as well.

It wasn't the sight of Jude that stopped her though. It was his horse.

The horse—if such a beast could be graced with that name—was huge, and just as sturdy and inelegant as Jude himself. In fact, the mount was downright ugly. A gray gelding that was fading to white in splotches and stripes, the poor thing now looked like an old carthorse dingy with grime.

Marissa took her time mounting and arranging skirts, giving herself a moment to recover. But when she looked toward him again, she couldn't help but wince.

"He looks as if he will be put out to pasture soon," she ventured as they walked their horses toward the road. "Perhaps you should find another mount."

He glanced down and patted the beast's neck. "He's only ten, and his gait is perfect."

"Oh."

Jude spared a look for her mount. "If I braid his mane, will you like him better?"

Her mare, a sweet, feisty girl named Cleopatra, tossed her head as if she knew she was the focus of attention. "It's only one braid!"

"She's lovely."

Marissa felt he was making some annoying point about her vanity, but she was distracted from her frown by the appearance of Harry and Aidan riding in. The men waved and nodded, as if they both agreed that Marissa and Jude were doing a good job of keeping up appearances.

Aidan's face looked younger in the warm sunlight, as it often did after a good ride. In London he never seemed happy.

"My brother," she murmured to Jude. "I'm happy you're a friend to him."

"What do you mean?"

"For a long while there, he only spent time with Harry, and that was begrudging."

"Ah. I suppose I have seen too much tragedy wrought from love. I did not find his story romantic, so he likes me."

Marissa nodded. The whole of the ton seemed to think Aidan nothing more than a dramatic figure to be used as a centerpiece at dinner parties. A young, handsome bachelor with a story that made the ladies swoon with sighed delight. The love of his life had been snatched from his arms by the cruel hand of death, and he mourned her to this day. What gentle heart could resist that story?

Aidan hated them all.

"You've been a good friend to him, I understand."

"Well, we have common interests. Between his ships and my father's investments, we often travel in the same circles."

"Really? Do you work for your father? I had no idea."

"I do. He enjoys dabbling in his own investments on occasion, and I enjoy having some industrious way to occupy my time. Idle hands make for the devil's work, you know." His gaze slid to her. "Perhaps you need more than stitching to keep you busy."

"Oh, aren't you clever?" She tried to leave it at that, but she found her body actually leaning toward his, curious to know more about this man. Marissa readjusted her posture and tried to look less fascinated. "Where do you travel then?"

"Well, France quite often, for obvious reasons. And all over Europe. Italy, Spain, Portugal. Constantinople was fascinating, of course."

"Constantinople? You've been there?" Well, there was no disguising her eagerness. She didn't even try. She could not imagine such an exotic place.

"I have." His eyes studied her, glinting with pleased assessment. "If we marry, I'd welcome your company when I travel. I'd be pleased to visit the Ottoman again."

She blinked several times, shocked and happy with his words. "Truly? I've . . . I've never considered. . . . Would I like it, do you think?"

His smile curved to a wicked angle. "You would love it."

She flushed at his words. The tone of them bespoke admiration and pride and a sure knowledge of her very nature. How could those simple words leave her flustered and overly warm? Marissa clutched her reins too tightly and shifted in the saddle. Cleopatra stepped nervously before relaxing into an easy gait again.

Marissa swallowed and urged her to a trot. She wanted to run, but the mare wasn't warm enough yet, even if Marissa was. She'd never been flustered by talk of travel before. Everything about Jude Bertrand was so very *different*. So unexpectedly intriguing. How did he make her need things from him that she didn't even want?

For instance, right now, she was staring hard toward the horizon, counting the seconds until she could push her mare to a full, hard run. The old church was only miles ahead, and she and Jude would be alone there. When they arrived they would dismount to explore the ruins. They'd disappear behind crumbling walls and overgrown orchards. Even a passing traveler would not be able to spot them.

Surely, he would kiss her, finally.

Finally.

Marissa reminded herself that she'd only known him for two days. And then she urged her horse to a gallop.

Chapter 8

Nothing.

He'd done nothing at all. Not a kiss. Not a stolen touch of her hip. Not a winking suggestion that she resume her exploration of his legs while they were away from the manor.

Jude had been a complete gentleman during the ride, and now the horses were happily walking the last few yards toward home.

Marissa's thoughts, however, had been less than ladylike. She still didn't think he was an attractive man, but she'd revised her opinion of his thighs.

Yesterday in the garden, his muscles had been just as hard as she'd expected when she'd touched him. Like stone, but stone that was warm and flexing and contoured into fascinating curves. Every shift of his body had felt like the pull and push of a mountain beneath her hand. And on his horse . . . my God, on his horse, his thighs had bulged and tightened and pressed with fantastic indecency against his breeches. Marissa had found her breath coming quick and shallow by the time they'd reached the ruins.

Yet, they'd done nothing but stroll. He'd been perfectly respectable, and Marissa was close to snarling with impatience. They were playing at betrothal. She'd earned a kiss!

The packed earth of the stable yard thumped beneath the horses' hooves as boys approached to take the reins. Jude dismounted with a grace that defied his large size . . . and the large size of his horse.

He reached to help her down, and his hands finally curved around her body, but they didn't linger. He let her go, and Marissa barely managed to not stomp her foot.

Frustrated, she only raised her chin higher. "Thank you for the ride, Mr. Bertrand. I had a wonderful time."

Hands behind his back, he walked with her along the side of the stable. "Why so cross then?"

"I am not cross."

"Really? I was about to start quoting from *The Taming of the Shrew*."

"And now you've called me a shrew. Lovely."

"You say that as if it were my last offense among many."

"Mm."

Jude took her arm and swung her gently around to face him. "What is it, *mon coeur*?"

"Why do you call me that? Your heart seems quite content to keep its distance."

"Does it?" He touched her temple, sweeping a strand of hair back. His fingers brushed the edge of her little riding hat, and she worried it had lost its jaunty angle. Did he not think her pretty enough? Did he not desire a kiss at all?

His eyes told her nothing as he watched her. "I had no idea you wanted it near," he murmured.

And he was right, of course. She wanted nothing to do with his heart, and she was suddenly afraid of the challenge she'd nearly issued.

"We'll be late for luncheon," she whispered, stepping back from the trap of his gaze.

He studied her a moment longer, his dark eyes keeping his thoughts secret, and Marissa let out a sigh of relief when he simply offered his arm. A kiss was one thing, but talk of his heart had been foolish on her part. She did not know enough about her own heart to have that conversation.

He led her into the manor without another word, and at the bottom of the stairs, he bid his farewell and bent over her hand. Marissa was holding her breath, anticipating the brush of his mouth against her skin, when someone called her name.

She looked up in surprise at the eager female voice and spotted her best friend rushing across the entry.

"Beth!" Marissa squealed over the top of Jude's bent head. "You're here!"

He released her hand, and Marissa stepped forward into her friend's embrace.

Beth's mother had been ill for nearly a year, so Marissa hadn't seen her at all during the past Season in London. She'd missed Beth so much that she felt tears prick her eyes.

In that moment, Marissa realized why she'd gone with Peter White. It hadn't just been wickedness or lust. She'd been lonely.

Beth's tight embrace said that she'd been lonely too. Marissa breathed in the familiar clean scent of Beth's dark hair. Their housekeeper made the soap herself, and it smelled like nothing else but Beth.

"Who is this?" Beth whispered in her ear.

Marissa let her go and turned to look at Jude.

"Oh, allow me to introduce Mr. Bertrand. Mr. Bertrand, this is Miss Elizabeth Samuel."

"Miss Samuel," he said. "It's an honor to meet you."

"Mr. Bertrand," she murmured, her voice quiet with shock.

"If you'll excuse me, I'll leave you two to your visit."

They both watched him walk away until Beth finally shook her head. "Good gracious, that man is quite frightening."

"Oh. Yes, I suppose he is."

"Did you go riding with him?"

"Yes." She felt the weight of Beth's curious gaze, but it was her own guilt that compelled her to blurt out, "He's very nice."

Beth just tugged her toward the stairs. "Come. Let's go to your room. You haven't written in a week. I want to know everything you've done."

Marissa thought that a singularly bad idea, but she pretended to agree.

"How many more proposals have you received?"

Marissa laughed too loudly and then peppered Beth with questions about her mother's health in order to keep her talking. Marissa didn't wish to speak of the past week. But mostly she didn't wish to speak of Jude. Beth wouldn't understand.

Marissa didn't understand it herself.

* * *

Dinner had been so lovely with Beth there to chatter with. And Jude as well, near enough to share an occasional smile if not a conversation.

After dinner, Marissa took Beth's arm and strode happily toward the music room, anticipating that the evening would only get better. She was wrong.

Beth's cousin had been far enough away from them at dinner that Marissa had been able to ignore her, but there was no ignoring her now. Nanette held court from her perch on a chair set close to the door.

"My darling Marissa!" she cooed. "I'm so happy to spend time with you again. This year has been so awfully dull, locked away from society."

Marissa gritted her teeth and offered a patently false smile. Nanette had lived with Beth's family for the past four years, and the two women should've been as close as sisters, as they'd come out the same year. But despite that the Samuels had taken Nanette in upon her father's death, she considered herself far above them. Her mother had been the sister of an earl, after all, and she herself was an heiress.

"I've made Aunt Samuel promise to get better. We simply cannot miss another Season! And we were so worried, of course."

"Of course."

Nanette leaned forward conspiratorially. "Did I tell you that Viscount Farington sent me lilies when he realized I would not be in London for the Season?"

"Mm," Marissa hummed, unwilling to say more. She knew that Viscount Farington had sent the flowers to both Beth and Nanette, but there was no point in clarifying it. Nanette would just wink and say that, of course, Viscount Farington had not wanted to be rude.

Beth sat tensely next to her cousin, not saying a word.

"Well," Marissa said, "You were both missed in London this year. Beth, did I mention that Mr. Dunwoody asked after you just yesterday?"

"He did?"

"Do you remember him? He says you met only once."

"Of course I remember. We danced. Such a graceful gentleman."

"So he is. My favorite partner of late."

Nanette trilled a laugh. "I wonder if he will spare me a dance as well! I shall decide if he's as lovely as you say."

Marissa frowned, but managed to refrain from rolling her eyes. Barely.

Still, she knew she wouldn't be able to hold back her irritation for long, so the sound of the men walking down the corridor was a great relief. Nanette would be too busy flirting to bother with the women much longer.

Marissa bent to whisper quickly in Beth's ear. "I hope you are ready to dance while you're here. Mr. Dunwoody was quite interested in your arrival."

Her friend's cheeks flared pink. A good thing, as her face had been quite pale. Now she looked less like a girl who'd spent a year at her mother's bedside and more like a youthful maiden.

Marissa waited impatiently for Mr. Dunwoody to appear, but she soon forgot that she was waiting for him and began watching for Jude instead. Would he be a gentleman tonight or a rogue? Would he smile mysteriously from the corner, or would he steal her away and kiss her?

Both, hopefully.

The night suddenly felt so uncertain. Her pulse leapt in uneven surges.

"Miss York," a man said. She knew the voice was too tentative to be Jude, but she still hoped it was him as she turned. The sinking of her heart seemed melodramatic in the face of such mild disappointment, but she smiled when she thought of what Jude would say to that.

"Mr. Dunwoody! Here is Miss Samuel, just as I promised! Did you get a chance to speak with her before dinner?"

"I did not." He bowed low over Beth's hand. "Miss Samuel, it is such a pleasure to see you again. I hope your appearance means your mother has improved?"

"She is much better, sir. Thank you." They smiled at each other for a long, awkward moment before Nanette nudged her cousin's elbow.

"Oh," Beth breathed, her expression melting into a combination of embarrassment and dread. "This is Mr. Dunwoody. Mr. Dunwoody, this is my cousin Miss Nanette Samuel."

"A pleasure," she purred with a graceful inclination of her head.

Mr. Dunwoody laughed nervously as he bowed, and when he rose, his eyes stayed on Nanette. "I meant to . . . oh!" He turned halfway back toward Beth. "I meant to request the privilege of a dance with you this evening, Miss Samuel. And with your lovely cousin as well, if she would deign to dance with a stranger."

Nanette tittered and touched his arm, and Mr. Dunwoody's smile widened to a grin.

Marissa gritted her teeth, but she told herself it didn't matter. Mr. Dunwoody liked Beth, and though Nanette always did her best to draw attention from her cousin, she wouldn't succeed this time, surely. When he walked away, Nanette observed how handsome he was and asked after his prospects. Then she proceeded to tell Beth that a gentleman without a title might be a fine catch for someone like her, but Nanette intended to be Lady Something-or-Other when she married. "Still," she laughed, "Mr. Dunwoody certainly seems a fine prospect for a dance partner in the meantime."

Marissa interrupted with a pointed look at Beth. "Beth, I believe my mother wanted to speak with you about designing a headdress for tomorrow's play. You're so amazingly creative! You will excuse us, won't you, Nanette?"

She pulled her friend up and led her toward the far side of the room. "I don't know how you live with that woman," she whispered to Beth. "She's intolerable."

"She's not so bad. At least when I sit next to her, the gentlemen flock around."

"Mr. Dunwoody did not need her presence to entice him. And, as always, you sell yourself too cheaply. Why, Malcolm James was very close to making an offer during your first Season."

"But he didn't." She shot Marissa a mischievous look. "It's all right. Nanette says I can be her companion if I never get an offer."

"She did not!"

"She did," Beth laughed.

Marissa stopped her for a quick hug. Beth was sweet and loyal, and if she didn't have the beauty of her cousin, she was very pretty at least. If only they did not have the exact same coloring . . .

Beth cleared her throat. "That Mr. Bertrand certainly seems fond of you. He watched you all through dinner."

"Did he?" She followed Beth's gaze to another corner of the room. She expected to find Jude watching her still, but he was looking down at the woman talking to him. Patience Wellingsly, the same woman who'd watched him so closely at dinner the night before.

"Doesn't he make you nervous? He looks like a ruffian."

Mrs. Wellingsly leaned into his arm, using the excuse of laughter to press herself close.

"Have you danced with him? I can't imagine he would recommend himself as a partner."

Marissa glared at the woman's hand wrapped so possessively around Jude's bicep. "What do you know about Mrs. Wellingsly?"

Beth looked surprised. "Her? Not much, I suppose. I know she's been widowed for a few years. And I believe she's very keen for whist." And big men who looked like ruffians, it seemed.

Marissa watched carefully, wondering why the gorgeous widow seemed so interested in Jude. Could they possibly be lovers? They hardly looked compatible. Mrs. Wellingsly, all pale beauty and delicate grace, looked like spun sugar next to him.

But she was obviously flirting, and Jude hadn't looked up once to see if Marissa was nearby.

"Hmph," she muttered, and Beth sent her a puzzled

look. "Come, let's find some wine. I'm sure my mother will start the dancing soon."

She managed to get through two glasses of wine and three dances without seeing Jude again, and while she told herself she was purposefully avoiding him, her irritation felt suspiciously like hurt.

Ridiculous. He meant nothing to her.

But when she spotted Mrs. Wellingsly in a half-shouted conversation with Aunt Ophelia, Marissa felt as if a tight band had just been released from around her chest. Wherever Jude was, he hadn't snuck off with that woman.

She spun around to see if she could find another dance partner, but found herself nearly colliding with Edward instead.

"Might I speak with you in my study?"

Frowning at his dark tone, Marissa followed her brother from the room. "What is wrong?" she whispered. "I haven't received another letter, if that's what you think."

"No," he muttered, "but I have."

"What letter?" she asked as he closed the door of his study behind her. Jude was there, and Aidan as well.

Not good.

"Cousin May wrote to warn she'd heard a rumor about you and Peter White having a private argument. It's dangerous to let it go on longer."

"But—"

"I will announce the engagement."

"But you promised me time!"

Edward folded his arms. "Engagements can be broken. But if this story spreads, there will be nothing I can do for you, Marissa. A betrothal to Jude

Bertrand will cause a stir and either smother the story or give it a less sinister turn. If you and Mr. White argued, it must only be over your growing affection for Jude."

Her brain tried to muster an objection, but in truth, it made perfect sense. Marissa looked toward Jude and met his serious eyes. He stepped forward, but she shook her head. She did not need his reassurance or influence. She would make this decision as an adult. "When shall we announce it then?"

"As soon as possible," Edward answered. "Tonight. I'll interrupt that harpist Mother hired. That should be dramatic."

"Yes. All right."

Jude cleared his throat. "If I might have a moment alone with Marissa?"

Her brothers both left, though Aidan stopped before her to place a hand on her arm. His eyes were dark, but she nodded his worry away. When he left, the door closed with a careful thump.

"This won't change anything for you," Jude said. "I'll still honor your plan."

"Thank you."

"But know that I honor mine as well. Scandal or not, I mean to marry you if you'll have me. And only if you'll have me."

"All this based on admiration for my overwrought nature?"

"Something like that."

He moved closer, and Marissa felt the room grow smaller, the air less cool. He stopped before her, and his hand touched her jaw as it had before. The last time, she'd thought he would kiss her, but now she had no idea what he meant by it.

"Will you do me the honor of accepting my hand, Marissa York?"

"I . . ." By God, everything he did was a mystery. "You understand that—"

"I do."

"All right. Then, yes, I suppose I do as well."

His mouth lifted in that already-familiar crooked smile. "I'm not sure you're a romantic at all," he said. Then he tipped her face up and lowered his head, and my God, he was finally going to kiss her.

He moved so slowly that she could feel her own breath rush between them. She kept her eyes open, worried he'd draw away if she didn't watch. But finally, finally, his mouth touched hers, and she sighed with stark relief.

His lips brushed over hers, a soft rasp that set her nerves tingling. He smelled good so close to her. That same spice she caught a hint of on rare occasions. He smelled like something she wanted to taste.

So she did, pressing her mouth more firmly to his. Jude rewarded her by parting his lips just enough to catch her bottom lip between his. Now there was a hint of wetness when she moved. Now it felt wicked and less than safe.

The tingling in her nerves spread out, chasing down her body with happy speed.

Marissa had been kissed before, and she knew how it was done, so she angled her head and licked his plump bottom lip, and then she had to do nothing but let him kiss her.

And kiss her he did, with tongue and mouth and nibbling teeth. Marissa found herself clutching his lapels in an attempt to keep him near. At any moment he could lift his head, and then when would he kiss her again? She'd waited so long already. . . .

His tongue rubbed a slow caress against hers, and Marissa moaned and strained toward him. His chest was so hard, and she could feel a faint roughness to his chin, but his mouth was nothing but warmth and sweet need. The kiss went on for long minutes, and soon enough she was thinking of couches and things that could be done on them. She was thinking of his thigh and what it might feel like under his trousers. Men had crisp hair on their thighs, she knew. And hot skin. And other interesting things in the vicinity.

So when he finally lifted his head, Marissa let him go, anticipating that something even better might happen. But nothing better did.

"That's as official as it gets, I'd say." His voice was deeper than normal, and much more rumbly.

Marissa fell back on her heels when she realized she was still poised on tiptoe. "Pardon?"

"Our betrothal. Shall we go share our joyful news?"

"I rather thought we'd stay here a moment and find ourselves even happier."

"Marissa! What kind of gentleman would I be if I tried to sway things in my favor by increasing your odds of . . . increasing?"

Her eyes slid toward the very comfortable-looking sofa on the far side of the room. It was far larger than the sewing-room couch. "You said there were other ways. . . ."

"Oh, Christ," Jude said to the ceiling. His neck stretched up when he raised his chin, and the shadowed darkness of his nascent beard caught her eye. Another thing that made him so much rougher than other gentlemen. Even when he was closely shaven, she could see the dark threat of whiskers beneath his skin.

Yes, he was altogether too rough. Yet he kissed like some sort of wicked angel.

"I'll never be fit for public presentation if you say things like that to me, Marissa."

"What do you mean?"

"Nothing," he muttered.

"Might we kiss more?"

Jude closed his eyes and shook his head. "Edward will come looking for us shortly, I'm sure. Anyway, it won't be good for my nerves."

Marissa felt like pouting, but she wasn't about to let Jude know. So she sniffed, "You make the oddest jokes," and pretended to straighten her skirts. "Are you ready, then?"

"I think I'm past offending, yes."

"Did you muss my hair?"

He made a show of tilting his head this way and that, then walked slowly around her, sending her body into tight awareness of his gaze. When he reached her front again, Jude stole a very quick kiss. "You look perfect." That easy kiss felt so natural that it startled her. And when she took his arm, she felt the same strangeness. Three days ago, she hadn't known him. Two days before, he'd been an unattractive acquaintance. Now he felt like a friend.

Like everything else to do with Jude, it made no sense, but there was no point poking at it with a stick. She should just be happy he was tolerable.

No one seemed to notice them when they entered the room. Even Beth didn't look up, absorbed as she was with watching Mr. Dunwoody dance with Nanette.

But Edward had been watching, and when Marissa gave him a small nod, he walked toward the musicians, his mouth set in too grim a line.

He held up his hands, and the music faded to a stop, the harp trailing out as if the song did not wish to end.

"Ladies and gentlemen, I have wonderful news tonight, and I'm thrilled you are all here to share in our family's joy. Mr. Jude Bertrand, an honorable and good friend of the York family, has asked for my sister's hand in marriage, and I was only too happy to give them my blessing." A murmur of shock trembled through the room. "Please join me in sharing congratulations with the happy couple." He gestured toward them, and the whole room turned as one. "We are all very . . . happy . . . with the arrangement."

No one seemed to notice her brother's awkward ending. They probably hadn't heard past their gasps and whispers. Every single face was etched in some measure of disbelief.

Smiling, clutching Jude's arm, Marissa looked around and caught Mr. Dunwoody's gaze. His face looked slightly crooked, torn between disbelief and horror.

In fact, several of the faces looking back at her could conservatively be described as horrified. Marissa tried to smile more widely, but embarrassment made her lips stiff. Embarrassment for herself, if she was being honest, but also for Jude. Nobody clapped. Nobody made noises of encouragement. Not one person could believe that

Marissa York would marry this man. And of course, under any normal circumstances, she wouldn't, and that knowledge was a rough stone lodged in her stomach.

But when she glanced up to Jude, he looked not the least bit discomfited.

"I'm honored," he said loudly, "that Miss York would even turn a smile in my direction, and I'm humbled that she has accepted my offer."

"Hear, hear!" Edward called, and the room had no choice but to follow suit. Aidan began to applaud, and the rest echoed him. Finally, the music started again, and Marissa felt faint with relief. It was done. And there was no doubt that talk of their engagement would overshadow any other talk drifting about.

Jude offered her a wink as a few brave souls approached, and his good humor helped to steady her nerves. Any other man she knew would be red-faced and fuming at this point. But Jude was steady as ever. In that moment, his brutish size seemed the least important thing about him. His strength was something entirely more than muscles and bones.

They accepted strained congratulations for a few moments before Cousin Harry clapped Jude on the shoulder with a hearty laugh. He was in on the plan, of course, but his acting had always been impeccable. Dear Harry was the star in every one of her mother's productions, and he played this role with aplomb as well. His hug was warm and genuine. His congratulations hearty but still surprised. The tension in the room eased, and Marissa found herself relaxing as she laughed and hung on Jude's arm.

For a moment it almost felt real. She was happy, and she'd be married, and she would love this man. And then Marissa caught sight of Beth's face, frozen with shock, and she remembered that this was all a terrible mistake.

Chapter 9

Marissa pushed the horse hard through the chilled dawn air, clouds of steam billowing from its nose to slide past her boots and disappear into the gray light. She didn't enjoy the hunt, she didn't like jumping, but this she loved. Speed. A horse running so fast that Marissa felt she might fly.

She wished she could fly.

There'd been no dancing after Edward's announcement had been made. There'd been a drama to rehearse and friendly gambling and charades, but no dancing. Marissa had used that as an excuse to retire early. Really, she'd been trying to escape the subtle questions and sly looks of forty people trying to puzzle out her relationship with Jude.

Beth had looked more than puzzled. She'd seemed downright frightened, and when Marissa had heard a soft knock on her door close to midnight, she'd pretended to be asleep. She couldn't tell Beth the truth. If Marissa was with child, she'd be sure that no one but her immediate family knew the truth.

She would not dishonor Jude in that way, nor the child.

The thought slackened her grip, and the mare began to slow. There was the faintest fog this morning, and while Marissa could see clearly twenty yards ahead, the world began to recede at that point, as if the earth ceased to exist once it got too far from her. That was a blessing today, so she let Cleopatra trot for a distance before slowing her to a walk and turning back. Today, her loneliness was welcome.

She wasn't with child. She was so sure of that, but no one believed her. She felt exactly the same as she had before that night, not even changed in the way that she should be. What did that say about her? Was she cold or callous? Was she missing some essential femininity that made one a woman? She'd always felt different, though not one person around her had seemed to notice. Not her brothers. Not her parents. No one . . . until Jude had come along. He saw her, truly, but she didn't know if she wanted to be seen.

It felt like a violation, sometimes, not being able to control what he knew of her. He didn't know her secrets because she'd told them. He saw them written on her in gilt script.

But out here in the fog, she was safe and alone, and her future was as fuzzy as the line of trees to the west. Even her cold skin was a relief from the hot blushes that had taken it so often of late.

Still, she could not stay lost forever, and the men were likely gone now on their morning hunt. If she could only find a way to avoid Beth as well . . .

Halfway back to the manor, hoofbeats approached.

For some reason, she knew it must be Jude, and she braced herself for his all-seeing eyes. He would likely ride up and take one look at her and ask why she was hiding in the fog and feeling sorry for herself.

Cheeky wretch.

She was ready for him when the horse finally materialized on the lane ahead. So ready that she felt a flash of disappointment when she saw the dark muzzle and pale white star on the horse's nose. It wasn't Jude's great ugly beast, so it couldn't be Jude on his back.

The figure raised a hand, and Marissa stifled a sigh. She knew that elegantly slim arm.

Mr. Dunwoody. *Damnation.*

She offered a somber greeting as he drew near.

"Miss York, I was hoping to find you on your ride this morning. The stable boy said you'd gone this way."

"Don't let me keep you, sir. I'm already returning as I can hardly feel my nose."

"Ah." His smile flashed for only a moment. "Please, if I might escort you back . . ." He turned his horse, and the gelding's elegant legs pranced in impatience. It was a beautiful horse, its lines as perfect as the seams of Mr. Dunwoody's coat. Marissa swept a wistful gaze over the gelding. She did so love beautiful things.

"Your betrothal came as quite a surprise."

"Mr. Bertrand has been a friend of the family for years now."

"Yes, well . . . I guess I did not notice him among your many admirers."

"Come, there were not so many."

"It seemed an intimidating horde to me." His

smile tried for self-deprecation but only looked worried. "Are you quite certain all is well, Miss York? After the argument with Mr. White and now this sudden betrothal, I can't help but worry."

"Worry about what, exactly?"

Now his familiar blush returned, and Mr. Dunwoody shook his head. "I apologize. It's none of my concern."

She should have corrected him, if only to be polite, but she couldn't. It *was* none of his concern.

The rigidity left his spine in tiny increments. Finally, he turned toward her with his normal smile. "All that aside . . ."

She smiled back, and wondered if she might ever have approached Mr. Dunwoody with her predicament. She couldn't imagine it. He looked so very . . . *young*. Almost certainly, he would've reacted to her story with horror and shock. He would've been disgusted or outraged. Under no circumstances could she imagine Mr. Dunwoody matter-of-factly asking if she'd bled yet.

Wincing at the thought, she faced the outline of the manor beginning to reveal itself through the white.

Beautiful or not, Jude Bertrand was a man who could see her through this haze. Her doubts about him had floated far away.

"Well then," Dunwoody finally continued. "May I ask what you think of Miss Samuel?"

Marissa's heart leapt. "Oh, Beth is wonderful. She's my dearest friend. She's kind and loyal, and I'm sure you noticed that she's an excellent dancer. So graceful."

"Of course. She's lovely and soft-spoken. Very nice."

"Yes."

"What of Miss Nanette Samuel? You must be close to her as well."

Her leaping heart landed in a heap atop her stomach. "Nanette? Um, yes, I have spent time with her as well."

"She's beautiful and so lively, wouldn't you say?"

"Mm." Her mind scrambled. If she spoke her true feelings, Mr. Dunwoody would likely discount them as the bitter words of a rival. But if she complimented Nanette, he would believe that too well. She took a deep breath. "Nanette is beautiful," she said, swallowing back her warnings. If he was smart, he'd be able to take her simple compliment for what it was. And if he were worthy of Beth, he would be able to see the truth himself.

"Yes," he murmured. "She is that."

Marissa gripped her reins tighter and hoped she'd done the right thing. But now she had another secret to keep from Beth.

Strangely enough, she found herself yearning to get Jude alone and tell him her troubles. A very odd feeling to have about a man, wanting to talk with him. Very odd indeed.

Chapter 10

Marissa hadn't come down to luncheon, and Jude was growing worried. The woman loved to eat, though she took such ladylike bites, people didn't notice that her last bite was often from a third serving. How she managed to stay so thin was beyond Jude's understanding.

He frowned down at the carpet as he paced along the hallway.

He'd sent Aidan to find out what the matter was, and her brother had come back to report she was taking a nap. Aidan had gone on his happy way, but Jude couldn't stop worrying.

Was she sick? Or was she regretting the betrothal? He didn't care to see the woman tortured. He truly believed they were compatible or he'd never have volunteered. Did she understand that?

Impatient with his maudlin mood, Jude decided to simply ask her the question himself and headed toward the second floor and Marissa's chambers.

She didn't answer the first soft knock, so he tried again, then wondered if waking her from a nap was counterintuitive to his goal. He had the feeling that Marissa York would not trip lightly from sleep.

"What is it?" she called just as he was turning away.

He tensed in surprise. "It's Jude."

Silence.

"I wanted to check on you."

She murmured something.

Leaning close to the door, Jude thought he caught the word "men," but he couldn't make out much more.

"Just a moment," she said more loudly.

And so Jude found himself standing in the corridor like a child awaiting punishment. A few eternal minutes later, Marissa opened the door and pulled him into her room.

And Jude gawked like a naughty boy.

She looked beautiful. Her normally styled-to-perfection hair was still braided, but the strawberry-blond braid hung down to curve over her shoulder. Her cheeks and lips were rosy as if she'd been curled beneath warm covers. Her eyes were heavy-lidded with sleep. He'd see her like this every morning if they married.

"Would you care for tea?" she asked.

"You're beautiful."

Her brow furrowed with skepticism as she touched the end of her braid with a snort. "You're either mad or a liar. I've been napping."

"Are you ill?"

Her hand went to her stomach, drawing his eye to the soft white peignoir she wore. "No. I only had trouble sleeping last night."

"The announcement?"

Gaze falling to his shoes, she shook her head.

"Not really. I can't tell Beth the truth. I don't want to avoid her, but I don't know what to say."

"Tell her that I kissed you and you couldn't refuse me. Those things are true, after all, if not in that order."

She snuck a tiny smile at that. "You want me to convince her that I love you?"

"Would she believe you?"

"I don't think so. I wrote to her a week ago, after all, and somehow forgot to mention you."

"A tragic oversight." Unable to resist the lovely picture she presented, he stroked the backs of his fingers over her rosy cheek. "Then why don't you tell her that I make you feel things you've never felt before. Would she believe that?" Her cheek grew warmer against his knuckles, and he was sure she leaned her face more fully into his touch.

Her gaze rose to meet his, eyes flashing green heat. "She might."

He couldn't kiss her. Not now. Not in her chambers when she wore that flowing white gown and nothing else. She'd be soft right now if he touched her. Soft and. . . . He dropped his hand and stepped back.

"I finished your book. You were right. The handsome gentleman did save the day."

Her eyes narrowed with irritation. "Mm. Who is that woman to you?"

"What woman?" He wondered if his face looked as dumbfounded as he felt.

"Patience Wellingsly. Is she your lover?"

"What?" His mind spun with the change of topic. "No. Of course not."

"Then why does she look at you as if she wants to be devoured?"

He shook his head. "Perhaps because I've refused to take a bite?"

She crossed her arms and glared at him. "I don't believe you."

"Marissa." His brain finally caught up to the topic, and Jude registered a shocking fact. Marissa York was jealous. Over him. "I have never so much as kissed Patience Wellingsly."

"Well then, that puts me a full minute ahead of her in your distribution of intimacy. A comforting lead."

He didn't point out that she was jealous. She'd only deny it. But there was one thing she might not deny. "Are you complaining about a lack of kisses, Miss York?"

"Well, what is the point of being betrothed if one can't even enjoy kisses? I was kissed more often before!"

"Were you? By whom?"

Her chin inched up. "Men."

"Are you sure?"

"Why do you keep saying that? What is this great divide in your mind that sets men apart from boys?"

This time when he stepped toward her, Marissa stepped away. Then she seemed to realize what she'd done and stood her ground, shoulders back and chin high. And when he kissed her, she leaned into him, fingers spreading open on his chest.

He didn't tease her this time, but kissed her fully. She tasted of sweet, hot tea, and she was soft. Very soft. The layers of thin fabric did nothing to conceal the feel of her curves when his hands touched her hips. She wore no corset. She wore practically nothing at all.

When she sighed into his mouth and pressed her entire body more firmly against his, Jude groaned and told himself to set her away. Instead he shifted her toward her bed. A natural instinct. An awful idea. But he was all instinct now, as her tongue stroked his in eager hunger.

Her passion had stolen his willpower away. Her hands eased beneath his coat and snuck over his chest. Her knee rubbed restless between his. Her soft noises seemed to wind around him and squeeze till he couldn't breathe.

He eased her toward the bed until her legs touched the mattress, then laid her slowly onto the goose down. "If I were a boy, I'd probably slide my hand beneath your neckline right now."

Her eyes popped open. "Oh!"

"I'd caress your breasts until I felt enough time had passed, and then I'd pull your dress up in bunches until you were sufficiently exposed. Does that sound familiar?"

She stared, wide-eyed, at him, her breath rushing past her lips.

"Then I'd rub your sex until it was slick enough for penetration. No more than that, mind you, because if I were a boy, my only goal would be mounting you."

"I see," she whispered.

"But I'm a man, Marissa, so I'll do this instead. . . ." Lying on his side, Jude made sure to keep his weight off her body as he kissed her again. Naturally passionate as she was—or perhaps just naturally impatient—Marissa slid her hands behind his neck and pulled him closer. He smiled against her mouth and murmured his pleasure, but he did not touch her. He only kissed, exploring her mouth, discovering what she liked and what she didn't, memorizing the texture of her tongue against his.

When she shifted restlessly beneath him, Jude finally broke the kiss and dragged his mouth down her neck. He sucked at her neck and nibbled her shoulder and kissed his way down her breastbone, his cock aching more with every taste. Her encouraging whimpers drove him wild. He wanted her making those sounds while she took him inside her. Wanted her begging him to give her more.

Jude took a deep breath and made himself calm. He wouldn't take her. Not until they were married. But he meant to *show* her, at least, that there was more to a man than dancing and tight trousers.

So he drew gently at the skin just above the ruffled neckline of her gown. Her belly sucked in, and her breasts pushed up. The delicate fabric showed the clear outline of her pebbled nipples, pushing against the silk. Jude stifled a groan.

She was a slim woman and her breasts were small, but by God, they were finely made.

His hands clenched the bedspread. He would not enact the very scenario he'd described.

"Jude," she whispered.

He ignored her plea and kissed his way along the line of the fabric. Her hands tightened in his hair and pleasure pulsed into his veins. She wanted this. She wanted *him*.

Jude eased one hand beneath her robe and curled it over her shoulder so that he could feather his thumb across the very top of her breast. She shivered and arched into his body.

This was a more difficult exercise in control than he'd imagined. And Marissa was showing no restraint at all.

Jude closed his eyes and counted to twenty; then, telling himself he could stop when he needed to, he finally pressed his lips to the thin fabric that covered her breast. He closed his mouth over her nipple, and Marissa gasped in a high, sweet voice.

Christ, yes. that was the sound he wanted. Those gasping, keening sighs. He sucked her nipple and coaxed more lovely notes, then scraped his teeth over her to hear even more.

He wanted so badly to tug her gown down and see the miracle of her naked body. He wanted to strip her bare and taste every inch of her skin. Then he wanted to bury himself deep within her for hours.

But more than anything, he wanted Marissa to think she couldn't live without him, as he was beginning to think he couldn't live without her.

He kissed her other breast as well, sucking at her nipple through the fabric until she was panting with lust.

Hands shaking with the effort of restraint, Jude lifted his head and kissed her mouth once more. Then he rolled to his back with a wince and closed his eyes. "That is the difference between a boy and man," he rasped.

"What? Why did you stop?" Unwilling to lie there passively, Marissa popped up on her elbow. "You haven't left me satisfied, if that's what you think!"

"Ha! Give me some credit. Half the joy of making

love is the pleasure of anticipation. I bet none of your dancing boys have ever taught you that lesson."

"But . . . but I do not need to be taught lessons! You are not my tutor!"

"No, I am only the man you paid no attention to until three days ago. I am no boy, Marissa, and I am no fool either."

She was silent so long that Jude finally forced his eyes open to look at her. She frowned down at him like a troubled nymph, her lips pink and swollen from a recent tryst in the forest. "I do not need you to tempt me, Jude. I like you well enough."

He cocked an eyebrow. "Well enough for what?"

Her lips curved into a smile. "Well enough that I did not want you to stop."

"We've discovered that at least."

She studied him for a long moment. "May I see your chest?"

"Pardon?"

"I'd like to see your chest."

"I'm not sure you'd like it. There's hair on it, you know."

"I know that!"

"What is it that you wish to see then?"

She narrowed her eyes in irritation. "Oh, I think I understand. You've seen women's breasts before, so why would you care to see more?"

There was no arguing with that nonsense, so Jude simply reached for his cravat. He pulled the ends free and unbuttoned his shirt down to the placard. She seemed satisfied with that and slipped her hand beneath the linen to touch his bare skin.

Jude stifled a deep groan. Her hand stroked a

tentative path over his chest and twisted knives into his soul.

"You are hairy," she breathed.

I will not pull her over me.

"But not frighteningly so. It feels rather nice."

And I will not slide myself atop her.

She explored up to his shoulders and down to the bottom of his rib cage. "You are so very wide compared to me."

Her palm slid over his nipple, and Jude clenched his teeth. And when her hand skipped down to the sensitive skin of his stomach, he sucked in a gulp of air.

"Sorry, does that tickle?"

"Yes." Yes, it tickled, but the jump in his heart-beat made his cock pound harder until his arousal felt more like pain.

"This is nice," Marissa murmured. "I like this."

Pain or not, he liked it too, and when Marissa laid her head on his shoulder and rested her hand over his heart, something more powerful than lust swelled inside him, and he closed his eyes and curved his hand over her head to keep her close.

"Mm," she murmured sleepily. "I finally see what you mean about not embarrassing yourself."

"Pardon?"

"Your trousers are quite out of sorts."

She sounded so ridiculously prim that Jude couldn't believe her words. Then he burst into deep, honest laughter. Marissa York was like no other woman he'd ever met. It was no wonder he was falling in love with her.

Chapter 11

Marissa hated Nanette, and she was beginning to hate Mr. Dunwoody as well. *And,* she decided with a petulant scowl, if she was going to hate people, she may as well add Patience Wellingsly to the list. The woman had no right to sit out in the sunlight on an autumn day and simply . . . glow.

Marissa had first thought her mother's suggestion of a grand picnic exciting. It was a beautiful, warm day, and a romantic picnic would add to the story of love at first sight that she and Jude were attempting to weave. Well, Jude was claiming he'd loved her at first sight. Marissa was smiling shyly and pretending to accept it all as her due.

"More punch, my darling?" he asked loudly as he rose to his feet. Patience Wellingsly watched from her blanket as he stood straight and dusted off his trousers. The woman's eyes showed a deep appreciation for such large thighs, and Marissa had to fight the urge to put a hand to his leg and lay claim to them.

"She is so beautiful," Beth sighed.

"I know. It's sickening."

"Do you think Mr. Dunwoody is in love with her?"

"Why would . . . ? Oh." She swung her eyes back toward the Samuel blanket, where Mr. Dunwoody sat straight and proper. "You should move over there. Talk to him. I daresay he'd be relieved to change subjects. One can only speak of Nanette for so long."

"Marissa!" Beth laughed, but her face soon turned miserable again. "No, I cannot move there now. It would be obvious I was only begging attention."

"Perhaps, but Nanette would do it and not feel the least amount of shame."

"Yes, but I am not Nanette. Unfortunately." She wilted down to the blanket to lie back and stare up at the sky, so Marissa joined her.

"Thank God, you are not Nanette. I'd not like you at all. It is so much more important that you be interesting and intelligent."

"Is that what you like about Mr. Bertrand?" Beth asked quietly.

Marissa's heart froze for several long seconds.

"It's only that I am so surprised! And please don't take this the wrong way, Marissa, but he hardly seems the kind of man you'd love. You never even mentioned him in your letters!"

"I . . . yes, I know. It happened quickly. And you're right, of course, he's not the kind of man to catch my eye. He's terribly brutal-looking, isn't he?"

Beth's hand found hers and held it. "I fear there's something amiss. You told me just yesterday that you'd never even danced with him."

"There are more important things than dancing."

"Like what?"

"He . . ." There were so many things she could say. He was kind and funny and strong, but Marissa knew she was not the kind of girl to jump into a quick marriage based on kindness. Better to take Jude's advice. "He kissed me," she whispered.

"And so have many others, by your account."

"Yes, but he kissed me and I thought . . ." She closed her eyes and imagined him leaning toward her. "I thought I might die with the pleasure of it."

Beth squeezed her hand. "Truly?"

"Yes. And he touches me like I'm priceless and . . . and base all at once."

Beth turned her head to look at Marissa. "I don't know what you mean."

"It's hard to explain."

"Harder still to understand. I've never been kissed. Not really."

"Perhaps if your morals were a bit looser?"

They both laughed and the tension was broken, and Marissa sighed with relief. Beth seemed satisfied with the answer, and Marissa felt . . . well, she felt strangely satisfied with the answer too. She didn't love him, and she didn't wish to marry him, but at least there were the kisses to look forward too. And the limbs.

"Do you know that men have hair on their chests?" she asked Beth.

Even from the corner of her eye she could see Beth's eyes go wide. "You mean laborers?"

"No, I mean all men. Beth . . . do you like Mr. Dunwoody?"

"I do. He's very handsome. And gentle. I think I

need a gentle husband. So many men are intimidating, aren't they?"

"Before dinner tonight, I'll come and help you pick out a dress, and then we'll get ready together. I'll have my maid style your hair, and we'll add a little rouge to your cheeks."

"My mother won't—"

"She won't even know. Nanette's cheeks don't get so pink from high spirits, do they?"

"No," Beth murmured.

"Then come to my room. You can be as shy as you like as long as you are prettier than Nanette."

"There's nothing to be done for that."

"She's only trying harder, and you are too kind to compete. But I am not kind at all," Marissa said with a grin, "so leave it to me. Will you?"

"I suppose," Beth murmured, but she sounded more loyal than certain. As if she suspected Marissa was up to no good.

Ridiculous, of course, but when Jude loomed over her with a glass of punch, Marissa knew she was caught. He took one look at her expression and grinned.

Yes, Jude had named her well. She was naughty indeed.

"Here," Marissa muttered, reaching a hand down the bodice of Beth's dress.

"Marissa!" her friend gasped as she tried to duck away.

"Elizabeth Samuel, men like bosoms, and yours are sheer perfection, if only you'd let them out." Once she'd plumped Beth's décolletage to her liking, she stood back. "Do you know what I'd give for bosoms like that? Mine make no kind of shape at all, no matter how tight my laces."

"Well, if they're so important, why have you had five offers and I've had none?"

"We each have our blessings. I have a swanlike neck, and you have wonderful bosoms. I show off my blessings, and you do not."

"Marissa!" She started to tug her bodice up, and Marissa slapped her hand.

"Don't you dare. Even if Mr. Dunwoody is blind, there are at least three other likely gentlemen here. I'll be surprised if they don't all ask you to dance. I've already spoken to Mother. She promises to have dancing after the play. Now hold still."

Marissa surveyed her work with a critical eye. Though Beth hadn't had any jewel-tone dresses, she'd brought this sky blue one from her last Season. She hadn't worn it more than once, because she'd felt too self-conscious, but Marissa had thought she'd looked beautiful. She did.

Marissa's maid had spent nearly an hour ironing Beth's curls into loose waves, and a touch of kohl at her lash line turned her plain brown eyes mysterious.

Marissa's own hair was pulled into a simple chignon as a result of all the time spent on Beth, but she didn't mind. She had her hands full of troublesome men already.

"Are you ready?" Marissa asked.

"No," Beth muttered as a faint knock sounded on the door. A maid entered, a note in her hand. Marissa's heart sank as she took it.

"Is it from Jude?"

Marissa lied as she opened it. She knew it wasn't

from Jude, but she couldn't let Beth know that. Instead she took the note to a corner chair and read it.

Mr. White wasn't giving up. He wanted to meet her one last time, to try to convince her of his good intentions. A meeting behind the stables at 10 PM, as if she were that foolish. He'd kidnap her or cause another scene. But what would he do if she didn't show up at all?

Damn that man. She felt helpless now, incapable of making a good decision and vulnerable to the whims of an untrustworthy scoundrel.

She folded the note and slipped it into a drawer of her dressing table. She'd have to consider it carefully. But right now she wanted Beth to emerge from this year of exile and enjoy herself.

"Come," she said with a forcibly bright smile. "Let us find you a gentleman. But remember what I said about kisses. A nice kiss is well and good, but keep trying until you find a kiss *magnifique*!"

"You're scandalous, Marissa!" Beth whispered, but she was still smiling a few minutes later when they entered the drawing room.

A freckled young man named Kenworth looked toward them, and his eye definitely settled on Beth, but she didn't seem to notice. Her focus fell on Mr. Dunwoody, who didn't look up from his conversation with Nanette.

Marissa's eyes locked onto Nanette too. "Oh, blast her," she said when she saw her dress.

Nanette had been in the room when they'd picked out Beth's dress, and she'd clearly meant to outdo her. Nanette was dressed in bright blue, with a bodice that came very close to immodesty.

"It's all right," Beth murmured. "It was a flawed

plan. I can't compete with Nanette. I'm better off waiting for her to marry before I set my cap for a husband."

Marissa disagreed. She wanted to shout that it wasn't true and Beth could marry whomever she liked. That they could both marry whomever they liked.

But there was no point flailing, so she only took Beth's arm and led her to another seat. "Next Season will be grand. You'll see." Except there was a good chance next Season wouldn't be grand at all, at least not for Marissa.

The play was so ghastly that Jude found himself enjoying it immensely. A vignette of *Othello*, with much shouting and wailing and gnashing of teeth. The death scene transcended awfulness and became sublime. Cousin Harry roared with perfect anguish, and the lady playing his wife died with many a tortured sigh.

Jude's mother would love these people, and he had a feeling that Lady York just might be persuaded to invite his mother for a visit. A secret visit, of course, but a friendly one, nonetheless.

"Bravo!" Jude shouted as the crowd burst into applause. He was about to rise to his feet when a feminine hand settled on the back of his neck. Expecting to find Mrs. Wellingsly standing behind him, Jude cringed as he turned. But when he saw that the fingers dragging over his neck belonged to Marissa, his body spread with instant heat.

She leaned down to speak into his ear, and her neckline caught his focus and held it, rendering him unable to concentrate on what she was saying. He'd opened his mouth against that skin earlier. He'd teased his lips over her collarbone. And he'd suckled her until she'd moaned with need. His earlier restraint now seemed an awful thing. If he'd only done what she'd wanted, he'd know what her breasts looked like, naked and flushed with lust.

Marissa started to stand again, and he shook his head. "I'm sorry, I didn't hear a word you said."

"I asked if you'd care to stroll about the garden before the dancing begins."

"God, yes."

Her polite smile spread into a smirk. "Were you staring at my bosom, Mr. Bertrand?"

"Surely not."

"You may stare as much as you like if it leaves you so starry-eyed and flustered."

"I live to please." He finally remembered he should stand in the presence of a lady and thanked God he hadn't stared at her much longer. Even her most casual movements seemed designed to enflame him.

"You're damned beautiful," he whispered as he rose to offer his arm.

"Why do you always say that?"

"Because I'm overwhelmed with it every time."

"Did you learn charm during your years in France?"

"Yes, but I'm not being charming."

"I'm too thin and only passably attractive, so it's definitely charm."

"My word, you're in a strange mood this evening. I didn't wish to interrupt you and Miss Samuel to find out, but are things still awkward with her?"

"No," Marissa sighed as he opened the terrace door and led her out. "No, I've convinced her that your kisses turned my head and overwhelmed my tender feelings."

"Ah, I can see why that has you out of sorts."

"That's not it either. It's just that Mr. Dunwoody fancied Beth until he saw her cousin, and now he can't see beyond Nanette's beauty. Beth is nicer and kinder and smarter, and now it's as if she doesn't exist. I want to strangle him!"

Jude stared at her for a moment, wondering if she was joking. But no, he could see the outrage in her wrinkled brow. "Marissa, are you complaining that Mr. Dunwoody enjoys flirting with pretty girls?"

"Beth is pretty," she muttered.

"I agree. But are you truly passing judgment on a man for being attracted to . . . fashion and fabric?"

She turned to him to glare. "He favored Beth until he met her cousin! It's not the same!"

"If you say so." He touched a careful hand to her hair. "I like your hair like this, *mon coeur.* It looks as though I could free it with a twist of my hand."

She touched her neck self-consciously, the anger leaving her face, and Jude bent to kiss her. He was slow this time, and careful, and Marissa seemed peaceful as well. They kissed for a long, quiet minute, but when he raised his head, Marissa laid her brow against his jacket as if she was weary.

"That's not all that's troubling me, Jude."

His stomach dropped. He put a hand beneath her chin. "What's wrong?"

"I received another note from Peter White."

"What's he done?"

"Nothing. He wants to meet tonight. At the stables."

"That scurrilous bastard. What time?" When Marissa

put a hand on his arm, Jude realized that he'd clenched both his fists in anticipation of pounding Peter White's face in.

"Jude, I want to talk to him. But I want you to come along."

He took a deep breath, trying to cool his own surprising temper. "What is there to say? If you like, I can go on my own. Convince him to leave you alone."

"With your charm?"

"Of course."

"You don't look very charming right now."

He shrugged one shoulder and tried to look less violent.

"No, I want to speak with him. It's too soon to be sure. . . . I didn't plan to say anything yet, but I'm . . . my stomach feels quite . . . achy."

"Morning sickness?" he asked, as half the blood seemed to rush from his head.

"No. Not that."

"Oh," Jude said. "I see."

"I'll know for certain in a day or two, but I thought if I told him, he might finally give up."

"Ah, yes. That's clever. He'll leave you alone if he knows there's no hope." Jude wondered if he was talking about himself or Peter White. But that was ridiculous. Jude hadn't given up hope yet. Babe or no babe, Marissa had started opening up to him. "I'll come with you. It's nearly ten now."

"Thank you." Instead of taking his arm, Marissa reached for his hand, and they walked like that through the quiet dark, each keeping their thoughts close.

Halfway to the stables, she finally broke the silence.

"What was it like when you lived in your mother's home?"

"Well, I knew nothing different at first. It was a home like any other, full of servants and visitors and parties. A happy place, though sometimes not ideal for a child. My mother would send me away to the country with my nurse sometimes, and I was dreadfully lonely without her. She's warm and full of wit and laughter."

"It sounds strangely ideal."

"Oh, there was the occasional fight with a neighbor child who called her names, but . . ." He shrugged those darker memories away. "But I was happy and loved."

He caught the glint of her eyes when she looked toward him. Her hand squeezed his. "When were you sent to live with your father? You were raised in his household, weren't you?"

"Yes." The heartbreak felt old as time now, and yet it still ached if touched.

"Jude—"

"It's neither tragic nor very dramatic. He married when I was three, and by the time I was eight, his family was established and he sent for me. My mother could hardly say no. He'd acknowledged me from the start, and she reminded me every day that I should be grateful for that generosity. And if he wanted to give me the life of a duke's son . . ."

"But the duchess?"

"Oh, she was as understanding as she could be, under the circumstances. Not loving, but not cruel either. It helped that I had been born before they met, I'm sure. And my half brothers treated me as an older cousin. We were close enough. I would've been overjoyed with the arrangement if I hadn't been so homesick."

Marissa stopped and turned toward him. Her hand touched his face, shaping to fit his cheek. "I'm sorry. I can't imagine being sent away."

"Most boys are sent to school at that age, you know. Earlier even."

"And I'm sure they all suffer from it. And your poor mother . . . I missed my brothers horribly when they were at school. She must have been devastated."

"We are close as ever. The story has a happy ending."

"I'm glad," she breathed, and Jude couldn't help but kiss her.

Their mouths met in desperation. A wildness unlike any kiss they'd yet shared. A threat hung over them. This charade might soon come to an end, and then they'd have no excuse to touch each other. No excuse to kiss.

But the charade shouldn't matter. He'd determined to convince her to love him and, pregnancy or not, he still could. She felt it too, after all, the threat of an ending. Her hands clutched him tight, and she kissed him as if she wanted to devour him before it was too late.

If it weren't for Peter White's imminent arrival, Jude would take her hair down. He'd run his fingers through the heavy red-blond locks and see her as no other man had. He'd carry her into the stables and lay her down and show her that she could not dismiss him.

He could overwhelm her with pleasure. He knew he could. A woman like Marissa would bloom under a wicked tutelage. But lust was a crumbling foundation on which to build a future. Lust would not support a year together, much less a life.

In that moment, he saw that he wanted everything, not just her lust.

So instead of sweeping her up into his arms, Jude set her back. "We'd best get this over with and return before we're missed."

"Yes," she said, though her voice was soft enough to get lost in the rustle of the trees around them.

She turned and trudged on without taking his hand.

"Marissa!" a voice hissed just as she drew even with the stable. "Is that you?"

"It's Miss York," she snapped back.

"Yes, of course. I meant no offense."

"What did you wish to speak with me about, Mr. White?"

"I feel as if we left things in an unfortunate state the last time we met. I desperately wish to rectify that, Miss York. I know you must have some feelings for me, else you wouldn't have—who in the world is that?" Peter White took a few frantic steps back.

Jude smiled.

"It's Mr. Bertrand," Marissa answered, her tone a bit too dismissive for Jude's taste.

"Well, what's he doing here?"

"He's here to be sure you don't cause offense, Mr. White."

"I would never seek to cause you harm, Marissa. You must believe me!" He threw his hands high in a dramatic gesture, and Jude tensed. He'd hung back to give them a semblance of privacy, but he was within two seconds of knocking Peter White to the ground if the man raised a hand in her direction.

"Be that as it may," Marissa continued in a cool tone, "I only met you here to insist you cease writing to me."

"I can't give up—"

"You must give up. You attempted to trick me into marriage after I'd twice refused your offer. You meant to take that choice from me, and I'll never forgive you for that."

"But you're ruined!" Amazingly, the man actually sounded sincerely concerned for her future.

"If you're implying that no man will want me, I'm forced to tell you that you're quite wrong. Mr. Bertrand has offered for my hand, and I've accepted."

"That's . . . that's not possible!" White's head turned toward Jude. "What kind of a man would take another man's leavings?"

Jude had been lounging against the side of the stable, but he stood straight at those words. "Pardon me?" he drawled as violence crept into his blood.

"Um . . ." White backed up again, stumbling a bit over a clump of grass. "Please understand. She may be carrying my child!"

Jude felt Marissa's touch and looked down to see her hand on his fist. "It is my opinion," he growled, "that only the lowest cur takes advantage of a woman and then abuses her for participating. Is that what you are, sir? A dog in need of putting down?"

"I—"

"Because if you think I will not beat you within an inch of your life, then you are stupid as well as immoral!"

When Marissa wrapped her hands around his

arm, Jude realized he'd stalked two steps closer to White. Almost within striking distance now. His hands shook with fury.

"Mr. White," she said quietly. "I am not carrying your child, so the matter is finished."

The man's eyes jerked nervously between Jude and Marissa. "Are you sure?"

"Yes. So please consider me a stranger. I do not wish to see you again."

"And," Jude added, "I promise you that if you breathe one foul word about her, I will hear of it, and I will kill you. Do you hear me?"

White seemed to sense that the immediate danger had passed, as he pulled his shoulders back and primly straightened his cuffs. "I do. Good-bye, Miss York. I only regret that my intentions have been misunderstood. I wish you the best in your fortuitous marriage."

Though Jude ached with the need to pounce, he let the man turn around and walk off into the night.

Marissa let out her breath in a long sigh. "My word, Jude. You are terrifying when you're angry."

"I cannot stand men like him."

She raised a knowing eyebrow.

"And not only because of my mother," he muttered.

"Were men cruel to her?"

"No, my mother is a good judge of character, but many of her friends were ill-used. Often it's how they came to be in that profession. Seduced by a gentleman, then cast aside like rubbish." He let Marissa turn him back toward the house.

After a few steps, she asked a very quiet question. "Is that what my brother does?"

"Who? Aidan?"

Not meeting his eyes, she nodded.

"No, I wouldn't call him a friend if he did. Aidan might be cold, but he's unfailingly honest. He does not love them and makes that clear."

"But they love him?"

"Only the very foolish ones, Marissa."

"He is just so cold now. And the stories I hear . . . I worry."

He was finally calm enough to feel that her hand trembled against his arm, and Jude pulled her to a sudden stop. "You're shaking. Are you all right?"

"Yes, I'm just feeling a bit . . . drained. I wasn't expecting to believe anything Peter White said."

"Did you?"

"Yes! And that's what so frightening. That he may have truly cared for me when he tried to force me into a future I did not want."

Jude made a sound of agreement as he wrapped her in his arms, but pain bloomed in his chest at her words. Is that what she thought of him, as well?

"Jude," she sighed. "You've been so good to me."

Closing his eyes, Jude breathed in the flowered scent of her hair, his whole body tightening with arousal as he drew her in. But he only held her, hoping he could calm her even as his mind raced. If he had to let her go, he'd do so with grace. Or at least pretend to.

"You're warm," she whispered, unbuttoning his coat to slide her hands against his shirt. For a moment it seemed an innocent quest for comfort, but she kept touching him in wide, slow strokes, and then she pressed her lips against his heart.

"Marissa," he said, meaning to remind her that someone would surely notice their absence soon, but then she whispered "Kiss me. Please?" and the warning died in his throat.

He kissed her, just as she'd asked, aware of her body melting into his as she met his sigh with one of her own. But Marissa was no longer content with just being kissed, and he could feel the racing emotion like another pulse beneath her skin. She kissed him hard and slid her hands along his waist, tugging at the fabric . . . and he suddenly felt the electric shock of her hands on his bare skin.

Stop, his brain said, but his body was still primed with aggression from the confrontation with White. His mouth refused to free itself. His throat refused to form a sound of warning. Instead he growled encouragement as she pushed his shirt higher and spread her hands wide.

Yes, this was what he wanted from her. Her arms holding him, nails digging into his skin to urge him closer. He wanted closer. He wanted in.

They were just past the small gazebo, a private little bower where they wouldn't be disturbed, the perfect place for a seduction, though he had no idea who was being seduced. Him or her or both of them.

Jude picked her up, just as he'd yearned to before, and he carried her into the gazebo as she kissed his neck, her mouth impossibly hot against his skin. The edge of his cravat kept her from exploring further, and he wanted to tear it off, throw down his coat and shirt, and let her explore as she wished. She was right, after all; he wasn't her tutor. He wasn't her master. He was her equal, and in that moment he regretted the control he'd exercised over his own lust. Who the hell was he to protect her from herself?

So he did it. Jude set her on a cushioned bench

and shrugged out of his coat. He pulled at the knot of his cravat, and tugged his shirt over his head.

Moonlight slanted through the latticed wood, throwing ribbons of light across her face. It was just enough to make out her hungry eyes as he sat down and pulled her onto his lap.

"Jude," she breathed, pressing kisses to his shoulder. Her hands ran eager paths down his arms and back up, then around to his back before touching his chest again. "My God . . ."

He held her by the waist and let her do what she wanted. Anything she wanted. She licked his neck and kissed his nipples and nuzzled her cheek against the hair on his chest. She whispered how large he was, and hot, and how much she'd wanted to do this. Her innocence was a starving thing, and in that moment, he was shocked she hadn't lost her maidenhead long ago. Passion seemed to have replaced the very blood in her veins.

"I want to see all of you," she whispered, the words a strange combination of lust and embarrassment. He would've said no if she demanded it, but she sounded so tentative.

Cursing himself, Jude reached for the buttons of his trousers, and Marissa slid back to give him room.

In that moment, the moon lit her whole face, and Jude froze. He wanted more than this lust, more than this night.

"Damn it," he growled. "I can't."

"Jude, please. We can—"

"I can't."

Her face fell, so he reached for her again. "Come here." He lifted her high enough to straddle him, then nearly moaned at the feel of her legs gripping his hips. Her bottom rested so close to his cock.

"I can't," he whispered against her neck. "I'm sorry." But when he sucked at her neck, she sobbed with need, and Jude couldn't leave her like that, no matter his intentions.

He gathered her skirts higher, and slid both hands beneath her chemise.

"Jude," she moaned as his palms settled against the hot skin of her buttocks. Good Christ, she was soft and sweet and warm.

He could free himself from his trousers and guide her onto his cock. And she would ride him, innocent or not. She'd ride him as his hands clenched the round cheeks of her bottom, and it would be the best moment of his life.

Sweat trickled down his temple as Marissa's hips moved restlessly against his hold. He urged her up, her knees pressing into the cushions of the bench, and Jude slid one hand along the seam of her body. The tips of his fingers slid along slick heat, and Marissa jerked hard against him, setting his heart into a gallop.

He circled his fingers over her, and she jerked again, her nails digging into his shoulders. His mouth watered at the feel of her wet flesh, at the way his fingers slipped along her. He couldn't resist pressing one finger in, just to feel what it would be like. The soft heat and squeezing tightness.

"Jude," she moaned. "Oh, Jude."

A shudder took her, or him. She pressed so tightly to his chest that he could not tell. All he knew was the feel of her and her thighs shaking as he stroked her, careful to concentrate his motions on that tight pearl of nerves.

She repeated his name like a desperate prayer, her hips rising and falling in a rhythm that left him clenching his jaw so hard that his teeth ached. His cock throbbed in time with her small movements. She wanted him. Wanted *it*. Wanted to be stretched and filled with his cock.

Now, he thought, meaning to unfasten his trousers and plunge inside her, but then Marissa's body drew tight, her breath gathering in, and she climaxed, sobbing and shaking in his arms, her thighs trembling and her sex pulsing around his fingers.

"Oh, Jude. Oh, God," she cried, her mouth pressed to his neck, the words echoing through his flesh.

Then she was still and limp, and Jude felt one awful step away from madness. Her breath shuddered over his jaw. "Jude?"

"Mon coeur," he rasped. "Do you finally feel better?"

Her gasp of laughter eased him back from his ravenous lust.

"That was . . . I've waited so long for that. Thank you." She pressed chaste kisses to his cheek and jaw. "Thank you. You're a miracle."

"I'd say the miracle is you."

"You'd be wrong. I've tried it myself and . . . um . . ."

He could not ponder that now. He could not tell himself what that meant and what Miss Marissa York had been doing in her bed at night. Not now. Later though.

He didn't dare mess her hair, so he stroked her back instead, and when his body had inched from madness to mere pain, he eased her back. "We've been gone a long while. We'd better—"

"Marissa!" a voice hissed from somewhere across the lawn.

Blast and damn.

"Oh, no!" Her eyes went wide with panic.

"Get up. Here, let me." He patted her skirts down and set her back a foot. "You look perfect." And she did, aside from the slight sway of her body as she fought for strength. "I, on the other hand . . ."

He snatched his shirt and tugged it on, stuffing it into his waistband as quickly as he could. As he fastened the buttons, Marissa found his coat and brought it to him as well.

"Shit," he muttered as he wound the damned cravat around and tried to tie it. The knot seemed to take forever to create. "How does it look?"

"I can't see. Let me—"

"There's no time. I suppose as long as I am not half-nude we must call it a victory. Come." He looked carefully back and forth, and saw no one, but once they'd both tiptoed down to the grass, the voice called again, louder this time.

"Marissa! Where are you? If you don't answer, I'm going to call for torches and guns!"

"Oh, blast!" she whispered.

"There's no hope for it." Jude gave her one last glance and found that she looked entirely normal. He'd have to feel outraged about that later. Right now he had a furious brother to face.

"Edward," he called, tugging Marissa along. "We're here."

"What the hell?" her brother cursed. "I was worried sick!"

Jude was taking a breath, prepared to accept full responsibility, when he noticed that Edward was waving a letter about.

"When I couldn't find you, I went to your room," he said as he advanced on Marissa. "And I found *this*!"

"How dare you look through my things!"

"I thought he'd taken you, damn it! You weren't idiot enough to steal out here and meet him, were you?"

Jude pulled her to his side. "She asked me to escort her so that she wouldn't be in any danger."

Edward rounded on him. "How could you do this without my support? You had no right!"

"There was no time. We met with him, and that was that. I can assure you he'll think twice about approaching her again."

"You shouldn't have let him go. I warned him not to set foot here again."

"I think his intentions were sincere, for whatever that's worth."

"Hm." Her brother's eyes swept down Jude's body. "There was a scuffle, I take it?"

Jude suppressed the urge to check his buttons. "Er . . . yes, but nothing too violent."

"Well, young lady," Edward continued, clearly dismissing Jude's mussed clothing as meaningless, "I suggest you retire to your chambers and think about what you've done."

Her cheeks darkened a bit, and Jude could imagine how pink they must be. "I am a grown woman. You can't order me about."

Edward's frown twisted into outrage, but Marissa

waved a hand before he could shout. "Oh, bother. I'll go. I feel quite spent as it is."

That cheeky minx. She ambled off toward the house while Edward and Jude both stared after her.

"That girl will be the death of me," Edward muttered, but Jude was quite sure he was going to be the one praying for mercy before the month was out.

Chapter 12

She'd managed to avoid Jude for a whole day without ever admitting to herself that she was hiding. She wasn't. She just felt . . . awkward.

Not quite anxious, and yet her heart would start pounding during quiet moments, and then she'd suddenly remember. What she'd done. What he'd done.

Perched tensely on the edge of her bed, Marissa put her fingers to her lips as if she could hold in the emotions that pressed at her throat. Excitement and fear and joy and regret . . . an intense combination. In that moment, she felt almost as though she were being chased. And as if she wanted to be caught.

But that made no sense, so she had no idea what to say to him or even how to look at him. It was simpler just to stay busy with Beth or her mother, or any of the other women doing singularly feminine things throughout the day.

But then that strange anxious yearning would rise. That niggling feeling that some knowledge lurked just past her notice. And then she would remember again.

Jude.

She'd known that men could bring intense pleasure. She'd discovered that quite accidentally two years before, though she'd been aware of *pleasantness* before then. But it was still so surprising that it could be Jude. Jude, whom she'd never so much as looked at.

If it had been some other man, she supposed she'd have simply simpered at him at their next meeting. Offered a blushing smile and a flutter of her lashes as well as a few heated looks. But she'd never even flirted with Jude, and how ridiculous she'd feel glancing through her lashes and giggling like a silly miss.

No, she had no idea how to face him now, and yet she had no choice.

A half hour before, she'd finally got her proof. There would be no child, and she had to tell him. It wasn't fair to drag this out longer. Assuming Mr. White did not spread tales, there'd be no need for a hasty marriage. No need for a marriage at all. After a few weeks, her family would quietly put it about that the betrothal had been called off. No one would be surprised. Her family name would remain unsullied, if more associated with melodrama than ever, and everything would return to normal. She might be damaged goods, but a secretly imperfect wife was a far cry from a fiancée already pregnant with another man's child.

So why was she sitting on her bed with her hands clenched in dread? Why wasn't she racing down to tell Jude the good news?

When her door opened, Marissa took a deep breath and let it out in a sigh that sounded suspiciously maudlin.

Her mother didn't notice however. "You wanted to see me, dear?"

"Yes, Mother. I'm now certain there will be no child, so you needn't worry any longer on that score. I understand that there may yet be consequences to my reputation, but if there are not . . . there'll be no reason for this betrothal to move forward."

"Oh, Marissa!" her mother yelped. "Oh, my sweet girl, this is wonderful news! Simply wonderful! I had not even dared to picture your wedding day to that man. His presence is so overpowering, is it not? And he's really not precisely respectable, despite the duke."

"Mm."

"Well, this is stupendous news. We'll wait a decent amount of time before calling off, of course, and there must be a reasonably interesting story, though I suppose we cannot cast Mr. Bertrand in a foul light after the kindness he's done us. Yes, we will have to tread carefully here, but reasonableness is so dreadfully boring!" She paused to take a deep breath, then swooped down to hug Marissa. "Oh, my darling, I'm so happy for you. You must be so relieved! I'll go tell the baron this very moment."

She always called Edward "the baron," unless, of course, calling him "my son!" evoked more drama. "I would prefer to tell Jude first, Mother. It's only decent. Would you wait a bit?"

"Yes, yes, you must tell him first. I'll tell the baron just before we go in to dinner. How's that?"

Nodding, she met her mother's thrilled smile with one of her own, though her heart felt heavy as lead in her chest and the smile only made it worse.

But as her mother breezed from the room, trailing a happy hum in her wake, Marissa forced herself to her feet and blamed her sick feeling on the circumstances. Of course she felt grouchy and out of sorts. 'Twas only expected.

She walked slowly down the stairs, each step marking four beats of her heart. She knew this because she found herself counting them, marking the time, slowing her pace to get it just right.

There was a small possibility she was stalling. But whatever her stalling techniques, the marble approached, and she was soon standing on it, and trying to decide which way to go. Her brother's study seemed a good bet, but Marissa found it empty. The library and drawing rooms were empty as well. Everyone was dressing for dinner, it seemed.

Marissa snuck a look up the stairs she'd just descended. It wouldn't be proper to go to Jude's room, but then nothing about their relationship was proper. He'd come to her rooms once already. And certainly making love with him last night in the gazebo hadn't been proper. Or whatever it was that they'd done the night before. Was there another name for that hot, tangled embrace? "Kissing" and "touching" were not up to the description.

For a moment, she was lost in that memory. It enveloped her and pulled her back into Jude Bertrand's arms. Her body seemed to rearrange its functions, until parts that normally lay quiet roused themselves to demanding life. And parts of her that normally worked with seamless skill, her knees, her lungs, her beating heart . . . they each seemed determined to ruin themselves.

She shouldn't sneak up to his room. It wouldn't be wise. But even after she took a deep breath and steadied her heart, she still felt compelled.

If she waited, she'd feel back to normal again, back to her anxiety and cowardice. So Marissa set her foot on the first step and started up. Only two heartbeats per stair this time, as she rushed toward something she should not do. This seemed a pattern for her, but there was no time to ponder that now.

She turned toward the south wing of the manor, and spotted a maid ducking out of a room.

"Mr. Bertrand is needed in the study immediately. Which room is he in?"

"The green room, miss."

Marissa hurried on. Down the hall. Around the corner. *There.*

She would have hesitated. Would have stood there and agonized for a few more moments, but what if she was seen?

Marissa tapped her knuckles frantically on his door. He must have been very close. She heard him say, "Yes?" even as the doorknob began to turn.

Certain someone else would peek from their room at any moment, Marissa slid through the opening while he was still swinging the door open.

"Jude," she whispered, pushing the door closed behind her. He was so close that she had to tilt her head back to see his face, and the scent of his skin wrapped around her as she pressed her back against the door.

But no, she wasn't pressing. It was Jude, hands

on her shoulders, pinning her gently to the door as he ducked down to kiss her.

His mouth was far more effective kindling than her memories of his kiss. As she opened her mouth to him, her blood swelled within her, putting pressure on her most sensitive parts. He tasted divine, and the thrust of his tongue made her legs shake with the memory of his fingers pushing inside her.

It had been so . . . naughty. As wild as she'd ever felt. As wicked as he'd named her.

Now she wanted to do it again. She wanted to stretch her arms above her head and let him touch her everywhere. Let him strip her dress from her body and see her nakedness. But she was in no condition for that, she suddenly remembered. And that was why she'd come.

Shaking with the strain of it, Marissa put her hand to his chest and turned her face away. Jude's mouth didn't give up its quest to distract her. He ducked his head and sucked at her throat, sending sparks of fire trailing down to her fingertips. "Wait," she panted. "Jude . . ."

When he lifted his head, his eyes were dark and drowning in want. For a moment, she was caught in their depths, sinking in. . . .

"You were hiding today," he murmured. "From me."

That sobered her, and her body suddenly felt real again and weighed down by the truth. "No. I only . . . I didn't know what to say. . . ."

"Nothing," he murmured. "Nothing at all." He kissed her again, and, sweet Lord, she wanted so badly to lose herself in it. Give up her body to that gorgeous weakness again.

But she pulled away. "Jude. We need to talk."

He straightened with slow deliberation, and his eyes lost their wild darkness by small degrees. "Ah. I see. Of course."

She felt too cool now, pressed to the wood with the distance between them measurable in lonely inches. They were two separate people suddenly, and now they always would be, and she hadn't realized . . . that kiss had been the very last. She shouldn't have turned away.

"I'm sorry," she said, and Jude frowned and stepped another few inches away.

"I'm not with child."

"You've bled?"

Her face flashed to a prickly burn. "Yes."

"A typical amount?"

"Good God, why do you insist on mortifying me?"

"I eavesdropped on my mother and her friends constantly as a child. This conversation is not new to me."

"It's new to me! I've never discussed this with anyone."

He shrugged. "Well? Is it normal?"

"Yes!"

"Then congratulations. You avoided disaster."

"As did you."

He inclined his head, his face giving no hint to his feelings.

"I do so appreciate what you've done for me. I don't know another man who would have offered the same."

"I am exceptional." Surely that was a hint of sharpness in those words?

Marissa curled her fingers against the wood,

wishing she had something to hold on to. "You *are* exceptional. An exceptional friend."

"Of course."

"And I'm sure you're relieved not to have to sacrifice yourself on my behalf."

"Oh, quite."

She would've thought he was angry if she hadn't witnessed his fury the night before. His face wasn't twisted with rage, it was simply a bit more stiff than normal. But there was no sign of a smile, crooked or otherwise.

Perhaps he was only . . . serious? Concerned? Marissa stared up at him, more confused than ever. "You'll probably want to leave soon?"

Now he frowned. "Why would I want to leave?"

"Because most of the guests are departing tomorrow. I assume you'd only planned to stay because you . . . might have been needed."

He watched her for a long moment, and his gaze dipped down her body so briefly that she wasn't sure she'd seen it.

"No," he finally said. "I hadn't planned on leaving soon."

She didn't like the way her pulse sped at those words. "But why?"

"Aidan invited me to stay as long as I like. I like it here. In fact, I'm considering renting a cottage."

"A cottage!"

"Yes, my only home is in London, and I enjoy this part of the country."

Her pulse tripped and stumbled now, panicking at his innocuous words. "Here? I see. Of course." She squeezed her fists harder, until the nails dug into her palms. "Well, I do thank you. Sincerely. And I enjoyed our time together."

One of his dark eyebrows rose to mock her.

"That is . . . I . . . well, I will see you at dinner, Mr. Bertrand."

His jaw jumped at that, and Marissa fumbled for the doorknob. Why did she feel she was doing something wrong? Why did she feel ashamed now, when she hadn't felt it before?

"Marissa."

She froze at the soft strength in his voice.

"We are still betrothed."

"I–I suppose we are. Until everything settles, at least."

"Agreed."

She was so flustered that she forgot any idea of stealth, and simply slipped from the room as quickly as she could. Only when she found herself standing in the corridor did she realize her mistake. Luck saved her from stumbling into another guest, but she didn't pause to savor it. Marissa sprinted around the corner, only able to force herself to slow when she could no longer see Jude's door.

This nightmare of hers was almost over, and as she walked sedately toward her room, chin held high, Marissa convinced herself that the sick feeling in her stomach was relief.

What else could it possibly be?

Chapter 13

"I just don't understand what he's still doing here," Marissa hissed as they ascended the steps of the Framershams' front entrance.

Aidan glanced down at her with an arch look. "He's my guest, and I am still here, so I gather that's why. The question, darling sister, is why his presence is causing you so much bother. Jude means nothing to you, or so you say."

It had been a week. A week of guilt and uncertainty.

Turning her head, she caught sight of Jude twenty feet behind her, gallantly escorting Aunt Ophelia up the steps. Cousin Harry followed with Beth and Nanette, and Edward had already swept Mother inside and out of the cold.

"He reminds me of something I should never have done. That's all."

"Well, I'm pleased you're capable of feeling regret, Marissa," Aidan drawled. "I wasn't sure you could. And I tell you, if I were your eldest brother, I would have turned you over my knee and paddled your backside for what you did."

She set her jaw and thought, *Hypocrite,* but she wasn't rash enough to say it aloud. Aidan's temper could crack like lightning, and she didn't care to face that storm in a public place. Once again, she felt the sharp loss for the brother he'd once been. "Of course I feel regret. I never meant it to affect any of you. I just want this incident to be over, and Jude reminds me that it is not."

"Good, because it isn't. It's not yet clear that the talk has died down, and we still have no idea what Peter White will say. If you're not feeling relieved, I'd say that's a sign of intelligence."

"Pardon me if I don't simper with gratitude at your assessment."

His bark of laughter was loud and harsh, but it was laughter, at least, and when he laid his hand over hers and squeezed, Marissa found that his eyes had softened. "You were born into this family, so you were bound to suffer a scandal or two. Let's hope this is the worst of them."

She longed to turn and hug him, but they were entering the hall now, so Marissa only smiled. "Will you dance with me tonight, Aidan?"

"I am here," he sighed. "I suppose I may as well dance."

"So gallant."

"As ever," he agreed, turning her for a kiss on the cheek before he walked away. She knew from experience that he was off to fortify himself for the evening with a few glasses of brandy. But Marissa was going to fortify herself with dancing.

A quarter hour later, and she'd already greeted the hostess and danced with two gentlemen she'd never met. The Framersham country ball was one of her favorites, for they always invited too many people and sent their footmen out in force with glasses of champagne punch.

In the mayhem, it was easy to lose sight of Jude and the reminder of the past two weeks of tension. Here, she was back to her old self, and when a beautiful young man approached her for the next dance, Marissa didn't have to fake her fluttering response. She'd met him twice in London, and his sky blue eyes and smooth cheeks had inspired several fantasies of kissing and more. So her enthusiasm was quite real when Mr. Erikson led her out into the center of the dancers. Her body tingled recklessly at the touch of his gloved hand on her back and the thought of him wrapping his arms around her. Oh, my.

When the dance called for separation, she took the opportunity to ogle his lean, graceful legs. But then something went wrong. The cut of his trousers was splendid, revealing the line of his thighs perfectly. But the line struck her as a bit . . . underwhelming. His coat was divinely constructed, but even with the expert padding in the shoulders . . . well, she certainly couldn't imagine Mr. Erickson picking her up and carrying her into a secret bower to make love.

Marissa forced herself to smile wider when he tossed her a flirtatious wink. It wasn't the carrying that mattered, after all. It was the kissing and the stroking, and surely none of that would be affected by the anemic color of his skin. That was only proof that he was always careful to wear a hat while riding.

His mouth looked made for kissing, after all, so

rosy and full. Yes, Mr. Erickson would give lovely, gentle, skilled kisses, she was sure of it.

But somehow as she slid past him and took the next dancer's hand, Marissa's thoughts of warm, skilled kisses twisted. Now she was thinking of being devoured. Of a mouth demanding that she open and yield. Of hands that lifted her into place and held her there for anything the gentleman might wish to do to her.

And when she swung back around toward her partner, he filled a disappointingly small area of her vision. But he *was* pretty. There was no doubt of that, and she could happily stare into his blue eyes for hours.

So that was what she focused on during the last steps of the dance. His eyes and the way they smiled at her, crinkling with delight at her attention.

By the time he escorted her off the dance floor, he seemed perfectly nice again. Not inadequate. Not disappointing.

Until she turned and found herself face-to-face with Jude Bertrand.

Her eyes traveled up and up until she met his dark gaze.

"Miss York," he rumbled.

"Mr. Bertrand."

"Are you enjoying the dancing?"

"I am. And you, sir?"

"Well, Miss York, I would enjoy this evening more if you would grant me the honor of a dance."

"I . . . pardon?" The dazzling width of his shoulders must've turned her head. "A dance?"

"Yes, a dance. With your beloved. Surely that can't be too much to ask?"

"Of course not. No."

"May I claim the first waltz then?"

Could he dance? She felt ungenerous when she thought of her toes, but more than anything, she was concerned for her poor heart, which beat a mad rhythm at the prospect of his hands touching her.

The first waltz. When would that be? A few moments from now? An hour? Marissa stared up at him, caught by his eyes. Finally, Jude offered that crooked half smile, and she realized that she'd missed it, missed that feeling of a secret joke that only they shared.

A throat cleared beside her. Marissa blinked and spun to face a gentleman who was offering a sheepish bow. "Pardon the interruption, but I believe this is my dance?"

"Oh, Mr. Jessup, of course." She took his arm with only a glance back toward Jude as she left, and did not let herself notice the delicate feel of the man's bones beneath her hand.

Jude Bertrand might be a friend, but he was not the type of man she intended to marry. Strong bones were nothing to recommend a husband. Nothing at all.

"You watch her," a soft voice said from behind him. Jude turned to see Patience Wellingsly smiling softly. She'd decamped a week ago, but she'd only moved to a cousin's estate a few miles away, so he wasn't surprised to see her.

"Pardon?" he asked.

"Your fiancée. You watch her. As if there were no one else in the room."

He inclined his head.

"I wish someone would look at me that way," she sighed.

"Come now, Mrs. Wellingsly. You're beautiful. Lovely. Don't tell me that men haven't looked at you that way."

"Not the right ones."

She looked so lonely in that moment, so lost, that Jude sighed and offered his arm to lead her to a pair of chairs against the wall.

"If you'll allow me to speak plainly . . . ?"

She looked surprised. "Of course."

"You've no business entertaining Aidan York if you want a man who'll cherish you. You're clever enough to realize that."

He watched her eyes slide toward Aidan. The man leaned against a wide column, looking bored and faintly disgusted.

"I know," she whispered. "It's only that I'm lonely. I've been lonely a long time." When she looked back to him, her face softened to tender sorrow. "Can't you understand that, Mr. Bertrand?" Her hand touched his, and she tried to hold it, but Jude eased his away.

"I'm sorry," she whispered, her eyes filling with tears.

Jude saw the circles under her eyes and the paleness of her skin, and he wasn't as angry as he might've been. "If you want a man to look at you that way, you want love, Patience, not the comfort of someone in your bed."

"Of course." Her elegant neck bowed.

"Tell me you're not in love with Aidan."

"No. Not him."

The hair at his nape prickled in warning. "You're not saying—"

"Do you love her?" she interrupted. "Miss York? She seems very young."

"She's an exceptional woman, and she'll be my wife. And that is all I intend to say to you about her."

"I understand. I apologize. Truly, I do. You're a good man."

He stood when she rose, and she walked calmly away, despite the tears swimming in her eyes. Christ. Did she believe herself in love with him? It seemed impossible. Yes, she'd pursued him in London, but he'd never even spent a moment alone with her.

Still troubled by the miserable solitude in her eyes, Jude watched her make her way across the room to the door beyond. From a distance she looked as cool and regal as ever. Up close she'd never looked so sad.

He knew that most of the ton wouldn't believe a woman as beautiful as Patience Wellingsly could be lonely. But Jude wasn't fooled. His mother's profession was made up almost entirely of incomparable beauties who had never truly been loved.

In fact, in a different time, with a different family, Marissa could easily have been one of those women, betrayed by her own lovely wildness.

The song that filled the room began to draw to a close, and Jude glanced toward the dancers to find that Marissa was leaving the floor on the arm of yet one more adorable pup.

She smiled up at the boy, both her hands wrapped around one of his arms. But when she looked in Jude's direction, her smile became a vicious glare.

Marissa was angry, and there was only one reason for that. She'd seen him talking with Patience.

Good. If he had to watch her dance and flirt with a thousand young gentlemen, she could face the truth that he was hardly undesirable himself.

Over the past weeks, he hadn't felt jealous. Not when she danced, not even when she stared at men's legs as if they were ham hocks laid out for her feasting. He hadn't felt jealous, because he'd known that, given time, he could turn Marissa's head in ways she wouldn't expect. He'd meant to tease her to the point of madness, draw out her natural lusts until she thought of no one but him. He'd meant to show her that looking at pretty boys was good fun, but the serious business of lovemaking was best left to men.

But now . . . now he was out of time. He'd rushed his seduction. Marissa had dismissed him. And he had no idea how to proceed.

Hell and damnation. He was stuck with *dancing.*

He watched Marissa stroll stiff-necked through the crowd of fashionable folk and knew he had no choice on the dancing. Any interaction would now be on her terms, not his. And he refused to give up on whatever small chance he might have of turning this false betrothal into a genuine marriage.

Marissa approached her brother and stole the glass of brandy from his hand. Her eyes cut toward Jude before sliding away.

Oh, yes. She was angry, and that cheered Jude immensely, but not so much that he forgot his mission. When he spotted her best friend hurrying by, he stepped into her path and offered a bow. "Miss Samuel."

"Oh! Mr. Bertrand!"

Her lashes fluttered nervously, and she blushed as she did each time he spoke to her. Miss Samuel was shy and soft-spoken, and he was beginning to understand Marissa's worry that she would not find a husband. She was pretty enough, but between her brazen cousin and the vivacious Miss York, Miss Samuel faded into the woodwork.

"Might I trouble you for a dance later?"

She stammered out an answer that seemed to be a yes, and Jude stepped out of her way to give her the chance to escape. Then he approached Marissa.

"I believe the waltz is next," he murmured. She stiffened and said nothing, and Aidan offered him a taunting smile.

"Lover's quarrel?"

"I'm not sure. Have I offended you, *mon coeur*?"

"Of course not," she snapped. "I'm only thirsty. Would you play the gallant and find me a glass of lemonade?"

"I assume 'lemonade' is code for wine?"

She was still drawing in an outraged breath when he retreated to find her a glass of wine. He found a lemonade too, just in case she'd been honest about that. But when he returned to her, she took the wine and left him with the warm and watery lemonade. She said nothing, and Aidan watched them both as if he were waiting for a play to begin.

Jude offered a quick glare, warning his friend to stay out of it, but he was Marissa's brother, after all, and he couldn't be dissuaded.

"So, have we picked a wedding date yet?" He smiled at the two sets of eyes burning a hole through him. "Everyone is aflutter about the match. I think we might charge for entrance to the nuptials, if we wanted. People are curious."

Marissa casually turned to look behind her, and she saw the same thing that Jude did. If the watching eyes were any indication, people really were curious. Marissa took the warning and smiled widely, but her words belied the grin. "Do you think they'd enjoy it if I boxed your ears?"

Aidan tweaked one of the curls that cascaded from the crown of her head and murmured something about what a fine lady she'd grown into.

Marissa maintained her smile even as she finished her wine. Quite an amazing feat. Jude was still pondering that skill when she popped the glass into Aidan's hand and turned toward Jude. "Shall we do this?"

He'd been so focused on her that he hadn't heard the strings singing out the announcement of the waltz. "Without a doubt," he said, with a little bow before he thrust the lemonade at Aidan and offered Marissa his arm. She kept her pace slow as they walked toward the dancing. He'd noticed that she tended to become deliberately proper when under stress.

"What has you so upset?" he asked softly.

"I am not upset. Not at all."

"I got the distinct impression that you were glaring at me earlier."

"Nonsense."

"Marissa—"

"If you want that woman," she began in a forceful whisper, "I can't fault you. She's beautiful. But I would ask that you at least wait until our betrothal has been broken!"

"I assume you're speaking of Mrs. Wellingsly?"

"You know exactly whom I speak of." They were nearing the couples poised to dance, and Marissa pulled him to an even slower stroll. "You two were cuddled together in the corner as if you were—"

"We were hardly cuddling. And I can't imagine what it matters to you, regardless."

"People will talk!"

"Ah, so you'd like me to be discreet in my affairs, while you openly flirt with every adolescent boy who dances a jig past your line of vision?"

"I've done no such thing!"

Her voice rang in his ears, and she blinked in shock before daring a glance around them. Everyone within a twenty-foot radius was staring. Even the conductor cleared his voice before he rushed the orchestra into the first notes of the waltz. Marissa and Jude stood at the edge of the dancers, facing each other. Her eyes got wider with each second.

Finally, Jude simply took her hand and placed it on his shoulder. It would only be more of a scene if she stormed off. She seemed to realize this as well and clasped his hand when he offered. They both wore gloves, and Marissa's back was protected from his touch by the shell of her corset. Not to mention the fact that they were both angry. But somehow all these prohibitions only heightened the sensations of holding her.

Her breath came too fast due to anger, and the rise of her breasts strained against her bodice. Her cheeks and lips seemed rubbed with rouge, they were so red, and her eyes glinted passion. Marissa York looked aroused, and Jude wanted to growl his lust right into the pretty shell of her ear. He hadn't been able to see her clearly in the gazebo, but this is how he would picture her now, furious and demanding and flushed. . . .

"Patience Wellingsly isn't my lover and she never will be."

"She looks at you like you're a candied treat." Her eyes swept down to his chest for a bare second. "Which is entirely ridiculous at your size."

Jude considered offering a quip about being a mouthful, but reminded himself that wicked as she was, she was not one of his mother's friends.

"I would not dishonor you that way, Marissa. I asked you to pretend we were truly betrothed, and I'll keep my side of the bargain at least."

Her face lost a bit of its stiffness as he spun her in a circle, just managing to avoid another couple. It was a slow waltz, thankfully, as he could not concentrate on their surroundings.

"What does that mean?" she asked.

"It means that I seem to have assumed the role of stranger in the past week."

She watched a spot over his shoulder. "I'm sorry."

"I volunteered to be used for your purposes. I understood what that meant. But I was foolish enough to think we'd become friends."

Now she looked at him. "I . . . we did. You're very kind. And funny. But you make me feel . . ."

His heart burned at what she might say. "What?"

"You make me feel . . ."

His blood seemed to strain toward her.

". . . ashamed."

The gravity she'd exerted over him was abruptly cut off, and everything inside him dropped into the pit of his stomach. "Ashamed."

"Only because I don't know how to treat you. I don't know what you are to me. Are we friends?"

He didn't answer. He couldn't.

"I'm sorry," she whispered again.

"I see. Well, if I inspire shame, I suppose I should do the gentlemanly thing and end my stay with your family."

"Jude, don't. It's my fault. I'm only being overwrought, as you've said of me. We are friends. Or I hoped we were. And . . . and I've missed our conversations."

He didn't know whether to accept her words.

"I've made a mess of everything this past month," Marissa said.

"You have."

Her shoulders dropped, and in her defeat her lower lip stuck out in a seductive pout. She looked at him with shiny green eyes that widened with a deep breath. And Jude knew that if they did marry, he was going to be in very big trouble. He couldn't resist this.

"Will you forgive me, Jude?"

The softness of his name put a hitch in his breath. He concentrated on the waltzing for a moment, as if he were really considering his answer. Finally he offered a smile. "I suppose I will. I'd be more sure of it if you'd stop by my chambers tonight and ask me again."

"Oh, hush!" she scolded as her pout turned into a reluctant smile.

"On my honor, I won't tell a soul. We'll only talk."

For a moment, a certain tilt to her chin made it seem as if she'd consider it, but then she shook her head with a laugh. "You're an awful influence on me, Mr. Bertrand."

"I do what I can."

"If you really wished to talk, perhaps we might share a bite of supper later? Mrs. Framersham always lays out some lovely choices."

"I'd be honored, Miss York. Truly."

By the time he escorted her from the dance floor, Marissa was laughing and teasing that he was a passable dancer after all, and Jude's plans were back in full force.

He was going to marry Marissa York, and she had no idea at all, poor thing.

Chapter 14

"He was a lovely dancer!" Beth said for the third time that morning. "I could hardly believe it."

Marissa nodded, though she couldn't honestly remember much of his dancing. Mostly she remembered the wide wall of his chest and the strength of his arms as he held her. They'd danced, she knew that. And there must have been other people dancing as well, but they hadn't been visible past his shoulders.

"Really," Beth continued, "he was quite charming. By the end of the dance, I'd forgotten how intimidating he is."

"Yes. He's really very civilized."

Beth gasped. "Oh, I'm sorry. I didn't mean it that way. I admit I was shocked when your brother announced—"

"No, it's fine. I thought the same things when I met him, I admit."

"But now I can understand your affection, and I'm so relieved that I see it now. He's very clever, and his eyes are quite lovely."

His eyes. Yes, they were lovely enough, despite their forbidding darkness. She glanced out the window to the small group of men waiting on their horses. Jude stood out as he always did. He was cut from steel, while the other men seemed molded of clay.

He looked toward the house as if he sensed her gaze. Marissa's body thrilled at the thought, and she shifted on her chair. He'd asked her to come to his room last night. He'd been teasing, but still . . . she could have. If she'd dared. He wouldn't have turned her away.

Marissa finished the last bite of eggs, and her eyes drifted toward the window again. Edward finally approached the group, only he wasn't on his mount. He stalked across the lawn like an animal.

"Miss York." The footman spoke quietly at her side. "The baron has requested your presence in his study. He asks that you come as soon as possible."

She met Beth's startled eyes, and Marissa's chest swelled with dread. "Of course," she murmured. As she laid her serviette carefully on the table, movement in the window caught her eye again. Aidan and Jude had dismounted and now followed Edward back toward the house. Her pulse leapt into racing panic, and she could hardly feel her legs as she pushed to her feet.

Possible horrors spun through her head. She dismissed the idea that her mother could have fallen ill. That hadn't been worry on Edward's face, or even grief. It had been fury.

So what could it be? It had to be her and her awful behavior. Had Peter White called their bluff and spread tales about her?

"Marissa?" Beth breathed.

Marissa forced a smile. "I'm sure it's nothing."

"I'll ask my mother to hold the carriage for a few—"

"Nonsense. Your mother is beginning to look tired. She should get home. Please don't delay your departure for me. Anyway, I'll see you in a few days at the next fete."

Beth gave her a long hug, and then Marissa made herself walk slowly through the entry hall and into the corridor that led to Edward's study. A brief swell of male voices rumbled over her, then ended abruptly with the sound of a door slamming. She turned the corner and faced the last few yards between her and the awful unknown. For a moment, her legs were too heavy to move. Her feet stuck to the carpet, holding her in place.

Something terrible had happened, and it was her fault.

This time she would not pout, whatever the solution might be. Marriage. A trip to the Continent. The nunnery. Marissa forced herself to take one step and then another, and she even managed to turn the knob before her courage gave out again. Every head in the room turned toward her. Her mother, her brothers, her cousin, and Jude. Five sets of eyes waiting for her to close the door. Again.

"It's as we feared," Edward said.

She slipped inside and shut the door as softly as she could.

"He's done it."

"Who?" she breathed.

"Peter White." His hand whipped up, waving a piece of paper. "He's sent his threat."

"Marriage? He still wants marriage?"

Edward's hand tightened on the note. "No. What he wants is five-thousand pounds."

Marissa and her mother gasped. Somehow, asking for money seemed even more crude than trying to force her into marriage. Marissa crossed the room and dropped onto the sofa to clasp her mother's hand.

"That's outrageous," Cousin Harry barked.

Jude clasped his hands behind his back. "Five-thousand pounds or he'll do what?"

They all looked to Edward, whose hand slowly fell to his side. He pressed his lips together and didn't answer.

"What will he do?" Marissa demanded.

Edward cleared his throat.

"Oh, just read the note, Edward!" she cried, unable to take the suspense a moment longer.

"Yes, do," her mother chimed in. Obviously, it would be impossible to gauge the appropriately dramatic action if one didn't know the details.

He cleared his throat loudly again, then snapped the paper out in front of him. "It has come to my attention that the Honorable Miss Marissa York was recently discovered in a scandalous embrace. If you care to protect Miss York's precious reputation, you will surrender five-thousand pounds at the location and time specified below."

"I presume," Jude drawled, "that the letter isn't signed?"

"It's not."

"Then how can you know it's from White?"

Edward's face turned red. His jaw clenched and jumped.

Aidan propped his back against the wall and crossed his arms. "That could be from anyone."

"He offers proof," Edward finally ground out.

"Oh, Baron!" their mother cried. "Just read the letter!"

His ears turned red as he looked down to the paper, and though Marissa had no idea what he might say, she started to raise a hand to stop him. She was too late.

"If," Edward ground out, "you do not provide the money as directed, I will reveal to society that Miss York has been compromised. As proof, I'll offer a description of a heart-shaped birthmark very high on Miss York's thigh."

A rush of sound seemed to enter the room with his words. Oh, part of it was certainly the gasps of those around her. Her mother, in particular, was letting out a distinctly warbling kind of wail. But there also seemed to be an ocean tide washing in and out of her hearing.

"Does he think we won't kill him?" she heard Aidan snarl.

"I made that quite clear," Jude responded with his usual calm.

Cousin Harry asked the most pertinent question, "Does anyone know where he's gone?"

The roaring waves swept in and out of her hearing until she finally identified the sound as rushing blood.

"He's close, I don't doubt." Edward's voice was hard as stone. "I assumed he'd gone to stay with the Brashears. His sister's family. They're only an hour or so away."

"Well, then," Aidan drawled. "Let's go pay him a

visit, shall we? Apparently he needs a demonstration of just how much more valuable his life is than a measly five-thousand pounds."

She heard the rustle and the mutter of men forming a mob, and Marissa realized she'd closed her eyes. She forced them open even though she wanted to hide forever. If she could only disappear from this moment, she wouldn't have to face the next.

Tucking her hands into her lap to stop the shaking, she spoke. "It might not be him."

Her words had no effect on the group. The preparations for murder and mayhem continued.

Beside her, Marissa's mother muttered a continual stream of sound, the emphasis falling on words like *blackmail* and *scandal* and *rapscallion*. She sounded equal parts horrified and enthralled, but Marissa was sure she also detected a *soupcon* of joy.

"It might not be him," she said more loudly.

One by one, the men ceased their violent planning and turned toward her.

"Pardon?" Edward said.

"Peter White. He might not be the one who wrote the letter."

Aidan rolled his eyes, as if she were a silly miss whose brain moved at a snail's pace. "Marissa, it's obviously him. Or an associate of his, at least."

Every face held varying degrees of confusion as they awaited her explanation. Every face except Jude's. He raised an eyebrow, and his eyes glittered with amused curiosity.

"There's a small possibility . . ." Her dry throat formed the words roughly, so she coughed into her fist and tried again. "There's a small possibility that someone else could've written that letter."

Realization took hold of Aidan's face first, then Edward's. Jude's eyes fairly glittered with laughter.

"Marissa," Edward growled.

"I would not like to see Mr. White unjustly murdered."

Aidan snatched the letter from Edward's hand and held it out toward Marissa. "He says he's seen your thighs, Marissa. So how could it be anyone but him?"

"Yes, well . . ." What in heaven's name was she to say to that?

Aidan's hand crumpled the letter, and the sound of it made her wince. "Is the description accurate?"

"I—"

"Is it accurate?" he shouted.

Strangely enough, his anger stoked her courage. She sat straighter, raised her chin, and met Aidan's furious green gaze with her own. "Yes, it's accurate. So before you string Mr. White up from the nearest tree, you may want to speak with Fitzwilliam Hess as well."

"Fitz . . . william . . ." Aidan stammered, his face growing alarmingly red.

Edward put a hand on his brother's arm. "Marissa, you're not saying . . . you said you were a virgin."

"I was." She didn't dare meet Jude's gaze. "Fitzwilliam and I only engaged in kissing. And such."

"And *such*!" Aidan yelled.

"Yes."

Their eyes were like flames against her skin, and Marissa felt a tickle of perspiration on her hairline. But it was nearly over. Nearly.

Edward dropped his head, hands fisting on his hips. "Is Hess even in the country? The last I'd heard he was on the Continent."

More voices joined in, debating the whereabouts of Mr. Hess. She glanced over her shoulder to note that her mother had fallen into a faint, her head hanging perilously over the side of the sofa. Possibly, she was truly unconscious this time.

It was now or never. Marissa chose a particularly faded rose on the study rug to focus on. "Also . . ." she said just loudly enough to stop the conversation. "There's a small possibility of a third gentleman."

At first, she thought the strangled huff was a male sob, and the sound startled her so much that her gaze lost its hold on the rose and flew up.

Jude stood, crimson-faced, hand covering his mouth. Was he . . . *crying?* He sobbed again, and despite the shock of her last statement, everyone in the study now looked at him.

Marissa's head swam with the idea that she might have broken his heart, and she was holding out her hand when he muttered "Pardon me," from behind his fingers and rushed for the study door. His eyes glinted with moisture. His neck burned red. She watched open-mouthed and horrified as he flew into the corridor and slammed the door behind him.

"What in God's name—" Edward started, but he was cut off by a roar of laughter trembling through the wood. Even from the study, one could clearly make out the echo of it bouncing down the passageway. Jude Bertrand was laughing his head off. At her.

"Why, I never!" her mother gasped, miraculously revived from her faint.

Marissa just stared at the door, stupefied. Jude's choked guffaws continued to sneak into the room.

Edward was the first to recover, and he wasn't

showing even a hint of amusement when he aimed his glare at her. "Christ Almighty, Marissa, this had damn well better be a joke."

She wished it was. If only everyone in the room found it as amusing as Jude did. "It was years ago, Edward."

His mouth opened, and his throat worked, but no words came out. She suddenly wished he were yelling. Aidan took care of that for him.

"Well, it's a damned good thing you have a fiancé, Marissa York, because it's clear you'll have to marry! With that many men under your skirts, it's a wonder you haven't been revealed before now!"

Her throat tightened at the disgust in his words. "Charles and I were in love. You should be able to understand that, Aidan."

Her brother's eyes narrowed and his nostrils flared, but he managed to hold on to his temper for once. "Charles. Charles LeMont?"

She dipped her chin in a faint nod.

"Didn't he marry three years ago?"

"It was arranged by his family. He didn't want the match."

"So," Aidan growled, "you told yourself it was all right to have an affair with a married man?"

"Aidan York!" she yelped, jumping to her feet. "I never would. Charles and I were in love before his betrothal, and we . . . we . . . it's possible we got a touch carried away when we were saying good-bye. And who are you to toss around such judgment, anyway?"

Edward said her name as a warning, but she shook it off.

"Oh, let's all stop treating him as if he were made of glass. He hates that anyway, or so he claims."

Her mother gave a little wail and collapsed back onto the sofa.

"Oh, Mother," Marissa sighed, though she was beginning to think she might try fainting herself. Because right now, she was standing in the center of an awkward mob, and they were all looking at her as if she were a monster.

Marissa slumped. "I'm—"

But Aidan cut off her apology. "Oh, for God's sake, she's right. Somebody else had better step in here, because I haven't got a moral leg to stand on."

Cousin Harry coughed uncomfortably, and everyone else shifted.

"Regardless," she finally continued, "I'm sure it's not Charles. He's never been anything but kind to me."

"Kind," Edward muttered, but Aidan was the one to hold up his hand.

"And Fitzwilliam Hess?"

"I don't know. I can't imagine it, considering his reputation."

"That's true," Harry volunteered. "He's quite the tomcat."

Marissa was sure she should've felt insulted, but all she could think was that it was no wonder he was popular with the ladies of the ton, with his skills. Still, Jude was more impressive.

As if drawn by her immodest thoughts, Jude reentered the study with a sheepish raise of his brow. "Apologies," he murmured. "Something caught in my throat." He glanced beyond Marissa's shoulder. "Is your mother well?"

"Yes," she answered without looking. Her mother moaned pitifully.

"So," he said brightly. "What's been decided?"

Edward dropped into his chair. "Your betrothal is no longer a charade."

"Ah. Lovely."

"Beyond that," Edward sighed, "things have gotten a bit complicated."

The silence that took the room felt like a physical weight, and Marissa sighed with relief when Edward waved a dismissive hand. "I need to think. Come back in an hour, all of you."

Marissa swept toward the door, not bothering to help rouse her mother first. Her mother could handle herself. Marissa, on the other hand, felt beset and bewildered, and she meant to escape while she had the chance.

She moved quickly enough to slip past Harry and steal from the room first, but Jude was there to open the door and offer a quick bow. By God, if he cracked a smile, she thought she might slap him. But Jude had controlled his amusement, and his face was serious when he rose.

"Would you have a few moments to spare, Miss York?"

"Oh, for God's sake! Yes, fine."

She followed him into the library, and rounded on him as soon as he closed the door. "How could you do that?"

"Do what?"

"You . . . you laughed! As if my utter humiliation were a farce."

"Marissa," his pleading tone didn't match the grin

starting to spread over his face. When she growled, he only smiled wider. "How could I not laugh?"

"It wasn't funny."

"Oh, *mon coeur.* It was the funniest thing I've ever heard."

"Jude!" she cried, stomping her foot before she realized she'd done it.

"I'd kiss you now if I wasn't sure that you'd bite me."

She would. She'd nip that obnoxious smile right off his face.

"Now I know why you're so good at it. Kissing. You've had loads of practice."

She was going to scream. She was going to stomp her feet and throw a tantrum and maybe toss a few books while she was at it.

"Do it," Jude said.

"Do *what?*"

"Whatever it is that's got your eyes blazing. You're throwing off sparks, *cherie.*"

"You shouldn't encourage me," she scolded, but once again, his encouragement had freed her. Her frustration fell away, as if she *had* kicked and screamed. She slowly lowered herself to the chair behind her.

Jude poured a glass of sherry and curled her fingers around the glass.

"Thank you. I can't believe this is happening. Again."

He dropped into the matching chair and crossed his legs, as relaxed as ever. "Care to explain what did happen?"

"With the men?"

"Yes," he said with a smile. "With the men."

She shook her head, but she so wanted to speak of

it. She'd never told anyone, and it had been torture to hold it in. "Won't you be . . . jealous?"

"Do I seem the jealous type?"

"No, you don't, and that's another thing I don't understand about you."

"I endeavor to intrigue. So . . . the men."

The men. That sounded so *sordid*. Or wicked. Or at least naughty. How did Jude manage to see so many unfortunate things about her? She sighed in surrender and gave up her resistance. She wanted to talk about it, and so she would.

"Charles knew he had to marry someone else."

"Charles?"

She shot him an irritated glance. "Yes, Charles LeMont. You missed that part while you were recovering yourself."

"Ah. Carry on."

"His family . . . they insisted he cultivate a political connection. But we fancied ourselves in love, and it was all very tragic and romantic."

"So you soothed your heartache in one another's arms?"

"Something like that. But it was all quite innocent, if such a thing could be. We were young, and we only wanted a few stolen moments. It was . . . lovely."

"Kisses and such?"

She blushed. "Yes. And then he married, and that was that. He's never so much as flirted with me since his wedding. So I can't imagine he'd send such a note."

"And then there's Fitzwilliam Hess. I needn't ask how you found yourself alone with him."

· "He's quite charming."

"So I've heard. So has everyone. He's infamous."

"Justifiably so," she said before she thought better of it.

"Ah, maybe I am jealous. You know that as a proper young miss, you're supposed to avoid infamous men, right?"

She thought of the way Fitzwilliam had touched her, and her face burned, but that didn't keep her quiet. "He could have ruined me, and he didn't. He just . . . he made me feel good. And *wicked*. And I would've done it again, if I'd had the chance."

She held her breath after that, waiting for a response. She had liked what she'd done with Fitzwilliam. For the first time in her life, flirting with a man had felt dangerous. *Risky*. When he'd flirted back, there'd been more than admiration in his eyes; there had been calculation, as if she were a code he'd wanted to crack.

She'd pretended not to notice it, just as she'd pretended not to know that he'd walked her far too deeply into the gardens at the Windsor ball.

Still, even with her sturdy powers of self-deception, she'd understood that stealing into the greenhouse with a known rake could not have a decent ending. And yet it had. Decent enough, at any rate. Fitzwilliam's self-preservation had protected her. He had no intention of being forced into marriage.

He'd explained that to her as he'd placed shivery kisses along her neck. "Don't worry," he'd whispered. "I won't ruin you."

And yet he had. The things he'd done to her in the dark. The secret places he'd put his mouth. The touches he'd demanded in return. . . .

Despite his promises, Marissa had been ruined,

because she'd only wanted more after that. More pleasure. More knowledge. But she'd been good. She hadn't snuck away with any more gentlemen, despite the wild curiosity for more embraces. She hadn't even shared more than a dance with Fitzwilliam Hess when she'd met him again.

No, she'd held her secret desires close and hidden . . . until that fateful evening with Peter White.

My God, what a waste that had been. Not pleasantly enjoyable like her night with Charles. Not unexpectedly amazing as it had been with Fitzwilliam. And nothing at all like the wild pleasure Jude Bertrand had shown her.

She glanced toward Jude and realized she'd pressed the tips of her fingers to her lips in memory. His gaze was focused just there.

"Yes, I'm quite sure I'm jealous, after all," he murmured.

She snapped her hand down to her lap, and nearly blurted out that she'd been thinking of him, not Fitzwilliam. But how would that be better?

"I did not know you then," she snapped.

"Ah, but you wouldn't know me now if you could help it."

What could she say to that? Hadn't she dismissed him as soon as the danger had passed?

He leaned forward. "Don't feel bad. Over the years, I've enjoyed some kissing myself. And such."

Marissa nodded and rose to leave, but somehow his words didn't make her feel better. In fact, she felt much, much worse.

Chapter 15

Jude Bertrand was in a foul mood. Bad enough that he was facing Peter White again. But he was also facing an uncomfortable truth.

He'd been perfectly confident in his seduction of Marissa York two weeks before. Yes, she was wild and wicked, but he'd been foolish enough to think he could turn her head with pleasure. He'd thought to show her exactly what that wickedness could lead to.

What an arrogant fool he'd been. Apparently she knew quite well that wickedness could be grand fun.

Jude suddenly found that her affection for untried boys was no longer amusing. He'd seen Fitzwilliam Hess a time or two. In addition to being an experienced lover, the man was exactly the type who caught Marissa's eye. Lean and pretty and polished to a goddamned glow. And this Charles fellow . . . Jude wanted to get a look at him as well, though there was no good reason to meet him, aside from torturing himself.

When Peter White finally slipped into the Brashearses' drawing room, Jude bared his teeth in a predatory smile. His smile widened when he saw that the cad's eye was still discolored and he was twisting his hands together in nervousness. Jude was just thinking about punching him in the nose when Aidan interfered by grabbing White's cravat and lifting him off the ground.

"What . . . ?" he croaked, grabbing for Aidan's wrist.

"Are you having trouble keeping your mouth shut?" Aidan growled.

"No! I . . . please . . ." When his face turned purple, Aidan set him down and gave him a shove for good measure. White stumbled back and caught himself on the wall.

"You'd better start explaining," Aidan said over White's coughing. "If I'm satisfied with your honesty, perhaps you'll escape this room with your life."

"I . . . I came to see her, I admit it. We met, but nothing happened!" His bulging eyes slid to Jude. "He was there!"

Aidan's voice offered no quarter. "The letter."

"W-which letter? I sent them. I did, but I was only trying to talk her into marriage. It was an entirely honorable communication, I swear on my life."

Jude finally spoke. "What of the last one?"

"What of it? She met me, and I had my say. I'm done with her. She's a faithless—" His gaze slid around the room, and Peter White closed his mouth with a snap.

The other men exchanged glances. Edward stepped forward to stand intimidatingly close to White. "Who else did you tell?"

"No one! Christ, do you think I'm mad? Even if I left my name out of it, everyone would know I was part of the story. I'd be struck from half the guest lists of the ton."

"But you threatened her." Edward leaned closer. "That night. You threatened to tell tales, and lo and behold . . ."

"I didn't do it! Please. I admit to seducing her, but I wasn't out to ruin her. I loved her, and I thought she was only being high-spirited. This wasn't my plan!" He jerked his hand to indicate the room and the men and the situation.

"I warned you that if I heard one word, I'd hold you responsible."

"I promise, if someone is talking it isn't me."

"What of your hosts?"

"I didn't say anything."

When Edward glanced over his shoulder, Jude jerked his head toward the far corner of the room and then joined Edward there.

"I think he's telling the truth," Jude muttered.

"He's the obvious suspect."

"He was sincere the night he spoke of his feelings for Marissa, and he's terrified enough to tell the truth now." They looked over to see Aidan looming over the crouched man. Peter White covered his head. "He's not a man brave enough to carry out a bribery scheme that would put him up against this family and the law."

White sobbed, and Edward rolled his eyes before he stalked back across the room. "The truth, Mr. White, is that regardless of who you did or didn't tell, my sister would not be in this situation if you hadn't behaved so dishonorably."

He peeked past his hands. "I know. I'm sorry.

This wasn't what I had in mind. I expected we'd be happily engaged by now."

"Get out of this district and don't return."

A flush crept over his face, but he nodded, and Edward turned and walked out.

As soon as they were free of the house, Aidan grabbed his brother's arm. "How can you be certain it wasn't him?"

Edward shook him off. "Jude is sure it's not him."

"Why?"

"He doesn't have the bullocks."

"Out of the three men we suspect, *he's* the one who ruined her. I should go back in there and strangle him now. He has no character. Hell, she's not even the first woman he's debauched!"

"His character is weak," Jude agreed, "but men have different weaknesses, do they not? He wanted her like a child wants a toy. He wasn't greedy for money. And at this point, his reputation is hanging by a thread. If that story gets out, he will be named. I don't doubt it."

Edward nodded. "Jude's right. White has nothing to gain and plenty to lose. And now, considering we have a whole legion of other possibilities . . ."

Aidan cursed and stalked toward the horses, leaving Jude and Edward to watch his retreating back.

"Well," Jude muttered. "He's handling this well."

"Marissa is right. We've coddled him since she died. Regardless . . ." He turned a dark eye on Jude. "We're off to visit the LeMont estate. I'd like you to return to the manor."

Jude stiffened. He wanted to see this Charles LeMont for himself. "Wouldn't you like another set of eyes? I'm good at reading people."

"I don't want to leave her alone, in case the threat becomes more malevolent. At any rate, it can't hurt for you two to spend more time together. It looks fairly certain you'll marry."

Jude stared into the distance. West, toward the York manor. An hour's ride and he'd be back with Marissa. And he wanted to see her a damn sight more than he wanted to set his eyes on Charles LeMont. What, exactly, did he expect to glimpse in the man, anyway? A resemblance to Jude that would give him hope?

Ridiculous. And pitiful.

So he nodded his agreement and set off for the lonely ride back. It seemed that he was about to get what he wanted—Marissa York as a wife—but he'd lost his certainty that he could turn this scandal into a happy ending.

The cold had finally set in, and the fire crackled and whooshed in the quiet drawing room. She and Jude were alone after a long, tense dinner with her mother and Aunt Ophelia and Cousin Harry.

Her mother had joined them in the drawing room, but she'd left a few minutes ago after several loud declarations of how weary she was.

"No, no! You two must stay," she'd protested, though neither Marissa nor Jude had offered objection. Finally, she'd yawned extravagantly and swept from the room, closing the door behind her.

Marissa knew what she was up to. Her mother had said earlier in the day that a marriage was inevitable, and Marissa would be wise to ensure that Jude didn't change his mind. "You know what to do," she'd whispered, poking Marissa in the thigh. "Clearly."

Her mother was arranging a seduction.

Too bad Jude didn't seem in the mood to be seduced. Marissa snuck a look at him, and found him in the same position he'd held five minutes before. One ankle crossed over a knee. His thumb under his chin and fingers poised thoughtfully beneath his bottom lip. His eyes stared into the fire as if it had transported him to another place. He held a brandy snifter, and that was different at least. Five minutes ago it had been full. Now it was empty.

Whatever her mother's expectations, Marissa had no powers of seduction. She'd only ever *been* seduced. All her experience lay in acquiescing.

So she sat, staring into the fire and trying to imagine her future. But the future seemed impossible to predict when the present felt so thoroughly muddled.

After the past week, she had no idea if Jude wanted to marry her any more than she wanted to marry him. *Did* she want to marry him?

The thought wound like a tightening snake around the muscles of her body, and Marissa leapt up to try to stave off the creeping sensation. "More brandy?" she asked, striding over to the table to grab it up.

"Yes, thank you."

The half smile flashed for the briefest moment as she bent to pour the brandy; then the smile was gone, replaced with this new, brooding expression that shut her out. Marissa looked at the blunt fingers holding the snifter, and her heart squeezed.

Jude wasn't even looking at her, so how in the world would she get him to *touch*?

"Did you see any suitable properties this week?" She hurried back to the table and poured herself a glass as well. "I mean, when you were looking for a house to let?"

"Perhaps. There's a likely place about three-quarters of an hour from here. Closer to Grantham?"

"That's a lovely area. Very green."

"Yes."

And here they were, awkward again, each sipping their brandy and looking toward the flames.

He'd come to regret his offer of marriage. She was sure of it.

Marissa wandered around the room, sipping her brandy and touching various objects, trying to look at ease. But her heart was fluttering with uncertainty. Her life was in suspension, stuck somewhere between her past and her future, and she wasn't sure she was even tethered to the ground. Her body felt too light and her mind far away.

"What's the matter, *mon coeur*?"

Marissa finished the last of her brandy and set the glass carefully down before she met his eyes. For once, she was too tired to be witty. "I think I'm supposed to seduce you, but you don't seem in the mood for it."

That got his attention. Jude's brow rose, and he dropped his foot to the floor. Perhaps he really did like her when she was outrageous. "I'm sure I'm always in the mood to be seduced," he said. "Who suggested it? I'll offer him a toast."

"My mother."

"Ah. Perhaps I won't mention it then. But I

should endeavor to keep my future mother-in-law happy. How did she think you should go about it, exactly?"

"Oh, hush. Did you not notice all the obvious efforts to leave us alone? She fears you regret your proposal." Marissa kept her voice light.

"Does she? And she believes you should seduce me into complacency?"

"More like satisfaction, I believe."

Now his eyes darkened, and she was gifted with a full, wide smile. Marissa's heart ceased to flutter and began to pound. Power surged through her. Maybe she *could* play the seducer.

"Satisfaction?" he purred.

"Perhaps."

His smile grew wider. "Come." He patted his knee, and though Marissa felt a spark of trepidation, she steeled her spine and approached. Only to stop at his shoulder.

"Impossible to seduce me from there, Marissa."

She wasn't sure that was true. Jude seemed able to seduce *her* from across the room. Then again, his knee beckoned, and it was attached to such a welcoming thigh. It would certainly be *easier* to seduce him from there.

Before she could lose her nerve, she scooted around him and perched on his knee. She didn't know how it felt to him, but the daring of the act sent wicked thrills shivering up her spine. She was sitting on a man's lap. In the hopes of arousing him.

Tapping her toes, she closed her fists and rested them on her legs. Now she was back to not knowing what to do. But her worries were baseless. Jude slid one hand under her hip and wrapped the other over her knee to pull her closer.

She grabbed him to balance herself, and Jude put his arms around her and pulled her down to his chest. Strangely, it didn't feel seductive. Her cheek was pressed to his shoulder, and he held her too tightly for her to wiggle up for a kiss.

"Shush," he murmured. "You don't need to seduce me."

Marissa lay stiffly against him, frowning at his throat. What did he mean, she didn't need to seduce him? Because he liked her or because he didn't care for her anymore?

"Jude . . ." When she placed her hand flat on his chest, the strength of his body made her heart ache. She wanted . . . *something* from him. But she no longer had any idea what it was.

"It's all right, *mon coeur.*" He stroked her back, and she finally relaxed into him a bit. His heart beat against her ear. "Are you reading a new novel?"

Frowning in confusion, she nodded.

"Tell me the story."

"What has that to do with anything?"

"It has nothing to do with anything, but I want to hear it."

After a few puzzled moments, Marissa shrugged and started the story. As she spoke, Jude stroked her back, then her arm; then his hand curved around the nape of her neck and rubbed small circles into her muscles. He laughed at the parts she'd thought were funny, and clucked over the drama of the six couples and their intrigues. And he touched her, always.

Marissa didn't want him to stop, so when she

came to the last part of the story she'd read, she continued on, weaving her own tale. She felt safe in his arms. Cared for. And *known*. It was so strange to consider a man a friend, and yet he was a friend. That was what she didn't want to lose.

She finally let the story drift away, but Jude's hand kept up its small caresses. In that moment, she wished they were married, just so they could climb beneath the covers of the bed and lie like this, with no stiff fabrics or stays between them. She wanted to press her hand to his bare chest again, and feel his skin against her cheek.

"I've been thinking . . ." he said, and her heart gave a small cry of pain. This was it. He was calling off. She held her breath and waited for the awful words.

"Is there any possibility your cousin could be behind this bribery?"

Her mind tumbled, tossed about by the strange topic. "What? Which cousin?"

"Harry."

"Harry!" She pushed up from his chest for a moment. "That's absurd."

Jude raised an eyebrow. "Is it? He knows all about your escapades."

"That's only because he's always here. He's like a brother, really."

"And yet he's not."

"He spent every summer with us. We are his *family*."

Jude eased her back down, and she went willingly, comforted by his warmth despite that he was the one saying such discomfiting things.

He put his hand to her neck and stroked his

thumb against her nape. "So he is almost like a brother, but not quite. Welcome in the family home, though it will never be his—"

"Yes. And?"

"Have you never considered that it could be painful? I have some experience with this, you know," Jude said, and Marissa felt suddenly chastened. Yes, of course he did.

"But you are not saying you resented them?"

"No, but I could have. And so could Harry."

"That's impossible. He's not that type of man. He loves us."

"All right. I only just thought of it. I haven't spent any time trying to feel him out."

Marissa frowned at the fire, troubled by his words. It was such a simple thought, that one could belong to a family and yet not belong. But it would never have occurred to her to have sympathy for Harry. Did he resent them? Surely not.

"It can't be him!" she blurted out. "What about the birthmark?"

"Ah. Yes, there's that. I suppose that settles it then."

"Yes. Good. It can't be him."

"I didn't mean to upset you. Harry seems a likeable fellow."

"He is."

"I was only grasping at straws."

They lapsed back into silence, and eventually, his easy touches soothed her trouble. Jude always did that for her, and her thoughts inevitably turned back to thoughts of marriage and this complex betrothal.

He pressed a kiss to the crown of her head, and her heart felt very strange in that moment. "Why wouldn't you let me seduce you?" she whispered.

"I don't need to be seduced."

"And I do?"

"Well, you need something, *ma belle.*"

My God, that was true, and Marissa couldn't do more than turn her face into his chest and laugh. If she shed a few tears in the process, no one ever knew. Not even Jude.

Chapter 16

Jude's mood of self-doubt had vanished by the next day. Oh, he wasn't more certain of Marissa's feelings for him. She'd cuddled quite sweetly into his lap, but the cuddling had started out as an attempt to secure his continued cooperation.

His only consolation was that Marissa was apparently having just as much trouble deciphering Jude's feelings, if she really thought he needed to be reminded how much he liked her. Seduction implied some resistance, after all, and he wanted nothing more than to take the woman to his bed and keep her there.

So, no, he was no more confident this morning, but he was already tired of his own brooding about. She'd love him or she wouldn't. There was no reason to get maudlin over it.

And jealousy . . . Jude had never understood jealousy and had looked on its victims as greedy, stupid men. But now he had a better understanding, not that he liked it any more. He wasn't jealous of Marissa's body, exactly. He just wanted to hoard all her pleasure for himself, even the pleasure she'd felt in the past.

"Fool," he bit out as he shrugged on his coat and stalked from his room. Hadn't he spent countless hours being pleased by other women? How had any of that affected what he felt for Marissa?

Despite the fact that he was done with his brooding, Jude wouldn't name his mood pleasant as he strode down the hallway toward the library. Aidan and Edward were supposed to have returned the night before, but it was now nine in the morning and there was no word. Had they discovered the culprit? Had they given him the thrashing he deserved?

By God, he wished he'd gone with them. Except then he wouldn't have spent that hour with the weight of Marissa's sweet body against him.

Jude reached the library and found it blessedly empty. After tasking a servant with bringing him coffee and breakfast, Jude positioned himself in the window nook and watched the stables. The breakfast room had a view of only the leading edge of the stable yard. From the library, Jude would see any sign of someone approaching.

But the first person he saw wasn't approaching the house, but leaving it. Harry hurried from the rear of the house with a packet tucked tight beneath his arm. He disappeared into the stables, and when he emerged a few minutes later without the paper-wrapped bundle, he looked around with a decided air of nervousness.

Jude frowned as he watched a young groom walk from the stables to mount an old gelding. The boy strapped the package behind the saddle and set off.

Something was going on.

Oh, there was nothing damning in a man sending a post, of course. Jude had sent a letter himself only two days before. But Harry had looked decidedly . . . furtive. And what did light-hearted Harry have to look furtive about?

Jude was still worrying over the scene a quarter hour later when the York brothers finally rode into view. He headed straight for the study and paced the length of it, waiting for the men to appear.

"What news?" he snapped as soon as Edward crossed the threshold. The man shook his head, and Jude cursed.

"Charles LeMont appears to have been away these past three weeks. He'll return tomorrow."

"Can you be sure?"

Edward pushed a hand through his disheveled hair and collapsed into the chair behind his desk. "We spoke to his wife. His sister took ill in Bath, and he went to visit.

Jude frowned. "And his wife didn't accompany him? That's suspicious."

Aidan walked in and tossed his coat onto a chair. "She's with child. Four or five months gone, I think. Handsome woman. She seemed eager to help."

Edward nodded. "I believed her. I don't think it's him."

"What story did you tell?" Jude asked as he resumed his pacing.

"Said we had a dying horse. Same illness that had taken one of the LeMont mares ten years ago and we couldn't remember his old stable master's treatment."

Aidan poured them all a serving of brandy before

slouching onto the sofa. Jude couldn't sit still to save his life. "Where the hell were you two?" he asked as he stalked over to glare out the window.

"We headed back," Edward grumbled, "but had to find an inn when it started to rain. Remind me never to share a room with Aidan again. He snores."

"That was you, old man." Aidan tossed back his drink, then tilted his glass toward Jude. "What's got you so foul? Courtship not playing gently on your soul?"

Jude ignored him and addressed Edward. "Is it Fitzwilliam Hess then?"

"Everyone we asked agrees that he's been on the Continent since the start of the Season."

"Perhaps he needs money?"

Edward shrugged. "He'd have plenty of targets to choose from. Certainly families more wealthy than ours."

"Could it be possible this is the way he supports himself? He's a wastrel by all accounts."

"A rich wastrel," Aidan interrupted. "I've dealt with some of the firms that handle his investments. He has no need for blackmail. His lifestyle is fully financed. I'm telling you that it's White!"

"Everything in life is not so black and white," Jude answered. "I spent my life around men active in one kind of transgression or another. I daresay I'm more familiar with the vagaries of the world than you."

Edward looked up. "But perhaps Aidan and I have a better understanding of honor among gentlemen." He said the words so casually, as if he didn't mean them as an insult at all. So Jude let them float away unanswered. He was a bastard. There was no denying that.

The silence stretched on. For a brief moment, Jude considered mentioning his suspicion of Harry, but he bit back the words. There wasn't even a hint of proof, and Marissa was right. Harry seemed a good, uncomplicated man. Jude would hold his tongue, but he'd keep his eyes open.

"Aside from White, who does that leave then?" Jude pondered. "Someone one of the men told? A friend?"

Aidan cleared his throat as if he were relieved to change topics. "One of their more recent lovers?"

"That would be strange pillow talk," Jude said.

"I've heard stranger."

Well, he had a point. Men talked with their mistresses. "Right," he murmured. "Not a wife, but a lover." He puzzled back over the men. Peter White had seemed genuinely chastened, not to mention terrified. And aside from the woman he'd ruined and scorned, Jude hadn't heard rumors of a recent lady friend. Perhaps Harry would know.

Jude knew nothing of Charles LeMont to say whether he kept a mistress or not. But Fitzwilliam Hess . . .

His head snapped up in alarm. "Christ. What about Mrs. Wellingsly?"

"What about her?" Aidan asked with a wary edge to the words.

"Didn't she and Hess have a flirtation last year?"

"Not that I noticed, but it seems likely enough. Still, I can't think why you'd suspect her. She inherited nearly half of her husband's estate. She doesn't need money, and I can't imagine she'd do something like this just to punish me."

Jude faced the window again. "No, but she might do it to punish me."

Despite the softness of Marissa's voice, it managed to fill the whole room. "Why would she want to punish you?"

Alarm flooded his body as he turned around. Marissa stood in the doorway, and her stiff face matched the even tone of her words perfectly. "You told me you'd never even spent a moment alone with her."

He held up a hand. "I—"

"You lied to me!"

"I didn't, Marissa, I swear. She . . ." He glanced toward Aidan for help, but the man smiled and made no move to assist. *Damn.* Jude could hardly call the man to the carpet in front of his sister. But tears glistened in her eyes now. "Listen," Jude pled as she started to turn away.

She froze but didn't look at him.

"The other night Patience Wellingsly confessed to some . . . tender feelings for me—"

"The other night?" Marissa snapped.

Jude looked up to the ceiling, but it was as unhelpful as Aidan York. "She implied that she was in love with someone. Possibly me."

"I see. Was she overwhelmed by your kisses?" Marissa was nearly shouting, and Jude would've enjoyed the spectacle if he wasn't feeling quite so panicked. Still, he assured himself, her jealousy was a good thing, as long as it didn't take too strong a hold.

"I told you I've never kissed her."

"Then it makes no sense." She flung a hand in his direction. "Why would she love you then?"

He'd taken a step toward her, but those words stopped him in his tracks. "What?"

"If you haven't so much as touched her, why would she be falling in love with you?"

That was far more than a question. It was an insult wielded with all the subtlety of a medieval mace. "You can't believe a woman would love me for any other reason?"

"How would I know?" Her words hovered in the air.

"Marissa," Edward said quietly.

Her brow wrinkled in a brief moment of confusion before the anger took over again. "What I believe is that you told me there was nothing between you and that woman, and now I discover she may be in love with you."

He'd told himself there would be no brooding today, but it was hard not to brood when it felt as if his chest was an open wound. He turned away from the woman who'd wielded the weapon and looked at Edward York. "I'll go see her. It's a small chance, but if we can put this to rest, all the better."

He heard the soft sound of his name on Marissa's lips as he passed, and felt the even more tentative touch of her hand, but Jude kept walking. Let her worry over what he thought of her; he'd spent enough time doing the same for her.

She thought him not worthy of affection, and her brothers thought him too low to understand honor. He'd always loved the York home, but for now he wanted nothing more than to walk away from it for a few hours.

Chapter 17

Jude paced the receiving room of the Wellingsly house, still furious with Marissa for her casual words. To assess that he was good for naught but physical pleasure and then throw that in his face.

But what right had he to be angry? His entire plan had centered around seducing her into affection. Yes, he'd hoped they had some small friendship as well, but seduction . . . that had been the very soul of his plan. So why did he feel so wronged to have it named?

He could not reconcile his anger, and it didn't help that he'd almost convinced himself that Patience Wellingsly was behind this blackmail fiasco. Had he sent her some false signal? He'd thought it nothing more than a simple flirtation. But she fell in love easily, and perhaps he should've taken more care.

"Damn it," he breathed, running a hand through his hair. The ride over had been damp and had done little to relieve his dark mood.

"Mr. Bertrand," she said, walking into the room with a wide smile. "What a pleasure."

"Mrs. Wellingsly." He managed a polite bow, but there was no mistaking the roughness of his voice. She started to stretch out both hands, as if to take his or even embrace him, but when she met his eyes, her hands fell. So did her smile.

"Is something the matter?"

"I wished to speak with you about a delicate matter."

For a split second, her eyes brightened, turning up a bit at the corners as hope started to bloom on her face, but then she gave her head a little shake. "I see. A delicate, unpleasant matter?"

"You know why I'm here, then?"

"I've no idea," she responded before sinking gracefully to a chair. He'd never seen her do anything with less than perfect grace.

Jude took the seat that faced hers and cleared his throat. "The other night, I felt you were about to confess something to me. Were you?"

She swallowed and tried on a pleasant smile. "I can't imagine what that would have to do with anything."

How was he to tell what she was hiding? He hardly knew this woman at all. Deciding he had little to lose, Jude offered an edited version of the truth. "I received a disturbing letter. An anonymous letter. I wondered if you had sent it."

"Me?" she gasped. "What kind of letter?"

"It was . . . the intent of it was to damage my relationship with Miss York."

"And you think I would want to do that?"

"At the ball, you implied some . . . tenderness for me, if I wasn't mistaken."

She stared at him, her face frozen, but her eyes bright as candles.

Jude flinched at the obvious pain in her gaze, but he did not temper his words. "Did you send the letter?"

"No." She didn't avert her eyes or shake with nervousness.

He inclined his head in acknowledgment, but he said nothing. As he'd expected, she couldn't tolerate the silence.

"I did mean . . . at the ball, I did mean you. But it wasn't . . ." Now she was nervous, swallowing hard, her hands fluttering for a moment before she pressed them to her knees. "I fancied myself falling in love with you."

Despite that he'd come here for an answer to that question, Jude still felt the shock of those words. It nearly rattled his bones. "Patience—"

"Don't," she interrupted. "After we talked, I realized I had assigned you an unwarranted affection. I'm lonely, Mr. Bertrand. And you are an attractive man. Something about you . . ."

An unfortunate amount of heat warmed his skin. Jude knew he was blushing, and he could not stop it.

"Something about you fascinated me. I wanted you so badly that I even turned my eye toward Aidan York, wondering if I might make you jealous."

Jude felt his jaw fall at that, but she waved off his shock with a little laugh. "Not that he's an unappealing companion."

"I don't . . . I'm sorry. I don't know what to say."

"You don't need to say anything. I'm a forty-year-old widow. I may still be as foolish as a girl, but I am at least mature enough to *see* when I'm being foolish. And you were right. If I really wish to find love, I must give up these childish affections. Surely there is someone for me. Perhaps a man who already has his children and will not mind a barren wife."

"Patience," he said. "You are as lovely a woman as I've met. Easy to love. And do you think I would love Marissa less if she could not have children?"

"Would you not?"

Jude didn't wish to probe his feelings for Marissa too deeply, but he knew the answer to this already. "Absolutely not. And if you hold yourself low because of such a thing, you dishonor your worth for no reason, madam."

"It's no matter," she said, but Jude handed her a handkerchief when tears spilled from her eyes. "I'm so sorry I put you in this awkward position, Mr. Bertrand. I promise that I wish you and Miss York only the best."

He believed her. Hell, maybe they were all fools in the face of these suspects, but Jude had no reason not to believe her. If she truly wanted to insert herself between Jude and Marissa, she would've at least confessed love.

If she had, what would Jude have said? Her admission that she was attracted to him had filled him with a twisted mix of appreciation and . . . discomfort? No, it felt like something more than that, and after he bid her farewell, he left the manor with a heavy step.

She wasn't the first woman to admit a strange attraction to him. Hell, Marissa herself had said nearly the same thing. He'd taken advantage of that very phenomenon with her and other women. He was strangely appealing, and he'd never minded that. He'd accepted it as his due.

Ten steps from his horse, Jude stopped in his tracks.

His *due*. His *place*. The role he fit in this world of polite people and impolite realities.

Jude's stomach dropped with a sickening realization: He did not think himself equal to these people at all.

"I'm sure this will turn out well."

Marissa looked up from her stitching to find Harry sitting next to her. She hadn't noticed that he'd sat down. "Pardon?"

"Jude will return soon with good news, I'm sure."

"Are you?" Marissa sighed. She wasn't sure at all. In fact, she was quite certain that if Jude returned at all, it would be with awful news. First that Mrs. Wellingsly wasn't the blackmailer. And second, that he'd discovered it quite nice to be around a beautiful woman who truly loved him. The more Marissa thought of it, the more sure it became. What man wouldn't want that? What man would prefer a childish girl who hurled insults and used him for selfish purposes?

Marissa blinked back tears. "Thank you, Harry."

"You just . . . if you don't mind my saying so, cousin, you look awful."

She didn't bother pretending insult. Harry wasn't as close as a brother, but he was certainly as close as a . . . cousin. He'd gone to school with her brothers, so his bond was stronger with them, but during the summers she'd learned to swim and ride and cheat at cards right along with him.

"You shouldn't worry so," he continued. "We'll watch out for you."

"Thank you, Harry." She studied him for a moment, trying to think what he was like as a man and not just as her cousin. But he was inscrutable to her, a true gentleman of the ton, never interested in more than horses and . . . well, he had a slight interest in sheep farming, but no head for politics.

She had never thought too much about him. He'd always simply been a fixture in her life. But Jude had begun teaching her to look beyond the surface of things, not that she was learning that lesson too well.

"Can I ask you something, Harry?"

"Of course."

"Was it ever . . . lonely for you? Spending so much time in our household?"

Harry frowned and shook his head. "What do you mean?"

"Well, between school and the time you spent here . . ."

"God, no. It was a relief. My mother is so dour, I can hardly bear the time I spend in her house even now. And I don't remember my father, I was so young when he died. Your father was far more than an uncle to me. An excellent man."

He had been an excellent man. Quiet, but not dour like his sister. He'd been a happy audience for the mischief his wife and children had got up to.

"I'm glad. You are such a good actor, I wondered if you were only pretending to be happy with us."

"Nonsense. Your family has been the only true family I've ever known."

Marissa looked back to her little pillow, the very pillow she'd teased Jude about two weeks before. The stitching was going quite nicely. If circumstances were different, she would have told Jude that and they would laugh together. She would have talked to him about her father, dead for seven years now. But she'd thrown Jude's friendship in his face this morning, as surely as if she'd slapped him.

"Thank you," she finally said.

Harry cleared his throat. "So, I believe Mrs. Samuel is trying to talk me into marrying one of the Miss Samuels."

That stopped Marissa's wandering mind. "She is? Which one?"

"I'm not sure she cares. She feels they've both been on the scene too long."

Well, Mrs. Samuel was a practical woman if nothing else. Beth had told her that her mother's only goal was to see both girls marry so that if she took ill again, they would be looked after. "And . . . do you favor one?"

"I hadn't much thought about it. Miss Nanette Samuel seems quite a handful. Not sure she'd make an ideal wife."

Marissa didn't know whether to feel hopeful for Beth or insulted that Harry was approaching this so heartlessly. But, she supposed, this was how most marriages were made. "Beth is my dearest friend, you know. She's a wonderful person."

"She is rather nice, isn't she? I suppose I shall consider it. She's modest and attractive, and I think we might match well."

She nodded, still torn by the strangeness of it all. "Don't you mean to find love, Harry?"

"I'm sure we'd come to love each other. I know our family typically approaches these things with a bit more fire, but I'm not quite as passionate in nature, I suppose."

Marissa couldn't help but smile. "Odd, considering your acting skills. Too bad you were born so respectably, Harry, or you might have trod the boards in London."

His expression twitched for a moment before he set it rights again. "I would've liked that, I think. Sometimes I do admit to feeling a bit superfluous."

"How so?"

"Edward holds all the responsibilities of the title. Aidan has his import firm. And I . . . I am merely pleasant entertainment. I've always enjoyed my time here, as I said, but I sometimes feel I should've made myself useful and entered the church."

"The church? Good God, I can't begin to imagine you as a parson."

He flashed a grin. "Mother was quite keen on the idea. I suppose I could've made a good show of it."

"Well, your sermons would've been lively. I can picture you illustrating all the parables with scenes from Shakespeare."

"You're right! Perhaps there's still time to take up the collar."

Marissa laughed, but then she took his hand between hers. "I do know what you mean, Harry. I've felt that same suspension myself. What have I to do but marry, after all? But you're a gentleman. You have your income. You can do what you like, you know."

"But what would I do?"

She shrugged. "Travel the world. Go to Africa. Visit the Orient. It's not as if you're some thread-bare relation. You're not forced to stay here."

"No, I suppose I simply like it. Africa, eh?" He seemed to think for a moment, then shook his head. "No, I like this family too much, I think, not to mention the comforts of England. And who would entertain your mother if I sailed away?"

"I daresay she can entertain herself."

They were chuckling over that when Jude walked into the drawing room, his hair wild from the wind and his face stony as a demon's.

Her smile fell as his gaze met hers and touched her with ice. She stood and felt the pillow drop to her feet.

"It wasn't her," he said simply, before turning to leave.

That was all. *It wasn't her.* Nothing about whether Mrs. Wellingsly loved him, or how he knew she hadn't done it, or what had happened when the woman had finally got him alone.

The horrid images that had writhed through Marissa's mind today all came to the forefront. Jude would've spoken privately with Mrs. Wellingsly, of course. He would've been forceful with her. She would've swooned into him. And then what?

Marissa strode toward the door to force him to answer her questions, but Jude wasn't in the hall.

She glanced up just in time to see his shadow round the corner at the top of the stairs, and she followed without another thought.

Patience Wellingsly was a delicate beauty with

polished manners and knowing eyes. She would never have called Jude ugly or insulted his appeal, not if she wanted him. No, she was the type of woman who knew how to stroke a man's ego. Marissa had never managed that skill, of making them feel important and masculine and needed. She could make a man feel lust, but what about love? That was a different thing entirely.

But Patience Wellingsly looked like a fairytale princess in need of rescue, and Jude had already proved himself capable of playing the valiant hero.

Marissa's gut burned with sick dread as she hurried up the stairs and into the south wing.

She rushed to his room, freed from having to worry about other guests. Only Jude and Harry had chambers here now, though a servant or two might talk. But Marissa was far beyond that kind of minor gossip now.

When she reached his door, she knocked, but couldn't wait for an answer and pushed his door wide.

Jude looked up from removing his cuff links. His coat and cravat were already missing. Now he was just a man in his breeches and boots and shirtsleeves. He looked wicked, and Marissa couldn't help but stop her mad rush and look him over.

"You must be missing your other male guests if you're reduced to ogling me."

She stared a bit longer just to make her point, then stepped inside and closed the door. "I want to know what happened with Mrs. Wellingsly."

"I'll wager you do."

She raised her chin. "Did you see her?"

"Of course I did." He set the last cuff link on the

dresser and tugged his shirttails from his breeches, momentarily distracting her.

"Well? What did she say?"

"She said she didn't do it."

Betrayal cut through her heart with a razor's edge. "You told her the truth?"

"No."

"Then how—"

Jude pulled his shirt over his head with such abruptness she felt the breeze of it across her face. His scent floated to her. That recognizable spice of some masculine soap, but tinged with sweat and horse now from his long ride. "I told her I'd received a disturbing letter, and I wanted to know if she'd sent it. Now if you'll excuse me, Miss York, I need a wash."

Miss York. That felt surprisingly painful.

She'd been dismissed. He turned to pour water from the ewer as if she weren't there. It must be icy cold, and yet he dipped a rag in the water and rubbed it against a ball of soap.

"I don't see why you believe her, just because she claims she didn't do it."

"Because we talked about more than that, and I believe she was telling the truth about it all."

The sick dread spiraled high at that, but it got wound up with excitement as she watched Jude swipe the soapy cloth over his neck and face, then down his chest and beneath his arms. Her sex tightened at the sight of the dripping water.

How very odd to watch this: Jude making the same movements she made as she washed. Such a pedestrian activity, but so fascinating to see him clean his strong chest and bulging arms. Milky water skimmed down his belly, tangling with the hair that trailed to his waistline.

She'd never observed him so naked before, and he looked very . . . different. Wide where she was not, narrow in places that her body had curves. His back formed a fascinating *V* until it straightened at his hips.

Marissa could hear her own breath as it quickened. He dipped the rag in the basin and washed himself again with clear water. Without looking at her, he reached for the buttons of his trousers.

"Does she love you?" Marissa blurted out.

He glanced toward her and dropped his hands. She thought he was being modest, but then he sat in a chair and began to tug off his boots. Not modest then. He'd forgotten his boots.

"Probably not."

She clenched her hands to fists. "Why must you speak in maddening phrases? What does that even mean?"

And why are you being so cold? That she left unasked. She knew why. She only wanted to know if it was permanent. What a silly question that was. *Do you think you'll be angry with me for very long?*

Jude stared at her as he tugged off his second boot and slipped his stockings off. The sight of his feet startled her. They were very large. In perfect proportion to his body, she supposed, as she'd never noticed them before. But now, naked, they were wide and strong, and his toes had *hair.* She fought the impulse to slip off her shoe and place her foot next to his. He would dwarf her, she was sure.

She tore her eyes away and found that he was still

looking straight at her. Holding her gaze, Jude stood and reached for the buttons again.

"Mrs. Wellingsly and I sat together." First button. "I asked what she'd meant by our previous conversation." Second button. "About love." Third button.

He turned to the side to face the basin again, and then Jude Bertrand slid off his breeches. She couldn't stop her gasp. He must have heard it, as it echoed in her own ears, but he didn't glance at her. He just reached for the rag. As if he weren't naked. As if she weren't looking at her first nude man.

He twisted a bit, and her wide-eyed gaze focused on his bottom. Pressing a hand to her mouth to stifle any further sounds of shock, Marissa devoured him with her eyes. His buttocks were tight mounds of muscle, with slight indentations that hollowed out the sides when he moved. The skin was so smooth and pale compared to the rest of his body, and her fingers twitched with the urge to touch him. To run her fingers down his spine, all the way to his arse. And then farther, down to his thighs, which curved out with strength and roughened with hair.

Water dripped down those thighs before snaking around his calves and soaking into the carpet. The spice of the soap grew heavy in the air, and it twisted around her, making her dizzy.

He grabbed a towel, and stepped onto it to avoid dripping any more water on the floor. The distraction of the towel momentarily kept Marissa from realizing that he'd turned toward her, but when she saw his front side, she pressed her fingers so hard to her mouth that her lips went numb.

Up to this point, she'd only had hurried glimpses of men in the dark. There'd been a basic understanding of shape and mechanics, but nothing more. But now she had a full view of Jude's manhood and all the . . . *accoutrement.*

His staff hung thick and heavy, the skin of it ruddier than she'd imagined. His bullocks hung beneath, tight and rounded. He must have washed already, because the dark hair around his shaft was wet, and his flesh glistened with water. As she watched, the shaft thickened before her eyes. She drew in a deep breath to try to calm her trembling heart.

"When I spoke with Mrs. Wellingsly," he continued as if nothing had interrupted the conversation, "she admitted she'd been considering the idea of falling in love with me."

Those might have been the only words that could've drawn her eyes away from his manhood. She focused on his face and the brutal cold in his gaze. "She did?"

"Yes." He drew the rag in a slow swipe across his chest. "She admires me. She wants me."

Marissa's eyelids fluttered with shock. Her stomach turned.

"But she's realized that she doesn't love me. Not truly. She only loves the idea of me."

Relief crashed over her, but the flood stirred up more fear. He'd be thinking of Patience Wellingsly now. How could he not? A beautiful woman who had confessed her admiration and desire . . . he must be wondering what it would be like to accept what she offered. He must imagine it. . . .

While she tried to fight the fear, Jude finished washing. He rinsed his whole body one last time, then reached for another sheet of linen.

"Mrs. Wellingsly sends her well wishes, by the

way. She said she was happy for the match. I think she meant it."

His eyes never left her as he toweled off, but Marissa's gaze roamed over his nakedness, taking it all in, noticing the way his shaft grew even wider and rose up in eager arousal. Just as it had when she'd touched his chest. When she'd kissed him and straddled his hips.

He wanted her. Still. Even when he was angry. And she wanted the chance to have more of him.

"So yes," Jude said, "I believed her. And if you're wondering if I touched her, the answer is no."

"I . . ." She forced herself to meet his gaze, which had gone black and fathomless with emotion. "I only feared that—"

"But I will touch *you,* Marissa, right now, if you don't leave."

"What?" She took a deep breath as a hint of trepidation sizzled through her excited body.

"I'll have you now and end this ridiculous farce between us. And we *will* marry. Understand that. If I have you, there will be a wedding."

Her eyes skittered over him as the nervousness chased her arousal faster. He would *have* her. If she let him. He'd lay her on the bed and press all that nude flesh atop her, and then he'd slide between her legs and—

"Turn around," he growled. "Stop looking at me like you want it and leave. Because we both know you'll regret it in the morning when you're stuck with me for the rest of your life."

"Jude—"

"Leave!" His voice exploded through the room, shaking the very walls, it seemed. He snarled and stepped toward her, and Marissa knew she should be scared, but she wasn't.

Still, she didn't want him this way, lusting and hating all at once. She would regret that, at least, if nothing else.

So she stole one last look at Jude's proud body, and she turned and walked away, even as her heart threw a tantrum inside her chest. It wanted him, and it resented the tight control of her mind. Marissa was beginning to resent it as well.

Chapter 18

There were only seven of them left in the house. Seven people in this house, and yet she hadn't caught even a glimpse of Jude since the encounter in his room. During breakfast he'd been out riding. For luncheon, Marissa had eaten in her mother's chambers while the seamstress finished the last-minute touches on the gowns her mother had sent for restyling. Then the afternoon had been spent sorting through old scraps that her mother insisted needed to go out to the village needy before the weather grew any colder.

But Marissa had been beset with nervous energy all day. The men had determined that there was nothing to be done but to pay the five-thousand pounds. They had no other suspects to interview. No leads to follow up. If Charles was at the ball tonight, he'd be pulled aside and quizzed as discreetly as possible. But the money would be left according to the instructions, and the men would take turns watching the hidey-hole for whoever came to retrieve it. This particular fete was popular, which was likely why it had been chosen. The suspect could hide among any dozens of neighbors or guests. There'd be no way to catch the blackmailer unless the trap worked perfectly.

And then what would happen?

Marissa paced across the drawing room as she worried. The warmth of the fire drew her in, then seemed to push her away on a tide of heat when she walked back toward the cold windows. Back and forth she went, forehead aching from the tightness of her frown.

She had no doubt the blackmailer would be caught, but the question was, could he be stopped? Could they convince him to set aside his plans and keep quiet?

There was no way to be sure, aside from murder, and her discarded virtue was no cause for killing.

And there was so much more to worry over, even beyond the blackmail. What was Jude thinking? What did he want? What would he do once this mess was over?

The drawing-room door snapped open, and Marissa spun around to greet Jude, but it was only her mother.

"Where is everyone?" Marissa complained.

Her mother tugged on gloves and went to sit in a chair pulled close to the flames. "It's so cold, I told the men to pile into the carriages first. We'll join them once the braziers have taken hold."

"Are they already outside then?"

"Most of them, yes."

Marissa craned her neck to peek into the corridor. "Jude?"

Her mother waved a dismissive hand. "I'm not

sure. But I want you to ride with me. There is still so much planning to do for the Boxing Day gathering. I refuse to allow last year's choir to return. My God, they were entirely dreary, weren't they?"

"The choices were a bit spiritual, Mother, but—"

"Horrid! This year, I think we shall have mummers. Won't that be enchanting? And fireworks! Oh, Marissa, it shall be spectacular!"

"Have you spoken to Edward about your plans?"

Another dismissive wave. "Bah. These parties only raise his stature in society."

"And deplete his coffers as well."

Her mother tittered as if it had been a joke, but Marissa didn't worry too much. She knew Edward budgeted a certain set amount for their mother's frivolities every year. On occasion he stepped in to replace, say, the fantastically expensive French red roses with more economical English roses, but with instructions for the florist to call them by a French name. He was smart enough to handle the dowager baroness.

And Marissa could not worry over Edward's pockets; she was busy worrying over Jude's nude body and whether she'd ever see it again. He'd been so angry. She'd meant to sit beside him in the coach and poke and prod until he revealed what he was feeling, but now it looked as if she'd be stuck with her mother.

She set her jaw, and when the footman bowed into the room and allowed that the carriages were sufficiently warm, Marissa waved her mother ahead. "After you."

She followed her to the lead carriage and managed a glance inside while her mother was boosted up and settled. No Jude there, just Harry and Edward and Aunt Ophelia. Though Marissa set her foot to the step, she then stopped and looked around as if startled. "Oh, pardon me, Mother. I just remembered that I need to speak with Aidan quite urgently!"

"But, Marissa!" her mother gasped as Marissa spun away and rushed for the second carriage. Before she reached it, she heard her mother sigh out "Well, Baron York, I suppose you shall have to help me decide."

Poor Edward.

But she'd managed to escape, so she couldn't summon much sympathy as she snapped open the carriage door and hoisted herself up. Her wrap trailed behind, so she hauled it in before dropping into the seat next to Aidan.

And across from Jude.

She pushed down her nervousness and met his eyes straight on. Her cheeks felt a little warm, but she thought she detected a hint of red high on his cheekbones as well, and that gave her the courage to raise one eyebrow. Jude glanced away and pretended to look out the window.

"Good evening, sister," Aidan drawled. She glanced over to see him sprawled against the seat with his eyes closed. He looked like an unrepentant rake, arms crossed and legs stretched out as if he were trying to catch a nap before the festivities.

"Late night?" she asked.

"I couldn't sleep," Aidan answered with a yawn.

"How did you sleep, Mr. Bertrand?"

"Well," Jude answered.

"Really? I found myself quite fitful. My mind would not stop racing."

"Sign of a guilty conscience?" he mumbled.

Aidan huffed a laugh. "That's generally my problem. Perhaps it's a family trait. Are you feeling guilty about this drama you've involved the whole county in, Marissa?"

"I did not involve them! And no, it wasn't guilt. 'Twas anger at Jude. Do you know that woman confessed that she had considered falling in love with him?"

Aidan squinted past one open eye. "Did she? That's a merciless snare, my friend. I'd tread softly."

"Aidan York!" Marissa snapped. "Jude is my fiancé!"

He closed his eyes again. "I thought you wanted free of him."

"I—" She looked from her brother to Jude, horrified that it had been put so bluntly. Jude's dark eyes narrowed at her hesitation. "It's not that. We both agreed that we would treat the betrothal respectfully."

Her brother grunted his disinterest.

Jude resumed his effort to ignore her, but Marissa couldn't leave it be. "I've only been trying to talk with you. Can you not spare me a few moments of your attention?"

"I'm no good for such niceties as talk," he growled.

"All right," Aidan said, pulling himself upright to bang on the ceiling of the carriage. The wheels slowed. "I can't spend forty-five minutes in here with you two. It's impossible to breathe in here with all the unspoken accusations clouding the air. I'll ride above. Behave yourselves."

He jumped out, and she was left alone with Jude, who sat glaring at the door Aidan had just slammed.

Electricity hovered between them, as if a great tempest were building above their heads. The carriage rocked and then began its journey again.

"Why are you being so cruel?" Marissa asked.

He didn't even look in her direction.

"I'm sorry if I wounded your feelings yesterday. It's just that . . . I don't understand."

"You made that clear."

"What?"

"That you don't understand Patience's attraction to me."

Patience. Oh, God, the sound of that name on his lips stung like sparks had landed on her skin.

"It's not just her. I've seen the way other women look at you. They look at you like . . . like you are the catch of the Season. Rich and titled and . . ."

"Handsome?" Bitterness burned in that one word.

Yes, she thought. *They look at you like you are handsome, and you are not.* But that was a truth she could not lay between them, despite that he'd already spoken it once. *You think I'm ugly,* he'd said. Her throat thickened with sorrow.

"You leave me so confused," she whispered.

He finally turned his eyes on her. She'd expected fire, but they were still ice cold. "I'll not list my worth to you, as if I were begging your approval. I offered you my name because I liked you, and I hoped to inspire the same admiration in you."

"I do like you! I've told you that."

"And yet you agonize over what other women might see in me. Do you really want to know?"

"I . . . I see that you are a good man, Jude. I do understand that."

"That is not what they want from me," he growled. "They do not want my heart, sweet Marissa, they want the man. They want my body. They want the things I can do for them and the way I can make them feel. I'm big and base-born, and they know that my mother was a whore, and they understand that I will be an animal in their beds." He paused, as if challenging her to respond.

Marissa felt her mouth open. She told herself she should speak, but what words could she possibly offer him?

"I have had that sort of admiration for a long while. I understand it perfectly, whether you do or not. And it never bothered me. Never. Not until I realized that I wanted more than that from you. But that's all you see in me too, isn't it? A big, ugly brute who can please you in private, but should hardly be acknowledged otherwise?"

"No!" she gasped. "That's not true!"

"It is true, but I can understand if you don't want to admit your own shallowness to yourself."

The sharp breath she drew hurt as it entered her lungs, as if it were so cold that it froze her very blood. "But I told you . . . I said you were my friend."

He jerked his hand aside as if he were flicking her words away.

"Jude, please. I know I said something awful yesterday, but it was only because I was . . . I was hurt."

Now that he was so focused on her, Marissa half-wished he would turn away again. Because even though he'd always seen things in her that others did not, he'd liked those things. He'd teased her and praised her and wanted to know more. But now she saw scorn in his eyes. And pain.

"Perhaps tomorrow," he said, "I will beg the same excuse for saying awful things. But tonight I wish to be left in peace."

Marissa held her tears back by sheer force of will. "I did not ask for any of this. I did not ask you to want me at all, much less offer to be my husband. You have no right to hold my feelings up and judge them. What you want or don't want from me is your burden, not mine."

For a moment, something broke through the ice of his gaze, something so raw that Marissa looked instinctively away, down to her clenched and shaking hands.

"You're right, of course," he murmured. "I apologize for trying to place on your back a burden you did not choose. How selfish of me."

His words did not relieve her pain. Instead, they drove it deeper, until the hurt pierced something hidden deep inside her.

She'd never been one for excessive introspection, but she did understand some things about herself. She'd never been quite the same as other ladies her own age. She didn't feel things as deeply as they seemed to feel. She'd claimed herself in love with Charles at some point, but in truth, it had only been attraction. And attraction was something she'd felt for many.

Likewise, she hadn't been stung too often by the words or opinions of others. But she could no longer deny the capacity to feel emotions as deep and true as anyone else, because Jude's pain had cut through her, and now the ache spread like a pool of blood through her chest.

Why? Because he truly was her friend? Or was it something more?

She'd claimed not to understand him or his appeal to other women, but perhaps she'd been naming it wrong the whole time. Perhaps what she couldn't understand were her own deepening feelings for him.

Jude had given up his scornful glare and now stared out the window at the passing night. Marissa watched him, unafraid that she might be caught looking. His face had struck her as unfortunate—and yes, ugly—when they'd first met. But watching him now, he only looked like Jude. His anger gave his jagged face a vicious cast, yet he wasn't frightening. His mouth was too wide, and yet it was the perfect width for kisses that devoured all her thoughts. His strong brows and dark eyes weren't the least bit gentle, but they seemed created for sending shivery thoughts down her spine.

He wasn't handsome, but something in him compelled her to want more than handsomeness. More than elegant legs and pretty flirtation.

And more from herself.

"Jude—"

"Leave me be, Marissa. *Please.*"

"But after tonight . . . if we need to marry—"

He shook his head, and what did that mean?

Marissa let her next words fall away and disappear, like floating ash dissolving into water. He did not even want to speak with her. He wanted nothing, just when she wanted so much more.

She bowed her head and told herself that all would be well. And if she were ruined, and Jude refused to marry her . . . it would be no more than she deserved. At least she had no sisters to pull down along behind her. At least it was just her, alone.

Chapter 19

The brightly colored crowd swirled before Jude like a flock of excited birds. He glared across the ballroom, unmoved by the lively sight.

He was too lost to appreciate the beauty of the scene. Lost in his unspoken worries that Harry could be behind this trouble. If it was Harry, the betrayal would break Marissa's heart.

But more than that, Jude was lost in his own past and the weight it pressed into his shoulders.

When he'd joined his father's ducal household, Jude had expected to feel like an outcast. Marginalized at the least, hated at worst. But he'd been pleasantly surprised by his welcome there. The duchess hadn't treated him like one of her own children, but she hadn't despised him either. As for his half brothers, he'd found two young boys who looked up to him as a large and foreign creature.

Much as the ladies of the ton did in his adulthood.

He could still remember that feeling of settling in at his father's home. He'd been homesick and heartbroken, but he'd also been relieved to have been so easily absorbed into the household.

He'd never lost that gratitude, he realized now. A courtesan's bastard was one thing, but a duke's bastard was another. Though he'd missed the warmth of his mother's home, and had luxuriated in it during the summer months he'd spent with her, he'd appreciated the mantle of respect that had come with being his father's son.

That respect had afforded him the confidence that permeated every fiber of his being. The confidence that allowed him to move through the ton and feel equal.

Or so he'd always thought. But Marissa had exposed a secret knowledge that he was not quite equal. Perhaps not less than, but most definitely different. That was a secret he could expose to himself and eventually live with, but the knowledge that he still felt relieved to be accepted . . . that was a bitter pill to swallow.

It was there in his attempt to seduce Marissa York into loving him. He saw now that seduction was simply a way to sneak beneath her defenses and trick her into feeling true affection. As if a lady would need to be fooled into taking him in.

He smiled bitterly and waited for her to circle around to his side of the dance floor again.

By God, she was a beauty. He told her so often, but he didn't think she realized that he wasn't speaking strictly of her looks. She was lively and smart and brave and passionate. And yes, a little shallow. But she'd been correct to tell him his pain wasn't her doing. That responsibility lay with him.

Sensing a presence at his side, Jude frowned to find Aidan there. "Is all in place?" Jude asked quietly.

"Yes. Edward has taken the first watch. I'm to meet him at the folly in an hour. Your turn will come next, then Edward again."

"We could be here all night."

"We could," Aidan agreed. Marissa appeared before them, her face slightly stiff as she danced a quadrille. "I'm getting the sense you've changed your mind about my sister. Will you call off?"

Jude shook his head.

"Well, you don't look like a man who's headed happily for the altar."

"Leave it. We argued. That's all."

"About Patience?"

"I said leave it!"

"For God's sake," Aidan muttered. "You're acting like a moon-eyed ass."

Jude gritted his teeth and glared so fiercely at the dancers that one gentleman shot him an alarmed look.

"In fact, you look almost as miserable as I was when I lost my . . . the woman I meant to marry."

Aidan never spoke of it, and the shock of hearing him talk of her swept some of Jude's mood away. "But she died," he said stupidly.

"Yes, but there was an argument. Before. We were estranged for a time . . . and then I never saw her again."

"Christ, I'm sorry."

Aidan rolled his shoulders as if loosening the memory from its hold. "Getting back to you—"

"I'd prefer not."

Aidan relented, finally, so they stood in companionably stony silence again, as good gentlemen of the ton often did. After a time, Jude realized the dancers had changed partners, and he caught sight of the man on Marissa's arm. "Who's that?"

Aidan followed his gaze and his face went hard. "The infamous Charles LeMont."

"Bloody hell." Just as Jude had suspected, Marissa's first love was a slender reed of a man. His golden locks curled in a perfectly tousled mess. His face was pale and smooth as a girl's. What a damned joke. "He practically violated your sister. Are you just going to let him dance with her?"

"Are you?" Aidan drawled, and Jude could've sworn the gaslight in the room went red for a moment.

He breathed deeply and told himself that creating a scene in the ballroom would be even worse than whatever whispered rumors the blackmailer might spread.

"Edward pulled him aside as soon as we arrived. LeMont seemed appropriately clueless before his wife hurried over to ask after our ailing horse. And he certainly looks harmless."

He did, even to Jude's jaundiced eye. Pretty, he might be, but there was nothing rakish about him, and he touched Marissa only when the dance strictly called for it. Not that Jude ceased his scowling. She was dancing with her former lover, knowing Jude would see her, knowing he'd be jealous. In fact, at that very moment, Marissa's eyes met his across the room, and she stared hard at him, with not even a hint of an embarrassed blush on her cheeks.

And Charles LeMont had seen her thighs. That was more than Jude could claim.

Frustrated with himself, he turned and walked toward the hall without a word to Aidan. Jude had never believed jealousy an appropriate response to any situation. It was a useless exercise practiced by prideless men. Either a woman wanted you or she didn't. Either she'd be true or she wouldn't. No amount of worrying or raging would change that.

And yet, here he was, fretting over Marissa as if she were a trinket he could possess.

He meant only to give himself some breathing room, perhaps have a glass of brandy to calm his nerves. But when he was only feet from escape, a woman stepped into his path, and Jude froze in shock.

"Hello, Jude," she said softly, her eyes crinkling in a smile.

"Corrine," he responded, as her name was the only thing making it through the churning shock of his mind.

"It's wonderful to see you."

"You've returned from Jamaica." Obviously.

"It was dreadfully hot there. I've no idea how my sister survives it." She sighed prettily.

A few heartbeats later and his mind was back in reasonable order. "Your sister and her family are well?"

She spoke a bit about the plantation she'd visited and what the island was like, while Jude tried to recover from the shock of seeing his former lover here, at a country ball in the middle of nowhere. Her black hair and brown eyes looked the same, but her skin had bronzed a bit on her journey, and she was thinner as well.

"I understand congratulations are in order," she finally said, her eyes falling to his chest as she shook her head. "I don't know why I'm surprised, but I am."

"Thank you. Have you not yet remarried? I was

certain you'd meet a dashing ship's captain and sail the world with him."

She laughed with a familiar husky sound that had once been enough to swell his cock with anticipation. She was, objectively, an average-looking woman, but she lived life with such joy that she enchanted everyone she met.

Corrine shook her head. "A ship's captain might make an ideal husband, actually, but I've yet to meet one who's dashing. I find them all rather grumpy and serious."

"Tragic."

"In the meantime, perhaps you will escort me for a dance. If your marriage is a happy one, this might be my last chance to insinuate myself into your arms. And I left so quickly for Jamaica that I already missed one last chance with you. I'd hate to miss this one as well."

There was a promise in those words, a hint that spoke of more than dancing. Jude offered a chagrined smile and began to excuse himself from the honor. He wasn't one to be led by his cock and didn't feel tempted, despite the current uncertainty of his and Marissa's future.

But he paused just before the words left his mouth. He remembered Marissa's steady look as she'd danced by in her former lover's arms.

"I'd be honored," he heard himself say as he bowed and offered his arm.

This was beneath him. Far beneath him. But as with his jealousy, he could taste the bitterness of it in his mouth, but he could not seem to spit it out.

He would dance with Corrine, if only to tell himself that he hadn't lost this battle. But the war . . .

the war was another matter entirely. Either Marissa would carry on with her life, or they would marry and he'd have a wife who thought she'd married beneath her.

So knowing it would help nothing, Jude escorted Corrine into the crowd just as a waltz began.

Breathless from the dancing, Marissa wound her way through the crowd to join Aidan and Jude. If she hadn't needed to speak with them, she might have avoided the men all night. Jude, at least, looked like an angry bull, anxious to gore at least a few of the guests before the evening was out. When she saw that Aidan stood alone, she wasn't surprised at the relief that loosened her muscles, but even then, she felt a pang of loss that she wouldn't be near Jude.

"Enjoying yourself, Marissa?" Aidan asked as he signaled a footman to bring a glass of champagne.

"I'm not sure how I could be. I only want this night to be over. Is Edward . . . ?"

"Yes. I'll be relieving him in half an hour or so."

"So there's been no word?"

"None."

The champagne arrived, but Marissa held it without taking a sip. "I danced with Charles."

"So I saw. Jude and I wondered if you were trying to tempt one of us to violence."

She rolled her eyes. "Charles is harmless. Which is what I wanted to tell you. The only topic he broached was his wife's pregnancy. He's elated. There was not even a hint of awkwardness between us. I'm sure it's not him."

"Perhaps he was hoping to wound you, speaking of the child he will have with another woman."

"No, I'm sure that wasn't it. He spoke of his wife with great affection. In the past, there was some tension between us, as if Charles was remembering our previous affection each time we met. But that's gone now. Or perhaps I am changed. . . . I don't know."

"Are you changed?" he asked.

She shook her head, unable to answer the question. Was she changed, or was she only cowed by all that had happened in the past month?

As she contemplated that question, Marissa caught sight of a familiar set of shoulders moving through the crowd. For a split second, she could not reconcile that they were Jude's shoulders, only because he was surrounded by dancers. But yes, Jude was dancing, and as he spun in time to the slow and sensual waltz, his partner came into view.

The woman was a stranger, which was another odd shock after the intimate confines of the hunting season. Her black hair was lovely and her brown eyes warm, but her face was unremarkable otherwise. At any other time in her life, Marissa would hardly have noticed her at all. Certainly, she would've sniffed at the idea of being threatened by her.

But this woman, plain or not, glowed with . . . *knowledge.* She moved with the rhythm of the music as if her body were a mystery only she understood. She knew the power of her large eyes and used them to full effect. And she knew Jude. Intimately. Marissa could see this with no effort at all. Patience Wellingsly had looked at Jude as if she wanted him.

But this woman looked as if she'd had him and knew she would have him again.

It was there in the secret tilt of her lips and the wicked quirk of one eyebrow. It was there in the curve of her fingers around his arm. Not tight and grasping, but easy and light. She laughed up at him, and Jude smiled.

That smile. That crooked half smile he saved for Marissa. He gave that stranger the smile that never ceased to make Marissa's heart skip a beat, and when the woman turned her head to the side, his eyes slid down her throat.

Everything inside Marissa's body went cold, even as her skin inched toward a burn.

Aidan said something, but she couldn't make out his words. "Pardon?"

"I asked if you wanted something else to drink."

"No, it's fine." To distract him, she sipped her drink as she watched Jude and his partner disappear into the crowd. She was left with watching the other dancers, just as she'd spent countless hours watching before. But tonight, the dancers seemed . . . shifted. Different in a subtle way. A year ago, she would only have seen the handsome gentlemen who showed a fine leg as they bowed through the moves of the country dances. Or the occasional lady whose dress Marissa coveted. She'd see the charming smiles and elegant hands. She'd mark the most beautiful couples and count them the luckiest.

But tonight, she saw the underpinnings of it all, like the sketch marks left under a watercolor painting, not meant to be seen, but caught with a close look.

There, to the right, a handsome young man danced with perfect grace, but he looked over the head of his beaming partner, not interested in her round, flushed face. A common enough scene, but made more tragic by the fact that they were newly married in a match necessitated by debts. The bride was happy. The groom made no bones about his dissatisfaction. He wanted everyone to know.

To the right, an elegant couple danced in matching misery. Their marriage had been heralded as the perfect match four years before, but he was now rumored to be frustrated with the lack of children. Apparently their beauty could not alleviate that disappointment. They were lovely, but they were not happy.

Farther away, toward the middle of the crowd, a man and woman who were both unfortunately short and boxy were engaged in a less elegant waltz, but their smiles radiated delight as he whispered things into her ear that made her blush and giggle. They'd been married nearly twenty years, Marissa knew, because their oldest daughter had just come out.

Ridiculous observations, easily visible even to a child, she suspected, but Marissa saw these truths for the very first time. Elegance did not make for a good husband any more than it made for a good bed partner. As a matter of fact, it was so inconsequential as to be meaningless in the face of a few years together.

Then again, couldn't she end up miserable with Jude as easily as she could with some handsome young buck?

Jude came into view again, and her heart pitched sharply down. He was an adequate dancer, not as fluid as some of the other gentlemen, yet Marissa wanted to be in his arms. No one else's. She wanted to ogle his legs, knowing she would see them stripped of wool cloth later in the evening. She wanted to pet his chest again, and kiss it, and this time she would lick him, as well, to see if that made him purr like a pleased beast.

That woman, that stranger, she probably already knew the answer to that. Instead of fury, Marissa felt despair, because she suspected this realization had come too late.

Jude looked up, face happy over something the woman had said, but when he met Marissa's eyes, his smile fell away in a slow wash, as if the sight of her was pulling it down.

And in that sad moment, Marissa realized that she loved him.

Chapter 20

The nearby trees created a constant storm of dried and dying leaves rustling and scraping in the wind. Jude could hear no footsteps or breathing, but there was no missing the jet-black figure that slipped up to the artistically piled rocks of the Greek folly.

Jude was surprised by the surge of fury he felt at the sight. He wanted this done and behind him, and it was only the smallness of the figure that kept him from knocking it to the ground with a brutal blow. Instead of throwing his fist at the shadow, he slipped a hand over its mouth and snatched the specter off its feet. A quick squeal snuck past his hand before he cut it off, but Jude wasn't surprised by the high pitch, nor by the softness of the body as it pressed into his. He'd known it was a woman right away, despite the dark cloak and deep night, and he felt a stark relief that it wasn't Harry.

The sack of money fell and bounced off Jude's foot as the woman struggled in his hold. She was a tiny thing, though, and he had no trouble pinning her arms down and reaching for the bag. She twisted harder as he pulled her into the trees. "Quiet. You're caught, and there's nothing to be done for it."

She cried out behind his hand and bucked against him.

"Come, woman. You'll only hurt yourself."

After a few more minutes of straining and wriggling, she finally gave in and slumped against him. Jude stopped to give his heart a moment to recover. He'd only settled into his watch five minutes before, and the shock of seeing a dark figure sneak toward the rocks had sent his pulse racing. The surprise of realizing it was a woman still confounded him. Was it possible Patience had lied?

The cloak had bunched up on her head, so he couldn't even glimpse the color of her hair in the faint light of the half moon. It could be Patience. She was a slender woman.

Christ, what a mess this was.

Jude slowly eased his hand down, and the forest filled with echoing pants as the woman pulled in breath after panicked breath. She was sobbing by the time he reached into his pocket for a rope to tie her hands. He tugged her arms behind her back and began to wind the rope around.

"Please, sir!" she whimpered.

Not Patience, thank God.

"Please, sir, it wasn't my idea, I swear it!"

Jude frowned at the cadence of her words. Even past the panicked sobs, he could tell she was a villager or servant. And in that moment, he knew that the mystery wasn't solved. They wouldn't know the culprit unless the woman could be persuaded to talk. And even then, what hold would they have over the blackmailer? None. He hadn't received his five-thousand pounds, so the tale would be told.

"Who do you work for?" he growled in frustration.

She wept harder, and shook her head in answer.

"God damn it! Who do you work for?"

"Please, sir. Please."

"Well, if you won't speak the truth, at least keep your mouth shut."

Wrapping his hand around her arm, Jude tugged her through the trees toward the lighter night beyond them. Aidan had already grown tired of the party, and when Jude had relieved him, he'd volunteered to wait in the garden instead of going inside. Jude saw the orange glow of his cigar when he was still forty steps away.

"I've got her."

"Her?" Aidan asked, pushing to his feet.

The windows of the manor cast a faint glow over the garden, so Jude tugged down the girl's cloak to get a look. She was no one he recognized, and Aidan looked her over and shrugged as well.

"We don't dare interrogate her here. If you'll call for one of the carriages, I'll meet you just past the gates."

"Good idea. I'll let Edward know."

The girl stiffened in his hands. "No! Please don't."

"You don't want to go with us? There's a simple solution to that, sweetheart. Tell us who sent you to retrieve the money."

She shook her head, then jerked straight. "I don't know who sent me!" she said brightly, as if the idea had just occurred to her. Jude rolled his eyes and led her back toward the woods.

"Then we'll spend the carriage ride discussing

his appearance, shall we? Perhaps one of us will recognize him."

"Don't take me away," she pleaded a few times as they walked. Jude ignored her in the hopes she would break and confess, but she didn't.

Though he was naturally sympathetic to women at a disadvantage, Jude spent the next quarter hour steeling himself against her pitiful pleas. Whether she was responsible or not, she'd played an essential part in this plot to destroy Marissa, and he would not let his tender heart affect the plan.

When the carriage finally rattled from the dark, the girl ducked down and tried to lunge toward escape, but Jude caught her on her second step and lifted her easily through the open door. He jumped in behind her and found that Edward had joined them as well. Jude tossed the money to him.

"Harry is going to gather up the women in a few minutes," Edward explained. "I didn't think it wise to usher everyone out in a rush." His eyes slid to the girl, now huddled in the corner of the seat. "Who is she?"

"She won't say."

Edward tugged her cloak back and frowned. "I don't think I know her, but she's a touch unremarkable, I suppose. Who are you, girl?"

She shook her head and tugged the hood back up. "Please let me go. I'm only a servant. I had nothing to do with this!"

Jude glared at her bowed head. "And yet you haven't yet asked what 'this' is, which strikes me as highly suspicious."

"Tonight could go very badly for you," Edward added. "A few years in jail, at least. But if you tell us the name of your employer, perhaps it will end well."

The girl looked up then, her eyes widening at the thought, but perhaps she was smart enough to see they were bluffing, because she shook her head again. In truth, it would go badly for her either way. If her master turned her out for giving away his identity, she'd be unemployable whether she went to jail or not.

Jude cocked his head and studied her, now that she was looking at them. He narrowed his eyes at the sight of her full mouth. She was pretty enough that this might not be about her position.

He considered Cousin Harry one last time as he offered his next conjecture. "Perhaps it is not a matter of who her employer is, but her lover?" She only looked momentarily confused, so he shook his head. "No, that's not it. Her accomplice is not her lover, so perhaps it's a woman behind this, after all."

"Ah," Aidan murmured when her face paled. "That's it then."

The girl pressed her lips together and dropped her head. She refused to say anything more no matter how many questions they peppered her with.

"Well," Edward sighed, "it's clear it must have something to do with one of you two."

"What?" Aidan barked, while Jude wondered again if it was Patience causing this trouble. But he was nearly certain it didn't fit her personality. He'd inherited a gift from his mother, to meet a person for even a few moments and form a good impression of them. She had based her whole career on that sense. Choosing the right man could mean the difference between life and death for a woman like her.

"What do you mean?" Aidan asked, nudging Edward's foot with his.

Edward barked a laugh. "If there's a woman out to destroy our family, surely you can see your fingerprints in this."

"That's the most—"

"Hold!" Jude shouted over Aidan's rising voice. "Edward's right that it could have something to do with one of us, but let's not forget the focus of this madness. Marissa. If it's a woman behind this . . . she could've come by her knowledge any way."

Her brothers exchanged uncomfortable glances.

"I'm talking of visits and changes of dress and bathing in the pond and—"

"Oh," Edward interrupted. "Of course."

"So how do we figure it out?" Aidan asked.

They all turned to look at the girl. As they studied her in silence, Jude's mind turned back toward Marissa. When he'd looked up from Corrine to catch her watching, he'd known that taunting her with Corrine had been a bad idea. The dance itself had been a happy waltz through the memories of their time together. He'd enjoyed it, but that enjoyment only made his gut burn with guilt now.

While he'd meant to tweak her pride, he'd seen more than indignation on Marissa's face. He'd seen sorrow. Sorrow he'd caused.

He was ashamed now. The characteristics he'd always liked about Marissa, the wild, free heart that was so at odds with her cool exterior . . . he'd started to resent her for those very things. He could hardly blame her for being confused. A few days ago, he'd teased her for her love of pretty boys, and now he derided her and called her shallow.

If his mother were here, she would toss her head in disgust and call him a fool. And she would be right.

Furious with himself, he turned that anger on this girl who was trying to harm Marissa. "We are almost to the York estate. You only have a short time left to confess what you know. I'll personally retrieve the constable as soon as we are settled, and then the matter will be out of our hands."

Though she took a shuddering breath, the girl said nothing.

"Tell us your mistress's name, and we'll let you go."

She was shaking her head when the carriage slowed and pulled to a stop.

"We're here," Edward murmured. "Let's get her inside and decide what is to be done. But if the girl is missed, it could already be too late."

Jude stepped heavily from the carriage and pulled the girl toward her temporary prison. For the first time, this family seemed more scandalous than his own, and he was quite sure he was no longer enjoying the drama.

Marissa raced through the house, heart and hands both trembling with anxiety. She knew nothing except that someone had been caught and brought back to their estate, which made no sense. Harry claimed that the men knew nothing more than she, and he seemed just as unconcerned as the baroness, who'd chattered brightly about intrigue on the whole ride home. Marissa was beside herself.

Her family's reputation was poised on the brink of ruin because of her actions, and the rest of them seemed to think it a farce. Maddening people.

Her slippers slid across the floor when she tried to make the turn. Marissa bumped hard into the wall, then kept going. She put her arm out to keep herself from tumbling around the next corner, and then she was at her brother's study . . . only to find the door was locked.

After wiggling the knob, she knocked impatiently. The quiet murmur of male voices stopped, and she was under the distinct impression that everyone, herself included, was holding their breath.

"Let me in!" she finally hissed.

The murmurs started again, and a few moments later she finally heard the click of the lock turning. Edward stuck his head out. "You shouldn't be here, Marissa. It's no place for a woman."

She fried to shove him out of the way, but his body didn't budge. "This is *my* scandal, Edward. Don't be ridiculous."

"Marissa—"

"Get out of the way!" She kicked him in the shin, which probably hurt her toes more than his leg, but he was so surprised that he gasped in horror.

"I want to know who it is, Edward!"

"We don't know who it is," he said, making a great show of rubbing his leg and looking hurt.

Jude would let her in. She knew it. So she called his name, and Edward rolled his eyes. "Oh, fine, you stubborn brat. Come in and see if you can make any more sense of this than we can."

He opened the door, and Marissa meant to search the room for the blackmailer, but as the door swung open, she spied Jude, only three feet away and reaching toward the door. For a moment, she thought he was reaching for her, and her heart jumped up to pound against her throat in delight. Maybe he didn't hate her. Maybe it wasn't too late.

But his hand dropped as the door swung open, and when she met his eyes, his gaze fell to the ground.

Marissa stared at his hard jaw and wide mouth, and she wished she had the right to touch him. To greet him simply and rise up on her tiptoes to press a kiss to his lips. But with all that lay between them now, she knew that even if they married, she wouldn't have that right. They would be like those other unhappy couples who danced together only once at each ball for appearance's sake. What would people see when they looked at Marissa and Jude? An unfortunate match, they'd say, likely blaming Jude's appearance and low beginnings.

Marissa felt a sharp pain where her heart had been pounding just a moment before. That future seemed unbearable, and as she stepped closer to Jude, Marissa reached out and touched his hand.

He frowned. His eyes rose. But before she could identify the emotion in his look, Edward slammed the door and locked it, startling her into dropping her hand.

"Well?" he said. "Here is our culprit, but she—"

"She?" Marissa asked, spying the huddled figure pressed against one arm of the sofa.

"Yes, it's a girl. A servant, we think, but she won't

reveal who her employer is, or anything else for that matter."

Marissa cocked her head to see beneath the cloak, but she couldn't make out anything of the shadowed face. "Remove the hood, please," she said loudly, but the girl only curled more tightly upon herself.

"She won't say anything," Aidan growled. "Not even when threatened with the constable, and that may turn out to be our only option."

She frowned at the girl, but was momentarily distracted from her study by the movement of Jude next to her. He walked away and stood looking out the window at the black night beyond, his back to the room. She wanted to follow him over to that private corner and ask if he could forgive her. It wasn't the time for such discussions, but her legs ached with the need to walk to him.

Impatient now, Marissa strode to the suspect and tried to pull her hood back, but the girl yelped and held tight to the fabric. "Oh, for goodness sake," Marissa huffed. "Let me see you."

A whimper emerged from the layers of cheap wool.

Edward said, "That's odd," and came to join Marissa. "She didn't put up such a fight with us."

A thought bloomed in her head. "She's a maid, you said?"

"Of some kind, I believe."

Marissa took a deep breath. "Take off the hood," she said one more time. The head shook again, and Marissa sighed in sorrow. "Take it off, Tess, or I shall have the men hold you down and I'll take it off myself."

The figure went still as a stone, while Edward looked at Marissa in confusion. "Tess?"

"My lady's maid. The one who went missing last month? We had to hire a new one, remember?" Edward still looked no clearer, but when Marissa reached for the cloak this time, the material slid free of the girl's hands and her brown hair was exposed.

"Tess," Marissa sighed heavily. It was her maid, and that explained the description of the birthmark on Marissa's thigh. Her embarrassing confession had been completely unnecessary. Though it had saved Peter White's life, she supposed, whatever that might be worth.

"How could you have done this?"

Tears spilled down the maid's cheeks, and she shook her head. "I'm sorry, miss."

"I was so worried about you. Mother said you'd probably run off to get married, but I was afraid something dreadful had happened!"

"I didn't meant to hurt you," Tess whispered.

"Well, you have!"

"I'm sorry! It . . . she . . ." Tess bit back her own words and ducked her head.

"Who?" Marissa barked. "Did someone pay you to do this? Who was it?"

Tess sobbed quietly and didn't volunteer another word. Marissa supposed at another time she would've admired the girl's steel, but right now she was far too betrayed for any generous thoughts. Marissa set her shoulders back and straightened her spine, trying to draw enough air to think, but all reasonable thought fled when she realized Jude stood at her shoulder.

"Are you all right?" he murmured, and when she turned to him, his arms opened and suddenly she was surrounded by him. Nothing else existed in that moment. Nothing but Jude's safe arms and spicy scent. His mouth brushed the top of her head, sending awareness tingling down her neck. He still liked her enough to pity her, at least, and Marissa felt tired enough to take prideless joy in that.

"I'm sorry," she breathed into his chest, knowing he would not hear it. Now was not the time, but she held on and let him stroke her back for a few more moments before she eased herself away. She was almost sure he hesitated before letting her go, but in the end it was probably her own imagination, because his face was still a stony façade.

Her brothers watched her with worry, but Marissa felt steadier when she turned back to watch Tess sob. "Who paid you, Tess? I assume you were paid, and didn't just do this because you dislike me?"

"Of course not!" the maid gasped. "I . . . I can't say any more. I can't."

"Why? Just tell me who did this and go. It's that simple. No damage done." She managed to make that lie sound quite genuine, Marissa thought.

"I can't!" Tess wailed. Marissa really couldn't understand her adamance. What did she have to lose? Was she being threatened? But what could be held over the head of a lady's maid?

"This is useless," Aidan muttered.

Edward agreed. "She's using information gleaned during her employment to blackmail you, Marissa. The constable will surely be interested in that. Perhaps she'll change her mind once she's been carted off. I'll send for him now. Jude?"

Marissa watched Tess, expecting her to waver at the thought of arrest, but the girl stared steadily at her lap, resigned to her fate. Marissa held up a hand to stop the men, then knelt down in front of her. "If you won't speak, then I'll have to go visit your family. Perhaps they know where you've been employed."

Tess's head flew up, eyes wide with panic.

"They're in Hull, are they not?"

She shook her head, face blanching.

"Yes, they're in Hull. I remember you went there to visit your mother last Easter. You must have written to let them know your new direction, because we haven't received any letters for you. That was one of the reasons Mother insisted you must be fine."

Tess stared, bug-eyed, at Marissa for a long time; then she looked to each of the men, as if one of them might save her. Apparently, she didn't find a friendly face, because her eyes filled with more tears. "If I tell you, she won't pay me. It's the only reason I did it, I swear. One hundred pounds . . . I still have four sisters at home. Even if I spend a year in jail, that money would . . ."

"It's too late now," Edward said softly. "Just tell the truth."

Silence swelled in the room until it became a relentless buzzing in Marissa's ears. The clock on Edward's desk ticked, and she wondered how she'd never noticed the sound before. Likely, her family was never this quiet.

Finally, Tess spoke. "At first, she paid me twenty pounds just to come work for her. Twenty pounds!"

"That's why you left?"

"I sent it all to my mum, I swear. It's not that I'm greedy."

Marissa nodded as if she understood.

"I should've known the woman was up to no good, but I thought maybe she'd admired your hair and such. . . ."

"Who?" Jude demanded.

Tess swallowed hard. "It was Mrs. Charles LeMont."

No one so much as breathed. The clock ticked even louder.

Tess seemed to relax, as if she knew her part was done.

"Mrs. LeMont?" Edward said. "That's ridiculous."

"She's pregnant," Aidan added.

Marissa shot them both a scornful glare as she rose to her feet. "And what has that to do with anything?"

Edward looked dumbfounded. "She's so nice."

"And," Jude added, "apparently jealous?"

Tess nodded. "Yes. She hates Miss York." The look she gave Marissa past her lashes was weighted. The maid was well aware that Charles and Marissa had been in love years before. Marissa had spoken of it, and the betrayal of that trust felt like a weight pressing on her chest.

"I don't understand. Surely he didn't say anything to his wife?" Marissa breathed.

"She told me nothing about it. Only that she wanted to know as much of you as I'd tell. I didn't say much, but she asked if you had any birthmarks, any features worth noting. I did not truly understand . . . and then, I only had to retrieve a bag tonight, and she said she'd reward me with a hundred pounds. I didn't mean anything by it, miss."

Whether she had or not, the damage was done. But at least they knew who was threatening them. "If she hates me so much, what is the chance that she will leave this be?"

She addressed the room at large, but no one answered. Edward glanced toward the clock. "I'd say this is best left till morning. It's nearly midnight already, and the LeMont estate is nearly three hours away. We'll leave at first light."

"And the girl?" Jude asked.

They all stared at Tess as she began to weep again.

Edward finally sighed. "I suppose we shall lock her in a room tonight and send her on to Hull in the morning. You're going home, Tess, so I hope that twenty pounds will count you settled for a time."

"Of course," she whispered.

Aidan wrapped a hand around her arm and lifted her up. "Third floor, I assume?"

Tess gave Marissa one last pitiful look before being led away. Marissa felt a twinge of pity for the girl who'd been her maid for four years, but Tess had known full well that she was being asked to do something wrong. No one paid a hundred pounds for charitable works.

"Why don't you try to get some sleep, Marissa?" Edward said. "We'll see what can be done tomorrow. If Mrs. LeMont is reasonable . . ."

Marissa didn't know the woman well enough to guess. She'd met her a dozen times over, but even before the marriage to Charles, there'd been nothing like friendship between them. She'd been a serious young woman who'd always seemed more comfortable with the married ladies. Marissa had run with the younger girls. And the gentlemen, of course. She couldn't fathom how Charles's wife had come to hate her.

She looked up from her thoughts to see that Jude had resumed his place at the window, and the rigid posture of his back screamed of a desire for solitude. Despite that, she considered going to him, to ask if they might speak in private. But what could she say? *I'm sorry I thought you ugly. I'm sorry I liked you and wanted you and still thought there couldn't be more between us.*

What if that only hurt him more?

Better to wait until tomorrow, when this drama was resolved. Better to know where they stood before she decided if she should take a step toward him or simply let him walk away.

So she left Jude staring out at the lonely night and went to find her own loneliness in her chambers. She only wished she knew if Jude was thinking of her as he stared out at the dark, or if he was praying for the chance to leave this mad place and never return.

Jude's muscles felt like tightening rope beneath his skin as he stared out at the black night. What had Marissa meant by that small touch? What had it meant when she'd clung so tightly to him?

Nothing, he told his injured heart. Nothing more than any other touch had meant. And there was so much more to worry over, but Jude couldn't seem to turn his mind to the problem at hand.

Edward sighed loudly, prompting Jude to face the room again. The man sat slumped at his desk, head in hands, the very picture of a troubled gentleman. When he raised his head, his weary gaze completed the portrait. "I'd best go check with Aidan," he grumbled. "Our servants' quarters are hardly equipped to hold prisoners."

He stood and set his shoulders deliberately back, as if to resettle the weight upon them. "I'll see you in the morning."

Jude raised a hand. "Good night."

He was turning back toward the window when Edward's voice drifted in from the corridor. "Harry," he said, "I'll be back in a few minutes to fill you in."

"But . . ." Harry wandered into the room, his face tight with confusion. "What in the world has happened? Did the girl confess?"

"She did." Jude poured Harry a drink and approached him with a carefully neutral expression. "The girl was Marissa's lady's maid, hired away by Mrs. Charles LeMont."

"Mrs. LeMont?" Harry sputtered. "But that makes no sense. The blackmail . . ."

"She was out to ruin Marissa's reputation because of Charles LeMont's previous affection."

"My God," Harry breathed. "All that because of young love?" Everything on his face sang of surprise, but Jude still felt uneasy. Harry was a born actor, after all.

Jude's neck prickled. His instincts had never failed him before. He raised one eyebrow. "Quite a feat for a gently bred woman to carry off on her own."

"Indeed." Harry's eyes didn't even twitch.

"Do you think she might've had help? Someone to arrange contact with the maid? Someone to help her plot?"

"I suppose it's possible." His forehead crinkled with thought. "One of the guests, do you mean?"

Jude cocked his head. "I was thinking someone closer still."

Harry's puzzlement held for a few more heartbeats, then his eyes widened as he met Jude's gaze. Blood rushed to his cheeks in a violent flush. "I say, sir! You are not accusing me in this, I hope!"

"Perhaps accuse is too strong a word."

"How dare you! I am her cousin. A member of this family! If anyone is set to benefit from this outrage, it's you."

A fair enough point, actually, but Jude was sure of himself, at least. "Ah," he said, "but I am not the one who's hiding something from this family, Harry. You are."

Jude felt a hard surge of satisfaction at the panic that flared in Harry's eyes. Without a doubt, Marissa's cousin was hiding something. Something important, it seemed.

"I d—don't . . ." he stammered. "I most certainly am not."

"Indeed you are. I can see it clearly on your face, not to mention there's the little scene I witnessed in the stable yard. Something involving that package you entrusted to the groom . . ."

Harry's face went so white that Jude felt a moment of sympathy. "You . . . you didn't . . . ?"

"Why don't you tell me the truth, Harry, else I'll feel it my responsibility to mention what I saw to Edward."

"It's nothing to do with this," Harry breathed. "I swear on my honor as a gentleman."

"The same honor that allows you to live beneath your cousin's roof and lie to his face? Tell me what you did. Perhaps you didn't even realize you were helping Mrs. LeMont."

"It's nothing like that! You must believe me."

Jude wanted to believe him, for Marissa's sake, if nothing else. "What is it then?" he asked quietly.

Harry shook his head. "Edward mustn't know. I owe him so much, and I've taken every precaution to protect the York name, I swear to you. It's only that I felt so unimportant. A useless extension of the family tree. For a time, I cared for Aidan. I was *needed*. But then . . ."

Jude felt more confused than ever. "What is it, man?"

"'Twas boredom, I suppose. I thought no one would know."

Jude wrapped his hand around Harry's arm to draw his attention. "What did you do?"

Harry's gaze met his, eyes wide with shock as if his own confession was a surprise. "I wrote a book," he murmured.

Jude shook his head. "You what?"

"I wrote a book. I never expected . . . but it was accepted by a publisher, and he wanted another. So I wrote a second book, and then a third."

Jude dropped his arm. "A book? What type of book?"

Harry's flush was back. He grimaced. "Nothing

edifying, I'm afraid. But I took great care to keep my identity a secret. I worry though. I never expected they'd be so popular. Still, the money goes to an account in my solicitor's name. No one will ever connect William Wicket to the York family, I swear. I'd rather die than bring dishonor on my cousins."

"William Wicket," Jude murmured. "Why does that sound familiar?"

"If I'd known they'd be so widely read . . ."

And then Jude realized. "The book," he said. "The book I read with Marissa!"

"Oh, God," Harry groaned. "Please don't tell the family. After everything they've done for me . . ."

The dark worry burning in Jude's stomach disappeared in an instant. His scowl turned to a laugh. "You write *love stories*?"

"Shh!" Harry shot a terrified look toward the door.

"That's not so awful. I quite enjoyed the story. What are you worried about?"

"The gossip. The tittering. The scandalized measuring of every line of every book . . . It would be awful."

Jude considered it a moment. "I suppose you're right. It would create a sensation."

"That's putting it mildly. Listen, I just sent off the last manuscript. I won't write any more, I promise. I feel disloyal asking you to lie to my family, but would you see fit to keep this to yourself?"

Jude shrugged. "I don't see why not. You're not hurting anyone. Aside from the tender minds of young Englishwomen, I suppose."

Harry swiped a shaking hand over his forehead. "I can't thank you enough."

"It's nothing. I apologize for my suspicions."

Harry shook off the apology and drained the glass of brandy Jude had handed him earlier. "Consider it forgotten," he rasped.

Jude was happy to oblige him. There'd be other worries to face in the morning, and the trip to the LeMont estate seemed the least of them.

Chapter 21

Jude rode through the early morning fog, ignoring the looks of the men traveling on either side of him. The mist bit into the exposed skin of his face, turning his cheeks to ice, but Jude didn't mind the cold. It matched his mood and helpfully froze his scowl into permanent place.

Aidan cleared his throat, but Jude continued to ignore him. They were nearly to the LeMont estate, if he could only keep their curiosity at bay for a short while longer.

"I say, Jude," Edward ventured, "are you in love with our sister?"

Jude, disturbed by the directness of the question, lowered his chin and urged his horse to a quicker pace.

The York brothers kept up, and Aidan pulled slightly ahead so he could look back and catch Jude's gaze. "Jude, are you in love with her?"

"Christ, what business is it of yours?"

"She's our sister."

"She's my fiancée! You've already given your

approval for our marriage, and that is where your involvement should end."

Aidan glared as if Jude had done something wrong. "Falling in love with a woman is a far cry from simply marrying her. We both know full well that there are plenty of couples who live separate lives. But a husband in love . . . that can be the start of endless troubles."

"This is a ridiculous conversation," Jude answered. "You've no idea what you're talking about."

"Yet you haven't denied anything."

"And," Edward added, "You've been decidedly foul-tempered for days. Scowling and snapping, yet when Marissa appears you become cool and silent."

Jude chose to remain cool and silent at that point, but Aidan wouldn't allow it.

"You're in love with her," he barked. "Admit it!"

"I'll do no such thing. You two are fools."

Aidan slowed his mount and let it draw even with Jude's again. He stared straight ahead and said quietly, "She doesn't love you, Jude. This can't end well. You're from two different worlds."

The sympathy in his voice didn't improve Jude's mood at all. *Two different worlds.* As if he hadn't lived half his life in a duke's household. He clutched the reins too tightly, and the horse shied and bumped Aidan's. Jude murmured something soothing and patted the horse's neck.

A good while later, Edward cleared his throat. "I want to thank you, Jude. Your suspicions were spot on. If you hadn't been here, Aidan and I would have blamed Peter White without exception."

"Once again, my base beginnings prove useful."

Edward cleared his throat again, but couldn't

seem to think what to say. Jude wished he could pull the petty words back and swallow them as easily as he'd so often swallowed his pride.

In the end, both he and the horse were saved by the landscape. They topped a small hillock, the drive of their destination came into view, and all three men pulled to a stop to stare down on it.

An uncomfortable visit awaited.

"Jude," Aidan tried again, but Jude held up a hand.

"Whether this story with Marissa ends well or not," he finally said, "I don't doubt there will at least be a moral in it. That's all I mean to say."

Aidan snorted and slapped him on the back, and the horses started down the hill in response.

"So . . . what if Charles LeMont is here?" Jude asked.

Edward set his jaw. "Then I suppose he will hear an unwelcome truth."

"She'll deny it."

"Of course."

When they reached the doors, Edward instructed the boy to walk their mounts. They didn't anticipate a long visit. Still, they found themselves pacing the morning room for a good half hour. The mistress was still dressing, the maid explained, seeming nervous in their presence. Jude supposed they must look forbidding, at best. He certainly felt as if he were attending a hanging.

Edward was right. Mrs. LeMont would deny it, and none of them were relishing the prospect of browbeating a woman. The maid had been a trying experience. What to do with a gentlewoman with a child in her belly? If she feigned illness, they had no defense against that. He had a sneaking suspicion this ambush would end with all three men gathered around the fainting couch, fanning their enemy and offering strong tea.

His stomach burned at the thought, and it wasn't alleviated by the sight of the smiling Mrs. LeMont breezing into the room. She rested one elegant hand on her rounded belly. "Gentlemen! What a pleasure to see you again so soon."

She was, as Aidan had said, a handsome woman. Dignified and glowing with good health. But as Jude moved closer, he saw that the flawlessness of her skin was enhanced by powder that did only a passable job of hiding the circles beneath her eyes. And though she smiled in happy welcome, her eyes glittered a bit too brightly. She was nervous, and no wonder. The maid had disappeared, and now there were wolves in her morning room. But he could understand that the York brothers had not been able to see past her belly. It was a distraction, and a sympathetic one.

"My husband is off this morning to oversee the clearing of a field, so I'm embarrassed to say you've missed him once again! You did find him last night though, right? Yes, of course, you did. I remember now."

"We did," Edward said.

"Has your horse not improved, then?"

"Mrs. LeMont . . ." Edward's voice was too serious to mistake it for anything less than somber, but her smile did not so much as fade at the edges. If Jude hadn't known the truth already, he would have suspected her involvement now. Edward cleared his throat. "We are not here about the horse."

"No?" That simple word rose at the end like a bird

taking flight. "Oh, forgive my rudeness, gentlemen. Let us all have a seat. Let me pour you a cup of tea."

Tea had been delivered upon their arrival, but the cups sat empty and untouched, and even after she waved them to the gathering of chairs, she did not reach for the pot.

"Mrs. LeMont," Edward tried again, "We have spoken to Tess."

"Tess?" she asked.

"The maid."

She shook her head in blank denial.

"The one you sent last night to retrieve the money. My money."

"What a very odd thing to say!" she chirped past her smile.

"Mrs. LeMont . . ." Edward said hopelessly.

Jude was done with this. "We know you were behind the threat to Miss York, so if you care for your dignity at all, you will cease this ridiculous playacting and tell the truth. This game is over, madam."

Her smile snapped away like a sheet popping in the wind. "Sir," she growled. "I do not know you."

"I am Miss York's fiancé, and that is all you need to know, I'd wager. I consider your threat to her as a threat to me, so here I am to see that it goes no further."

For a moment, her face was frozen in vicious outrage. All the color in her skin gathered in two spots of scarlet high on her cheeks.

"Perhaps," Jude murmured, "We should take this up with your husband?"

There was her weakness. Her outrage melted into stark fear over the course of several long seconds.

The mad brightness in her eyes suddenly revealed itself as swimming tears, trapped by her lashes. "Don't," she whispered.

"Madam," Edward said, leaning forward a bit, "You must stop this dreadful assault against my sister. I don't know what you think she's done to you—"

"He loves her," she hissed, and Jude felt the shock of those words as if she'd just stripped him bare.

It took more than a few heartbeats for Jude to realize that she wasn't speaking of him.

"He has always loved her."

Edward frowned. "Your husband?"

"If he finds out about this, he will hate me. Please . . . ."

Edward handed her a handkerchief, and Jude felt a brief moment of vertigo. All the niceties must still be observed, even if the lady was a blackmailer. Among his mother's circle, things would've been handled with a bit more honesty.

Jude interrupted the tender scene as she dabbed at the corners of her eyes. "To put this more bluntly, madam, you dislike Marissa, so you decided to ruin the reputation of the York family and steal from them as well?"

"No! It's not that I wanted to steal from you, but I thought the culprit would be less . . . *identifiable* if money was involved."

"But you did mean to ruin the family? Or her, at least."

She stiffened, and her jaw trembled with outrage. "It's not fair! He's my husband. He took me as his wife! I always suspected that he was hesitant to love me. At first I didn't know why. And then I saw them. . . ."

"What do you mean?" Aidan barked.

She jumped and pressed the handkerchief to her mouth as she calmed herself. "At a harvest feast. I looked up at him and caught an expression on his face . . . yearning. Heartbreak. And when I followed his gaze . . . there was Miss York, strolling by with some other gentleman."

Jude scowled. "And you blamed her for that?"

"Who else was I to blame? My husband? I love him! And she seemed so cool, as if his love hardly affected her at all. I knew that one cruel word from her could've cut him loose, but she was always kind enough to keep him enraptured."

"Still—"

"I asked around, and I found they had been sweethearts. I saw the way she was with other men. So flirtatious and bold. I knew . . . I assumed she and Charles had . . . and then . . ." She glanced up as if jarred from a secret thought, but when her gaze fell on Jude, her eyes hardened. He knew he looked scornful, but he could not help it.

"Don't look at me that way. I could've lived with it. I told myself it was my imagination. I let myself believe my own eyes had lied. But then he . . . then he whispered her name. He whispered her name in my bed!"

Heat burned through Jude at that. Jealousy and a horrible, sudden sympathy for this woman's heart.

"He didn't even realize it. He called me by her name, and he didn't even realize." Her soft words broke on a sob, and Edward shot Jude a glare as if he had done something awful.

Aidan rescued him by being just as hard-hearted. "So you decided to have your revenge?"

"I love him," she wailed. "And when I discovered my condition, I felt desperate that he should love me as well. I will be the mother of his children. How could he not love me? I hired Tess away, thinking I could at least reveal some of Miss York's secrets to him. Tear her down with idle gossip. Then when I heard the recent whispers about her, and well, it seemed too good to be true. I just wanted him to see her for what she was! I wanted him to scorn her. To *hate* her."

Jude leaned back in his chair, relieved that the whole story was finally out. "Where have you spread your lies?"

"Nowhere. Not yet."

"Not yet?" Edward asked.

Though the woman's hands shook with startling force, she did not look away. "I . . . Tess, the maid . . . she told me your sister had some intimacy with Fitzwilliam Hess, but if you promise not to tell my husband, I swear to you, I'll never say anything."

"For God's sake," Aidan roared. "Are you threatening us even now?"

"Please!" she cried. "I'm sorry, but I love him! If you tell him what I've done, he'll never forgive me. Please, just give me that. You may cut me dead at the next ball, but please do not tell Charles." She was sobbing now, both arms wrapped around the firm bulge of her pregnant belly.

"What you are doing is unforgivable," Edward said.

She nodded frantically, eyes shut.

"Christ," he bit out. "Do you swear you will never so much as imply a foul hint about my sister?"

"I swear. On the life of my child. Just grant me this mercy."

Jude was inclined to be done with this mess, and when he glanced at Aidan, he found that the other man had averted his eyes. Despite his bad temper, Aidan had a good heart, and no taste for cruelty toward women.

Edward, of course, had the softest heart of all three of them, and he actually started to reach toward the woman's hand before he caught himself and sat back. "All right," Edward finally said. "You will have to earn your husband's attention in some other way. I won't tell him."

"Thank you," she sobbed, her body curling in as if she meant to protect her child. "Thank you. I'm sorry. I don't . . . I feel I've gone a little mad."

Well, Jude had heard that tale about pregnant woman often enough from his mother's friends. They laughed over their moods and manic tempers later, but he did not think Mrs. LeMont would laugh over this.

Aidan walked out, and Edward followed, but Jude hesitated for a moment.

He almost left without saying a word, but then she looked up at him with a question on her face.

"Your husband," he said carefully. "He danced with Miss York last night. And she told me she's never seen him happier."

Her brow crumpled in doubt. "She did?"

"She said he spoke of you and the babe and nothing else."

Her face cleared, and for a heartbeat or two, she looked hopeful, so Jude left her with that. He understood what it was to love someone who could not love you. He hadn't resorted to criminal activity, but surely he'd made a fool of himself at least.

There should've been some satisfaction amongst them as the men remounted their horses and turned toward home. They'd averted disaster, after all, saving the York family both their reputation and their five thousand pounds. But they were a trio of long faces as they rode down the drive of the LeMont estate.

"Well," Aidan said. "There will be no scandal, so it seems we will not be brothers after all."

"I'm sure you're relieved that my services will no longer be required."

"Jude, I never meant that. I'm humbled that you agreed to marry Marissa in the first place. But now . . . she simply doesn't share your feelings."

Jude stared out at the horizon and didn't say a word. This time, the brothers did not push him. Speaking of love was one thing, but a broken heart was another matter entirely.

Chapter 22

Despite the cold that turned her fingertips to ice, Marissa wandered through the garden. The roses were being pruned, and she wanted to supervise the gardeners, but more than that, she could not bear sitting and stitching and waiting for the news.

Her mother's constant chatter hardly helped her nerves, so Marissa had left her to gossip away to deaf Aunt Ophelia. Harry had long since gone off for a ride.

She could breathe out here at least, in the crisp tang of autumn, and her blue cloak tossed dramatically in the wind, satisfying some blood-born need for dramatic effect. She'd get windburn if she wasn't careful. Her pale skin couldn't take such abuse.

She was reaching for her hood to pull it up when she noticed a man from the corner of her eye.

Jude.

He stood beneath the tree where they'd lain together, and he watched her with a direct stare that made no excuse for his gaze. In that instant, she felt nothing but a deep, dark satisfaction that he watched her as if he owned her. Then she realized what his presence meant. Her steps were slow as she walked toward him, and he strode out from the shade to meet her at the edge of the roses, bringing too soon an end to her reprieve.

"Did you see her?" she asked.

He nodded.

"And?"

"She was jealous of you."

"That makes no sense. Charles married *her*."

"She feels he's still in love with you."

Marissa didn't pretend not to understand. She was sure he had still loved her, a little, when he'd said his vows. But not for a long time now, surely. "I don't think that's true, Jude. Not anymore."

"I told her as much."

"And . . . she admitted it all?"

"She did. On the condition that we not tell Charles."

Marissa frowned viciously. "But he should know what kind of woman he's married to. She's deceptive and conniving and—"

"She's in love with her husband and pregnant with his child." His brow was creased with worry. "She said at first she only meant to tell tales about you to Charles. I'm not saying I would be bosom friends with her, only that she is in pain."

Though she was still furious with the woman, Marissa considered what it would be like. To be married to Jude and know that he loved another. It wasn't hard to imagine going mad with frustration and aching. "You're certain she was sincere?"

"As certain as I can be. And her fears are well-founded.

If her husband finds out, whatever love they've built together might crumble."

"I suppose I shall have to let it be, then."

Jude nodded. "Fair or not, she felt as if she were living with your ghost between them."

"Are you actually attempting to turn my anger into guilt?"

Jude smiled and offered his arm, with a bit of the old easiness between them. Marissa took his arm with a feeling of tentative hope as they walked along the outer edge of the garden. Maybe he was not done with her.

"Not guilt," he said, "but I admit to a sympathy for the poor woman. I was furious when I arrived, and only maudlin when I left. Do you really think he's come to love her?"

She nodded and wondered how to broach the more difficult subject of her own feelings. This was the time, when no outside obstacles existed between them. This was the moment to set her fears aside and speak honestly.

But her fears clawed up inside her and invaded her mind. There was no more danger. No need to marry. Jude was free, and she'd given him every reason to change his mind about this match. She needed to convince him that it was more than a farce. More than a desperate means of saving her from ruin.

Marissa needed to tell him what she really felt.

She'd had hours to plan a speech, but she hadn't used those hours wisely. She'd worried and fretted and paced and frowned. But she hadn't thought of the right words, and as she struggled with them now, Jude spoke instead, and his speech made hers impossible.

"I'll leave in the morning." Five simple words, but they told her everything. She was too late.

"You . . . You're leaving?"

"We'll still carry on with the betrothal, of course, but I'm no longer needed. You are saved. I'll let you and your mother sort out the details of the break, and how it will be presented."

Her limbs went numb and heavy with the weight of his announcement, and his arm seemed the only thing supporting her. Marissa curled her fingers tighter around his sleeve. "But . . ."

"I trust you not to paint me in too dark a hue." He smiled at her then. Actually *smiled*, while Marissa was trying not to fall to the grass.

"Yes," she whispered. "Of course. You've been so kind to us. We wouldn't dream of casting you as the villain."

"Well, your mother might not be able to resist, for drama's sake, but I know you'll watch out for me." He smiled again, and she felt dizzy at the sight.

"Jude . . . I wish . . . That is to say—"

"No, don't say anything, Marissa. I owe you an apology. I've behaved abominably these last few days. What I said and did . . . it was inexcusable, and I hope you can forgive me."

She spun toward him, squeezing his arm too tight. "Of course I can."

"I'm glad." When his mouth offered that crooked half smile, she thought he might say something different. Ask for another chance at winning her hand. But he said, "Perhaps I did overstay my welcome, and the spirit of Othello infected me. Though not with murder, of course. Just madness."

A joke. He was joking. She made herself answer his smile.

"I've never been a jealous man, Marissa. I liked you too well for my own sanity, I think. But I've found my bearings again, so I hope that we might still be friends."

"Of course," she breathed.

"Perhaps we might stay in touch."

Stay in touch? How could he say that so casually? Did he feel nothing for her anymore?

"I'll send you my favorite novels, even, and this time you may tease me."

"I would like that," she lied, staring up at his wide mouth and damaged nose and wicked eyebrows. What had once been vulgar was now sensual. What had seemed obtrusively brutal was now simply masculine. She had touched that wild, thick hair and found it smooth beneath her fingers. She had kissed those lips and found them more tender than any other man's.

He could have been her husband, and now he wanted to be her *friend*? Did he hate her so much? So much that in a few days' time he could go from standing naked before her, daring her to touch him, to offering a friendly farewell and the promise of a witty letter or two?

She realized then that if the threat of scandal still hung over her head, she would never have let him free of his promise to marry her. Love or not, she would've held him to it. Given time . . .

"I'm sorry," she blurted out, reaching to clasp his

hand between hers. "I'm so sorry for what I said! Jude, please—"

"Don't." His smile slipped finally. For just a moment, she saw his hurt, the hurt she'd done to him. His gaze slid to the ground, and when he looked up again, the pain was gone. But she'd *seen* it. "Don't," he repeated.

He turned to continue their stroll, and what could she do but let go her death grip on his hand and walk beside him?

"I'm off to Italy for my father," he offered in that pleasant voice. "There's a vineyard he admires. He may purchase it."

"Italy? You'll leave now?" The evenness of her tone stunned her.

"Best to sail before the winter storms set in."

"Of course."

"How will you occupy your time, Miss York? With stitching?"

Marissa frowned at the grass, troubled by his teasing. Everything he said indicated that he was over his little affection for her. But she'd seen that moment of pain in his eyes. And her own eyes burned with it. "But what if . . ." Her throat choked on the words. If she confessed her new and tender feelings for him, he would have to say something, but she had no idea what that something might be.

He might still like her, but not well enough to marry. He might confess that familiarity had bred contempt. He might say that he had loved her for a moment, but she had brushed it aside to dry and wither. Or he might love her still.

The last seemed a small possibility, and her own feelings felt so large and vulnerable in comparison.

He'd confessed to liking her, after all, and nothing more than that.

His voice interrupted her painful thoughts. "I'll say my farewell."

She looked up, startled, and found that they were standing before the conservatory door now. Their walk was done. Jude smiled down at her.

"But you said tomorrow."

"Today I must pack and send letters to my father and to the vineyard. Perhaps I'll invite my mother for a visit in Italy. She loves the sun there."

"Your mother . . ." Marissa latched onto the topic, desperate to keep him talking. To keep him standing there, his arm solid beneath her fingers. "Where in France does she live?"

"She lives on a quiet little street at the outskirts of Paris."

"Is that where you were raised?"

"Yes." He knew what she was doing. His voice had lost its playfulness, and he glanced toward the door with a hint of impatience.

But she couldn't give up. The moment she stopped talking would be the end. The end of his visit, yes, but more than that it would be the end of them together.

"Does she have a . . . a companion right now?"

Jude relented and offered a slight smile. "No. She only keeps male friends on her own terms now. She's still beautiful, but she says she's too old to worry over pleasing men."

"She sounds very wise."

"Yes. She goes to the . . ." She'd had him for a moment. But Jude caught himself midsentence and shook his head. "We'll speak about this some other time."

"When?" she asked in a voice that sounded too much like pleading.

"I'm sure I'll return soon. How could I resist?" But she read the insincerity in his words. They were meant to make her smile. There was no promise in them. He didn't mean to come back.

"Good-bye, Marissa," he said.

The sound of her name urged her up to her toes, and Marissa dared to press a kiss to his mouth.

He was stone beneath her lips, rigid and cool. He did not warm to her, did not open. And Marissa blinked back tears as she settled back to the earth, her mouth burning with shame.

He looked away from her and reached to open the door. She stood there for a moment, but Jude stared out at the gardens instead of at her. He wanted her to believe this farewell meant less than nothing to him.

And in those few heartbeats, she did.

Chapter 23

After dinner, Marissa escaped to her room as soon as she was able. She'd never have entered the dining room at all if not for the hope that Jude would be there.

She'd told herself that if he came to dinner it would be a sign. A signal to her that he might still care. After dinner, she would be brave and request a stroll through the conservatory.

But Jude hadn't come down to dinner. And it had been all Marissa could do not to burst into tears over the barley soup. He was gone already, really. And she missed him with a fierceness that turned every morsel of food dry and bitter in her mouth.

It had been up to Harry to create cheer over dinner, and between him and Marissa's mother, the talk had been lively. Marissa had managed a few smiles for Harry's sake. She felt guilty for having even discussed that he might have been disloyal. Harry had been the one to stay by Aidan's side during those first awful days of grieving. And when

Aidan had gone off to London to drown his sorrows, Harry had been there to ensure Aidan did not end up murdered in a slum somewhere. Marissa was not supposed to know these things, of course, but she'd stolen looks at Edward's correspondence.

So she should never have doubted Harry, and her regret kept her with her family through dinner, at least. But now, at nine o'clock, she stood impassively in front of her mirror and let her maid ready her for bed.

If she were married, the maid would brush out her hair and leave it loose. She would dress Marissa in layers of scandalously transparent fabric, and then tuck her into bed to await her husband. Jude would be the man to join her, and he would slide his big, naked body against hers and let her do whatever she wanted with him.

He'd never tell her no. He'd egg her on and dare her to be naughty. And she would be. With him. *For* him.

But when her maid tucked her beneath the covers, there was no anticipation in it. The door closed, and the room snapped to darkness, and that was the end of her day. She was alone in her cold bed, with no husband.

What if she married someone else? Would that be less lonely? Perhaps her problem lay only in her age. She should've been married by now. Perhaps her feelings had nothing to do with Jude.

Lying in the dark, Marissa stared at the ceiling above her. It was just another shade of black. There was nothing to see, but Marissa *imagined*. She imagined that another body lay next to her. A man.

She imagined him as Charles LeMont. Then as

Fitzwilliam Hess. She even imagined Peter White and Mr. Dunwoody.

She wanted to turn toward none of them. In fact, her arms hugged her body at the thought. Charles could not have understood her passion. It would've intimidated him. Even during their bout of innocent groping, he'd been . . . surprised. "You should not let me," he'd murmured several times, though he'd shown no interest in controlling his own questing hands. He'd wanted to remind her of her virtue even as he helped tarnish it.

And Peter White had been the same. *You should have stopped me.*

She knew the type now. Mr. Dunwoody could not have been much different. They wanted women to be delicate creatures who could be *persuaded,* not beings who yearned and wanted.

Fitzwilliam Hess hadn't minded that, at least, but he would've made an awful husband, all the same. How to turn to a man in bed when you could not trust a word from his mouth?

But Jude . . . Jude she could imagine beneath her covers, the weight of him on the mattress pulling her closer. If he loved her, Marissa could touch him with impunity. She could ask him anything. Explore everywhere. He would not think less of her. He would think more.

And beyond the bedchamber, he would be her friend. He was clever and kind and so comfortable in his skin. "I know who I am," he'd said more than once. And he had known, at least until she'd asked why a woman would love him. What an awful thing to ask a man who was eminently lovable.

She was the unlovable one, the one with the cold

heart and arrogant presumptions and casual dismissals of a good and decent man.

Good and decent, yes. Too good and decent for her. He'd spent time with her in close quarters, and now he was done. She wanted to imagine that he'd grieve when he left. She wanted to pretend he would sail away and miss her and return someday to declare his unrelenting love. But in truth, he'd go to Italy and spend time with beautiful dark-eyed women who looked at him and saw a man and nothing less.

He'd do things with them that he'd never done with Marissa. He'd be lost to her.

Tears dripped into the hair at her temples. She scratched away the tickling feeling and sniffled her self-pity.

She did not want to give him up. She wanted to be his friend and lover. She wanted him to never belong to another. She wanted to hang on his arm and growl at any woman who came near.

Marissa wanted to fight for him. If she had to fight Jude himself, then so be it. He'd liked her well enough before. He could learn to like her again.

Heart pounding at her own daring, Marissa slipped from her bed and stole to her chamber door. Though it felt like midnight, it wasn't yet ten, and she stayed at her door for a long minute, listening for her family. The hallway seemed bright as day when she finally snuck out, and the stairway a mile across as she hurried toward the south wing of rooms.

She didn't know why she was so nervous. If she ran into one of her brothers, she'd simply raise her chin and inform him she was trying to save her betrothal. If she came across her mother, the woman would be giddy with the shock of scandal and lust. Harry would say nothing to stop her, and Aunt Ophelia would likely squint and order a cup of hot milk from the strange maid sneaking about.

All in all, this was an excellent family to have if one wished to engage in secret trysts.

Marissa reached Jude's door undetected and felt almost let down by the quietness of it all. But before she had a chance to breathe a sigh of relief, she realized she was about to meet her most formidable obstacle. Jude had been impervious to her feelings earlier. And unlike the men of Marissa's family, Jude seemed to grow cool with anger, not hot.

She could understand yelling and fist banging and slamming doors. But Jude's cold stare made her want to cower. She wondered if he'd learned it from the duke.

She wondered if she was stalling again.

Forcing herself to be brave, Marissa raised her hand. For a split second, she considered not knocking at all. Knocking would give him the chance to say no and send her away. But barging in would be worse than rude. It would be cowardly.

Marissa set her shoulders and knocked.

"Yes?" Jude responded immediately, his voice clipped and distant.

Before her bravery could run dry, Marissa turned the knob and opened the door.

Jude sat at the writing desk, a pen in hand, neck bowed as he scratched some last line. A forbidding frown drew his brows low, and the scowl stayed in place when he glanced up.

But she took comfort in the way his pen dropped

from his fingers when he saw her standing there. "Marissa."

"I don't want you to leave," she blurted.

"Pardon?"

Marissa shut the door behind her, realizing that even with all her worrying, she still had no plan for what to say. "I don't want you to leave," she repeated, unable to find any other words.

"I can't stay here forever, Marissa."

"But you'd planned to. You were looking for a house. You meant to stay a long while!"

He stared at her as if he couldn't quite make out her voice.

"You meant to stay, and now you say you're not angry with me, and yet you're still leaving."

"You were right. It's better if I go."

"Why?"

He turned back to the letters on the desk and spread his hands wide over them. His shoulders rose with a deep, slow breath, then slumped when he exhaled. "What do you want from me, Marissa? We've said our good-byes."

"What if . . ." Her pulse sped to an impossible rhythm. "What if I say I've reconsidered the plan?"

"What plan?" The words were tight with impatience. He wanted her to leave. She took three steps farther into the room.

"The plan. My plan. Your idea was much better, I think, to treat our courtship as a true betrothal. Can we not simply go back to that?"

"Marissa . . ." He dropped his head into his hands and buried his fingers in his hair. "I do not have the will to puzzle this out tonight. I'm exhausted."

"But you will leave in the morning, and then . . . then it will be too late."

"Too late for what?"

It was easier to approach him when he wasn't watching her. Marissa crossed his room and watched his shoulders tighten as she neared him. But he didn't look toward her. He simply steeled himself, as if he were waiting for a blow.

"Too late for me to apologize. I—"

"You already apologized, and I said I was sorry as well. Can we not—"

"But," she interrupted, "I haven't apologized for how stupid I've been. How blind. Jude, I don't want you to go." She dared to put her hands on his shoulders. "Stay."

His head lowered a bit. As if she had defeated him. "To what end? Your games have grown too dangerous. I wasn't trying to tempt you to indiscretion. I was trying to . . ."

She slid her hand up. He wore no cravat or coat, so the skin of his neck was bare to her. He was so warm. Nearly feverish. She curled her fingers to the shape of his muscles. "Trying to what?" she whispered.

Jude shook his head.

She could not resent that. She'd been trying to coax him, but she was the one who'd come to say her peace.

"Jude? I want . . . I want you to stay because I think I'm in love with you."

She felt the flinch of his muscles as if they were her own, but when he spoke, his voice carried not a hint of emotion. "You're wrong."

"I'm not."

"You decided you might love me now, because the drama has passed and I'm leaving. That's the only reason."

"No."

He turned so quickly toward her that the force knocked her hand away. "You're not in love with me, and this game between us is done."

"I haven't been playing a game," she insisted. His stubborn expression didn't budge, so Marissa went to her knees on the carpet and took one of his hands between hers. "Jude, listen—"

"Don't do that. Get up."

She held tighter. "Whatever my faults, whether I'm shallow or wicked or selfish, when have I ever lied to you? When?"

"Get up."

"This isn't a game, Jude."

He stood and pulled her to her feet as well. "It is a game. Don't you understand that?"

Marissa's whole body turned cold for a split second, as if she'd moved through a draft in the room. "What do you mean?"

He let go of her arms and pushed past her to stalk across the floor.

"Jude? What do you mean that it's a game?" Her frozen body was thawing now, and shaky pain revealed itself. "You were *pretending*?"

"No!" he snapped. "I wasn't pretending anything. I liked you, and I thought I could help you."

"And nothing more?"

"Oh, there was more. I thought if I teased you enough, if I made you want me, then you might marry me happily. And look. It worked."

Marissa choked back the tightness of tears in her throat. "I don't understand."

Jude began to pace, his hands moving in brutal gestures as he spoke. "I wanted to trick you into liking me, Marissa. I knew I could do it. You're passionate and curious and *alive*. But I don't want that anymore. I want something more."

"Something more than me?"

"Something more than lust and whatever affection can be gleaned from that. I've had lust, Marissa. I am not so hard to want, despite what you may think."

That snapped her back out of her fear. He hadn't lied to her. He'd never made any bones about his intentions. What he was confessing wasn't the truth about what he'd done. He was confessing that she'd hurt him.

"So you needn't be surprised by your lust," he snapped. "I'm not. That was the entire point."

"I know you are not hard to want, Jude. Believe me, I know that. But I know you are worth more than lust too. I'm so sorry for what I said. It wasn't that I thought no one could love you—"

"You have no idea the difference between love and lust. You've said so yourself."

"When?"

"When you spoke of Charles and your affair."

"I was seventeen! I am a woman now, and I can see beyond your body!"

"I certainly hope so, as you don't much care for it."

Marissa blinked at his muttered words. She looked him up and down and shook her head in utter shock. "Jude Bertrand, are you pouting?"

His eyes snapped to her. "Pardon?"

"Are you pouting because I don't think you're pretty?"

"Don't be ridiculous," he growled, but she caught a hint of a flush creeping up his neck.

"Ha. I think you are. That's fine, because I *don't* think you're pretty, so there's no need to mutter it like it's a secret."

"Thank you for your honesty!"

Marissa crossed her arms and glared at him. "What woman would ever think you pretty? You're big and wide, with legs and arms like tree limbs."

Jude growled. "Perfect."

She moved closer to touch a finger to his jaw. "You've a face like an ancient warrior, as if it's seen far more battles than waltzes. And hands better suited for battering opponents than playing the piano."

He turned his face away. "Touché."

"You are not pretty, Jude. And I want you more than I've ever wanted any pretty man. You are strong, and looking at you makes me feel *weak*. For you." She tried to spread her fingers over his cheek, but he stepped away.

"Weakness is nothing to build a life on, Marissa. This was all a mistake. I wanted you, and I thought being wanted in return would be enough."

"It's not?"

"No, it's not! I've been satisfied with being accepted for too long. I would ask more than that from my *wife*."

Marissa almost gave an easy answer. Reassurance was a simple thing, because she felt so much for him, but just as she was taking a deep breath, the torment on his face stole her words.

His eyes glinted with an impossible mixture of regret and pride. "For a dozen years, it's been enough for me to be my father's bastard. To be welcomed as an exotic diversion. To be *accepted*. And I tried to win your love in the same way. Do you see that? To slip in beneath your defenses and lull you into *accepting* me." He snarled the word, rage curling his lip. "But I am not a bastard child anymore. I am a *man,* and I ask for more than that."

His anger should have frightened her, but she found that she needed to touch him. His words didn't scare her, because she had his answer. She could give him what he demanded. She already had.

Marissa stepped close, one last time. If he stepped away again, he'd find his back to the wall. "Would you ask for love?" she whispered.

"Yes."

She put her hand to his chest, amazed that it could already feel familiar. "And admiration? And respect?"

Jude closed his eyes, his chest expanding under her hand as he drew in a deep breath.

"And would you want lust too, I hope?"

"You're saying foolish things."

She slid her hand around to his back and laid her cheek to the spot she'd touched. His heart raged beneath her ear. "I love you, Jude."

"Don't say that, *mon coeur.* Don't."

"I love you, and I'm weak with wanting you."

"That is lust," he insisted, his words hoarse at the edges. "It's only lust."

"And my yearning to talk with you, to be alone

and hear your thoughts? Is that lust as well? I underestimated you, Jude. I dismissed you. And now you're doing the same to me. I love you as a man, and I want you as a husband."

"Marissa," he said. His hands settled on her shoulders, poised to pull her tighter or push her away. She didn't know, and she suspected Jude had no idea himself.

"I want this betrothal to be real, Jude. I want you to take me as your wife. And out of all the pretty men I've danced with and all the lust that's burned in my heart, I never wanted that from any of them."

He drew a sharp breath as if he'd speak, but no words passed his lips.

"Do you still like me?" she asked, squeezing her eyes shut in preparation. There was every chance he'd seen her true self and changed his mind. What an irony that would be, for Jude to decide, in the end, that she was too ugly for him.

But perhaps she could turn his own techniques against him.

Marissa rubbed her cheek against the thin linen of his shirt. He was so warm beneath the material, and she wanted to feel that warmth on her. In her. And perhaps his lust would keep him near long enough for him to see that she had changed and grown wiser. Become more than just a girl who loved dancing.

His hands tightened on her shoulders, and she pressed her mouth to his collarbone and her belly to his hips. "Do you still like me a little, Jude?" His strong jaw flexed, and Marissa put her mouth to that hard edge and gently bit down.

His body jerked against hers.

Marissa hummed sympathetically against his skin. "You reap what you sow. You teased me, flaunting your body in front of me, and now I want to have it."

"Stop," he barked, setting her back from him. "I don't need to be teased into wanting you, damn it. I take myself in hand every night out of lust for you."

Her sex tightened with sharp need. She knew what he was saying. She could *picture* it. "So take me."

"I won't. You'll change your mind, and then where will we be? You never wanted me for a husband, and I refuse to live fifty years looking at regret in your eyes."

"Bah! That's nonsense. When have you ever known me to regret anything?"

His scowl softened, as if he were actually considering her question. "You regret Peter White."

"Well, that's true. But to be specific, I regretted Peter White's *failures*." Marissa could've sworn she saw his mouth twitch into a momentary smile. "You wouldn't give me any cause for regret, would you, Jude?"

"I would disappoint you in countless ways."

Shaking her head, Marissa reached for the ties at the shoulders of her gown. "I'm shallow. If you keep me happy in a few small ways, what more would I ask?"

"Don't do that," he growled.

Marissa backed away from his advance and pulled the ties loose. "You did it to me."

When she slipped her shoulders free of the flowing arms, Jude froze. "Don't. Please."

"Don't be a coward," she said, to him or to herself. And then she dropped the gown.

For the first time in her life, Marissa was completely naked in front of a man. He hadn't admitted any lingering affection, and that vulnerability left her with the urge to hide behind her hands. But she didn't.

She could make him like her again. She'd use her body as he'd once planned to use his.

Jude's gaze slipped over her nakedness. He swallowed hard. And then he stalked toward the door.

He was only two feet from escape when Marissa darted past him and barricaded the door with her body. Her nude body.

Jude could feel his face twist with anxious shock. "What are you doing?"

"Seducing you," she answered. It seemed an odd choice of words for sprawling naked against a door. All the same, he *was* being seduced. Her small breasts and slim waist, and my God, the golden curls that hid her sex . . .

"I—" he started, then lost the words in his study of her body.

"I love you," Marissa said. "I want to marry you. And I'm willing to use my body to trick you into feeling some affection." His heart twisted to hear her say those words. He felt true pain when he took a deep breath.

"I don't want to be tricked," he finally managed to say, darting a quick look at the doorknob next to her hip.

Marissa straightened, drawing her feet closer together and sliding her hands down the door.

"Marissa, don't. Just don't." He was begging. He wanted more than this, and yet this was *all* he wanted.

Instead of granting mercy, she stepped away from the door and stopped only a foot from him. He supposed if his body had been more willing, Jude might've been able to retreat, but Marissa's nakedness stole his will and he couldn't move.

She curled her arms slowly around him, her touch blooming from the faint line of her fingertips to the warm bands of her arms going around his ribs. Finally, her whole, hot body took him over, pressing tight to his front. All Jude managed to do was raise his hands high enough to avoid clutching her to him.

"No," he said, shaking his head. "I won't do this. We'll wait. And if we marry . . ." *If we marry.* My God, those words cut jagged holes in him. Was that possible, after he'd steeled himself for the loss of her?

"No, Jude," she whispered. "I'll have you. Now. Please? Take off your clothes. I want to feel you against me."

He shook his head, but his cock had long since responded to the sight of her, and it throbbed eagerly at her words.

"Fine." Marissa pulled his shirt free from his trousers and pressed her belly to his.

"Oh, good Christ," he moaned. The feel of her skin, hot on his, became his whole world in that moment.

"You've made me wait too long already," she whispered. "You've reduced me to throwing myself against you. At least ease this ache you started."

"Hush," he ordered, starting to forget why he fought her. Why? She slid her arms around his waist and pressed her breasts tighter to his chest, and Jude finally lowered his hands to her back. He spread his fingers wide over her naked spine.

"I don't want to do this," he murmured.

Marissa shivered beneath his hands. "It feels like you do."

God, he did want to give in. But more than that, he wanted to have her forever. "Let me leave, Marissa. I won't go to Italy. I'll find a house, and I'll court you properly. We can take our time. You can be sure. You *must* be sure."

She stretched like a cat, and his hands slid naturally down her back, shaping the precious lines of waist and hips. She was just so damn *naked*.

"Oh, Jude," she purred. "I love that."

Love. The word taunted him, and anger swelled in his chest again. But anger combined with a naked woman to enflame him in a different way. Instead of rage, he felt blind lust.

He kissed her then, tasting her for the first time in so long, dragging his hands down her body with intoxicating freedom. All of her was exposed to him. All of her was *his*.

She pressed close, her nails digging into his back, and kissed him with as much hunger as he kissed her. He could just unbutton his trousers and have her. Right now. Slide deep and true and make her his forever. Everything in his body and soul yearned toward that, a force he could feel, pulling every fiber of him toward her.

She wanted this. Wanted *him*. Why couldn't that be enough?

Jude let go of her and pushed her away, running

a hand through his hair in violent frustration. "No! We'd have to marry—"

"All this talk of being a man," Marissa snapped, hands flying up in frustration.

She gestured from his head to his toes, but Jude's eyes lost track of her hand and focused on her breasts again. The nipples tight and flushed . . .

"Well, I need a man, Jude! Now. *Tonight.*"

"Forever, Marissa," he growled. "You understand that? Coming to my bed is the same as marrying me. I won't let you go."

She raised her chin and held his gaze. "You're neither my tutor nor my guardian, so stop treating me like a child. Take me, and damn your caution."

Her eyes blazed with anger and lust. Jude knew his did too. And she was right. She wasn't a child, and she proved that by walking to his bed and laying herself out. Like a sacrifice or a feast. His pulse hammered.

She trembled a bit, like a leaf fluttering, and everything inside him shook as well.

This was a mistake, but she was offering herself and he *ached* for her, had been aching for weeks. Her eyes dared him to refuse. Challenged him.

Jude growled like an animal and pulled off his shirt.

It took him only a few moments to strip, and his lust grew as she watched him with triumph in her smirk. And then he was sliding into bed with Marissa, her skin an impossible beauty against his.

She was right. A man would not run from the love of a woman like her. A man would take his chances, and damn the risks, even if it was the worst mistake he'd ever made.

* * *

Marissa's body was a strange jumble of heavy pleasure and anticipation that made her feel afloat. Jude's body became her world. He was pressed against her and hovering above her, and she could see nothing but his dark eyes as he stared down at her.

The hair of his chest was crisp against her naked skin, and when he slid closer, his manhood pressed against her hip. The fit of their bodies felt natural and fantastically strange at the same time. A thing she'd always known but had never had.

She put her hand to his neck and drew him down to her.

His kiss was no seduction this time. It was a claiming, slow and deep. He was in her body, his tongue exploring her heat, and she dug her nails into his neck to pull him deeper. Everything about him made her yearn for more. His size, his heat, his flexing muscles and scratchy jaw. He was a fascination and a danger all at once. A danger that belonged to her. A fascination she could explore to her heart's content.

She slid a foot along his calf, murmuring with pleasure that she could. When Jude shifted, she insinuated her leg between his and turned toward him. *Now* they were touching. Now they matched. His shaft pressed against her sex. Her breasts rubbed his chest as they kissed. And Jude sighed with the same relief she felt.

He pulled back to look at her. "You are a fantasy," he said as he cupped a gentle hand over her breast. "Here, in my bed, turning to me."

"I love you," she whispered. "There is nothing of fantasy about that."

"Speak for yourself."

But she couldn't speak. She was too busy arching into his exploring hand. He teased her nipple for long, delicious seconds before smoothing his hand down to her hip and back up again. When she twisted impatiently, his hand returned to her breast, just as she'd wanted it too.

"You know what you want, already, *mon coeur*?" His soft words danced over her.

"I'm precocious."

He put just the right amount of pressure into his teasing, and Marissa groaned her pleasure.

"You certainly are. Soon, I shall have nothing left to teach you." When she arched hard against his hips, Jude gasped. "In fact, I think you're teaching me how to perform as a boy again."

Caught between a laugh and a groan, Marissa rubbed her body more firmly against his, and his shudder filled her with power and lust. He might know more of making love, but she could still make him shake with lust for her. How could she not feel powerful?

Ducking her head down to taste his neck, Marissa did some exploring with her hands as well. His chest and ribs, his hips, so narrow and unyielding compared to hers. Everything about him was a new world. She wanted to know it all.

The muscles of his stomach jerked from her touch like she'd burned him. She knew the feeling. Half her body felt afire already.

Heart pounding, Marissa smoothed her hand down his stomach. She touched the crisp hair that surrounded his sex, and then her fingers brushed his shaft. Again, his body jerked away, but then he settled, his chest still as he held his breath. She held her breath too, and curled her fingers around the thick width.

"You're so hot," she whispered. "Is my hand too cold?"

"No," he bit out.

Marissa smiled and tightened her hold. "Does it feel good, then?"

"Yes."

"And this?" She stroked him, keeping her hold firm.

"Yes. You . . . needn't ask again. It's all yes, Marissa."

She chuckled, testing a light hold on him, then tighter. He felt heavy in her hand, and powerful, and Marissa was curious enough to scoot back and push off the bedclothes. She was warm now, after all, and she wanted to see him.

"You will unman me," he groaned, as she watched her hand stroke his cock. She trailed her fingers down to his bullocks as well, then drew her hand up to circle the crown.

Jude groaned and bent to suck her nipple between his teeth. That kiss spiraled through her, tightening her sex and reminding her of where her need was centered. Touching Jude had aroused her to the point that she whimpered and writhed as his teeth scraped her.

She rubbed her leg restlessly against his, needing to draw him near. "Jude," she breathed. My God, she wanted him so badly. What she'd felt in the past had been nothing but mere curiosity. This was *need*.

Jude seemed to realize she was done with her teasing, he kissed her with a pressure that eased her to her back, and then it was his turn to explore. But Jude wasn't touching out of curiosity, he was touching to arouse . . . and succeeding splendidly. He trailed kisses to her neck, then sucked there as he shaped her hip with his hand. Her impatient squirming seemed a hint he could easily read though, for his hand moved down to her thigh.

When he raised his head, she thought he'd kiss her again, but instead he looked her over. "What's this?" His thumb feathered like a kiss over the top of her thigh. "The cause of so much trouble."

She looked down to see the faint pink mark she'd had since she was born. It looked so harmless and innocent, but the heart-shaped discoloration had caused her to confess so many wicked things.

"I'm honored to finally be amongst such a small band of brothers."

"Hush!" she scolded.

Jude chuckled against her neck and distracted her from her outrage by cupping his hand over the hair between her thighs.

"Oh," she sighed, tilting her hips up in shocked welcome.

"So pretty," he murmured, as his fingers slowly stroked. "So warm and lovely and . . . slick."

Marissa eased her knees open so that he could do those wonderful things he'd done that night in the gazebo. Yes, she was slick, and she knew what that meant. Slippery sliding and wonderful thrusts.

And Jude didn't disappoint. He stroked her until she was shaking, and then he finally slid one thick finger inside her.

She thought she might scream with the pleasure of it. Maybe she did scream a little, as she dug her heels into the bed and ground her hips against his hand. Jude kissed her hard, and his mouth absorbed her cries of need. It felt so good, his finger working in and out, but she knew what would feel better. She knew what she wanted. But he seemed infuriatingly content to continue his torment.

Just as she reached the peak of desperation, Jude pressed another finger in, and the pressure caught her breath in a stranglehold for a moment.

How much larger would his thick shaft feel? How much more satisfying?

She tore her mouth from his. "Please."

Though his breath quickened against her neck, he didn't respond. If he could ignore her plea, he couldn't possibly be as desperate as she was, but Marissa knew a quick way to rectify that.

Hard as it was to tear her mind from his thrusting hand, Marissa let go of her hold on his arm, and curled her fingers around his cock instead.

His rhythm faltered; his teeth scraped her neck. And when she stroked him slowly from tip to base, Jude gasped, and his whole body thrummed like a taut bow.

That power again, this time tightening around the fingers deep inside her. She was triumphant. And whimpering like a kitten.

And when Jude drew his fingers from her body, she wrapped her arms around his waist to pull him over her. He came willingly, thank God, and when his cock rubbed her sex, she arched into him, moaning as he slid against her.

Oh, God, yes. That was good. So good. And even

better when the head notched against her and he eased inside.

"Oh," she whispered, "Jude," because she wanted her body to know it was him she took inside. Jude, who stretched her sex tight as he slowly sank into her.

He drew out a little, then eased farther in, and Marissa wrapped her arms so tight around him that she could hardly breathe.

"Shh," he murmured. "Relax, *mon coeur.*"

"I can't!" She was breathing too hard, overwhelmed with all she wanted from him.

"Marissa." His voice dropped. "Marissa." He reached back to tug one of her hands free. Then the other.

He tucked her fisted hands into his and lowered them to the bed. Marissa squeezed her eyes shut and tried to slow her breathing.

"Shh," Jude whispered. He pressed a kiss to one of her eyelids and then the other.

She sobbed and drew her legs high on his. When she wrapped her ankles around him, Jude thrust deep and true, and sank himself fully inside her.

She arched, pushing her head back in stark relief. She was filled with him, just as she'd wanted.

Jude eased slowly out, and when he thrust back in, Marissa opened her eyes to see him above her. He looked fierce and frightening. As fierce as she felt inside her heart as she tightened her fists and tilted her hips up to meet him.

"Breathe, Marissa."

"I can't! I just . . . I want you so much."

"You have me, *mon coeur.* I'm yours."

"Please," she pled. "Jude, I . . ."

He kissed her cheeks, her mouth, her jaw. "Here,

love." Her eyes were still closed when he turned her. Suddenly she was above him, and he was still snug inside her. "Here," he said, "I'm yours."

Marissa drew a deep breath and pushed up on her hands. The weight pushed her body more firmly against him, and she sighed her satisfaction.

He let go of her wrists, and Marissa put her palms to his chest and looked down at Jude. He was gorgeous beneath her. Not pretty, not even handsome, but a gorgeous sight as she raised her hips and then took him deep.

Oh, yes. She could breathe again, though Jude seemed to be having trouble now. His hands gripped her hips as she began to ride him, and his breath came fast and hard.

Marissa felt that power again, the power she held over him, but this time it mixed up with his power over her. He filled her. Pushed inside her. Forced her body to stretch and take him in.

And she loved it. She loved him.

She tried moving faster, then in slow, torturous increments. Jude let her do what she wanted, and it was all as lovely as she'd dreamed. Her thighs began to shake, but she couldn't stop. It wasn't nearly enough. Jude's eyes narrowed, his jaw clenched, and he slid one hand along her thigh until he touched her sex.

"Ah!" she cried out, her hips jerking with the shock of that electric touch.

"That's it," he murmured. "Have me."

She took him harder, as his thumb pressed that spot where all the tension built. "Oh, God. Jude." This was the culmination of every sensation she'd been chasing for years. The wickedness, the tightening, the wild licks of pleasure, the fullness of her very core. This was everything.

The tension became an aching weight that pulled her into herself. Marissa closed her eyes and dropped her head, concentrating on the miracle of her own body. And it *was* a miracle, the way her pleasure pulled at her soul, becoming something close to pain. She cried out in desperation, and then she broke. Her soul or her body, something inside her broke and released all her joy and pleasure with such force that she screamed as she slammed her hips into Jude's. She needed him impossibly deep, and he must've sensed it, because his hips rose to meet hers with brutal force as she sobbed and shook against him.

When the pleasure finally let go its grip on her, Marissa collapsed to Jude's chest, to pant and shiver against him. His big hands stroked her back as he hummed a soothing sound against the top of her head.

"You're amazing, Marissa."

"I've never . . . I've never felt anything like that."

"Ah. Finally."

"Jude!" she gasped, slapping his arm, but he was laughing against her. When she began to laugh too, his chuckles came to an abrupt stop. She couldn't help but laugh harder, aware of the way her muscles squeezed him.

"Christ, woman."

She rubbed her cheek against the hair of his chest, finding that his skin was damp with sweat. He smelled good and felt even better, pressed damp and hot against her.

She squealed when he flipped her to her back and surged deeper into her.

"I've told you I need no teasing, *mon coeur.* You're driving me mad."

He *looked* mad, wild-eyed and flushed with passion. Marissa wrapped her legs around his hips and took him as deep as he needed to be. He kissed her with the same hunger she'd felt moments before. And when he finally reached his climax with a last desperate thrust, Marissa felt tears leak from her eyes.

He was her friend and her lover, and he'd be her husband as well.

"I love you," she whispered into the wild mess of his hair.

When he sighed, the weight of his body settled more fully onto her, but it was a happy weight, not one she wanted to squirm away from. He set his forehead to the pillow and shook his head. "I couldn't resist, and now you will regret this."

"I could never regret this. Never."

He pushed up a little, raising his head to look into her eyes. After a moment, weariness settled into his features. "It's too late regardless. I'm yours now."

I'm yours. The beautiful opposite of what Peter White had said to her. *You're mine now,* he'd crowed, as if she were a purchased treat. The difference, it seemed, between a boy and a man. Just as Jude had promised.

But she could not like the sadness in his eyes. Her vision went blurry. She felt a tear slip free and slide down her temple.

"I should not have given in," Jude sighed.

Marissa hit his shoulder. Hard. She felt his whole body tense against her, and then he rolled free, making her gasp with the strange feeling of him withdrawing from her body.

"Whatever your regrets," he said softly. "We'll marry."

"Those are your regrets, not mine!" she shouted. "I regret nothing. I will wait for you to like me again. I will demand it, do you understand? You will love me someday, damn your stubborn hide."

Jude slowly rose up to his elbow to give him a better vantage point from which to glower down at her.

"Oh, don't look so dark. You're stuck with me now. I will use you until you surrender. You'd do well to make the best of it."

She was about to sit up and reach for the covers, but he stopped her with the gentle brush of his thumb over her cheek. "You're trying to turn my own pleasure against me? Trick me into loving you?"

"You can hardly judge me for the very thing you meant to do. Only *you* are the fickle one it seems. So easily turned away from your affection." Her breath skipped and jumped in her throat as she tried to hold back more tears. "Don't . . . please don't tell me I'm too late, Jude. I only just realized how much I love you. It isn't *fair.*"

His hand cupped her chin as pain twisted his mouth into a brief scowl. "How can you be sure?"

She blinked away more tears, angry when they escaped and let Jude see how much she hurt. "All I know is that I have no idea what you're thinking, but I'm willing to tell you what I feel. I love you, and you may not like me at all."

"Ah, God, Marissa." His thumb traced shivers over her bottom lip. "Don't be a fool. I love you."

She swallowed hard, but a small sob of relief still escaped. "You do?"

"Of course I do. I love you. And that's why I can't stand the thought of having less than everything."

Marissa felt more tears fall, and she ignored them, even when Jude kissed them away. "And your regrets?"

"I regret nothing." He slid over her again, kissing her, and she was just wondering if she might dare spending the whole night in Jude's room when the hard crack of knuckles on the door invaded the quiet.

Jude was reaching desperately for the bedcovers when the door opened with tragic speed.

"Sorry to disturb you," Harry said, his voice still coming from the hall, thank God. "But Marissa has gone missing and—"

She met Harry's eyes at the exact moment his voice died an ugly death in his throat. Jude had half-succeeded with the covers at least, though she suspected Harry had seen far more of Jude than he'd ever expected to.

"Harry," Jude started, but Harry just shook his head and backed out.

"Oh, never mind. So sorry. I'll just . . ."

"God damn it," Jude barked as the door closed with a crack that sounded eerily like impending doom.

"Good thing you didn't regret it," Marissa muttered.

"Jesus, woman, you are a magnet for scandal."

"I know. Who will ever marry me now?"

Finally, the fierceness left his face, and Jude smiled, then laughed. "You may break my heart and ruin my reputation, but I already know it will be well worth it." He offered a kiss that left Marissa sighing with satisfaction.

"How long do you think we can stay here?"

Jude shook his head. "You're too wicked for your own good. It's time to pay the piper. Again."

"*Again*. This is getting tiresome. At least when we're married, I won't have to face the prospect of being called to your study."

"I'm not so sure about that."

Amazingly, despite the drama awaiting her below-stairs, Marissa laughed and teased as she dressed. Jude kissed her and promised to meet her at her room so that she needn't enter Edward's study alone. Fifteen minutes later, Marissa was presented before the exhausted eyes of her family. She only just managed to look somber in the face of their shock.

Chapter 24

Caught in the snare of the silent room, Jude realized that from the start, this had been the inevitable outcome: Marissa perched on a chair before her brother's desk; Jude standing behind her, struggling to look regretful; both of them still weak with the intensity of their lovemaking.

Her maid had put some effort into making her presentable, but Marissa's mouth was swollen and pink, and there were at least two distinctively reddened patches on her that weren't quite covered by the high collar of her gown.

Jude hoped he looked almost normal. He'd combed his hair, but it was still wet from the grooming, and there'd been nothing to do for the stubble on his jaw that made him look a rakish debaucher.

Marissa cleared her throat. "So . . ."

"I take full responsibility for everything that happened," Jude interrupted.

Marissa looked over her shoulder and raised an eyebrow. "Oh, do you? Funny, if it had been up to you, you'd be halfway to Italy by now. Alone."

Jude aimed a quelling look at her, but she'd already turned around, so it did no good. "I'm a guest in this house," Jude continued. "And I apologize for abusing your hospitality so . . ."

"Strenuously?" Marissa ventured.

"Oh, for God's sake!" Edward shouted, banging the flat of his hand against the desk. "Marissa Anne York, you are behaving outrageously!"

She shrugged. "I suppose. But we are engaged, so I'm not sure what all the fuss is—"

"The fuss," Edward ground out, "Is that this *gentleman*—"

The word carried enough scorn that Jude felt his shoulders tense in defense.

"—promised not to dishonor you further, regardless of the status of your betrothal. Which, by the way, I understood that neither of you intended to carry through."

Jude swallowed his anger and bowed his head in acknowledgment. "I can't deny that I broke my word."

"I suppose I shouldn't be surprised, considering," Edward growled.

Clenching his jaw, Jude shot a look toward Aidan, but his friend watched him with a steely eye and offered no sign of sympathy. "I assume you refer to the details of my birth?"

"You made a promise," Aidan snapped

Jude squeezed the back of the chair until his hand went numb. This was what he'd always known and never admitted. That one misstep would see respectable friends turn against him. "And what has that to do with my circumstances? A well-born man has never been a fool for the sake of love? Neither of you has ever broken a promise over a woman?"

Oh, Aidan lost his steely-eyed look then. Sharp, jagged fury transformed his face into an animal's.

Jude faced him and stood his ground. "Do not throw my birth at me, then pretend outrage in the face of the truth. You are no better than I, damn it. Not at all."

A moment hung between them, a moment where Aidan might say something unforgivable. At the very least, Jude expected they would come to blows. But in the end, Marissa stood and rounded her chair to stand next to Jude. She put her arm through this.

"You two men were forgiving enough of *my* dishonor, and I daresay I have an impeccable bloodline. And my fall was seen to by a gentleman of the ton, I might add." She cocked her head. "Actually, all of the men in my past have been pure-blooded gentlemen, have they not? So Jude is absolutely right. This has nothing to do with his birth, and it dishonors you both to bring it up."

Aidan's face did not relax. His fists remained clenched. Marissa didn't seem intimidated. "Jude was gentleman enough to take your sister off your hands when it was convenient," she said. "Your hypocrisy boggles the mind."

The scene hadn't changed. Jude still stood before two rightfully enraged brothers, but the tension eased from his chest, replaced by a suspiciously maudlin warmth. Her words sounded sincere. She didn't regret loving him. She didn't regret his birth.

Jude tried very hard to maintain a serious expression. "Marissa has agreed to marry me in truth."

"Oh, my word, no!" her mother shouted.

"Mother," Marissa gasped, but Jude could see that the baroness was not the problem.

Edward was the man of the house, and he looked only marginally less furious than he had moments before. "I don't understand, Marissa. You've made your feelings clear from the start. You cared nothing for him."

"I was a fool. Such a fool that even Jude did not believe me. However, I did my best to convince him, and eventually he . . . succumbed."

"I see." Edward offered Jude a dark look.

"Oh, don't look at him that way. What was he to do? Push me out into the corridor naked?"

Jude put a hand over hers. "Marissa."

"Oh, I am done with all this. I am no better than I should be, and Jude does not mind that at all, and I love him."

"But no!" the dowager baroness squealed. "My darling girl . . . it was lovely of Mr. Bertrand to offer to help, but to marry him for *love* . . . I cannot imagine."

Marissa shot her mother an impatient look. "You'll get used to it, Mother."

"Well . . . this is all very strange!"

"It is," Jude agreed, and the baroness's feathers unruffled a bit.

She looked back and forth between the two of them. "I suppose we must make the most of it, as circumstances have already . . . progressed."

Aidan cursed again while Edward shook his head in disgust.

Her mother clapped her hands together with a sound like a shot. "We shall plan a spectacular wedding for just before Easter! Do you think your father might attend, Mr. Bertrand? What a coup that would be! I daresay—"

"I'm sorry, Mother," Marissa said. "But the wedding cannot wait until spring for obvious reasons. It might be more of a spectacle than even you would care to present."

Her mother's eyes dipped to Marissa's belly, and she actually took a moment to think it over. "Oh, I suppose you are right."

"Wait a moment!" Edward shouted. "I have not agreed to any of this."

"Oh, stop it, brother," Marissa scolded. "In a month's time, I will no longer be your problem."

"A month, you say?" His face lost some of its tension.

"Perhaps even less."

Her mother fluttered about, trying to convince them all that she could not possibly plan a wedding within a month's time. But when Jude assured her that his father would likely attend no matter the short notice, she settled into wedding plans with an enthusiasm that overtook the rest of the discussion.

"I'm due in Hull in a month," Aidan growled. "I've a new ship being outfitted."

Their mother quivered with outrage. "You will be at the wedding, Aidan York. She is your only sister, and she is blossoming into womanhood!"

The whole room went silent. Amazingly, no one laughed, though Marissa clearly came close.

Though Jude's mood had become impossibly light, he could see that neither York brother was at peace, so he offered a little bow to the room. "If

I could beg a moment of privacy with Edward and Aidan . . ."

"Oh, of course!" the baroness chirped. "Marissa and Harry will come to the sewing room to look over the latest fashion plates that just arrived from London."

Harry had been sitting quietly in a corner, looking painfully embarrassed by the whole situation, but he brightened at the thought of escape. "Yes, of course! Anything I can do to help!"

"Mother," Marissa complained as she was ushered out, "there's no time for a grand wedding." Just before she was pushed out the door, she dug in her heels. "Wait!"

She rushed to Edward and gave him a tight hug.

"You're incorrigible," he growled, but when she smiled at him, his scowl twitched up for a split second.

"I'm happy," she whispered.

"You're sure?"

"Absolutely."

"Then I shan't lock you in your room until the wedding. If you promise to behave yourself."

"I'm sure I'll try the best I can."

Edward's face reddened again, but Marissa's smile widened. She stopped to kiss Jude's cheek before floating from the room, and on that note, he faced the York brothers with far more happiness than the situation called for.

"Well," Aidan said, "You got what you wanted."

"Your sister loves me." He said the words, and they felt real on his lips. Jude found himself truly believing it for the first time. "You may find it as difficult to fathom as I do, but it's true."

Edward snorted. "And you think that will last?"

He gestured at Jude as if his very being made the words a joke.

"Don't underestimate her," Jude said. The words were quiet, but he saw the way they hit Edward. "I would not love her if she weren't strong and intelligent and capable of seeing me for who I am."

Edward ran a weary hand through his hair while Aidan escaped to the sideboard to pour himself a drink. After shooting a dark look at Jude, he poured two more drinks and offered one to each of the men.

Jude took his glass and stopped Aidan with a hand on his sleeve. "I apologize for speaking so callously. And . . ." He cleared his throat. "I apologize again to both of you for betraying my word. If it's unforgivable, I can accept that. But I'll marry your sister, regardless."

Edward looked up at the ceiling for a moment; then he shook his head and stood to offer his hand. "You did this family a priceless service. I can't resent that it might actually turn out for the best."

Jude shook his hand. "Thank you."

"Congratulations."

Aidan did not slap him on the back and claim that all was well. Instead he slumped into a chair and drained his whole glass in one swallow. "As you once made clear, the line marking decent and dishonorable is a shaky, twisting thing. You were right then, and you are right now. And who has honor ever served, anyway?"

"I'll treat her well," Jude said quietly.

"I can see that." Aidan waved a dismissive hand and pushed to his feet. "Well, welcome to the blasted family. You'll fit right in, clearly."

Both men seemed content to leave it at that.

Jude felt a small sense of relief. He'd stepped into this room knowing he would marry Marissa, regardless of their objections. Still, his heart pounded with satisfaction as he escaped to find his bride.

Marissa loved him, and she was bright and brave and, yes, a tiny bit shallow. And he loved her.

The rest of society could go to hell. What did it matter what the rest of England thought of him, if Marissa loved him for the man he was? He needed nothing more than her.

And soon enough, it would be official. The family had given their reluctant blessing. The danger of public scandal had finally passed, and now Jude was looking forward to a lifetime of private debauchery.

A month suddenly seemed a long time to wait.

Chapter 25

The ceremony was, by all accounts, lovely. Marissa could remember nothing of it but Jude's hands around hers, and his happy eyes and secret smile. And then he'd kissed her and they'd left the chapel in a shower of good wishes and flower petals. It was done.

Once again, the rush to the altar had proved unnecessary, but Marissa would not have put off this day for anything.

She glowed. She knew she did, and it was confirmed by the whispers around her as they entered the wedding ball and were presented as man and wife.

"The bride . . ."

"So beautiful . . ."

"Like an angel . . ." No one said anything about the groom. But to Marissa he was far more an angel than she. One of God's warrior angels, perhaps, equipped with a great steel sword instead of a harp. He was fierce and gentle and so protective that he'd only let her sneak into his room twice more in the month since she'd convinced him to stay.

Infuriating man. He'd finally started bolting his door against her. But she'd have him tonight, and the knowledge burned bright in his gaze each time their eyes met. She'd have him tonight and every night she wanted.

Suddenly, Marissa regretted that her mother had forgone the traditional wedding breakfast in order to host a ball. Marissa had been thrilled with the idea of dancing with Jude on their wedding night, but now she wanted nothing more than for the festivities to be over. But her mother would never forgive an escape before the dancing. What if there were no grand toasts or romantic exhibitions of marital bliss? And what would be the point of the tiny children wandering through the crowd dressed as cherubs? They would float through the room with no couple to bless.

Marissa caught sight of a white feathered wing bobbing by, and she cringed. Both she and Edward had tried to dissuade their mother from the cherubs, but no mortal force could change her mind. And so here they were, in a play as great as one might see on stage. Peacocks called from the yard, and Marissa could only hope they didn't freeze to death in the cold night. They weren't visible in the dark, but it was the idea of the thing, or so she'd been informed.

Marissa leaned over to say hello to Aunt Ophelia, despite that the old woman appeared to be asleep.

"Eh?" her great aunt cawed as she popped upright in the chair.

"I asked how you liked the ceremony, Aunt Ophelia!"

The woman squinted up at Marissa. "Oh, I liked it very much."

"I'm glad."

The wrinkles in the old woman's face folded deeper when she smiled. She smiled so rarely that Marissa found herself laughing with delight. Perhaps Aunt Ophelia was sweeter than she seemed.

"Yes, I liked it very much," Aunt Ophelia repeated. "And a lucky thing to get you married off before you worked your way through next Season's crop of gentlemen."

Marissa's grin froze. "Pardon?"

"Nothing wrong with a little slap and tickle, girl. But you've got to be a bit more circumspect. Girls were more clever in my day. I was beginning to think your wits as ill-used as your virtue."

"I . . . Aunt Ophelia . . . *Pardon?*"

But the old woman just slumped back into her nap. Marissa was about to shake her silly when she was stopped by a hand curling over her shoulder. Still dumbfounded, Marissa looked up to find Jude smiling down at her. She spared one last confused look for Aunt Ophelia before rising.

She managed an uncertain smile.

"My father," he murmured as he turned her around to face the duke.

Marissa shook off her shock and offered a curtsy. "Your Grace," she said, feeling a more genuine grin stretch her mouth. She'd met the duke the night before, but she was still surprised by the sight of him. The Duke of Winthrop, one of the loftiest peers in England, looked exactly like Jude.

She blushed when she considered how many times she'd thought of Jude as a groundsman or blacksmith. What a fool she'd been. The duke was not as tall as Jude, nor quite as solid, but there was no denying that Jude had inherited the man's face, right down to the wide mouth and square jaw.

The duke teased her for her blush, and she let him think she was shy and nervous, though Jude watched the exchange with an incredulous expression.

"Just a moment, m'dear," the duke said, patting her hand. "I've a surprise for you, if only I could find him."

When his father turned away, Jude leaned in close to brush his lips against her ear. "You'd think," he murmured, "after loving a woman like my mother, he'd be able to recognize a wicked woman when he saw one."

Grinning, Marissa raised up on her toes so that Jude's mouth would rest against her neck. He obliged her with a little nibble, then called her a distracting wanton and stepped away. She was still smiling when the duke returned with a young gentleman in tow.

"Look who arrived just in time for the ceremony!"

"Melbourne!" Jude responded, clapping the newcomer on the back.

"Please," the duke continued, "Allow me to present my son, Viscount Melbourne, soon enough the duke himself, I don't doubt."

"Father," the man said flatly.

"Melbourne, I'm pleased to introduce you to your new sister, Mrs. Marissa Bertrand."

She curtsied deeply, studying him through her lashes as he bowed. This son must look like his mother. He was handsome enough. And elegant. And Marissa wished for nothing more than to send him away so that Jude could do a bit more nibbling.

But she managed to be gracious as she spoke with both gentlemen for ten minutes. The whole crowd watched the exchange. Half were likely curious about the relationship between Jude and his father. The other half were taking note that the young viscount would someday need a wife.

If they knew that Jude and Marissa were sailing to France before their honeymoon in Italy, there'd be even more talk. A duke was one thing, but a French courtesan was even more interesting. Or so Marissa thought, anyway.

While Jude and his brother were reminiscing about something decidedly male—a fishing hole of some sort—there was a grand flourish of violins, and Marissa looked up to find her mother gesturing furiously from the potted ferns that hid the orchestra.

"Jude, I believe we're wanted."

"Ah, yes. That plant does seem excessively eager. Pardon us, Father. Melbourne."

They emerged from the ferns a minute later, flanked by a cadre of cherubs. Edward, who was in the midst of introducing them to the crowd, choked and stumbled to a halt when he saw the great flock of wings. Marissa wished she could simply disappear into the floor, but Jude appeared to be greatly enjoying himself. She elbowed him several times, but his grin never faltered.

As he refused to share her humiliation, Marissa distracted herself by looking over the crowd. Beth and her cousin were right at the front, and Mr. Dunwoody, that fickle idiot, stood at Nanette's side, smiling down at her. Interestingly enough, Cousin Harry stood at Beth's side. Marissa would have thought nothing of it, if not for their recent conversation.

Before she could ponder it further, the room erupted into applause at the last of her brother's words, and the flock of cherubs ushered Jude and Marissa out to the dance floor.

Marissa threw off her thoughts, ignored the loose feathers floating in the air, and put her arms around her husband.

"No regrets yet?" he asked as they stepped into the music of the waltz.

"Aside from my fear that I'll slip on an angel feather and break my neck, no regrets at all. And you?"

"You know I've wanted this from the moment we met."

"When did we first meet?" she teased him.

She'd only been joking, but Jude's face turned intent when he looked down at her. "Aidan had dragged me here for some hunting. I don't care for the hunt, but I came along anyway. And when I walked into the music room, there you were, dancing with your cousin. You smiled at something he said, and then you caught sight of some gentleman walking past, and all your bright prettiness turned wicked and warm."

"Stop," she laughed.

"It's true. And I thought to myself, there is a woman who wants pleasure."

"Jude!" She blushed and slapped his arm; then she realized that the whole crowd chuckled in response. They were being watched. "You're awful," she whispered.

"Perhaps. But I was right, wasn't I?"

Finally, a few other couples joined them in the waltz, and Marissa could lean a little closer to her husband. "I do want pleasure," she answered. "Badly."

"Wench. Don't tease."

"But I've so yearned for a good ride these past weeks."

Jude groaned and glared around the room. "How many dances must we grant them?"

"No more than three, I should think."

"Excellent."

Marissa watched Mr. Dunwoody as he hurried by with a glass of punch. He looked . . . delicate and weak-chinned. The thought made her smile.

Jude leaned in close again. "Once we are established, I shall have to hire pretty footmen to entertain your eye."

"What? I wasn't ogling anyone."

"Mm-hm."

"I wasn't! Anyway, I thought you were a jealous man now."

He pulled back to smile down at her. "No. I'm not jealous anymore. Look as much as you like. Just no touching, if you please."

"Ah. The same goes for you, husband."

"I have no need to look at other women," he said with a cocky smile.

"We'll see. In a few years' time, you may find yourself yearning for a glimpse of a real bosom. Or two."

Jude threw back his head and laughed so loudly that the whole ballroom paused to look. Every smile was happily indulgent.

"Your bosom," he finally said, "is more than enough for me."

"What a meager appetite you must have," Marissa murmured. "By the way, if I'm not mistaken, I believe Aunt Ophelia just called me a witless tart."

Jude must have assumed she was joking, because he only shook his head as if he didn't understand the joke. Oh, well. Marissa didn't understand it either.

They were in the midst of their second dance when Marissa saw that Beth was dancing with Harry and that Harry had put on his most charming smile. Was he following through with his thoughts on courting one of the Samuel girls? Marissa's heart cheered with happiness that Beth might someday be her cousin. She would not marry some man from the south and disappear for months at a time.

But there was a shadow to that thought as well. Harry did not love Beth, and Marissa wanted Beth to be happy.

"Do you think," she whispered to Jude, "that a marriage might be happy if two people are not in love?"

"This is a bad time to bring that up, sweet wife."

"I was speaking of someone else."

"Well then . . . I'm not sure. I'd hoped that if we married, you would come to love me. I think it does happen. I saw Charles LeMont and his wife in Grantham the other day."

"You did? Did she run away weeping, I hope?"

Jude rolled his eyes. "They didn't see me. But they looked happy. Very happy."

"I suppose I should be thankful for myself, at least."

"Be thankful for her," Jude said softly.

"Yes, I think you're right. I'll be thankful for her

and for Charles." Jude was such a good man. She fought the urge to lay her head on his chest. Not yet. Not till much later.

When the dance ended, Marissa headed straight to Beth to tease her about Harry. "Your cousin has always been so kind to me," Beth responded with nary a hint of pink in her cheeks.

"Mm. He has a thousand pounds a year, you know. He shall make someone a good husband someday."

"He will indeed. Such a thoughtful man."

But Beth wasn't paying any attention at all. She was too busy frowning at Mr. Dunwoody, who was too busy fawning over Nanette to notice Beth's stare. One of the cherubs wandered up to pretend to shoot an arrow at Mr. Dunwoody's heart. Wretched little feathered beast.

Marissa spotted Edward walking toward her and latched on to the distraction. "Ah, there is my brother looking far too serious, as usual. Have you danced with him yet, Beth?"

"Aidan? No, but he promised to find me later."

"I meant Edward," Marissa said, as her brother stepped up.

And then something very odd happened. Her friend jumped as if she'd just been poked, and her eyes flew to Edward. As Edward was leaning close to Marissa to complain about the cherubs, Beth's face turned a miserable shade of red.

"No, not him," she answered too loudly.

Edward looked up. "I apologize. I've interrupted your conversation."

"No!" Beth yelped. "It's nothing!"

"Edward," Marissa drawled. "You must dance with Miss Samuel tonight. Have a little merriment."

An eerie peacock cry drifted above the music, and Edward scowled. "Yes, of course," he muttered, then offered a little bow in Beth's direction. "I believe there is a quadrille coming up. I hope you'll do me the honor, Miss Samuel."

Beth stared at him, mouth agape, and didn't offer a response, but Edward was too distracted to notice. "Pardon me. I believe I just saw a peacock wander down that corridor."

"Inside?" Marissa gasped, craning her neck toward the doorway. She narrowed her eyes, wondering if this had been part of her mother's plan all along. It seemed highly likely. A few shrieking ladies would add to the excitement of the ball, and why not add a few colorful feathers to the down already floating above the dancers?

"My mother has truly—" But when Marissa swung back toward Beth, she found that her friend had vanished.

Marissa stood there, too puzzled to move. Surely Beth's reaction had been decidedly odd. She tried to think of other strained moments between her friend and Edward, but she could picture nothing. No interaction at all, which was even stranger than Beth's blush.

Before she could formulate a theory, Marissa was accosted from behind. The brief touch of a warm mouth on her neck identified the man at her back.

"Time for our third dance," he whispered, and Marissa felt her cheeks heat. The riddle of Beth's awkwardness would have to wait until after tonight. After her honeymoon, even. She turned to Jude and happily took the hand he offered. In a few moments, they'd be in their bedchamber with no mysteries to solve, no wandering birds, and no angel feathers floating between them.

Heaven.

No feathers awaited them, but there *were* rose petals. Everywhere.

"Mm," Marissa sighed as she peeled a petal off Jude's stomach and planted a kiss there. "You smell so pretty."

"I . . ." His breath hitched when she placed another kiss lower down. ". . . endeavor to please. As always."

"I admit," she breathed against the faint path of hair beneath his navel, "I was convinced the roses were my mother's doing. I didn't suspect you at all."

"I . . . only wanted to . . ."

"Relax, my love," she drawled. "Breathe." She touched her lips tentatively to the head of his manhood and smiled at the way his breath went ragged. It ceased altogether when she licked him. He tasted . . . warm. And friendly.

She smiled at the thought and tasted him a few more times to be sure. Yes, definitely friendly.

Marissa wasn't quite sure how to go about this. It seemed a very different task than when Jude had offered his own scandalous kisses during her last stolen visit. But when she closed her mouth over his shaft he made a sound of tortured pleasure, and his hips jerked toward her.

Oh, my. Delighted—and horribly aroused— Marissa took him deeper into her mouth, marveling at how smooth he was on her tongue. This was pure wickedness, and she was well aware of the wetness between her thighs as she slid her mouth down his cock. When she drew up and then took him deep again, Jude moaned. The sound was like a hand stroking her sex, and Marissa moaned as well. Every slide of his shaft over her tongue made her wiggle with eager arousal. He grew larger as she sucked.

"Christ," Jude murmured, and she looked up to see him watching, eyes narrowed in fierce concentration. "Come here, love," he whispered.

She ignored him, taking him deep into her mouth again, but he slid his hand into her hair to stop her.

"I have grander plans for our wedding night. If I spend like this—"

She licked her lips. "Oh, can you do that?"

Jude groaned and let his head fall to the pillow. "You will ruin me with happy looks like that."

"But you must let me—"

He pulled her to his chest and kissed her. "Yes, I will let you, cheeky girl. Tomorrow. Or later tonight? But not now. Now, I want to . . ."

His hands stroked down her arse, and when his fingers delved into the seam of her body, Marissa pressed her hips into his cock with a moan of need.

"God, but you're wet," he whispered. "Already."

"I liked doing that," she confessed. She felt a shudder run through his body.

Jude rolled her to her back and covered her, kissing her with such an intensity that he stole her breath away. But when he entered her in one merciless thrust, she gasped in a desperate gulp of air.

"I love you," she whispered as she wound a hand into his hair. "Forever."

Here, in their bed, Jude was a man, and she was a woman, and there was no thought of gentility or elegance or society. Out there, her life might be shallow and pretty. Here, they were base and honest and wild together. And Marissa would not regret that in a thousand years.

Here, Jude was beautiful, and she was the beast that would devour him if she could.

"Forever," he whispered back, and it was the prettiest thing she'd ever heard.

Books by Bestselling Author
Fern Michaels

Available Wherever Books Are Sold!
Check out our website at **www.kensingtonbooks.com**

More by Bestselling Author
Hannah Howell